£ 2.00

Billy Hopkins, who is better known to his family and friends as Wilfred Hopkins, was born in Collyhurst in 1928 and attended schools in Manchester. Before going into higher education he worked as a copy boy for the *Manchester Guardian*. He later studied at the Universities of London, Manchester and Leeds and has been involved in school-teaching and teacher-training in Liverpool, Manchester, Salford and Glasgow. He also worked at universities in Kenya, Zimbabwe and Malawi. He is married with six grown-up children and now lives in retirement with his wife in Southport.

Billy Hopkins' novels have been warmly acclaimed:

'How wonderful to have a book like this. A book . . . that pulls the reader back to that different world . . . A glimpse of a lost reality' *Manchester Evening News*

'Heartwarming fictional memoirs' *Bolton Evening News*

'In one moment you cannot help but chuckle, in the next you are wrestling with a lump in your throat, hoping that no one will notice' *Warrington Guardian*

'Literature's version of L. S. Lowry . . . Evokes the sights, sounds, atmosphere and cohesiveness of the Lowryesque community' *Lancashire life*

'A good read' *Times Educational Supplement*

Also by Billy Hopkins

Kate's Story
Going Places

Our Kid

and

High Hopes

Billy Hopkins

headline

OUR KID first published in Great Britain in 1996
by The Limited Edition Press

First published in 1998
by HEADLINE BOOK PUBLISHING

HIGH HOPES first published in Great Britain in 2000
by HEADLINE BOOK PUBLISHING

First published in this omnibus edition in 2004
by HEADLINE BOOK PUBLISHING

A HEADLINE paperback

10 9 8 7 6 5 4 3 2 1

ISBN 0 7553 2658 X

Typeset in Times by Avon DataSet Ltd,
Bidford-on-Avon, Warwickshire

Printed and bound in Great Britain by
Clays Ltd, St Ives plc

Headline's policy is to use papers that are natural, renewable and
recyclable products and made from wood grown in sustainable
forests. The logging and manufacturing processes are expected to
conform to the environmental regulations of the country of origin.

HEADLINE BOOK PUBLISHING
A division of Hodder Headline
338 Euston Road
London NW1 3BH

www.headline.co.uk
www.hodderheadline.com

Our Kid

For Clare

'Give me the child for the first seven years, and you may do what you like with him afterwards' Attributed as a Jesuit maxim, in *Lean's Collectanea* vol. 3 (1903) p. 472

'If only it were true!' Jesuit priest, 1998

Prologue

Another Bloody Mouth to Feed

'Come on now, Kate. Y're no' really tryin',' said the midwife. 'Pull on the towel and push! Push!'

'I am bloody well pushing,' Kate shouted back. 'I can't push any harder. Pull and push. It's like rowing a boat on Heaton Park lake. You'd think God would have thought of an easier way of having kids.'

'It won't be long now, luv,' said Lily Goodhart, her next-door neighbour, wiping Kate's glistening forehead.

'That dose o' castor oil should speed things up,' said Nurse McDonagh. 'Anyway, it's no' as if it's your first wean.'

'Aye, but it never gets any easier, no matter what they say,' said Kate.

A sudden contraction convulsed her.

'Glory be t'God, that was like a red-hot poker going through me!' she gasped.

'Bite on your hanky when it gets too bad, Kate,' said the nurse. 'We don't want the neighbours to hear. And your kids are in the other bedroom. Is your husband no' around?'

'No, I told him to take himself off to the pub outa the road. He'd only be in the way. Besides, he doesn't like trouble, y'know.'

'Lucky for him! Just the same, I think he should be here, just in case we have to fetch Dr McDowell. Lily, you'd best go across to the pub and bring Tommy over.'

'Eeh, I don't think he'll like that,' said Lily.

'Never you mind whether he likes it or no'. Tell him he's needed over here. Dinna come back without him.'

'Very well, if you say so,' said Lily doubtfully as she left the little cramped bedroom.

'I do hope we don't have to bring no doctor. I'd be so embarrassed, like . . .' said Kate after Lily had departed.

'But he's a *doctor*.'

'It doesn't matter. He's a man, isn't he? I don't want no man – not even me husband, for that matter – to see me like this. And anyroad, I think . . .'

But the nurse did not discover what it was she thought, for Kate was racked by another agonising spasm and was busy stifling a scream.

'Come on now, Kate,' urged the midwife. 'Nearly there! Now, pull and push! Pull and push!'

It was eight o'clock on that Sunday night in 1928. Tommy was already on his third pint and a feeling of bonhomie and goodwill had begun to flow over him. He felt completely at home and in his true element.

'This is the place for me,' he said to Jimmy Dixon, his bosom pal. 'This is where I really belong. The vault of Tubby Ainsworth's. Best bloody pub in Collyhurst.' Its real name was the Dalton Arms, but hardly anyone called it that.

The thick tobacco smoke and the excited babble of twenty male voices talking at once combined to produce in Tommy a deep sense of contentment and comradeship. In here, he felt safe and away from all those goings-on at home.

He took out a packet of Player's Weights, extracted the last remaining cigarette, tapped it slowly on his yellow, nicotined thumbnail, and struck a match. Puffing contentedly on his fag, he looked up from his cards and gazed round the vault, taking in the picture of the pasty-faced men in their flat caps and woollen mufflers which they wore like a uniform.

'Eeh, what a bloody fine bunch o' working men they all are,' Tommy said.

'Whadda you mean? Working men! Most of 'em are on the dole!' said Jimmy.

'Doesn't matter, they're the salt o' the earth. Except for that bastard Len Sharkey over there,' he added quickly as his eye lighted on his hated enemy, guffawing as usual with his mates over some joke or other.

They took a long pull at their pints.

In the main, then, Tommy was happy. A pint, a pal and a bit of peace – that was all he wanted. That wasn't asking too much, was it? But that Sunday night, he had more. It was his lucky night. He was on a winning streak, having just pegged twelve on the cribboard with a double pair royal. No doubt about it. He was well on the way to taking not only the game but the shilling bet that was riding on it. Mind you, Jimmy Dixon was a real Muggins and wasn't quick enough to add up even his own score, never mind Tommy's. But what the hell! Friend or no friend, a shilling was a shilling in this rotten old world. He downed the rest of his pint and stood up.

'My twist, Jimmy. Same again?'

Jimmy drained his own glass. 'Aye, ta. Don't mind if I do, Tommy. And see if you can't buy me a bit o' bleeding luck while you're at it.'

Tommy pushed his way through the men standing at the bar.

'When you're ready, Tubby. Pint o' usual for me and a pint o' bitter for Jimmy there. Oh aye . . . and ten Weights as well. Must have a smoke for the mornin'.'

'Right, Tommy. Pinta best mild, pint o' bitter, an' ten Weights. That'll be one and eleven altogether,' Tubby Ainsworth said, drawing the pints.

Tommy paid up, collected the beers and his cigarettes and returned to his seat at the card table.

'All the best!' said Jimmy.

'Bottoms up!' rejoined Tommy.

It was at that precise moment that his peace of mind was shattered. As he tilted his head back to drink, he saw through the bottom of his glass the shawled figure of Lily Goodhart hurrying towards him.

'Bugger it! Don't turn round now, Jimmy, but have you seen who's coming?'

'No. How the bloody hell could I?'

'It's Lily Goodhart, me next-door neighbour. And I know why she's here.'

As Lily threaded her way through the unyielding male bodies, she was greeted by various cat-calls.

'Women not allowed in the vault!'

'Men only in 'ere.'

'Go and fill your bloody jug at the snug.'

'S'all right,' she said. 'I just want a word with Tommy there.'

She went up to the card table. Tommy put his pint down.

'Yes, what is it, Lily?' he asked irritably – put out by her appearance in the vault and the fact that all eyes were on him. Especially those of Sharkey, who seemed to be enjoying yet another horse-laugh with his cronies.

'It's time, Tommy,' she said in an urgent whisper. 'It's Kate. I think you'd better come now. Her waters broke and the pains are coming faster. I don't think it'll be long now.'

'Bloody hell. No peace for the wicked – not even in the bloody pub. But what do they want me for? Kate told me to bugger off out of the way.'

'I think it's in case there's complications, like, and they have to call the doctor.'

'A doctor! I can't afford no two quid for a bloody doctor. Besides, I've heard they kill more than they cure with their bloody instruments.'

'I'm only telling you what they told me.'

'All right, Lily. I'll finish this game first. Mind you, I can't see what bloody use I'll be. She'd be better off if I just stop where I am. How long's the midwife been there?'

'Over half an hour. I think she's doing her best to hurry things along, like. Anyroad, Tommy, I'd better get out of the vault afore these men here chuck me out. But I promised to come and fetch you. Shall I wait for you?'

'Look, Lily, there's no bloody need for that. I've said I'll come when I've finished the game, and I will.'

'All right. If you say so.'

As if for protection, she pulled her shawl tightly around her shoulders and hurried out.

Tommy returned to his card game, but his heart was no longer in it. Lily's visit had put him off and he lost his concentration. He missed an obvious run of four and several other chances on the next deal. Jimmy Dixon wasn't as daft as Tommy thought and was quick to take advantage of the distraction. He soon caught up, and after a few more deals beat Tommy with a final flush of five, giving him a total of 121. Jimmy picked up his winnings and put them in his pocket.

'Hard luck, Tommy. I really thought you'd beat me there. Never mind, old son. Have another pint to wet the new baby's head. Pint o' best mild, isn't it?'

'Shouldn't really, Jimmy – the baby's not been born yet. But . . . er . . . go on then. Y've twisted me arm. Better make this the last one, though.'

Deep down he was feeling queasy at the thought of having to listen to Kate in the throes of childbirth.

Jimmy came back with their pints and they each took a long swig.

'Ah!' sighed Jimmy, smacking his lips. 'There's nowt to beat a drop o' good ale!' He leaned forward and adopted a confidential tone. 'How many kids have y'had now, Tommy?'

'I think I've bloody well lost count. Let's see.' He counted off on his fingers. 'There's our Flo, Polly, Jim, Sam and Les. How many's that?'

'Five.'

'That's right. Two girls and three boys and this new one'll make six if the little bugger makes it. But I'd best be off, Jimmy. Better go and see what's happening, I suppose. With any luck it'll all be over by the time I get there.'

He swallowed the rest of his pint and got to his feet.

'Thanks for the beer, Jimmy – though I won't say thanks for that bloody game o'crib. I'll win that bob back from you next time, you'll see.'

He headed towards the door to a chorus of ribald remarks from the Dalton Arms regulars.

'About time you was castrated, Tommy!'

'Y'ought to get yourself doctored!'

'Y'want to tie a bleeding knot in it, Tommy!'

Tommy turned to face the source of the last remark.

'And you want to keep that big mouth of yours shut, Sid Hardcastle, afore I fill it for you.'

The speaker went quiet, because he knew that,

although Tommy looked harmless enough, being only a small, bald man with knock knees, he had a vicious temper and was perfectly capable of carrying out his threat. He hadn't worked and survived in Smithfield Market for thirty-odd years without picking up something about the art of pub brawling.

As Tommy was going out of the door, Len Sharkey said in a loud, sarcastic voice:

'I don't know about *Tommy*. Tom-cat's more like it, eh, lads?'

His cronies rewarded him with a loud belly-laugh. Encouraged, Len added:

'Catholics are all the same round here . . . breed like bleeding rabbits.'

Tommy stopped, turned, and walked over to Sharkey. He looked up into the other man's face.

'Whadda you mean by all that? Tom-cat, Catholics and bleeding rabbits?'

'Piss off home, Tommy. I don't want no trouble. We was only joking.'

'Sharkey, you're full o' Malarkey. And I wanna tell you summat. We've got some big fellas in the market.'

'Oh, yeah. So what?'

'I've never come across a fella as big as you. You must be over six foot.'

'Six foot three,' answered Len proudly.

'I've never come across a fella as big as you, with so much muscle. I take me hat off to you,' Tommy continued, whipping off his cap.

Len preened himself.

'But you must be the only fella in Collyhurst with no balls.'

Then, without warning, in one swift, flowing motion, he nutted Sharkey with the skill of Dixie Dean heading one home for Everton. Len went sprawling across the floor, and it was a good job there was sawdust down, for his nose began to pour blood as he lay there. There was a momentary pause, and then all hell broke loose. Len's mates began shouting abuse – 'You mad bastard!' 'You crazy sod!' – as they helped their leader to his feet. Jimmy Dixon was over at Tommy's side in a flash, restraining him from further action.

'Calm down, Tommy lad. Take it easy, mate,' Jimmy said.

'Right!' shouted Tubby Ainsworth, pointing to Tommy and Len Sharkey. 'You're both banned! I won't have no fighting in my pub. Now bugger off home, Tommy, for Christ's sake. They want you over there!'

'It's OK, Tubby,' said Jimmy, trying to cool the situation. 'He's going now. I'll see he gets on his way.'

He walked Tommy to the door.

'You'd best get home, Tommy lad, and get someone to see to that cut on top o'your head. But, by God, that Len Sharkey's been asking for a good hiding for some time now. He'll not be so free and easy with his mouth in future.'

'He'd no right saying all that, Jimmy. All that stuff about Catholics. I'd have murdered the get if y'hadn't stopped me. And now Tubby's banned me. Me – one of his best customers.'

Jimmy laughed. 'Banned you, be buggered! If Tubby banned everybody who'd had a fight in the vault, he'd have an empty pub. No, take it from me. He'll have forgotten it by tomorrow. I'll call over after, Tommy, and see how you've got on.'

Leaving the smoky atmosphere behind, Tommy emerged from the pub into the Collyhurst evening air. It was half past nine and not quite dark, but already the lamplighter was going his rounds down Collyhurst Road.

Tommy crossed over the road, cursing Len Sharkey for making him lose his rag like that. With his strange, shambling gait, he hurried along by the side of the River Irk – known simply in the district as the Cut.

As he approached the iron bridge which led to the Dwellings, he spotted Polly playing 'Queenie-o-Co-Co, who's got the ball?' with a lot of other kids. 'See I haven't got it!' 'See I haven't got it!' they choresed as they offered alternate hands for inspection.

'Come on, our Polly,' he ordered. 'Time you was in. And bring Jim with you. It's past his bedtime.'

'Aw, Dad. Can't we stay out a bit? S'only early.'

'No you can't. Up you go.'

'Yes, but Dad . . .'

'Will y'do as you're told, y'cheeky little sod. And less of your ole buck. Now get up them bloody stairs afore I land you one. It's time you packed up them bloody daft games. You're thirteen and you'll be starting work next year. You should be giving help at home, not playin' out here. Your mother's not well, y'know.'

'Yeah. I know. She's got that stomach ache again. It's through eating all them kippers on Friday. But we're out 'ere 'cos they chucked us out when the nurse came. Sam and Les are already in bed, though.'

'I should bloody well think so. But now it's time the two o' you was in. So up the Molly Dancers!'

Reluctantly, Polly collected her ball and her younger brother. Squeezing past a courting couple who were at it on the steps, she followed her dad up the stairwell until they reached the landing and the lobby which led to their tenement – number 6, Collyhurst Buildings.

★　★　★

The door was ajar. Inside, they found Lily stoking up a big fire at the black-leaded kitchen range. Flo, the eldest daughter, was filling a large iron kettle from the tap in the corner of the room.

'It's a boy, Dad,' announced Flo. 'Seven pounds. And he's lovely.'

'Oh aye,' sighed Tommy, resignedly. 'I thought it might be a boy the way your mother's been eating all that apple pie lately.'

'How d'you mean?' asked Lily.

'Well, fancying apple pie means a boy, and cherry pie, a girl. S'well known, that, in Lancashire. But by God, another boy, eh! Another bloody mouth to feed! That's six kids we've got.'

Nurse McDonagh, all bustling and businesslike, appeared from the bedroom carrying a brown paper parcel, which she thrust into the fire.

'What's that? It's not the baby, is it?' asked Jim, his little face aghast.

'Never you mind what it is, young man,' Nurse McDonagh said. 'And no, it's no' the baby. The very idea, indeed!'

She turned to Tommy.

'So the prodigal son has come back to the fold, eh? And you look as if you've been in the wars, as well.'

She fished in her medical bag, pulled out a small bottle of iodine, and applied a little to Tommy's wound. Tommy winced.

'It's only a scratch. Not worth botherin' about.'

'Dinna fash yoursel'. I'm no botherin' that much. If you daft men want to punch each other's heads at night, it's no skin off my nose. More like skin off your heid, I'm thinkin'!'

'You're a hard woman, Nurse.'

'Ye've got to be in my job. But you took your time gettin' here. Timed it just right, didn't you? Like the last time – arrivin' home when it's all over. Typical man! You think when you've put your wife in the puddin' club, that's you out. Your contribution to the birth process!'

'Now, you know very well I'd have been no use to you. I know nowt about bringing kids into the world, except that you need a lotta hot water.'

'Aye, and I suppose you think that's for mixing with your whisky to make yoursel' a hot toddy! All things considered, though, I think maybe you were better taking yoursel' off to the pub and keepin' outa ma way.'

'But how's Kate? How's me wife doing? Is she all right?'

'You've no need to worry on that score. I thought at one point we might need the doctor, but everything's turned out fine, and mother and son are both doing well. You've got a strong, healthy wife there. She had her baby without any fuss – hardly made a sound. The only noise was from your son, and judging by the strength of his lungs, there's not much wrong with him either.'

'I know I picked a good 'un when I picked Kate,' he said proudly.

'Well, anyway, I've cleaned things up as best I can. And now I suppose you'll be wanting to go in and see the bairn. I don't see any way I can stop you.'

'I should bloody well hope not,' he said indignantly.

'I don't suppose there's any harm as long as you don't go breathing your beer fumes and germs all over the baby. Not too much noise, either,' she said, looking pointedly at the younger end of the family. 'Now, I'm awa'. I've got another case over the road – a lot more urgent than yours. I'll call in again tomorrow morning to see how things are. See that Kate gets a good sleep tonight.'

She began packing up her mysterious black bag, and Polly asked:

'Is that what you brought the baby in?'

The nurse gave her an old-fashioned look, hesitated, looked as if she were going to say something, then changed her mind.

'In a way it is, I suppose.'

'We had a listen at your bag before, and we didn't hear no baby in there,' said Polly.

'Don't be daft,' said Jim. 'Everyone knows that babies are brought by an angel. Don't you know nowt, Polly?'

'How d'you make that out?' asked Polly.

'Well, when one person dies, another one gets born.'

'Straight away?'

'No, stupid. When a person dies, he has to go up to this room in the sky where he has to wait for, I dunno, maybe a hundred years until it's his turn to get born again.'

'I dinna ken what they're teachin' 'em at school these days,' said Nurse McDonagh, shaking her head.

Tommy gave the nurse a sealed envelope.

'Ta very much for all you've done, Nurse. Though I think we should be getting a discount for quantity.'

'That'll be the day – when a Scotswoman gives a discount!' And with those words, Nurse Flora McDonagh departed from the scene.

Less than a minute after she'd left, a little voice from the second bedroom piped up:

'Dad, can we come out? We want to see the new baby.'

'You little buggers should be asleep,' said Tommy. 'Not listening to all that's goin' on out here.'

'Go on, Tommy. Don't be so miserable,' said Lily Goodhart reprovingly. 'Let 'em see the baby. It's not every day that they get a little brother.'

'Aye, I suppose you're right, Lily. Go on then. We may as well all go in together – though it'll be a bit of a squash in that little bedroom. All right then, you little buggers. You can come out. But just for a minute.'

In a wink the two young 'uns, Sam and Les, were out of the bedroom, dressed in their everyday shirts which served also as their nightwear.

'Right!' said Tommy. 'In we all go.'

He knocked gently on the front bedroom door and called softly:

'Kate, is it all right if we come in?'

All held their breath to catch the answer.

'Yes. S'all right, Tommy. You can come in now,' said Kate.

He opened the door quietly, and all seven of them traipsed into the room and gathered round the bed. Kate was sitting up, smiling and looking radiantly happy, whilst the newborn baby – oblivious to all the fuss going on around it – slept soundly in the large wooden drawer which served as a cradle.

'How do, Kate,' said Tommy. 'How y'feeling?'

'Oh, I'm not so bad, Tommy. Not so bad. But what's that stuff on your head? You've not been fighting again, have you?'

'No. S'nowt to bother about. I bumped into Len Sharkey, that's all. You're the one to worry about – not me.'

'Did you pay the midwife, Tommy?'

'Aye, I did that. Ten bob as usual. Is that right?'

'Aye, that's right. Same price as last time. Well, what d'you think? Another boy, eh?'

'Aye, another boy,' he replied, with feigned brightness. 'That's four we've got now. And this one's just as welcome. Just as welcome. He's got to be fed. We'll look after him and see he's all right.'

He took a peek at his son but couldn't think of anything to say. To him, all babies looked alike. Wrinkly and red-faced – like miniature Chelsea pensioners without their uniforms. But he felt he had to say something.

'Well, he seems to have everything,' was the best he could manage. 'It's bloody marvellous. He's even got fingernails! Did y'put a penny on his belly button?'

'Aye, I did that.'

'What's that for?' asked Flo.

'That's to flatten it,' said Kate.

'A bit like when they put pennies on a dead person's eyes,' said Polly.

'Well, not quite . . .' replied Kate.

Meanwhile, the three boys stood silent, taking in the scene: the big brass bedstead, the heavy dressing table with the swivel mirror, the large jug and basin, and the huge mahogany wardrobe with Dad's pot hat on the top – the one he took down for funerals.

'Do you want to see your new baby brother?' Kate asked.

They nodded, and Kate folded back the blanket a little to give them a better view.

'He looks like a big red tomato,' observed Jim. 'Though on second thoughts, p'raps he's more like a beetroot.'

Jim had recently started a Saturday-morning job helping Joe Ogden, the greengrocer.

Sam and Les looked on. They weren't too keen on a new baby sharing their things and their space, but as compensation they wondered if they could make use of this tiny doll-like creature as a prop in one of their games.

'Are we goin' to keep him? And will he be able to play out with us?' asked young Sam.

He had in mind the idea of using the baby on Guy Fawkes night, not only to augment their collection of money but as a possible real-life effigy to put on the fire.

'Course we can keep him. He's ours now,' said Kate. 'And he'll play out with you when he's a bit bigger.'

'I think he's got your hair, Tommy,' Lily announced.

'Well, some bugger has,' said Tommy. 'But it doesn't matter about his hair as long as he's not skenny-eyed or hare-lipped or anything like that.'

'I think he's the loveliest baby I've ever seen,' said Polly. 'What are you going to call 'im, Mam? What about Rupert? That's a lovely name; it's the name of a prince, you know.'

'We don't want no princes in this house,' said Kate. 'Though I really haven't had no time to think about names much. I usually leave that to your father. What do you think, Tommy?'

'I've named them all up to now,' replied Tommy. 'But I think we've just about run through the Litany o' Saints. So I don't mind what you call him as long as it's not summat like Marmaduke or Archibald . . . or Winston like that bastard Winston Churchill.' Tommy had never forgiven Churchill for the Dardanelles.

'What do you think, our Flo?' asked Kate.

'Well, the boss at work has ever such a lovely name,' said Flo. 'His name's William Armstrong . . . And then there's that poet they learned us about in school – William Wordsworth, I think he was called. It was a poem all about daffodils. "I wandered lonely as a cloud" – summat like that. Why don't we call him William? It's ever such a nice name.'

'Aye. I like the sound o' that,' said Kate. 'It's got a nice ring to it.' She pronounced the full title in her best imitation of a posh-voiced flunkey announcing an important dignitary at a royal banquet: 'William Hopkins! Yes, I like it,' she declared. 'As long as he doesn't get called "Willy" or "Billy".'

'I don't like the name William,' Polly proclaimed petulantly. 'I think it sounds dead sissy. And anyroad, if you're going t'give the names of poets and all that, what about Rupert Brooke? He's a poet too, isn't he? They're learning us a poem by him at school. Something about "If I should die . . ." '

'Oh, bloody hell,' said Tommy, putting both hands on top of his head. 'She's got death on the brain! The kid's only just been born and already she's talking about dying.'

'Now, I've told you before,' said Kate. 'We don't want no Ruperts and no princes in this house.'

Flo said: 'Besides, he'd get called Rupie.'

'Yeah, loopy Rupie!' added Jim.

Polly pouted. 'Everybody's always laughing at me in this rotten house! I'm fed up, I am. If Flo says anything, oh yes, that's all right. But not if I say it. Everybody just picks on me.'

'Will you stop causing trouble, our Polly. You're an awkward little bugger. You should learn to keep *that* shut,' said Tommy, indicating his mouth.

'Then why can't we give him two names?' Polly insisted, not to be talked down. 'What's wrong with Rupert William?'

'Listen, you little madam,' retorted Kate. 'Two names is for toffs. All our kids have just the one name and that's enough. Anyroad, there'll be no more arguments. It's settled. His name's William and that's the end of it.'

The others gave murmurs and nods of agreement. Not that their opinion mattered once Kate had made up her mind.

'There's something none of you have noticed,' Lily declared. 'Today is Sunday, and you know what they say about a Sunday child: *The child who is born on the Sabbath*

16

day/Is lucky and happy and good and gay.'

'P'raps he's going to win Littlewoods or the Irish Sweepstake,' said Tommy.

'I think you may be right,' said Kate. 'I spilt some sugar the other day, and that's a sure sign that we're going to have some good luck.'

'Let's hope so,' Tommy said. 'Now then, the nurse said we wasn't to tire you, Kate. So I think that'll do for tonight. All told, it's been a very busy day – you might even say a productive day, especially for you. But not a bad night's work, eh – even if I say so myself!'

'Cheeky bugger,' retorted Kate.

He looked at the big alarm clock on the dressing table, and, thinking about the market, continued: 'Anyroad, I've got to be up at four o'clock tomorrow morning. Someone's got to earn the money now we've another mouth to feed. So come on, you lot. Say good night and off to bed with you.'

After their good nights, they all left. The three boys got into their big bed, top and tail fashion, in the other bedroom, and the two girls climbed into theirs in the same room.

'I'll be on my way now, Tommy,' Lily said. 'Me family will be thinking I've fell in the Cut. I haven't seen 'em all day. I'll call in again tomorrow to see how she is and if there's anything she wants.'

'Ta very much, Lily, for all you've done,' Tommy said. 'We couldn't ask for a better neighbour. You're a brick . . . the best.'

'Oh, don't mention it, Tommy,' she said. 'That's what neighbours are for.'

When everyone had left, Tommy decided to go on to the front landing of the Buildings for a last smoke. It was a bright night and the Cut was bathed in moonlight, giving it a beautiful romantic aspect. Lighting his fag, he looked out towards Collyhurst Road. It was closing time at Tubby Ainsworth's and he could hear the last customers shouting their slurred good nights. From below, he heard a familiar voice calling him. It was Jimmy Dixon, about to go into his ground-floor tenement.

'Aye, aye, Tommy. How did you get on?'

'Oh, not so bad. I've had another boy.'

'Another boy, eh? It must be all that bloody Boddies you've been supping. We'll have a pint o' two to celebrate in Tubby's tomorrow night. G'night, mate.'

'G'night, Jimmy.'

Another son, Tommy said to himself. God, look at these here hovels – stone-flagged floors and walls dripping with damp. Three rooms and a lavatory between two adults and six kids. Not much of a place to bring 'em up. The landlords have a bloody cheek charging us five bob a week rent for these holes. They slung these tenements up in the 1880s and called 'em artisans' dwellings. Well, I don't know what the bloody artisans thought about 'em but I know what this here bloody market porter thinks about 'em. Slums for the working class, that's what they are. Only fit for the bloody cockroaches that share the dump with us.

Then there's the Cut over there. Looks a bit of all right in the moonlight. Like a picture postcard. But it's nothing but a bloody sewer, and everyone round here dumps their shit in it – especially that dye works up the road. 'Is it any wonder the kids round 'ere get scarlet fever with all them bloody colours,' he added aloud, seeing the irony of it.

But this is no bloody place to rear a family, he thought. As for this latest little bugger . . . What chance does he stand here in Collyhurst? I think we'll have to flit. There's got to be something better than this, though I don't know where.

He ground out his fag and went in to get some sleep.

Chapter One

A Mixed Infant

Billy was six and he knew how to whistle. He had many other accomplishments, of course: he could read, tell the time, throw stones, catch a ball, and climb the railway fence. But his whistle was the thing he was most proud of; he simply puckered up his lips, blew, and out came the one and only tune he knew: 'The Stars and Stripes Forever', which he'd heard on his Dad's HMV wind-up gramophone. 'Whistling Rufus', Mam called him. Only that morning when he'd been on their veranda lavatory, she'd called through the door:

'Come on out, Whistling Rufus – come an' wet your whistle.'

She had a funny way of saying things like that. Why, at breakfast, when he was eating his Quaker Oats, she'd said:

'That's right. Get that down you; it'll stick to your ribs.'

The idea of all that gooey porridge clinging to the inside of his ribs didn't appeal to him at all. But then her list of wise sayings was endless:

'Crusts make your hair curly.'

'Fish makes you brainy.'

'Stew puts a lining on your stomach.'

All true, of course, because Mam was forty-seven and knew everything.

Whistling Sousa's march, he set out for school and soon crossed the bridge over the Cut, which that morning was flowing a sickly yellow. He waited on the edging of Collyhurst Road and, like he'd been told, looked both ways, finding the speed of the horses and carts easy to judge but not so the post office vans which came tearing out of the recently built depot. He made it safely to the other side, however, and stopped just outside the Rechabite Hall and looked up at the big sign-board emblazoned with the words:

ORDER OF RECHABITES: FOUNDED 1835
TEMPERANCE MISSIONARY HALL

Billy thought about the truly wonderful Christmas party they'd had in there the previous night. But at the same time he felt a twinge of guilt on account of the sin he'd committed by attending it.

Now, it was common knowledge amongst the Catholics of Collyhurst that the Rechabites – despite the fame of their kazoo and comb-and-paper band – were misguided heretics who were bound to go straight to hell for not believing in the right religion. At Holy Mass only yesterday, hadn't Father O'Brien, the parish priest, warned everyone about the dangers of false religions and the worship of false gods. From his pulpit, he had thundered:

'Remember, my dear brethren, that God has said, "Thou shalt not have strange gods before me!" Any Catholic who takes part in the worship or prayers of a false religion is guilty of a grievous sin and will be doomed to hell for all eternity.'

On the other hand, it was common knowledge amongst the people of Collyhurst that the Rechabites organised an annual children's Christmas party of breathtaking magnificence. For those children who were lucky enough to get a ticket, the party was undoubtedly a never-to-be-forgotten affair. And Billy had a ticket! Given to him by Dad! It was the equivalent of a Cup Final ticket for an adult, and how his dad had come by it was anybody's guess – certainly not for any feat of sobriety. Perhaps he'd won it in a game of crib, or found it outside Tubby Ainsworth's pub. But Billy wasn't interested in the whys and wherefores – he had a ticket, and that was good enough for him!

The party was due to start at six o'clock. Before Billy was allowed to put a foot outside the tenement, Mam washed him and scrubbed him until he shone like a polished red apple. Then on with his best jersey, navy-blue trousers with striped elastic belt, long stockings with the colourful tops, and finally his black leather boots which Dad had buffed and buffed until they were gleaming. Mam issued dire warnings about not losing the cup and saucer he had to take, and about being on his best behaviour. At last a spotless, luminous Billy set out with a final piece of advice ringing in his ears:

'Eat their cakes an' jelly, son,' Mam had said. 'But try not to join in their prayers and hymns if you can help it. That's a good boy.'

Over at the Rechabite Hall, ten tables had been laid with colourful paper covers, serviettes, crackers and party hats – the latter being the well-made, expensive variety – not the cheap, flimsy kind. The eyes of all the children, however, were focused not on the tables but on the open kitchen doors through which they could see the waiting banquet. Around the sides of the hall stood the Rechabite Sunday-school staff smiling in welcome but dressed in sombre clothes as if going to a funeral.

So that's what heretics look like, thought Billy. But what's making them smile like that?

Seated at the tables, sixty boisterous kids – nearly wetting themselves with excitement – all looking unnaturally clean and laundered, and holding a motley collection of crockery of different shapes, sizes and colours, waited impatiently for the festivities to begin. At six fifteen, a tall, bearded gentleman in a black suit – not unlike the pictures of Abraham Lincoln that Billy had seen at school – appeared on the stage, clapped his hands for attention and intoned in his best church voice:

'It does my heart good to see so many bright and shining little faces here before me. The Lord Jesus has said: "Suffer the little children to come unto me." And this is what we are doing tonight, for the dear little children of Collyhurst have indeed come unto us to celebrate the birth of our Lord and Saviour, Jesus Christ. But before we begin our feast, my dear children, let us stand, bow our heads and thank the great Lord above for his munificence.'

For the young listeners, this speech was not only incomprehensible but unbearably long, for they were eager to get on with the serious business in hand, namely the dispatch of all that seductive food sitting out there in the kitchen. The kids of Collyhurst, however, had learned a pragmatism that John Dewey would have been proud of. They knew which side their bread was buttered on, and if to get at all those lovely comestibles they had to take part in a few curious rituals, so be it.

Billy was worried, though, about that word 'suffer' the Lincoln character had used. He'd met the word before, in 'Suffered under Pontius Pilate', and he wasn't too happy about what these Rechabites had in mind.

All present bowed their heads. Surreptitiously, Billy made a cross with his two index fingers, like he'd seen in a Dracula picture, to ward off evil spirits.

The Rechabite intoned solemnly:

'O let Israel bless the Lord: let him praise and exalt him above all for ever. We give thanks to Thee, O Lord most holy, Father almighty, God everlasting, for this bounteous food which Thou hast placed before us in celebration of the birth of Thy son, Jesus Christ. Impart unto us, we beseech Thee, O Lord, the grace to quench within ourselves the fire of evil desires; grant that no flame of guilt lay waste the souls of Thy servants here present tonight. Amen.'

This strange incantation was enough for Billy. Lucifer had been summoned up as the unseen guest.

But now the food was brought on, and any thoughts of Lucifer were temporarily suspended. For some time, the only sound in the hall was kids chomping their way through mountains of food. And what food! They had never seen such a spread! Potted meat sandwiches, quickly gobbled up, followed by mince pies, chocolate cake and a choice of three kinds of jelly – the whole lot being washed down with copious quantities of sweet, milky tea served by the funereal Rechabites from large metal tea-pots.

When the repast had been devoured, it became time to pay the piper, and the price was the singing of hymns – Rechabite hymns and only just short of devil-worship. The kazoo band assembled on stage and began to tune up like the Hallé Orchestra. A large grubby chart containing the words of the heretical hymns was rolled out on display. The band struck up with its tinny zuzzing sound and they were off. With great gusto, the Rechabites and their followers sang out, their voices ringing to the rafters.

The first one, 'Stand up! Stand up for Jesus', sounded

particularly depraved, but there followed others equally wicked, like 'Fight the Good Fight' and 'Tell me the old, old story'. As not a single one of these had ever been heard in St Patrick's Church, Billy became more and more convinced that his soul was turning blacker and blacker with every note he sang.

There was a temporary respite from all this, however, when silent films were shown on an 8 mm projector, featuring celebrities like Charlie Chaplin, Harold Lloyd and Buster Keaton. The memory of the hymn-singing episode was soon lost in laughter at the antics of Charlie and the deadpan face of Buster.

Like any good production, the party had a finale. An authentically dressed Father Christmas ho-hoed his way into the hall and proceeded to give out presents of all kinds of games and toys. The fact that they were distributed by a sinful Rechabite Santa – or was that Satan? – was irrelevant since they were lavish beyond the Collyhurst kids' wildest dreams. The red-robed figure must have been mad. With wild abandon he handed out boxed games of ludo, lotto, draughts, tiddlywinks, and snakes and ladders.

But like all the other delights that evening, they had to be paid for. This time with the prayers of this misguided religion.

What would Father O'Brien say if he could see me now? thought Billy. He could hear the priest's voice echoing in his head: 'Prayers of a false religion . . . grievous sin . . . doomed to hell for ever.' Meanwhile, the staff had lined up on the stage – like the cast at a pantomime taking its final bows – for the concluding ceremony.

Now the sinfulness of the hymn-singing was compounded by the recitation of Rechabite versions of well-known prayers, like their unauthorised phrasing of the Lord's Prayer which contained various words different from those Billy was used to: 'Our Father *Which* art in heaven' instead of the orthodox and correct 'Our Father *Who* art in heaven'. And sin of sins – surely the work of Old Nick himself – there was a postscript at the end, which instead of finishing at 'deliver us from evil. Amen' actually went on with 'For Thine is the kingdom, the power and the glory, For ever and ever. Amen.' As Billy uttered this final sinful supplement, he felt sure that he'd sold his soul to the devil for a set of snakes and ladders.

Maybe he had. But then it really was a very good set.

Now Billy awoke from his reverie and continued his journey. At Dalton Street, he was joined by his two best friends, Teddy Smith and Joey Murray.

'Hiya, Billy,' said Teddy. 'Goin' to school?'

'Course I am!' replied Billy. 'D'you think I'm wagging it or somethin'?'

Teddy's pants had more patches than pant, his shoes were scuffed dusty grey, there were great spuds in his stockings, and he had a snotty nose. Just the same, he was well-liked – after all, he was a very good fighter and a very good stone-thrower.

Joey Murray was better dressed because his dad had a job with a pension at the new post office depot and consequently had a position to keep up.

'What a stink!' said Teddy as they passed the Phillips rubber works. 'It's nearly as bad as the Cut.'

'Aye, but not as bad as the boneworks over there,' remarked Joey.

'I wonder what do they do at the boneworks,' said Teddy suspiciously.

'Dunno,' said Billy. 'But me mam says they make glue out of bones.'

'Whose bones? They don't use dead people, do they?' Teddy asked in horror.

'No, I think they use mainly horses. But I suppose they must use people sometimes – if there's a shortage,' said Billy, always a mine of information.

They passed under the big railway arches at Aspin Lane.

'I played in the Cut yesterday,' said Teddy. 'It was dead smashin'. We was all throwing stones at the rats. I hit one a beauty.'

'I'll bet y'had it for your Sunday dinner,' said Joey.

'Oh no we didn't,' replied Teddy defiantly. 'Me mam got a sheep's head from the butcher's, so there!'

'Oh yeah,' replied Billy. 'Well, me and our Les climbed over the railway fence an' went picking coke an' cinders on the tip. An' after, we followed a cart out o' the gas works; it was piled up with coke – warm an' steaming, like. We picked up some really big pieces what fell off. We got nearly half a bag for me mam. But me dad wouldn't half belt us if he knew we'd been on the tip.'

At Sharp Street Ragged School, Teddy asked:

'Why do they call it the Ragged School, I wonder?'

'P'raps it's because all the kids who go there are ragged,' said Billy.

'Like you, eh, Teddy?' said Joey.

'Don't be such a cheeky sod, Joey, or I'll belt you one,' said Teddy, giving him a friendly cuff.

'Hey, I saw a dead body yesterday,' said Billy. 'In a coffin.'

'Did yer heck,' said Teddy. 'Where?'

'In the Fannings' toffee shop. It was their lad; I think he'd swallowed a huge tube o' summat. They said he'd died of a tube o' colossal. That's what it sounded like,

27

anyroad. He looked dead beltin' in his coffin'; he was smiling, like, as if he'd just heard a good joke, an' he was dressed up in altar boy's clothes. Funny, that, 'cos they're not Catholics.'

'I wonder what it's like bein' dead,' said Teddy. 'I'll bet it's smashin'. Like being in the pictures all the time an' watchin' Mickey Mouse an' with as many toffees as you can eat.'

'You might have to go to purgatory first,' said Joey, 'if you've done a lotta sins.'

'How long for?' asked Teddy.

'About ten billion billion years,' replied Billy pessimistically. 'That's what Miss Gibson says, anyroad.'

At Dantzig Street, there was a newspaper boy yelling in a street-seller's sing-song voice: 'News! Latest News! Hitler next German Chancellor! Gordon Richards now champion jockey! Loch Ness Monster seen again!'

Teddy couldn't help having a go at the paper boy's strident call:

'News! Latest new-ew-ews! Donald Duck dead!' he bawled in an uncannily accurate imitation.

They arrived at the Salvation Army hostel, where they crouched down with knees bent to peer into the basement dining hall at the down-and-outs slurping their soup at the long wooden tables. There was a powerful pong of stew and steaming underpants and singlets coming through the open windows.

The three boys poked their heads in and shouted: 'Get your hair cut!'

Immediately one of the derelicts left his place at the table and came running towards the window, bawling:

'Get away with you. Cheeky little buggers.'

They ran off quickly up Angel Meadow, chanting as

they did so a rhyme that was compulsory for Collyhurst children passing that way:

'*Jack, Jack, turn around/Turn your face to the Burial Ground.*'

'Jack' was the revolving air-vent on the top of the CWS Tobacco factory, whilst the Burial Ground was St Michael's Flags – an ancient parish cemetery now being used as a recreation ground.

'Are there any people buried under there?' asked Teddy, pointing to the stone flags now worn smooth by the feet of two centuries.

'Miss Gibson said there are thousands and thousands,' said Billy. 'They all died of some collar disease.'

'How do you die of a collar disease?' asked Teddy, anxiously fingering his neck.

'I dunno. I suppose it's when your collar's too tight. But don't ask me!' said Billy, getting a little impatient. He could see himself being cast in the role of medical consultant just because he'd seen a dead body. 'I don't know everything!'

'Is it haunted, do you think?' asked Teddy nervously.

'Don't be daft, Teddy,' answered Billy. 'Course it is. Must be. I wouldn't come down here on a dark night. Not for anything. You'd see all the ghosts come out moaning an' clutching their collars.'

At the bacon warehouse, they followed their usual routine with the man at the bacon hoist:

'Got any rickers, mister?' Billy called out.

'Got any knickers, mister?' Joey shouted cheekily.

'Here!' said the man, throwing out a whole lot of small, flat pieces of wood which the boys then put between two fingers and clicked like castanets. Rattling their rickers, they turned the corner into Sinclair Street. Straight into trouble!

There, lying in wait for them, was their hated and feared enemy, the skenny-eyed kid. His squint seemed to have given him the distinct advantage of being able to look in two directions at once, like the swivel eyes of a chameleon. He was about thirteen years old, and his close-cropped, basin-barbered head and the area around his mouth were painted with a hideous purple ointment – the standard treatment for ringworm and impetigo at the school clinic. In his hand he held a large catapult, which he pointed at the three youngsters.

'Right, what've you gorr on yer? Empty your pockets or you get this,' he snarled, indicating the fully loaded catapult.

The three boys took out all their prized possessions and placed them at the feet of the highway robber. The booty consisted of one yo-yo, one piece of chalk, one tin soldier, three pairs of rickers, two marbles, a piece of string, and one Uncle Joe's mint ball.

'Whorrabout money? Where's yer money?' the robber demanded.

The three lads shook their heads in reply.

'Right,' the young thug said. 'Next time I see you lot, you berra 'ave money!'

The three victims were then allowed to go on their way. Trembling with fear, they reached the sanctuary of the yard of St Wilfred's Mixed Infants.

The school was accommodated in a large hall which served as a church on Sundays and a place of learning on weekdays – curtains being the only means of separating the classes. As the boys arrived, Sister Helen of the Santa Maria Order was ringing her large handbell to start the school day.

Sister Helen! Beautiful Sister Helen! What mixed

thoughts her name conjured up in Billy's mind. When he had first started school two years previously, he had looked up to her as a saint. Even in appearance she resembled his statue of St Thérèse of Lisieux, the Little Flower of Jesus, which he had won for answering catechism questions.

After his mam, Sister had been his favourite person. When all was said and done, she had been the one who had taught him to read when he was only four; the one who'd called him in from the playground to tell him that he had made such progress in his reading that he was to be promoted. She had said:

'William' – only teachers, priests and others in authority ever gave him his full title – 'you are the first in the class at reading and so you are to come off cards and start on a real book!'

The book in question was all about a family where the dad wore a suit and a tie, the mother a lovely silk dress, and they had a pretty little daughter named Kitty who spent all her time playing with their pedigree Collie dog called Rover. They all lived together in a big house with a large garden in which the dog would run about freely whenever a member of the family gave it the command: '*Run, Rover, run.*' At which they exclaimed to each other with obvious pride: '*Rover is running. See Rover run.*'

Again, Sister had been the one to award him countless religious prizes for his ever-widening religious knowledge, until his drawer at home had become a veritable Aladdin's cave of crucifixes, rosary beads, holy pictures, statues of major saints, holy water fonts, and enough medals to make an African general jealous.

Yes, Billy had placed Sister on a pedestal, and from his lowly position, he had sat at her feet and worshipped her and hung on to her every word.

But the relationship was too fervent and did not – indeed, could not – last. One dark day, he found that his heroine had feet of clay. She used bad language! He found her out in lesson time. She was teaching nursery rhymes, and the children had had all the usual stuff about amorous Georgie Porgie and the neurotic Miss Muffet when Sister turned to a new one which went:

> *Curly locks, Curly locks,*
> *Wilt thou be mine?*
> *Thou shalt not wash dishes*
> *Nor yet feed the swine;*
> *But sit on a cushion*
> *And sew a fine seam,*
> *And feed upon strawberries,*
> *Sugar and cream.*

Billy could not believe his ears. The term 'swine' was a very bad swearword in Collyhurst, as in the expression: 'Bugger off, you little swine.' And here was the holy nun using the 'S' word in a nursery rhyme! Billy had reported the obscenity to Mam, but she had merely laughed and told him not to worry.

Nevertheless, in his mind, the reputation of his heroine had become tarnished. And there was worse to come. His suspicion about her tendency to use profane words was confirmed when towards Christmas he heard her employing yet another 'S' word. She was teaching a carol all about some king called Wenceslas who was having problems with snow and ice. Everything had been going fine until she reached the fifth verse, when he heard her sing:

> *In his master's steps he trod,*
> *Where the snow lay dinted.*

Heat was in the very sod
Which the saint had printed.

Everyone knew that the word 'sod' was a major term of abuse, as in the phrase: 'You cheeky little sod' or the command: 'Sod off!' Once again, Billy reported the matter at home. And once again, Mam laughed and advised him not to worry. He found this very difficult to understand, for on the odd occasion when he had tried using these words himself, he had been given a swift clip round the ear and told not to be such a cheeky little bugger.

In his turn, he let Sister down. In the playground one day he made a disgrace of himself by failing to make it to the lavatory in time. His brother Les had to be called out of class to take a weeping, wet William home for a change of pants. So ended a beautiful relationship.

At the age of six, Billy was promoted to Miss Gibson's class. Sarah Gibson was a dark-haired, frosty-faced spinster about forty years old, her powerful pebble glasses giving her the look of a bullfrog. On her upper lip there was a hint of a moustache, whilst on her cheek she had a large hairy mole. In her class, he devoted nearly all of his time to the hard grind of the three Rs and the acquisition of basic literacy and numeracy. Day by day, he fought his way through book after book and table after table until he had reached the dizzy heights of his five times. In religion, he had completed the initial training for his First Confession and First Communion whilst at the same time battling through the Penny Catechism until his store of religious emblems had grown to the point where he was considering opening a shop specialising in the sale of sacred objects.

There was no doubt, though, that his favourite lessons

were fairy tales and poetry – especially the nonsense verses of Lewis Carroll:

> *'Will you walk a little faster?' said a whiting to a snail,*
> *'There's a porpoise close behind us, and he's treading on*
> *my tail.'*

and:

> *'The time has come,' the Walrus said,*
> *'To talk of many things;*
> *Of shoes – and ships – and sealing wax –*
> *Of cabbages – and kings –*
> *And why the sea is boiling hot –*
> *And whether pigs have wings.'*

They also recited poetry all about 'The house that Jack built' and the maiden all forlorn who had a cow with a crumpled horn.

Came the day when Miss Gibson thought she would round off the afternoon lessons with a half-hour of class entertainment.

'Who would like to make a start?' she asked. 'Will anyone here sing or dance for us?'

Her request was met with complete silence. Most of the children of Collyhurst had learned at an early age the first rule of survival: never volunteer for anything – unless you're going to get paid for it!

'Come along, children,' she said impatiently. 'Surely someone can do something.'

Unable to stand the tension any longer, Billy raised his hand.

'I can dance like Fred Astaire, miss,' he said.

'Come along then, William. Let's see this dance of yours.'

He went to the front of the class and executed a kind of tap dance à la Fred Astaire but more economical, as Billy used only one foot – his right. When he felt that his audience had had enough, he stopped to assess their reactions. He need not have worried. Miss Gibson said:

'That was very good, William. I think it deserves a round of applause. Come along, children.'

The clapping and the admiration which followed were meat and drink to Billy – especially that of June Gladwin, his sweetheart, who sat in the front row watching him admiringly. He sat down triumphantly.

'Now, I'm sure there must be somebody else who wants to do their little party piece,' Miss Gibson said.

Silence, while most of the kids tried to puzzle out what she meant by 'little party piece'.

'Come along now, children. Surely there must be someone else,' she coaxed, sounding a little desperate.

For Billy, this lack of response became unbearable, and he wondered if he should volunteer his services again to solve Miss Gibson's embarrassment. He remembered a little act of his which always caused great laughter and amusement at home with Mam and his two sisters when they were fooling around with the latest craze from America, the Shimmy – danced to a pop song of the day, 'I wish I could shimmy like my sister Kate'.

He raised his hand again.

'I know another dance if you want, miss.'

'Very well, William. You seem to be the only one who's willing to do anything today. Let us see this other dance.'

Billy went out to the front and began his rendering of the Shimmy. This involved raising both arms above his head and wiggling his hips voluptuously in the style of Miss Dorothy Lamour doing a hula-hula dance in the

South Sea Islands. Miss Gibson took one look and frowned.

'Sit down,' she commanded. 'That is disgusting.'

Billy sat down deflated – bewildered that his perform-ance could cause happy laughter in one place and disgust in another. There was no understanding the adult world!

Perhaps the Shimmy was associated with sin in Miss Gibson's mind, because before they finished school that day, she said:

'Remember, children, that tomorrow morning our young curate, Father Conroy, is coming over to hear practice confessions. Remember to have a sin ready to tell him, and don't forget all that I have taught you.'

After the usual prayers, Miss Gibson dismissed the class.

On the way home, Billy and his friends – boys and girls – gathered together in a little secluded corner near the Burial Ground to play their favourite game – Truth or Dare. The boys consisted of Teddy Smith, Joey Murray and Billy, whilst the girls – also a trio – were Patsy McGivern, Wendy Killick and June Gladwin. Patsy McGivern was a brown-eyed belle with dark hair arranged in a neat fringe across her forehead; Wendy a rosy-cheeked girl with fair hair plaited in two long tails; but the greatest beauty of all was June Gladwin, with her gentle blue eyes, her long light-brown tresses which cascaded down her back, and a lovely little smile that could melt a heart of stone. Billy was hopelessly in love with her.

The game started with Joey Murray asking the questions.

'Truth or Dare?' he enquired of Teddy Smith.

'Dare!' said Teddy, always ready for action.

'I dare you to climb up that lamppost, swing round it, spit twice, and then come back to your place.'

Teddy executed the deed with the skill of a Hollywood stuntman and was back in his place in a flash.

'Truth or Dare?' to June Gladwin.

'Truth,' said Billy's heroine.

'Is it true you love Billy?'

'Yes, it's true,' she said, blushing. Billy's heart leapt for joy.

'Truth or Dare?' to Wendy Killick.

'Dare,' she answered.

'I dare you to hug me,' Joey said.

Typically selfish, thought Billy.

Then came his turn:

'Truth or Dare?'

'Dare,' answered Billy boldly.

'I dare you to kiss June Gladwin,' said Joey obligingly.

Billy carried out the command readily by giving June a smacker on the cheek.

'Awwww!' exclaimed the other two girls admiringly. 'He went and did it!'

Joey now turned to Patsy McGivern: 'Truth or Dare?'

'Dare,' she said, not to be outdone by her friend Wendy.

'I dare you to show us your knickers!' said Joey.

A long-drawn-out 'Awwwww!' came from the three girls. Then, 'We're telling on you . . .' And on that shocked note, the game broke up.

Disconsolately, Billy and the other two boys began the journey back together until they reached the forge, where they parted company. Billy wanted to watch the horses being shod, but the other two had to get back to help with babies at home.

Through the open top half of the smithy door, he watched fascinated as the blacksmith and his mate hammered and shaped the white-hot metal into a horseshoe, which they then nailed on to the horse's hoof.

Why, he asked himself, doesn't the poor horse feel the hot shoes being nailed on to its feet?

Still puzzling about this, he set off for home. But as he turned into Collyhurst Road, there was the skenny-eyed kid! For the second time that day! Waylaid by the wretch who seemed to have a grudge against the rest of the world.

'Stop! You're not going past! Worravyer gorrin yer pockets, kid?' he demanded.

'Nothin'. Honest to God. You took everythin' this morning.'

'I told you to get some money for the next time I saw yer, din't I?' he said. 'An' you 'aven't got it, 'ave you? So just for that, you get this.'

He wrestled with Billy and pulled him to the ground. Then, kneeling on him, he took from his pocket a box of ointment – the very same evil-smelling purple ointment which was smeared on his own head and mouth.

'Try some of this, you little bastard,' he snarled, rubbing the foul stuff on Billy's face and head. 'Now let that be a bloody lesson to you, you little sod. Next time, 'ave some money or else you'll get some more!' the juvenile footpad growled.

Released from the bully's grip, Billy wept and wailed his way down the length of Collyhurst Road, causing passers-by to tut-tut in sympathy.

'What've they done to you, son?'

'What's that horrible purple stuff on your face, son?'

'They should set the coppers on to 'em.'

These sympathetic noises only served to make Billy howl the louder. He reached his own door at last and for good effect turned up the volume of his bawling by several decibels as he crossed the threshold. Mam was black-leading the grate with Zebo when she clapped eyes on him. He made such a sorry sight, she almost went berserk.

'Who in God's name has done that to you? And what *is* that awful stuff? Whoever done this should be locked up! If I get my hands on the swine . . .'

Billy never did find out what she'd have done to the skenny-eyed kid because she was too busy putting pans of water on the gas rings. In double-quick time, she began washing his hair so vigorously that she got soap in his eyes and his ears, thus causing a fresh outburst of blubbing. Then it was all over and his natural colour was restored. As a special treat for being so brave, she cut him a very thin slice of Mother's Pride, covering it generously with 'best' butter.

That night the family gathered round the table for their evening tea of 'tater-ash' – Lancashire hot-pot covered over with a golden pastry crust. The conversation turned to the bullying and brigandry of the skenny-eyed kid and the effect it was having on 'our kid', who had now become frightened to walk home from school on his own.

Billy's hero was his brother Jim, who was now thirteen years of age and in his last year at St Chad's Elementary School in Cheetham. Every night after school, he could be seen running home down Collyhurst Road to do his paper round at the Fannings' corner shop. In the evenings however, he had been receiving boxing instruction for some considerable time at the Welcome Boys' Recreation Club just near the Dwellings. Now, when he heard this conversation at the dinner table, his ears pricked up.

'What time does this cock-eyed kid start his bullyin'?' he asked Billy.

'After school lets out – at half past three.'

'Right. We let out at four o'clock. So if I run fast . . .' said Jim, working out some calculation. 'OK. Leave it to me,' he said finally. 'An' I think it's time I started givin' you boxing lessons so you can look after yourself.'

After tea, there occurred a rare event. Dad climbed on to a chair and, reaching up to the very top shelf of the built-in wall cupboard, took down his most prized possession – the one which had a picture of a dog listening to a loudspeaker horn on its lid. His portable gramophone! Nobody, but nobody – except himself – was ever allowed to operate this piece of amazing technology. In fact, the machine was only brought down on very special occasions, for example when Dad was in an unusually happy frame of mind, or alternatively when there had been perhaps a minor family crisis and someone needed to be cheered up. This particular evening seemed to slot into the latter category. The trouble was that there was only a limited selection of records to choose from. But that evening, Dad played the complete repertoire. There was, of course, 'The Stars and Stripes Forever', and in addition Waldteufl's 'Skater's Waltz', Arthur Tracy's street-singer's 'Marta', Harry Richman's 'King for a Day', Sandy Powell's monologues ('Can y'hear me, Mother?') and the top songs of 1934 – recently purchased by Billy's two sisters – 'Sing as We Go' and 'Isle of Capri', both sung by Lancashire's own Gracie Fields.

Billy's favourite was still 'Underneath the Arches' sung by Flanagan and Allen, because it reminded him of that Christmas two years ago and his wonderful first visit to town with Flo and Polly when they had bought the record at Woolworth's. He would never forget that trip – not as long as he lived. He had been just four years of age, and his two sisters had met him after school at the top of Angel Meadow. Together they had walked down Thompson Street and Oldham Street, and the sheer splendour of the scene – the bright lights, the gleaming store windows, the honking of the traffic, and the visit to meet Father Christmas in Lewis's store – had so filled him with awe and wonder that he could only gaze open-mouthed at the fairyland world to which he had been transported. On the way back, they had bought black puddings as a special treat for Mam and Dad, plus, of course, the record. As these thoughts went through his head, Sam and Jim began their Flanagan and Allen act, singing and strolling about the tenement.

Mam brought him back to the land of the living.

'Come on, tough guy. Time for bed.'

The day of drama ended on a happy note. As Mam was tucking him into bed, she asked him the question she always liked to ask:

'What are you?'

And he gave the James Cagney answer she wanted to hear:

'A smart guy and a tough kid!'

'Now,' she said, 'time for sleep. Before you close your eyes, say the prayer our Flo learned you.'

He began, 'Now I lay me down to sleep, I pray the Lord my soul to keep; And if I die before I wake, I pray the Lord my soul to take.' And as a postscript, he added: 'And by the way, God, if I meet the skenny-eyed kid tomorrow, will You please fix it so that I can run faster than him!'

The next day began like any other. The journey to school had become a routine. Billy whistled as he strode across the bridge. His two friends joined him at Dalton Street, and they shouted their usual 'Get yer hair cut' through the Sally Army's window, and collected more rickers from the bacon man at the hoist.

The skenny-eyed kid, however, was nowhere to be seen that morning.

School started off as usual, but on this particular morning, religious instruction was devoted to role-playing confessions with Father Conroy. As Billy watched his adorable June Gladwin go in first, he wondered what sins this lovely blue-eyed creature could possibly have committed. How could an angel sin? The class of children waited their turn to be called to the confessional box – each one anxious not to make a mistake, each one ready with a sin. As the queue went down, their nervousness went up. Like waiting to be shot, thought Billy. Too soon, Miss Gibson called:

'Next – William Hopkins.'

His heart fluttering, Billy entered the confessional box and began:

'Bless me, Father, for I have sinned. This is my first confession.'

'Good boy, William,' said Father Conroy. 'Now the sin part. Tell me a sin.'

'Please, Father, Joey Murray asked Patsy McGivern to show him her knickers.'

There was a long pause before Father Conroy continued. He appeared to be weeping, because he had a handkerchief up to his eyes and he was making little snorting noises. Billy didn't think that Joey's sin was that serious.

'Now, William, tell me *your* sin,' Father Conroy said when he had recovered his composure.

Billy didn't really have another sin ready, as they'd been told to prepare just one for practice. He thought very quickly and came up with:

'Please, Father, I did the Shimmy dance.'

He didn't know what it was, but Father Conroy had started crying again.

Billy began the walk home after school feeling very nervous and apprehensive. This journey back – fraught with danger and possible violence – was beginning to resemble a walk through a dark African forest with wild animals lurking behind every bush. He passed the corner where he had been attacked – now forever associated with assault and evil-smelling ointment. He strode bravely alongside the Cut, whistling his tune to cover up his nervousness – when suddenly, he was there! The skenny-eyed kid! Legs astride, catapult in hand.

'Right, kid,' he rasped. 'Empty yer pockets. Where's yer money?'

Billy was about to answer but didn't get a chance. For without warning, the bully was sent reeling by a blow of the ox-felling kind. Jim stood over him and said:

'If I ever see you near our kid again, I'll give you the hiding of your life. Now scram!'

Jim then continued his run to Fanning's so as not to be late for his paper round.

Now it was the turn of the squint-eyed mugger to howl. But before the young thug could obey the order to scram, Billy got in the final word:

'Listen, kid! That was me brother and he's a boxer, see. You pick on me and you pick on me family.'

And he stepped over the prostrate body and swaggered home, whistling 'The Stars and Stripes Forever'.

The following Monday, Billy set off for school as usual. At Dalton Street he was met – as usual – by Joey Murray. But there was no sign of Teddy Smith.

Later that morning, Sister Helen called a meeting of the whole school and announced that Teddy Smith had drowned in the River Irk whilst throwing stones at the water rats. He had fallen in at a deep part of the Cut, where the swift current had swept him away into the sewers.

On the way home, Joey and Billy stopped at the railings of the Cut. They looked down at the river, which was a dirty grey cesspool of filth and garbage containing rusty bedsteads, decayed mattresses, twisted bicycles and decomposing dogs. But over near the bank, there was a tiny section of the river where the water swirled and eddied in a whirlpool of technicolour dyes, and as it pirouetted over stones and rocks, it seemed to be enjoying a fit of bubbling laughter.

'Poor Teddy,' said Billy. 'I wonder if he's down there watching Mickey Mouse, and with all the toffees he can eat.'

Chapter Two

Honeypot Street

Moira McGurk was giving her favourite lesson on the British Empire.

'You see, boys,' she began. 'When David Livingstone went to Africa, he found that many tribes had not even discovered the wheel – they didn't even have calendars . . .'

'Then how did they know which year it was, miss?' asked Billy.

'Well, William,' she answered. 'They remembered each year by calling it after some big event that had happened in that particular year. For example, if they had had millions of locusts, they might call that "The Year of the Locusts". Now, what do you think they would call it if they had no food?'

This was something the Red Bank kids could relate to.

' "The Hungry Year",' suggested Carrots Campbell.

' "The Year of Famine",' said Billy.

'Good, good,' said Miss McGurk. 'What about a year with no rain?'

' "The Thirsty Year",' said Joey Flewitt.

'Excellent,' said Miss McGurk. 'Or "The Year of the Drought". Now then. What about this year – 1935? What could we call this year?'

The class was stuck for a moment.

'Something that happened in May. You were all given special mugs. Think of King George and Queen Mary,' she prompted.

'Ah, I've got it,' said Henry Sykes triumphantly. ' "Silver Jubilee Year"!'

'Good lad, Henry,' said Miss McGurk. Then, warming to her subject, she asked: 'But what would you call this year for you and your family – personally? I mean, it might be "The Year Your Grandad Came to Stay" or something like that.'

'Please, miss,' said Stan White. 'For our family, it's the year me Dad ran off with our lodger.'

'Yes. Yes,' she said, doubtfully. 'But we don't want to hear about that. You mustn't tell us about that here!'

'Please, miss,' said Billy. 'It's the year we did a flit from the Dwellings to Honeypot Street.'

'You mean a "moonlight flit",' said Stan White.

'No I don't,' replied Billy defiantly. 'We moved in the daylight when everyone could see us.'

'Now stop it, you two!' said Miss McGurk ominously. 'But anyway, nice people don't say "flit", William – when they mean "remove" or "move house". What does "flit" really mean, does anyone know?'

'Please, miss,' said Carrots. 'It's that stuff me mam squirts to kill the bugs in the wallpaper.'

'No, no,' said Miss McGurk. ' "Flit" is what little birds do when they fly lightly from one branch to another.'

Exactly, thought Billy.

The overcrowding in the Collyhurst tenement had become too much. Mam and Dad had talked and talked about it for months. It was time to move. Through her half-sister, Hetty, Mam got wind of an empty house – rent eight and six a week – at number 17, Honeypot Street, Red Bank, on the other side of the railway. She didn't waste any time but went straight over to see the landlord and put down the key-money. It was as simple as that and the house was theirs.

On Wednesday 2 October 1935, Rolls-Royce announced their new 50hp, twelve-cylinder Phantom III saloon costing £1,850. It was also Dad's birthday and the day they upped sticks and began their move. For the whole weekend before, the family – aided by a sorrowful Lily Goodhart – had been employed on the job of wrapping up their most fragile possessions in newspapers: the holy statues, the glass-domed shades, the picture-frames, and the oddments of crockery not immediately required.

'Eeh, I'll miss you all when you've gone,' sighed Lily. 'I don't know what I shall do, I really don't. I think we might flit ourselves; we've heard about some nice houses on that new estate in Benchill.'

'You can always come up and see us, Lily. We're only on the other side of the railway, you know,' said Mam.

Now, in Smithfield Market, Tommy had a mate, Sid Lawson, who had a horse and cart. After he'd bought him about ten pints of beer, he agreed to 'flit' them. It would have been cheaper to have paid a removal firm to do it, but that was by the by. With the help of Jim and Sam, the two men loaded up the furniture and the other few bits and pieces, securing the whole lot with a few stout ropes. They set off to make the three-mile journey by road whilst the rest of the family walked by a shorter and quicker route – each one carrying a different household item. Mam had two heavy shopping bags of groceries; Flo the bucket and mop; Polly a sweeping brush and dustpan; Les the gramophone – God help him if he'd dropped it – and Billy the large iron kettle. They made a strange sight as they processed down Collyhurst Road past all the familiar landmarks.

'Goodbye, Rechabite Hall!' said Billy.

'Goodbye, Fanning's shop!' said Les.

'Goodbye, Welcome Boys' Club!' said Polly.

'And goodbye, River Irk, and also you, Teddy Smith,' said Billy. 'Are you still down there in the pictures with your toffees?'

They climbed the seventy-seven steps and crossed over the huge railway bridge.

'It's like climbing the stairway to heaven,' said Flo breathlessly.

'S'more like climbing up Mount Everest, if y'ask me,' Mam gasped.

They trudged along by the railway fence on Barney's waste ground, then turned the corner and there it was: Honeypot Street and the start of a new life!

'Why do they call it Honeypot Street?' asked Billy. 'I don't see any bees around here.'

'Well, what about Angel Meadow then?' said Les. 'You didn't see any angels there, did you?'

'And we didn't see no meadows neither,' added Polly.

Billy had to admit they had a point.

At the beginning of the street, they were welcomed by a pack of mangy-looking mongrels which, disturbed by the unusual sight, barked and growled at their heels whilst a small gang of ragged, snotty-nosed urchins called after them:

'Eh, look at this lot. It's a Whit Friday procession.'

'No it's not,' said a bigger one. 'It's a strike by the railway cleaners.'

The family ignored them and walked on past a bakehouse which boasted the sign: 'NATHAN COHEN:

BAKER & CONFECTIONER' and from which there wafted the delicious aroma of hot crusty loaves and freshly baked bagels.

'That'll be useful,' said Mam, indicating the bakery.

'But we don't eat Jewish food,' said Polly.

'You'll eat what you're given and like it,' said Mam.

As they progressed along the street, they chanted together the countdown of the odd numbers: 25 . . . 23 . . . 21 . . . 19 . . . 17! Number 17! Their house at last! The five of them gazed up at it in awe. After Collyhurst Buildings, it was a palace! It was one of three houses raised above street level and was approached by six steps.

'Eh, we're going up in the world,' said Billy.

'First thing we do,' said Mam, 'is donkey-stone them steps. We can't have the neighbours talking about us. That's your job, Polly, d'y'hear?'

'Why does it always have to be me? I always get the rotten jobs,' complained Polly, though deep down she was secretly proud to be given such an important task so early in the 'flitting' process.

Half an hour later, Dad, Sid and the lads arrived with the furniture. Watched by prying neighbours from behind their curtains, the Hopkins family began unloading their possessions.

'Right, our Flo,' said Mam. 'Start by getting our old curtains up to the front bedroom window.'

'But suppose they don't fit?' said Flo.

'Don't make problems,' said Mam. 'Get your father to nail them up for the time being. We don't want them nosy neighbours over there watching us undress for bed, do we?'

'What about us?' said Polly. 'What if they're watching me and our Flo?'

'Who'd want to watch you?' answered Mam. 'Anyroad, you're at the back of the house.'

'Yes, but there might be somebody in the back entry looking up at us,' said Polly.

'Listen, Miss Yes-But, get on with the unpacking and stop arguifying,' said Mam. 'And you, our Sam, see if the Gas Board have turned the gas on, and if they have, get the kettle on. We could all do with a cuppa tea. I'll start mopping out the scullery. If there's one thing I can't abide, it's dirt.'

The house was in chaos, with half-opened tea-chests everywhere, wrappings strewn about the floor, ornaments and chairs and bedding all mixed up higgledy-piggledy. As a first priority, Dad and Jim had gone upstairs to assemble all the beds with a spanner. When disorder was at its peak, there came a knock at the door.

'I wonder who that can be,' Mam snapped. 'It can't be anyone we know; we've only been here five minutes. Go and see who it is, Polly.'

Polly came back: 'It's one o' them nosy neighbours you was talking about. Mrs Sykes from next door,' she said.

'Hush. They might hear you,' said Mam. 'Ask her to come in.'

Polly returned with Mrs Sykes and a young boy about Billy's age. She was a big, heavy woman with asthmatic breathing problems.

'Hello, Mrs 'Opkins. I heard you was coming,' she panted. 'I'm Mrs Sykes from next door. And this is me son, Henery. I just thought I'd pop in and ask if there's anything I can do for you. A bit a shopping or summat.'

As she spoke, she flicked glances about the room, noting the disarray and taking an inventory of their possessions like an eagle-eyed bailiff from the Assistance Board.

'That's very nice of you, Mrs Sykes,' said Mam. 'But we're all right, ta. I brought a lotta food with me for emergencies, like. We're just brewing up. Would you care for a cup?'

'Oh no, Mrs 'Opkins,' she wheezed. 'I don't want to put you to no trouble. I thought I'd better let you know about the shops in the street and that, though.'

'That's right thoughtful of you.'

'We always shop at Ormeroyd's,' Mrs Sykes went on. 'It's a nice clean shop and Elsie Ormeroyd is ever so obliging if you're a bit short o' the ready, like, and you want to put it in the book. There's Sidebotham's at the other end, but we don't trust that shop.'

'You mean Sidebottoms?'

'Yes, that's right. Only they like to be called Siddy-both-ams, not Sidebottoms. Anyroad, we don't like 'em.'

'Oh, and why is that?'

'There's always a funny musty smell in there, like – sort of mouldy, if y'know what I mean. I think she keeps the firelighters next to the bread. Besides that, she has one o' them there notices which says: "Please do not ask for credit as refusal often offends." Y've probably seen 'em.'

'Oh, I don't think we want no tick.'

'We've also got a chippy at the end of the street if you're stuck for summat t'eat,' she continued, ignoring Mam's protestation. 'There's a nice pub as well – the Queen's Arms, which we all call Capper's on account of that's the name of the lan'lord. We gen'rly go in there at weekend for a gill or two; they're all very nice, friendly people as goes in there. I dare say you'll get to know it all when you've been here a bit. Anyroad, I can see you're busy so I won't take up no more o' your time.'

'That's very good of you, Mrs Sykes. It's as well to

know we've got neighbours like you,' said Mam.

'Don't mention it, Mrs 'Opkins,' she said. 'And my Harry, me husband, is a rag-and-bone merchant. So he can get you one or two things that you might need. For a start, I've brought you this donkey stone. I'm sure you'll want to do your steps.'

'Ta very much,' said Mam. 'I was just saying to our Polly that the steps needed doing, wasn't I, Polly?'

'Yes, Mam, you was,' said Polly obligingly.

Throughout this conversation, Billy and Henry Sykes had been eyeing and weighing each other up, like two boxers in the ring assessing the other's strengths and weaknesses. Billy quite liked the look of Henry, who seemed friendly enough and not a bit like the runny-nosed brats they'd seen at the bottom end of Honeypot Street.

Mrs Sykes and her son made their way to the front door and Mrs Sykes took one last look over her shoulder to make sure she hadn't missed anything.

'Remember now,' she said. 'If there's anything . . . anything at all.'

The door had no sooner closed behind her than Mam said:

'I do hope 'er next door isn't one of those who's always coming in and out, 'cos I believe in keeping y'self to y'self. And who the hell does she think she is, anyroad? Does she think we're one o' them there rough families who have more dinner-times than dinners? We're a respectable family in this house, we are. For a start, there'll be no tick as long as I'm in charge. I believe in paying my way, I do. None of this here putting it on the slate. As for fish and chips! There'll be none o' that muck in here – not as long as I've got a pair of hands to cook with.'

'You're right there, Mam,' said Polly.

'And what was all that there stuff about a pub? She must think we're drunkards or summat. Then the cheeky bugger starts telling us to donkey-stone our steps when we've only just bloody well got here.'

She turned to Polly:

'Get out there and get them steps cleaned – now! Be sharp about it! And no buts.'

'Look at this, Mam,' shouted Polly some time later, when she had completed the step-cleaning chore. 'We've got a lovely parlour. It's got wallpaper with lovely blue flowers. We can have parties and all that.' Polly's interest in parties was not unconnected with the fact that she had recently acquired a boyfriend, a certain Steve Keenan, and it was beginning to look serious.

'We can't afford no parties – what with a rent of eight and six a week,' said Mam. 'Don't mention parties to your father, for God's sake – you know what he is.'

'Yes, but . . .' began Polly.

'There you go again.'

'Sorry, Mam. I'll try to stop arguing and I'll try to help out a bit more. This house means a new life for all of us. And p'raps me and our Flo could start our own little sideline, like. But honest, I'm dead happy we've come here. Me and our Flo have even got a whole bedroom to ourselves at last.'

'I know. It's been a good move. We should've done it years ago. There's no bathroom, mind you, and the lav's outside in the yard. But considering the smells, specially when your father's been on the beer, it's probably best out there. And then you can't expect to have everything, can you?'

'We'll freeze to death out there in winter,' complained Polly.

'Good. It'll stop you from sitting out there reading the lavatory papers. And that reminds me – get one o' the lads to cut up some newspapers and tie 'em on the nail out there. Enough about the lavatory. We've got a good living room with a posh gas mantle – you've only to pull that there chain and it plops on. Isn't it marvellous what they can do nowadays? And just look at that range! I'll be able to bake me own bread in that oven. That's another job for you, by the way, our Polly.'

'What, me baking bread?'

'No, y'daft ha'porth – black-leading the oven and the grate.'

'Aw, Mam. That's not . . .' Then she remembered. 'Sorry, Mam.'

'And it's not a bad scullery either,' Mam went on. 'It's got a big slopstone and a good gas stove. Eeh, I'm proper glad to be out o' them Dwellings – though I'll miss Lily Goodhart. We'll probably spend the rest of our lives in this house. In fact, I'm sure we will.'

'I do hope so,' said Polly. 'I do hope so.'

Whilst all this talk was going on, Billy and Les were charging through the house, inspecting and commenting on every room and facility.

'Eh, our Les,' shouted Billy happily. 'Take a look at this yard. Have you seen how big it is? We can play football in it. I could even make a cart or a guider here.'

'Yeah,' said Les. 'And what about the cellars? We can hide in the dark down there.'

'I don't fancy that much,' answered Billy. 'It's dead dark, and besides, it's cold and damp.'

As the two boys scampered about the house, little did they know how much time they were to spend down there in the years ahead.

Chapter Three

We're in the Money

The family settled into a new routine, and a year later Collyhurst Buildings and the Cut seemed like another world, a million years and a million miles away.

It was a Saturday morning in July. Billy had recently had his eighth birthday – not that anyone had noticed. Today he awoke at his usual time, around seven o'clock, and lay in bed thinking. Saturday! His favourite day of the week. No school, of course. Instead he would be going to the matinée at the local flea-pit. But more important, it was money-making day!

All the family seemed to be at it! What Dad did for a living, Billy wasn't too sure. He only knew that Dad got up very early in the morning and went off to Smithfield Market, where he carried things about on a cart. But beyond that, Billy was pretty vague. There were two things, though, he was sure about. Dad was always bringing home lots of fresh fruit and vegetables. And fish! Loads and loads of it! To the point where he felt that he had eaten so much of the stuff his true home was not Red Bank but Dogger Bank! The other thing Billy knew for sure was that after work, Dad drank enough beer to float a battleship, and if he went over his limit – as he usually did on a Saturday – it was best to keep well out of his road or else!

The rest of the family were also on the money-earning trail. Jim had started work in a warehouse on Salford Docks, whilst Sam and Les had their paper rounds at Blount's, the newsagent's on Cheetham Hill Road.

But it was Flo and Polly who had hit the jackpot with their sideline. They worked as seamstresses for Northcotes, the fur-coat manufacturer, on Oldham Road, and one of the perks of the job was being allowed to take home any useless fur remnants left lying around the factory. With typical Collyhurst acumen they had spotted a golden opportunity and had built up a lucrative business making fur mittens at fourpence a pair from the unwanted scraps. Already they seemed to have kitted out most of the residents of Honeypot Street, and several streets beyond. A few months previously, they had boldly introduced a new line in Cossack hats, using larger fragments of fur – which the family had to assume were true waste scraps and not deliberate errors made by fellow workers hoping for a share of the profits. The hats had been an immediate winner, as people had soon realised that they could double as tea-cosies when not being used as headgear. So popular were the hats in winter, the neighbours had begun to look like extras in a Chekhov play. Billy's part in this Russianisation of the Red Bank residents had been to hire out his hands – at the reasonable charge of a farthing a pair – as templates for children's gloves. He had to make a living too.

Apart from this, Billy had his own ways of coining it – in the heating and lighting business. It had taken him some considerable time to build up his clientele and win their goodwill. The thing was, he had his eye on a beautiful model yacht which he had seen displayed in the big plate-glass window of Baxendale's store on Miller Street. For several weeks now he had drooled over this magnificent boat, and had even spent one or two hours sketching it in his drawing book. To raise the seventy-five shillings required to secure this glittering prize, he had worked out that he would need to put aside one shilling and sixpence a week for one whole year, and already he was halfway to reaching his goal. In his mind's eye, he could see himself at the end of the year proudly carrying the boat under his arm up to Queen's Park lake, to launch the vessel on her maiden voyage to the applause and envy of all his friends and brothers.

'I now christen this ship the SS *Jolly Jim*. May God bless her and all who sail in her!' said King Edward. He could dream, couldn't he? He emerged from his fantasy world and went down to breakfast.

Mam also had her dreams. That same morning, she looked at her bank book. With compressed lips, she carried out a complex mental calculation, counting with her fingers on her chin and throwing away imaginary numbers into the air – as she had been taught at the Board School many years ago. It had taken almost twenty-five years of scrimping and saving to put aside the amount she had. She checked the total – £42.17.3d. She prided herself on being a good manager; that is, being able to make a little go a long way. In her world, the worst insult for a housewife was to be called a bad manager – one who spent more than the family earned and who relied on tick to buy the groceries. Hire purchase was something those funny Americans did, and certainly nobody in the working class – nobody who wanted to be thought respectable, at any rate – would even dream of buying on the never-never. Anyway, today Kate was going to spend a good part of her nest egg. She didn't know how Tommy would take it. Sometimes he didn't take kindly to the idea of her buying something as important as furniture without first asking him.

But, she thought to herself, I know how to pacify him all right. An hour in bed with him this afternoon will soften him up. I'll tell him about it after we've done it; that's when he's in a good mood – the daft ha'porth – and he'll agree to anything.

Kate's attitude to sex was simple – it was a duty women had to put up with in order to satisfy a man's bestial nature and keep the peace. She took no pleasure, and indeed expected none, for herself. On the other hand, she saw no harm in occasionally exploiting the situation and making use of Tommy's Achilles' heel – though in fact, she thought naughtily, his weakness was situated at the other end of his leg.

After a breakfast of toast and tea, she called Flo and Polly together.

'I want you to come to town with me this morning,' she said.

'What for?' asked Polly, her usual agreeable self.

'I'm going in for a new three-piece suite, and I want you to help me pick one out.'

'Oh, that's smashing, Mam,' said Polly. 'I've seen some lovely ones in Dobbins, that new store on Oldham Street.'

'We're not going to no Dobbins. We're going to the Co-op in Downing Street where we'll get a sensible suite and the divvy as well. Should be a lot of divvy on furniture.'

'Oh, that'll be really good,' said Flo. 'We can make that room look lovely. And me and our Polly have got a few pounds saved from selling our mittens. You can have some of that to buy a few bits and bobs to finish off the room.

Y'know – pictures, mirrors and oilcloth, and all that.'

'And p'raps we can have a few friends round as well, if we've got a nice parlour,' said Polly – though she wasn't too keen on Flo mentioning their 'mitten money', as she had earmarked her own share for her bottom-drawer. Her two-year courtship with Steve Keenan had developed into a full-blown romance, and they were now officially engaged. Hence her desire for parties, and the chance to bring him home to introduce him to all her family and friends.

Billy had already met this boyfriend for a few minutes, and those moments were indelibly imprinted on his mind.

It had been one early Sunday morning – was it only two weeks ago? – that he had been coming down the stairs still rubbing the dreams from his eyes. Suddenly there had been a rat-a-tat-tat on the front door. After drawing back the two bolts, he had opened the door and there, silhouetted against the newly risen sun, had towered the apparition of Douglas Fairbanks, the aviator star of *Dawn Patrol*. The colossus had been rigged out in full battle regalia of leather suit, helmet and goggles. Billy had simply gaped open-mouthed. And the giant, god-like creature had spoken in a deep, sonorous voice:

'Hello, young man. You must be Billy. I've heard a lot about you from your sister Pauline.'

Mam had appeared and had said in her poshest, up-market voice:

'Oh, good morning, Mr Keenan. Won't you step h'inside for a moment. Polly won't be too long.'

'Many thanks, Mrs Hopkins. That's fine. Please call me Steve, by the way.'

The hero had actually stood waiting in their living room whilst Polly had been putting the finishing touches to her outfit. Why, even Dad had cringed and deferred before this well-spoken visitor. But then he always did when he felt he was in the presence of anyone 'higher-up'. If he'd had a forelock he'd have tugged it.

'So, young Billy,' said Steve. 'Pauline tells me you're very clever at school.'

Billy's chest swelled with pride and he took an immediate liking to this tall, handsome stranger.

'What's your teacher's name?' he asked.

'Miss McGurk.'

'Is she kind or is she nasty?'

'A bit of both, I think.'

'What's your favourite subject?'

'I've got two really – composition and sums.'

'You'll not go far wrong with those. You can write a book and then count all the money you'll make from it, eh?'

Polly, looking like Amy Johnson, had come downstairs then, and the couple had greeted each other fondly. But none of that kissing or anything. Not in front of Mam and Dad.

'We'll be off now, folks,' Steve said. 'We're going for a run over to Scarborough.'

'Where's Scarborough?' asked Billy. It might have been on the other side of the world for all he knew.

'On the east coast of Yorkshire. It's about two hundred miles there and back,' he'd replied nonchalantly.

Two hundred miles! said Billy to himself. I was right. It *is* on the other side of the world!

Douglas Fairbanks and Amy Johnson had then mounted Steve's 250cc BSA motorbike and roared off into the unknown.

Now Billy was brought back to the present by Mam's reaction to Polly's suggestion of a party.

'Now I've told you before. You'd better not let your

father hear you talking about having friends round,' she said. 'He'll throw a fit.'

Tommy was a very strict father and ruled the household with an iron hand. All the kids were afraid of him because they knew how easily he could flare up, especially after the pub. Sometimes, like dogs with hypersensitive hearing, they sensed his approach long before he arrived, and when he walked through the front door, a hush fell over the living room.

'I'll be careful, Mam,' said Polly. 'Don't worry.'

'What'll we do with our Billy?' asked Flo. 'All the lads are out and he's there in the back yard by himself.'

'Well, we can't take him with us,' said Polly. 'It'd take too long to get him cleaned up.'

Billy came in from the lavatory.

'Listen,' said Mam. 'We're going into town. Why don't you go and play with Les and Sam?'

'They won't let me go with 'em. They've gone off with their gang to Queen's Park. They told me to scram.'

'Why've they done that?' asked Mam.

'They said I'm a telltale just 'cos I told you when they went swimming in their bare skins in Cauley's Millpond. When I try to go with 'em now, Alfie Rigsby – 'e's the boss of the Honeypot Street gang – says: "Eh, Sam and Les. Tell your kid to scram. He'll tell on us".'

'P'raps it's because you are a telltale! You're telling on 'em now! You should learn to keep *that* shut,' said Polly, pointing to her mouth – a mannerism learned from her father.

'Well, Billy,' said Mam. 'What are you going to do with yourself while we're in town?'

'I've got a very busy morning ahead of me,' replied Billy. 'First my religious work with the Jewish people. Then Henry Sykes is coming round and his dad's brought him an old kitchen door that we're gonna chop up for firewood. When we've sold the bundles of wood, we should have enough money for the pictures and some toffees.'

'All right,' said Mam. 'See that you do your chopping in the back entry, though – not in the yard. Your father'll go mad if he sees a mess. Now, we'll be back about twelve o'clock to make the dinner for your father coming in. See that you behave yourself.'

The three females of the Hopkins family put on their best coats and departed to catch the 62 bus to town.

Billy went into the house and checked the time. Half past nine and time to start the Saturday-morning routine – fires and lights. The quickest money he'd ever made.

He went first to the easiest job of the day, at the Beth Shalom Synagogue on Cheetham Hill Road. Rabbi Greenberg was in charge, an oddball who'd claimed last week that, according to his Jewish calendar, the date was 5696. But his money was good. The rabbi was already waiting, and as soon as Billy arrived, he indicated the electricity control cupboard. Billy stood on a chair to reach the panel of light switches, and, on a signal from the rabbi, flicked them all on, flooding the synagogue in bright illumination. That was it! He was told to return just before one o'clock to switch them all off again.

It's a mad world we live in, he said to himself, quoting one of his mam's favourite sayings.

Next in line was the firelighting end of the business – equally puzzling but equally rewarding. First port of call was in Stock Street to Mrs Gluckman, a superstitious old soul if ever there was one.

'So, come in then, William,' she said. 'The fire's already

set. Try to jump over the step though, or we'll have bad luck.'

Billy was ushered into the front room, where an ancient Jewess at least two hundred years old lay propped up on pillows on the bed. There was an overpowering smell of camphor oil and embrocation. Casting a professional eye over the arrangement of newspapers, firewood, clinkers and coal, he selected a lump of coal, which he placed on the pyramid in the grate with the delicate touch of a master-craftsman.

When he was sure that all was in order, he applied the match and the fire ignited. That was not the end of it, however, for he now had to apply a blower to encourage a good, healthy blaze. There were on the market metal blowers, but none of his customers had ever taken the trouble to afford one and it was necessary to get by with a makeshift device consisting of a shovel balanced on the bars of the grate with a large sheet of newspaper placed across it. Suction from the chimney then activated the blaze, but great care had to be taken to avoid setting the paper blower itself alight – a disaster which had happened to him on one or two occasions. For this simple service he was paid the princely sum of threepence.

As he left the room, he took a surreptitious look at the decrepit old woman, who reminded him of a hideous old witch in a Grimm Brothers' fairy tale. At that moment, the old crone sneezed loudly. Mrs Gluckman shot over to her like a rocket and tugged both her ears in an upward direction.

'To long, lucky years,' she recited piously.

The old woman's ears might be long, but they weren't so lucky, thought Billy as he prepared to leave. Still, it was none of his business. He shrugged his shoulders, pocketed his wage and walked happily along the lobby whistling 'We're in the Money'.

'Stop!' cried Mrs Gluckman, holding up her hands in horror. 'Shaydem! Shaydem! Demons. Whistling attracts them, didn't you know that? Aren't there enough things to go wrong in this house without inviting them in?'

She ran back into the house and emerged with a large packet of Sankey's salt, which she sprinkled liberally about the lobby and the threshold.

'That should fix 'em!' she said.

'Sorry about that, Mrs Gluckman,' said Billy. 'See you next Saturday.'

I'll never understand adults, he thought as he strode off. What's that other thing me Mam says: 'There's nowt so quare as fowk.'

On from there to Mrs Levy. Another fire. Another threepence.

'I'm well on my way to buying a yacht,' he remarked to Mrs Levy as he was leaving.

'With your head for business, I'm not surprised,' answered the woman.

His final domestic job involved quite a long walk to Elizabeth Street, to the house of old Mr Benjamin Hymans, who always wore his skull cap and prayer-shawl on Saturdays and who always haggled over the price. This week was no different.

'Come in, Villiam,' he mumbled as he shuffled back into his kitchen. 'So, this veek I need two fires. Von in the kitchen for me and von in the bedroom for Becky, my vife, who is not very vell. So it should be cheaper for two. Vat d'y say? Fo'pence for two.'

'Sorry, Mr Hymans,' Billy said. 'The best I can do is fivepence – a cut price – specially for you as an old customer.'

'Then we split the difference,' said Benjamin. 'Fourpence ha'penny.'

'It's a deal. Just for you,' said Billy. 'But please don't tell the others or they'll all want a cut price.'

This last job finished, Billy ran like the wind to get back and join his pal, Henry, in the firewood-production end of the enterprise.

Billy and Henry were experienced woodchoppers. They had never counted how many bundles of firewood they had chopped but it must have run into many hundreds – even thousands, who knows? Their method of breaking up a kitchen door was simplicity itself. Though they lacked a knowledge of basic mechanics, they knew that the weakest part of an object was its centre point. So, resting the door against a wall, they were able to break it apart by heaving a very heavy stone on to its middle. Once the door had cracked into two parts, it was child's play to break it down further by leaning the pieces against a big stone and jumping on to the wood with both feet, preferably wearing heavy boots.

The final stages required tools, and Billy went inside the house to fetch his dad's hammer and pincers. An axe – or better still a hatchet like those Indians had in *Last of the Mohicans* – would have made the job easier, but beggars couldn't be choosers. He and Henry worked hard with skill and dedication, splitting the kindling with the claw end of the hammer. Inside an hour, they had twelve bundles all neatly tied up and ready for sale. They placed the firewood in the wooden cart they had made earlier in the year from a soap box and a set of pram wheels. Mr Sykes's profession really had proved most fruitful in the matter of supplying raw materials for that particular joint enterprise.

With a full load on board, they set about the business of selling the morning's production.

Their first call was on the Hardman family at the bottom end of Honeypot Street. It was not a success. There were ten kids in the Hardman family, five dogs and Billy didn't know how many cats. The Hardmans were also noted for their strong on-going relationship with the police: almost every other day, a representative of the law seemed to call at their home to pay his respects. Billy knocked at their door nervously, afraid they might drag him in and eat him for dinner. His knocking triggered off hysterical weeping from several babies and ferocious barking from a pack of hounds somewhere in the bowels of the house. Eventually, after much rattling of chains and the sound of bolts being drawn back, Wally Hardman – looking like one of the meths drinkers Billy had seen on Barney's brickyard – appeared, restraining a big, snarling Alsatian that obviously fancied Billy as a tasty tit-bit.

'Yeah. Whaddya want?' demanded Wally.

'D'you want to buy any firewood, Mr Hardman?' Billy asked anxiously. 'Only a penny a bundle.'

'Me! Buy firewood!' bawled Wally Hardman. 'Bloody 'ell! That'll be the day! If we want firewood, son – which we don't – we just tear out one o'them bloody railway posts growing at the end o' the yard. Now go on! Bugger off! Try somebody else!'

They walked on and reached old Mrs Finkelstein's house. Here they had better luck – but they had to bargain a little with her.

'Very well, lads,' she said. 'So I'll take three bundles already. Threepence, you said. But what about a bit o' discount for an old lady? Say tuppence for three.'

'Sorry, Mrs Finkelstein. No discount,' said Billy. He'd

learned the ways of Cheetham Hill at a very early stage in his career as a salesman. 'Business is business. But I'll tell you what I'll do. Today's Saturday and you're not supposed to light fires yourself, right? So I'll light yours for you for an extra penny. I usually charge thr'pence for lighting a fire. Today I'm feeling generous, so give us fourpence for the lot and we'll call it square.'

The old lady thought for a minute. Billy was right – the going rate was threepence to get a youngster to come and light the fire on a Saturday. She made a rapid mental calculation and came to a prompt decision:

'All right. If you light the gas stove as well, it's a deal. You should be in business, Billy,' she said. 'Oh, and by the way, would you untie the bundles for me? We're not allowed to do that ourselves on a Saturday either.'

Billy thought she was asking a lot for the extra penny but puzzled by all these do's and don'ts, he went into her house, lit a burner on the stove, applied a match to the fire and collected fourpence. On the way out he asked:

'Tell me, Mrs Finkelstein. Why do Jewish people have so many rules about this and that?'

'So, we're not allowed to work on the Sabbath; it's in the Old Testament. There are thirty-nine things we're not allowed to do; lighting a fire and untying things are just two of 'em.'

Billy joined Henry, who was waiting in the street.

'Thank God,' he said, 'I belong to a nice, simple, straightforward religion like the Catholic Church. No daft rules for us!'

Further along the street, they called on the Priestleys – a very religious Catholic family made up of mother, father and three children – two daughters and one son. The daughters were fairly grown-up: Jean, aged sixteen, was very pretty, always bright and cheerful, and had been seen once or twice lately in the company of Billy's brother Jim; Teresa, aged fourteen, never smiled because she was going to be a nun. David, the only son, was eleven years old.

The family was obviously a cut above the rest of the street, as the father smoked a pipe and possessed a clarinet which he kept on top of a cupboard. No one had heard him play it, but that wasn't the point. To top it all, he wore a trilby instead of a flat cap like the other men. When it came to the social ladder of the street, Billy had often tried to puzzle out just where his own family stood. It wasn't easy to work out. He knew they were higher than the Hardmans. But the Priestleys? Billy's dad smoked lowly Player's Weights, and the only musical instrument they had in the house was Les's mouth organ, which probably didn't count. Then again, their house did have six steps and three feet of a sort-of garden at the front. So he supposed they cancelled out the pipe, the clarinet and the trilby. On balance, he thought, that made them about equal. But if that was the case, it meant that the Sykes family was top of the street, because they had not only six steps and three feet of garden, but also a piano – out of tune, admittedly – which Henry's dad had saved from the rubbish tip. Billy gave up trying to solve the sociological problem; it was too complicated.

Mrs Priestley was a very solemn but friendly lady, who gave the impression of being very efficient and someone who would stand for no nonsense.

'Come in, William,' she said. 'You too, Henry. What is it you're selling? Firewood? And at a penny a bundle! That's a lot cheaper than the shop. I'll take them all. Take your cart out to our back yard and put the wood in the shed.'

Billy and Henry could hardly believe their ears and

their luck as she handed ninepence to them.

As they were going out, Mrs Priestley looked at Billy and asked:

'Why are you wearing that big scarf on a hot day like today, William? It's summer and I'm sure you don't need it.'

'That's to hide me dirty neck,' said Billy truthfully.

And for some reason that he never understood, the whole family – except for Teresa, of course, who succeeded in holding herself back – broke out into paroxysms of laughter as if they had heard the funniest joke in the world. Even Mrs Priestley smiled. Forever after that, Billy was regarded as a natural comedian by the Priestley family, and whenever he appeared they broke out into amused smiles and waited for him to say something funny.

'P'raps they're not used to telling each other the truth,' Billy said to Henry.

They left pushing their empty cart before them and with one shilling and a penny in their pockets from the firewood end of the enterprise.

'We're in the money! We're in the money!' they sang laughingly as they strutted up back Honeypot Street to their back doors.

'That's sixpence ha'penny each,' said Billy. 'We can go to the matinée at the Shakespeare; it's Buck Jones in *McKenna of the Mounted*. Should be smashing.'

'I'd rather 'ave Ken Maynard,' sighed Henry. 'But I suppose Buck Jones will 'ave to do. Have we got enough for a toffee apple?'

'Of course we have,' replied Billy, the accountant. 'We can afford not only a toffee apple but some pear drops and all. See you after dinner, Henery.'

Billy ran back to the synagogue to complete his duties there. He was a trifle early when he arrived but he always liked to get there a little ahead of time to watch and listen to the closing ceremony. He went in through the main door and up to the gallery from where all the ladies observed the proceedings. Standing behind them, he had a first-class view.

There were one or two men wearing wide-rimmed fur hats – might be some additional business here for Flo and Polly, thought Billy – embroidered silk caftans, white half-length stockings and, strangest thing of all, slippers! But the great majority of the men were dressed like black-bearded undertakers, with long, untidy tufts of hair straggling out from under their black homburgs – which, horror of horrors, they were wearing in church! – whilst on their feet they wore white plimsolls. Over their 'mourning' suits, they had draped black-and-blue-striped bedsheets, and four of the worshippers began processing down the main aisle carrying a large canopy above Rabbi Greenberg. As all this was going on, the whole congregation, sounding as if they were in great pain, wailed sorrowfully and pitifully in Yiddish. Young skull-capped boys then went out in turn to a central altar where, under a shawl held by one of their friends, they chanted in sing-song fashion from a large parchment scroll. After each reading, the congregation rocked back and forth and chorused what sounded like: 'Whadda shame!'

These curious rituals were rounded off by the rabbi taking a collection, placing the proceeds in a large red handkerchief and whirling it around his head three times, at the same time intoning Jewish prayers to which the people responded once again with their exclamation: 'Whadda shame!' perhaps referring to the shameful way in which the rabbi was treating their good money. The day's ceremonies concluded with the blowing of a very long and very old horn whose strong, piercing sound almost blasted Billy out of his perch in the gallery.

The tantivy signalled the end of the strange and weird service, and the congregation filed out of the synagogue. When the last one had departed, Billy went downstairs to meet the rabbi, who showed him to the control panel once again. A quick flick of the switches, off went the lights and the job was done! For this he collected eightpence – a small fortune for a small job of work.

'It's a mad, mad, mad world,' said Billy aloud to himself. 'And I'm buggered if I can make any sense out of it!'

He strode triumphantly down Derby Street with a jingle of coins in his pocket, a dream of a yacht in his heart and a song of joy on his lips.

About the time that Billy was doing his fire and light round, Tommy, his dad, was finishing a seven-hour stint of portering in Smithfield Market. He had worked hard and fast until gone eleven o'clock, when the pace had finally slowed down and the market had become relatively quiet.

That'll do for today, he said to himself. Not a bad day. Nearly fifteen shillings and a good lot o' stuff to take home. I think I've earned meself a drink o' two. He made his way to the Hare and Hounds on Shudehill, and as he went in he was met by that lovely, familiar, inviting smell of beer and tobacco smoke and the buzz of the market porters' heated arguments about football players and racehorses.

'Pint o' the usual?' said Geoff Docherty, the landlord, as Tommy walked through the door.

'Aye, ta,' said Tommy. 'Who d'you fancy for the Steward's Cup today, Geoff?'

'I like the look of that Solerina,' said Geoff. 'Might be worth having a little flutter on it.'

Two hours and six pints later, Tommy thought it was time to be making tracks. As he wobbled his way back, he thought about the nice dinner Kate would have ready on the table for him.

I like Sat'day, he said to himself. Life's not so bad now we're in Honeypot Street. I'll go home now and have a kip after me dinner. P'raps Kate might get into bed with me if the kids go out. Now she's forty-eight there's no danger of kids no more, thank God.

Thinking of kids suddenly reminded him that he'd promised her he would try and mend Les's boots on his shoe-last – though he usually made a pig's ear of it and had to take them to the cobbler in the end.

'Aye, I'll do them right after me dinner,' he said aloud. 'It'll save a few bob.' A sensual thought struck him. 'That should please her. It might just get her in the right mood.'

Speeding up his erratic walk a little, he planned the details of his campaign for a Saturday-afternoon seduction.

Tommy and Kate had certain signals to indicate to each other a willingness or otherwise to have sex. He was still somewhat shy on the subject. Despite all their kids, for example, he'd never seen Kate naked. When he came to think of it, she'd never seen him naked either. And when it came to asking for his oats, he hadn't the cheek to come straight out with a direct request like he imagined the toffs might do. He had to be more subtle and throw out hints in suggestive remarks. At night, he might say:

'I don't think I'll be long out o' bed tonight, Kate. I want to be up early.'

Kate knew what he meant by 'up', and if she felt in the mood she would answer:

'Go on up then, Tommy, and I'll join you.'

For an afternoon session, he would say:

'I'm feeling tired, Kate. I've had a hard day. I wouldn't mind going to bed for a bit.'

If Kate was willing, she would answer:

'Aye, I wouldn't mind getting off me pins for a while and lying down for a bit meself.'

Thinking these salacious thoughts, Tommy felt a stirring in his loins and, swaying a little, hurried back to Honeypot Street.

Billy reached home well after one o'clock and found Dad reading the *Daily Dispatch* while Mam and his two sisters prepared his favourite dinner – chips and egg. They had bought some tripe and onions from the UCP shop in town for Dad. They sat down to their meal, and whilst Billy made chip and egg butties, Dad slurped his tripe noisily.

'I've had a little bet on a horse called Solerina, Kate,' announced Dad. 'Only a bob each way. A tip from Geoff Docherty.'

'That'll be the day, when you win summat,' she said.

They continued eating. After a while, Dad said:

'I see here in the paper that some writer-fella called McMahon has tried to shoot King Edward.'

Dad often read out choice items of news from the paper to Mam. It was his way of educating her and keeping her up to date on current affairs.

'I hope they caught him,' she said.

'Aye. They caught him red-handed, all right. With a bloody loaded revolver in his hand.' Changing the subject, Tommy asked: 'Where are the lads, then?'

'Well, our Jim's upstairs, getting himself all spruced up to take that Jean Priestley from across the road out rowing on Heaton Park lake this afternoon.'

Jim was now sixteen and had discovered girls. Which

explained why he had become very fastidious about his personal appearance, spending a lot of time shining his shoes, brilliantining his hair and examining his face in the mirror for spots. It had to be said, though, that the green suit he had bought from Weaver to Wearer left something to be desired in the matter of taste. He was earning quite a decent wage – about 17s.6d. a week – as a labourer in a bonded warehouse on Salford Docks. In the evenings, however, he continued his boxing lessons at the Welcome Club, and had now achieved a creditable standard, and had won several cups and medals. He had also been giving Billy lessons in the art of self-defence for a couple of years – since the skenny-eyed kid incident – and he too had reached quite a good level for his age. Fortunately, though, there had been no footpads on Red Bank and so Billy's boxing skills had never been put to the test.

'Aye,' said Dad. 'What about the other lads?'

'They've all gone out to Queen's Park for the day, sailing their boats,' said Mam. 'Oh, and Tommy, me and the girls've been out this morning doing a bit o' shopping to beautify the front room, like. I'll tell you about it later. I think you'll be pleased.'

'Aye, we're definitely going lah-de-dah, Kate,' he said. 'A posh parlour. What next? The neighbours'll soon be calling us stuck-up if we're not careful.'

He began to lead up gradually towards the subject uppermost in his mind – the one that had been gnawing at him since he'd left the pub.

'Well, it's Sat'day. What's everybody doing today?' he asked brightly, looking round the table.

'Me and Polly are going out to tea at Patty Bristow's. Then we're going to the pictures at the Temple,' said Flo.

'And I'm going to the Shaky with Henry Sykes to see Buck Jones,' said Billy.

Tommy's hopes began to rise.

'I thought I might mend Les's best boots after me dinner and then go and lie down for a bit,' said Tommy, throwing out the hint.

Still thinking about her three-piece with its brown rexine cover and brass studs, Kate took the bait and said warmly:

'Aye, that'll be good if you mend Les's boots. You've been promising to do that for weeks. And, er . . . I wouldn't mind a rest meself for a bit, after all that walking about I did this morning. And I thought, if you fancy it, we might go for a drink tonight in Capper's.'

It's on. I'm on a winner here, thought Tommy. He could hardly wait to get the boot-mending bit over with. He went into the scullery to his tool-box. It was then that he made the discovery!

'Have you seen me hammer and pinchers?' he asked Kate.

'No,' said Mam. 'Why, aren't they there?'

She turned to Billy, who had gone white to the lips.

'Have you had 'em, Billy?' she asked anxiously.

'Yeah, I had 'em,' mumbled Billy. 'But, er, I thought I put 'em back. They must still be in the back entry.'

He ran out to check, followed closely by his dad.

In the entry, there was no sign of any tools.

'You stupid little bastard!' yelled Dad. 'I'll give you losing me 'ammer.' And he hit Billy a smack across the face that knocked him off his feet. 'You stupid, stupid little get,' he bawled, now beside himself with rage, and continued to smack Billy across the legs mercilessly, propelling him back across the yard. 'I'll bleedin' show you who's boss in this bleedin' house,' he bellowed, removing the belt from around his waist. He was about to strike when Kate got between them.

'Don't you bloody well dare hit my son with that bloody belt or you'll get a taste o' this,' she screamed, brandishing the poker. 'Now I'm warning you, Tommy. I'll swing for you, God help me, I will.'

Then Dad took the whimpering Billy by the scruff of the neck and thrust him into the cellar, slamming the door behind him. Sobbing uncontrollably, Billy sat in the dark on the cellar steps whilst the screaming and the shouting continued unabated in the scullery.

'I never wanted the bloody kid in the first place,' Tommy roared. 'Now he's messing up me life losing all me tools. He deserves a bloody good hiding to teach him a lesson. You're too bloody soft with 'im.'

'Oh, shurrup, you bloody big bully,' Mam screeched. 'I'll buy you a bloody hammer and pinchers if that's all you're worried about.'

Jim's voice could be heard shouting angrily above the fracas:

'Listen, you. If you ever hit our Billy like that again, you'll have me to reckon with. I don't care if y'are me father. I'll thump you, mark my words.'

Billy listened to the rowing and the wrangling through the cellar door. Gradually, very gradually, the commotion died down. After half an hour or so, Mam called softly through the door:

'Are y'all right, our Billy? Y'can come out now. The big bully's gone to bed to sleep it off.'

Filled with self-pity and still racked by involuntary sobs, Billy emerged from the gloom of the cellar.

'I'm not staying in this house. I'll run away and join the circus,' he said tearfully. 'I'm going to see me pal next door.' And he ran out of the house.

Henry came out of the back door as soon as Billy called his name.

'Are we going to the Shaky then?' he asked.

'No, I'm not going now,' replied Billy. 'I'm running away from home.'

'I'll come wi' you,' said Henry without hesitation. 'Where'll we go?'

'Dunno,' said Billy, still choking back the occasional catch in his voice. 'What about them gypsies you see at the fair on the croft sometimes? P'raps they would have us.'

'We could run away to Africa. Stow away on a boat,' said Henry.

'Yeah, and they'd never see us again. Then they'd be sorry. We might even get killed by the Fuzzy Wuzzies and then when we were dead they'd be crying when they saw us in our coffins in altar boy's clothes and then it'd be too late. And I'd be dead glad,' said Billy. But the thought of his own death and funeral nearly started him off whimpering again.

'Wait there,' said Henry, 'and I'll get some of that cold toast left over from our breakfast this morning, and we've got a big bottle of dandelion and burdock.'

'We'll run away to Barney's,' said Billy, 'and join the army with Mad Jack. They'll never find us there.'

The two friends set off together across Barney's wasteground until they reached Mad Jack's cabin. Here was a man they admired and looked up to. He was dressed in a ragged army greatcoat secured around the waist by a piece of string, whilst on his head he wore a faded military cap at a lop-sided angle matching his disfigured, lopsided face. On his arm he wore three faded stripes. Sergeant Mad Jack was a shell-shock victim from the Great War, and he lived with his flea-bitten, one-eyed dog in a ramshackle hut which he had built with his own hands out of oil drums and corrugated-iron sheets in an attempt to create a replica of his dugout. He cooked his own food – usually bacon and sausage plus a potato baked on the end of a fork at a coke fire at the entrance to his shack. Here was true happiness!

'I'll bet his dad doesn't belt him for losing his hammer,' Billy said to Henry. 'He can come and go as he pleases, like that poem they're learning us at school:

> *'Give to me the life I love,*
> *Let the lave go by me.*
> *Bed in the bush, with stars to see,*
> *Bread I dip in the river.*
> *There's the life for a man like me.*
> *There's the life forever.'*

'Yak,' exclaimed Henry. 'Don't think I fancy bread dipped in a river. It'd be all soggy, like – a bit like them pobs me dad had to have when they took all his teeth out.'

Bubbles of spittle appeared round Mad Jack's mouth and he broke out into one of his babbling fits, having an imaginary conversation with unseen companions:

'Yes, Lieutenant Marsh. Yes, sir. Very good, sir. Jerries at three o'clock in no man's land. Take aim. Fire. Got that one, sir. Get your 'eads down, lads. Here comes a whizzbang!'

'Private Billy and Private Henry reporting for duty, Sarge,' said Billy, saluting.

'Have you two lads taken the shilling?' Mad Jack asked.

'Yes, Sarge,' they answered in unison.

'*On Saturday I'm willing,*' Jack sang. '*If you'll only take the shilling, To make a man of any one of you.*'

'Have you been over the top today, Sarge, into no man's land?' asked Henry.

'Any chep not going over the top when I blow my

whistle will get a bullet in the back of the head,' recited Mad Jack in a public-school accent.

Billy and Henry ate their toast, offering some to Mad Jack and his derelict dog, both of whom gladly accepted their visitors' hospitality. When it came to the dandelion and burdock, though, Billy didn't fancy drinking any of it after Mad Jack and his dog had had their swig. As they sat there sharing their fare and their conversation with the Old Contemptible and his mongrel, they really felt that they had run away and left their homes forever. They were never, never going back as long as they both lived. Though exactly why Henry had run away was not entirely clear.

'How's the weather been, Sarge?' asked Billy.

'*Raining, raining, raining,*' sang Jack. '*Always bloody well raining./Raining all the morning/And raining all the day.*'

' 'Ow many Jerries have you shot today, Sarge?' asked Henry.

'*If you vant to see your Vater und der Vaterland,*' sang Jack. '*Keep your 'ead down Fritzy boy.*'

After about an hour of this, Henry said: 'It'll be getting dark soon, Billy.'

'D'you fancy staying the night in Jack's dugout?' asked Billy.

'I would, Billy,' said Henry, 'but we allus have beans on toast for tea at home on Sat'days. What d'you think, eh? Is it time to go back yet?'

'Yeah, OK then. I think we've taught 'em all a lesson. I think that's enough. They won't try hitting me again. 'Cos if they do, I'll run away again. Next time to Africa. Come on, Henry, we'll go back.'

After saying goodbye to Mad Jack, who gave them a smart military salute, they wandered home and parted at Henry's back yard gate.

* * *

Billy went in by the rear door and found Mam, his two sisters and Jim, along with Jean Priestley, sitting round the table waiting for him.

'Where've you been, our Billy?' Mam asked. 'We thought you'd run away to the circus and left us forever. While you've been out, Mrs Priestley, Jean's mam, has been over to see us. And guess what? You left the hammer and the pinchers at their house in their shed. So all that ranting and raving was for nowt. And that big bully upstairs can go to hell. I won't be talking to him for a while. You can be sure about that.'

When he heard all this, Billy's lip began to tremble and he almost started blubbering again at the thought of the terrible injustice he had suffered. However, he managed to control his tearfulness and Flo said:

'We've talked it over while you were gone and we've got a nice little surprise for you. We've all changed our plans and we're going to take you to the Rivoli.'

'You've never been to the Rivoli, have you?' said Polly. 'It's the poshest picture house in the whole o' Manchester.'

At this news, Billy's eyes filled up once again, at the idea of such kindness after all the brutality.

'What's on?' he asked tearfully.

'Freddie Bartholomew in *David Copperfield*,' answered Mam.

They went – six of them – to the first house, in the best seats at the front of the balcony. Sixpence each for the grown-ups and threepence for him. The cinema was more like a royal palace than a picture house. Such magnificence! The only cinema he'd ever visited had been the Saturday-afternoon matinée in Collyhurst where the seats were hard wooden benches. Now, here in the Rivoli – fragrant with exotic perfumes – there was subtle, subdued lighting and silk illuminated pendant drapes on a giant stage which gave the whole place an air of mystery and elegance. Before the big picture started, a theatre organ played the popular number of the day: 'The Way You Look Tonight' after which the organist announced:

'And now for the song made famous by Lancashire's own star comedian, Mr George Formby.'

There followed the most popular song of all, 'When I'm Cleaning Windows'. This was high living indeed! The theatre lights began to dim and the organ, still playing as if protesting at the interruption, descended miraculously into the orchestra stalls. The huge velvet curtain opened slowly and noisily on its track rods, revealing yet more layers of silk curtain which rolled back one after another until at last there was the silver screen.

As for the film! Billy sat in a trance as he was transported into the fantasy world of Dickens' favourite child.

They were about ten minutes into the film when Billy turned to Mam and whispered:

'Who was Betsy Trotwood, Mam?'

'That was David's father's aunt, d'y'see?' she replied – a bit too loudly for Billy's liking.

A lady behind spoke up:

'Excuse me,' she said.

Here it comes, Billy said to himself. She's going to tell us to hush up.

But he was quite wrong, for the lady continued:

'Does that mean she's David's great-aunt, then?'

'Correct,' Mam answered authoritatively.

'Wasn't Betsy married?' asked the lady's husband.

'Yes, she was. But her husband died in India,' Billy's all-wise mam answered.

'Then why is she called *Miss* Betsy Trotwood?' another gent asked triumphantly.

'Because she didn't like her husband so she decided to go back to her maiden name. Now d'you understand?' said Mam.

It looked very much as if a full-scale debate and discussion might soon develop, but an usherette came and, flashing her torch, ordered silence.

As Dickens' story unfolded, four of Billy's companions wept unashamedly with tears overflowing and even Jim gave an occasional sniff as they watched Basil Rathbone being heartless and cruel to Freddie Bartholomew. What a coincidence that Billy should witness such hard-heartedness on this day of days. Mind you, Mrs Murdstone was weak and did little to stand up to Basil Rathbone and defend little David. Not like his own mam, who was brave and defied bullies by threatening them with pokers. And then David didn't have a brother like Jim either.

Ninety minutes later, they left the cinema cleansed and purged, having identified closely with the characters and the story. Aristotle would have been pleased to see that his cathartic principle had been so roundly vindicated.

'What did you think of it all, then?' asked Mam.

'I thought it was the best picture I've ever seen in all me life,' replied Billy.

'And what about the picture house itself?' asked Polly. 'I told you it was the poshest place in all Manchester.'

'It was all right, I suppose,' answered Billy. 'But I didn't think much o' their seats. They was dead hard and narrow.'

'How d'you mean?' asked Flo, puzzled. Then it dawned on her. 'You forgot to turn the seat down, y'daft devil!' she exclaimed. 'You've sat on that upturned seat for over two hours!'

And they laughed and laughed as they walked home. Then for a minute or two they all went quiet, until suddenly one of them remembered and set the others off. So they laughed all the way back.

Chapter Four

Oh No! Not Another Sermon!

'No man can serve two masters,' Canon Calder had said. 'Ye cannot serve God and Mammon.'

Billy didn't see why not. Yesterday he had served Mammon, and today, Sunday, he'd serve God. Simple.

The day after the flare-up, Dad was abashed and abased. Earlier that morning Billy had heard him – an habitual early riser – come upstairs to Mam with a cup of tea as an olive branch.

'I've brought you a nice cuppa tea, Kate,' he said humbly.

'Don't bother. I don't want no tea from you, thenk y'very much,' she had retorted. 'Drink it yourself, Mussolini. You're nowt but a big bully like . . . er . . .'

She was temporarily stuck for a word, but then it came to her.

'Like . . . er . . . Basil Rathbone!' she shouted triumphantly.

Uh-oh! thought Billy. War's been declared!

Immediately he felt sorry for Dad, as he was about to get the fish-eye treatment – God help him! The whole family knew what it was like when Mam decided to freeze somebody out. It was all a question of how long she would keep it up; she had been known to go for a whole week, like the occasion when Dad had been particularly loathsome after a marathon drinking session. Billy hoped it wouldn't last that long this time. Still, there was nothing he could do about it.

He put on his best pants, thumbed his braces over his shirt and went downstairs to have a cold-water 'swill' at the scullery slopstone. He had to go to the nine o'clock children's Mass at St Chad's on Cheetham Hill Road.

In the living room, he found that Dad had already made and raked the fire, put the big kettle on the hob, and was busy blacking and buffing all the family's shoes. He wore a contrite and hangdog expression.

'How are you, our Billy?' he asked anxiously. 'I've blacked your boots and you can see your face in 'em now.'

'Ta, Dad,' answered Billy, ready to let bygones be bygones.

'What d'you want for your breakfast, son?' Dad asked gently.

It was hard to believe that this man, who only yesterday had been a roaring, raging bull, had now become this quiet, subdued character cleaning shoes and enquiring about his breakfast.

'It's Sunday, Dad,' Billy answered. 'An' I'm going to Communion. I always have my breakfast when I come back.'

'Righto, son. Then just have a cuppa tea. It's freshly made.'

'Can't, Dad. The rule says "fasting from midnight", and if I swallowed even one tiny drop o' water, I couldn't go.'

'No one'll know. Just us two. And I'll not tell.'

'No good, Dad. God'd know and then I'd go to hell for

ever and ever. Miss McGurk said.'

'That seems a bit unfair. Just for a drop o' water.'

Mam came downstairs looking as if she'd sucked half a pound of lemons.

'I've done all the shoes, Kate,' said Tommy ingratiatingly.

'So I see,' she said icily, looking straight through him. Addressing Billy, she said:

'When you've had your swill, our Billy, your Sunday jersey and your stockings are laid out on y'bed. And tell the others to get a move on or we're gonna be late.'

Mam was in the Catholic Mothers' Union whilst Flo and Polly were both members of the Children of Mary. Every Sunday the three ladies of the family and the three younger boys went to the same Mass, though the lads preferred to make their own way there. As for Jim, he supposedly went to a later service but Billy knew that secretly he went to a nearby croft and played pitch-and-toss.

There had even been a time when Dad had started going to Mass. How much praying he did was very much in question, for he always returned with detailed accounts not only of who was there, but of what they had been wearing, together with scathing comments on their moral and financial standing.

'I saw that Mrs O'Brien there – all done up to the nines,' he would say. 'Mutton dressed as lamb. I wouldn't mind but they've not got two bloody ha'pennies to rub together, that lot. As for him, he wants to try doing a day's work for a change.'

When they told him that he went to church to pray, perhaps he thought they meant 'prey'.

As Billy was about to go through the back door, Dad called out:

'Whilst you're on Cheetham Hill, Billy, you can take the accumulator to Forman's radio shop for an exchange. Here's a bob and y'can keep the change, son. I backed a winner yesterday, y'see,' he added by way of explanation.

Here was real generosity, as the refill for their big Cossor wireless cost only a tanner. At this price, Billy thought it was almost worth getting belted.

'Mind y'don't spill acid down your new stockings,' said Mam. 'And don't wiggle the accumulator about or you'll get the programmes mixed up and we'll be getting Hilversum when we want the BBC.'

After dropping off the used accumulator at Forman's, Billy went into St Chad's Church, where Mass was about to begin. The front rows were reserved for the pupils and teachers of the school, the remaining rows being occupied by the various church organisations – the Children of Mary, the Men's Confraternity, and the Mothers' Union. The high altar was bedecked with a profusion of beautiful summer flowers – roses, carnations and lilies – and the various brass ornaments gleamed in the candlelight.

The sanctuary bell signalled the beginning of Mass. Mr Thomas, the headmaster, led the school prayers, the rest of the congregation joining in:

'O my God, I offer this Mass; first to give Thee supreme honour and glory; secondly to thank Thee for all the blessings I have received from Thee.'

Billy followed the Mass with the others.

The whole congregation rose to its feet when, in clear, ringing tones, Canon Calder announced:

'A reading from the Holy Gospel according to Matthew: "Jesus said to his disciples: 'You have learnt how it was said: An eye for an eye and a tooth for a tooth. But I say this to you: offer the wicked man no resistance. On the contrary, if anyone hits you on the right cheek, offer him the other as well . . .' " '

Then the Canon sermonised movingly and passionately on the theme of loving your enemy.

'In the Lord's Prayer, we all say: "Forgive us our trespasses as we forgive those who trespass against us." But do we mean it? Do we understand it? Do we apply it in our daily lives? Turn the other cheek! It means you must not bear hatred for your brother in your heart! It means you must openly tell him, your neighbour, of his offence; this way you will not take a sin upon yourself. You must not exact vengeance nor must you bear a grudge. It means you must love your neighbour as yourself no matter what he has done.'

Billy wondered if Mam was taking any of this in, and he could not resist taking a quick peek to see if she was listening, but her deadpan expression gave nothing away. Oddly enough, though, his brother Sam had a strange look in his eye, and appeared to be paying unusually close attention.

Wonder what's got into our Sam? Billy asked himself. Let him try turning the other cheek in St Chad's school yard and he'll find out what'll happen!

At the Consecration – the gravest part of the Mass – the warning bell sounded. Billy had never seen what happened at this juncture because Mr Thomas always made everyone bow down their heads as he intoned: 'My Lord and My God!'

Finally, '*Domine non sum dignus*'. Billy struck his breast three times and joined the line of kids queueing up at the altar rail. Canon Calder, in his magnificent silk vestments, bearing the chalice, progressed along the kneeling figures, repeating, '*Corpus Domini nostri Jesu Christi custodiat animam tuam in vitam aeternam. Amen,*' over and over again as he placed the consecrated host in the mouth of each communicant. The wafer felt large and tasteless on Billy's tongue, and in his dry mouth it stuck to his palate, but although he was tempted to release it with his finger, he knew that to do so would mean eternal damnation and suffering in the fires of hell. Miss McGurk had said so. So he buried his face in his hands and, freeing the host with his tongue, managed to work up enough saliva to swallow it. Then he joined the congregation in the prayers after Communion.

After Mass, Billy picked up the spare accumulator from Forman's and, having rolled his stockings down, carried it gingerly in his right hand, away from his legs. He crossed Cheetham Hill Road to make his way home and had walked only a few yards down St Chad Street when he was joined by David Priestley, who'd been one of the altar boys who'd served the Mass.

'Hello, Billy,' he said. 'I'll walk back with you, if that's OK.'

'Sure. But it'll be best if you walk on the side away from the accumulator.'

They walked on a little while in silence until Billy asked:

'How d'you like serving on the altar?'

'Oh, it's really great. The Canon even gives us a little cash at the end of the week, if we've served our full quota.'

At the mention of cash, Billy's ears pricked up. He was still thinking about that yacht.

'What d'you have to do to be an altar boy?'

'Well, if you fancy it, you'd have to learn the Latin, but I can teach that to you if you're really interested. I know there is a shortage of servers at the moment. The Canon was saying we need a few more.'

'I'm not sure I have the brains to learn all the Latin that's said in the Mass.'

'Sure you have. Say this: "Dominus, have the biscuits come?"'

'OK. "Dominus, have the biscuits come?" So, what is it – a daft game?'

'No, no. Now say: "Yes, and the spirits too."'

'Seems barmy to me, but OK. "Yes, and the spirits too."'

'You've just had your first Latin lesson. Try it. I say: "Dominus, have the biscuits come?" and you say. . .'

'Yes, and the spirits too.'

'Got it first time. Now I'll tell you a daft joke. There were once three men. Now, two of them were Irishmen – one called Carey and the other Christy; the third man was a Jew called Abie. They all wanted to open a shop and so they applied to the town hall for a licence. After a week, the two Irishmen got their licences but Abie got nothing. "How did you two manage it so quickly?" he asked the Irish fellas. "We went to Mass and prayed," they said. "Why don't you do the same?" So Abie went to Mass, and when it came to the Kyrie, the priest turned to the people and said: "*Kyrie Eleison. Christe Eleison.*" Straightaway, Abie stood up in the church and shouted: "Never mind 'Carey a licence' and 'Christy a licence'! They've already got licences! It's Abie who needs the licence!"'

Billy laughed heartily. 'That's a good'un,' he said.

'That's your second lesson,' said David. 'I'll tell you what. Come with me on the altar tomorrow at half past seven Mass. You won't have to do anything and we'll see if you remember the Latin you've just learned.'

'OK, I'll give it a go. But which people speak Latin anyway?'

'It's a dead language.'

'You mean it's spoken by the dead, by ghosts?'

'No, no,' laughed David. 'I mean that it's no longer used by normal living people.'

'I see. Just us in the Catholic Church.'

Billy was trying to live up to his reputation in the Priestley family of being the street comedian.

'I'll soon be learning the language properly,' said David. 'I've just heard that I've passed the scholarship.'

'The scholarship? What's that?'

'It's a test you can take when you're about eleven, and if you pass you go to a grammar school. I'm going to Damian College.'

'What's wrong with St Chad's? It's good enough for me.'

'Nothing wrong with St Chad's, but I'd like to be a priest one day, like my uncle in Aberystwyth.'

'With a name like yours, what choice do you have? But can't you be a priest from St Chad's?'

'You could – but it wouldn't be easy. Better to go to grammar school first and then to a seminary. If you stay at St Chad's you'd leave at fourteen and go out to work.'

'I think that's what me dad wants me and me brothers to do. He says that the best jobs are at the Wallworks factory on Red Bank.'

They had reached home.

'I'll call for you tomorrow about seven o'clock. Make sure you're ready,' said David as he crossed the street.

Inside, Billy's mam said:

'I hope you didn't spill no acid on your stockings.'

'No. I rolled me stockings down but I spilt a tiny bit on me leg.'

'That's all right then. As long as you didn't spill none on your new stockings.'

He handed over the accumulator to Dad – who was

apparently still in the dog-box – and he made a great show connecting it up to the wireless as if it was a complicated operation like brain surgery.

Billy sat down at the table with the others for the special Sunday breakfast which Mam and his sisters had already prepared. For a while there was temporary silence as they all concentrated on the serious business of tucking into their bacon and egg.

' "Hunger's the best sauce",' announced Mam after a while, quoting one of her many sayings. 'Oh, and by the way, our Polly,' she continued. 'I noticed you weren't at Communion this morning. Why was that, may I ask?'

'Oh, Mam!' exclaimed Polly, turning red. 'I think that's my business!'

'I know why she didn't go,' said Billy darkly.

'Oh, and why was that, clever clogs?' asked Mam, now very interested.

' 'Cos she's on a diet!'

Everyone laughed except Polly, who got to her feet angrily.

'You've been going through my things,' she snapped.

'I saw him go into your room,' said Sam maliciously. 'And he was in there a very long time.'

'That's not very nice,' said Flo. 'Our room's supposed to be private. Have you really been going through our things, our Billy?'

Now it was Billy's turn to go red.

'No, I haven't,' he protested. 'I haven't been going through your rotten things.'

But Billy was telling fibs! He had indeed been in their room and had pried through their things. On Friday, his mam had asked him to take up their clean clothes, and whilst in there, he had become fascinated by all their

92

belongings. On their dressing table he'd noticed the couple of books Polly had been reading. One, called *Release the Real You!*, asked:

> *Do you know what to say but don't know how to say it?*
> *Cat got your TONGUE?*
> *Do you wish to be SILVER-TONGUED?*
> *Then amaze your friends with this miraculous new method!*
> *WHO you are and WHAT you are depend on your*
> *COMMAND OF LANGUAGE!*
> *SPEAK THE KING'S ENGLISH CORRECTLY!*

The other book was entitled *A Slimmer, Slender You! A Diet For The Modern Miss.*

Billy had skipped through the books quickly, for his interest had been drawn to his sisters' clothes – especially their underwear, which they had left lying about the room in their hurry to get out to work. There was something about the room that was essentially feminine: perhaps it was the smell of face powder and cream, or perhaps that strange, mysterious perfume. Whatever it was, he found that he was enjoying a new and inexplicable pleasure in examining the various items of female apparel – silk slips, suspender belts and girdles, bras and lace panties. He had experienced the same peculiar thrill a couple of weeks back when he'd looked at women in their undies in the Empire mail-order catalogue. Was it sinful? It must have been because he'd enjoyed it, and therefore he'd had to tell it in Confession.

'Bless me, Father, for I have sinned against the sixth commandment,' he'd said.

'Oh? In what way?' Father Maguire, the curate, had asked.

'I looked at women in their corsets.'

'I see, my son. And exactly where did you see these women?'

'On page 216 in the Empire catalogue,' said Billy, always ready to supply detailed information to anyone interested.

The priest had given him a penance of five Our Fathers and ten Hail Marys. Billy had never unravelled the mystery of how the priests managed to arrive at these numbers, and how they assessed the value of each sin in terms of prayers. Maybe they had a ready reckoner drawn up by the Pope. As he recited his act of contrition, the priest had said: '*Ego te absolvo in nomine Patris, et Filii, et Spiritus Sancti. Amen.*'

Then he'd added:

'And pray for me, my son.'

Perhaps he has the same problem, said Billy to himself. Perhaps he's even been lookin' at the same catalogue.

Now his mind came back to the breakfast table, however, and he said:

'Mam told me to take up your clean clothes and I just happened to see your book on the table.'

'It's true,' Mam said. 'I did ask him.'

Billy was saved any further recriminations by the appearance of Jim, who came downstairs for his breakfast. As he was sixteen, working and a man, there was no pressure on him to go to Holy Communion. He was his own boss.

Billy seized the opportunity to go upstairs to change out of his best things and make his escape. In Back Honeypot Street, he met Henry, who had acquired a huge lorry tyre – courtesy of his scrap-dealer dad. Henry didn't appreciate how lucky he was to have a father with access to such rich booty. For the next half-hour, they took turns at crouching inside the rim and pushing each other down the slope of the street until the tyre crashed into a wall at the bottom.

After a while, Jim, dressed in his hideous green suit, appeared on the street.

'I'm just going on Barney's tip for a game of pitch-and-toss,' he said. 'You can earn a tanner between you if you dog-out for us.'

'I thought you were supposed to be going to eleven o'clock Mass,' said Billy mischievously.

'Nah. I went last month. That's enough for me. Come on, the two o' you. Watch out for the rozzers and if you see one coming, whistle as loud as you can.'

'OK, our Jim,' said Billy. 'We was getting tired of that game anyroad.'

'Huh! Funny!' said Jim.

On the tip Jim joined a number of his mates in the illegal game of pitch-and-toss, which involved gambling on the outcome of tossing five ha'pennies into the air. Why it should be illegal was anybody's guess but, if anything, its illicit nature was one of its chief attractions. Billy and Henry left off their tyre game and climbed into good spots in two withered trees on top of the hill. From these vantage points, they kept a sharp lookout, like two eagles surveying their territory from high up in their eyries. Each time the coins were tossed into the air, there was an excited shout from all the young men, engaged in their own particular form of Sunday worship. An hour later, Jim came down the hill, whistling. A sure sign that he'd won. He threw a thr'penny bit to each of his sentries.

'That'll do for today,' he said. 'Right, Billy. Time for your boxing lesson in the back yard. Let's go!'

Pushing the two of them inside the tyre along the back street, Jim started to sing:

> '*Red stains on the carpet*
> *Red stains on the stairs . . .*'

'That's supposed to be "Red sails in the sunset",' called Billy from inside the tyre. 'We've got the record by Gracie Fields. What're you singin' them words for?'

'It's because of that murder by Dr Buck Ruxton,' Jim shouted back. 'Didn't you hear about it? He cut up his missus and her maid. He was hanged at Strangeways a few weeks ago. There's another one we sing about him as well:

> '*When you grow too cold to steam*
> *I'll have you to dismember . . .*'

'That should be "When I grow too old to dream",' called out Henry.

They reached their back doors. The young 'uns disembarked, and Henry managed, with Jim's help, to push the giant tyre into his own back yard.

Jim went inside the house while Billy waited in the yard. Five minutes later Jim appeared in full boxing regalia – shorts, shirt and canvas shoes – and carrying two pairs of boxing gloves. He tied one pair on to Billy's fists, leaving his own on loosely.

'Right,' he said. 'What are the four things ever to be remembered?'

'Death, Judgement, Hell and Heaven,' replied Billy promptly.

'No, daftie. In boxing!'

'Oh, right! The rules, the stance, correct punching and active defence.'

'Good lad! You're not behind the door. Now, why do we box?'

'To score points. To hit the opponent more than he hits you.'

'OK. Take up your position like I showed you.'

Billy took up his boxing stance, with his left foot a little forward, the toes of both feet pointing to the right.

'Good,' said Jim. 'Feel the floor with the balls of your feet. That's it. Now take up the peek-a-boo style that I learnt you. Carry your hands high, close to your cheeks, and punch from that defensive position. That's it! You've got it!'

Billy went into his shadow-boxing routine with all the skill of two years' practice.

'Elbows in! Chin into your left shoulder! Great! Light on your feet like you was dancing. Good! Good!'

Jim started to dance around, from time to time holding out an open glove for Billy to punch into. Billy's reflexes had been well trained, and every time Jim proffered a glove, he gave it a sharp, swift jab, varying the routine with the occasional uppercut.

'You've done well, our Billy. I can see you now in the ring against Jock McAvoy.'

'Don't act daft, Jim.'

'OK! OK! Remember – a boxer is a kind o' liar. A feint is a lie. You pretend you're gonna hit your opponent in one place, he covers the spot, and what d'you do?'

'You punch him on the other side instead!'

'Right! A punch that starts out as a left jab then turns into a left hook – that's a lie! Like starting with a straight "I" then making it into an "L". Making openings – that's what it's all about, see! You start a conversation with your left fist – say three or four quick jabs – so that your other fist can come out of its shell and hit your opponent like a rocket. Got it!'

'Got it!'

'Right! Let's get Bennie out.'

Bennie, short for 'Benito', was Jim's own invention. It was a special apparatus consisting of a mattress wrapped around a post which had been sunk in a bucket of concrete. An obese human figure had been painted on it in white, and superimposed on this Jim had put numbers on all the vulnerable spots (jaw, ribs, solar plexus, stomach).

'OK, Billy, get down in the Benny Lynch crouch. That's it! And duck, bob and weave! Duck, bob and weave! You've got it! Ready! When I call out the numbers, let's see you hit 'em! Right, 7–2–1!'

Billy dodged from side to side and let fly with a left jab, a straight right and a left hook – all on target on the wretched inanimate Bennie.

'Good! Good!' Jim called excitedly. 'Now 4–2–1!'

Like quicksilver, Billy hit a right uppercut, a right cross and a left hook. Poor Bennie! He was taking a hammering!

'That's enough with Bennie,' said Jim. 'He can't hit back. So you can now have a go at me!'

Jim fastened two small pads to his knees and knelt to bring himself down to his brother's height.

'Okey-doke,' he said. 'Let's see you hit me!'

The two of them moved around the yard – Billy dancing lightly and Jim shuffling around clumsily. Billy tried to land a punch but in vain, as his brother was too quick for him in his ducking and his dodging. Billy's punches simply bounced off his gloves. Jim then moved forward and, with the speed of a cobra, gave Billy three rapid light jabs in quick succession – one-two-three.

'Just stop for a minute,' he said. 'If you were standing on railway lines and the train came, what would you do?'

'Jump to the side, of course.'

'Right. Well, do that when your opponent comes

forward at you. Weave to the side and watch for an opening. If you're ever in a fight, it's not just a matter of who's strongest or biggest, it's more a question of who's got the most skill and the most determination. Spirit is what counts! Remember that. One day you'll thank me for these boxing lessons, because you'll know how to take care of yourself. You'll see!'

'Ta for the sermon, our Jim. That's the second I've had today.'

Mam appeared at the back door.

'Come on, you two. Time for dinner.'

Lowering his gloves, Jim turned in her direction.

'OK, Mam. We've just finished.'

Like lightning, Billy landed three quick light jabs to his head – rat-a-tat-tat.

'Always keep your guard up, Jim! And you did say look for an opening, didn't you!'

'Y'cheeky little bugger,' said Jim, laughing.

Together, they went inside.

Whilst Billy was having a wash at the slopstone, he heard Dad giving Mam the nearest thing to an apology.

Thank God! Billy said to himself. At least they've started talking again. He hated the strained atmosphere in the house when Mam went into one of her 'freezing-off' moods.

'I'd had a skinful, y'see, Kate. Too much o' the bevy,' Billy heard his dad say.

'There's nowt wrong with having a drink, Tommy, but you always go too far. I know a man needs his pint and his smoke, but within reason is what I always say. Otherwise, you'll drink us out of house and home.'

'Aye, you're right there, Kate. Never no more. I'll not touch another drop.'

'I'll believe that when I see it,' she said.

She called up the stairs.

'Right, you lot. Dinner is served.'

The rest of the family – with the exception of Polly – appeared and sat down to Sunday dinner, the main meal of the week. Mam believed firmly in having a good table, and this meant a fully stocked one rather than a balanced diet. Her family wanted something solid down 'em – none of that rabbit food for dinner. The Sunday midday meal was a family ritual which never, never varied. Roast beef, Yorkshire pudding, cabbage – or sprouts or cauliflower, whichever happened to be in season – green peas, boiled potatoes, and one – and only one – roast potato each, the whole lot being covered by a generous helping of 'Ah, Bisto!' gravy. This first course was consumed and savoured in reverent silence and with near-religious dedication, so beautifully cooked and tastily flavoured was the fare. Pudding time, however, was the time for talking, and as Flo and Mam brought in the rice pudding, the three youngest boys chorused:

'No skin on ours!'

'I'll have their share,' announced Jim promptly – a bit too promptly.

Mam was almost sure that at some point in the past, Jim had put the young ones off the skin by telling them it was human skin and only fit for cannibals, but she couldn't prove it.

'Where's our Polly?' asked Dad. 'She was actin' a bit funny this mornin', wasn't she?'

'Oh, she's all right. Just a funny mood. It's her time of the month,' Kate whispered. 'Anyroad,' she continued, 'she's gone off to Southport with Steve on his motorbike. They said they'd be back for a bit o' tea about six o'clock.'

'Oh, aye,' answered Dad. 'Then we'd best get the good cups out.'

'You mean the ones with the handles,' said Billy.

There was a few moments' silence as they turned their attention to the rice pudding. Jim had already reached the stage of scraping the skin from the large dish.

'I see in the *Empire News*, Kate, that the GPO have started a speaking clock on the telephones,' announced Dad.

'Isn't it marvellous what they can do nowadays. How does it work?'

Dad made funny shapes with his hands, as if trying to explain the intricacies of the telephone system.

'Oh, it's too complicated, Kate. Y'wouldn't understand it.'

'I see,' she said, looking straight at him.

'I've heard one of them clocks on the telephone at work,' said Jim. 'There's a woman keeps giving the time over and over again. She says: "At the third stroke, it will be three twenty-five precisely." She goes on and on all day long.'

'What a boring job!' remarked Les.

'What if she wants to go to the lavatory?' asked Sam.

'She has to take the phone in with her!' said Billy, not to be left out of the speculations.

'That means she has to sit there with the phone in her hand, telling people the time,' added Les. 'I definitely wouldn't fancy that for a job.'

'Anyroad,' said Dad. 'Over a quarter of a million rung up to ask the time during the first week.'

'Eeh,' observed Flo. 'She must have been hoarse!'

'And wouldn't you think the toffs with telephones could afford clocks of their own like ours?' remarked Mam.

Dinner over, Flo and Mam sided the table and washed

up, after which the family dispersed to their various Sunday-afternoon recreations. Sam and Les went out to join in the never-ending activity of their gang; Jim announced that he was taking Jean Priestley rowing on Heaton Park lake – postponed from the previous day; Flo said she would be going out to tea again with her friend Patty Bristow; and Billy that he would be spending the afternoon reading his comics – *Chips*, *Film Fun* and the *Rover*.

As for Kate and Tommy, they too had a postponed appointment.

'Right, our Billy. No noise, d'y hear me? Me and your father's going for a lay-down for an hour. Then you and me'll go and see your Auntie Cissie and your Uncle Eddy over in Greengate. So think on.'

For the next hour and a half, peace and tranquillity reigned over the Hopkins household.

Chapter Five

No Green in Greengate

To reach the Greengate district in Salford, Billy and his mam had to cross Cheetham Hill Road and pass by the terrifying towers of Strangeways Prison with its massive twenty-foot walls.

'Our Jim said this is where they hung that fella for cutting up his missus and her maid,' said Billy.

'He's not the only one that's been hanged here. Not by a long chalk.'

'I hope his ghost isn't still hanging about,' Billy said with an involuntary shudder. 'I don't think we should hang about neither. Come on, Mam, let's hurry up!'

Over Great Ducie Street and past the assize courts they walked, passing street after street and row after row of shoddy back-to-back houses – every one the same – criss-crossed by a pattern of foul-smelling back entries and mean, squalid little courts. There were no green fields in Greengate, not even blue skies – a permanent half-fog drifted over the place. The smoking, huddled houses were dominated on all sides by dark, gloomy factories – notably the Greengate Rubber Works – and the services which attended them: the goods depots and the gasometers. The viaducts interweaved with the railway lines and with the canals below, and here and there they passed a church or a Methodist chapel, whilst at every street corner there was the inevitable dingy little pub.

At last they reached Cable Street, where Auntie Cissie and her brood resided. At number 11, they found the front door already wide open, so Mam called down the lobby.

'Cissie! Are y'in? It's Kate! I've come to see you!'

The voice which responded was so strident, so piercing, it could have shattered glass or bent steel.

'Chuck thy cap in, Kate, and come inside!' Auntie Cissie screeched. 'Well, I'll be buggered!'

Reassured by this warm welcome, Billy and Mam went down the lobby and into the living room. Cissie was an extraordinarily thin, scrawny woman. It was difficult to understand how such a loud, shrieking sound could have emanated from such a bony frame. She was about forty-five years of age and obviously overjoyed to see her sister, for she clasped her in a long, affectionate embrace. Then she turned her attention to Billy and said:

'Hasn't he got big? I'm sure he's grown another foot since I last seen 'im.'

Billy looked down at his shoes.

'No,' he said. 'Still got only two.'

'I can see we've got a bloody comic in the family and all,' she said. 'Anyroad, I won't kiss him, 'cos I know little lads don't like to be kissed.'

Billy was truly grateful for this omission, especially as Cissie's three young daughters – Rose, Violet and Iris – were busy sniggering at something. He saw that they were pointing in the direction of his genitals from the corner of the room where they had been engaged in dishing out tea to their numerous dolls. Their dog, Scamp, appeared to be part of the conspiracy as it began nuzzling his crotch.

Seated by the fireside was Uncle Ernie, Cissie's husband – a morose, grumpy-looking individual who was engrossed in raking, poking and rearranging the coal on the fire. Billy could have given him a few pointers. Ernie acknowledged their presence and existence with a typical Lancashire greeting which was brief, economical and to the point.

' 'Ow do,' he said, and spat a great wet gozzler into the fire.

'You'll put t'bloody fire out doing that!' Auntie Cissie squawked.

Mam and Auntie Cissie retired to the kitchen for a private, sisterly chinwag, and Billy, not wishing to be left alone with the taciturn, expectorating Ernie, the giggling girls and the perverted dog, followed them.

He didn't understand much of their whispered conversation and confidences but he caught intermittent snatches:

'We've had some right times, you and me, Kate, since we was in service together.'

'We have and all, Cissie. A few heartaches and a few laughs.'

'That's all life is, isn't it? But how's Tommy treating you, Kate?'

'Mustn't grumble, Cissie. He doesn't ask for it much, if y'know what I mean. He's earning good money in the market, gives me thirty-five bob a week – so it's not so bad. We manage. We keep our heads above water. I even bought a new three-piece t'other day at the Co-op. What about Ernie in there?'

'He's all right. A bit of a miserable bugger but, like Tommy, he's not allus wanting to have it off like some men do. He gets good money at the rubber works but he doesn't half stink when he comes in at night! But never mind him. How's your Flo and Polly getting on nowadays?'

'Not so bad, Cissie. Our Polly's walking out with a very nice young man – well-off and a very posh talker. But I hope she settles down soon, 'cos she's a bit of an awkward bugger. Our Flo's lovely, but no prospects as yet. There's plenty of time, though; she's only twenty-four. She might as well enjoy herself while she's still young – that's what I say.'

'You're right there, Kate.'

Cissie adopted a conspiratorial tone and whispered:

'Eh, whatever happened to that there Bridget Sharples who lives in your street – the one who...'

She glanced over in Billy's direction, but he was absorbed in a copy of the *News of the World* which had been left lying on the kitchen table. He was reading the various headlines: *Sex-crazed choirmaster tells his story; 'They tempted me,' claims vicar; Climbed into nudist colony – lost his trousers.*

'... the one who, you know, had that illegible baby?' said Auntie Cissie, trying in vain to keep her voice down.

'That wasn't her first, you know,' Mam whispered. 'She'd had another one by another fella, about three year ago.'

'Tut-tut-tut. Get away. Just goes to show, a slice off a cut cake is never missed, eh?'

'You're right there, Cissie. They say you don't open t'oven door for just one loaf.'

'You'd think a girl like her would have used one of them contraspective things.'

'Aye. But I've heard that they put a hole in 'em every so often to keep the population up.'

'Tut-tut-tut. It's this here bloody Baldwin gover'ment. You can't trust the higher-ups, can you?'

'It's allus been the same, Cissie. They're all in a click and they're all twisters.'

'And what about your Billy, there? They say he's the brains of the family, eh?'

'Eeh, I tell you, our Cissie – he comes out with some things for his age. I get that worried, I do. I'm sure his brain's gonna burst one day!'

'You want to be careful there, Kate. You want to make sure that all the goodness of his body doesn't go into his head, 'cos then it can come out in his hair, specially if it's too long like it is now. You should allus make sure he gets a good haircut or y'might find his body goes weak and then he'd get poorly very easy. That'd be my advice t'you.'

'I think you're right there, Cissie. I'll have him at the barber's tomorrow. Anyway, I think we'd better be off now. We've got two more visits to make – to me mother's and to our Eddy's.'

'Eddy's!' said Cissie. 'You'll find they've got problems there all right. Mona'll tell ya. I won't keep you, but it's been right nice seeing you – just like old times.'

As they made their way down the lobby, Mam called out, 'Ta-rah, girls! Ta-rah, Ernie!'

When they reached the front door, Auntie Cissie shoved a shilling into Billy's hand, and in his mind's eye, his yacht hove into view.

Grandma McGuinness lived in a little two-up, two-down in Viaduct Street, opposite the railway goods yard. Mam knocked on her door and a voice in the house croaked:

'Who is it?'

'It's Kate, Mam. I've come to see how you're getting on,' Mam shouted through the letter box.

'Hang on! I'm coming,' Grandma said.

The door was eventually opened by an old lady who

was swathed completely from head to foot in black, with a simple cameo brooch at her neck; she was the image of the old Queen Victoria in mourning for her beloved Albert. They returned to the sitting room where Grandma sat down heavily in her rocking chair and returned her attention to the glass of stout she had been nursing.

'Take your coats off, and if y'want a cuppa tea, Kate, y'know where the stuff is. And bring this lad here that there bit o' roast beef left over from me dinner. He looks to me as if he needs feeding up. Why, he's just a bag o' bones.'

'S'all right, Mam,' Kate bawled in Gran's earhole. 'We've only just finished our dinner and we'll not take our coats off 'cos we can't stop. We're going over to our Eddy's.'

'I don't know why y'bother coming if y'can't stop. But bring that bloody bit o' beef for this here lad anyroad and stop arguifying.'

Billy was presented with a large piece of beef covered in fat and gristle. His stomach heaved.

'Get that down you and shurrup,' his gran said. 'And as for you, our Kate, you spoil yer kids, y'do. They won't eat this and they won't eat that. Not like our Hetty's kids – they'll eat anything.'

Billy looked round frantically for some way out of the impasse, searching for, as Jim would have put it, an opening. Mam pointed to a boat-shaped teapot on the mantelpiece.

'I notice you've still got your Coalport teapot, Mam.'

Grandma's gaze was momentarily diverted towards her most valuable possession, which had pride of place amongst all the ornaments. Billy seized his chance and, with the speed of a Joe Louis, thrust the fatty beef into her aspidistra plant-pot. Jim would have been proud of him.

'That's proper porcelain is that, Kate, and it's stopping where it is. As you well know, it belonged to me grand-mother, Mary Molly McGinty, and it was given to her by her father, Sean McGinty, as a wedding present in Dublin in 1815.'

'Have you ever had tea in it, Gran?' asked Billy.

'I have not, young man,' she answered haughtily. 'It's a family heirloom is that and not for drinking tea out of. When I'm kicking up daisies, Kate, it'll come to you as me eldest daughter.'

'I'm sure I'll take care of it as you've done. But don't talk like that, Mam. That day's a long way off, I'm sure,' Kate said. 'Anyroad, we just come over to see if you're all right and if there's anything you want.'

'That's right; you just leave me 'ere. I dare say I won't be troubling you all that much longer. And there's nothing I want. I can look after meself. I like to be independent, I do. But tell our Eddy when y'see him that I'm very upset with him. I don't like the way he's knocking and bashing Mona about. If he can't behave himself and start looking after her, 'e needn't bother coming to me funeral. I don't want him there weeping over me coffin. Just tell him from me to think on. Oh, aye, and tell him I'm running out o' stout and to get me a drop in when he goes to the boozer tonight.'

Mam washed up a few dishes for Gran, including the one which had borne the vanished beef. Billy's brothers, when faced with dollops of Gran's inedible blubbery beef, had opted for the same solution. One day, somebody would clean out that plant-pot and discover a new species of meat-bearing aspidistra which shed steak instead of leaves.

Eddy, who lived appropriately – by either accident or design – in Brewery Street, facing Boddington's, was a rough diamond and a bully of the first order. All his life he had worked at tough jobs – as railway carter, market porter, slaughterman and meat packer. For Billy, however, his most remarkable feature was his right hand, which was missing a couple of fingers severed at the top joint some time previously in mysterious industrial accidents. He constantly bullied and badgered his wife, Mona, for her inability to provide him with offspring, with the result that she had developed not only a nervous tic but a high-pitched, plaintive whine.

Mam knocked on Eddy's door.

'Anybody in? It's Kate come to see you!'

The door was opened by Mona, a short, dark-haired woman on whose face was etched a permanent expression of anguish and apprehension, as if she was expecting to be struck a blow at any moment. Grimacing a painful smile, she said sorrowfully:

'Come in, Kate. It's so good t'see a friendly face again. Eddy's out at the moment – at the boozer as usual. I think he must have hollow legs; I don't know where he puts it all, I don't.'

'How do, Mona,' replied Mam. 'How are things with you?'

'Not so good, Kate. Not so good. It's your Eddy. He's all right when 'e's sober – he can be charming – but he's terrible when he's had a drop.'

'Why, has 'e been knocking you about again?'

'He has that, Kate. Something terrible,' she whimpered. 'Only yesterday he come in and . . . Hey up! He's here!' Mona cringed visibly. 'I better get his dinner out of the oven,' she wailed.

Eddy appeared obviously the worse for drink. He was

swaying and his eyes were bloodshot.

'How do, our Kate,' he said drunkenly. 'What's this bleeding woman been saying about me? Where's me bleeding dinner, you? Yer bleeding useless get!'

'Here's your dinner, Eddy. It's a bit dried up now from being in t'oven so long,' Mona stammered, placing his meal on the table.

'I'll show you what I think of yer bleeding dried-up dinner,' he bawled. Taking the plate, he flung it against the wall. The plate shattered into a thousand pieces and the amorphous mess slithered slowly down the wall.

'Oh, Kate,' Mona sobbed. 'What am I going to do? What am I going to do?'

'Go on, cry, you stupid bitch, cry! You'll piss less,' Eddy snarled.

It was time for Mam to act.

'Look you, you drunken pig!' she bawled at him. 'I won't have you using that dirty language in front of our Billy here. I'm ashamed of you as a brother. Now get to bed!'

Through his alcoholic haze, Eddy noticed for the first time that Billy was indeed in the room, witnessing his drunken, barbaric behaviour. Eddy nodded stupidly at his older sister and mumbled:

'Sorry, our Kate. I didn't see him there. I'll get meself off to bed. But *she's* no bloody use to nobody. Neither use nor ornament.'

Eddy stumbled off to bed, almost falling on his face as he went through the bedroom door. The three of them were left alone. Mona and Mam began cleaning the dinner from the wall.

'It's not my fault that I can't have kids, Kate,' wailed Mona. 'He's no right to treat me like this.'

'He'll be back to his charming self when he's slept it

off,' said Mam. 'But I wouldn't stand for it no more. You can either set the cruelty man on to him or you can leave home. If it were me, I'd leave.'

'I think you're right,' said Mona.

'Well, Mona, I've got to be getting back to make the master's tea. But think on what I've told you.'

On the way back, Mam said to Billy:

'You know, your father's not so bad really. You see, it's his work; they're a rough lot in the market and they all drink. He could be a lot worse!'

Mam turned the key in her own door.

'Eeh, I'm right glad to get back to civilisation!'

Billy fully agreed with her, for after that to-do at Uncle Eddy's, his own home and his own family really did seem like civilisation.

In the scullery, they found that Dad had already half-prepared the high tea which they had on Sunday nights: a magnificent salad – as befitted a Smithfield Market worker – consisting of lettuce, spring onions, tomatoes, radish, cucumber and beetroot, with a wide choice of condiments like pickles, piccalilli and chutney, plus, of course, the obligatory mayonnaise. In addition there was usually boiled ham or corned beef, but this Sunday, seeing there was a guest, there was a delicious middle-cut of West's red salmon – though it was for the adults only. To mark Sunday as something extra special, the bread was sliced diagonally into thin triangles instead of the customary weekday rectangles.

It wasn't long before young Sam and Les – prompted, no doubt, by healthy appetites – came in looking for food.

'The only time we see you two,' Mam said, 'is when you're hungry. I'm not kidding. You use this house like a Blackpool boarding house. What do you get up to in that Honeypot Street gang of yours?'

'We're collecting wood for Bonfire Night,' replied Les.

'Glory be t'God! Not already! It's three months off!'

'Aye. But we're gonna have a bigger blaze than Derby Street this year,' said Sam.

Shortly after that, Jim returned from his romantic boating expedition, and a little later Steve and Polly arrived looking as if they'd just flown in from Australia.

'Hello, Steve,' said Billy. 'When are you going to give me a ride on that motorbike of yours?'

'We'll see,' replied Steve. 'One of these days. I don't know when. But we'll see.'

That seemed pretty vague to Billy and so he didn't pursue it. He'd only been trying it on, anyway.

'Good evening, Mr Keenan . . . Steve,' said Mam, in her posh voice. 'Would you care for a little swill?'

'A swill, Mrs Hopkins? Sorry, I don't . . .' Steve said, glancing anxiously towards the table, which had been set out for tea, then quizzically towards Polly for a translation.

'You know, a wash, like. To freshen up,' explained Polly.

'Oh, that would be lovely, Mrs Hopkins,' said Steve, looking distinctly relieved. 'Is it upstairs?'

'No,' replied Polly apologetically. 'You have to use the slopstone in the scullery. Sorry.'

'No problems,' said Steve. 'That's fine.'

The great man went into the scullery for a swill and then joined the family at the table.

'Why can't we have salmon?' complained Sam.

'Because! That's why!' replied Mam. 'Eat what you're given and shurrup!'

'What d'you do for a living, Steve?' asked Dad as he made a large butty of salad and salmon – much to the embarrassment of Polly, who had raised her eyes to heaven in supplication.

'I'm an engineer at Avro Ansons, Mr Hopkins. We make aeroplanes,' answered Steve modestly.

Billy had always suspected that Steve had something to do with the aviation business.

'That's very useful,' said Mam.

'It will be if there's a war,' said Jim.

'I don't think there's going to be no war,' said Polly. 'Not according to that Hitler in Germany.'

'There'll be a war all right,' said Dad as he poured his tea into his saucer, blew on it and slurped it noisily. 'Mark my words! I wouldn't trust that bloody goose-stepping Hitler fella as far as I could throw him.'

'I'll get the dessert,' said Polly, now looking pale and drawn.

The Sunday dessert was usually pineapple chunks, but today, in honour of the important guest, there was tinned peaches and cream as well, but once again, for adults only.

'Why can't we have peaches too?' asked Sam, always the disgruntled one and a bit of a socialist to boot.

'You be happy with them chunks,' said Mam. 'A family in Africa'd be glad o' them.'

'But that's where they come from!' said Sam.

'Will you stop being so obstroculous,' Mam said. 'And while we're about it, let's change the subject as well,' she continued. 'All that miserable talk about war! Have you visited a picture house lately, Steve?'

'No, Mrs Hopkins. Not lately. I'm waiting for the picture house to visit me. It will one day.'

'How d'you mean?' asked Jim.

'The BBC have started transmitting the first talking pictures,' said Steve, 'on something called television.'

'Get away,' said Jim. 'Never. S'not possible.'

'Oh, it is,' replied Steve. 'The first broadcast covered

only a distance of ten miles from Alexandra Palace to Olympia, but it worked, though we're told in the paper that the announcer, Leslie Mitchell, looked as if he had two black eyes.'

'Isn't it marvellous what they can do nowadays? What will they think of next?' said Mam. 'Pictures in your own home. But I don't think I want one of them big screens and one of them projectiles in our front room.'

'You won't have to,' said Steve. 'Your set will be no bigger than that wireless there.'

Up to this point, Dad hadn't said a word, because he didn't understand the concept of television. He was also busy removing a piece of tomato skin from his upper denture, which he had taken out of his mouth to facilitate the operation. Polly had turned a funny colour. But now, when he had cleared the irritation, Dad felt it was time to deliver his opinion.

'It'll never work,' he said. 'Not in a month o' Sundays!'

Billy was sure he was right. Dad always was.

After tea, the family formed the usual big half-circle round the hearth, with Dad in the big chair near the wireless where he could operate the controls. In deathly silence, they listened to the news, which was all about Adolf Hitler recognising Mussolini's occupation of Abyssinia, King Edward opening a memorial on Vimy Ridge and England winning the Davis Cup.

'There's nowt else on,' Dad said. 'Not on a Sunday night. Nowt but religion! And that Mr Middleton and his bloody garden!'

If Dad said there was nowt on, there was nowt on. For when it came to judging wireless programmes, there was none better. Performers were either 'in' or 'out'. If somebody was awarded the accolade of a thumbs-up, he'd say: 'He's a good 'un!' or, alternatively, 'He's a good turn!' But if the thumb was turned south, he'd mutter, 'Bloody rubbish!' or 'Should be shot!' Henry Hall, Gracie Fields, George Formby, Arthur Tracy and Robb Wilton were all 'in', but Vic Oliver, Jack Warner, Harry Roy and, most especially, the languid, public-school Western Brothers with their 'Keep it up, chaps! Keep it up!' were definitely 'out'.

Dad switched the wireless off and the family was allowed to make conversation. Billy was the first to seize the opportunity.

'I met David Priestley today and he wants me to go on the altar with him.'

'Oh, aye,' Mam said. 'That'll be nice, but it means you'll have to get up early every morning.'

'That's all right. He also said he'd passed his scholarship and was leaving St Chad's to go to another school called Damian College.'

'That's a very good school,' said Steve. 'He must be a clever lad.'

'Oh, he is and all,' said Mam. 'I was talking to his mam after church this morning and she says he wants to be a priest.'

'D'y'ever fancy going to a higher school, our Billy?' asked Polly.

Dad responded for him.

'No, that's not for the likes of us. I believe in doing right by the lads and getting a good trade in their hands.'

'You mean like yours,' asked Kate contemptuously.

'No, not like mine. I never had a chance. But I'll tell you this, Kate – I've worked hard all me life and can look anyone in the face.'

'And look what you've got to show for it,' Mam snapped back. 'Nowt! If our Billy's got brains, he should get the chance to make something of himself.'

'Book-learning never did nobody no good,' replied Dad. 'Are they any happier, these bloody clever dicks, with their heads full of nowt but theories?'

'Education can lead to a better-paid job,' said Steve. 'Besides that, you know what they say: "Don't hide your talent under a bushel." '

'I don't want none o' my kids getting above themselves, being lah-de-dah and giving themselves airs and all that. A good apprenticeship at the Wallworks is worth more than all that book rubbish they learn 'em at them stuck-up schools.'

'That's what I want to do,' said Sam, chipping in. 'Billy's not the only one in this house with brains, y'know. But I want to start earning good money, not waste me time at one of them daft schools.'

'Me and all,' added Les.

'Y'see, Steve,' went on Dad, 'I want me kids to be nice, friendly people who can get on with others and not to be thinking about money all the time.'

'I agree with you, Dad,' said Polly, looking pointedly at Steve. 'I don't think it's right to try and alter people. You've got to take people as you find 'em.'

'Money isn't everything, I know,' conceded Steve. 'But just the same, the very top jobs, the interesting jobs, the well-paid jobs go to those who are well educated.'

'I think the big pay,' said Jim, 'the *really* big pay, goes to those at the very top of the tree, like our champion boxers – Jock McAvoy, Benny Lynch, Eddie Phillips. But I don't know what we're arguing about here, 'cos Billy's only eight and it's at least another three years before he can even think about scholarships and all that. A lot can happen in three years.'

How right he was!

* * *

The family discussion broke up when Dad said:

'I think I'll just slip out to Capper's for an hour and a game o' crib.'

'I thought you'd stopped drinking,' said Mam.

'Just a quick one,' said Dad. 'I won't be late as I've got to be up early again tomorrow.'

He went into his getting-ready-for-Capper's routine – a performance which the family always watched with fascination.

He went to the slopstone and soused thoroughly, snorting and snuffling and splashing water in all directions like an elephant. Next came the ritual dressing. He rolled up a brown silk scarf into a long sausage, put it round his neck, crossed it in front and secured the ends in his braces. He did not wear a tie. That was for Saturdays. Instead, he closed the top of his striped woollen shirt with a collar stud. On with his jacket, and then the final touch. He warmed his cap at the fire and placed it carefully on his head. Grooming completed, he went out. There was always a sense of relief when he left.

Jim also went out – in his case to some unknown destination, probably more games of pitch-and-toss, since it did not get dark at this time of year until after ten o'clock.

With Jim gone, things went dead for Billy.

'I want to go to the pictures, Mam,' he announced.

' "I want" doesn't get,' replied Mam automatically. 'Besides, it's Sunday and there are no pictures, except maybe Jewish ones.'

'Then I wanna go to the Jewish pictures,' he whined.

'They're in Yiddish, so you won't understand 'em.'

'It don't matter. I WANNA GO!'

Steve picked Billy up and hung him by his braces on

the coat hook on the living-room door.

'I suppose you think you look like Christ on the cross,' said Sam.

'Why have y'put me up here, Steve? Come on, don't keep me in suspense!'

'Right,' said Steve. 'You're up there for being cheeky to your mother. What's the fourth commandment?'

'Honour thy father and thy mother.'

'OK, remember that, and also that the most important people in the world for you are your mother and father and your family. Always show respect to them and you won't come to any harm. With your brains and your talent, you could get to the top one day, but you won't get anywhere if you give cheek. Got it?'

'Oh, no! Not another sermon! That's the third I've had today. From up here, I feel as if it's me as should be giving the sermon,' said Billy, laughing. 'Come on, Steve, let me down!'

'Only if you promise to behave yourself.'

'OK, OK,' replied Billy. 'I promise to behave if you promise to take me for a ride on your motorbike!'

'This brother of yours is a real wheeler-dealer,' said Steve to Polly. 'OK, Little Lord Fauntleroy. It's a deal! But we leave the date open.'

Steve took him down.

'He's learned all this bargaining and making deals,' said Mam, 'working amongst the Jewish people on Sat'day morning. Maybe he should go into business.'

There was an hour before bedtime, and the three younger lads settled down to scanning their comics avidly, as if they might find the answer to the riddle of the universe in one of them. The *Rover*, the *Hotspur*, the *Skipper* and the *Adventure* were passed around from hand to hand whilst Mam turned her attention to the 'Bullets' competition in *John Bull* – not that she'd ever won anything. Steve and Polly retired to the front room for a bit of courting.

Around ten o'clock, the three young lads were given their marching orders, and together they trooped out. Before going up the stairs, they paused outside the front room to eavesdrop on the courting couple, making mock kissing and hugging gestures as they did so. Through the door, though, they could hear Steve and Polly talking earnestly, and, judging from the sound of it, there was an almighty row brewing.

'You've got to live and let live, Steve. You can't change human nature,' Polly was saying angrily. 'You've got to remember that it takes all sorts to make a world.'

'I'm not trying to change you. I'm just saying that everybody can improve themselves – me included.'

'Yes, you may have opinions about that, but you're always pushing 'em down people's throats – like y'did with me dad tonight.'

'I did nothing of the sort. We were having a friendly discussion, that's all.'

'I think you look down on us, y'know. The way me dad eats, the way I speak and the way we live. You're always correcting me! I think you just turn your nose up at other people. And another thing. I didn't like the way you hung our Billy up on that door tonight.'

'It was just a bit of fun, that's all. I think you're just talking rubbish.'

'Oh, rubbish, is it . . .'

The three lads fled up the stairs as it suddenly sounded as if the lovers were coming out of the room. From the top of the stairs they heard Polly storm at Steve:

'Go and find someone who speaks proper. And you

can take your lousy ring back. I don't want to see you again!'

'There goes me motorbike ride!' said Billy.

They heard Polly run up to her room, and the sobbing which followed. Poor Steve left quietly by the front door, and a few moments later they heard his motorbike roar off down Honeypot Street.

As Billy lay in bed, he couldn't help reciting quietly to himself: '*This is the man all tattered and torn,/That kissed the maiden all forlorn . . .*'

But his thoughts soon turned to happier things – to a beautiful, graceful yacht gliding across Queen's Park lake. And tonight there was added a second dream: he saw himself going up on to the school stage at St Chad's to the applause of all his teachers, friends and family to be told by Mr Thomas that he had passed the scholarship to – what was the name of that school again? – Damian College. Then he was asleep.

Chapter Six

Monday-morning Blues

Monday came, and the morning sky was grey, grey as Greengate on a sunny afternoon.

Billy rose early and was ready when David Priestley called to take him to St Chad's Church for 7.30 Mass. As they were setting off, Mam called from the scullery:

'On your way back from church, I want you to call at the Jewish bakery and buy threepenn'orth of reject bagels or buns or whatever they've got.'

In the vestry of St Chad's, David showed Billy how to put on a cassock and a cotta, making a few fussy adjustments as if dressing a dummy in Lewis's window.

'There,' he said finally. 'St William of Cheetham.'

The two boys lit the altar candles, and processed with Canon Calder, the parish priest, into the silent old church. At that time in the morning it had an eerie atmosphere, their footsteps on the terrazzo-tiled floor echoing round the empty building. Empty, that is, except for two devoted worshippers: old 'Brother' Kelly, whose private 'silent' devotions sibilated round the near-deserted nave; and silver-haired Sally Sweeney, who was noted for her dedicated attendance at all church services, including weddings and funerals. Especially funerals, which were her favourite.

The Canon's voice reverberated round the hollow church as he intoned the beginning of the Mass:

'*In nomine Patris, et Filii et Spiritus Sancti. Amen.*'

David responded with a fluency born of long practice. Five minutes into the Mass, he caught Billy's eye and gave him a broad grin and a meaningful nod. The priest turned to face the congregation of two.

'*Dominus vobiscum.*'

'Dominus, have the biscuits come?' Billy said quietly.

Giving a big wink in Billy's direction, David responded, '*Et cum spiritu tuo.*'

'Yes, and the spirits too,' Billy mouthed.

A minute later, the priest whirled round and raised his arms.

'*Kyrie eleison.*'

Sotto voce, Billy replied, 'Carey a licence,' whilst David, grinning even more broadly, answered correctly: '*Kyrie eleison.*'

'*Christe eleison,*' said the priest.

'Christy a licence,' said Billy, adding under his breath, 'But it's Abie who needs the licence.'

The rest of the ceremony passed without incident, and Billy watched and imitated everything that David did, enjoying the experience immensely.

'At the end of the week,' David said, on the way home, 'the Canon gives us sixpence if we've served our quota. Then there's tips from weddings and funerals. Funerals are the best, 'cos not only do you get good tips but also a ride home in a big black limousine.'

'It seems quite easy, David.'

'I told you it was easy. And it will get easier still as you go along. Just follow in my footsteps and you'll be OK.'

'I'll try to do that,' Billy said.

They parted and Billy went to the Jewish bakery. He waited around for twenty minutes or so, then bought a big bag of bagels and seeded buns for threepence.

At home, he found the usual breakfast chaos. His brothers argued and bickered amongst themselves whilst Mam made toast, one piece at a time, by holding a round of bread, speared on an ordinary dinner fork, up to the bars of the living-room fire. Every weekday morning it was the same. She burned the thumb of her right hand, while the boys fought and squabbled noisily over who was first in line for the piece of toast due to come off the assembly line.

'The next one's mine!' wailed Sam as Mam threw a finished piece on to the table.

Jim was too fast for him and snaffled the toast with practised ease.

'Workers first,' he said.

Sam's whining reached fever pitch:

'Aw, that's not fair, Mam. I've been waiting I don't know how long for that piece. It was my turn and now he's rotten well swiped it.'

'Shurrup, the lot of you,' yelled Mam, her thumb resembling a well-done steak. 'Shurrup. I've only got one pair of hands.'

'I'm fed up of this rotten house and this rotten lot. That was my piece of toast.'

'Shurrup, I said,' Mam shouted, and she winged Sam a beauty across his left cheek.

Sam's whingeing took on a new urgency.

'Go on,' he howled, turning the other cheek. 'Hit the other side now!'

Mam duly obliged by landing a second slap right on target.

It was at that juncture that Billy, bearing buns and bagels, arrived like the relieving US cavalry.

'I saw you in church yesterday listening to that sermon,' Billy said as he deposited the provender on the table. 'You shouldn't do everything that the Bible tells you, 'cos sometimes it tells you some funny things like if your eye looks at something bad, you're supposed to pluck it out. Next thing we know, you'll be walking around like Lord Nelson!'

There was a loud knocking at the front door.

'Glory be t'God!' said Mam. 'Who can that be at this time o' the morning? I hope it's not her-next-door on the cadge for sugar or summat. Go and see who it is, our Les.'

Les was back in a minute.

'It's the postman. He sez he has an unstamped letter for us. There's a double surcharge or summat on it.'

'Now who can that be from?' Mam said, puzzled.

She went to the door to find out. The boys heard the postman say:

'Sorry, Mrs Hopkins. There's no stamp on it, though someone's tried to draw one in pencil there in the corner. Anyroad, the charge is double, I'm sorry to say. That's twice three-halfpence, making threepence due altogether.'

Mam took three pennies from her purse and paid up. She came back into the living room still perplexed, carrying the surcharged letter.

'It's addressed to "Master Samuel Hopkins". Here, it's yours,' she said, handing over the letter.

Billy and Jim had gone strangely quiet and were grimacing at each other as Sam, wearing a confused expression, opened up his mysterious letter.

'Well, what does it say?' Mam asked.

'It says: "Dear Sam, You are daft and potty. From your brothers Billy and Jim."'

'You daft devil, Billy,' said Jim. 'I told you to put it in the letter box of the door, not the pillar box at the corner of the street.'

'Right, you pair of daft buggers,' said Mam. 'You can both pay me threepence each for worrying me like that.'

This incident was only one of many against Sam, who had been cast in the role of family scapegoat. The other boys enjoyed baiting him, because he never failed to oblige them by reacting in exactly the way they had hoped. One of Dad's gramophone records began, 'And it's Pom! And it's Pom! Pom! Pom! Pom!' Whenever they were short of entertainment, they had only to chant, 'And it's Sam! And it's Sam! Sam! Sam! Sam!' for him to reward them by throwing a fit of purple rage. He was also the most faddy kid in the family. And that was saying something, for they were all a fussy lot as Grandma McGuinness had rightly asserted. Jim was chief tormentor, especially in the matter of food, for it usually meant an extra helping for him. Whenever there was meat pie for dinner Jim always sang – *sotto voce*, of course:

> *'Our John Willie's got scabby eyes,*
> *A dirty snotty nose,*
> *And he makes meat-pies.'*

On cue, Sam would begin yowling:

'I can't eat this pie now, Mam. Our Jim's put me off.'

This morning's breakfast scene was no different from usual.

'Right,' said Mam. 'No more toast. I'm fed up burning me hand. Get stuck into the buns!'

Jim was leaving for work, but as he hurried through the door, he found time to say:

'See all those little bits of things on the buns?' indicating the poppy seeds. 'Rats' droppings from the bakery!' Then he was gone.

'Can't eat 'em now!' Sam wailed. 'I'm fed up in this rotten house. If it's not our Jim putting me off everything, it's everybody going on about Billy and how brainy he is. Right, I've tried all that stuff about turning the other cheek. From now on, it's gonna be "An eye for an eye, and a tooth for a tooth"!'

After breakfast, Billy looked at the clock. It was already quarter to nine. He hadn't realised how much time he'd spent at church and queueing up for bagels. Being late at St Chad's was serious and meant the strap. Mr Thomas's rules were inflexible; no exceptions – no excuses.

Henry Sykes had told Billy that if you put a single horse-hair on the palm of the hand, there was no pain. This morning, in anticipation of the strap which was sure to follow, he took precautions, extracting a strand from their horse-hair sofa before running as fast as his legs would carry him to try to beat the nine o'clock deadline. He arrived at the school gate at 9.02 and found the headmaster waiting with a queue of latecomers already lined up.

'Right, all of you. In to morning assembly,' he ordered.

Billy was lined up with six others on the stage in front of the whole school.

'Now,' announced Mr Thomas, 'Charles Dickens has a character called Mr Micawber who says "Annual income twenty pounds, annual expenditure nineteen pounds nineteen and six, result happiness. Annual income twenty pounds, annual expenditure twenty pounds and sixpence, result misery." In this school, arrival eight fifty-nine, result happiness; arrival nine oh one, result misery.

'Now, in this world, being on time, being punctual, is one of the most important things in life. A great French king once said: "Punctuality is the politeness of princes." But there is a lot more to it than just politeness. Oh, yes. Everything depends on being on time: the rising and setting of the sun, the moon, the stars, the tides. Our great British industry and our commerce all depend on it. The factories and the mills must start on time; the trains, the trams and the buses all must run on time. If you go to catch the nine o'clock train and you arrive at five past, it's too late, lads. The train has gone! Remember this, boys: "Punctuality is the soul of business." I read the other day that a man called Lucas said: "People who are late are often so much jollier than the people who have to wait for them." That might be true where he comes from, but not here, not in St Chad's school!'

He turned to the first latecomer:

'White, you were late every day last week. What's your excuse this time?'

'Please, sir, me mam forgot to wind the alarm clock up.'

'Remind your mother then. Hand out!'

Thwack. White shrugged his shoulders impassively.

'Next. Hardman, what's your excuse?'

'Please, sir. Please, sir, I had to go to the lavatory and I had to wait me turn.'

'Be first in the queue next time!'

'But please, sir, I have five brothers and I'm the youngest.'

'No excuse. Hand out!'

Thwack. A cry of 'Ow! Ow!'

'Tarpey! What have you to say for yourself?'

'Please, sir, I had to wait for me mam to finish patching me keks.'

'We don't say "keks" in polite society, we say "trousers". Anyway, it won't do. Hand out!'

Thwack. A yelp.

At last it came to Billy's turn to have his excuse assessed.

'Hopkins, you're not usually late. What excuse?'

'Please, sir, I served half-past-seven Mass and then I had to get the family breakfast from the Jewish bakery.'

'Not good enough. You should set off earlier. Hand out!'

Surreptitiously, Billy managed to stick the horse-hair on to the palm of his right hand. Mr Thomas brought the tawse smartly down and then, spotting the hair, looked Billy straight in the eye.

'It doesn't work, lad,' he said. 'Now hold out your other hand for trying to deceive your headmaster!'

Smarting from the burning pain, and blowing and shaking each hand in turn, Billy joined the main body of the school for prayers.

'Oh Lord, send me here my purgatory,' he recited with the others.

After prayers, Mr Thomas gave his little talk, as he did every morning.

'There was once a father with six sons. One day he made them all bend down and he covered them over with a big sheet. Then, even though they hadn't done anything wrong, he started belting them with a big strap. He didn't know which one he was belting as they were all hidden under the sheet. Very unfair, you all think. But when he'd finished, he took the sheet off them and said: "Let that be a lesson to all of you for the rest of your days. Life is very unfair and it's no good moaning about it. You have to learn to take the knocks and the blows even when you haven't done anything and you don't deserve them. Remember – that's life!"

'Now, we've come to the end of another school year.

Today the school will break up at dinnertime instead of the usual four o'clock.'

The school could not restrain a loud cheer in spite of the glares and cuffs of the supervising teachers. For most of them, school was a prison with no court of appeal and no time off for good behaviour. The lucky kids, they thought, were those who were off sick or in hospital with TB.

'We shall return to school after the holidays on Monday the thirty-first of August. During the holidays, keep out of mischief and try not to get yourselves killed.'

Then, in military fashion and in time to Miss McGurk's rendering of 'Christ the Lord is risen today!' on the old battered piano, the various classes filed out to their classrooms.

Seated two to a desk and in absolute silence, Billy's class waited for Miss McGurk to make the trip from hall to classroom. In this five-minute period, the ink monitors seized the opportunity to make their rounds, filling the ink-wells with their watery, freshly made-up ink. Then their mistress arrived.

Miss McGurk was the most feared and hated teacher at St Chad's. She was an Irish teacher of the old school – stern, unbending and often cruel as a disciplinarian. She was about forty years of age and she wore flat, sensible shoes and carried with her everywhere a massive leather handbag. On her lip – unlike Miss Gibson – there was no hint of a moustache. No hint. It was a definite moustache. All the kids in the class, except the very tough ones – like Stan White – lived in mortal fear of her, and some of them were nervous wrecks, their fingernails bitten down to the quick. On her desk she had a brown strap always hot from use, and she hit out on the flimsiest pretext and sometimes when there was no pretext. It was rumoured that in the locked drawer of her desk she had a green strap which she had had specially made up for her in Ireland. When it came to straps, this, it was said, was the jewel in the crown, the mother of all straps. Punishment with this piece of Irish leather was reserved for specially evil crimes, like swearing, farting, playing with oneself or making too many blots or mistakes. Some of the kids were mental defectives or of very low intelligence. It didn't matter. She made no allowance for handicaps.

She began by calling the register to make sure no one had escaped. At the same time, she checked on Mass attendances, which were recorded on a chart on the classroom wall. She lifted the lid of her desk and took out a box of Sharp's toffees and a tin of chocolate biscuits. The kids in her class watched her every move like dogs waiting for their meal. The first name always to be called was one of her special favourites.

'Flewitt!'

'Nine o'clock Mass and Holy Communion, miss.'

'Excellent, Joey. Here you are – one toffee and one biscuit. And another gold star for you!'

Flewitt went out to the front, collected his reward and stuck a small star on the long row of gold stars he had already accumulated against his name.

'Hopkins!'

'Nine o'clock Mass and Holy Communion, miss.'

'Very good, William. A toffee, a biscuit and a gold star.'

Billy accepted his prizes and placed his star on his row of mixed gold and silver honours.

'Sykes!'

'Nine o'clock Mass, miss.'

'Why weren't you at Communion?'

' 'Cos I swallowed a little bit o' water, miss.'

'You were quite right not to go, Henry. Listen, class. There was once a little boy who swallowed a drop of water when he was brushing his teeth and he thought it didn't matter so he went to Communion anyway. On the way home from Mass, he was knocked down and killed by a bus. Where do you think he is now?'

'Burning in hell,' the class chorused – all impressed and moved not only by the story of the little boy's tragic death but also by that bit about the boy brushing his teeth, since none of them possessed a toothbrush – as the school dentist would have confirmed.

'Right, Henry. One toffee and a silver star. White!'

'Never went, miss.'

'Not "never went", White, but "didn't go"! Why didn't you go?'

'Miss, since me dad left us, me mam sleeps with me uncles and they never wake up in time.'

'You mustn't tell us about your uncles here. And you must learn to get up yourself. Get out here and hold out your hand!'

The brown strap whacked White's hand.

'Now go and put a black star against your name.'

Stan White did so. When it came to his personal record of stars, White was all black.

In St Chad's school, there were many tough kids. None came tougher than Stan White, who had raised swearing and blaspheming to an art form. His dad had run off with a younger woman the year before, and his mam had had to go on the game in order to support her young family. Stan was nearly nine and already streetwise and the senior male in his family. Not only was he cock-of-the-class, he could fight many of the older boys in the two classes above. He was scared of no one and was incorrigible. At playtime he would, for a ha'penny, let anyone have as many whacks at his hands as they wished with a strap that he had stolen.

Only one punishment scared him – Miss McGurk's ladder! It was the equivalent of walking a pirate's plank. The classroom had a high ceiling with a trap-door to the loft. Leading to this there was a ladder permanently in position.

'Up there in the roof,' Miss McGurk had told them, 'it is very dark and there are hundreds and hundreds of rats ready to gnaw the very eyes out of any boy who's sent up there. If I find anyone in this class being sinful and wicked, up there he goes, I promise you!'

It was the one threat that worked, for even the hardest kids in the class quaked at the thought of being made to climb that ladder.

'You never go to Mass,' barked Miss McGurk at Stan White. 'Call yourself a Catholic? A Whit Friday Catholic is all you'll ever be. Who knows what a Whit Friday Catholic is? Hands up!'

The very term 'Whit Friday' was enough to trigger off powerful memories in Billy's mind.

Whit Week walks! These were an annual affair and a most important event in the school's calendar. Every year, about three or four weeks before Whit, all the Hopkins boys were taken to Mays', the pawnbroker's and outfitter's on Rochdale Road, to be kitted out: new shoes and stockings, grey breeches, a brightly coloured elastic belt with a hooked clasp, a new white shirt and a silk tie, a beautiful navy-blue blazer with an embroidered emblem on the pocket, and to crown it all, a new cap with the letters 'SC' emblazoned on the front. Billy didn't know how it was all paid for – perhaps by weekly payments, but then his mam didn't believe in the never-never.

Whit Monday was for Protestant processions. If it was sunny, the Protestants said: 'God knows his own!' and if it rained, 'God waters his little flowers!' Catholics used the same expressions – it was one of the few things they had in common.

Whit Friday was reserved for the Catholics, and for them it was a public demonstration of faith. Churches from all over the Salford diocese blew the dust off their banners, statues, crucifixes and display floats, and brought them out of storage. These were decked and covered in a profusion of beautiful flowers, ribbons and gaily coloured silks.

When the St Chad's processors gathered outside the school in preparation, Billy stood open-mouthed with awe and wonderment at the utter splendour and beauty of the people and the pageantry of the occasion.

Here were the scrubbed-faced young boys – Stan White among them – newly suited, hair gleaming and plastered flat with barber's hair oil, and each with a bright-red sash tied around his torso like an ambassador; the small girls in their brightly coloured silks; the young ladies in their bridesmaid's dresses and long white gloves; the teachers with their unaccustomed well-groomed, shining look; and the parish priest in black suit and gaiters, silk topper and silver-headed cane.

And when the proud banners bearing the St Chad's legend, and the silken streamers held by the beautiful maidens were raised, when the statue of Our Lady of Lourdes was lifted on to the decorated carriage and the Children of Mary took up their positions, when the schoolchildren were arranged in military order by the teachers, then Billy's heart swelled and overflowed with pride that he belonged and was part of such an august body of people!

The band struck up with 'Colonel Bogey' and they were on their way!

Down Cheetham Hill they flowed like tributaries as other churches joined them, and other bands struck up with rival tunes. Forward marched the glorious procession, swelling to even greater lengths as church after church merged. St Chad's, Corpus Christi, St Anne's, St Boniface's, St Malachy's, St Patrick's. Was there no end to these churches from such far-flung places as Blackley, Miles Platting and Ancoats? On down Corporation Street, along Market Street, the thronging crowds cheering and shouting tumultuously – 'Keep your 'ead up, son!' and 'Swing yer arms, our Billy!' – as they made their way majestically to Albert Square. From time to time a proud mother would break away from the cheering bystanders and rush out to her son or daughter to give advice and thrust money or sweets into their hands.

Finally they reached Albert Square, where a vast multitude – beyond anything Billy had ever seen or imagined – had assembled. Then the strains of 'Faith of Our Fathers' broke out and that massive crowd stopped its excited gabble, men and boys removed their hats and, standing to attention, everyone joined in the hymn – many moved to tears and sobbing at the sheer emotion of the scene.

> Faith of our Fathers, living still
> In spite of dungeon, fire, and sword;
> Oh, how our hearts
> beat high with joy
> when e'er we hear that glorious word!
> Faith of our fathers! Holy Faith!
> We will be true to thee till death,
> We will be true to thee till death.

★　★　★

Then there was the anti-climax of the slow and somewhat wistful march back to school, and the final dismissal. Back home to Honeypot Street to be told to get 'them new clothes off sharpish' and to see them stored in the wardrobe, where they had now become the new Sunday best. So, rather deflated and dejected, they went back to their normal routine and play, though without much enthusiasm.

In the pubs in town, however, heavy drinking and sentimental speeches were the order of the day. There were declarations of undying faith and loyalty to the Holy Mother Church from men, and sometimes women, who had not been near a church in years. A wrong word, though, in the wrong ear and a powder keg would be ignited and drunken brawls would explode: 'No man is going to insult my church or my religion! Take that, y'idiot!' Thus was born the expression 'Whit Friday Catholic'.

'Please, miss,' said Billy now, in answer to Miss McGurk's question. 'It means someone who never goes to church but says 'e's a Catholic on Whit Friday.'

'That's right, William. Someone who claims once a year to be a Catholic – usually in a pub in order to start a fight.'

Miss McGurk set the class to learning about baptism from the catechism whilst she sat at her high desk and tackled the daily calculation of register totals. It was a task she did not find easy, and she squirmed and shifted position several times, inadvertently revealing a little of her thighs as she did so.

White, who was sitting in the front row and

immediately in front of her, had a first-class view. Suddenly he turned to the class, leered and said in a loud whisper:

'Blue today, lads!'

'Who said that?' she snapped angrily. 'Was it you, Sykes?'

'No, miss. Honest to God, miss.'

'Don't take the name of the Lord thy God in vain. Then it must have been you, White!'

'Me, miss?' he exclaimed in feigned innocence. 'Not me, miss. I wouldn't look up your clothes, miss. Honest!'

'Well, it was either you or Sykes. Was it White who said it, Sykes?'

'I think it might have been, miss. But I'm not sure,' said Henry, not wishing to take the blame for something he hadn't done.

'Right, White. I've had enough of you and your impudence. Up the ladder you go. See what colour the rats are, since you're so interested in colour.'

White had indeed turned white.

'Please, miss, I won't do it again. Honest. Please, miss.'

Miss McGurk was adamant and unforgiving.

'Up you go, White. You filthy beast!'

Stan began the slow ascent up the ladder whilst the class, spellbound with horror, had become still and silent.

'Keep going, White!' she bawled. 'Right to the top!'

White was now terror-stricken at the thought of the rats waiting in the loft above.

'Please, miss. I promise never to look up your clothes again. I promise I won't tell anyone the colour of your knickers. Honest to God, miss. Please, miss.'

'Very well. You may come down this time. But if I ever catch you doing anything like that again . . . I promise you . . .'

Stan returned to his place, but when an opportunity arose, he turned to Henry, showed him a clenched fist and whispered:

'You wait till playtime, Sykes. You're gonna get thumped for tellin' on me.'

Miss McGurk turned to the class, who were still mesmerised by the Stan White drama.

'Right,' she said. 'You're supposed to have been learning your catechism. What is Baptism? You, Flewitt!'

'Baptism,' answered Flewitt, 'is a Sacrament which cleanses us from original sin, makes us Christians, children of God, and members of the Church.'

'Good. Does it have to be a priest that baptises you or can anyone do it?'

'Anyone can do it in an emergency,' answered Billy. 'You could even use tea or beer if there was no water handy.'

'Right. But let's hope that it doesn't come to that. Now. What do we promise in Baptism? You, White!'

'We promise in Baptism, miss,' he said, 'to renounce the devil and all his work and pimps.'

After religious instruction, Miss McGurk turned to her favourite subject and her favourite method of torturing her charges – mental arithmetic. She began:

'I went to the greengrocer's and I bought: three cabbages at a penny three farthings; two pounds of potatoes at twopence halfpenny; a pound of apples at twopence three farthings; a pound of carrots at a penny halfpenny; a pound of onions at a penny farthing. Right. How much change did I get out of half a crown? You, Campbell!'

The hapless Campbell was one of those pupils with no fingernails, and as far as he was concerned, mental arithmetic may as well have been advanced calculus.

'Please, miss, I don't know. Would it be fourpence ha'penny?' he said, making a wild stab at the answer.

'It would not. Get out here!'

Carrots Campbell went out to take his punishment like a man – as did many others in that lesson. The one thing they seemed to be learning was fear and the arbitrary nature of pain and punishment. Maybe Mr Thomas had been right.

Cuffing and clouting also accompanied the handwriting lesson – and handwriting meant copperplate script with lots of whirls, curls, loops and flourishes. Great store was set by having a good hand. The trouble was that writing was done with standard issue pens and the watery ink which the monitors had put into the inkwell of each desk. Nibs had a dual purpose, since they could be used either for writing or for dart-throwing, and, even though they inevitably wore out, it was impossible to obtain a replacement, with the result that attempts at calligraphy often resulted in scratches and ink blots.

'Handwriting time!' Miss McGurk announced. 'Copy the first two verses of "Daffodils" from your poetry books into your English exercise books!'

In fairy tales, King Midas had the misfortune to turn everything he touched into gold. For many of the St Chad's kids, everything they touched turned into an ink smudge. They already had grubby hands to start with, and they seemed to drip ink from the ends of their fingers like monsters in a science-fiction story. Add to this the fact that many of them trembled with nervousness and it was easy to understand why their exercise books were a mass of blots and blotches. Miss McGurk did her best to help by walking up and down the rows administering blows with shouts of 'You donkeys! You dafties! You dolts!' causing the ink-drippers to be even more nervous and prolific. 'Campbell,' she yelled. 'Your writing looks as if a swarm of ants has escaped from your inkwell and walked all over your exercise book without wiping their feet!'

Creative writing followed.

'See that funny mark on the blackboard?' she asked. 'Tell me what it reminds you of! You first, Shacklady!'

Shacklady was a mental defective with a hare-lip and a ferret-like face, and in all fairness he should have been in a special school.

'It reminds me of a funny mark on the blackboard,' he answered.

'Out here!' she bawled. 'I'll teach you to be funny in my class!'

The brown strap swished and found its mark – twice.

By this time Billy was panicking and put his hand up in desperation.

'Please, miss, it reminds me of a man looking out to sea watching the white, screaming seagulls skimming the tops of the waves.'

Tears sprang to Miss McGurk's eyes. She went to her capacious handbag and pulled out a Sharp's caramel.

'Here you are, William,' she said. 'For you. You should go a long way one day.'

'Yeah,' said Stan White. 'To Timbuktu.'

'Out here, White!' said Miss McGurk.

At playtime, the kids were turfed out and the teachers retired to their staffroom to recover their strength and their spirits. St Chad's playground resembled Strangeways prison yard with its high wall topped with broken glass embedded in cement. There was normally a teacher acting as a warder on duty, but as this was the last day of term, they had all gone to celebrate the event with a glass of sherry in the staffroom.

Billy was playing a game of 'Which-hand-is-it-in?' with Henry when Stan White strode up to them, held out his fist and said:

'Right, Sykes, you're in for a good thumping for telling on me.'

'Oh no you don't,' said Billy. 'Leave him alone. McGurk made him tell.'

'Keep outa this, Hockey. It's nowt to do with you. S'none of your business.'

'Henry's me pal. So I'm making it me business.'

As soon as he said this, an excited and expectant shout went up from the other kids in the vicinity: 'A fight! White and Hockey! A fight! A fight!'

White pushed his shoulder against Billy's and snarled:

'Wanna start something, Hockey? I can lick you easy.'

Billy pushed back and said:

'Oh, yeah. Y'couldn't lick a toffee apple.'

'I'm warning you – you gonna get a knuckle butty. I'll mollycrush you.'

'Oh, yeah. You and whose army?'

'Scram, Hockey, afore I spit in your eye.'

'You're just a big mouth, Whitey. If your mouth was any bigger, you wouldn't have no face left to wash. That's all y'are – just one big mouth!'

'Say that again, Hockey, and I'll paste you.'

'Big mouth! Big mouth!'

In an instant the two boys were grappling with each other and rolling over and over on the stone flags, clinging to each other like wild cats. Panting like two steam engines, they tugged and tore at each other's hair and jerseys, and Billy forgot all his boxing lessons as he tried to gain the upper hand on his savage, flailing opponent. By some miracle, he managed to roll away, get to his feet and adopt his Len Harvey stance. Now his blood was up.

'Get up, Whitey, and fight fair.'

White struggled to his feet, and as he did so, Billy rapped him on the forehead with three rapid straight jabs – rat-a-tat-tat.

White's face registered complete amazement, as well as a purplish swelling above his right eye. With a roar, and with arms opened wide as if to embrace him, he charged at Billy. As they wrestled about, White kicked Billy in both shins and followed this with a head-butt. Billy's nose began to bleed, but he managed to land a right hook on White's jaw. Then he felt himself being held back by a strong hand on the scruff of his neck.

'Right, you two. Enough,' shouted Mr Woodley, the deputy head. 'Go and wait outside the staff room for Mr Thomas.'

Holding his head back, Billy stemmed the blood from his nose with his hanky and, accompanied by White, whose face was looking none too good, went to await Mr Thomas's dispensation of justice.

As the two boys waited, they could hear through the half-open door of the staff room the voice of Mr Kinsella, who was in charge of Standard 5 and the most popular teacher in the school:

'For the past ten years, I've been a jailer in a children's prison. It's been my job to clamp down their bubbling energy and to chain them to their desks for six hours a day. You can see in their eyes that they hate school, for it's only when the bell rings at four o'clock that their eyes light up with delight at the thought of getting away from our clutches for a few hours. Did you notice how they cheered when they were reminded that today is the start of the long holidays? We pump rubbish into one ear and watch it come out the other. What's that old rhyme again?

Ram it in! Cram it in!
Children's heads are hollow.
Jam it in! Slam it in!
Still there's more to follow!'

'Most of the kids from this school are going to be "hewers of wood and drawers of water",' argued Miss McGurk. 'I treat them all with loving kindness but I think it doesn't do to go putting ideas into their heads.'

'But that's what we get paid for,' replied Mr Kinsella.

'I think Miss McGurk's right,' said Mr Thomas. 'I see our job as bringing a little order and discipline into their disorganised lives and . . .'

He noticed Billy and Stan White standing at the door.

'What have you two been up to?' he asked. 'As if I can't tell. Who won? Never mind, I don't want to know. As it's the last day of term, you can go. I think you've punished each other enough. The school nurse is coming round the classes just now so you'd better let her have a look at your injuries. Now, be off with you.'

Heaving great sighs of relief at the unusual leniency, the two boys went back to Miss McGurk and the last lesson of the day. It was the one they hated most – music!

Before the dreaded lesson began, the school nurse came into the class and did a quick check on all the kids' heads, looking for any lice or nits that might be lurking there, or ringworm that might have developed since her last visit. Billy always wondered why the nurse never examined Miss McGurk's hair for nits, as she was just as likely to have acquired a few from her wards.

When it came to his turn, his nose-bleed had stopped and so special attention was not required. But the visit of the nurse had at least delayed the start of the music.

On the blackboard, Miss McGurk had painstakingly

drawn music staves on which she had written various notes of music – quavers, semiquavers, crotchets, dotted crotchets, minims, dotted minims – all Double Dutch to the kids in her class.

'We shall start by clapping out the rhythms you see I've written up on the board. Ready! Now!'

The class began clapping but they could tell it wasn't right by the way she screeched at them:

'No, no, no! You set of donkeys! You imbeciles! Try saying it with me! Ta. Ta. Ta. Tay. Ta-a-a-tay. Ta-ta-ta-ta tay.'

But to no avail. The kids just did not understand what they were required to do. Miss McGurk flipped her lid.

'Right. We'll try again,' she screamed in an apoplectic frenzy. 'Anyone fooling about gets the green strap!'

'Ta-tay. Ta-tay. Ta-tay,' chorused the class nervously.

'Ti-tee. Ti-tee. Ti-tee,' chanted White, unable to resist the challenge and curiosity of a new experience offered by the much-vaunted green strap.

'You've asked for it, White. Get out here!'

She went to her desk drawer and withdrew the dreaded green strap. There was a gasp of excitement and horror at the sight of the Irish tawse which, up to this point, had existed only in myth and legend.

'Hold your hand out, White, and see how you like this!'

White held his hand out to the side and, with professional proficiency, waggled it about in a jerky, see-sawing motion, making it very difficult for Miss McGurk to hit the target accurately. The first whack was slightly off course and clipped the tips of his fingers, causing even that hardened character to cry out in pain. The second stroke, however, missed his wobbly hand altogether and struck Miss McGurk on the thigh, sending her into a paroxysm of rage.

'Out! Out! Get out! Go home! You vile wretch! And don't bother coming back!' she shrieked.

Whitey slunk to the classroom door, but before he disappeared he gave the whole class a cheeky grin and a broad wink.

'See you next term, miss,' he said as he departed.

After he had gone, the class was joined by boys from Standard 6 and 7, and the real music began as they worked their way through their repertoire of sea shanties. They sang them all with great gusto and enthusiasm: 'Hearts of Oak', 'Shenandoah', 'A-roving', 'Drunken Sailor' and the great favourite with them all, 'Bobby Shaftoe'.

'One day,' said Miss McGurk, 'some of you will join the Royal Navy and maybe have the privilege to fight for the British Empire and all that she stands for. Remember these shanties then, boys, and cherish them.'

Thus ended the term and the academic year at St Chad's Elementary School.

Chapter Seven

Say it with Flowers

When the school bell finally rang, there was a mad rush to escape. Woe betide any member of the public who got in the way of that tide of young humanity which erupted from the school gates like lava from a volcano.

Billy ran all the way home, as his energetic morning had given him a tremendous appetite. Monday meant nourishing lentil soup made up of the stock from the remainder of the Sunday joint plus a mixture of sundry vegetables. Mam had had an energetic morning too, for Monday meant wash-day in the front cellar. Somehow she always managed the miracle of preparing a lunch for five people at the same time as washing, mangling, wringing, drying and ironing the clothes for eight.

'What have you been doing to your nose?' she asked as they sat at the table. 'Have you been fighting?'

'Yeah,' Billy answered. 'I was nutted by Stan White.'

'You should be taking lessons from your father then – not from Jim. Your dad can show you what to do in a dirty fight.'

'P'raps you're right.'

'Anyroad,' Mam continued, 'your hair needs cutting badly.'

'I'd rather get it cut properly.'

'Stop acting daft,' she said. 'I want you to go and get your hair cut this afternoon. Your Aunt Cissie says it'll help you keep your strength up. Your father allus likes Larry's on Cheetham Hill – specially as it only costs fourpence.'

After dinner, Billy set off for the barber's but not to Larry's. Billy knew another barber – Lenny's, on Rochdale Road, who charged only threepence provided you didn't cry out during the comb-and-scissors bit. He walked along by the railway fence, over the big bridge until he reached the top of the steps, from where he spotted a big lorry way below pulling out of the dyeworks yard. The big truck was heading slowly towards Collyhurst Road, where it would have to stop. Billy leapt pell-mell down the steps and reached the bottom in time to catch up to the lorry as it was crawling the last thirty yards to the major road. Just in time to steal a ride on the back for that short distance. The vehicle manufacturers had thoughtfully provided a rail for the purpose at exactly the right height. Gleefully, feeling like a trapeze artist at the circus, Billy hung on to the back.

This is smashing fun, he thought, as the lorry crawled out of the compound.

Suddenly there was a rapid change of gears and the lorry accelerated at breakneck speed down Collyhurst Road, with Billy clinging for dear life on to the back. Instinctively, he sensed that to release his grip meant certain death. His head would have smashed like an egg on the cobbled road rushing giddily behind and away from him.

Screaming desperately for help, he grasped the metal bar in a grip of iron as the vehicle tore at full speed down the road. Streets, shops, pubs, factories became one dizzy blur in a crazy, nightmare whirl through Collyhurst. Completely unaware of his hysterical stowaway passenger swinging wildly on the rail at the back, the driver, in carefree mood, whistled 'Pennies from Heaven' as he took his load, the last of the day, on its routine journey back to the depot.

Billy's screams rang across the district, alerting pedestrians and bystanders on the pavements. But always too late to signal to the driver.

The huge truck changed gear to negotiate an incline, and as it did so, it began belching suffocating exhaust fumes into Billy's face. The acrid smoke got into his throat and his lungs. He felt himself losing consciousness. He could not hang on much longer. His grip was weakening.

'Move over Teddy Smith and make room for one more at the picture show,' he said aloud to himself. 'And save me a few toffees as well!'

But Billy's time had not come. By some miracle never fully explained or understood – perhaps his Guardian Angel had applied the brakes – the lorry stopped its ride of death. Simply stopped at the corner of Roger Street. Billy dropped off the back like a wet dishcloth, got to his feet and fled down a side street howling like a wounded animal.

He managed to totter into Lenny's shop, where he got himself a good haircut. Throughout the whole shearing operation, he was strangely silent, not even uttering a sound when it came to the scissors-and-comb bit, and earned himself a penny discount.

Home for the ritual hair-wash which always followed the school nurse's inspection and a visit to the barber's. Mam went at the task with passionate fervour.

'Just look at the dirt rolling out!' she exclaimed. 'Have you ever seen such muck? I'm not kidding, you could grow taters in your hair, you could!'

Billy enjoyed the sensual experience of having his scalp massaged, but then followed the part he hated most.

'Close your eyes and get your head down!' ordered Mam.

He set up a howl of protest when she poured a large jug of hot water over his head. She always managed to get a considerable quantity down his earhole, an occurrence which was to have long-term repercussions.

After the hair-drying stage came the hunt for any lice or nits that had miraculously survived this intensive decontamination. This had all the excitement and drama of a big-time African safari. Operation Dragnet began! The search for the parasites called for specialist equipment, and a fine-tooth comb was brought out and tugged through the tangled locks to trap any hardy and unwary survivors hiding with their offspring in the undergrowth. Short work was made of them as Mam, now the female White Hunter, cracked them on the comb under her thumb nail with dramatic commentary and cries of: 'Here's a big 'un! Gotcher!'

Feeling thoroughly purged and purified, Billy escaped into the street for an afternoon of freedom and frivolity. No school! No teachers! No Miss McGurk! A shiver of sheer pleasure and ecstasy ran through his body at the thought of the five weeks of liberty which lay ahead.

There was no such thing as being bored in Honeypot Street, as there was always something going on – a wedding or a funeral, an attempted suicide, an ambulance, a street-singer or a knife-sharpener, a chimney on fire, or a family fight that could be heard several streets away.

But most enthralling of all for Billy were the street games, with the flagstones, the red pillar box and the lamppost serving as props.

Billy and his pals played only with boys. After all, who wanted to join in with the girls, who were always playing sissy games like 'Hospitals' or 'House' – especially if they could borrow somebody's baby. If not that, they were always skipping to daft poems like:

> *Who's that coming down the street?*
> *Mrs Simpson's sweaty feet!*
> *She's been married twice before,*
> *Now she's knocking on Eddie's door.*

Boys' games were more intelligent, even though they changed with the seasons. Last month, yo-yos had been the thing, and the month before that whips-and-tops, but the current game was alleys – what the posh people called 'marbles' – which were ranked in status according to colour and killing-power – blood-reds being the most scarce and the most valuable. Billy was the proud possessor of six murderous 'bloodies'.

But the real favourite amongst his pals was bowling their hoops, or 'garfs', along the street – propelling them with a stick round impossible obstacles. Billy and Henry were the envy of all the other lads, as their garfs were bicycle wheels with pumped-up tyres.

'Watch this, Henery!' Billy called to his pal as he executed a particularly difficult bit of garf-guiding in and out of a set of bricks specially laid out for the purpose. He had completed the obstacle course when he was thrown off his stride by the roar of a motorbike coming down the street. It was Steve Keenan on his BSA.

'Righto, Billy,' called Steve above the noise of his engine. 'I promised you a ride on my motorbike. How about now? You still want a ride, don't you?'

'Do I!' exclaimed Billy. 'Let's go and tell me mam!

Quick, afore you change your mind!'

Mam wasn't too keen on the idea at first. She eventually came round but insisted on a big clean-up and a change into Sunday best.

'But I'm going on a motorbike – not to church.'

'Doesn't matter. Someone might see you!'

Steve made him put on a helmet and goggles and they went out into the street, where a gang of admiring kids were inspecting the motorbike. Their eyes nearly popped out of their heads when they saw young Billy 'Biggles' appear.

'By Jove, you young chaps, kindly stand aside, will you,' ordered Billy. 'My chum and I here are just going for a jolly old spin before tea, don'cha know!'

He sat astride the pillion and Steve started the engine.

'We'll go for a ride to Heaton Park. Hang on tight!'

With a roar, the two of them rode down Honeypot Street, leaving behind a gang of goggle-eyed kids.

'This is the greatest day of my life!' Billy called out as they sped along Cheetham Hill Road.

Street after street, shop after shop seemed to whizz by as the bike zipped through Cheetham Village and past the halfway house – a journey which took ages by bus and eternity on foot. In no time they had reached Heaton Park gates, but instead of turning in to the park, Steve steered the bike into a very affluent housing estate. They stopped outside a detached red-bricked house.

'Come in and meet the rest of the Keenan family,' he said.

Billy had seen one of these houses before – in his first reading book at St Wilfred's. He'd never thought he would ever go into one. Steve opened up the garden gate and wheeled his bike along the path.

They found Steve's parents and his sister, Constance,

sitting on deckchairs on the patio at the back of the house.

Mr Keenan Senior, in his early sixties and well over six feet in height, was a distinguished-looking gentleman with a silver George V beard. He was smartly dressed in flannels, white shirt and blue tie, and looked as if he had just stepped off a film set. Steve's mother was wearing a blue flowery summer dress, whilst Constance had on a smart tweed two-piece costume.

Straight out of the Beacon readers, Billy said to himself. The only thing missing is that pedigree dog.

As if it had read his thoughts, a beautiful sheepdog bounded into the garden and began licking his hand.

'This is Pauline's youngest brother, Billy,' announced Steve.

'How do you do?' said Constance. 'So nice to meet you.'

'Don't listen to her,' said Steve playfully. 'She's a teacher and doesn't know anything.'

'Glad to know you, young man,' said Steve's George V father.

'Now, Billy,' said Mrs Keenan. 'What about a nice glass of cold home-made lemonade on this hot afternoon?'

'Ta very much,' he answered. 'That ud be smashing.'

'With ice?' she asked.

'No, ta,' he replied, not used to being treated in this royal fashion. And anyway, ice-cream didn't go with lemonade.

He sat quietly in the deckchair that was offered to him, not daring to speak in case he said the wrong thing or put his foot in it. His mam had always told him: 'Speak only when you're spoke to and then your mouth won't get you into trouble.'

Mrs Keenan returned with his lemonade in a tall glass with a striped straw sticking out of it. Here was a new world, a new style of living.

This I could get used to, said Billy to himself, imitating one of his Jewish friends' expressions.

As the conversation flowed Billy swivelled his head from person to person. He listened to their adult talk about the weather, about the news, about the cost of the living, about Mussolini, about Constance's planned holiday in Italy, about the dog, and about the garden.

'I must say, Mother,' Constance observed, 'your petunias are looking very colourful this year.'

'Yes, aren't they? And they go on flowering for such a long time throughout the summer. That's why I like them.'

'Petunias are very nice,' said Mr Keenan, not to be left out. 'But my favourites are geraniums – they're always so bright and cheerful.'

'Do you have a garden, Billy?' asked Mrs Keenan.

'We do have a little patch at the front of our house where me dad's growing thistles, dock-leaves and dandelion and burdock. And me mam has a window-box in the back scullery – but I think she's growing water-cress. Either that or shamrocks.'

To Billy's bewilderment, this contribution to the horticultural discussion caused great amusement – especially to Mrs Keenan, who laughed till the tears ran down her cheeks.

'Steve told us you were a comedian,' she said, dabbing her eyes.

'I've even got the red nose for it,' Billy said.

'It looks quite sore, Billy. How did it happen?' asked Constance.

'Yeah,' replied Billy. 'I had a scrap at school today with the class bully. A lad called Stan White. He give me a Wigan kiss.'

'A Wigan kiss?' asked Mrs Keenan.

'Yeah, he tupped me with his head. Butted me, y'know.'

'I do hope you managed to hit him back,' said Mr Keenan.

'Oh, yeah. I socked him a beauty with a right uppercut.'

'Oh, I am glad to hear that,' said Constance. 'We mustn't let bullies get away with it, must we? Not in school. Not on the political scene. Not anywhere!'

I like her, thought Billy. It's not her fault she can't talk properly. And I like this family, their garden and their dog. I hope our Polly stops acting daft and marries this fella and gets to live in a house like this.

'Well, I'll have to take this young chap home, as I promised not to keep him out too long,' said Steve. 'If there's time, though, I thought we might take a little excursion before I drive him back. Come on, Billy 'Laugh-a-Minute' Hopkins, let's go!'

As they got up to leave, Mrs Keenan thrust a shilling into Billy's hand.

'You're worth a guinea a box. Here you are. Buy yourself something.'

'Ta very much. I've been very pleased to meetcha,' he said, and he meant it. 'By the way, what kind of dog is this?'

'It's a Collie type,' said Constance.

'So am I!' said Billy. 'And what's 'is name?'

'Why, it's Rover!' replied Constance.

'Thought so!' said Billy, as he waved goodbye.

They went back in the direction of Heaton Park.

'I've got a surprise for you,' Steve called over his shoulder, and they drove into the park until they reached an open space. Steve parked and locked his bike.

'Come on, Billy. Let's hire a motorboat!'

First a motorbike! Then a motorboat! Billy's heart turned somersaults at the thought of riding around the lake in one of those mechanised boats-for-two which he had seen but had never hoped to ride in. More than that, Steve actually trusted him enough to let him drive!

With both hands holding the steering wheel in a tight grip, Billy guided the chugging craft around the island and into the wide expanse that was Heaton Park lake.

After a while, Steve asked casually:

'How's Pauline today?'

'She was all upset last night, but she was OK when she went off to work this morning.'

'Yes, but how did she seem? I mean, did she look happy or what?'

'Oh no, she didn't seem happy. But she can be moody sometimes,' said Billy, more interested in the small family of ducks he had narrowly avoided decapitating.

'I wonder if she'll see me again.'

'I'm sure she will.'

'Perhaps if I wrote her a letter she might come round to seeing me once more . . .'

'I know how to get round our Polly – sorry, I mean Pauline.'

'Tell me, O great wise one!'

'Easy! Flowers! Especially roses. She loves them. That's your answer! Send her roses.'

'You think they might work?'

'I know they will.'

They finished their tour of the lake confining their attention and their conversation to more mundane, nautical matters. At the quayside, the lake attendant held their bobbing boat steady with his hook whilst they clambered out.

'Come on, young 'un,' said Steve. 'Time to get you home or I'll be in deeper trouble with your sister!'

On the way back, Steve stopped off at a florist's on

Queens Road, and a few minutes later he emerged with a beautiful bunch of red roses wrapped in cellophane.

'Billy,' he said, 'I want you to give these to Pauline for me. Tell her I need to have a reply by tomorrow night. I'll come by Honeypot Street at about half past four to get her answer from you. You can be our go-between.'

'Go-between!' said Billy. 'That's a new word on me, or is it two words?'

Steve dropped him off outside number 17, remounted his mechanical steed and sped off.

Billy rushed into the house bearing Steve's peace offering. He found Polly sitting at the kitchen table in earnest conversation with Mam.

'Polly! Polly!' he blurted, not stopping to catch his breath. 'I've been for a ride on Steve's motorbike and we went on a motorboat as well on Heaton Park lake. And I met all his family. And he's sent you these. And he says I'm to be your go-between.'

'Really?' she answered haughtily. 'Calm down! Come upstairs and tell me all about it.'

In her room, she put the bouquet on the dressing table.

'Just look at these flowers he's sent, Polly,' Billy said. 'Aren't they smashing?'

'Sending me flowers doesn't change nothing,' she said, not too convincingly.

With her young brother looking over her shoulder, Polly read the card attached to the cellophane:

> *O my Luve's like a red, red rose*
> *That's newly sprung in June:*
> *O my Luve's like the melodie*
> *That's sweetly play'd in tune.*

'That poem's a belter,' said Billy. 'But that Robbie Burns fella didn't know how to spell, did he?'

'Never mind all that. I don't want nowt to do with them. They'll all have to go back anyway. I can't be bribed with a few flowers. Steve's just trying to get round me, that's all. What did you think of his family, anyroad? Didn't you think they were a bit stuck-up?'

'Oh, no. Not a bit! I like 'em. They all talk very posh; his mam and dad sound as if they've each got a plum in their mouth, and their Constance as if she's got two. But they can't help it if they talk funny. And I still like 'em. They're nice and friendly.'

'What about Steve? D'you like Steve? How did he look? Was he happy? Was he depressed? Did he talk about me?'

'I think he's great. I like him no matter what you say about him. He's very kind and he thinks the world of you, our Polly. He was talkin' about you nearly all the time. And he did look a bit depressed, like, 'cos he's missing you already. Not only that, he's nice-looking and all. Reminds me of Douglas Fairbanks without his moustache.'

Polly looked pleased.

'And what about me?' she asked. 'Who do I remind you of?'

Billy thought for a minute or so. He had to be careful here.

'Ginger Rogers. Definitely. Only her hair is sort of gold and – er . . . yours is light brown. But, yeah. Ginger Rogers!'

'Ginger Rogers! D'you really think so?' Obviously enjoying the game of 'Look-alike', she asked, 'What about our Flo? Who's she like?'

'Gracie Fields!' answered Billy promptly.

'What about our Jim?'

'Easy. He's the spitting image of James Cagney. Sometimes he thinks he *is* James Cagney. Combs his hair like him, and dresses like him. But what about me then? Who am I like? I suppose you're going to say Freddie Bartholomew.'

'No, no,' she said. 'He's much too sissy. No, you're more like that lad in *Treasure Island*. Jackie Cooper, I think his name was.'

Billy felt ten feet tall, as it so happened that Jackie Cooper was one of his favourites.

'Oh, there's one thing I've been wanting to ask you,' he said. 'Why have you changed your name to Pauline? I like it 'cos it sounds real posh. But what was wrong with Polly?'

'I think the name Polly's horrible. Whoever heard of a heroine called Polly? It rhymes with Dolly, and Golly. And besides, it's the name of a parrot.'

'You're wrong, Polly. Look at the heroine in that song "Sweet Polly Oliver". And what about my name? Sometimes kids call me Silly Billy. Then there's our Flo. I won't say what her name rhymes with.'

Polly laughed, and she really did look like Ginger Rogers.

'Honestly, do you like the name Pauline or are you just saying that to please me?'

'No, honestly, I do like it. You're named after one of the saints – St Paul. And at school they've learnt us not only that song "Polly Oliver" but another one called "Pretty Pollie Pillicote". So what more do you want?'

'Oh, I do like talking to you, our Billy.'

'Remember, I'm your go-between,' Billy replied. 'What do you want me to tell Steve tomorrow?'

'Well, William Go-Between,' she said. 'Just tell Steve the flowers were lovely. He'll know what I mean.'

* * *

Three months later, Steve and Pauline were married at St Chad's Church. Billy and his friend David Priestley served the Nuptial Mass, and their tips were wildly generous.

A week after the wedding, Billy – accompanied by his brothers, Jim, Sam and Les, plus, of course, his pal Henry Sykes – launched a beautiful yacht called *Jolly Jim* on Queen's Park lake.

Chapter Eight

A Momentous Year

When 1939 began with a death, Billy knew that it was going to be a memorable year. After talking for so long about it, old Grandma McGuinness finally carried out her threat and went to join her stout-drinking cronies in the great snug in the sky.

From the top of the wardrobe, Dad took down his pot hat and brushed the dust from it. Uncle Eddy wept non-stop from the moment he heard the news.

She was laid out in her coffin in front of her living-room window. Just before the funeral, Auntie Cissie and Mam took Billy in to view the corpse.

'Ooh, she does look well!' said Auntie Cissie. 'And what a lovely dress she's got on.'

'Aye, we showed her one of them shroud things just before she died,' said Mam.

'And what did she say?'

'She said, "I'm not wearing that bloody thing. I wouldn't be seen dead in it." '

'But what a lovely smile on 'er face,' observed Auntie Cissie.

'I never seen her smile once when she were alive,' said Billy.

'It don't matter, Billy,' said Mam. 'She's happy now, wherever she's gone.'

'Pr'aps she doesn't realise she's dead,' said Billy.

'Then she's in for a bit of a surprise when she wakes up tomorrow,' said Auntie Cissie.

'Not half,' said Mam. 'It'll be enough to give her a heart attack.'

'I just hope she never found all that meat in the aspidistra plant-pot,' said Billy.

'Did you have any money on her, Cissie?' asked Mam.

It sounded like a bet, and Billy half-expected to hear something like 'Aye, a bob each way', but instead Cissie said:

'I had a tanner a week with the Royal London club man. What about you, Kate?'

'I've had a bob a week on her for the last thirty years – ever since I was in service.'

'You must have a tidy sum coming to you then.'

'Aye, not so bad. Enough to rig out the whole family for the funeral.'

'Who did you get to do the funeral then, Kate?' asked Cissie.

'I got the Co-op. No sense in missing the divvy,' said Mam. 'Besides, they do a lovely send-off. You've probably seen their advertisement: "A funeral you will really enjoy." '

A week after the funeral, Ikey Goldstein, the second-hand furniture dealer, came round to value Grandma's bits and pieces. As Mam was the eldest child, it fell to her to administer the estate and arrange for the sale of the goods and chattels.

'There's no call for all this Victorian and Edwardian furniture any more,' he said. 'It's too old-fashioned.'

'Aye, I suppose it is,' sighed Mam.

'I mean, look at that mahogany dresser and that marble washstand, not to mention the old grandfather clock. All too big and too heavy for the modern home.'

'How much would you say then altogether?'

'I like you, Mrs Hopkins. I can see you're a straight-forward woman. So, all right. For you I'll do a very big favour. I'll risk ruining myself. Say ten pounds for the lot.'

'Ten pounds! That's ridiculous!'

'So, I should need another dresser – another wash-stand! My shop's full of 'em. Well, I'll tell you what I'll do. I'll make it twelve pounds ten and that's my very last offer. I must be going mad – giving money away.'

Then he saw the teapot on the mantelpiece.

'Wait a minute, though,' he said. 'Let me have a look at that.'

He turned the boat-shaped pot over with an expert hand and read out loud:

'ANSTIC, HORTON AND ROSE, 1805. Never heard of them. It's just an old teapot worth a couple of bob, that's all.'

'I'm not selling that,' Mam said. 'It's a family heirloom.'

'It's my crazy day. Fifteen pounds for the lot with the teapot thrown in.'

'I'm very sorry. Just give me the twelve pounds ten. I'm not selling the teapot. It's been in the family too long.'

Ike had been in business long enough to know when it was pointless arguing. This was one of those times. He paid over the money and arranged for his van to collect the stuff the next day.

Mam worked it out that each one of Grandma's children would receive two pounds ten. But as it happened, Auntie Cissie had no need of the money. Two weeks after the funeral, her fate, her future and her fortune were tragically transformed when Ernie, her husband, was knocked down and killed by a lorry reversing into him at work. The company admitted liability. The record compensation of £4,000 was, by any standard, immense. Billy's dad, who was earning £3 a week, worked it out at thirty years' wages.

Cissie bought a 'little gold-mine' of a shop which had the monopoly of supplying groceries to three blocks of nearby flats. She also bought a complete range of new furniture, including a Bluthner upright piano which no one knew how to play, and the whole family appeared dressed in the latest Kendal Milne outfits.

Unfortunately, just around the corner was the Golden Lion, and Cissie, along with her new-found friends, spent more time drinking in the pub than tending the shop. It wasn't long before the drinking sessions extended late into the night, with the result that the shop failed to open until around midday. The residents of the flats were not slow to weigh up the situation and began to help themselves to the free milk and bread which had been delivered to the doorstep of the shop.

'You see,' explained Mam to Billy one day as they were returning from a visit to Cissie's 'gold-mine'. 'Money doesn't always mean happiness.'

Back in Honeypot Street, it was all happening.

One night in February there was the usual silence as Dad listened to the news.

'Pope Pius XI is dead,' said the announcer. 'He died early this morning at his residence in the Vatican. The Pope was noted for his outspoken attack on the evils of Nazism.

'The Home Office,' continued the broadcaster, 'has announced plans today to provide free shelters to thousands of homes in the London districts most likely to be bombed. The steel-built shelters are made in sections and can be erected by two people without skill or experience.'

'Does that mean there's going to be a war, Tommy?' asked Mam.

'Most definitely. Never mind what that Chamberpot fella with the umberella says.'

'Glory be t'God! I hope you're wrong, Tommy. And all that stuff about shelters. Does that mean we're gonna get bombed?'

'Them poor buggers in London will. But not us. The bombers won't be able to get this far.'

To the Hopkins family, it certainly looked as if war was coming. Flo had given up sewing in the fur-coat factory to begin war work tending a conveyor belt at the Dunlop Rubber Company. Les, who had just left school, was working as a raincoat maker at Louis Epstein's on Cheetham Hill. Mainly military raincoats, he'd said.

'With you two working in rubber,' said Mam, 'it's no wonder this house is beginning to smell like a blooming factory. Why can't you get a decent, clean job like our Sam's?'

Sam was now sixteen and had been working as a lift attendant for over a year at Dobbin's, the new super store on Oldham Street. He was required to wear a page-boy's uniform complete with pill-box hat, and he certainly looked very smart.

The previous Saturday afternoon, the whole family – Mam, Dad, Les, Flo, Jim and Billy – had gone into town to listen to Sam at his work. They had crowded into his lift and had heard him call in a loud, confident voice:

'Mind the gates, please! Watch the gap!'

'Any chance of a lift, brother?' asked Jim.

They had more or less occupied the whole lift as it rode up and down the floors.

'Ground floor,' said Sam in his very poshest voice. ' 'Orticulture! 'Ardware! H'ironmongery!'

'Eeh, don't 'e sound posh?' said Mam. 'Like a real toff.'

'First floor,' Sam continued. ' 'Aberdashery! Perfumery! Lingerie.'

'You mean "corsets and suspender-belts",' said Billy.

'Here, where did you get to learn about such things?' asked Dad. 'You shouldn't know about things like that at your age.'

'Second floor. Men's wear. Shirts. Underwear.'

'You could do with a new pair o' long johns, Tommy,' said Mam.

'Oh, Mam, you're embarrassing us,' said Flo, red-faced.

'Don't you be so stuck-up,' Mam said. 'There's nowt wrong with sayin' long johns in a lift.'

'Top floor,' announced Sam. 'Beds, bunks and bassinets.'

'I allus knew he'd get to the top one day,' said Jim.

'Go on,' said Dad. 'Take us down to the bottom and we'll hear it all again.'

'It does my heart good to hear him,' said Mam. 'In charge of so many people. And he talks so nicely. No one would ever guess he comes from Collyhurst.'

The family rode up and down five times, encouraging Sam with their comments and their praise. On the sixth ride up, Dad turned to the gentleman who had managed to squeeze into the lift.

'This is my lad, y'know, what's doing all this announcing.'

'Oh, really,' said the gentleman. 'And I'm the manager of this store and I've been wondering when you are going to finish riding the lift and let some of our other customers use it!'

Shamefaced, the family left the store. It was already lighting-up time and so they wandered across Oldham Street towards Tib Street Market, which was a hive of activity on a Saturday night.

As they crossed the street, Dad said to Billy:

'Now that job that Sam has. That's a really good job, that is. Steady, secure and you don't have to dirty your hands. Sam gets twenty-five bob a week and he likes the job. Just riding up and down all day and announcing things.'

'It probably gets a bit boring, though,' said Jim. 'Just saying the same things over and over again. I know I wouldn't fancy it.'

'Just the same,' said Dad. 'He's bringing money in. And not wasting his time in one o' them colleges. Take a leaf out of his book.'

'That's right,' said Les, who didn't usually join in these intellectual discussions. 'Look at me. Only fourteen and already earning seventeen and a tanner just putting glue on raincoats with me finger.'

'If you like it,' said Jim, 'you just stick it out. But don't expect our Billy to give up his chance of education for seventeen and six a week. You'll probably end up with your finger sticking up in the air for good.'

They had reached Tib Street Market, a maze of narrow streets choked by stalls and hawkers' barrows, crowded with a happy-go-lucky throng of Saturday-night shoppers all pushing, jostling and shouting, intent on having a good time.

A simple-minded-looking youth in a grubby raincoat emerged from the crowd. 'Wanna buy a pup?' he asked, holding out a tiny, emaciated, shivering puppy. 'Only one and a tanner!'

There was no chance whatsoever of Dad ever buying a dog, especially one so disease-ridden as the one being offered. He had allowed a black cat, named Snowy, as a big concession, but beyond that he was not prepared to go.

They came to the first stall, lit by a bright, hissing naphtha flare, where a red-faced man with long flowing hair was extolling the virtues of his sulphurous ointment and his foul-looking medicine.

'This ointment and this medicine are the result of a secret recipe stolen by Buffalo Bill from the Apaches. The ointment will cure anything. Boils, pimples, ulcers, blisters, abscesses and carbuncles. It's so pure you can eat it! Just watch this!'

He took a great dollop of the glutinous yellow ointment in his hand and swallowed it, washing it down with a swig of the medicine.

'You said it will cure anything, but will it cure piles?' a lady asked.

'This will cure piles on your bum and piles on your carpet.'

'You mean haemorrhoids?' said a male by-stander, anxious to show off his knowledge of medical terms.

'This ointment will cure fibroids, haemorrhoids, rheumotoids, adenoids and asteroids. If you've got an "oid" this will fix you up!'

They moved on to the linoleum stall. How fascinated Billy was by the histrionic performance of the salesman as he emphasised each point by striking the lino with the flat of his hand.

'This lino has been laid in the kitchen of the Duke o' Devonshire. (SLAP) We've got these offcuts (SLAP) at a special price. I'm not asking a pound (SLAP), not even ten bob. (SLAP) Give me seven and six!'

On to the crockery stall, where the salesman performed impossible juggling acts with his Chinese porcelain.

'These eighteen-piece sets are five pounds in Kendals! I'm not greedy. I'm not asking even a pound. Not fifteen bob. Not ten bob! Who'll give me five bob? What, nobody? You bloody mean lot. Go on then, I'll give 'em away. Give me 'arf a crown! One for the lady over there, Bert!'

So, on to the home-made toffee.

'Only the best stuff goes into this treacle toffee. Try one. Go on, it's free.'

'A perfect night's entertainment,' said Jim. 'Who needs the wireless or the pictures when you've got this lot for free?'

At the corner of Swan Street, against all Mam's principles, Dad bought fish and chips for everyone, and they walked down Miller Street eating them straight from the paper.

'I wonder why fish and chips always taste better from newspaper,' said Flo.

'Not every newspaper,' said Dad. 'Only out o' working-class papers like the *Daily Mirror*. I wouldn't fancy eating them out o' the *Manchester Guardian*.'

They walked on for a little while, munching away happily. Then Jim dropped his bombshell.

'By the way,' he said nonchalantly, 'I've joined the Royal Navy. I report to HMS *Exmouth* training ship next week.'

'You've done what?' exclaimed Mam incredulously. 'What made you go and do a thing like that?'

'You daft bugger,' said Dad. 'If there's a war, you'll be right in the thick of it.'

'War or no war, I would have joined anyroad,' said Jim. 'I want to see something of the world.'

'It'll be the bloody next world, if there's a war,' said Dad.

'I want to go and visit all those places I've seen in the school atlas,' said Jim. 'Singapore, Hong Kong, Sydney, Cape Town.'

'What makes you want to go mixing with a lot of bloody foreigners? What's wrong with here?' said Dad.

'There's more to life than just working in a warehouse on Salford Docks and living in Cheetham Hill. There's a great big world out there and I want to see it.'

'How does that song go?' asked Mam. ' "*I joined the Navy to see the world./And what did I see? I saw the sea.*" '

'It'll be the bloody bottom of the sea if Adolf Hitler has anything to do with it,' said Dad.

'I'm gonna miss you, our Jim,' said Billy. 'Who'll show me how to box now?'

'Don't worry, old son,' said Jim. 'I'll be back afore you know where you are. I'll get plenty of leave. And if I do get to see those far-away places, I'll bring you back some smashing presents, you'll see. And as for boxing, you don't need any more lessons now. You can stick up for yourself if you watch out for the head-butters and the dirty fighters.'

'I suppose so,' said Billy, not convinced and beginning to feel thoroughly miserable. After all, his brother, his friend, his mentor, and his hero was leaving. Somehow, his fish and chips had lost their flavour, and at the next litter bin, he dumped them.

The following day was the start of the Easter holiday. Billy went to spend a few days with Steve and Pauline, who lived in Prestwich in a small, comfortable semi-detached house – a wedding present from the Keenan family. Steve and Pauline now had two small sons, Oliver and Danny, who even at the tender ages of two and one, regarded Billy as the family comedian – the one who was always good for a laugh. The house, which was on an estate of new, red-bricked residences set in wide, clean avenues, had all the latest amenities, including lawns at front and back, a through lounge, a modern kitchen and, wonder of wonders, a bathroom with an inside lavatory!

On Saturday afternoon Billy found Steve digging a great hole in the back lawn.

'What's happening, Steve?' he asked. 'Why are you ruining your lovely lawn with that big hole?'

'This is to build an Anderson air-raid shelter,' replied Steve. 'In case there's a war.'

'But me dad says that even if there is a war, the German bombers will never reach us here.'

'Since when is your dad an expert in modern aerial warfare? Take it from me, Billy, if the war starts, the Germans have got the bombers all right.'

'Which ones could reach here?'

'There's the Dornier 217 for a start, and then there's the Heinkel 111. All part of Goering's Luftwaffe when it starts a Blitzkrieg.'

'What's that, Steve – a blitz-what-you-said?'

'It means a lightning war – a massive air attack to bring a quick victory.'

'Do you think there will be a war like that here, Steve?'

'I'm almost sure there'll be a war, but we'll be ready for them. Hitler won't just walk in here as he did in Czechoslovakia. At Avro's, we're working flat out every hour that God sends. Winston Churchill seems to think there's going to be a war. Neville Chamberlain is doing his level best to avoid one, but I don't think he'll succeed in the end.'

'I notice that everywhere I go men are building shelters and filling sand-bags,' said Billy.

'Better to be safe than sorry. There's no doubt the

whole country is getting geared up for a big fight. But never mind about war for a minute. What about you and your scholarship? I hope you're going to try for it – war or no war.'

'I'd like to, but I don't think me Dad wants me to go. He says it's a waste of time and I should get a job at fourteen like the others.'

'Take my tip. You have a go. It could change your whole life, believe me. Imagine yourself as a teacher, say. Taking the boys for cricket and football. Teaching them to understand things. Taking them out on school trips. Treating them like human beings – unlike some of the teachers we have in schools today. Apart from that, look at the long school holidays. Don't be daft, Billy. Go for the scholarship if you can.'

'You've convinced me, Steve! I like the idea of being a teacher. Especially after all that talk about holidays. But I've got to pass the scholarship first. I'm not even sure me dad's gonna let me sit for it.'

Pauline was trying to join the middle classes. She was most anxious to be accepted by her neighbours, and spent much of her time cleaning and polishing the steps, the brasswork, the windows, the paintwork, and even the brickwork, as well as trimming the hedges and mowing the front lawn. She had even taken to organising middle-class birthday parties for her children. At these shindigs, Billy was appointed as unpaid entertainer and funny-man.

On Oliver's second birthday, Billy prepared for his act in Pauline's bathroom. He put on the Nazi armband Mam had sewn up for him, then made up his Adolf face by combing his hair across his forehead and applying burnt cork to produce the effect of a small, square moustache; finally, using Pauline's lipstick, he painted small swastikas all over his face. He checked the final effect in the mirror, and, after satisfying himself that all was in order, strode downstairs to await his cue to begin his performance.

When the moment came, Billy marched into the lounge doing a goose-step, and with his right arm raised in the Nazi salute. Most of the kids at the party were too young to understand the full significance of the political satire and innuendo which was put before them, but that didn't matter. There was a howl of approval and much applause as Billy entered the room to begin his Adolf routine.

'*Achtung! Achtung! Mein namen ist Adolf Hitler! Vat ist mein namen?*' called Billy.

'Adolf Hitler!' all the kids yelled back.

'Gut. I am ze king of all ze vorld. Vat am I?'

'King of all ze vorld,' they shouted.

'I vant peace! Vat do I vant?'

'Peace! You vant peace!' they chorused.

'*Ja!* I vant peace. A piece of Poland! A piece of Czechoslovakia! A piece of Belgium! And a piece of . . .'

Grabbing Oliver and holding him up in the sky, he finished:

'And a piece of zis little boy!'

There were squeals of delight from all the kids.

'What are those funny things on your face?' called out Angus Greenhalgh, the precocious little four-year-old who lived next door.

'*Ja.* I am glad you ask about zese funny things on my face. Who knows vat is wrong mit me?'

All the kids shook their heads.

'*Kommen.* Someone must know vat these svastikas mean.'

No one knew.

Finally Billy delivered the punch line:

'Zese svastikas mean I am haffing ze German measles!'

The kids squealed their pleasure even though they didn't get it. It wasn't what he said; it was the way he said it. But the middle-class mothers who were there with their children seemed to like that one.

Finally the party was over and the guests all departed, leaving a chaotic aftermath. Pauline and Billy sat down, exhausted from all the effort expended in feeding and entertaining ten toddlers. There had been only one complaint, from Angus Greenhalgh, who had gone home weeping and wailing:

'I wanna Unca Billy like theirs! I wanna Unca Billy!'

Billy was still a pupil at St Chad's Elementary School, where little had changed – Mr Thomas saw to that. It was the same class of kids, the same ink-drippers, and the same impudent rascals like Stan White. But now, by simply getting older, they had been elevated to Standard 4 under the tutelage of Miss Susan Eager, a buxom young Irish teacher who went in and out in all the right places. The work – at least for some of the brighter ones – had moved on to a more difficult and challenging level.

Miss Eager was something of a slave-driver. One day she announced to the class:

'Some of you could go on to do great things if you worked hard. Think about taking the scholarship this May, because if you pass you could become doctors, dentists, solicitors, priests, and the very clever ones amongst you could even become teachers. But that requires very special ability. Those of you who wish to enter for the scholarship should take a form home today and bring it back completed and signed by your parent or guardian.'

In sums, her charges hacked their way through a jungle of long multiplication and division, of fractions both vulgar and improper, of decimals – 'I can't see any point in 'em,' said Henry Sykes – and finally of endless arithmetical problems about baths – something which not one boy in the class possessed – whose careless, stupid owners had left both taps running with the plug pulled out.

In English, they waded through the swamp of punctuation where crocodiles and alligators in the form of commas, apostrophes and semi-colons lurked in the undergrowth, ready to snap up the unwary. In spelling, they learned to tackle the imbecilic, illogical patterns of English words. Miss Eager made everyone learn her favourite rhyming verse:

I take it you already know
Of tough and bough and cough and dough?
Others may stumble, but not you
On hiccough, thorough, laugh and through?

Well done! And now you wish perhaps,
To learn of less familiar traps?
Beware of heard, a dreadful word
That looks like beard and sounds like bird.

And dead: it's said like bed, not bead –
For goodness sake don't call it 'deed'!
Watch out for meat and great and threat,
They rhyme with suite and straight and debt.

And cork and work and card and ward,
And font and front and word and sword,
And do and go and thwart and cart –
Come, come, I've hardly made a start!

A dreadful language? Man alive,
I'd mastered it when I was five.

Billy learned the finer points of writing compositions on any given subject, from 'What I did in my holidays' to 'My ambitions in life'.

'When you write compositions,' said Miss Eager, 'remember the interrogative pronouns that I told you about last month. Do you remember what they were?'

'Yes, miss,' answered Joey Flewitt. 'Please, miss, they are what, why, who, how, where and when.'

'Well done, Joey,' she said. 'They are what Rudyard Kipling called his six honest serving men. Now you must always use as many of these as you can in the very first sentence of your composition.'

'Please, miss,' said Joey. 'Can you give us an example?'

'No,' said Miss Eager. 'You can all make one up for me. Now!'

The class got their heads down, and for the next ten minutes there was no sound but the scratching of nibs on school exercise paper, and the sucking of pens. Finally, Miss Eager said:

'Right, that's enough. Let's hear what you've written. We'll begin with you, Henry Sykes.'

' "On Saturday afternoon, in our scullery, me dad kindly give me a tanner for cleaning his shoes." That tells you when, where, who, what, how and why, miss.'

'That's not bad, Henry. Next Campbell.'

' "At home last week, me dad hit me with his belt very hard because I said bugger off to my brother." Where, when, who, what, how and why, miss,' said Carrots Campbell proudly.

'I suppose you couldn't help bringing in a bit of swearing. But apart from that, it was correct. Next you, White,' said Miss Eager.

' "Last night at two o'clock in the morning, me mam crept into bed very quietly with uncle number three because she needed the money." '

'How many times have I told you not to bring tales about your mother into my classroom?' said Miss Eager. 'The English is correct but I want no more of those stories, do you understand?'

'Yes, miss. But they're all true, miss, and so I can't help it.'

'Very well. We'll let it go. Now let's hear yours, William.'

' "Many years ago, there lived in the village of Redbank two hunchbacked brothers, Kevin and Desmond, who were both woodcutters, but sadly, they were always down in the dumps because of their humps." That would be the beginning of a fairy tale, miss.'

'Excellent, William. I'm not altogether sure about the rhyming couplet, but full marks. Now I shall collect all the others in and mark them at home tonight. Since you have all worked so hard this morning, I shall read you a story.'

How Billy loved those stories she read to them – from books published by some coloured family called Blackie and Sons. Stories from Hans Andersen and the Grimm Brothers with opening sentences like: 'There was once a man who had five sons. One day, he called them together and said . . .'

But today, Miss Eager's story was from Greek legend.

' "Many many years ago, there was a great king called Dionysius who lived in great magnificence at Syracuse. One of his courtiers named Damocles tried to win his favour by flattery, telling him constantly how marvellous it must be to be king.

' "If that's what you think," said the monarch. "Come to my banquet and try sitting on the throne. See how you like it."

' "In the midst of the feast, the king told him to look

up at the ceiling. There Damocles saw, hanging above him by a single hair, a naked sword. Damocles was so terrified that he went on his knees and begged Dionysius to let him move to another place which did not involve such danger.

' "Now you see," said the king, "that I am under constant threat and my power hangs by a single thread." '

'That also warned Damocles not to be such a flatterer,' said Miss Eager. 'We use the expression "a sword of Damocles" whenever there's an ever-threatening danger.'

'Is it a bit like Britain today, miss,' asked Joey Flewitt, 'with war and all that hanging over us?'

'Exactly right,' said Susan Eager. 'The sword of Damocles is hanging over all of us at the present time.'

Religious instruction still loomed large in the school curriculum, mainly because teachers' efficiency and thus their security of tenure depended heavily on the successful outcome of an annual religious inspection. The rote-learning and memorisation of the Penny Catechism continued unabated, and Miss Eager employed every method she knew, from persuasion, bribery and pleading to unbridled use of the strap, in order to cram Catholic doctrine into her pupils' unwilling heads. What was more, the answers had become harder, deeper and perhaps more philosophical.

'Which are the four sins crying to heaven for vengeance?' she asked one day.

'Wilful murder,' said Stan White, thinking about his dad.

'Sin of Sodom,' said Joey Flewitt. 'Please, miss, what is the Sin of Sodom?'

'Never you mind,' said Miss Eager, blushing. 'What's the third, Campbell?'

'Oppression of the poor,' replied Campbell, whose family was on the means test.

'Defrauding labourers of their wages is the fourth,' said Henry Sykes, thinking about his Mam, who had refused to give him his spends last Saturday when he'd given her old buck.

'Next week,' announced Miss Eager, 'we shall be having our religious inspection, and a priest specially sent by the Bishop of Salford will be coming to test you. We shall have to go over the catechism many times. We will begin by revising the eight Beatitudes. Right, you, Henry Sykes, what's the third Beatitude?'

'Blessed are they that mourn; for they shall be comforted,' said Henry in a confident voice.

White farted. The whole class roared with laughter and approval. Miss Eager blew her top.

'White! Get out here, you filthy creature,' she screamed.

Thereupon six of the strap followed – all of which, as everyone knew, were totally ineffective on Stan's elephant-hide hands.

'Now, get back to your place, you disgusting animal, and keep quiet.'

'What is the fifth Beatitude?' she asked softly of the class.

'Blessed are the merciful,' answered Billy; 'for they shall obtain mercy.'

'Very good, William,' she said. 'And the Eighth – anybody?'

'Blessed are they that suffer persecution,' said Stan White; 'for theirs is the kingdom of heaven.'

On the day of the religious inspection, Miss Eager was on edge. As she said the early-morning prayers, she appeared unnaturally cheerful and she smiled too much.

'I shall want Flewitt, Hopkins and Sykes at the front and White, Campbell and Shacklady at the back,' she said. 'And woe betide anyone who lets me down or gives daft answers!'

'Why do we have to be at the back, miss?' asked White.

'In the hope the religious examiner won't notice you, that's why.'

A few minutes later, Mr Thomas entered the room with the religious inspector – a tall, fresh-faced young man who exuded enthusiasm from every pore.

'Let me introduce Father Mulhearn,' said Mr Thomas, addressing Miss Eager. 'Father is one of our more, shall we say, progressive thinkers with very modern, up-to-the-minute ideas on methods of inspection.'

'How do you do, Father,' said Miss Eager, all coy and simpering.

'Pleased to make your acquaintance,' said the great man, offering a limp hand.

The class waited in trepidation for the stranger to make the first move. Miss Eager sat at the side of the room with that peculiar, fixed smile frozen on her face. The priest's first words struck everyone – including the teacher – rigid.

'Let us imagine,' he began, 'that we are going to have a football match against the devil. Who shall we have on the devil's team and what position will they play?'

There was a long silence as the class tried to take this in. There was nothing in the catechism about the devil and his angels being allowed to play soccer. The smile on Miss Eager's face had changed and her expression was beginning to resemble that of Our Lady of Dolours.

Carrots Campbell was the first to respond.

'Lucifer in goal.'

'Mussolini and Hitler on the wings,' shouted Shacklady.

'Good. Good,' replied the priest.

'Dracula and Frankenstein in defence,' called Henry, joining in the spirit of the team selection.

Miss Eager sat frigidly at the side with a look that reminded the class of the Agony in the Garden.

'We need half-backs,' said the oddball cleric.

'How about Herod, Pontius Pilate and Boris Karloff?' suggested Billy, getting into the swing of things.

'Now the Evil Ones just need a good centre-forward,' said Father Mulhearn.

'I've got it,' shouted Stan White. 'Me dad. He'll play a blinder for the devil.'

'Right,' said the priest. 'That's the opposition. Now who are we going to have on our side? God's side. First who shall we put in goal?'

'Christ,' said Joey Duckett. ' 'Cos he's a Saviour.'

'Nah,' said Billy. 'Let's have one o' the apostles, 'cos as fishermen they'd be better in the nets.'

'Angels Gabriel and Michael on the wings,' said Henry.

'Holy Ghost as centre-forward,' said Campbell. 'He'd be much too tricky for 'em. Besides, they wouldn't see him 'cos he's invisible.'

'St Peter in charge of defence, as he'd thump anyone who tried to get past him,' said Shacklady.

'St Jude for lost causes and St Veronica as she'd wipe the floor with 'em,' threw out Billy, feeling that this football-team idea was ridiculous.

Miss Eager had gone into some kind of trance.

'Joan of Arc with St Peter in defence, and finally the Little Flower of Jesus as inside-right,' suggested Henry.

'Why the Little Flower?' asked the Father.

'Dunno,' said Henry. 'But I've allus fancied the Little Flower.'

By this time, the inspector was beginning to feel that his progressive approach had gone far enough.

'Very well,' he said. 'Enough of all that. Now let's see if you know your catechism. What are the twelve Fruits of the Holy Ghost? And don't say apples, bananas, oranges and so on.'

The class laughed politely. Miss Eager seemed to be coming back to the land of the living and looked encouragingly towards Billy and Joey Flewitt.

'Charity, Joy, Peace and Patience,' recited Joey.

Miss Eager nodded enthusiastically – now smiling brightly.

'Benignity, Goodness, Longanimity and Mildness,' said Billy.

Miss Eager positively beamed.

'Faith and Modesty,' added Henry.

Miss Eager smiled broadly, but then looked worried, for Stan White had put his hand up.

'Yes. Finish them off,' said the priest heartily, pointing to Stan.

'Please, Father. Incontinence and Ignominy.'

'That'll do for today,' said the visitor abruptly. 'Thank you so much, Miss Eager, for letting me take your class.'

After the inspection, Miss Eager said:

'White, see me after school! Flewitt and Hopkins come out here. For answering so well, a bag of toffees each and I hope you'll share them with your friends.'

She hugged the two boys to her shapely breasts – one each. Billy wasn't sure whether he liked it or not. Perhaps it was because he was having to share with Joey Flewitt.

A week later, Miss Eager spoke to the class:

'Only two boys are entering for the scholarship this year. That is not very good. What happened to you, Flewitt?'

'Please, miss, me mam and dad want me to leave school

at fourteen and help me dad on his second-hand stall on Bradford Road Market.'

'What a waste of a good brain! At the last test you were second in class, only one or two marks behind William. You could easily pass.'

'Me dad says there's good money in buying and selling second-hand things.'

'Very well,' she said. 'If that's what your dad thinks. Then we're left with just William and Henry, both from Honeypot Street.'

Little did Miss Eager suspect the planning, plotting and conniving which had gone into Billy's application form. At the weekend his dad had set his face completely against the idea.

'Shall we let our Billy take the scholarship, Tommy?' Mam had asked.

'Not bloody likely, Kate,' he'd said. 'He can bloody well leave at fourteen like the rest of 'em and start getting a good trade in his hands.'

'Look, all the others could have gone to college but for you, Tommy. You've been too fond of the bevvy. Our Billy's our youngest. Why don't we give the last kid a special chance?'

'I don't want no kid o' mine getting above himself. Getting too big for his boots. Our sort have got to stick together, 'cos we allus get the rough end o' the stick.'

'But one day he might become a doctor or a teacher – even a priest.'

'Then he'll start talking and acting posh. Giving himself airs and graces, being lah-de-dah and all that. Then he won't be one of us no more. He'll be a toff.'

'And what's wrong with that? You'll be proud of him, specially if he starts bringing in a bit o' money when you're old and grey.'

'If he becomes a toff he won't want to know us. Anyroad, he's not going to no college, and that's the end of it.'

But that Monday morning, Mam had come to Billy and said:

'I've been talking to 'er-next-door, and their Henry's going in for it, so I don't see why you shouldn't and all. So here's your form – Steve and Polly helped me to fill it in – all signed, sealed and delivered. You go and do your scholarship and never mind your dad. I'll see to him when the time comes, but it's best you say nowt to him for the time being. It'll be our little secret.'

'Who says I'll pass anyroad?' said Billy.

Once Susan Eager knew that Billy and Henry were entering the lists, she piled on the pressure. Both boys were kept back after school for extra coaching, and as if that weren't enough, she gave them masses of homework in sums, in punctuation, in composition, in problem-solving, in dealing with trick questions.

'Noses to the grindstone,' she insisted. 'Study Chapters One and Two of Fowler's *The King's English*, do all the sums on pages sixty and sixty-one in the London Arithmetic, and write a composition on "Keeping a Pet". I shall want them all by Monday morning.'

'But that means we can't go out to play, miss,' said Henry.

'Forget play,' she said. 'The honour of St Chad's is at stake.'

'But all work and no play makes Jack a dull boy,' said Billy.

'And an empty sack cannot stand up,' she said. 'And the devil finds work for idle hands. So get on with it.'

Billy began working and studying so hard that Dad

began to suspect something was going on.

'That lad's brain's going to explode one day,' he remarked. 'Doesn't he know that you never learn nowt from books?'

'Come on, our Billy,' said Mam. 'Stick at it. I'll see you get some more fish for your dinner tomorrer.'

Came the morning of the scholarship.

'Do your best writing, son,' said Mam. 'Wear these rosary beads round your neck and don't forget to use your blotting paper or you'll have smudges.'

Armed with a new ruler, a pencil, a sharpener, a new Waterman's fountain-pen – a present from Flo – a small bottle of ink and a large piece of blotting-paper, Billy met Henry and together they took the 62 bus to Heath Street Municipal School. Both lads were highly nervous and uncomfortable in their single desks in the strange surroundings – especially since there were no familiar faces, no holy pictures, no crucifixes and no statues.

The teacher came round with the test papers and soon they were so busy adding, subtracting, multiplying and dividing that they forgot where they were. The second paper was Problems, and they quickly became engrossed in calculating areas for wallpapering, volumes for bath-filling and finances for housekeeping. The afternoon was taken up with punctuation, spelling, grammar and finally writing a composition on the proverb 'All that glisters is not gold'. Billy had read a poem about a cat that fell into a tub of goldfish. He thought he would write about that. He remembered what Miss Eager had said about the tragedy of the cat being a lesson to everybody not to be taken in by false riches. He had a bright idea. He recalled what Mam had said about Auntie Cissie – 'Money doesn't allus mean happiness.' He began writing:

A few years ago, in the town of Salford, there lived an old man and his wife but they were very unhappy because they were always short of money. One day, the old woman found a mangy stray cat and so she took it home, fed it and looked after it. The next day, she found that the kitten was really a fairy princess who was so grateful for all the care the old woman had given her, she granted her one wish.

'Please give me some more money so that we can be more comfortable,' the old woman pleaded.

'Your wish is granted,' said the fairy.

The next day, her husband – the old man – was knocked down and killed whilst on his way to work and the old woman received thousands of pounds in compensation. She now had so much money she didn't know what to do with it. So she got drunk every night in the pub with all her friends. But even though she had so much money, she was very miserable and so she learnt the lesson: 'All that glisters is not gold.' The End.

Henry and Billy went home with their heads spinning after a full day of writing non-stop. But the big challenge came the following day with the intelligence tests. At top speed, the two boys tackled question after question on opposites, analogies, sentence completion, deciphering codes and reasoning.

It was dinner-time when the tests finished and they returned to St Chad's, where Miss Eager conducted a thorough post-mortem and inquisition.

'What did you put for this, and what did you put for that?' she snapped. 'That sounds right! And that sounds right! I do believe the both of you may have passed!'

That night the boys got back to Honeypot Street with

their brains in a whirl. There was only one cure! They went to the Rivoli to see Walt Disney's *Snow White and the Seven Dwarfs*. As they licked their giant cornet ice-creams, they both thanked God it was all over.

But was it?

A month later, both boys were invited to attend with their parents for interview at Damian College, Regina Park. Mrs Sykes and Billy's mam accompanied them on the bus ride across Manchester.

'You can only do your best,' said Mam to the two lads.

Before going into the interview, the youngsters were taken into a small examination room, where a brother in clerical cassock gave them a piece of paper and told them they had fifteen minutes to study the question and then write a short paragraph on the subject given.

'Bring your effort into the interview with you,' said the brother.

'Perhaps me dad was right,' said Billy to Henry. 'It's not worth all this trouble to get into this snooty school.'

He looked at the test paper which said: '*Write on what you understand by the sentence "Uneasy lies the head which wears the crown."* '

For fifteen minutes they wrote furiously.

Henry was called in first. Ten minutes later he emerged and gave Billy a big wink.

'Nowt to it.'

Billy was next. Heart thumping, he went into the office, where the head – a tall, white-haired brother, was seated at a desk with a lady and another cleric.

'Now, William,' boomed the head. 'Tell us something about yourself. How old are you?'

'I'll be eleven on the eighth of July, sir.'

'Good. And why do you want to come to this school?'

'Me friend David Priestley comes here, sir, and 'e says it's very good, sir.'

'Priestley? Priestley? Ah, yes. In Upper Four. A clever young chap. Nice to know he recommends us, eh! And tell me, William, what do you want to be when you grow up? Apart from being an adult, that is.'

'A writer, a teacher or a priest, sir.'

This appeared to be the right answer, for they smiled and nodded approvingly.

'Good. Very good,' said the white-haired head. 'Now we should like you to read us your effort on the subject we set you: "Uneasy lies the head that wears the crown." '

'Yes, sir,' said Billy, and he began to read his composition.

' "There was once a man called Dionysius who was made King o' Syracuse. The royal hatter measured him for a crown and said, "Six and seven-eighths, sire, is your hat size," and he made him a crown that was a perfick fit. As Dionysius sat on his throne, his subjects flattered him. "O great King, you are the greatest ruler of the world," they all said. The king became so swelled-headed that the crown began to hurt his head. The hatter came back to inspect and he said, "Your hat size 'as gone up to eight and a half, sire." And no one could get the crown off his head. He had to go to bed that night still wearing the crown. All his subjects said to each other when they retired, "Poor man! I wouldn't fancy being king tonight. Uneasy lies the head that wears the crown." '

'Don't be a teacher or a priest,' said the white-haired man in a fit of laughter. 'Be a writer! Tell your parents we'll let them know the results in July. Now good morning, William. Size eight and a half, eh? That's a good one.'

Chapter Nine

Red-Letter Day

On Saturday 8 July 1939, the day was bright and sunny and Billy had been up since the crack of dawn, as this was to be a big day – a proverbial red-letter day. Not only was it his eleventh birthday, but it was also the day of Capper's annual pub outing to Blackpool. What was more, the icing on the cake was that Mr and Mrs Sykes, along with Henry, had agreed to make up a little Honeypot Street party on the trip to the coast.

At eight o'clock the two families, wearing their specially bought summer outfits, met outside the pub along with the other day-trippers to await the arrival of the 'chara'. Suddenly from around the corner it came, a motorised magic carpet that was to transport them to the wonderland of Blackpool.

'It's here! It's here!' shouted the two boys, hardly able to contain themselves.

'Look at the size of it, Henery! It's massive!'

The golden Fingland coach pulled up outside the pub and the Queen's Arms regulars, along with a motley collection of relatives who had been kept hidden in various cupboards for most of the year, boarded the single-decker bus – all laughing and chattering in holiday mood. John

Capper, the landlord, ever anxious to slake the thirst of his patrons, loaded on his gift of three crates of ale and countless bottles of stout. Finally the white-coated driver in his peaked hat climbed aboard, turned the ignition key, and the great diesel engine roared into life.

Along Chapel Street they sped, leaving the murky factories and the grey streets of Salford behind. Billy sat with Henry, who had 'bagsed' the window seat. Behind them sat Mrs Sykes and Mam, whilst Mr Sykes and Billy's dad were in front.

As the coach ate up the miles, Henry and Billy were mesmerised by the ever-changing scenery, and places with foreign, strange-sounding names like Irlams o' Th'Height, Blackrod and Whittle-le-Woods. The two mothers behind them, however, were less interested in the ever-receding parade of houses, shops, pubs, fields and cows, and more concerned with matters medical. What Dad referred to as an organ recital.

'How have you been lately, Jessie?' Mam asked.

'Oh, not so bad, Kate. I've been under the doctor for the last three month. And he's told me if I don't pull meself together, I'll never get on top of it.'

'Why, what's been the trouble?'

'Me legs again. It's with having kids.'

'Ooh, I am sorry to hear about that. What's been wrong with your legs?'

'First,' she said, 'I had inflation of the veins which turned into bellicose ulcers. But, thanks be t'God, they're non-malicious.'

'Phlebitis?'

'Oh no, there's no fleas in our house. I've scrubbed it from top to bottom, I have. You could eat off my floor.'

'I weren't implying anything, Jessie. Not for a minute.

But you've been having a lot o' trouble with Harry there, and all, haven't you?'

'Oh, aye. He were in hospital for a bit. He was having terrible abominable pains. And they had to give him all sorts o' tests. They fed him one o' them there barium meals.'

'They're funniosities, these men. I'll bet if you'd given him that for his tea at home, he wouldn't have touched it.'

Billy caught these snippets of clinical conversation, but as most of them were lost on him, he turned his attention to the two dads sitting in front.

'I never thought Portsmouth would beat Wolves in the FA Cup, Tommy,' said Harry Sykes.

'They more than beat 'em, Harry,' said Dad. 'Four–one was more like a massacre, eh?'

'Aye, I reckon you're right there, Tommy. Talkin' of massacres, who do you fancy for the big fight on Monday?'

'I think it'll go to Len Harvey, Harry. He's got a better punch than Jock McAvoy. Len's one of our lads, y'know. Manchester born and bred.'

'Well, would you believe it?'

There was a temporary pause as the two men studied the fleeting Lancashire countryside. Then Dad said:

'That was a terrible thing what happened the other day to them sailors trapped in that submarine in Liverpool Bay, eh, Harry?'

'The *Thetis*? Terrible, Tommy. There was nowt anyone could do to get 'em out in time.'

'Poor buggers! They tapped messages in Morse code on the sides. Only eight got out alive. But seventy-one dead!'

'Horrible, Tommy. Just horrible! But you know there'll be a lot more than that killed if there's another war.'

'War! I tell you, Harry, I'm more worried about the

bloody IRA at the moment. Bombs in London and bombs in bloody letter boxes. It's not safe to post a bloody letter no more. Thank God they caught five o' the buggers last week.'

'Aye. They gave each of 'em twenty years in Strangeways for their trouble.'

'Twenty years! I'd have hanged the bastards if I'd had my way. Bombing us when we're facing those two bloody dictators in Germany and Italy.'

'You think there's gonna be a war then?'

'I don't think, Harry. I'm bloody sure. The signs are all round us. We've doubled the Territorial Army, we're digging shelters everywhere, we're turning out hundreds of planes every month, and we've even got plans for evacuating all the kids. There'll be a war all right, make no mistake.'

'But the new Pope, Pius XII, has called for all the leaders to meet him at the Vatican.'

'He might as well save his breath, Harry. Eh, did you see that they've banned throwing darts in Glasgow pubs. Too dangerous, they said. Either the Scotch gets are too pissed to see straight or they're throwing 'em at one another.'

'The best way to beat these German bastards,' said Harry Sykes, 'is to send in the Black Watch with a set o' darts each. And watch the Jerries run.'

'Or better still – send in the Beefeaters.'

Dad looked out of the window.

'There it is, everybody,' he called. 'The Tower! Over there on the horizon!'

Everyone turned their eyes to the distant view of Blackpool's famous landmark.

'Eh, do you know what that reminds me of, Kate?' called Dad.

'Never you mind what it reminds you of,' replied Mam. 'Keep that sort of thing to yourself.'

'I was goin' to say a salt cellar or a vinegar bottle in a chip shop,' said Dad. 'There's nowt wrong with that.'

'Aye, I know you too well,' replied Mam.

The Tower was the cue for the communal singing to start.

'*Oh, I do like to be beside the seaside,*' they all sang. '*Oh, I do like to be beside the sea.*'

Twenty minutes later the bus pulled into Bloomfield Road parking lot behind the football ground.

'This is it, folks – Blackpool!' announced the driver. 'And it's turned out proper nice for you. But I'd like y'all back here by seven o'clock as the traffic will be heavy on the way back. Now off you go and I hope y'all have a reet champion day.'

The laughing, carefree passengers disembarked and went their separate ways. The little Honeypot Street party strolled blissfully down Lytham Road, heading – as if guided by some primeval instinct – for the sea.

'Eh, Henery, just look at the tower now,' said Billy. 'Not so long ago it was just a tiny thing in the distance. Now it looks like something built from a giant's Meccano set.'

By the Manchester Hotel they turned the corner, and there it was! The sea, and miles and miles of Blackpool's legendary golden beaches.

'First thing we do,' said Mr Sykes, 'is get these two lads buckets and spades.'

They crossed the road and over the track, and nearly jumped out of their skins when a passing tram suddenly gave a loud, piercing shriek. They reached the promenade safely and Billy's mam said:

'Right, you two lads, stand there, breathe out and get rid of all that Manchester muck from your lungs. Now get snuffing up this good seaside air. That's what we've brought you for. Go on, snuff up!'

Billy and Henry stood there holding on with both hands to the promenade rail and taking deep breaths. When Mam judged that they had completed the lung-clearing exercise, then and only then did the party go down on to the sands.

'Last in the sea is daft,' called Dad, now in boyish mood as he took off his boots, peeled off his socks and rolled up his trouser legs. There was a mad, childish scramble not to be last, and five minutes later the six of them were paddling in the Irish Sea.

'That sun's very hot,' said Mam. 'You men had better cover up your heads or you'll get burnt. Especially you, Tommy.'

The four males tied knotted handkerchiefs around their heads, and the picture and their joy were complete.

'Doesn't the sand feel lovely under your feet – so soft and soothing, like,' said Mrs Sykes.

'And this salt water'll do your bunions a power o' good,' said Mam.

They returned to the spot where they had left their shoes and clothes. Whilst the adults just lay back, snoozed and generally enjoyed relaxing and doing nothing, Billy and Henry got down to the serious business of building a medieval citadel in sand.

After about half an hour Dad said:

'I wouldn't mind wetting me whistle over there in the Manchester.'

'Trust you to be thinking of booze,' said Mam.

'I think it's the best idea I've heard all day,' said Mr Sykes.

'Go on then,' said Mrs Sykes. 'After all, Kate, we are on holiday.'

'Right then, you two lads,' said Mr Sykes. 'Here's a coupla bob. Get yourself some ice-cream and we'll be back in two shakes.'

After their parents had gone, Billy bought two giant cones from Pablo's van and Henry and he settled down to licking them into extinction. Like two consultant engineers, they continued constructing a castle complete with bailey, barbican, keep, gatehouse and, most import-ant of all, elaborate moat.

As they added more details, a shifty-looking middle-aged man approached them.

'That's a great castle you've built there, lads. It's got everything. If you're interested in castles, there's one on exhibition in the Tower. Have you seen it?'

'No, we haven't,' said Henry.

'Come on then,' the man said. 'I'll take you to look at it.'

'But our mams and dads will be back in a minute – they've just gone for a drink over there,' said Billy.

'Oh, you'll not be gone long,' said the stranger. 'We'll be back in no time. I've got my car parked up there.'

'I don't think so,' said Billy. 'Besides, that's me dad just coming across the sands.'

The man darted a quick look in the direction Billy had indicated and hurried off.

'Who was that man?' Dad asked when he got near.

'Some bloke who wanted to take us in his car and show us a castle in the Tower.'

'Listen,' Dad said. 'Never, never talk to strangers. Now let that be a warning to you. There's some right funny people in this world. Anyroad, the tide's almost in and it's dinner-time. What do you say to fish and chips in Woolworth's café.'

'Smashing, Dad,' said Billy. 'But first we want to see the tide go over our castle.'

The two boys watched their artistic handiwork, their city in sand, slowly but surely being enveloped and destroyed by the incoming tide.

'I can understand how old King Canute felt,' said Henry.

After a magnificent repast of fish, chips, bread and butter and a pot of tea, served up as only Blackpool could, the little group decided to spend the afternoon strolling along the Golden Mile.

'Have you seen the sign over that café?' asked Billy. 'It says "Jugs of tea for the sands". Seems like a waste of tea pouring it into the sand like that.'

'Stop talking daft, our Billy,' said Mam.

At a stall on the front, Mr Sykes bought hats for everyone – pirate hats for the boys, cowboy hats for the men and 'Kiss-me-Quick' sailor hats for the ladies. Dad bought a dozen sticks of rock and a bright-red carrier bag to take them home in.

'Isn't it marvellous how they get the name to go right through the rock?' said Mam. 'How do they do it, Tommy?'

'It's very complicated, Kate. You wouldn't understand it.'

'Oh, aye,' she said.

The first stop on the Mile was to have their photos taken for the family albums at the cut-outs of fat women with big bosoms.

'If you two go to Damian, I only hope the head doesn't see them photos,' said Mrs Sykes. 'Or he'll throw you out on the first day.'

The next stall was Gypsy Rose Lee, the fortune-teller.

'Go on, it's only a bit o' fun,' said Mam. 'Let's have a go.'

Mr Sykes went in first. After five minutes he came out,

shaking his head and chuckling to himself.

'Hey up, Jessie,' he said. 'You'd better watch out. She says I'm going to get married again, to a younger woman.'

'Over my dead body,' replied Mrs Sykes. 'Anyroad, who'd have you? You're just a rag-and-bone man.'

Mam and Dad went in together, and when they emerged she said:

'Good news for me, anyroad. I'm goin' to live to ninety-two, God help me!'

'A lot o' bloody rubbish,' said Dad. 'She said we're going to flit in the next two years. We've no intention of moving from Honeypot Street.'

Mrs Sykes reported next:

'She says me health is going to get better and I'll get over me asthma. But when I asked how long I was going to live, she said she didn't give predictions like that. Waste of half a crown, if y'ask me.'

'It's only a giggle,' said Mam. 'Let the two lads have a turn. Here's half a crown, our Billy, ask her to do the two for half-price.'

The two boys went into the dimly lit tent and could just make out the figure of the old gypsy in the gloom.

'Cross me palm with silver,' she said.

'Can you do the two of us for half a crown?' asked Billy. 'We're only young.'

'Very well. You pay half the price and I give you half of your future. You,' she said, pointing to Henry, 'will lead an exciting life in the next two years, but after that I see only clouds.'

'P'raps you're goin' to join the RAF and be a pilot, Henry,' said Billy.

'Or work in the CWS Tobacco Factory,' replied Henry.

'What about me, Gypsy Rose Lee?' asked Billy.

'You're a poet and don't know it,' said Henry.

'For you, I see a strange life,' said the gypsy. 'Many children and you live in Africa. That is all you get for half a crown.'

When they came out of the tent, Billy said:

'Daylight robbery! She says I'm going to have a lot o' kids and be a missioner in Africa. The Pope would never allow it, 'cos missioners can't get married.'

At the next stall, there was a man labelled 'The Memory Man' who could remember the past and tell the future for the price of a tanner a question. He offered a prize of a shilling if he couldn't answer.

Mr Sykes paid over his sixpence and asked:

'Who won the FA Cup in 1909?'

'Too easy,' answered the blindfolded oracle. 'Manchester United beat Bristol City one goal to nil.'

'What was the name of the woman who tried to stop the King's horse in the 1913 Derby?' asked Dad.

'The woman's name was Miss Emily Davison, aged forty, and she died four days after; the King's horse was named Anmer.'

'Bloody amazing,' said Dad. 'Go on then, for another tanner: will there be a war?'

'The war will start this year and it will last five years.'

'Righto,' said Billy's mam. 'I may as well have a tanner's worth. When will the world end?'

'The world will come to an end on the seventh of August 1945 in the biggest fireball the world has ever seen.'

'You're wrong there, for a start,' said Kate. ' 'Cos Gypsy Rose Lee has just told me I'm goin' to live till I'm ninety-two! So there! I want the shilling prize money.'

'You'll have to come back on the eighth of August 1945 for that,' said the voice.

'Bloody twister!' said Mam.

They spent the rest of the afternoon exploring all the different stalls and listening to the various spiels, each one extolling the virtues of the product in question and claiming it as the greatest discovery of the twentieth century. Tommy and Harry Sykes, however, seemed to get caught up at the newsagent's shop, which displayed hundreds of saucy postcards.

'Hey up, Tommy. Have you seen this one? She's saying, "You Union Men are all the same – sticking out until you get what you want!"'

'There's one here where the wife is saying to her husband, "Fancy being jealous of the milkman – he's in and out in five minutes!"'

'Are you two going to spend all day reading dirty postcards or what?' asked Mam.

'Right, Kate,' said Dad. 'I think we just about read 'em all now. All hundred of 'em. What we doing next?'

'Me and Jessie thought we might have a tram ride up to Cleveleys and have a look round up there and a bit o' tea whilst we're there.'

The rest of the visit was spent at Cleveleys. At six o'clock they took the tram back to Blackpool for the coach home. Too soon, their day trip had come to an end.

On the journey back, the weary holiday-makers were strangely quiet and subdued after such an exhausting, fun-filled day. The only sound to be heard was the gentle snoring of a few passengers who had dozed off, and the comforting throb of the coach engine. At Adlington, the chara made a last stop at an old coaching inn to allow passengers to empty and re-fill their bladders and to exchange stories of the day's events. Dad came out of the pub after five minutes.

'Here y'are lads, a bottle o' lemonade each and a packet

o' Smith's Crisps. Mind you don't eat the blue paper inside – that's the salt!'

When they set off again, the short stop seemed to have galvanised the passengers into action and given them a new lease of life, for they began a fresh round of community singing – working their way through their repertoire of 'The Man Who Broke the Bank at Monte Carlo', 'Cleaning Windows' and 'Leaning on a Lamppost', and finishing most appropriately with 'My Little Stick of Blackpool Rock'. The hat was passed round for the driver, and as Mr Sykes handed him his money, the trippers gave him a chorus of 'For He's a Jolly Good Fellow'. An hour later, the bus came to a halt outside the Queen's Arms.

'Harry and me'll just go in Capper's and have one for the road,' said Dad.

'Which road?' asked Mam. 'You've just finished with the road. It's the road to hell you're drinking for, if you ask me.'

'Don't spoil a nice day, Kate. We'll be home in 'alf an hour.'

Billy's red-letter day had almost come to an end. But not quite.

When they got back into the house, there, leaning up against the tea-caddy on the mantelpiece, was an official-looking letter. Mam didn't like receiving typewritten letters, and it was with a worried frown that she sat down in her rocking chair to read it. She hadn't got very far when she burst into tears.

'It's about Damian College,' she said.

'I've failed me scholarship,' Billy said. 'I just knew it.'

'But you haven't,' she said. 'That's just it. You start at the college on Monday the fourth of September!'

'Oh Mam,' exclaimed Billy. 'I can't believe it. Me at

Damian College! But what will Dad say when he finds out? He won't like it.'

'You leave your father to me,' said Mam. 'I know how to keep him quiet.'

'I must run and tell Henery!' said Billy. 'It's only half past nine; they'll still be up.'

'Henery, I've passed! I've passed!' he called excitedly when Henry opened his front door. 'What about you?'

But one look at Henry's face gave him his answer. A bit like Miss Eager's when Stan White had answered in religious inspection.

'I didn't make it, Billy,' he said simply. 'We've had a letter and all. So it's St Chad's for me and Damian for you.'

'It's all right, Henery. Just 'cos we go to different schools doesn't mean we can't still knock around together.'

'Dead right,' Henry replied.

But somehow they didn't believe each other.

Chapter Ten

Back To St Chad's

Day after day in that summer of 1939, the news bulletins talked about 'dark clouds gathering over Europe', but for Billy, in Manchester, there was nothing but blue skies and glorious sunshine. It was warm that August and there was a great chorus of birdsong from the rooftops – even in Honeypot Street. In this idyllic atmosphere, there was only one dark spot on his horizon, and that was the fact that Henry would not be accompanying him to his new school.

'Y'know, Henery, you must've just missed passing by a few lousy marks. I'm really sorry, I am, 'cos we could've travelled to school together every day. Now I'll have to go on me own and I won't know nobody there.'

'I know, Billy. And I only wish I'd passed. But I'm not bothered no more 'cos me dad says I can join him in the family business. There's a lot of money in the rag-and-bone trade.'

Throughout that month, Henry and Billy played together in Honeypot Street. Besides the usual games of kick-can, alleys, garfs, yo-yos and spinning tops, they had found a new challenge. Henry's dad had presented them with a large bike – the sit-up-and-beg type – commonly

201

called a bone-shaker. Neither of them could reach the pedals from the saddle, but they had devised a way of riding side-saddle by placing the left foot on the pedal at the same time as sticking the right leg through the triangular gap under the crossbar. They had both become very skilled at propelling the bike by pressing the right foot forward and then back-pedalling with the left; so skilled, in fact, that they were able to attain a high speed up and down the street.

On her way back from Ormeroyd's corner shop one day, Mam had called out:

'That's very dangerous riding that bike side-saddle like that. If you break your legs, don't come running to me moaning about it.'

Their favourite activity, however, was sailing their model yachts on Queen's Park lake. This meant a whole day's outing, with lots of banana sandwiches, a large bottle of sarsaparilla and threepence for an ice-cream.

To get there they had to tramp across Barney's – stopping, of course, to chew the rag with Mad Jack, who was still in residence in his ramshackle oil-drum cabin. Then along Queen's Road to Hendham Vale.

'What a beautiful name!' remarked Billy to Henry.

From there it was but a short walk to Queen's Park. The scene which met them at the lake resembled a miniature Henley regatta, with throngs of noisy, excited youngsters all intent on launching and sailing a wide variety of models ranging from motorboats, catamarans, and steamers to square-riggers and three-masters.

Hurriedly removing stockings and plimsolls, which they hung around their necks for safe-keeping, Billy and Henry paddled through the cool, clear water pulling their yachts behind them like Gulliver hauling in the Lilliputian navies.

'If only it could be like this for the rest of our lives!' sighed Billy.

'This must be what paradise is like!' added Henry.

But such happiness could not last forever. It was on one of these joyous days that the letter arrived. Billy returned from Queen's Park lake to be confronted by his dad waving a piece of paper at him.

'We've had a letter from that there college of yours,' Dad shouted, almost triumphantly. 'It's all off!'

Billy's heart skipped a beat.

'How d'you mean, all off?'

'See for yourself,' said Dad, handing him the letter. With trembling hand, Billy took it and began to read:

Dear Parent or Guardian,

I write to you as parent of one of our new boys due to begin studies here on Monday 4 September. You will appreciate that, in order to maintain the high standards of the school, we expect our pupils to dress appropriately and to be furnished with all necessary equipment in order to be able to take full advantage of the facilities offered by the school. Overleaf you will find a list of essential requirements which we expect our boys to possess on the first day of term, together with the name and address of the school outfitters.

Yours most sincerely,
Adam McGrath, OD.
Headmaster

Frantically, Billy turned over the page to examine the school's requirements. When he saw the length of the list, he was filled with dismay. No wonder Dad had said it was all off – the list was formidable. It included a full school uniform, plus sports equipment – a complete football outfit, cricket gear, gym clothes. The inventory seemed endless. Further, the school outfitter was located in King Street, Manchester, notoriously the most expensive part of town. When he had finished reading, Billy knew it was hopeless.

'How much would it all cost?' he asked in despair.

'How much? How much?' Dad echoed. 'I'll tell you how much. About twenty-five quid! That's how much! If we can all do without food and not spend a penny for the next ten weeks, we could just about afford it.'

'It may as well be twenty-five hundred or twenty-five thousand then,' said Billy.

'The best thing you can do,' said Dad, 'is to forget these daft ideas of going to this lah-de-dah school. Go back to St Chad's; leave at fourteen and get a good job like our Sam's at Dobbin's, or apprenticeship at the Wallworks.'

Throughout this speech, Mam was strangely quiet and offered no comment.

She's as shattered as I am by this blow, thought Billy.

'There's one consolation,' Billy said at last. 'At least me and Henery will be going to the same school after the holidays.'

But Mam was more shattered than he thought, for she still said nothing. Instead she wore an odd look – one he'd never seen before – and she was counting her fingers on her chin as if involved in some bizarre mathematical exercise.

That night, Billy went to bed despondent. The dream of going to that posh college had been all very well, but it was time to come down to earth. How could his family ever afford such huge sums of money for uniform and sports equipment?

No, it was back to St Chad's for him. And in three years' time he could leave school and start bringing in some money, instead of taking it out. Perhaps a job like Sam's. It might be good fun riding up and down in a lift, announcing things. And then it would be nice to see Miss Eager again. She would be disappointed, of course, after all her hard work. But that was too bad. After all, that was what life was all about, wasn't it? He could still beat Joey Flewitt in class and it would be great to be going to school with Henry again. Now, whose class would he be in at St Chad's? Why, Mr Kinsella's! Only the most popular teacher in the school, that's all. That was good, wasn't it?

But if it was so good, why was he weeping as he went to sleep that night?

Chapter Eleven

Uncle To The Rescue

The next day it was raining heavily.

'What rotten weather!' Billy said aloud to himself. 'What a rotten day! And what a rotten life!'

He went downstairs and was surprised to find the house deserted. Everyone had gone to work, but Mam was usually there when he appeared for breakfast.

'Strange! I wonder where she's got to?'

He looked at the old clock on the mantelpiece and was taken aback to see it was ten o'clock, for he didn't normally sleep as late as that. He made himself a small pot of tea, and hacked into the loaf, producing a lumpy slice of bread over which he spread first a thick layer of margarine, then a liberal coating of raspberry jam.

'You always make a big mess o' the loaf when you cut into it,' Mam had said. 'And you can have either maggy-ellen or jam, but not both.'

Today, the way he was feeling, he didn't care. As he bit into his thick jam butty, he wondered what he and Henry could do with themselves on such a wet day.

The front door opened suddenly and in strode Mam.

'Right,' she said decisively. 'Get your best clothes on. We're going to town. As for the college – it's on again! I'll show your father what's what and who's who.'

'But where did you get the money from? Twenty-five quid!'

'Never you mind about that. I've just been talking to that Mrs Priestley, her-across-the-road, and she says you don't need half of them things on that list. For a start, there's no cricket until next summer; so that lot can wait. I won't have no son of mine losing his chance to make summat of himself just for a few quid. Hurry up and get changed. We're off to King Street.'

Billy ran upstairs to change into his Whit Friday clothes for the trip to the tailor's.

Where had she got the money?

Then it struck him like a bolt out of the blue. When he'd looked up at the old clock on the mantelpiece that morning, he'd felt somehow that something wasn't quite right, something was missing, but he couldn't quite place it. Now he knew! The family heirloom! Grandma's ship-shaped teapot! It was gone!

He went downstairs.

'What's happened to the teapot?' he asked.

'Gone to uncle's for safe-keeping.'

'Which uncle? Uncle John or Uncle Eddy?'

'Your Uncle Abie.'

That day in Wippell's of King Street, Mam spent £12 on equipping Billy with gym shorts and singlet, grey woollen stockings with blue turnovers, grey worsted shorts, two white poplin shirts, a silk blue-and-gold tie, a royal-blue blazer with the gold school crest on the breast pocket, and a matching cap with a metal badge just above the peak.

Billy gazed at himself in the full-length mirror and saw a strange, snooty-looking kid looking back at him.

'Is that really me?' he asked.

There were tears in the corners of Mam's eyes as she gazed at him proudly and said:

'It's you all right, our kid. And you really have joined the toffs! We'll show 'em.'

Next port of call was Timpson's shoe shop for new black, low quarter shoes – none of your boots this time – a pair of white galoshes and, strangest purchase of all as far as Billy was concerned, a pair of hard-toed football boots.

'While we're out getting fitted up and kitted out,' Mam said, 'we've got one last place to visit.'

Billy wondered what and where it could be, since they seemed to have everything. When they went into Cheetham Town Hall, he was even more puzzled. Then he saw the notice on the door:

OFFICIAL DEPOT FOR ISSUE OF GAS MASKS

Billy and his mam were given various gas masks to try on, but they found it impossible to refrain from laughing as the celluloid visor and the metal snout gave them an inhuman look.

'You look like a Martian, Mam.'

'And how do you know what a Martian looks like, since you've never seen one? Anyway, you look like a pig.'

The masks gave off a nauseating smell of rubber, and testing them by placing a card over the snout and then sucking in steamed up the visor and almost suffocated them.

'I think I'd rather be poisoned by the gas,' Mam said.

Toddlers were also being fitted out, with Mickey Mouse-type masks, whilst very young babies were being placed in huge black rubber contraptions which looked like divers' helmets and which terrified the lives out of the poor little things.

'There's nowt funny about this exercise,' said an official. 'Please sign for your mask and then read the notice on the wall. If there is a war, you must carry your gas mask everywhere with you.'

They did as they were told and started to read the notice:

POISON GAS:
If poison gas has been used, you will be warned by means of hand rattles. If you hear hand rattles do not leave your shelter until the poison gas has been cleared away. Hand bells will tell you when there is no longer any danger from poison gas.

'It's beginning to sound serious,' said Mam.

The school uniform and the other items were put away to await the fateful day when Billy would go to his new school. Meanwhile, he and Henry returned to their sailing pursuits and street games. Their latest craze was jumping down the stone steps in front of the house. Billy held the record of five, but Henry was always threatening to take it away from him by attempting six. That Sunday morning, Henry decided to have a go, and taking a deep breath he said:

'I'll do it. I'll do it. I'm not scared.'

'Go on then, let's see you. You keep saying you'll do it.'

Henry jumped. It was a mistake. He landed badly and bashed his forehead against the concrete gate post, and when he saw the blood, he let out a yell that could be heard several streets away.

'I'm bleeding to death,' he bawled, and ran inside to get help.

★ ★ ★

Billy rushed into his own house to tell Mam of Henry's mishap.

'Mam! Mam! Henery's cut his head open and . . .'

But he got no further, for his dad landed him a clout across the head and shouted:

'Be quiet, you daft little bugger!'

The family was gathered round, looking at the wireless set and listening to some miserable fella saying:

'. . . no such undertaking has been received and that consequently this country is at war with Germany. This is a sad day for all of us, and to none is it sadder than to me. Everything that I have worked for, everything that I have hoped for, everything that I have believed in during my public life has crashed into ruins.'

'He's not the only one it's a sad day for,' said Billy. 'Henery's just crashed into ruins as well by jumping down the steps.'

And everyone seemed to find it funny. Poor Henry!

Chapter Twelve

Scholarship Boy

Came the day that Billy had been dreading. His first day at Damian College! He donned his new uniform and felt very self-conscious in his new get-up. He looked new and he smelt new.

'Everyone will be looking at me, Mam,' he said.

'Nonsense,' she said. 'No one will even notice you. Besides, David Priestley said he'll go with you on your first day to show you the ropes. So stop worrying.'

For that first day, Mam had made up sandwiches and coffee in a new thermos flask. Billy brought out his new school set of pencils, pen, ruler, compass and protractor. He gathered everything together. It was then he made the discovery.

'We've forgotten to buy a satchel. What am I supposed to carry all these things in? A paper bag?'

'Oh, bugger it,' said Mam. 'I thought we'd got everything. It's the one thing we didn't think of. I'll get you one this week as soon as I get the time to go into town again.'

'But what am I going to do today? I've got all these things to carry, and there's my gas mask as well. Mustn't forget my gas mask.'

'Wait a minute,' she said. 'You can use that big strong

carrier bag what we bought on our trip to Blackpool.'

'But it's bright red, and on one side it's got a big picture of George Formby saying "Turned Out Nice Again" and on the other a dirty big Union Jack.'

'It doesn't matter just for a few days. No one will ever notice.'

'Oh, all right. If you say so,' said Billy doubtfully.

David Priestley called for him at half past seven and they set off together. On the 42 bus, the conductor said:

'What've you got in the bag, lad – your ukelele? If it's Blackpool you want, you're going the wrong way.'

'Take no notice,' said David. 'Come on, I'll show you where Regina Park and the school are. Don't be nervous, Billy. You'll be all right. I was just the same on the first day – as nervous as a kitten. But you'll soon pick up the new routine.'

They passed through two huge iron gates, not unlike those Billy had seen on the front of Strangeways, and into a large quadrangle. There it was – Damian College! A massive, towering, frightening red-bricked building with hundreds of windows. In the yard there was a great crowd of boys all dressed in school uniform – some obviously new like himself and looking very edgy and ill at ease. And a few looking petrified like the proverbial lambs. About the place there were also many adult-looking students in similar smart – but not so new – uniforms. The big fellows completely ignored the young ones. As they walked through the school gates, David Priestley glanced over towards his own form-mates, who were laughing and pointing at Billy's red carrier and at David, who had now turned the same colour as the bag.

'I'll leave you here, Billy,' he said abruptly. 'I have to join my own friends over there. You'll be OK now.'

Eventually, a master in a cassock appeared and blew a

whistle. They were shepherded – new boys first – into a large hall with a stage over which there was a giant shield with the school motto in large letters across the top: ASTRA CASTA, NUMEN LUMEN – which meant 'The stars my camp, God my lamp'. The new boys were lined up trembling with fear, caps in hand, satchels on backs – with the exception, of course, of one who carried a red bag. The rest of the school was brought into the hall and arranged in ascending order of age, with the big adult-types at the back.

On to the stage came the all-male staff, wearing black gowns.

'If they were hanging upside down from the ceiling,' said Billy to the tall, thin boy next to him, 'they could be a scene out of *Mark of the Vampire*.'

In unison, the staff sat down and Billy waited in trepidation for Bela Lugosi to appear.

He hadn't long to wait. On to the stage he swept – the star of the show. As he did so, the whole staff rose as one to its feet. He was a giant, majestic figure wearing thick, dark glasses, and more terrifying than Lugosi himself. Adam McGrath, alias Brother Dorian, OD, gazed down on the boys as if they were ants, and even though there were over three hundred boys in the hall, you could have heard the pin. The new boys watched the performance, hypnotised.

Brother Dorian took out a small silver snuff-box, sprinkled a little snuff on to the back of his wrist and sniffed the powder deliberately up each nostril. From somewhere deep down in the folds of his black cassock he extracted a huge silk handkerchief, into which he blew his nose with a deafening explosion. Looking like a human giraffe sniffing down his nostrils at the mortals beneath, he glared at his juvenile audience. Slowly and meticulously he proceeded to fold the handkerchief into a long sausage, which he used to polish under his nose with a side-to-side sawing movement. Lingeringly, he put the kerchief back into his cassock, removed the heavy spectacles, fixed his eyes solemnly upon his insect-like students and addressed them in deep, sepulchral tones.

'Be under no delusions . . .'

Thinking that a delusion might be some kind of sword of Damocles, Billy looked up anxiously at the ceiling to make sure he wasn't under one.

'The world is now poised on the edge of an abyss,' the silver-haired colossus continued. 'Yesterday, war was declared on Germany. One third of our school has been evacuated to Blackpool and you who remain here in Manchester must be prepared for the might of the Boche and Goering's Luftwaffe to be turned on us. It may not be tomorrow, nor even the next day. But make no mistake – come he will. We in this country must be ready for him. But I hear you ask . . .'

Billy looked round to see who had asked, but the school seemed to be listening stony-faced.

'Yes, I hear you ask,' continued Brother Dorian. 'How long can Herr Hitler and his group of wicked men whose hands are stained with blood and soiled with corruption keep their grip on the docile German people? It was for Hitler to say when the conflict would begin, but it will be for us to say when it will end. Today is not the end. Nay, it is not the end of the end. It is not even the beginning of the end or the end of the beginning. But of one thing you can be sure – today, we begin to begin.'

The staff behind him looked perplexed at this statement.

Billy was almost sure he had heard a song on the wireless with very similar words: 'When they begin the beguine' or something like that.

'Now let us pray,' said Brother Dorian.

After the prayers the school was dismissed, but the new boys were told to stay behind in the hall, where a roll-call was taken and they were allocated to their forms. Billy found himself in a form with the curious title of Three Alpha, and one of the bat-like masters – a particularly corpulent individual – herded them off to their form-room, with Billy making futile attempts to hide his conspicuous carrier bag. There, the master assigned each one of them to an individual desk and told them to print their full names on the cardboard badges which he had supplied.

'These badges must be worn on your lapels for the first month,' the fat man said, 'until we get to know you. Woe betide anyone who loses his badge.'

Carefully, the boys set to work. When the task was completed, the master addressed them again.

'My name is Ronald Puddephatt. If I see even a flicker of a smile on anyone's face at the mention of my name, they'll be for it.'

The boys sat staring ahead, poker-faced.

'For my sins,' he continued, 'I am your form master and your English teacher. Right, let's begin. Each of you will now introduce himself to the rest of us by giving his full name and telling us something about himself.'

'We shall start with you,' he said, pointing to a fair-haired, spotty-faced boy in the front row.

It was during this session that Billy came to a full understanding of how different this new school was from the dear, dear old St Chad's he had left behind.

'My full name,' said the boy indicated, 'is Rodney Arthur Potts, and I live with my parents and four older sisters in a detached house in Fallowfield. My father owns a chain of grocery shops in the Manchester area; you may have seen one or two of them about the place.'

'Next, Cash.'

Cash was an ugly, buck-toothed, thick-set, heavily built lad who looked a little older than the rest of the class.

'My full name is Robert Edward Cash,' he drawled. 'You will note that my name could be abbreviated to R. Eddy Cash. Ready Cash, do you see? My father thought this rather droll, as he is a financial consultant on the Royal Exchange.'

'Next, Hopkins. Aren't you the boy with that hideous red carrier bag? Where on earth did you get it from?'

'Yes, sir. P-please, sir, me dad got it with some sticks o' rock when we went to Blackpool in the summer.'

'Did he indeed! And why, may we ask, have you not acquired a satchel like the rest of the form?'

'Please, sir, me mam forgot to get one o' them satchels. But she says she's gonna gerra new one tomorrer.'

'Yes, all right. Go ahead. Tell us about yourself.'

'Please, sir . . .'

'And stop saying "Please, sir". You're not at your elementary school now.'

'Yes, sir. Me name's Billy 'Opkins and I come from Cheetham Hill and me dad's a porter.'

' "Hopkins" isn't a name,' remarked Cash. 'It's some sort of disease, isn't it, sir?'

'You stupid fellow,' said the master. 'You're thinking of Hodgkin's disease. No, this name is altogether different. It's the name of a famous poet, but we can hardly call our new boy here "Gerald Manley", can we? Perhaps George Formby would be a more appropriate name, eh? Anyway, this poet wrote, "*Glory be to God for dappled things –/For skies of couple-colour as a brindled cow*", but in that beautiful poem, Hopkins, your namesake makes no mention of red carrier bags bearing the face of George Formby and the Union Jack.'

'Perhaps Gerald Manley was his grandfather,' volunteered Tony Wilde, another new boy.

'I doubt it,' said the teacher, 'since Gerald Manley was a Jesuit priest! But one thing is obvious, my dear Hopkins, we are going to have to do a *Pygmalion* job on you. Does anyone know what I mean by that?'

'Isn't that the name of a fillum, sir, with Wendy Hiller and Leslie Howard?' said Billy.

'It is indeed,' said the master. 'Has anyone here been to see it?'

'Not bloody likely,' said Billy.

'Get out here, Hopkins. You must be introduced to my method of dealing with unruly little boys.'

'But, sir,' protested Billy, 'I was only quoting a line from the fillum. I read about it in the *Evening Chron.*'

'The fact that George Bernard Shaw swears is no excuse for you to emulate him. Now turn your face over to the side.'

Mr Puddephatt made Billy stand by his side and then tilted his face at an angle, leaving him in that position.

'Excuse me, sir,' said Billy. 'That fillum was on in town but we can't go to see it now 'cos the gover'ment's closed down all the picture 'ouses in case the Germans drop bombs on 'em.'

'They won't remain closed forever, boy. Now keep your head tilted.'

The next boy, Robin Gabrielson, had a face resembling one of the angels painted on St Chad's altar. His head was a mass of black curls and his eyes seemed to dance when he spoke.

'Don't tell us you're the son of an archangel,' said Puddephatt after Robin had introduced himself.

'No, sir. My father is a tea merchant. He buys and sells tea in the Manchester district. We live here in Rusholme, not too far from the school.'

'Sounds very impressive,' said the master. 'Next boy!'

'Me name's Nodder, sir.'

Before Nodder could continue, however, Mr Puddephatt moved at lightning speed and delivered a stinging slap to Billy's face, which was still inclined at the angle where he had set it.

'That is known in the school as the Puddephatt Slap. Sit down and remember it! Now, Mr Nodder, you were about to enlighten us with a few details about yourself. Incidentally, I do hope you're not related to the infamous murderer, Frederick, who was hanged at Lincoln last year.'

'No, sir. Me name's Norbert – Norbert Nodder. Me friends call me Nobby. And me dad's a driver on the 95 bus with Manchester Corporation.'

'Neither the number of the bus nor the particular corporation he drives for is of any interest to us here,' said the teacher. 'But I trust, Mr Nodder, that you're not going to nod off to sleep in my class. Anyway, I shall call you Fred. Next boy.'

'Me name's Richard Smalley, but at me last school everyone called me Dick Smalley. And me dad's a cleaner for the LMS Railway.'

Not a muscle on Puddephatt's face moved as he said:

'Dick Smalley? Yes. Yes. A most interesting name. But in this class you'll be called Titch, which has a less phallic ring to it, I think.'

The boy sitting behind Titch had an even more unfortunate name.

'I'm called Oliver Hardy, sir,' he said apologetically.

With a menacing scowl, Mr Puddephatt quelled the roar of laughter which had been suppressed since Titch had announced his appellation. When the noise had subsided, he said:

'Go on, Olly.'

'My dad's got his own window-cleaning round and my brother's learning to be a priest at a college in London.'

'A window-cleaning round, eh? Another George Formby aficionado. Perhaps you should buy a bag like that of Hopkins.'

By break-time, Mr Puddephatt had managed to get round the whole form of twenty-five boys, hearing introductions, making what he thought were facetious comments and dishing out nicknames. Antony Wilde, a tall, thin boy, became Oscar, whilst a rather tubby, bespectacled boy named William Bunnell was awarded the sobriquet Bunter.

At the end of the session, Mr Puddephatt said:

'It is quite evident that a number of you are going to have to learn the King's English. For some of you, English is a foreign tongue. But remember this, to quote from Shaw's *Pygmalion*: "Your native language is the language of Shakespeare and Milton and the Bible", and I'm going to make sure you speak it correctly if it's the last thing I do. It is vital that you read and read and read. I shall insist that you get through at least one book per month. Now, here is your first piece of homework. You will begin by studying the first tale in this book that I am about to present to you, and I shall test you on it in our very next lesson.'

He pointed to Cash. 'I'm appointing you form monitor, as you seem to be the oldest and perhaps the most sensible boy here. Give out the books.'

'Yes, sir. Thank you, sir,' said Cash as he distributed copies of *The Arabian Nights* around the class.

'Secondly, by tomorrow – and not by tomorrer,

Hopkins – you will each write either a limerick or an epitaph based on one of the names of a member of this form. You may work in pairs if you wish. I look forward to hearing them. Class dismissed.'

As the boys filed out of the room, Cash mimicked Billy's introduction:

' "Me name's Billy 'Opkins and Ah coom from Cheetham 'ill and Ah bought me red bag in Blackpool, Ah did. And me dad's a porter." Good God, how have these working-class peasants got into one of our schools? And his father's a porter, don'cha know? I do hope he's not one of those black chaps who carry boxes on their heads for explorers like David Livingstone.'

He roared with laughter at his own joke. A few of the rich boys who were near him joined in, mainly to avoid becoming targets of his sarcasm themselves.

Robin Gabrielson overheard the jibes and immediately took Billy's side.

'Look, Cash, we're all new here today and we're all feeling edgy and nervous. We've got to make the best of it and try to make friends – not enemies. So lay off. And if you're so high and mighty, why didn't your father send you to a public school?'

'As a matter of fact,' said Cash, 'my father did consider Downside, but I preferred to remain at home.'

'S'all right, Robin,' said Billy. 'Cash don't worry me. I've dealt with tougher guys than him in me time. But what do you make of this Mr Puddephatt then?'

'Who does he think he is, making fun of our names?' said Tony Wilde, joining in. 'We're not even allowed to smile at his stupid name. I think I shall call him "Pussycat".'

'I think I'd rather have "Puppyfat",' said Billy.

The laughter which this suggestion occasioned decided the issue.

After the break there began what seemed like an endless procession of masters, each trying to sell his subject, rather like the stallholders on Tib Street Market – French, Latin, maths, physics, history, geography, art and physical education.

At the end of that first day, Billy went home with his head in a whirl and feeling distinctly unhappy.

'I don't think I'm going to like this school,' he said to Tony Wilde who, since he lived in Moston, used the same 53 bus home.

'I feel just the same,' said Tony. 'I don't think I can put up with Puppyfat for a whole year.'

When Billy reached home, Mam was waiting for him with a cup of tea.

'Well, how was it – your first day?' she enquired anxiously.

'I'm missing St Chad's, Miss Eager, Henry Sykes, Joey Flewitt and even Stan White already. And please, please, Mam, can we go out now afore the shops shut and buy a satchel?'

'No need,' she said. 'I've already done it!' and she produced the most beautiful leather satchel.

'Thank the Lord for Grandma's teapot!' he said.

The next day Billy went proudly to school with his new leather satchel firmly strapped to his back. He didn't feel quite so bad on this second day, as he now knew what to expect, and he had made a few tentative friends in Robin Gabrielson, Tony Wilde, Titch Smalley, Nobby Nodder and Olly Hardy.

Things could be worse, I suppose, he said to himself.

In the first lesson of the day, Puppyfat wasted no time.

'Right, yesterday I set you some homework. I hope for your sake that you've done it or it'll be the Puddephatt Slap for some of you. So let's hear your efforts. We'll start with you, Oscar.'

'Yes, Mr Puddephatt.

> *'An unfortunate lad, Rodney Potts,*
> *Was plagued by an outbreak of spots,*
> *Zam-buk he applied oh so thickly,*
> *Which made him look even more sickly,*
> *But won him the name "Join-the-dots".'*

'Quite good, Oscar,' said Puppyfat. 'And your reply, Potts?'

'Very good, sir.

> *'A beanpole whose name was Wilde.*
> *Said "No, it can't be denied,*
> *When challenged to fight,*
> *I take off in flight,*
> *And burst into tears like a child." '*

'Touché,' said the master. 'Now let's have your effort, Gabrielson.'

'Mine is an epitaph for Titch Smalley, sir.

> *'Titch Smalley's dead, and here he lies,*
> *Nobody laughs and nobody cries;*
> *Where his soul's gone, or how it fares,*
> *Nobody knows, and nobody cares.'*

'That's a very grave statement,' said Puddephatt. 'No doubt you have a reply to that, Titch?'

'Yes sir. I knew he'd written that and so I've written an epitaph for Gabrielson's tombstone.

> *'Here lies Robin who came from heaven*
> *And left this world in thirty-seven,*
> *Where he's gone, no one can tell,*
> *We only hope it isn't hell.'*

'You really are a bunch of malicious boys,' the master said happily. 'Your effort now, Cash.'

'Very good, sir. Mine's about Billy Hopkins.'

'Yes, I thought it might be,' said Puddephatt. 'Let's hear your masterpiece.'

> *'A slum-kid named like a poet,*
> *Was stupid and didn't even know it.*
> *He carried the flag,*
> *On the side of his bag,*
> *And thought he would hide it, not show it.'*

'I am not sure Gerald Manley would appreciate your wit, Cash,' said the teacher. 'Do you have a reply, Hopkins, to this onslaught?'

'Yes, sir.

> *'A lad by the name Eddy Cash,*
> *Thought he was really quite flash,*
> *But when faced with a fight,*
> *He quickly took flight,*
> *And broke the school's hundred-yard dash.'*

'And that's where I think we'll finish,' said Puddephatt. 'We'll hear the rest next week.'

* * *

As David Priestley had predicted, Billy soon fell into his new routine, and the days passed quickly. He travelled into school on the 42 bus with David, and at night he made the long bus ride home with Oscar Wilde on the 53. The days turned into weeks, and before he knew it, November had come round, and St Chad's and the scholarship exam seemed like ancient history.

At school, the learning went on relentlessly. He found geometry particularly difficult, mainly because of the bad teaching of Brother Campion, who had the rare gift of making the simplest proposition sound like Einstein's theory of relativity. Further, he had devised a cruel and inflexible means of punishing those who had the audacity not to understand his gobbledy-gook.

'Let me introduce you to Paddy-whack,' he said, flourishing a large gym shoe above his head. 'If you get two out of ten for your homework twice running, he will make his acquaintance with your backside.'

Billy had already had one two-out-of-ten for his attempt to answer a question he did not understand: '*Show that if the mid points of the sides of an equilateral triangle are joined, the resulting triangle is also equilateral. What fraction of the whole triangle is it?*' That weekend he made a superhuman effort to solve the problem and produced work of incredible neatness, but it was wrong again. On Tuesday morning he met Mr Paddy-Whack, and received two swipes on his rear which made it difficult for him to sit down for the rest of the day.

'There's only one thing for it,' he confided to Oscar on the way home. 'I shall have to get help at weekends from my brother-in-law, who's a draughtsman at Avro's.'

Indeed, it was Steve Keenan who gave Billy what little spare time he had to help him solve his problems and unravel the mysteries of Euclid's theorems.

Soon, classroom personalities emerged and two distinct groupings began to form. The Cash group, made up largely of fee-payers and well-to-do pupils, sneered at the other set, which consisted mainly of working-class scholarship boys. There was no doubt which of the two divisions Mr Puddephatt favoured.

One day towards the middle of November, the master was called out of the room by a telephone call.

'Cash, whilst I'm out, stand by my desk and take the names of any boys who make a nuisance of themselves.'

As soon as Puppyfat had left the room, Billy called out:

'Who do you think you are, Cash?'

'He thinks he's a teacher,' said Robin.

'He thinks he's rather flash, does Cash,' said Oscar, unable to resist quoting Billy's immortal verse.

'You think you're a teacher, Cash. Here's a piece of chalk for you!' shouted Titch, and he threw a small morsel at Cash's head.

'And another from me!' called Nobby Nodder.

At that moment Brother Dorian was walking by, and as he entered the room a deathly hush fell over the class.

'Where is Mr Puddephatt?' he asked sternly.

'He had to leave the room for a few minutes, sir,' answered Cash, 'and he left me in charge and told me to take the names of troublemakers.'

'And have you?' asked the head. 'I would very much like to know who was making all that row just now.'

'Yes, sir. I've taken down the names.'

Cash handed Brother Dorian his sheet of paper.

'Right, the following boys will now go down to the gym and wait for me. I will not tolerate such hooliganism in my school: Hardy, Hopkins, Gabrielson, Wilde, Nodder and Smalley.'

'I just knew there'd be trouble,' said Titch.

'Not many people know,' said Olly, 'that if you relax your whole body on the first stroke of the cane, you won't feel any pain.'

Trembling, the six boys made their way down to the gym. After five agonising minutes, Brother Dorian strode in swishing and testing out a long cane.

'Line up,' he said. 'Gabrielson, you first. Out here and touch your toes.'

Robin went forward and bent down as if about to play a game of leapfrog. The five waiting boys watched spellbound. Brother Dorian took up his stance, raised the cane high in the air, and brought it down with a loud swishing sound. There was a thwack as the cane bit into the flesh of Robin's bottom. The scream which started up from Robin's throat was quickly stifled. The torture continued, and as the second blow was on its way down, Robin reached instinctively to his backside and the cane struck him across the back of his hand, immediately raising an ugly, livid, purple weal.

'Stay down, boy,' called the head. Robin received a total of six strokes, and when he straightened up there were two large tears glistening in the corners of his eyes but he made no sound.

'Next, Hopkins.'

Slowly and fearfully, Billy went forward to take his punishment. No sooner had he bent over than the first blow landed. To his surprise, he heard the crack as it struck but he felt no pain. There followed five more strokes. Still no pain. He stood up, and it was then that a searing, burning sensation hit him, as if someone had applied a red-hot poker to his buttocks. The whole of his rump was aflame. He could hardly breathe let alone move out of the gym because of the agony. He forced the tears back and painfully made it to the door.

Outside, he waited with Robin for the others to emerge from the torture chamber. They heard the pistol shots of the stick as it struck buttocks, and the screams of torment as each in turn underwent his flogging. When all was over, the six boys climbed painfully back up the stairs.

'That theory of yours, Olly,' said Oscar, grimacing, 'about not feeling anything. Well, it needs looking at again.'

'That's what was claimed in the book where I saw it.'

As they re-entered the form room, a strange, unearthly silence fell over the class and looks of admiration followed their return to their desks. Cash, however, could not look the heroes in the eye.

Chapter Thirteen

What's In A Name?

At the end of November, Jim came home on leave. He had completed his initial course on the training ships *Exmouth* and *Drake*, qualifying him as a naval gunner, and the navy had finally posted him to the battle-cruiser *Renown*. Before sailing off, he had been given a week's furlough, and he intended to make the most of it.

When Billy saw him after so many weeks' absence, his heart filled with pride at the sight of this handsome hero-brother in smart, immaculate nautical uniform.

'He smells so clean and fresh and soapy,' he said to Mam.

'And he insists on ironing everything himself,' she replied.

Jim gave Billy the job of rolling his cigarettes. Billy would gladly have gone through fire or swum the Atlantic, let alone roll his cigarettes. He got down to it, delighted and honoured to have been entrusted with such an important task. He opened the sealed tin, releasing the pungent aroma of fresh Virginia tobacco, sprinkled the requisite amount into the little machine, inserted the Rizla paper, licked the adhesive strip, and lo and behold! A cigarette! He must have made almost three hundred in this way – enough to keep both Jim and Dad going for some considerable time.

Jim spent half his time at Auntie Cissie's shop, where the unorthodox lifestyle seemed to appeal to him. He spent the other half in the company of Jean Priestley, who had developed into a most beautiful raven-haired young lady. But he still had lots of time for his youngest brother.

'Well, our kid,' he asked one day, 'how's it all going at that new school of yours?'

Billy poured out all his sorrows about Puddephatt, about Brother Campion and his Paddy-whacker, about Brother Dorian and the flogging, but most of all about Cash and his snooty, mocking ways.

'But you've made some friends, I hope.'

'Yes, a few.'

'Then you're lucky, old son. Have they given you a nickname yet?'

'No, not yet. But Mr Puddephatt said he'd call me George, after George Formby.'

'When your mates give you a nickname – not this Mr Puddephatt – then you'll know you're in and that you've been accepted.'

'What's your nickname in the navy, Jim?'

'Oh, they call me the Champ, 'cos of my boxing. But when I first got there, it was just the same for me in Devonport Barracks. Everything was strange and unfamiliar. If you've got a few good mates, though, you can face almost anything and anybody. And things do change and get better in the end, you know.'

'Right now, I wouldn't mind going back to St Chad's and me old mates.'

'No, that's the one thing you cannot do. You can't go backwards. Forget St Chad's. There's only one solution to your problems, you know,' he said calmly, lighting up one of Billy's cigarettes. 'The question is: do you have the guts to do it?'

'Just tell me what to do and I'll do it.'

'Take on Cash and beat him.'

'You mean – fight him? Jim, you must be joking. He's older, he's bigger and he's about a stone heavier.'

'You know what we say in boxing: "The bigger they are, the harder they fall." Tell you what I'll do. I go back Sunday night, so on Saturday afternoon I'll give you some pointers. On Monday you challenge this Cash character to a scrap with gloves in the gym. Then you fix him good and proper.'

Jim was as good as his word, and on the Saturday afternoon he met Billy in the old familiar back yard.

'OK,' he said. 'We don't need Bennie the Dummy today. I'll move around the yard and when I stick out my glove, you hit it. Now take up your stance and your peek-a-boo style. Let's go!'

Together the two brothers danced around, and every time Jim showed an open glove, Billy struck it with the rapidity of a lizard snapping up a fly.

'You've lost none of your speed, and the way you hit, you've got golden hands,' said Jim. 'Remember to keep moving all the time, though. See, when you punch, your opponent concentrates on avoiding it. If you punch and move, by the time he gets set you're not there.'

'What about breathing?' asked Billy.

'When you're boxing, breathe fast and keep bobbing and weaving. You've got to get yourself fit by running and skipping; that's what I do.'

'And smoking?' chipped in Billy, unable to resist the jibe.

'Yeah, yeah, yeah. OK, St William. I hear you. But most important, watch your opponent's eyes.'

'Why his eyes?'

'Because they tip you off when he's going to try for a punch; there's a slight movement of the eye and that's your signal to make sure you're not there when he goes for it. And keep looking all the time for an opening.'

'He's a very big lad, Jim. What if he gets a punch in first? He'll flatten me.'

'Make sure he doesn't. Block him with your elbows, like this. And keep your defence up. When you've let out a punch, move quickly to the side, or duck and then let in a sneaky one-two-three. Look for his weakness all the time.'

'Right, Jim. I'll remember it. But I hope you'll send me some grapes if I end up in hospital.'

'You won't. You'll be too fast for him. He won't be able to get near you. Your best plan is to take it easy in the first round, watch his style and look for his weakness; in the second, give the poor lad a bit of false confidence; in the third, finish him off! Think at all times and keep your head.'

'That's the one thing I'll try to keep.'

'Right. Enough talking. Let's go for a run.'

And the pair of them set off across Barney's.

The end of Jim's leave came all too soon. On the Sunday evening, the whole extended family descended on Honeypot Street – Uncles Eddy and John, Aunts Cissie, Mona and Hetty, Steve and Pauline, who had left the children in the care of Steve's mother, and a few friends, including the beautiful Jean from across the street. The great crowd went off to Capper's pub to commemorate the send-off in Tetley's ale. At ten o'clock, they all returned with innumerable bottles of beer to the Honeypot Street home to tackle the mountains of tongue-and-pickle sandwiches which Mam had prepared beforehand.

Between bites of bread and swigs of ale, the gathering sang their way through their whole repertoire of nautical songs: 'The Sailor with the Navy-Blue Eyes', 'All the Nice Girls Love a Sailor', 'Sons of the Sea', 'The Fleet's in Port Again, Yo-Ho', 'The Fleet's In'. As time went on, the songs became more and more sentimental and sad: 'We'll Meet Again', 'Yours', 'If I Had My Way', and Jean Priestley gave a soulful rendition of 'I'll Pray for You While You're Away'.

Jim, as the centre of attention, sat there with a happy grin on his face, enjoying and savouring every moment.

For a brief moment the spotlight turned on Billy.

'Come on, our Billy,' said Dad. 'Time you was in bed! Up the Molly Dancers!'

'Hey, Tommy, don't be such a miserable old sod!' shouted Uncle Eddy. 'Leave the little bugger alone. He can stay up just this once, can't he?'

Dad, who was a little afraid of Uncle Eddy, deferred.

'Go on, then. Just this once.'

Uncle Eddy thrust half a crown into Billy's hand.

'Here, you clever little bugger,' he said. 'Tek it for your eddication. Grammar school, eh? What're they learning him at this bloody posh place then, our Kate?'

'Eeh, I tell you, our Eddy, he's that clever I get worried, I do. There's so much stuff going into his head. There can't be room for it all. I'm afeared that one o' these days his head's gonna burst like a sausage in a frying pan. And you should see the things they're learning him! Foreign languages and all! Hey, come here, our Billy, and say a few words in algebra for your Uncle Eddy.'

After the knees-up came the sad part. Quiet, unassuming Uncle John had gone on to Cheetham Hill and ordered two taxis – a thing almost unknown in that district. The assembly crammed into the cabs and escorted Jim to London Road station. There, at two o'clock in the morning at the main platform, stood a huge train crowded with sailors. The wooden signboards attached to the last carriage announced its destination: MANCHESTER–PLYMOUTH EXPRESS. How that signboard conjured up romantic pictures in Billy's mind! Of battleships with their massive fourteen-inch guns, cruisers, destroyers; of sea-battles with German pocket battleships; and of U-boats and E-boats being sent down to Davy Jones's locker.

Then came the parting.

Billy watched with a lump in his throat as his mam hugged Jim close to her and said quietly:

'Look after yourself, son.'

Dad took Jim's hand and was about to shake it, but he changed his mind and instead took him in a tight embrace.

'All the best, son. Take care.'

Billy looked at his brother's dear, beloved face, and realised that soon he would be gone.

'Come here, our kid,' Jim said, and gave Billy a big bear-hug. 'You look after Mam and see she's all right. And see you win that fight at school. Remember all I've told you.'

The family withdrew a short, respectful distance to let Jim be with Jean Priestley. He spent the last five minutes talking earnestly to her, and finally took her in his arms and gave her a long, lingering kiss.

'Goodbye, Jean,' he said quietly. 'I'll be thinking of you.'

He boarded the train and stood leaning out of the window. The train began to move off, taking him away. They watched him still grinning and waving as he got smaller and smaller, until they could see him no more. All around them were other relatives straining for a last glimpse of their loved ones – still waving their goodbyes to the hundreds of sailors disappearing into the distance.

Finally, the train was gone and the family and Jean Priestley were left alone – sad and deflated – to make their melancholy way back to Honeypot Street.

Billy was very tired the next morning and could hardly open his eyes. It made no difference. He still had to go to school.

The daily routine at Damian College ground on as usual until break.

'Good God!' exclaimed Cash. 'Just look at Silly Billy Hopkins. He looks like something the cat's dragged in! Can't you peasants in Cheetham Hill afford beds, Silly?'

His cronies around him rewarded him with the usual supportive guffaw.

'For your information, Cash, my name is Billy. You will either stop calling me Silly Billy or I shall be forced to take it out on your ugly face.'

This fighting talk attracted a small group of third-formers who were eager to enjoy the witty exchanges.

'My dear Silly, if you would only wash your neck, I'd wring it.'

'Cash, you're a dimwit, and furthermore, you've got buck teeth.'

'Who cares what his teeth cost?' said Titch, who was listening to the exchange.

Cash grabbed Titch's lapel and examined his name tag.

'Keep out of this, Smelley, or whatever your name is. It's none of your business. It's between Hopkins and me.

'Hopkins,' he continued, 'you're a nasty little insect, and if you're not careful, I shall stamp on you.'

'You'll either apologise for that remark, Cash, or I'll be

forced to teach you a lesson you'll never forget.'

'I can't believe my ears! Why, you little runt! As the Arabs say: "May the fleas of a thousand camels infest your armpits"!'

'You're not the only one who's read *Arabian Nights*, Cash. "May your left ear wither and fall into your right pocket"!'

'Hopkins, you are asking for a severe beating. Did anyone ever tell you that you have a face like a cake left out in the rain?'

'Cash, I would say the same about you if you had a face.'

'That's the last straw, you little pipsqueak. I can swallow you in one bite.'

'And if you did, Cash, you'd have more brains in your belly than in your head.'

'Are you looking for a fight, Hopkins?'

'Cash, everyone in the form knows you're all talk. Like an over-ripe banana – yellow outside and squishy inside.'

'Hopkins, you little tin-ribs, I challenge you to a fight in the gym!'

'You're on, Cash! Let's go and fix it up with Brother Brendan right now.'

The big fight was arranged for Thursday at 4.15 in the gym.

'Are you sure you know what you're doing, Billy?' asked Oscar.

'No, I'm not. But it's too late now.'

'What kind of flowers do you like?' asked Titch.

'I think Billy will pull it off,' said Robin. 'Brains will always triumph over brute force and ignorance.'

Every night until the fight, Billy skipped in the back yard and went for a run across Barney's.

'I must get myself really fit if I'm going to beat Cash,' he said to Mam.

The big fight had been well publicised. There were notices on the boards of 3A and 3 Alpha.

DON'T MISS THE BIG FIGHT IN THE GYM
THURSDAY 28 NOVEMBER AT 4.15
CASH, THE FIGHTING FINANCIER FROM
FALLOWFIELD
VERSUS
HOPKINS, THE BATTLING BARD FROM
CHEETHAM HILL

Brother Brendan had made a professional job of setting out the boxing ring. At four o'clock every place was taken and the atmosphere was at high voltage. Many third-formers had postponed going home, and a few of the teachers, including Mr Puddephatt, Brother Placid and Brother Campion, were there to witness the event. Robin, Oscar and Titch Smalley had agreed to act as Billy's seconds. Cash had Rodney Potts and a couple of other rich kids as his.

At 4.10, the two contenders, fully kitted out in shorts and singlets and wearing boxing gloves which seemed much too big for them, put in their appearance. There were loud cheers from all the spectators. Next to Cash, Billy looked truly diminutive, and the fight had all the hallmarks of a David-and-Goliath battle.

At 4.15, Brother Brendan announced the fight.

'For the boxing championship of the third forms, we have in the right corner, Ready Cash of Fallowfield.'

There were loud cheers from his supporters.

'Go on, Eddy, show him who's who.'

'Give him one for me, Eddy!'

'You're too strong for him,' shouted Potts.

Cash nodded his head and smiled in acknowledgement and agreement.

'And in the left corner,' the brother continued, 'we have the Bard from Cheetham Hill, Billy Hopkins.'

'Teach him a lesson,' said Oscar, none too convincingly.

'I'm sure you can do it, Billy,' called Robin confidently.

'You can only do your best,' said Titch dubiously.

'The contest will be fought by Queensberry Rules over five rounds,' announced Brother Brendan. 'When you hear the bell, come out fighting. Let's have a clean fight.'

The bell rang for the first round. Billy hardly heard the cries of excitement. Taking up his boxing stance and his peek-a-boo style, he walked to the middle of the ring.

'Weigh him up in the first round and find his weakness,' Jim had said.

Billy slid to his left and feinted. Cash's body moved to avoid the punch that never came. Billy moved to the right and jabbed. Once again Cash moved back to evade the blow. Billy was moving smoothly and was in control.

Cash rushed Billy, who moved back and made a rapid move to his left and feinted again. Cash's short arms moved to block the punch that should have come. But there was no punch. Billy, busily sizing him up, smiled at Cash, who went red with anger, rushed again and threw a wild left hook. But Billy was no longer where Cash thought he was. The rush sent Cash headlong on to the ropes.

Billy was already in the middle of the ring, and he beckoned to Cash to come and get him. Enraged, Cash lowered his head and rushed like a bull in a tournament, and Billy, with the graceful movement of a matador, danced to the side and instead of punching Cash propelled him into the ropes, where his head became entangled.

The bell for the end of the first round sounded. Billy had learned all that he needed to know about his opponent. Cash lost his temper easily, relied on brute force to win and occasionally lowered his guard.

As he sat in his corner, Robin Gabrielson wiped his brow with a wet flannel.

'You're doing OK, Billy,' he said, 'but don't let him land one of those vicious punches on you or you won't get up.'

'Keep ducking and diving, bobbing and weaving,' said Titch.

'You make it sound like a cotton mill,' said Oscar.

Over in the other corner, Cash's seconds were giving frantic advice.

The bell rang for the second round. Now what was it Jim had said about the second round? 'Give the poor lad a bit of false confidence' – that was it.

Billy danced to the middle of the ring. With a snort, Cash charged, and this time he landed on Billy's chest a lucky thump that was heard all round the gym, followed by an elbow in his opponent's face.

This is definitely not part of the plan, thought Billy.

Winded and gasping for breath, he could hardly move. As Billy panted and tried to regain his composure, Cash smelt blood and moved in for the kill. Like a man possessed, he swung stiff punches, each connecting with a different part of Billy's body. A right-handed blow sent Billy reeling against the ropes.

Brother Brendan approached anxiously.

'Do you want to throw in the towel, Hopkins? There's no shame. You've put up a very good show.'

'No, sir. Please, no towel. It's nearly the end of this round.'

Then his forehead started to weep blood. He tried to stem the flow with his glove. Whatever happened, he had to avoid those vicious swings of Cash's if he was to stay on his feet. He danced around lightly, staying out of reach. Cash moved clumsily like a great elephant, and so it was not so hard. Cash kept up the pressure but Billy was an impossible, moving, dancing target. Then blessed relief. The bell rang.

'He's tired,' said Mr Puddephatt to Brother Placid. 'Hopkins should throw in the towel. Cash is much too big and heavy for him. Our Cheetham Hill poet has done awfully well for such a lightweight, but he should know when he's beaten.'

'Give him one more round and then I think Brother Brendan will have no alternative but to stop the fight.'

In Billy's corner, Robin was busy stemming the blood with a wet flannel and styptic pencil.

'Are you sure you want to go on, Billy?' he asked.

'Look, Billy,' said Titch, 'be a pal. Throw in the towel. I can't stand seeing you hit like that. Just 'cos he got us the stick from Dorian – well, it doesn't seem worth it.'

'He's right,' said Oscar. 'Pack it in, Billy, and call it a day.'

'The odds are against you, Billy,' said Titch. 'It's a well-known fact that the heavyweight always triumphs over the lightweight.'

'We're on your side, Billy,' added Oscar, 'but I think Cash is too big and heavy for you.'

Billy noticed the purple weal on Robin's wrist; he remembered the caning from Brother Dorian, the snide remarks about his Blackpool bag, the insults to his Cheetham Hill background and to his father's job.

'Oh, no!' said Billy. 'It's not over till the final bell.'

Third round.

With a smirk on his face, the over-confident Cash made his play and rushed at Billy like a tank. He wanted to hit and hit. His hands had become lower than before. Billy jabbed and crossed with a right. Though the jab was on target, the right cross missed. But it was enough. The leering expression on Cash's face had changed to one of utter amazement and consternation.

Billy recovered his posture and was in charge again. A jab. Another one. He moved back and threw in a one-two-three combination, and all three punches landed on Cash's head.

'Good jabs, Billy,' called Robin.

'Give it to him,' yelled Titch.

'Let him have it,' shouted Oscar.

'You've got him now,' called Robin. 'I knew you had it in you to beat him.'

Billy now moved like a ballet dancer, and as he pirouetted, he flicked left jabs on Cash's head. Cash was hurt and his legs started to wobble.

'Timber!' called Oscar.

'He's going down!' shouted Titch.

Billy moved in and delivered a right uppercut. Cash went down on one knee – shaking his head in disbelief.

Brother Brendan moved in quickly and signalled the end of the fight. He raised Billy's right hand above his head and said:

'The boxing champion of the third form. The Battling Bard from Cheetham Hill, Billy Hopkins.'

Then someone from 3 Alpha called:

'Well done, Hoppy!'

Billy turned round to face the speaker.

'Thanks,' he said.

Now he had his nickname.

Chapter Fourteen

Mind Your Language

Before that first term ended, Billy had a piece of good news and a piece of bad.

The bad news was that, in the terminal examination, he came twentieth out of twenty-five. This was a blow for a boy who had been accustomed to being first in class.

'*Could do better. Must try harder*,' said his report.

'There was never a truer word spoken,' Billy said, as he handed his card to Mam.

The good news was that Puddephatt had been called up into the army.

'I shall be taking the King's Commission,' he announced one morning towards the end of term, 'in the Royal Artillery.'

Not even Puddephatt could stop the cheer that went up.

'I take it,' he continued, 'that the cheer is because you appreciate that my contribution to the war effort will help bring hostilities to a speedier conclusion. And not because you are pleased to see me go.'

At the break, the boys agreed to take a collection for a parting gift. A set of bound copies of the works of George Bernard Shaw was decided on.

'But what can he do in the Royal Artillery?' asked Tony Wilde.

'I heard on good authority,' said Olly, 'that fat men in the army are put in the Pioneer Corps and employed on clerical duties.'

'They could fire him as a human cannon-ball on to Berlin,' said Robin. 'He'd wipe out the whole city.'

'Or they could tie a rope to him,' said Billy, 'and float him high in the sky as a barrage balloon – after they'd filled him with gas, of course.'

'No need for the gas, Hoppy,' said Titch. 'He's full o' hot air as it is.'

After Christmas, the study and hard work began in earnest and the procession of subject specialists stowed, stacked and stuffed their esoteric knowledge into the heads of their reluctant recipients. In Latin, the boys learned about the nominative, the vocative – O Chair! O Table! – the dative and the ablative; in physics about batteries, bunsens and Boyle's Law; in maths about powers, percentages and Pythagoras; in art about painting and perspective; in history about Perkin Warbeck and Lambert Simnel; in geography about cotton, coal and anthracite.

War or no war, the endless, relentless cramming process went on.

Not all was gloom in the classroom, however. French was taught by a bad-tempered brother called Placid. One day, Billy had to translate: '*Jean et Paul marchent sur le plancher; ils ne marchent pas sur le plafond; ils ne marchent pas sur les murs; ils ne marchent pas sur les fenêtres.*'

'John and Paul walk on the floor; they do not walk on the ceiling; they do not walk on the walls; they do not walk on the windows. But sir,' said Billy. 'Flies do.'

Which seemed to amuse all and sundry except Brother

Placid, who blew his top. But such was schoolboy humour. And then there was the case of the Rodney Potts translation.

'Translate the following sentence,' said Placid.

He wrote up on the blackboard: '*Non, merci, ma cherie. Je ne vais pas acheter un appareil cinematographique.*'

Poor Rodney did his best to make sense of this incomprehensible language, and read out his English version:

'No sherry for me, thank you. I'm appearing at the cinema.'

They played the 'Knock-knock. Who's there?' game in French.

'*Toc-toc. Qui frappe la porte?*'

'*Henri.*'

'*Henri qui?*'

'*Henri soit qui mal y pense.*'

Music was taken by a bumbling, absent-minded, slightly deaf middle-aged man, Brother Maurice, a brilliant musician. The boys loved him. He introduced them to his favourite traditional English folk-songs, with a few Irish, Scottish and Welsh thrown in. How Billy loved singing the various descants and rounds which the brother taught with great verve and enthusiasm.

It was in early 1940 that Tony Wilde revealed his talent for making up unauthorised versions of some of the songs. These compositions had to be quite subtle, in that they had to avoid arousing Brother Maurice's suspicions. The result was that the brother was never altogether sure that he'd heard aright. One of the most popular songs with the boys was 'Come Lasses and Lads'. The third verse was where Oscar had done his work, changing it from:

> *'You're out!' says Dick;*
> *'Not I,' says Nick,*
> *' 'Twas the fiddler*
> *played it wrong.'*
> *' 'Tis true,' says Hugh.*
> *And so says Sue,*
> *And so says everyone.*

to

> *'Take out your dick!'*
> *'Not I,' says Nick,*
> *'The fiddler'll*
> *play with my dong.'*
> *' 'Tis true,' says Hugh.*
> *And so says Sue,*
> *And so says everyone.*

No doubt the adults, had they discovered this ribaldry, would have found it disgusting. But Billy and his twelve-year-old companions thought that it was the funniest thing they had ever heard and considered their Oscar to be something of a genius.

The most momentous event in the school that year was the appointment of a middle-aged lady, a Miss Sybil Barrymore, to Puddephatt's English post. She was a gushing, bubbling bundle of energy and enthused about everything in sight.

'What a beautiful day it is today,' she rhapsodised at lunch to the brothers seated round their refectory table. 'I am so uplifted that I feel as if I'm floating on a little cloud. And how particularly crisp, green and lettucy the lettuce looks today!'

In her first English lesson with 3 Alpha, she gave out

copies of *Treasure Island* and prattled on about Robert Louis Stevenson whilst the form sat spellbound by this female phenomenon.

'What a great writer he was!' she babbled. 'And do you know, boys, he was ill with tuberculosis for most of his life? He wrote *Treasure Island* simply to amuse his stepson, and the book became a best-seller in the 1880s. Let us now read it aloud around the class. Each of you will take turns so that I can see how well you enunciate and articulate.'

The lesson went smoothly – each boy giving of his best in order to impress this elegant lady of letters.

When the last boy had read, she said:

'Excellent, boys. Really excellent. I can see many of you will get jobs with the BBC. Class dismissed. But would the following boys kindly remain behind: William Hopkins, Norbert Nodder, Richard Smalley.'

'We're in trouble again,' said Titch.

'I'd like to talk to you three about your English,' she said. 'Can you meet me here in the form room during the lunch break at, say, one o'clock?'

'But we allus play footer at dinner-time,' said Nobby.

'Then you must forgo your footer for once,' she snapped.

Just before the appointed time, the three boys waited for her in the form room.

'I wonder what she can want,' said Billy.

He didn't have long to wait, for at that moment Miss Barrymore sailed into the room.

'I shan't beat about the bush,' she said. 'I am concerned about your powerful Manchester dialects.'

'What's wrong with 'em?' asked Nobby.

'Oh, there's absolutely nothing wrong with them. All three of you speak the dialect perfectly. That's the trouble.

But I want to help you to do something about it. You, William, show a distinct talent for language. What a pity it isn't English.'

'I can't see nowt wrong with the way we talk,' said Titch.

'Eeh, I don't want to learn to talk posh,' said Billy. 'Me mam and dad wouldn't like it.'

'I'm not going to try to teach you to talk posh. On the contrary, I can teach you to speak not posh but properly, if you will give me the chance. In six months I can teach you RP.'

'You mean the language of the dead?' asked Billy.

'No, not RIP, but simply RP – Received Pronunciation – the accepted way of talking.'

'I can't see any point in it,' said Nobby. 'The way you talk doesn't matter.'

'That is where you are so wrong,' she said. 'The way you speak can affect your whole life, the kind of job you will get, the kinds of friends you will make, even the kind of wife you will eventually marry. The way you talk does matter, believe me.'

' 'Ow d'you make that out?' asked Billy.

'Listen,' she said. 'I'll give you an example. How would you like it if you went to the doctor and he said: "Hey up – chuck th'cap in, and coom in and get sat down. 'Ow've you bin, luv? Eeh bah gum, you do look proper poorly." '

The boys laughed at her mimicry.

'Doctors don't talk like that, miss,' said Titch.

'Exactly,' she said. 'I want to try a little experiment. Here's a list of occupations. I want you to tick the job you think best fits the way I read this extract from *Treasure Island*. In other words, what's the job of the person reading it. Ready?'

'Right, miss,' they said, enjoying the game.

'Number one: "Ah remember 'im as if it was yisterday, as 'e coom ploddin' to th'inn door, 'is sea-chest followin' be'ind 'im in an 'and barrer; a tall, strong, 'eavy, nut-brown man; 'is tarry pigtail fallin' over t'shoulders of 'is soiled blue coat; 'is 'ands ragged and scarred, with black, broken nails; and t'sabre cut across one cheek, a dirty, livid white." ' Her first reading was in a powerful Manchester dialect.

'Well?' she asked. 'Which occupation have you picked?'

'Comedian,' said Billy.

'Street sweeper,' said Nobby.

'Coalman,' said Titch.

'Now I'll read it again.'

This time, she did so in an exaggerated upper-class accent.

'Which occupations this time?' she asked.

'Prime Minister, but it sounded a bit like Cash and all,' said Billy.

'Duke of Windsor,' said Nobby.

'A butler,' said Titch.

Laughingly, she said:

'Now listen to the same passage read with Received Pronunciation.' And she read it in a clear voice.

'Teacher,' said Billy.

'Lawyer,' said Nobby.

'News reader on the wireless,' said Titch.

'So you see,' she said, 'how we associate certain occupations with accent and dialect. We'll finish this little session by reading a very short play I have written for you. William, you take the part of Herbert; Norbert the part of Henry; and Richard the part of Howard.'

The boys began to read her script.

Billy: 'Ello, 'Enery. 'Ello, 'Oward. 'Ow are you?

Nobby:	'Ello, 'Erbert. 'Ello, 'Oward. 'Ave you 'eard 'Arry 'Opkins 'as gone on 'oliday?
Titch:	'Ow 'appy for 'im. 'As 'e gone to 'Arrow again?
Billy:	Honestly, I 'aven't 'eard.
Nobby:	I 'ope 'e 'asn't gone 'untin' on 'is 'orse again.
Titch:	I 'ope not. Last year 'e 'ad an 'orrible accident.
Billy:	Yes, 'e 'ad it when 'is 'orse refused to jump a 'igh 'edge.
Nobby:	'E 'ad to go to 'ospital, 'adn't 'e?
Titch:	'Ow 'orrible!

'Thank you,' said Miss Barrymore. 'I rather think I 'ave taken on an 'ard up'ill task!'

The boys agreed to meet Miss Barrymore for half an hour every lunch-time, and gradually they began to slough off their unwanted dialects. She was a hard taskmistress and she believed in repetition – over and over again.

> *Moses supposes his toeses are roses*
> *But Moses supposes erroneously.*

> *Round and round the rugged rock,*
> *The ragged rascal ran.*

After countless sessions of reciting selected tongue-twisters, Billy learned how to aspirate.

'Say them ten times a day,' she said, 'until it's second nature to pronounce the 'aitch'. Push a lot of air out and do not let your tongue touch the roof of your mouth.'

But Billy had a further problem. He had to be very careful not to speak this new language at home.

'That little bugger's getting above himself,' said Dad. 'He'll be thinking he's better than us soon. You mark my words.'

'I don't think so,' said Mam. 'Anyroad, he's got to learn to talk proper if he's going to make summat of himself.'

As the nights became colder, Billy found he could no longer do his homework in the bedroom but had to tackle his geometry and his Latin and the myriad other subjects in the living room, where he had to compete with the wireless, constant chatter, and the numerous visits of friends, neighbours, relatives and customers for gloves and Cossack hats.

'Why can't we have a fire in the front room, Mam?'

'Because. That's why. You know very well we only have a fire in there at Christmas. D'you think we're made of money?'

Then there was Henry Sykes. He called one night in October.

'D'you fancy coming out for a game o' footer, Billy?' he asked. 'Me and the other lads are trying to get a bit of a team together to play Derby Street.'

'Sorry, Henery. I've got piles and piles of homework.'

'OK, Billy,' said Henry sadly. 'Be seeing you then.'

'Sometimes,' Billy said to his mam, 'I wonder whether all this learning's worth it.'

'It's worth it,' she said simply.

Chapter Fifteen

A Bit of Excitement

'Some war!' said Billy to Mam. 'Here we are, August the twenty-second, and nowt's happened.'

Dad overheard and, looking up from his paper, addressed the wireless set:

'Nowt's happened! Hitler's taken over all bloody Europe, we've had Dunkirk, we've had the Battle of Britain and Jerry's in Paris. And he says nowt's happened!'

'You know what I mean,' said Billy. 'All those things are taking place somewhere else. Here in Manchester there's been nowt exciting.'

'No, and we don't want nowt exciting, thank you very much,' said Mam. 'Don't tempt providence, our Billy.'

'Yeah, but at school they're making jokes, calling it the Bore War and saying Hitler's Blitzkrieg should be called his Sitzkrieg. Anyway, all the kids who were evacuated in 'thirty-nine are coming back home.'

'We've had our share of excitement in this house,' said Dad. 'Take last December. Look at the way our Jim in the *Renown* chased across the Atlantic to Rio after the *Graf Spee*. He made it scuttle itself in Montevideo, didn't he? And he helped to sink the French fleet last month. So what more d'you want?'

'I just feel sometimes that the war's happening to other people all the time, that's all.'

'Let's hope it stays that way,' said Mam.

Billy had spoken too soon, for on Wednesday 4 September, the Luftwaffe carried out night raids on twenty-one British towns, including Manchester. The RAF replied by bombing Berlin, causing fires that could be seen fifty miles away.

'We'd better get ourselves organised,' said Mam, as she sat with Billy in the dark cubby-hole in the coal cellar. 'We'll catch our death o' cold if we have to come down here every night.'

That first raid lasted only three hours and little damage was done in the centre of the town, but there was the promise of more to come. The next day, as Billy walked back from Ormeroyd's corner shop with Dad's Player's Weights and his *Evening Chronicle*, he read the front page headlines and reports:

HITLER PROMISES TO BREAK US!

In a speech yesterday to the German nation, Hitler said: 'The British will know that we are now giving our answer to the impudent raids of the RAF. If they attack our cities, we will erase theirs. We will call a halt to these night pirates. The hour will come when one of us two will break up, and it won't be Nazi Germany. If the British throw two or three thousand pounds of bombs, we will unload 150, 180, yes, 200 thousand . . .' Apparently he intended to continue the progression of figures, but the shouts of the crowd halted him.

'It looks as if our Billy's going to get his excitement after all,' said Dad when he read the headlines.

Blackout curtains were put up to the front cellar windows and a new mantle was fitted to the gas bracket down there. Mattresses were placed on the floor and the Hopkins family prepared to dig in. In fact, provision for only three was needed, as Flo was on permanent night work with the Dunlop Rubber Company, whilst Les and Sam were out every night on duty as ARP messengers.

Next door, the Sykes family had made similar preparations and were ready for the Blitzkrieg which Adolf had threatened. The two families were able to communicate with each other through the adjoining cellar walls. Billy had made a special 'knocking' hammer which was beautifully decorated and was most effective in calling their neighbours' attention.

'Are you there, Jessie?'

'Aye, we're here again, Kate.'

'Are y'all right, Jessie?'

'Not so bad, but being in this cellar's not doing me asthma no good.'

'Who's with you then?'

'There's just me and our Henery. Harry won't get out o' bed. He says if he's gonna die, he'd rather go in his bed than in the coal cellar.'

'Same with Tommy. He's still in bed too. He says, "What has to be will be and if your name's on the bomb it'll hit you no matter where y'are."'

'By gum, that's true. So why are we here in the cellar, Mrs Hopkins?'

'Well, you won't know your name's on it till it hits you, will you?' said Mam.

This philosophical poser seemed to stump Mrs Sykes, for she went quiet after that.

Billy often wondered himself about this notion of names on bombs. He could imagine some Luftwaffe corporal over there in Germany carefully chalking his name and address on the side of a large hundred-pound bomb: 'With love to Billy Hopkins, 17 Honeypot Street, Cheetham. Special Delivery. By Express Air Mail.'

'It's a frightening thought, Mam,' he said, 'to think that up there, floating above us in the clouds, there are some men trying to kill us.'

The raids began to increase in frequency and duration. Regularly at six o'clock, the siren sounded.

'There it goes. Moaning Minnie! You can almost set your clock by it,' said Mam. 'Come on, our Billy. Down we go. Bring your homework with you. You'll just have to do it down there.'

The raids usually lasted until dawn. Early on, Billy would get on with his Latin and geometry whilst the heavy bombers droned overhead. Around ten o'clock, after a cup of cocoa made during a lull, it was time for shut-eye on the mattress.

One night all was quiet and calm, a heaven-sent respite from the waves of bombers passing above. Suddenly they were awakened by the sound of heavy gunfire, which was so loud it seemed to be in the cellar with them.

'God help us!' cried Mam as she awoke with a start. 'That's near!'

Then they traced the source of the gunfire. It was their black cat, Snowy, walking gingerly across the upturned tin bath!

On Friday 29 November, the sirens burst out as usual at six o'clock, and Billy and his Mam took up their places in the front cellar. There was something different about this raid, though, for the deafening sound of gunfire – of the real kind – began almost immediately and the dull explosion of faraway bombs was heard within the first five minutes.

'It says on the wireless that the Jerries are giving London a miss tonight and heading up north,' Dad called down to them. 'Manchester's gonna get it tonight. I think I'd better join you two down there.'

'What about all that stuff about your name being on the bomb?' asked Mam.

'Aye,' he said. 'But there's no sense in me writing it meself, is there?'

The raid lasted twelve hours. All night they listened to the thud of bombs dropping somewhere to the north of the city.

'Some poor buggers have been getting it up there,' said Dad.

'I wonder how our Polly is,' said Mam. 'She lives up that way, doesn't she?'

'I'm supposed to be staying with 'em this weekend,' said Billy. 'I'm going up there after breakfast, so I can see how they are.'

He took the 62 bus up Cheetham Hill to Heaton Park and was unprepared for the sight which met him. As he stepped off the bus, he saw devastation everywhere. A great area of the new housing estate where Pauline, Steve and the two children lived had been flattened and left a smoking ruin. Billy ran to Pauline's lovely new house to find Steve nailing boards to windows and doors.

'Steve, Steve,' he cried. 'What's happened? Where's Polly and the kids? Are they all right?'

'They're all OK, but we've had one hell of a night, Billy. Jerry has well and truly plastered this area. God knows what he was after. Pauline's in the garden round the back trying to put a few things together.'

In the back garden, Billy found Polly and the two boys packing up a few suitcases of the belongings they had managed to get out of the house. She was weeping quietly.

'Oh, Billy,' she sobbed. 'We've lost everything, and we're all lucky to be alive.'

'Tell me what happened, Polly, for God's sake.'

'During the night the bombers dropped those aerial landmines – the ones that come down by parachute. Twenty-five people have been killed and I don't know how many injured.'

'Where were you during all this?'

'We were in our Anderson shelter for almost twelve hours. I suffered a dislocated jaw because of the blast but Steve seemed to know what to do.'

'I'm so sorry,' he said. 'But at least you're all OK.'

'We're not badly injured like a lot of other people. But we've lost our new home. It's unsafe to live there now as the foundations have been rocked by the explosions.'

'What'll you do now? You can always come to us in Honeypot Street.'

'No, we'll go to one of the emergency centres set up by the WVS, and then we'll be found a new home.'

'Is there anything I can do?'

'No, nothing. You'd best get back and tell Mam and Dad what's happened here. We'll come down to see them later today.'

As Billy turned away to go back to his bus, young Oliver said:

'Unca Billy. Make us laugh!'

But he couldn't, because of the tears in his eyes.

The air raids on Manchester did not let up. If anything they intensified, and a second evacuation of children from the big cities was being organised. This time Billy was included.

'You'll have a smashing time,' said Mam, trying to be cheerful. 'You'll be going to Blackpool of all places. You've allus been lucky; that comes of being a Sunday child.'

Towards the end of the Christmas term, Brother Maurice came round during the music lesson as the boys were singing 'Come Lasses and Lads' and, cupping his hand to his ear, listened to each boy individually.

'He suspects something,' said Billy to Robin Gabrielson.

At the end of the lesson the brother said:

'I should like to see the following boys before they go: Gabrielson, Hardy, Hopkins, Nodder, Smalley and Wilde.'

'Trouble again,' said Titch to no one in particular.

Billy could almost feel the pain again on his backside.

'Right, boys,' said Maurice. 'I've selected you to form a little choir for the school concert on the last day of term, Friday the thirteenth of December. It's bound to be a very lucky day.'

'Why is that, sir?' asked Billy.

'Because thirteen is my lucky number,' he said. 'We shall put in twenty minutes' practice every lunch-hour.'

'I wonder when we'll get time for dinner,' said Nobby to Billy.

'If you want to learn to sing and speak English, you'll have to do without dinner,' replied Billy.

For Billy, the school concert was a most unusual affair because not only Mam but also Dad had agreed to attend – his very first visit to the school. In the first half, the school orchestra, conducted by Brother Maurice, played, in its inimitable off-key style, various pieces of light classical music. At the interval Billy went back-stage to check a few details of their appearance in the second half. When he returned to the auditorium, he found Mam and Dad already engaged in conversation with Tony Wilde's parents.

'The fall of France was a disaster,' said Mr Wilde.

'Just terrible,' said Dad. 'And did you see the way Jerry went up Champs Elsie. Must've been a terrible sight for the French.'

'It's to be hoped the German SS brigades never get over here,' said Mr Wilde.

'You've never said a truer word,' said Dad. 'Them Gas Peter fellas would love to get their hands on Churchill.'

'Sorry, not with you,' said Tony's dad.

'Y'know, the SS fellas.'

'Oh, you mean the Gestapo. But you're too right there, Mr Hopkins. The SS seem to be without normal feelings – a bit like what we hear about the Japanese.'

'The Japs have already signed an agreement with Hitler. Mark my words, they'll be worse than the Jerries if they ever go to war against us. Y'know they worship their Emperor, Hi-de-hi, as God.'

'Hi-de-hi?'

'Y'know, that Mickey Doo fella.'

'Oh, you mean the Mikado?' said Mr Wilde.

'That's right. That's what I said.'

Mam, meanwhile, was chatting with Mrs Wilde.

'We've been having one or two air raids round our way,' Mam said.

'Oh, aye,' said Mrs Wilde.

'First they dropped them Fairy lights – the ones that make it all bright as day.'

'Oh, aye.'

'Then they dropped them there incondescet bombs to start fires.'

'Oh, aye.'

'And me daughter what lives in Heaton Park has just been bombed out. It was a good job she and her family was in one of them Hans Andersen shelters.'

'Oh, aye.'

Billy interrupted Mam's one-way conversation.

'How are you enjoying the concert so far, Mam? What did you think of the orchestra?'

'I enjoyed it – listening to 'em practising and tuning up their instruments. And when they get the tune right, I think they'll be very good.'

The second half of the concert was a tear-jerker. Five of the boys, looking like cherubs in altar boys' gear, hummed softly whilst the chief cherub, Robin Gabrielson, gave a heart-rending solo performance of Schubert's 'Who is Sylvia?'. But the item which had the mothers in tears and the fathers swallowing hard was the boys' *pianissimo* performance of Ivor Novello's 'Keep the Home Fires Burning' whilst a handsome sixth-former, dressed in full military uniform, rifle on shoulder, recited the lines from *Richard II*:

> *This royal throne of kings, this sceptred isle,*
> *This earth of majesty, this seat of Mars,*
> *This other Eden, demi-paradise,*
> *This fortress built by Nature for herself*
> *Against infection and the hand of war,*
> *This happy breed of men, this little world,*
> *This precious stone set in the silver sea,*
> *Which serves it in the office of a wall,*
> *Or as a moat defensive to a house,*
> *Against the envy of less happier lands.*
> *This blessed plot, this earth, this realm, this*
> *England.*

At the conclusion, Brother Dorian took the centre of the stage to deliver the final speech.

'My dear parents, this is a sad day for us all. The might

of Goering's Luftwaffe is now being turned on us civilians. Night after night, hour after hour, raider after raider dumps bomb after bomb upon us and our homes. We in Manchester have suffered, but I tell you now, we have not suffered one half as much as those poor citizens of Coventry who were bombed mercilessly on the night of the fourteenth of November. We are all in the front line now. I read in my newspaper today – and it may be of some comfort to you to know it – that it takes one ton of bomb to kill three-quarters of a person. At that rate, it will take Hitler many years to wipe out Manchester.

'But we must stand rock-like together, shoulder to shoulder, and when the blast of war blows in our ears, then we must imitate the action of the tiger, and go forward together as one man, a smile on our lips and our heads held high.

'And soon you must part from your children. They are our future, our seed-corn. Without them there is no tomorrow, and they must be protected from the evils of that guttersnipe, Shikelgruber. But rest assured about this: I shall try to love them all as if they were my own. Let us therefore look to the distant horizon, raise our eyes to the golden light on the hillside, and filled with confidence and courage, our resolve unshaken, we shall not fail.'

This moving speech was met by thunderous applause from the assembled parents.

'Ooh, he does sound like Winston Churchill,' said Mam on the way home.

'Where d'you think he got the bloody speech from?' observed Dad shrewdly. 'And how, I should like to know, are we supposed to stand rock-like together and at the same time go forward like bloody tigers with smiles on our bloody faces?'

★ ★ ★

The decision to send Billy to Blackpool was reinforced just before Christmas. Manchester suffered its worst blitz on the nights of 23 and 24 December when the centre of the city was almost blasted out of existence.

The sirens sounded at dusk on Christmas Eve right on time.

'Time, gentlemen, please,' said Mam. 'Here we go again.'

'You're just like the landlord o' the Queen's Arms,' said Dad. 'And you keep a good cellar.'

As soon as they had descended to the cellar, Billy knocked on the cellar wall with his home-made mallet.

'Are y'all right, Jessie?' called Mam.

'We're not so bad,' called back Mrs Sykes. 'We're all down here tonight. What a bloody way to spend Christmas, eh? I think we're for it again, Kate.'

Shortly after she had spoken, the fiercest anti-aircraft barrage they had ever heard began, as chains of shells burst high in the sky, creating a curtain of steel.

'Hey, Billy,' shouted Henry, 'there'll be tons of shrapnel for us tomorrow from that lot.'

They heard off in the distance the cracking explosions of bombs followed by a succession of staccato reports like machine-gun fire. From dusk to dawn there was hardly a period of more than two minutes when bombs were not falling on the city.

'The town's getting it tonight,' shouted Mrs Sykes. 'Look out your cellar window, Kate. Thompson Street goods yard's gone.'

They turned off all the gaslights and opened the window, and there across the railway sidings, silhouetted against the skyline, was their beloved city of Manchester – a raging inferno.

'The whole bloody world's on fire,' said Dad.

'It's like that scene in *Gone with the Wind* where the whole town is in flames and Scarlett O'Hara rides up in a carriage,' said Mam.

'If we had a fiddle, we could play it like Nero did when Rome was burning,' added Billy, showing off his classical knowledge.

'I'm just glad you're getting out of this next week,' said Mam. 'You'll be a lot safer in Blackpool.'

'Hey, Kate, it's Christmas Eve,' called Mrs Sykes. 'How's about a bit o' carol-singing?'

'Right, you're on,' Mam called back. 'What d'you suggest, our Billy?'

'How about a nice German carol – "Silent Night"?'

At dawn, the all-clear sounded, and Billy and Henry spent that Christmas morning collecting shrapnel, which they found in great abundance scattered in the cobbles of Honeypot Street.

Despite the pounding their city had received, the Hopkins family enjoyed a magnificent dinner on Christmas Day, thanks to Mam's culinary skills on the living-room range, and Dad's special connections in Smithfield Market. At three o'clock they gathered round the wireless set to listen to the King's broadcast to the Empire from Buckingham Palace. When he had finished, Dad said:

'After that rousing speech, what about cheering ourselves up and giving ourselves a good laugh. Let's have a listen to Lord Hee-Haw.'

Carefully, he fine-tuned the wireless set to 31 metres.

'Jairmany calling. Jairmany calling,' drawled a nasal voice. 'This is Reichsender Hamburg, Station Bremen on the thirty-one-metre band.

'Merry Christmas to all you British citizens, especially those of you living in the big cities. We do hope you enjoyed our little Christmas gift to you. No doubt you have finished your Christmas dinner of scraggy chicken and the few paltry rations your government allows you. Are you aware, people of Britain, that your well-fed Winston is at this very moment puffing away at a good Corona and sipping his Napoleon brandy after a lavish banquet with your stuttering King at Buckingham Palace? Hard luck on you working cheps, what?

'During the week, your Air Ministry announced that many German bombs were dropped at random. Honest injun, we do offer our special condolences to the denizens of that unfortunate city. Sorry we had to pick on your town, cheps, but there really is nothing left worth bombing in Coventry. And all you people of Manchester must be very busy sweeping up the mess our gallant Jairman airmen have left behind. By the way, do you know your Town Hall clock has stopped? We know that because we are the ones who stopped it. Sorry about that, old man. However, we here in the Jairman Reich do hope your Christmas goes with a bang. But in the words of your coloured singer, Mr Albert Yolsen, "You haven't seen anything yet". We conclude this transmission by wishing you all a Heppy New Year – even if it's a short one.'

'I do feel sorry for all them poor people what live in Random,' said Mam.

'That bugger Hee-Haw should be hanged,' said Dad.

So 1940 came to its close.

'Well, our Billy, I hope you've had all the excitement you was wanting. Let's hope 1941 is a quieter year for us all,' said Mam.

'I'll drink to that,' said Dad.

If only they'd known.

Chapter Sixteen

I Do Like To Be Beside The Seaside

During the Christmas holidays, the college had sent one of its letters listing the clothes it deemed essential for an evacuee, and for over a fortnight Mam had been busy washing, ironing, and sewing name tapes on the huge pile of garments the school insisted on.

'I've never had pyjamas before, Mam,' Billy said.

'It's not the only thing you've never had before. Looking at this list, anyone'd think you was going on safari to Africa. It's a wonder they've not asked for mosquito nets and a sun helmet. Anyroad, I've packed your bucket and spade as well, in case you go on the sands.'

'I'm not going on me holidays, Mam. I'm being evacuated.'

'I know that. I'm not daft. But take 'em just the same. You never know when they might come in handy. I'm also giving you some sandwiches, a bar of Cadbury's and a bag o' fruit in case you get hungry on the journey. Oh, aye, and when you meet your new "mother", make sure she gets your ration book, and here's a nice bag of chocolate biscuits to give to her when you get there.'

On that first Monday of 1941, they made the bus

journey across Manchester together – Billy loaded up with a satchel and his gas mask on his back, a small suitcase in his right hand and his red Blackpool bag in his left.

On the 42 bus, the familiar conductor said:

'Off to Blackpool again, then, eh, lad? I told you last time you was going the wrong way.'

'Not this time I'm not. Anyroad, I'm not supposed to say where I'm going; it's a state secret.'

'Do I look like a Jerry?'

'If your right ear was a bit bigger, you would definitely look like the Jerry we have under our bed.'

'Cheeky little bugger,' said the conductor good-humouredly. 'You should be on the music hall.'

Outside the college gates there was a fleet of six double-decker buses waiting to take them to Victoria Station on the first leg of their journey, and a great crowd of schoolboys with their tearful mothers issuing last-minute instructions and advice.

'Don't forget your gas mask!'

'Don't lose your money!'

'Change your underpants twice a week.'

Billy reported to Miss Barrymore, who ticked off his name on her clipboard. He gave her his ration book and she handed him a set of labels with his name printed on them.

'You look like a post-office parcel,' Mam said as she helped to tie the labels on to his raincoat.

'I don't mind – as long as they don't stick stamps on me face and sealing wax down me ears,' he said, trying to make a joke and keep the parting cheerful.

'Keep well lapped up, son. Have you got your hanky? Don't use your sleeve like that. Don't forget to wash your neck and behind your ears or you'll leave a tide-mark.'

'I won't. I promise.'

'And don't stick your head out o' the train window or you'll get it sliced off. And don't forget to write every week and let us know how you're getting on. You'll be all right with your pals.'

'Time to get on your bus, boys,' Miss Barrymore called.

'I'll have to go now, Mam.'

'I won't kiss you. Not in front of all your pals. And I won't cry neither,' she said, two big tears glistening in the corners of her eyes.

'Thanks, Mam.'

'But there's nowt wrong with a big hug for a smart guy and a tough kid,' she said, suiting the action to the words.

'Ta-ra, Mam.'

'Ta-ra, son. And look after yourself.'

Billy boarded the bus and went upstairs to join his pals. He watched Mam out of the window and could see her looking up so sad and forlorn as the bus pulled away from the kerb.

Five minutes later, they were moving rapidly along Oxford Road towards the railway station.

'Old Hoppy's brought his George Formby bag,' called Oscar, grabbing the carrier bag. 'And look! He's brought his bucket and spade for the sands. Isn't that nice?'

'So what!' Billy replied. 'We are going to Blackpool after all. In case you didn't know it, Oscar, there's a beach there. You might find a bucket and spade useful yourself.'

'The day I need a bucket or a spade, Hoppy, I shall hire yours for threepence.'

'Hey, look at Potts's gas-mask case,' shouted Titch. 'It's dead posh. That must've cost a bomb, Potts. Let's have a look at it.'

'My eldest sister bought it for me for Christmas,' said

Potts. 'It's got a red velvet lining and a little zipped pocket for my ear plugs.'

'And what about your teddy bear and your little drum?' said Titch. 'I hope you haven't left them behind.'

'My mother said I had to take no notice of boys who were rude and tried to make fun of me. So I shall ignore you, Smalley,' said Potts.

At Victoria Station there was chaos as thousands of children in crocodile columns each headed by a Pied Piper marched across the concourse to the 'Evacuation Specials', which stood ready and waiting to take them off to their rural and seaside destinations.

Guards' and teachers' whistles shrilled at the same time, adding to the confusion of both schoolchildren and train drivers. Amidst the hissing steam, teachers ran hither and thither through the whirling mass like sheep-dogs, trying to head stray children back into their designated places.

The Damian College contingent found their way to the Blackpool platform and a single blast of Brother Dorian's whistle gave the signal for them all to climb into the compartments of the non-corridor train. A final register check was taken by the form teachers and they were off, clattering out through Salford and Pendleton.

'This is a great adventure into the unknown,' said Oscar.

'I hope it's not an adventure into trouble,' said Titch.

Soon they were out into open country, doing at least ten miles an hour – crawling at a snail's pace through Lancashire's rustic regions.

'If we go any slower,' said Robin, 'we shall be going backwards.'

Then the train did start to go backwards, and a great cheer went up from every compartment.

'We're going back,' said Billy. 'Hitler's surrendered to our Beefeaters.'

Finally the train stopped, and there they remained for a whole hour. 'Why are we waiting?' sang the whole train, followed by an old First World War favourite, 'We're Here Because We're Here'. An inquisitive matronly cow came to the embankment fence to inspect them.

'There's one of Hoppy's brindled cows,' said Oscar.

'And there's a scarecrow in the field,' added Nobby.

'That's not a scarecrow, Nobby,' said Billy. 'That's the farmer.'

While they waited they made weak jokes to pass the time and to cover up their nervousness about what fate had in store for them. Eventually the train began to move, but oh so slowly.

'Why do we have to wear these stupid labels, I wonder?' asked Robin. 'I feel like a turkey with its weight and price tagged to it.'

'It's so people will know who we are,' said Titch.

'But we've got mouths and we can talk. Why do we need labels?' asked Oscar.

'In case we're killed and need to be identified,' said Titch gravely.

'Who'd want to kill us?' asked Billy.

'The Germans, of course. That's why our destination is kept secret,' answered Titch. 'They might want to machine-gun the train.'

'Might be true,' said Robin. 'Look at the way that evacuee ship was sunk last year. I forget what it was called.'

'The *City of Benares*,' said Billy. 'I read about it in my dad's paper. Over three hundred were drowned.'

'Many of the rich people have tried to get their kids out of the big towns,' said Oscar.

'That's what happened to Cash,' said Nobby. 'He went to boarding school in the end.'

'That wasn't because of the war,' said Robin. 'It was because Hoppy beat him in the ring.'

'Anyroad, if the Germans decide to bomb us,' said Titch, 'we're a sitting duck right at this moment 'cos we've stopped again.'

Someone in another compartment started up community singing again, and choruses of 'Ten Green Bottles' and 'Ten Men Went to Mow' rang out across the countryside.

Three hours later, they reached Preston.

'You know,' said Billy, 'I did this journey by bus last year and it took only an hour and a half all the way to Blackpool. Today it's going to be almost four hours.'

'I want to go somewhere,' said Titch, 'and there's no toilet on this train.'

'Pee out of the window,' suggested Robin.

'I can't make my thing reach that high,' he answered.

'I've got the same problem,' said Oscar.

'I've got the answer to our prayers,' said Billy. 'Do it first in my bucket and then chuck it out of the window. The pee, I mean, not the bucket.'

'Me first,' said Titch.

'Me second,' said Oscar.

'For you, Oscar,' said Billy, 'it's threepence. Remember?'

'I can see you were brought up in Cheetham Hill,' he said.

There was a loud yell from the compartment behind.

'Who the hell's throwing tea out of the window?' an angry voice enquired.

Titch popped his head out.

'Well, we haven't thrown any tea,' he called truthfully.

Just then, the sudden thunderous roar of a train going the other way made him jump out of his skin and pull his head back into the compartment.

'That were a close thing,' he said. 'I nearly lost my head. But blast it, I've got a piece of soot in my eye.'

One after another, using their handkerchiefs, they all tried to remove the dirt from Titch's eye, but to no avail. By the time they reached Blackpool's Central Station, his eye was red, swollen and watering and he looked like Tommy Farr after his fight with Joe Louis.

Outside the station, Miss Barrymore took another roll-call to make sure no one had run away. Then she ordered her form into the coaches for final allocation to their new homes and their new parents. Before they set off, three ladies from the WVS boarded the bus bearing lots of small carrier bags.

'We're very sorry, boys, to hear about the air raids on Manchester,' said the first lady.

'We're very sorry to see you taken from your homes like this,' said the second. 'But we have these little parcels of emergency rations – a tin of Spam, a tin of baked beans and a bar of chocolate – to tide you over the next few hours until billets are found for you.'

'We're very sorry we couldn't do more for you,' said the third, 'but we wish you all the very best of luck and we hope you'll be happy here in Blackpool.'

'They're very kind ladies,' said Nobby. 'But what does WVS stand for?'

'Didn't you notice,' said Billy, 'what each one said? WVS stands for "We're Very Sorry".'

'Oh, that explains it,' said Nobby.

The coach moved away from the station.

'Anyone got a tin-opener?' Billy called out.

No one had.

'Ah well,' he said. 'We'll just have to wait till we get one.'

Attention now turned to the business of finding new homes.

'This is the part which worries me most,' said Titch. 'With my kind of luck, I'm bound to end up with a couple of loonies or a mad scientist or something.'

'Stop being so cheerful,' said Billy. 'You might get someone really nice like Sweeney Todd or Boris Karloff.'

The bus wound its way slowly round the streets and avenues of Bispham, stopping every so often so that Miss Barrymore could match boys to billets.

The selected foster-parents waited anxiously at their doorways to see what they had let themselves in for, and what kind of kid destiny would deposit on their doorstep. Would he be thin, fat, tall, short, spotty or bespectacled? Cheeky or well-behaved?

'You two boys, go here,' Miss Barrymore said consulting her clipboard and choosing boys at random. 'And you three go over there.'

Nervously, the boys remaining in the bus watched and waited their turn, wondering what kind of folk fate would ordain for them.

'It's like a raffle or a lottery,' said Oscar.

'More like a cattle market,' said Robin.

Eventually the coach stopped outside a large, luxurious villa and an extremely ugly, cross-eyed lady wearing a pinafore and a hair-net emerged to collect her quota.

'One only here,' called Miss Barrymore.

Every boy tried in his own way to look invisible by avoiding eye contact: some gazed off into space, some looked at the floor, some became suddenly engrossed in the books they weren't reading.

'No volunteers,' she said. 'Then I must use my prerogative. I choose you, Hardy.'

'Aw, miss. Please pick on somebody else. Not me!'

' "Many are called, but few are chosen",' she replied. 'Be brave, Hardy, for that is what your name means, and you share it with the great sea-captain, Sir Thomas, who was Nelson's great friend.'

'Yes, miss, if you say so.'

'Also, Olly, remember your other great friend, Laurel,' said Oscar. 'And it looks as if you've gotten yourself into another fine mess.'

Slowly, the reluctant Olly, carrying his case and his gas mask, got up from his seat and, accompanied by his form mistress, dragged himself across the road to his new 'mother', who promptly embraced him and gave him a big kiss, which delighted the busload of boys, sending them into convulsions of laughter.

'Kiss me, Hardy,' Titch called.

The laughter, however, was tinged with a certain amount of relief at their lucky escape.

Two hours later, Miss Barrymore was down to the last five boys, who were now beginning to look tired and dishevelled. The bus drove on, passed a cemetery, turned left into Kincraig Avenue and stopped outside some small semi-detached houses. Billy noticed standing at the gate of number 1 a pretty, dark-haired girl of about twelve years of age who was studying the proceedings with great interest.

'I hope I'm billeted there,' said Billy. 'Now that is what I call a real foster-mother.'

'You should be so lucky,' said Robin.

'I have you five boys left and only four billets,' Miss Barrymore said. 'Come along and we'll see what can be done.'

Mrs Rivers at number 7 was a round, motherly woman with a kind face.

'I'll take two,' she said, as if ordering pints of milk.

'Thank you, Mrs Rivers,' the teacher said. 'It's much appreciated.'

She consulted her clipboard.

'Tony Wilde and Nobby Nodder – you're here with Mrs Rivers. Say good evening to your new mother.'

'Good evening, Mrs Rivers,' the two boys said.

'Come on then, lads,' said Mrs Rivers. 'Bring your things and we'll go inside.'

'Right, I have just you three boys now and then I'm finished, thank the Lord. Let's go and see if we can persuade Mrs Mossop at number 9.'

Mrs Mossop was a serious-looking, unsmiling woman, aged about forty-five. She wore steel-rimmed glasses and her hair was arranged in a bun. She waited impatiently at her door.

'I asked for two girls,' she said. 'Not all these boys.'

'I'm afraid we have only boys in stock today,' said Miss Barrymore. 'Girls are being billeted on the South Shore. But these are three very nice boys.'

The boys did their best to look nice, which wasn't easy since they had been on the road for over eight hours. Robin put on his best angelic expression. Mrs Mossop seemed unimpressed.

'I used to be a nurse,' she said. 'And I can tell you – they don't look very nice to me. That little squidgy one there looks as if he has conjunctivitis, which is very, very contagious. And I have two children of my own to think of. The other two don't look too clean either. They don't have nits or anything like that, do they?'

'I'm sure they don't,' said their teacher. 'They were all medically examined and certified clean before we let them out of Manchester. As for young Smalley there, he's got some dirt in his eye, that's all.'

'What about bed-wetting? I hope they don't wet the bed. I wouldn't stand for that. I've heard some terrible stories from other landladies.'

'These boys have all passed their scholarship – besides which, they're all over twelve years of age. But even if they did wet the bed – which they don't, I can assure you – you would get a special enuresis allowance on top of all the allowances you'll already be getting for three.'

'Aye, but boys eat more than girls, don't they?'

But the mention of money seemed somehow to have done the trick and changed things a little, because Mrs Mossop said:

'Oh well, I suppose I've got no choice. I really did want girls but these three'll have to do. All right then, I'll take them.'

Miss Barrymore entered the details on her pad and then heaved a great sigh of relief.

'Now perhaps I can see to my own accommodation,' she said. 'Best of luck, boys. I'll see you at our new school tomorrow.'

The bus drove off and the boys were left with their new mother.

Inside the house, they saw two young children – a podgy boy who looked a little overweight for his age, and a rather tubby girl who was studying them closely. Mrs Mossop said:

'This is my daughter, Beryl, who is now eight, and this is my darling little boy, Neville, who is six. Say how-do-you-do to our visitors, children.'

'How do'y' do?' said Beryl with a strong, adenoidal twang.

'How do you do,' said Neville, like a trained parrot.

'I'm Billy,' said Billy, taking the initiative, 'and this is Robin and Titch. Is Mr Mossop in the army?'

'I can see you're a nosy boy and no mistake,' she said. 'But no, if you want to know, my husband, Donald, is on war work at Salford Docks. He gets home leave every six months or so. Now are you satisfied?'

'Yes, thank you, Mrs Mossop.'

'Anyroad, yours is the back bedroom,' she said. 'It's a bit small but I'm sure you'll be all right. The three of you will have to share the double bed, as I only expected two evacuees.'

'Fine, Mrs Mossop. We'll be OK,' said Robin, his usual optimistic self.

'You can take your things up now and unpack. Go and get a wash in the bathroom but don't make a mess. I hope you brought your own soap and towels with you. When you've finished, come down and I'll give you something to eat.'

'Yes, Mrs Mossop, we brought soap and towels. And we've got some food to give you as well – tins of Spam from the WVS and some chocolate biscuits from my mother in Manchester,' said Billy.

'Well, I'm glad somebody appreciates all that we're doing for you here in Blackpool.'

Upstairs they shared out the wardrobe and drawer space and began putting their things away – which was not a very big job as they hadn't brought all that much with them. They had been occupied in this way for about ten minutes when young Beryl knocked at the door and said:

'I have a letter here for William.'

'A letter for me?' said Billy, perplexed. 'I don't know anyone here.'

'But someone knows you,' replied Beryl. 'It's from

'Doreen Aspinall who lives at number one.'

'That must be the girl I saw leaning on the gate,' said Billy. 'How does she know my name?'

'I told her,' said Beryl proudly.

Billy took the letter, which was sealed in a blue envelope and addressed in a large hand 'To William'.

'Very odd,' he said.

'Maybe it's a proposal of marriage,' said Titch.

'You're not very far out. Listen to this,' said Billy, reading the letter. ' "*Darling William, I am sorry to hear that you have been bombed out. Will you go with me? I love you. From Doreen Aspinall. P.S. We are having a game of Truth or Dare outside my house tomorrow night and you and your friends are invited.*" '

'Talk about fast worker! How come she loves you and not us?' asked Titch.

'I thought I was the one with the film-star face around here,' said Robin.

'You are. You are,' said Billy. 'But we didn't say which film star.'

'How's about Charles Laughton as the Hunchback of Notre Dame?' suggested Titch.

'Anyway, for Doreen Aspinall it must have been love at first sight,' said Billy.

'Ah, she probably just feels sorry for you 'cos you look so pathetic,' said Robin. 'Are we going to accept?'

'What do you think?' said Billy. 'Of course we're going to accept. I haven't played that game since infant school but I think I can still remember the rules. I suppose they're the same here in Blackpool. Come on, though, we'd better go down and eat.'

Downstairs, Mrs Mossop had prepared a meal of mashed potatoes and cabbage.

'I'm sorry, Mrs Mossop,' Billy said. 'I don't eat cabbage.'

'Can I have yours, Hoppy?' asked Titch.

'And why, may I ask, do you not eat cabbage?' enquired Mrs Mossop.

'It's ever since I saw a whole load of caterpillars on some cabbages. You can't be sure they've all been washed off.'

'On second thoughts, I won't have any cabbage either,' said Titch. 'Could we have some of the Spam, Mrs Mossop?'

'You'll have none of that Spam today. I've put that in the larder for a rainy day. And you'll all have to get used to eating what's given to you. Don't you know there's a war on?'

As they tucked into their mashed potatoes, she stood over them and said:

'We'd better get a few things straight as long as you're in this house. First, I am the one to say what food we'll eat – not you. Secondly, you do not help yourself from my kitchen; in there I'm the boss, d'you understand?'

'Yes, Mrs Mossop,' they chorused.

'We share our food with you and so it's only right that you should share any food you get with us.'

'Yes, Mrs Mossop.'

'And you can stop calling me Mrs Mossop. Call me Auntie – it's more friendly.'

'Yes, Mrs Mossop – Auntie.'

'I've got some other rules as well. I don't want you in this house during the day. During the week don't come back here before five o'clock. As I said, the house is a bit small; we have only this kitchen, a lounge and three small bedrooms and so I can't have you cluttering up the place.'

'What do we do about dinner when we're at school?' asked Billy. 'Do we take sandwiches?'

'I haven't time to be making sandwiches. Besides, I

can't afford them on the allowances I get. You can take any toast that's left over from breakfast. I'm sure you can get by on that.'

'Yes, Auntie. What about weekends?' asked Robin.

'I'll try to make a Woolton Pie on Sundays.'

'Woolton Pie? What's that, Auntie?' asked Billy.

'It's a pie made of carrots, turnips and potatoes.'

'Sounds like good fodder,' whispered Robin.

'And at weekends I don't want you under my feet either – so you can play outside.'

'What if it's raining, Auntie?' asked Titch.

'Then you can go to the garden shed and play in there.'

'Maybe we could keep out of your way by going into the bedroom,' suggested Titch.

'You may not. You must not go upstairs until it's time for bed. And you must never, never go into my bedroom or the children's. Is that clear?'

'Yes, Auntie.'

'I didn't ask for three boys, as you know. So the best thing you can all do is keep right out of my road.'

'You mean "seen and not heard",' said Robin.

'No,' she said. 'I mean both. Not seen. Not heard.'

'What about the bathroom?' asked Titch. 'Are we allowed in the bathroom?'

'There's a toilet out in the garden which you can use during the daytime.'

'What about baths?' asked Robin. 'What do we do if we need a bath?'

'There's not enough hot water for all of us. My back boiler's not big enough. You must take your bath after me and the children have finished.'

'You mean in the same water?' asked Billy incredulously.

'I do, young man. We've got to save water and energy.

Don't you know there's a war on?'

'I think we're beginning to realise it,' said Billy.

'Anyway,' she said, 'I hope you'll all be very happy here. If you're not, it'll be your own fault, because I'll do my very best to make you feel at home.'

'Are we allowed to go out for a walk now?' asked Titch nervously.

'I don't mind what you do as long as you don't come bothering me and as long as you're back by nine o'clock.'

'Thank you, Auntie,' said Robin. 'Right, boys, let's go.'

As soon as they got outside, Billy said:

'The bloody old battleaxe. We may as well be in Strangeways. And we've not even committed a crime.'

'And there's no bail,' said Robin.

'I knew we'd be in trouble as soon as we left Manchester this morning,' said Titch. 'I felt it in my bones.'

'You thought we were going to be machine-gunned by German planes,' said Billy.

'Living with this Mrs Mossop is nearly as bad,' said Titch.

'I'm still hungry,' said Billy. 'Let's see if we can find a shop open and buy a bar of chocolate.'

'A bar of chocolate!' said Robin.

'Don't you know there's a war on?' they chorused.

Chapter Seventeen

Keep A Diary

The next day, the boys reported to school, which had been accommodated in a domestic science college. There they sat between the gas cookers, the sink units and the baking tables whilst Miss Barrymore tried to inspire them with a love of Shakespeare and an appreciation of *Julius Caesar*.

' "*Let me have men about me that are fat*",' she intoned. ' "*Sleek-headed men and such as sleep o' nights.*" '

'She won't find any of those if they come from Mrs Mossop's place,' said Titch.

At the end of the English lesson, Miss Barrymore said:

'Last night I had a brilliant idea for all of you. A famous lady once said, "I always say, keep a diary and some day it'll keep you." '

'Who said that, miss?' asked Oscar.

'A certain Mae West in a film called *Every Day's a Holiday*.'

'But why should we keep a diary, miss?' asked Robin.

'We are living in such an exciting time in history, you should try keeping a record of all that is happening to you. You can also note down all your secret ideas. Who can tell? One day you might be studied by future generations just as we today study Samuel Pepys. If you're interested, you couldn't do better than begin reading an exciting sea-story entitled *Two Years Before the Mast*, by R.H. Dana.'

'If you wrote secret things in it, miss,' said Billy, 'someone else might read them.'

'Oh, no, never,' she answered. 'A diary is a very private thing indeed and no one should ever read another person's secrets. Anyway, it's just an idea. It'll give you food for thought.'

'Talking of food, miss,' said Titch. 'Do you think we could ever have dinner here in the school?'

'I'm afraid not,' she said. 'There are complications with ration books, and although it's a domestic science college, they don't have the facilities to provide food for big numbers. Besides, we are allowed here in the mornings only, as they require their premises back in the afternoons.'

'Does that mean we have only half-day schooling then?' asked Oscar.

''Fraid so,' she said, 'but we have to be grateful we've been given even the mornings, because this place was designed to teach cooking, baking and the other culinary arts.'

'Fancy being taught in a domestic science college!' said Robin. 'The smell of all this grub around the place will drive us mad.'

'Water, water everywhere,' said Titch, 'and not a drop to drink.'

'What I wouldn't give for a piece of my mam's apple pie right now!' said Billy.

At break-time, the boys swapped horror stories with their friends.

'Your Mrs Rivers looked nice and friendly, Oscar,' said Billy.

' "Looked" is the right word. She hasn't spoken to her

husband for two years because of some argument they had about who should wash the pots,' answered Oscar.

'How do they manage?' asked Robin.

'They talk through their young daughter, Mavis,' said Nobby. 'She's a cracker, about our age, by the way. Mr Rivers says, "Mavis, tell your mother there's too much salt in this porridge", and Mrs Rivers says, "Tell your father to like it or lump it." '

'What happens then?'

'He lumps it,' said Oscar.

'What about you, Olly?' asked Billy. 'How are you getting on with your beauty queen?'

'I think I must've got the best billet of you all,' said Olly. 'She's a very rich widow, she's got a car, a chauffeur and everything. She has no kids but she's always wanted a son. So now she's got one, and I'm it!'

'Trust you to be lucky,' said Titch. 'If it were raining soup you'd have a big bowl and I'd have a toasting fork.'

'It's not quite so straightforward,' said Olly. 'She has some peculiar habits.'

'Like for instance?' asked Oscar.

'She smokes a pipe for one thing, and for another, she keeps cuddling and kissing me. Last night she tucked me in and sang me nursery rhymes. It's a well-known fact that women who smoke pipes are not to be trusted.'

'There's nowt so queer as fowk,' said Billy.

'The best billet of the lot,' said Rodney Potts, who'd been listening to their conversation, 'is mine.'

'I suppose you landed up in the Imperial Hotel,' said Titch.

'No,' he said. 'I'm in Brother Dorian's bungalow at Cleveleys along with Miss Barrymore, two other teachers and twelve boys. The food is great and we're well looked after.'

'I'll bet it was your dad pulling strings,' remarked Nobby.

'Or pulling out his wallet,' said Oscar.

'Rubbish,' said Potts. 'It was the luck of the draw.'

'Maybe,' said Titch. 'But first you've got to have the money to buy a ticket.'

In the afternoon, after their meal of cold toast, the three boys wandered along the promenade. The gold of the Golden Mile had turned to grey. The stalls which had so recently been the occasion of so much happiness and gaiety were now boarded up and lifeless. On the beach there were miles and miles of barbed wire to keep potential German invaders at bay. There were airmen everywhere, particularly Polish pilots, who could be distinguished by the small silver eagles chained to their lapels. Even the Tower had had its tip lopped off as it had proved a danger to the many aircraft buzzing around the skies. Even as they strolled along that afternoon, Bolton Paul Defiant fighters zoomed at head-top height along the beach, swooping over the piers at dizzy, breathtaking speeds.

'One of these days, one of those crazy pilots will have a nasty accident,' remarked Billy.

Then, drawn by the sound of a juke-box playing 'Tumbling Tumbleweed', they went into an amusement arcade.

'Anyone got any money?' asked Billy. 'I'm still hungry.'

Between them they managed to raise three penny pieces.

'What's the money for?' asked Robin.

'Over there there's one of those machines with little cranes for lifting toys and things out. And that one has bars of Fry's chocolate. Let's try our luck.'

Billy inserted the first penny and, sticking out his

tongue to aid his concentration, manoeuvred the crane until it picked up a small chocolate bar. Just as he thought he had grabbed it, it slipped out of the grip and fell back amongst the other trinkets.

'Damn and blast it,' he said.

'Here, let me try,' said Titch.

He could do no more than steer the chocolate a little nearer to the edge.

'This requires a professional touch,' said Robin, putting in the last penny.

His efforts left the bar balanced precariously and tantalisingly just over the outlet.

'That's the last coin,' said Robin. 'What do we do now, Hoppy?'

'Confucius he say, "When fate not go your way",' said Billy, narrowing his eyes, ' "give fate little nudge." '

As he spoke, he hit the machine with his backside and the chocolate rolled out.

'Hoi, you lot,' shouted the attendant. 'I saw that. Bring that bloody chocolate back.'

Too late, they were gone. As they walked along the front eating their prize, they were joined by an English airman.

'I saw all that, boys,' he said. 'Are you hungry? Is that it?'

'You're telling me,' said Titch.

'Come on,' said the airman. 'I'll buy you some food.'

'Food?' said Robin. 'What's that?'

Together the four of them went into the self-service restaurant above Woolworth's store.

'That's right,' said the airman as they slid their trays along the bar. 'Enjoy yourselves. Chips and fish, bread and butter and a pot o' tea for the three of you. Just what the doctor ordered. My name's Kevin, by the way.'

To say the boys ate heartily would be the understatement of the year. They pitched in and devoured the meal as if they hadn't eaten properly for a couple of days – which they hadn't.

Kevin watched them with an amused smile.

'I thought you were hungry when I saw you trying to capture the chocolate in the arcade. Look, I can't stay now. But I like your company. You remind me of my young brother at home. Would you like to go to the pictures with me tomorrow? I'll pay. They're showing *Stagecoach*, starring John Wayne, at the Regent.'

'That'd be fantastic,' said Titch, 'because we're going to be free every afternoon.'

'OK, Kevin,' said Robin. 'It's a deal. See you tomorrow.'

'Right,' said Kevin as he got up to leave. 'I'll meet you outside the cinema at two o'clock tomorrow.'

'At last, a friendly face,' said Billy.

When they got back to their billet at five o'clock, Mrs Mossop had prepared a meal of baked beans – their own – on toast. They tucked in ravenously despite the fish and chips earlier.

'I knew it,' she said. 'Boys just wade in and shovel it down. I don't think I can afford to feed you lot on the pittance they're paying.'

'Sorry, Auntie,' they said.

After tea they went upstairs to prepare for the game of Truth or Dare. Billy spent much time trying to tame and flatten an errant lock of hair which insisted on sticking up like a feather on an Indian brave. Feeling happy, nervous and excited, they went downstairs.

'I know where you three are going,' Mrs Mossop said. 'You're going out swapping spit with those girls in the avenue.'

'Hope so,' Robin whispered to Billy.

'I wonder if it's the same game as I used to play many years ago,' said Billy.

'We'll soon find out,' said Titch nervously.

They called next door for Nobby and Oscar. Nobby appeared immediately.

'Let's go,' he said.

'What about Oscar?' asked Titch.

'I dunno,' said Nobby. 'He says he's not interested in girls. He prefers to stay in, reading.'

'Maybe the love bug hasn't bitten him yet,' said Billy.

Outside the gate of number 1, four girls were already waiting.

'Hello, William,' said Doreen of the long black tresses. 'This is Mavis, who lives next door to you; this is Sally, who lives opposite; and this is Ruby, who is fourteen and works at the Milady toffee factory.'

Mavis was a fair-haired girl with bright, clear blue eyes and a freckled complexion – obviously the healthy, outdoor type – whilst Sally was an auburn-haired beauty with dark-brown eyes and a ready smile. Ruby was also pretty, with a friendly face, but what distinguished her from the others was her grown-up figure with its definite shapely bust – which the boys weren't slow to notice.

The evacuees smiled and nodded shyly.

'I'm Billy but everyone calls me Hoppy; and this is Robin, Titch and Nobby. But Mavis and Nobby already know each other as they live in the same house.'

'Right,' she said. 'It's nice to have some boys from Manchester as a change from all the lads here in the avenue. Do you know how to play this game?'

'I played it a long time ago,' said Billy, 'and I think I can remember it.'

'We all stand in line against the fence – first a boy, then a girl, then a boy again, like that.'

The participants arranged themselves according to the instructions, and Doreen started off the proceedings. In the first round, everyone cagily opted for Truth.

'Hoppy, is it true you've never kissed a girl?'

'No, it's not true. I once kissed a girl when I was in infant school.'

'Mavis, is it true you like boys a lot?'

'Yes, it's true.'

When Doreen had gone round everyone with her questions, Billy said:

'It *is* the same game that I used to play years ago, when I was a mixed infant.'

'Then you've not learnt very much,' said Ruby. 'We'll have to see if we can teach you a thing or two here in Blackpool. I'll start the second round.'

Doreen opted for Dare.

'I dare you to show Hoppy what a real kiss is like by giving him a film-star kiss.'

Doreen wrapped herself around Billy, put both hands behind his head and gave him a long, lingering kiss as she had seen Katherine Hepburn do with Cary Grant.

'Wow! When's the wedding?' asked Titch.

Having seen what happened with a Dare, Robin thought he'd better play it safe and chose Truth.

'Coward!' said Ruby. 'Is it true you've never felt a girl?'

'True!' said Robin, turning bright red under the streetlamp.

Courageously, Titch selected Dare.

'I dare you to put your right hand on Sally's breast.'

Titch did as he was instructed.

'But there's nothing there,' he said. 'It's as flat as a billiard table.'

'Thank you very much,' said Sally. 'Don't you be so cheeky. There is something there.'

When it came to Sally's turn, Ruby said:

'I dare you to feel Titch's thing.'

Sally placed her hand at the strategic place.

'But there's nothing there,' she said, getting her own back. 'It's as flat as a pancake.'

'What do you expect,' said Titch. 'After all, my name is Dick Smalley.'

Nobby was next in line.

'Let's see how daring you are. I dare you to put your hand here,' said Ruby, indicating her breasts.

Nobby put his hand on his own chest and said:

'Nothing to it.'

That night in Blackpool, the boys' sex education had begun. The second lesson was the very next day.

As the boys were leaving their classroom at lunchtime the following day, they passed the wing where a lesson in baking was just about to finish. As they listened to the teacher, their mouths watered.

'So, girls,' the teacher was saying, 'always keep pastry light and fluffy. The secret is in the amount of fat you use and the method of rolling. Our efforts today at shortcrust mushroom pie should be ready in about ten minutes. We'll have a short coffee-break and then finish. Now remember where you left your dish in the oven, as we don't want to get them mixed up, do we?'

The class laughed politely at the thought of this happening.

'Dear me no,' said the teacher. 'We don't want to go home with someone else's pie, do we?'

No sooner had the class filed out to the common room than Billy said:

'This is where my Cheetham Hill training comes in handy. Quick, boys!'

With the speed of lightning, they whipped into the classroom, opened the oven doors, helped themselves to a mushroom pie each and were out of the room before the cookery students had even poured their coffees.

They walked along the front, munching voraciously at the stolen pies.

'Do you realise that a hundred and fifty years ago we'd have been sent to Botany Bay for this?' said Titch.

'It would be worth it for these pies,' said Robin.

'Yes,' said Billy. 'But there's something worrying me.'

'What's that?' asked Titch anxiously.

'That teacher was right. These pies needed another ten minutes.'

Just before two o'clock, the boys arrived at the Regent cinema to find Kevin already waiting. He paid for four seats in the stalls, and as they settled down – Kevin on the outside of the row next to Billy, with Titch and Robin on the inside – offered round a bag of sweets.

'Chocolate eclairs,' he said. 'Only the best is good enough. And this should be a really exciting film.'

'We're really looking forward to it,' said Robin.

'Let me see your hands,' Kevin said, taking Robin's right hand into his own. 'They're so soft. I'll bet none of you has ever done a real day's work. Look at mine.'

Titch examined the palms of Kevin's hands.

'They're rough,' he said. 'You must do very hard work for the RAF. Look at my hands; they're soft like Robin's and Hoppy's.'

Kevin examined Billy's hands as well.

'It's time you three did some work for a living,' he said.

The big picture began and soon the three boys were transported to Monument Valley as the stagecoach bearing its five passengers made its hazardous way across Indian territory. Soon the passengers were joined by the Ringo Kid in the person of John Wayne.

'Gosh, isn't this exciting?' said Kevin, taking hold of Billy's hand. 'Don't worry, though. John Wayne will look after them.'

Billy became completely engrossed in the action of the story, which began to reach a climax when the Indians attacked the coach and it was only because of the Ringo Kid's bravery that the day was saved. As the coach rolled into Lordsburg escorted by the cavalry, Billy felt the imprint of a button on his hand and became aware that his right hand was being used to massage Kevin's testicles.

He snatched his hand away, got up, and said:

'I'm just going to the toilets and also to see the manager.'

Two minutes later he was back with the manager, but Kevin's seat was empty.

'Where's he gone?' he asked.

'Dunno,' said Titch. 'When you went to the toilet he got up very quickly and walked out. What did you say to him, Hoppy?'

'Whatever it was,' said Robin, 'we just lost our meal-ticket.'

'Worse things happen at sea,' said Billy.

Later on that night, when they were in the bedroom, he told them what had happened. For hour after hour they plagued him for further details.

'Eh, what was it like?' asked Robin and Titch over and over again.

'The nearest thing I can think of,' said Billy, 'is a peach. It was like massaging a large soft peach.'

'Eh, was it heck. What was it really like, eh? What did it really feel like, eh? Did it? Did it heck!'

When news of the event got round the school, Billy was a celebrity for some time afterwards as the whole schoolboy body latched on to the catchphrase.

'Eh, what was it like, eh? Like massaging a peach? Was it heck! What did it feel like, eh? Did it heck!'

Boys continued to trot out the phrases long after the event which had occasioned them had been forgotten.

Psychologists have claimed that somewhere between the ages of eleven and thirteen a young boy experiences a gradual awakening of his dormant sexual desires, which grow in strength until they amount almost to an obsession. Under normal circumstances, this might be true, but for our three boys at number 9, Kincraig Avenue in 1941, circumstances were far from normal. They did, however, have one obsession – food! They spoke of and thought of little else.

The subject even invaded their dreams, and they had nightly visions of Christmas turkey, roast potatoes and plum duff.

'Last night,' said Titch, 'I dreamt of a bakery and tray upon tray of hot, crusty bread soaked in creamy butter. It was so real you could even smell the grain and the flour.'

'That, I suppose,' said Billy, 'is what is called a wheat dream.'

Billy even began to eat cabbage.

'What about the caterpillars?' asked Titch.

'Good protein.'

Ideas far removed from the topic of food became immediately associated with eating.

'Fancy going for a stroll?' asked Robin one evening.

'Sure,' replied Billy. 'But where are we gonna buy a roll at this time of night?'

'What's that book you're reading, Hoppy?' asked Titch.

'It's a book about spies.'

'What kind of pies? Apple or rhubarb?'

They tried every way they knew to supplement Mrs Mossop's meagre fare. Doreen stole food for Billy from her mother's larder, Sally became Titch's provider, and Ruby brought bags of Milady toffees for Robin. The boys' two-and-sixpenny postal orders which arrived from home every Friday became their lifeline.

'I'm beginning to feel like that music-hall singer, G.H. Elliott,' said Robin one Friday as they came out of the sweet shop. 'You know, the one they call the chocolate-coloured coon.'

'Me too,' added Titch. 'I've eaten so much Cadbury's I look like the chocolate soldier. We've been here now for three months and I think we're suffering the torture of slow starvation.'

'It's time we did something,' said Billy. 'I didn't want to bother my mam and dad at home 'cos they've got their own troubles, what with the bombing and all that. But I think I'll write them a letter.'

'You mean complaining?' asked Robin.

'No, not so much that,' said Billy. 'I could ask them to send us some food or something. My dad can get fruit in Smithfield Market.'

'That would be really fantastic,' said Titch.

One day, two weeks later, they got back to Kincraig Avenue from one of their frequent visits to the amusement arcades at about four o'clock.

'We're not allowed back in until five o'clock,' said Titch. 'What about a game of cricket against the lamppost?'

'Great idea, Titch,' said Robin sarcastically. 'What do we use for a bat or ball, since they're up there in the bedroom.'

'What're you so scared about?' said Billy. 'She can't

stop us going to get our own things. I'll go up and get them. I'd like to see her stop me.'

Boldly he went into the house by the back door. As he crossed the threshold, he was met by the most delicious whiff of meat stew, and there at the kitchen table sat Mrs Mossop with her two children tucking into a meal of Lancashire hotpot complete with golden pastry crust.

'What do you mean bursting in on us like that?' she screamed. 'You're not allowed in until five o'clock and you know it.'

'Sorry, Auntie,' he said. 'Just want to get our cricket things from the bedroom.'

'Hurry up and get out,' she yelled.

Billy did as he was told but not without a backward glance at the meal, which was still steaming on the table.

That night the boys were given their usual meal of bread and jam. When they went to bed, Billy wrote furiously in the diary which he kept locked in his case under the bed:

'*Came home early today. Entered house at four o'clock. Found Mrs Mossop having secret meal of Tater Ash. She was very angry as she was CAUGHT IN THE ACT!*'

'Did you ever hear from your mam and dad about the parcel you wrote for?' asked Titch.

'I had a letter from them to say they had sent some fruit. Jaffas, my dad said. Eat them slowly, my Mam wrote, 'cos they're like gold. But they never arrived.'

'They've gone astray,' said Robin. 'A lot of things have gone missing because of the war.'

'More like one of those thieving temporary postmen,' said Titch, always ready to look on the bright side.

'Well, parcel or no parcel,' said Billy, 'I don't intend letting Mrs Mossop starve us. We'll wait our chance.'

Their chance came on Friday night.

* * *

It was one of those rare occasions when Mrs Mossop was going out for the evening – on the town! During the day she had been to the beauty salon for a hair-do and a facial. She had removed her glasses and looked almost pretty.

'I shall be back about ten thirty,' she said. 'I'm leaving you boys in charge and you are on your honour. Look after things whilst I'm out, and maybe tomorrow you'll have a nice omelette for dinner.'

'Real eggs?' asked Billy. 'Or the dried variety?'

'Dried, of course,' she said. 'What else is there?'

Whilst she was out, the boys and her two children played a game of Monopoly with much cheating and much arguing about rents, mortgages and going to gaol, until it was time for bed. At ten o'clock the two young ones were duly retired and the three boys were installed in their double bed top and tail. The five youngsters filled the house with the singing of all the patriotic songs they knew, beginning with 'God Save the King', through the Polish national anthem and 'Rule Britannia', and finishing with 'There'll Always Be an England'.

'Did you notice,' said Robin, 'in that last song, there's no mention of Scotland and Wales?'

'Perhaps they've had their chips,' said Titch.

'Are you going to read us a bedtime story before we go to sleep?' shouted Neville.

'OK, just one,' called Billy. 'And then it's time for shut-eye.'

He went through to their bedroom and read them the story of 'The Frog Prince' by the Brothers Grimm.

'That's it for tonight,' he said, as he got up to go. 'Time for sleep now.'

As he was leaving, he noticed some very tiny blue

stickers on their dressing-room mirror. 'Jaffa', they read.

'Where did you get these?' he asked.

'Mummy said it's a secret and we weren't to tell. But they were on the big oranges she gave us.'

'I see,' said Billy. 'You were very lucky to get a Jaffa orange. Don't you know there's a war on?'

That night he made another entry in his diary.

At about eleven thirty Mrs Mossop came home, and she wasn't alone. The boys were still awake and they heard the sound of a man's voice – a foreign voice.

'Do you think it's a spy?' said Titch. 'Do you think Mrs Mossop works for the Germans?'

'Grow up, Titch, and don't ask daft questions,' said Billy. 'Of course she does.'

Half an hour later, Mrs Mossop went into her bedroom. And so did the man.

'Now's our chance,' said Billy, 'to get some food. Titch, you listen at her bedroom door and give the word if you think she's coming out. Robin and I will go downstairs and see what's in the pantry.'

The three of them listened at her door to make sure she was fully occupied, but all they could hear was the creaking of bed springs and Mrs Mossop moaning as if in pain.

'Whatever she's doing,' whispered Titch, 'she doesn't sound as if she's enjoying it.'

Robin and Billy went down to the kitchen, where they noticed a Polish pilot's tunic draped on one of the chairs.

'It's nice to know that Auntie is doing her bit for the war effort,' whispered Robin.

They managed to filch a good piece of cheese and a hunk of bread. As they lay in bed consuming their feast, Billy said:

'Another entry for my diary. At this rate I'm going to need a bigger book.'

In the afternoons, the trio continued to frequent the arcades, looking for coins which punters might have dropped on the floor or left in the slots of the apparatus. Over the months they had become extremely skilful at manoeuvring prizes out of the crane-grab machine and other tests of mechanical skill. They had also come to know every tune in every juke-box: the Ink Spots' 'I Don't Want to Set the World on Fire', Flanagan and Allen's 'Let's Be Buddies', Tommy Trinder's 'All Over the Place' and many others.

They had also invented an extremely dangerous game called 'Race Against the Sea'. The game was most exciting when the sea was rough and choppy, and required good timing as it involved running down the wooden promenade steps when the tide receded and then running back up to beat the returning wave. The winner was the one who could run furthest down the steps, and the game was made more hazardous by the fact that the steps were wet and slippery. On one of these occasions Billy ran down almost to the bottom, but as he turned to come back, he skidded on the greasy surface. The sea showed no mercy and a great wave enveloped him, soaking and almost drowning him in the process.

There was nothing for it but to find shelter in the warmth of Woolworth's café, where they found they could just about afford one cup of tea with the twopence they had left. Completely saturated and dripping sea-water everywhere, Billy sat huddled near a radiator.

'We can't go back until five o'clock,' said Robin. 'So you'd better make that cup of tea last.'

The hands of the clock moved extremely slowly and it seemed like eternity before it was time to go back to the billet. When they finally got there, there was more trouble waiting. Mrs Mossop was on the warpath. As Billy went into the house, shivering and sneezing, she was standing there, hands on hips.

'I've just been cleaning out the bedrooms and I've found this,' she said ominously, indicating Billy's diary.

'But that was in my locked case under the bed,' he managed to stammer between sneezes.

'Well, you left it open this time,' she yelled. 'And just what do you mean by "Caught in the Act", you cheeky little bugger. If you were my child, I'd give you a bloody big slap in the chops.'

'You have no right to pry into my things,' said Billy. 'That diary was private.'

'And so is my life,' she bawled. 'Who I choose to get in bed with is my business, not a little snotty-nosed evacuee's. How dare you write in your diary, "Tonight, Auntie brought home an airman and together they went climbing and exploring the North Pole." And later there's this: "Where did Auntie get the Jaffa oranges?" '

'Well, where did you get them from?' asked Robin, joining in the fray.

'I bought those from Thomas Talbot's Fruit Market on Waterloo Road.'

'And I suppose they went over to Palestine to get them,' said Titch.

It was then that Billy collapsed in a heap, shivering uncontrollably.

'Why, he's ill! Quick! Help me get him to bed,' exclaimed Mrs Mossop, her nurse's instincts coming to the fore.

Billy remained in bed for ten days, suffering from a severe bout of influenza. During that time, Miss Barrymore came to visit him:

'You have been very ill,' she said, 'and you have lost a great deal of weight.'

'I was already a tin-ribs to start with, miss,' he said.

'This is the billet where the lady was most reluctant to take you, isn't it? I feel partly to blame for all that's happened. I should have been along to see how you were getting on much earlier than this.'

That afternoon, Billy and his form teacher had a long heart-to-heart about the billet and the treatment they had received at the hands of 'Auntie'.

'I'm not sure about that idea of keeping a diary, miss,' said Billy.

'It's a good idea,' she said. 'But you must always make sure it's kept under lock and key. You never know, one day you might include some of the details in a book.'

A week later, Mrs Mossop was requested to attend at the school to meet Brother Dorian. The trio were called out of class to go to his office. There they found Auntie, wearing a smartly cut suit, and a hat with a veil, but looking distinctly uncomfortable. She was left in no doubt as to whose side the head was on.

'Come in, the little soldiers,' boomed Brother Dorian.

There followed not so much a trial as an inquisition.

'Tell me, Mrs . . . er . . . Messup. What do you give these young growing boys for tea? Perhaps muffins with butter, or crumpets? Perhaps eggs, cheese, meat, that kind of thing?'

'Well, no,' she said falteringly. 'I make them a nice tea of bread and jam or lemon cheese.'

'Yes, yes, I see,' he said, making Auntie's food sound like Oliver Twist's workhouse gruel. 'And what about supper? Perhaps hot-milk chocolate or cocoa with a biscuit or two?'

The three boys exchanged 'is-he-kidding?' glances.

'Well, no,' she said. 'I don't give my own children anything before bed. Besides, we couldn't afford all those things on the allowances you pay to us landladies.'

'No, no, quite,' he murmured. 'Talking of allowances, I notice on the returns you have been submitting that you have been claiming the special enuresis allowance. Which of these boys wets the bed?'

Mrs Mossop had turned red.

'I can't really say. But I did once find the bed slightly wet,' she said.

'Quite. Quite,' he said. 'Well, thank you for coming, madam. I think I have the picture now.'

Turning to the boys, he said:

'Wait outside the door now, you brave little soldiers. England should be proud of you.

'Now, Mrs Messup, I am going to take the three boys away from you.'

'Mossop, sir. Very well, then. But perhaps you could send me two nice girls in their place?'

'Be under no delusions, madam. Under no circumstances would I even contemplate such a thing. I do not consider you a fit person to take care of young evacuees.'

'Well, I must say! I did my best for them. I looked after them, I did.'

'Tell me, madam, do you consider half-starving them was looking after them? Do you consider keeping them out of the house until five o'clock every day in all kinds of weather to be looking after them? I am in two minds whether to advise the evacuation authorities to prosecute you for falsifying the returns you made.'

'I don't know what you mean.'

'You claimed the enuresis allowance when you knew perfectly well it was false,' he roared angrily. 'These young boys are away from home, and they come from good homes, let me tell you. They are young and vulnerable and it is an easy thing to take advantage of them. The generous allowance you received was for their sustenance, not your profit. Now I advise you, madam, to go before I change my mind about prosecuting you. I shall find a new billet for them this very day. Good day, madam.'

'Well, I've never been so insulted in all my life!'

Mrs Mossop stormed out of his office and glowered at the three boys, who had heard every word of the discourse, as Brother Dorian had intended.

'Now, my young warriors,' he said. 'I want you to go back to your billet with Miss Barrymore and collect your things. I am moving you all to my bungalow at Cleveleys. I think you will find the fare we provide a distinct improvement on what you have been used to with that wretched woman. Go along and I shall send Miss Barrymore to you immediately after lessons.'

'Oh, thank you, sir,' they said together.

'At last things are looking up,' said Robin when they got outside. 'According to Potts, we've got the best billet in Blackpool.'

'About time too,' said Billy, 'after the lousy time we've been having with Auntie. Going to live with Brother Dorian is bound to be better.'

'You know,' said Titch, 'whenever I hear you two talking happily like that . . .'

'It makes you feel happy too, I suppose,' said Robin.

'No,' said Titch. 'That's when I feel most worried.'

'You're just a born Jeremiah,' said Billy.

'Not at all. I just feel that if things are going to get better, it's only because they're going to get worse later on.'

Chapter Eighteen

Out of The Frying Pan . . .

In the spacious living room of Martindale Bungalow, the three boys, feeling distinctly ill at ease, sat stiffly together on the edge of the *chaise-longue*. Brother Dorian was standing, whisky and soda in hand, with his back to the fireplace.

'You three young, brave warriors have come through the fire, and now you must become hardened like tempered steel, ready to face up to all the trials and tribulations that you will meet on the road of life. Are you ready for such challenges?'

'Yes, sir,' they said, not altogether sure exactly which challenges he was referring to.

'One of our generous old boys,' he continued, 'has kindly given us the lease of this magnificent bungalow together with all its elegant period furniture for as long as we require it. I feel it is our solemn duty to so bear ourselves that should we be here for a hundred years, men will still say, "Neither the furniture nor the residence had a single mark upon them." Do you agree with these sentiments?'

'Yes, sir,' they chorused enthusiastically.

'You will sleep in the main house, and I have reserved

for this purpose the top attic room, which has a truly panoramic view of the sea. I trust you will find this to your satisfaction.'

'Yes, sir,' they chanted eagerly.

'I have also arranged for all our boys to eat and spend their leisure hours in the capacious garage at the back of the house. In charge there we have a most worthy fifth-former in the person of Pablo Garcia, who has my full authority and acts on my behalf. You will find him firm but fair and you must obey him in all matters. Do you agree to this arrangement?'

'Yes, sir,' they sang in unison – at the same time wondering what would have happened if they had said 'No, sir, these arrangements are unacceptable.'

'You will find the food here plain but wholesome and a great improvement on that provided by your Mrs Massey.'

'Mossop, sir,' said Billy. 'She was called Mossop.'

'Mossop, Moscrop, Mossman, Mussell – no matter. You will find our comestibles a distinct improvement. We have an excellent cook in Brother Brendan, who will make sure that your need for sustenance is well met. Does all this meet with your approval?'

'Oh, yes, sir,' they said fervently.

'Very well. I shall conduct you to the garage and introduce you to Pablo.'

The garage was large enough to accommodate a fleet of cars. The far end had been converted into a mini games area with a small billiard table and a darts board, whilst at the near end there was a large oak dining table with monks' benches at either side and a large carver chair at the head.

'This is Pablo Garcia, our head boy at Martindale,' said Brother Dorian, indicating a tall, dark, heavily built youth. 'Three more for you, Pablo. That gives you a total of fourteen. Can you cope?'

'No problem, Brother,' Pablo replied. 'I can cope.'

'Then I shall leave you now in the capable hands of Pablo, who will show you our facilities and explain our routines. Good afternoon, boys.'

'Good afternoon, sir, and thank you, sir,' the three boys said.

When he had gone, Billy turned to his two companions.

'We're going to be OK here,' he said. 'It's much better.'

'I just knew things were going to get better,' said Robin. 'Everything has turned out for the best.'

'I hope you're right,' said Titch doubtfully.

No sooner had he spoken than Pablo took out a large scout knife and threw it at the garage door just behind Billy's head, missing him by a hair's breadth.

'I did not say you could speak,' he said with a most peculiar smile on his face. 'In this place, I am boss and you speak when I say so. Do you hear me?'

'Yes,' they mumbled.

'Louder!' he cried. 'Say, "Yes, Pablo, we hear you." '

'Yes, Pablo, we hear you,' they shouted together.

'Told you there'd be trouble,' whispered Titch.

'Did you speak then?' demanded Pablo, recovering his knife from the door.

'Not me,' replied Titch. 'Not a word.'

'Understand this,' said Pablo. 'If you want to play darts or billiards, you ask permission and then you sign the book. Got it?'

'Got it,' they said.

'At mealtimes, I bring the food from the main kitchen. You eat when I say so. Got it?'

'Got it.'

'You step out of line and you don't eat. Give me cheek – you don't eat. Break any of the rules – you don't eat. Say, "Yes, Pablo." '

'Yes, Pablo.'

'May we please play darts and billiards this afternoon, Pablo?' asked Billy.

'Yes,' said Pablo. 'But first, you go down on one knee – all three of you – and say, "May we please, Pablo?" '

'May we please, Pablo?' they asked from the kneeling position.

'Very well,' he said. 'You're getting the idea. Now sign the book, join the others at the back and wait your turn. I have to go into Blackpool for Brother Dorian's snuff and I shall be gone for a couple of hours.'

'Thank you, Pablo,' the three boys said.

'Bassett, I'm leaving you in charge and I'll want a full report when I get back.'

When Pablo had gone, there was an audible sigh of relief – a cork-out-of-the-bottle effect – as the fourteen boys tried to make up their daily quota of conversation like Trappist monks suddenly released from their vows.

As the trio played a game of '301' at the darts board, Billy said:

'Thought you said this was a good billet, Potts. That Pablo is a bloody big bully.'

'Not so,' said Potts. 'He sounds tough but he's always very fair. You'll see.'

'It's more like a gaol,' said Robin. 'We just need a couple of warders, a few Alsatians and a solitary confinement cell, and we're there.'

'And James Cagney and George Raft,' added Billy, 'and don't forget the electric chair.'

'We could try digging a tunnel,' said Titch, 'but with my kind of luck it'd come up in Brother Dorian's bedroom.'

'Anyway, the food here is good,' said Potts. 'You'll see at dinner tonight.'

'Dinner at night?' said Billy. 'What kind of weird place is this we've come to? Next thing you'll be saying supper is tomorrow morning.'

Dinner was at seven o'clock in the evening, and the fifteen boys – all with good healthy appetites – were standing around in anticipation of the 'off' signal. In front of Pablo's place at the head of the table, the soup plates and the thick 'paving-stone' slices of bread were piled up ready for the feast.

'Come and get it!' called Brother Brendan from the kitchen in the big house.

'Right. Bassett and I will bring the food across,' said Pablo. 'The rest of you wait at your places.'

The trio sat down at one of the benches in readiness.

'If he catches you sitting down,' said Potts, 'you don't eat. You have to wait until Pablo gives the word before you sit down and before you can begin.'

Pablo and Bassett soon came back carrying between them a large, double-handled cauldron of hot, delicious-smelling soup.

'Make way! It's fish soup!' called Pablo as they set the heavy dish down at the head of the table.

The diners stood at their places, their tongues hanging out, their mouths watering at the prospect of getting that lovely concoction inside them.

'First – grace!' announced Pablo, throwing his scout knife quivering into the table. 'For what we are about to receive, may the Lord make us truly thankful.'

'Amen!' they all replied impatiently.

'Sit!' he ordered.

Then, skilfully and carefully, he ladled the soup into the plates, which were then passed from hand to hand down the table. Next came the slices of bread, and when all had been distributed, he said:

'You can begin!'

Fourteen spoons were lifted and were about to descend as one when suddenly Pablo called:

'Wait! There's one slice of bread left.'

'You have it, Pablo,' said Potts ingratiatingly. 'You've earned it.'

'No,' he said. 'Justice must not only be done, but must be seen to be done.'

Wresting his knife from the table, he cut the slice into fifteen small squares – each about the size of an Oxo cube – and distributed one each to the assembled company.

'Never let it be said,' he stated, 'that I, Pablo, took more than my fair share. Now, once again – you can begin.'

It was then that Billy saw the fish eyes floating on the surface of his soup. He thought for a moment of caterpillars and cabbage. He hesitated. He closed his eyes and made a decision.

Bugger it! he thought I'm too hungry to worry about it.

The boys fell into their new way of life, and although they found it difficult at first to adjust to Pablo's hard manner, they found that Brother Dorian's early assessment of him as 'firm but fair' was about right. They weren't too keen on his knife-throwing exercises, but these were severely curtailed after an incident one Saturday morning.

'See that small round mark on the door, Hoppy,' he said, pointing to a knot about the size of a penny.

'Yes, I see it, Pablo.'

'Throwing underhand, I'll get the knife right into it. Watch!'

He threw the knife low down, but instead of hitting the mark with the point of the blade, he struck it with the hilt. The knife bounced out of the door and embedded itself in his shin. Pablo uttered no sound. He looked in surprise at his leg, reached down, calmly removed the knife and went off to get a plaster. Billy noticed that after that there was a definite reduction in knife-throwing.

Not so spartan was Rodney Potts. On the same Saturday morning, Potts came into the garage, holding his hand to his forehead and grimacing in pain as he approached Pablo.

'I have the most terrible headache, Pablo. May I please be excused from football practice this afternoon?'

'Come off it, Potts,' said Pablo. 'You're making it up. You're like a shy bride on her wedding night.'

'Honestly, Pablo, it's true. I do have a headache.'

'S'probably a brain tumour,' said Titch cheerfully.

'Yes, that's what it looks like,' said Robin. 'Why, there's even a big bump at the back here.'

'Nonsense,' said Billy. 'That's where his mother dropped him. Or maybe it's proof that he comes from the apes. You're the missing link, Potts.'

They came home from football later that day and were sitting around the table waiting for their cream of onion soup.

'So, then, Pottsy,' said Titch. 'How's the brain tumour?'

'Cut it out, Smalley,' he said.

'I would, if I were a surgeon,' said Titch.

'Don't worry, Pottsy,' said Robin. 'We'll see you get a good funeral.'

'Or he could give his body for medical research,' said Billy.

'If you're not careful, Pottsy,' said Titch, 'people will start to call you big-headed.'

'Anyway,' said Pablo, 'you missed the football, Potts, and in my book that means death. Which do you prefer – burial or cremation?'

'Just stop it – all of you!' cried Potts, rushing away from the table.

Later that night, Billy realised that they had over-stepped the mark with the hypersensitive Potts when they found him kneeling by his bedside, his missal open, reciting the prayer, Litany for a Happy Death.

'*O Lord my God, I now, at this moment, readily and willingly accept at Thy hand whatever kind of death it may please Thee to send me, with all its pains, penalties and sorrows.*'

'Listen, Potts,' Billy said. 'It was all a daft joke. No one really meant it. You'll live till you're a hundred.'

'No,' said Potts. 'I'm ready to die and I shall phone my dad tomorrow and tell him to arrange the funeral.'

'Don't be so stupid, Pottsy,' said Robin.

'It's all gone wrong,' said Titch. 'There'll be trouble.'

Titch was right. For once his pessimistic prediction came true.

The following night when Billy, dressed only in pyjamas, was coming out of the downstairs lavatory, he saw in the main hallway a small knot of boys, with Brother Dorian towering in their midst. He was brandishing a long cane above his head.

'Pull the chain and close the lavatory door, boy,' he bellowed. 'Then come over here.'

Shaking with fear, Billy joined the little assembly.

'Now, this evening,' began Brother Dorian, 'I have had a most distressing telephone call from Potts's father. He accuses you, Hopkins, of persecuting and tormenting his son. Is this so?'

'Yes, sir,' said Billy, now paralysed with terror.

'He claims that you have convinced his son that he is about to die of a tumour on the brain. Is this true?'

'It's not true about the tumour, sir, but Potts did think he was going to die.'

'Did you think you were going to die, Potts?'

'Yes, sir. He asked me if I wanted to be buried or cremated.'

'I cannot allow this kind of thing to go on under my roof,' roared Brother Dorian. 'I am going to give you, Hopkins, a thrashing you will never forget. Bend over.'

As Billy was in the act of touching his toes, he thought back to the last time he'd had the stick – to the agony, to the purple weals left on his backside. This time would be infinitely worse, as he was wearing only thin cotton pyjamas. His fingers reached his toes.

'Stretch tighter, boy. Tighter.'

Billy winced, steeled himself and waited for the first stroke to descend.

'Wait, sir,' said a voice. 'I cannot allow you to do this.'

It was Robin.

'Cannot allow! What on earth do you mean, boy?' raged the brother.

'Everybody here present was involved,' said Robin. 'So you must punish us all.'

Titch and the other boys exchanged glances on hearing this. They did not look altogether happy about Robin's suggestion.

'Explain yourself, Gabrielson.'

'It was just a prank, sir. A joke that went wrong. We had no idea that Potts would take us seriously.'

'I support Gabrielson, sir,' said Pablo. 'We were all involved. You must punish us all.'

'I see. I see,' said Brother Dorian. 'Get up, Hopkins.'

His heart still thumping, Billy straightened up.

'Now, Potts. Why did you name Hopkins if so many others were involved?'

'His was the first name to come to mind,' said Potts.

'Potts, you are a great sissy!' boomed the brother. 'A girl! A spoiled brat! It's time you grew up and faced up to the world. As for the rest of you, these games must stop. I shall overlook it this time. Now be off with all of you before I change my mind.'

'Oh, thank you, sir. Thank you, sir,' they all murmured as they began climbing the stairs.

'Wait a moment!'

They froze.

'Tell me, Potts. What did you decide in the end? Burial or cremation?'

'Burial, sir.'

'That's good, Potts, since cremation is forbidden by the Church.'

Back in their room, Titch said:

'That was a close shave. I like the way, Robin, you volunteered us all for the stick. That was very brave of you. If you ask me, you've spent too much time reading all that public school stuff in *The Fifth Form at St Dominic's*. Next time, volunteer your own backside. If you want to be brave, let it be your own funeral, not ours!'

'I owe you one, Robin!' said Billy. 'What courage! What bravery! What madness!'

In the warm spring of that year, there was little to remind them that a major world war was being fought in far-off lands, and that only a few miles away Goering's Blitzkrieg continued unabated. The air above them was filled with friendly aircraft and the boys had become expert in aircraft identification: Avro Ansons, Bothas, Paul Defiants, Hurricanes and Spitfires – they could recognise them all with hardly a second glance.

After the brain tumour incident, the trio became more friendly towards Potts and began to include him in their activities.

'He's spent too much time in the company of women,' said Robin. 'Remember, he's got four older sisters at home, molly-coddling him.'

As Potts was drawn into their games, he in turn became less selfish and less turned in on himself. One day, he even told them a joke.

'This man met a girl at a party and he took her into a dark corner and asked her for a kiss.

' "No, I won't," she said.

' "Why not?" he asked.

' "Because I've got scruples," she said.

' "That's all right," he said. "I've been vaccinated." '

'Is that it, Pottsy?' they asked.

'That's it,' he said anxiously, searching their faces.

The three boys all laughed, perhaps over-long.

'That's not bad, Pottsy,' said Billy. 'Not bad at all.'

Sometimes they walked around the superb golf course at the back of the bungalow, looking for lost golf balls. Occasionally, when their searches were proving fruitless, they hid in the bushes and waited for the odd ball to come bouncing over the horizon – its arrival thoughtfully announced by a distant figure calling out, 'Fore!' Then they would snatch the ball up and run for all they were worth to the beach, leaving the unfortunate golfer to drop another ball at the cost of a penalty stroke.

Most of their evenings were spent on the beach, constructing masterpieces in sand, and now that there was a team of fifteen working on the projects, whole cities were shaped rather than single castles. The joy of building their town was only exceeded by the sheer ecstasy of destroying it in an imaginary raid over Berlin. Holding Titch aloft like an aeroplane, Billy and Robin carried him over the unsuspecting city.

'Target in view, skipper.'

'Roger, Titch, old boy.'

'Starboard a little, skipper. Now port a little, skipper. Steady! Steady-y-y! Bombs gone!'

A brick would be dropped mercilessly on a building which had taken all of two hours to create, and the fantasy air-raid would continue until the city had been razed. Then the boys would break out humming the RAF march-past as the young bombers headed home to their well-earned celebration in the local pub and the love and admiration of their WAAF girlfriends.

One day – out of the blue – Billy had a letter written in an almost illegible scrawl from his dad – a rare event indeed, since Tommy found it inordinately difficult to put pen to paper, having left school at the age of ten.

Well, Billy, so you have moved in with Brother Dorian so I am coming over to see how you are getting on next Saturday with a special present for him I will be on the nine o'clock train from Manchester so please meet me hoping this finds you as it leaves me.

Your loving Dad.

Billy hadn't seen any of his family for over three months, and so it was with great eagerness that he went down to Central Station to meet him. The train was only one hour late and then there he was – Dad, dressed in his funeral best, complete with pot hat, hurrying down the platform to meet him. He was clasping a large brown paper bag to his chest.

'How do, son,' he said. 'I won't give a hug or anything like that as I've got summat precious here for you and your Brother Dorian.'

'How do, Dad,' said Billy, falling into the vernacular. 'S'great to see you again after all these months. But what've you got in the bag?'

'Shhh!' he whispered. 'Eggs! Three dozen of 'em! Eggs! Like bloody gold. In fact better'n gold 'cos you can't eat that stuff.'

'I haven't tasted an egg since God knows when,' said Billy. 'They're scarce, aren't they?'

'Scarce! Scarce!' Tommy said, appealing to the unseen listener he seemed to carry on his shoulder for moral support and confirmation of his arguments. 'I should bloody well think they are. They're worth more than a bloody penny-black. They queue up for hours in Manchester just to get one.'

'Then where did you get 'em from, Dad?'

'Ah!' he said, tapping his nose with his finger and addressing his phantom audience. 'He wants to know where we got 'em from. But what we say is "Ask no questions and you'll get told no lies." Anyroad, come on, let's get out o' this station.'

'It's too early to go up to Cleveleys,' said Billy. 'They'll still be having their dinner up there – what they call lunch.'

'Then what do you say to a plate of fish and chips and a pot o' tea at Woolworth's?'

Billy's heart turned over with joy, not only at the prospect of the promised meal, but because it was so good to see Dad's simple manner and to have him around again; he seemed so normal after all the bizarre experiences of the previous few months.

In later years, Billy might have enjoyed grander meals

– champagne dinners and the like – but there was never anything to equal the feast of that day in Woolworth's – eaten to the background music of Deanna Durbin singing 'Waltzing, waltzing, high in the clouds'.

Whilst they were tucking in, Billy took the opportunity to catch up on family news.

'Our Jim's been given another ship – HMS *Fiji*, a new type of cruiser,' said Tommy. 'Our Sam's joined the Marines. He got fed up going up and down in that lift. Les's still in the ARP messengers and our Flo's still at Dunlop's. Oh, aye, and she's got herself a fellah at last – a sergeant in the army. Polly and Steve have another house in Cheetham Hill – not as good as the one that was bombed. But beggars can't be choosers, can they?'

'And what about Mam?'

'She keeps us all going in spite of some terrible air raids we've been having. We get down to the cellar quick now – and no messing.'

'Tell her ta for all those postal orders she's been sending me. I'd have starved without them. One of these days I hope to get back to Manchester again.'

'You're best stopping where y'are with the raids we've been having. There's hardly any of the town left.'

After dinner, they strolled together – father and son – along the front towards South Shore.

'Is there anything you need here, our Billy?'

'I don't think so, though one thing that would be useful would be a bike; it would save a lot of tram fare. My two pals have both got bikes and we could ride together. Maybe Mr Sykes could find a cheap one that we could do up.'

'I'll see what I can do.'

They reached Tommy's favourite Blackpool pub, the Manchester, and the tempting smell of XL ales was too much for him.

'Wait outside a moment, Billy,' he said. 'I'll just pop in and have a quick one.'

After a minute he came out again.

'No,' he said. 'I've changed me mind. I won't go to see Brother Dorian with the smell of beer on me breath.'

They continued their walk until they reached the Pleasure Beach.

'Most of it's closed up for the duration,' said Billy.

'But not all of it,' Tommy said gleefully, now in boyish mood. It seemed to be the effect that Blackpool had on him. 'Come on, our Billy. Let's have a go on this.'

He bought two tickets and together they clambered aboard a car to ride the Big Dipper. At a crazy, breakneck speed they hurtled around the roller-coaster, leaving their stomachs behind at every turn and every sudden, precipitous plunge into empty space.

'Wheee!' squealed Tommy in delight, now a young child again, but still clutching his precious cargo of eggs.

After their suicidal ride round the perimeter of the Pleasure Beach, they took the promenade tram-car to Cleveleys.

As the tram lurched its way northwards along the front, Dad seemed to get more and more jumpy.

'This is like going to see the bloody Pope or King George,' he said. 'I need a drink for this kinda thing but I can't even have that. Anyroad, I've brought me peace offering.'

'Don't worry, Dad. You'll be all right. Just be yourself. He's only human like the rest of us.'

'That's just what he's not. Human like the rest of us. He's a brother. Doesn't smoke or drink or do any of the things that make life worth living. Anyroad, what do I do? Do I shake hands with him or kiss his ring, or what?'

'He's not a bishop, Dad. Just say good afternoon.'

'And he talks like Winston Churchill. He's probably a friend of his.'

'Give him the eggs. That'll keep him quiet.'

The tram passed the Norbreck Hydro.

'For a minute there, I thought you lived in that bloody big castle. It wouldn't have surprised me.'

'No, that's been taken over by Lord Woolton. That's where they do all the work on the ration books for the whole country.'

'Then the Germans should drop a bomb on that bloody place for a start. That lot in there are starving us to death with their coupons for this and coupons for that.'

They reached Cleveleys and the bungalow and Billy took his dad up to the front door and rang the bell. Dad removed his pot hat and held it in his right hand whilst he held the bag of eggs in his left. The door was opened by the great man himself.

'Good afternoon, sir,' said Billy. 'This is my father who has come from Manchester to have a word with you.'

'Delighted to make your acquaintance, Mr Hopkins. An honour and a privilege,' boomed Brother Dorian.

'Very happy to shake your hand, sir,' said Dad. 'And I've brought you a little gift for your dinner table, sir.'

'How generous of you! How magnanimous of you! And how appreciated it will be! What is it, by the way?'

'Three dozen eggs, sir.'

'Three dozen eggs!' echoed the brother, taking the eggs quickly before Dad could change his mind. 'I can't believe it, Mr Hopkins.'

He inspected the eggs.

'Why, these are almost as valuable as Fabergé eggs.'

'These are the best new-laid,' said Dad with a puzzled frown. 'Where do these Farberjay eggs come from?'

'They're from Russia,' said the brother.

'Oh, I see,' said Dad, relieved. 'These are from English Leghorns. We don't deal in foreign eggs at Smithfield Market.'

'Yes, I see,' said Brother Dorian, equally puzzled. 'William here is a fine young chap and we all think very highly of him. He gets on very well with all his school companions, don't you, my boy?'

'Yes, sir,' said Billy dutifully.

'Anyway, come along into the drawing room, Mr Hopkins, and we'll have a chat. William, take the eggs to Brother Brendan, there's a good fellow.'

The two men went into the drawing room and were in there for over half an hour. Billy tried to overhear what they were saying but in vain – the door was too thick. Eventually they emerged.

'So nice to have met you, Mr Hopkins, and so interesting to hear about your family, especially your son on HMS *Fiji*. We must listen out for news of him. I am sure he will distinguish himself again as he has obviously done aboard HMS *Renown* with the vital part he played in the sinking of the *Graf Spee*. Good afternoon, Mr Hopkins, and if you are ever in the area again, don't hesitate to call. And thank you so much for the eggs. I'll make sure the boys get the benefit of them.'

'Thankee, sir,' said Dad. 'And God bless you and all you're doing for these lads.'

Billy accompanied his dad to the tram stop.

'The old bastard,' said Dad when they got outside the door. 'He was drinking Guinness and smoking all the time we was talking, and the old get never offered me a bleeding drink or a bleeding smoke. The bloody old skinflint. Then the bastard says he'd rather have bleeding Russian eggs. Well, I hope them good English eggs bleeding choke him. Make sure you get some of 'em from the bastard, our Billy.'

'I will, Dad. Don't worry. Ta-ra, Dad,' Billy called as the tram pulled away. 'Love to everyone at home. Make sure you get a drink on the way back.'

'Have no fear on that score, son. I will,' he shouted. 'And I'll see Mr Sykes about a bike for you. Ta-ra.'

He was gone. Billy walked sadly back to the bungalow. Neither he nor any of the boys got to see a single egg on their dining table.

Chapter Nineteen

Blitzkrieg

About a month after his dad's visit, Billy was playing a game of pontoon with Robin when Brother Dorian made an entrance into the garage. An immediate hush fell over the room, reminiscent of a scene in a cowboy film when the stranger walks through the swing doors and up to the saloon bar.

'William,' he said. 'I should like to see you in the drawing room; it's a personal matter.'

'Trouble,' whispered Titch.

Billy wondered what the matter could possibly be. When Brother Dorian summons you, he said to himself, it usually means something's wrong.

'You have a brother serving on HMS *Fiji*, do you not?' asked the brother. 'Only the ship has been in action at Crete and it, along with a number of other ships, has been sunk. Let us listen to the news bulletin.'

He switched on the wireless.

'*This is the BBC Home Service*,' said the announcer. '*Here is the news and this is Wilfred Pickles reading it. Crete has been evacuated and more than fifteen thousand troops have been withdrawn to Egypt. The losses inflicted on the enemy's troops and aircraft have been enormous but we regret*

to announce the loss of the two cruisers HMS Gloucester *and
HMS* Fiji *and also four destroyers including HMS* Kelly,
*commanded by Lord Louis Mountbatten, who is reported to be
among the survivors now in Alexandria.'*

Brother Dorian switched off the wireless.

'I am sorry you have received such bad news, William.
We can hope and pray that your brother is amongst the
survivors now in Alexandria. I shall get everyone here to
say a special prayer for him.'

'Yes, thank you, sir,' said Billy, bewildered and overcome at the thought that Jim might be dead.

He returned to the garage and told his friends of his
news.

'I'm sure he has been saved, Billy,' said Robin. 'From
what you've told us about him, he sounds as if he's a
lucky type.'

'You'll see,' said Titch, untypically hopeful. 'He'll be at
Alexandria with all his mates.'

All that week, Billy could think of nothing else. His
mind went back to the 'skenny-eyed kid' days, to the 'daft
and potty' letter to Sam, to the boxing lessons in the back
yard, to the games of pitch-and-toss and the rides in the
big tyre, to the send-offs at the end of Jim's furloughs, to
the way he waved goodbye from the train at London
Road. And as he reflected on all the good times in the
past, he wept for the brother who might be lying at the
bottom of the Mediterranean.

'Cheer up,' said Pablo. 'Remember – no news is good
news.'

Then the letter from home arrived. With shaking
fingers, Billy tore open the envelope. He scanned the first
page of his mam's writing – hungrily, desperately.

Everything was all right! Jim had been saved and was
amongst the survivors at Alexandria. Furthermore, he

was being sent home on compassionate leave and would be in Manchester within a fortnight.

A fortnight is only two weeks, or fourteen days, but that particular fortnight in 1941 seemed like forever.

'Do you think time can stand still?' Billy asked Titch.

'Depends,' said Titch. 'If you're watching a good film it flashes past, but if you're in a lousy Latin lesson it doesn't move.'

Billy went about his daily routines – working in lessons, eating Brother Brendan's thick soups, doing homework, playing on the beach and on the golf course, cheating at cards in the evenings; still the days went by at a snail's pace.

But time runs through the longest day, and one Friday afternoon the endless period of waiting came to an end.

He came cycling up to the gate – on a Raleigh bike. Jim! He hadn't changed – same stupid grin and in the same immaculate uniform, except now it was decorated with all kinds of service stripes, gunnery emblems and war ribbons. His brother! They shook hands and then grabbed each other in a powerful bear-hug.

'How've you been?' asked Jim.

'OK,' said Billy, his eyes glistening. 'And what about you?'

'Not bad,' he said. 'I should be OK. After all, I've just come back from a sea cruise – with a tour of the Greek islands thrown in.'

'Whose is the bike?'

'It's yours,' he said. 'I brought it on the train and cycled up from the station. Dad bought it for you from Mr Sykes for a couple o' quid.'

By this time a number of the boys had appeared and were looking curiously at this brotherly scene.

Pablo came forward deferentially and asked:

'Are you the brother who served on the *Fiji*?'

'That's right. That's me.'

Billy stepped back and simply basked in the reflected glory. Brother Dorian and a couple of the other brothers came out and enquired if he was *The* brother. When it was confirmed that indeed he was, Brother Dorian said:

'We are honoured to have you here. Let there be no misunderstanding that we citizens at home fully appreciate the suffering, the conflict and the sacrifices which you and your shipmates have so recently undergone.'

'Thank you, sir,' said Jim politely.

'Won't you come into the drawing room and tell us exactly what happened at Crete?'

'Certainly, sir,' said Jim. 'But it would be nice if all these young boys here could come too, as I'm certain that they would be interested to hear.'

'Of course they may,' said the brother. 'Come along, boys. Everyone into the drawing room. It's not every day we get the news straight from the horse's mouth.'

All the residents crowded into the drawing room and all eyes were on Jim as he told his story.

'The destroyer *Greyhound* was sunk first. The *Gloucester* and the *Fiji* were ordered to pick up the survivors. But the *Gloucester* was hit, set on fire and started to sink fast. We had to leave her or we would have lost contact with the rest of Admiral Cunningham's fleet. We managed to survive nearly twenty bomber attacks before we ran out of ammunition.'

'What kind of plane attacked you?' asked Pablo.

'We were hit by bombs from Messerschmidt 109s, but there were also many, many Stuka dive-bombers coming at us.'

'What kind of gun do you operate?' asked Brother Brendan.

'I was operating a Pom-Pom, with my mates, of course. I tell you, when the Stukas came screaming down at us, we could almost see the eyes of the Jerry pilots.'

'What did they look like?' asked Titch, shivering.

'They looked as if they had been drugged.'

'And tell me, James,' said Brother Dorian, 'what happened next?'

'I spent over twelve hours in the sea, clinging to wreckage, until me and my mates were picked up by the destroyer *Kipling* and taken to Alexandria.'

As Jim related his experiences to the admiring group, Billy looked on, his heart filled with pride – as much pride as he had felt when Jim had given the skenny-eyed kid his come-uppance. Now he could see from the glances he was receiving from his fellows that his own status at Martindale Bungalow had taken off into the ether.

When Jim had finished relating his adventures, Brother Dorian said:

'On behalf of us all, I must express our deepest appreciation and gratitude for a truly fascinating account of the action off Crete. The glorious defence which our forces put up can only command admiration in every land. If we in this island can keep up the same spirited defiance, it can only result in the annihilation of the savage Hun.'

After this ringing, stirring speech from the headmaster, the group broke up.

'I have a favour to ask you, sir,' said Jim.

'Ask away,' said the brother.

'If you could agree, sir, I should like to take my young brother back to Manchester with me, as we shall be having a family gathering to celebrate my homecoming.'

'Why, certainly,' he said. 'By all means. We shall expect to see him back here after the Whitsun holiday.'

When he heard this, Billy's cup overflowed. Had he been able to look into a crystal ball, however, he might not have been so happy.

The party for Jim's home-coming was a grand affair. All the uncles and aunts, plus the beautiful Jean Priestley and the Sykes family, gathered together for the customary booze-up in Capper's and the sing-song and sandwiches back at Honeypot Street. Dad even made a speech.

'I'd just like to thank y'all for coming tonight to celebrate our Jim's safe return. A lot o' sailors was killed at Crete and he's very lucky to be here with us tonight, and I thank God for sparing him.'

'You mean his time hasn't come,' said Auntie Cissie.

'His name wasn't on the bomb,' said Mam.

'P'raps that bugger Hitler didn't know how to spell it,' said Uncle Eddy.

'Anyroad, Jim's here with us tonight and I raise me glass to him and say: good luck to you, son, and God bless you and I'm proud of you.'

Overcome with emotion, Tommy had to sit down.

'Come on, our Kate, give us a song,' called Uncle Eddy.

After much protesting, Mam was persuaded to sing her favourite song, 'Keep Right on to the End of the Road.'

'Go higher! Go higher!' Dad kept calling proudly as she sang.

'What about a song from you, Dad?' said Billy. 'Give us "Dolly Gray".'

'Y'can have her,' he said. 'Bloody hell! How old d'you think I am? That song's from the Boer War. I won't sing that, but I will sing this.'

In his high, cracked voice, he gave his rendering of

'Don't Dilly-Dally on the Way', with the crowd joining him in the chorus. This seemed to encourage other would-be soloists, for after that followed versions of 'Miner's Dream of Home', 'Nellie Dean' and 'Goodbye!'.

Whilst all this was going on, Billy managed to exchange a few words with Henry, his old pal.

'How's it goin', Henery?'

'Not so bad, Billy. I leave school next year.'

'Great. What are you gonna do?'

'I'm gonna work with me dad on the rag-and-bone cart. Me dad says I can earn nearly two quid a week.'

'Lucky you, Henery. Me – I've got to go on studying at school till I'm sixteen.'

'How're you getting on there?'

'Not so bad now. I didn't like it at first but I'm getting used to it. Right at the very beginning, I was nearly last in class.'

'You last!'

'Yeah – well the work was so different. But at the last exam I came twelfth out of twenty-five, so I'm getting better.'

'If I know you, Billy, you'll be near the top before long.'

'And if I know you, Henery, you'll be a millionaire before you're thirty.'

'I should live so long!' he said, imitating their Jewish neighbours.

The next day was Sunday, and in the evening Billy and his mam and dad took Jim to London Road station for a quiet send-off.

'Not like the old days, Jim,' said Dad, 'when we poured you on to the train in the middle of the night.'

'Thank God for that,' said Jim. 'We used to have terrible

hangovers when we got back to the ship. Hardly a fit state to fight a war.'

'Anyroad, you're not going back to fighting for a bit,' said Mam.

'Will you get another ship, Jim?' asked Billy.

'No, I don't think so. After Crete and all that time I spent in the water, it won't be long before I get my ticket.'

'You mean – leave the navy?' said Billy.

'That's right,' he said. 'I'll get an honourable discharge.'

'What'll you do then?' Billy asked.

'I could join the Merchant Navy or something like that, but I'll cross that bridge when I come to it.'

'Ta-ra, son,' said Mam. 'Now you look after yourself, d'you hear?'

As the train pulled away from the platform, Mam said:

'I'm not kidding. I've said ta-ra that many times to that many people, I'm beginning to sound like a record with its needle stuck.'

At ten o'clock that night, Billy went up to bed, leaving his mam and dad downstairs listening to Sandy Macpherson at the organ; Les was out as usual on ARP messenger service. As he lay there in the darkness, he heard way off in the distance first the gentle hum-hum of aircraft engines, then the very faint whistle of bombs, followed by muffled explosions. There had been no air-raid warning and so Billy wondered if he were hearing things. Hardly daring to breathe, he listened again. There was no mistake – the sounds were still there.

'Mam,' he called, 'I think you'd better come up here and listen to this.'

She did so cupping a hand to her ear and straining to listen.

'By gum, you're right,' she said. 'I can hear 'em. It's a raid.'

She called downstairs.

'Tommy, they're here. The Germans. A raid. Come up here and listen. It's the bombers.'

Billy got up quickly, dressed and went into the cellar. Soon afterwards, Mam joined him.

'Best to get under the stairs,' she said. 'It's the part of a house that's always still standing after it's been bombed.'

They sat together in the dark on the cold stone steps. Thirty minutes later the sirens sounded and Dad joined them.

'They're a bit bloody slow in sounding the warning tonight,' he said.

'I must have a word with her-next-door,' said Mam.

Billy knocked on the wall in the customary manner.

'Are y'all right, Jessie?' called Mam.

'Aye, we're all right, Kate,' she answered. 'I think they're after the railway tonight, the bombs are that close.'

'Look after yourself, Jessie.'

'Aye, you and all.'

'Are y'all right, Henery?' Billy yelled.

'I'm OK,' replied Henry. 'You remember that fortune-teller in Blackpool?'

'Yeah, so what?'

'I think I can see them clouds she was talking about.'

Billy and his mam went back to their place on the steps.

The bombers came closer and closer, louder and louder, and the guns all around the district opened up with their distinctive '*Crump! Crump!*'

'I wonder where our Les is,' was all Mam could say.

Then the air attack really began. Deafening explosion after explosion. The bombs whistled with the shriek of death as they hurtled across the rooftops, detonating on the nearby Red Bank sidings.

'It's the railway they're after all right,' said Dad. 'The bastards know it's the main line between Manchester and Sheffield.'

'Tommy! Tommy!' cried Mam hysterically. 'We'd better get out to the big shelter afore we all get killed here.'

Dad was on the step above him, and Billy could hear his slippered foot trembling near his head. The thunder-claps and the bangs now bursting around them became louder than a dozen storms rolled into one. The three of them passed beyond fear and resigned themselves to death.

'By God,' Dad shouted. 'We'd better get out or we're dead. I'll put me shoes on!'

He got up and went upstairs into the living room. At that moment, there was a hellish, terrifying screeching across the house and there followed the mother of all explosions. The whole world shuddered – the house seemed to lift up and sway over to one side. Then came the overpowering, nauseating smell of cordite, filling their mouths, throats, nostrils with choking, suffocating soot and dirt.

'God help us, Tommy, we've been hit! Are you all right? Are you still there?'

'I'm all right, Kate,' he yelled. 'I was saved by the kitchen door. Never mind me bloody shoes! Let's get out afore the whole bloody place falls on us!'

During the short lull they got out of the ruined, devastated house and hurried towards the public shelter. They were not prepared for the horror outside.

'It's a bloody nightmare!' Dad shouted.

It was a fitting description of the ruins which were now all around them. It was still dark, but in the moonlight they could see that the shape, the landscape, the very geography of the district had been transformed in a few short hours. They struggled through the debris, clambered over crumbled walls and the remains of buildings until they reached the comfort, if not the security, of the large shelter under a raincoat factory.

There they found mayhem – a scene like that of the trenches in the First World War – with corpses and wounded lying higgledy-piggledy about the place. One man sat on the floor moaning and holding his face, which had been gashed and torn by flying debris; another lay with his face bleeding from the glass of his spectacle lenses which had been blown into his eyes. Others sat staring, bewildered – in a state of shock.

At dawn the all-clear sounded. The survivors emerged from the basement like moles blinking in the light. There was a pall of smoke hanging over the area, and some of the houses were still burning. Everywhere they looked, there was destruction and desolation.

The family walked back to the place where their house had been and found only a heap of rubble and charred timbers. Sitting nearby on a low wall was Mr Sykes.

'They're both gone, Mrs Hopkins,' he said flatly.

'Good God! What's happened?' she asked.

'During the night, I heard screams of women and children and I went out to see if I could help. It was then that that bomb – the one which has wiped out your house and mine – hit us. A direct hit, as you can see. Jessie, Henery. Both gone. They were in the cellar. They couldn't have known a thing. Blew them to smithereens. The ambulances have taken what was left of their bodies away.'

He continued to stare off vacantly into space. No tears. No emotion. He was mesmerised and unable to take in the enormity of the disaster which had befallen him.

Heartbroken at the loss of his old pal, Billy took off his woollen scarf and wrapped it around Mr Sykes's neck, but the man didn't seem to notice.

Dear old Henry – dead! Henry, who'd shared so many games, so many exploits, so many dreams!

'No career in the rag-and-bone trade for Henry,' Billy said tearfully to Mam.

'And Jessie's had her asthma cured good and proper,' replied Kate sorrowfully.

'We've lost our home and our good friends all in a few short hours,' said Dad. 'If that bomb had fallen just a couple of yards shorter, it would've been us taken away in them ambulances.'

'Somebody up there must like us,' said Mam. 'Either that or our name wasn't on that bomb.'

As they left Honeypot Street, Billy glanced back. The last view he had of the place where he had spent such a happy boyhood was Mr Sykes sitting expressionless and alone on that low wall.

The family moved to an Emergency Rest Centre to await re-housing. Back safely from his ARP duties, Les found them two hours later and gave an account of the hair-raising time he had had during the night, cycling around the district which had been disintegrating and falling about his ears.

'You'd best get back to Blackpool,' said Dad to Billy. 'You'll be safer out of this lot. You never know, Jerry might be back tonight.'

It was a very sad farewell when Mam went with him to Victoria Station.

'Ta-ra again,' she said. 'One o' these days, all this lot'll be over and I might find myself saying hello just for a change. And here's a photo of the Sykes family I found in me handbag. You might like to keep it to remind you of happier days.'

As he sat on the train, Billy looked at the photograph and his eyes filled with tears. It was a picture of the two families posing together in the cut-outs on Blackpool promenade – oh, so long ago, before the horror of war had rained death from the sky. He recalled how he and Henry had run away to join Mad Jack's army on Barney's, how Jim had pushed them home in the big tyre, their boat-sailing adventures on Queen's Park lake, how they had sat the scholarship together and the look of bitter disappointment on Henry's face when he found he hadn't made it, and how he had defended Henry against Stan White's bullying in the schoolyard. Well, Henry wouldn't have to worry any more. This time, though, there had been nothing Billy could do to save Henry from being blown to bits by a German bomb. But for a quirk of fortune, a slight deflection of the wind, it would have been him, and not Henry, lying on that mortuary slab in Monsall Hospital. How cruel was fate, which seemed to pick its victims so mercilessly and so haphazardly. As the thoughts went through his mind, the tears ran down his cheeks.

A WAAF sitting opposite him in the compartment regarded him with concern.

'Are you all right, son?' she asked.

'Yes, thank you,' he replied. 'Just sad at having to leave home.'

'I know the feeling,' she said. 'Only too well.'

When he got back to Cleveleys, Billy reported to Brother Dorian all that had happened.

'Oh, you poor boy,' said the brother, embracing him. 'And your poor family. Tomorrow at morning prayers, I shall tell the school about your tragedy.'

He was as good as his word.

The whole school was assembled in the large hall of the domestic science college.

'Out of the depths I have cried unto you, O Lord,' intoned Brother Dorian.

'Lord, hear my voice,' responded the school. 'And let Thine ears be attentive to the voice of my supplication.'

'Eternal rest give unto them, O Lord,' said the brother.

'And let perpetual light shine upon them,' replied the school.

'May they rest in peace.'

'Amen,' chorused the school.

'And now I have to give you solemn news concerning one of our boys. William, would you please come up here on the stage where we can see you?'

Billy walked slowly and reluctantly on to the stage.

'Let this boy be an example to us all. He returned to the bosom of his family, believing it was safe to do so, but behold the disaster which has befallen him. Last week, Hitler's Luftwaffe flew over Manchester like vultures looking for carrion and rained down havoc and annihilation on the houses beneath – destroying this unfortunate boy's home and killing the family of his neighbours. Be under no delusions. Death can strike at any time. Consider Snake Hips Johnson in the Café de Paris, which is deep under a cinema – so deep that the noise of an air raid above does not even reach the revellers below. There he was, Snake Hips . . .'

Here the brother did a hula-hula dance.

'. . . swaying his hips from side to side in lecherous gyrations, thinking he was safe and immune from the conflagration which raged above. But the bomb searched him out all right. Snake Hips was killed along with thirty-two others and with over sixty injured.

'Stay here in Blackpool, boys, where you are safe from harm and under our care. Very well, William. You may return to your place.'

Shortly after the bombing, Billy wrote a poem for the school magazine.

SIRENTIME

The sirens burst out on a sleeping town
And people withdraw to shelters deep down.
The buzz of a plane is heard in the sky
And innocent people get ready to die.
Thud! Thud! Thud! drop the bombs with a quiver
And children in cellars start to tremble and shiver.

Soon the city's aglow with buildings on fire
And for some folk out there, it's their funeral pyre.
Crump! Crump! Crump! goes the sound of a gun
And so it goes on till the rise of the sun.
But we must pray hard for a glorious end,
Therefore to God, all our prayers do we send.
O please, please God, grant us a boon,
Let the end of this havoc come very soon.

Life ticked over peacefully and uneventfully at Martindale Bungalow until a certain day in August 1941.

One evening when all the boys were occupied with their various games, Johnny Bassett burst into the garage with astounding news.

'The old bugger's started giving us baths. I've just had one and he spent an awful long time washing my balls. There's a roster on the bathroom door, so you lot can check when it's your turn!'

The trio rushed into the house to consult the list and to find out when they were due for the treatment.

'Bloody hell,' said Robin. 'You and I, Hoppy, are down for tomorrow.'

'My name isn't down,' said Titch.

'Perhaps he doesn't fancy you,' said Billy.

They listened at the bathroom door, and over the sound of splashing water they could hear – if somewhat muffled – Dorian's deep, sonorous voice.

'How's that, my boy? Do you like that, boy? Let me wash under there, boy.'

'My God!' Billy said. 'What are we going to do?'

That evening, dressed only in pyjamas, Robin went down to see the brother to tell him that he had a touch of the flu and wished to be excused baths for the time being. It seemed to work, for five minutes later he was back.

'I've been excused for a week,' he said, 'but if you're going down to see him, Hoppy, for God's sake watch your step. He's gone off his head.'

Also dressed only in pyjamas, Billy went down to see the head.

'I have a very bad cold, sir. I think I must've caught it from Gabrielson, sir,' he said.

'And I suppose you want to be excused baths too. Is that it? That will be no problem, William. You just get off to bed.'

Brother Dorian stood up and caught him in an embrace, hugging him close and at the same time cupping his hand under Billy's genitals.

'Good night, my boy. What beautifully shaped testicles you have. Would you like to take hold of me there?'

'No thank you, sir.'

'Very well, my boy. Perhaps tomorrow, then.'

Billy escaped to his room, where Robin was waiting for a report.

'Did he try it on?'

'Yes, he did. And with you, I suppose.'

'Yes. What are we going to do?'

'I don't know what you and Titch are going to do, but I'm off.'

'How do you mean, "off"?' asked Titch.

'I'm going back to Manchester now – tonight!'

'But how . . . ?'

'I've got my bicycle with a dynamo and I reckon I can ride it to Manchester in about four or five hours. I'll get my dad to write to Brother Dorian and tell him I'm not coming back to Blackpool. That I'm needed at home. Anything.'

'Why not go tomorrow and I'll come with you,' said Robin.

'No fear,' said Billy. 'Dorian wants to see me tomorrow. I'm going before he puts sex education on the timetable and makes the practical part compulsory.'

'Right, I'm coming with you,' said Robin. 'I've got lights on my bike too.'

'What about me?' said Titch.

'He's not asked to see you – yet,' said Billy.

'It's only a matter of time,' said Titch. 'I'm so small, he hasn't seen me. But wait till he notices me and I've had it.'

'You haven't,' replied Robin. 'But you'll get it.'

'Then I'm coming too. The three musketeers!'

At midnight, when the house was quiet, the three boys sneaked downstairs. As they passed the head's bedroom, they could hear him snoring loudly. He turned over and snorted. The boys froze. Billy put his finger to his lips and pointed downstairs. Hardly daring to breathe, they tiptoed down to the hallway and into the kitchen, where they helped themselves to a few provisions for their journey.

'I reckon the old bugger owes us this food,' said Billy,

'for all those eggs we didn't see.'

They crept out to the garage and retrieved their bikes from the small shed at the back, then very, very quietly wheeled them out on to Briarwood Drive.

'Let's go!' whispered Billy.

Through the night they pedalled. Kirkham – Preston – Leyland – Chorley – Horwich – Bolton – Salford – Manchester.

They rode and rode through the darkness until their legs seemed to belong to other people. The journey took not four hours but eight, and they finally cycled into the centre of their beloved Manchester at eight thirty the next morning.

'God knows what my dad'll say,' observed Titch.

'Same here,' the other two said.

'Are we all agreed,' said Robin, 'that we say nothing about Brother Dorian to our parents?'

'Agreed,' said Billy. 'There's no point. They probably wouldn't believe us anyway.'

'Agreed,' said Titch. 'There'd have to be a big inquiry and it would land him and us in big trouble.'

'Anyway,' said Billy, 'I'm going home to a new address somewhere in Crumpsall, and first I have to find it. It sounds really posh – forty, Gardenia Court! I can hardly wait to see it.'

Chapter Twenty

Gardenia Court

'Gardenia Court' Mam had written, '*off Smedley Road, off Queen's Road.*'

Billy rode down Queen's Road, checking off various landmarks: bus depot, Harrigan's Dance Academy, Clifton Street, Smedley Road.

'At last,' he said aloud. 'This is it.'

He pedalled down the road and there, at the end, he beheld what seemed like a whole city of tenement blocks: Hyacinth House, Hazlewood House, Hawthorn House.

What lovely-sounding names, he said to himself. What a pity they're all slums.

He freewheeled down Hazelbottam Road and then he saw it – opposite a large shirt factory – a dirty, dilapidated building all on its own. GARDENIA COURT, the sign said. He turned left into the approach road and was attacked by a pack of snarling mongrel dogs, which barked furiously and determinedly at his back wheel.

He dismounted and walked a few yards along the pavement. There, sitting on a low wall, was a buxom girl in her early twenties, singing to herself.

'Baa baa black sheep,' she mumbled, saliva gathering on her lips.

'Excuse me,' said Billy. 'Do you know where the Hopkins family live?'

'Ockins,' she babbled. 'Ockins.'

'Right,' said Billy, getting the picture. Then, more kindly, 'What's your name?'

'Annie,' she sputtered.

He walked a little further into the cul-de-sac which ran by the side of the tenement block. He looked up at the filthy grey building with its mean, ugly verandas, which seemed to be used mainly for hanging and draping out the washing. Sitting at the bottom of one of the stairways were two shabbily dressed boys, about his own age, playing cards.

'Excuse me,' he said. 'Can you tell me where I can find number forty?'

'Oh, h'excuse me,' replied one of them, mocking his accent. 'Well, h'aren't we posh, then? Whadda y'think we are – a bleeding information desk?'

'Try the next hovel,' said the other lad.

'Hovel?' said Billy. 'What's that?'

'Are you bleeding daft or wha'?' said the first one. 'Hovel. The stairway. The entrance.'

'Right, ta,' Billy said.

He hoisted the bike on to his shoulder and entered the stairwell. 'Hovel' was indeed the right word. The first thing that hit him on the ground floor was the vile stench of stale urine and pickled herrings. On the first floor his nostrils were assailed by a second, more powerful smell – that of sour cabbage mixed with onions cooking. The third floor was worse, with its stink of rancid cheese and human excrement.

'Shut your bleeding mouth, yer stupid cow!' roared a gruff male voice from number 38.

'Don't you bleeding well talk to me like that or you'll

get this bleeding frying pan on yer 'ead,' screeched a female voice.

Finally, he reached number 40 on the top floor. He gave a rat-a-tat-tat with the brightly polished knocker.

Mam came to the door and gazed at him uncom-prehendingly.

'Yes?' she said. Then she recognised him.

'It's our Billy. What in the name of God are you doing here? You should be in Blackpool.'

'Well, I'm here now,' he said. 'I'll just bring my bike in and I'll tell you all about it.'

Once inside, and after a breakfast of bacon and dried-egg omelette, Billy said:

'Many of the boys are coming back from Blackpool now that you're not getting as many air raids. Not since Hitler's been kept busy in Russia. We can't see the point in being evacuated any more.'

'I see,' she said. 'But it's a bit sudden, like, isn't it? I mean, why didn't you write and tell us you was coming?'

'I couldn't,' he said, continuing the lie. 'Me and me pals decided to come back to start the new term in Manchester. Half of Damian College is still here, remember. You'll have to get Steve Keenan to write a letter to the school explaining how I'm needed at home.'

'Oh, I see. Well, I just hope you and your pals know what you're doing.'

'What about this terrible place we've come to, Mam? It's worse than the dwellings in Collyhurst. The Priestleys got themselves a nice house in Wythenshawe.'

'I know, they was lucky. We didn't have no choice after being bombed out. We was just told to take it or leave it. So we had to take it. It's a bit small, I know, but we do have a little bathroom and we've got hot water for the first time in our lives.'

'But what a rotten district! And who was that funny girl I met coming in?'

'Oh, that would be Annie. She's bit simple, like, but harmless enough.'

'Then there were those lads playing cards in the next hovel. They looked a right pair.'

'That'll be Mick Scully and Vinny Buckley. You'd better keep well away from them two or you'll have your father after you.'

'Why, what's wrong with 'em?'

'They've both been away in Borstal for the last three years – that's what's wrong with 'em. They've only just come back.'

'Planning their next job, I suppose. What about that couple underneath us? He's bawling his head off and she's screeching like a lunatic. Her voice is worse than Auntie Cissie's.'

'That's Mr and Mrs Pitts, and she *is* a lunatic. They're allus at it – fighting like cat and dog all the time. She's either screeching at him or the kids or both. It's worst on Friday nights when he's had a drop too many. But not all the neighbours are as bad as that, thank God. On the bottom floor there's a very nice family – the Weinbergs.'

'That explains the smell of pickled herrings I got a whiff of as I came up. But you know, Mam, we're back where we started in Collyhurst. And there at least we had a view of the Cut and the railway. Here, from that veranda, we're just looking at another block of flats.'

'There's allus the view at the back.'

'Oh, aye, a great view of the Smedley Shirt Factory.'

'Well, our Billy, we'll just have to grin and bear it, won't we?'

'We'll bear it, but it doesn't mean we have to grin about it as well.'

★ ★ ★

After a year of bearing it, the family became resigned to their lot and to their wretched existence in the squalid tenement block. How they looked back wistfully to those wonderful days in Honeypot Street before the war when, despite the lack of bathroom and hot water, they had had space and privacy.

'Life is like a game of snakes and ladders, Mam,' said Billy. 'Just as you think you're getting somewhere, down a snake you go.'

'But then there are always ladders just around the corner,' she said.

'That's not what I've found up to now. You go down one snake only to find it leads to an even longer one.'

'You are an old grumps.'

Misery makes strange bedfellows, and the occupants of the Gardenia Court block were a miscellaneous set of people ranging from the respectable to the criminal, the reasonable to the insane. The one thing they all had in common was their joylessness.

If anything, though, when it came to misery, the Weinbergs on the ground floor were in a class of their own, for not only were they poor, they were Jewish into the bargain. This combination made life intolerable for them. Successful Jews had long since moved on to the affluent northern suburbs of Manchester, such as Heaton Park or Prestwich. To make matters worse, the Weinbergs had three daughters they had to find husbands for. The girls were pretty enough, but in their straitened circumstances, how were they going to capture nice Jewish boys with well-paid jobs if they couldn't offer a decent dowry? The whole family went about with permanently melancholy expressions and they rarely spoke to or even acknowledged the existence of anyone else on the block.

During that first year, Billy spent much of his time looking out from the veranda at the flats opposite and the people walking below.

One afternoon, he saw Vinny Buckley and Mick Scully sitting on a wall opposite the flats.

'Hey, Billy,' called Vinny Buckley. 'Come down here. We wanna talk to you.'

Having nothing better to do, and being a little curious, Billy went down and joined them.

'There's bugger-all to do round 'ere,' said Mick Scully. 'If you get bored just looking out from your veranda, why don't you come out on a job with us? We'll show you how to have a good time round 'ere.'

'Yeah, it's dead belting,' said Vinny Buckley. 'Anything for a bit of excitement.'

'Better not,' said Billy. 'I don't want no trouble with the coppers.'

'Neither do we,' said Mick Scully. 'We just make sure we don't get caught.'

Billy's dad was going past on his way back from work.

'Billy,' he shouted, waiting at the foot of the stairway, 'come over here quick.'

Billy did as he was told.

'Get upstairs,' Dad said. 'And don't let me see you talking to them two again, d'you hear? They're both up to no good and they'll drag you down with 'em if they can. You think on what I've said.'

But Billy was thoroughly dejected at the cramped conditions they had to put up with and the dismal district which surrounded them and hemmed them in. Nobody seemed happy. Nobody smiled. To while away the time, he took to spitting out the stones of the beautiful, plump plums his father had so abundantly supplied, to hit marked objects on the pavement three floors below. Like the game of 'Bombers over Berlin' on the Cleveleys beach, he pretended to be on a raiding mission with the RAF over a German city:

'Left a little, skipper. Now a little more. Steady-y-y. Bombs gone!'

Then he spat with deadly accuracy.

When feeling particularly fed up, he generously tried to share his despondency with the neighbours below by hitting the tops of their heads with the odd plum stone, and then withdrawing his own head inside quickly so that they were never sure where it had come from. On one occasion, when the Weinberg sisters were looking especially glum and down in the dumps, he tried to cheer them up by unselfishly releasing a large, succulent Victoria, which landed plumb on target. The bombing diversion had to stop, though, when Mrs Weinberg complained to his mam.

'I'm not kidding, our Billy, you must be going off your chump dropping plums on the poor people underneath. It's time you grew up.'

'It was only a bit of fun.'

'And talking of growing up, it's time you got out of them short trousers and into long pants. You're beginning to look like a big scoutmaster. And another thing – I think I can see a few hairs on your chin. It's time you tried having a shave.'

'Me? Shave?'

'Yes, you! Ask your dad tonight if you can borrow his razor.'

'What! You shave!' Dad exclaimed that evening. 'I didn't think you were that grown-up. But aye, you can borrow me razor. D'you know what to do?'

'I think so, Dad. You work up a lather with your brush and your shaving stick and then you scrape it off with that Gillette thing.'

'That's it,' he said. 'A good lather is half the shave. Should come off easy. That there fuzz on your face is only bum-fluff.'

Billy went into the bathroom and carried out the whole operation meticulously. He manufactured a great mountain of soapy lather, which he then worked into his face with his dad's shaving brush. He scraped off the foam very carefully and dried his face. The fuzz was still there! He repeated the whole operation, applying even more soap the second time. Again he scraped. No joy! He went out of the bathroom.

'Dad, this razor of yours doesn't work. Look, the fuzz is still there.'

'That's funny,' Dad said, examining the razor. 'Wait a minute, though, you little daft bugger. You've forgotten to put a blade in the holder.'

Early in 1942, Les was called up into the army.

'Everyone seems to be in uniform except me,' said Billy to his mam one day.

'If this war goes on, you'll be called up as well – just like our Les. Anyroad, what do you want to be in uniform for?'

'I want to do my bit for the war effort.'

'I think it's the girls you're thinking of. I suppose you think you'll have 'em all running after you.'

As usual, Mam was right. The following week Billy joined the Air Training Corps and was given a uniform.

Feeling somewhat self-conscious in his blue tunic, he set off one evening. On his way he passed Buckley and Scully at the foot of the stairway.

'Don't forget what we told you, Billy. Any time you want to join us, just let us know. We'll show you the ropes. You'll find it a bit more exciting than playing at soldiers or whatever you do at that ATC rubbish.'

'Better not,' answered Billy, hurrying off. 'I've got to get to the Training Corps parade.'

A couple of weeks after donning his uniform, he got a girlfriend by the name of Phyllis Hood. She was an extremely tall girl with a figure like a broomstick, but she had the most beautiful, doll-like face. For hour after hour he stood with her at the bottom of her hovel, talking, romancing and serenading her, though in order to reach her lips for a kiss, he had to stand on a higher step. The affair came to an end after a month when she found another boy who didn't have to stand on the step.

Apart from the uniform, Billy enjoyed his time in the ATC. How proud he felt when their commanding officer called out, 'Squa-a-a-dron . . . 'Shun!' It was almost like the real thing. Training involved parades, march-pasts, visits to airfields and, on one memorable occasion, a flight over Cheshire in an Avro Anson. There were also aero-nautical studies – Morse code, radio technology and, most important, navigation. It was in this last subject that Billy acquired a deep interest and a fairly high level of competence. He learned to calculate precise latitude and longitude on a map, magnetic north, angles of deviation, wind speeds, and how to plot a flight path.

'I hope this war lasts long enough for me to get into it,' he said. 'I'd like to be a navigator in a bomber.'

'Well, I hope it doesn't,' Mam said. 'Anyroad, you've done enough bombing with them Victoria plums on the Weinberg girls.'

Not long after Billy had joined the ATC, Jim was given his honourable discharge from the navy. At first he was cheerful and happy at the idea of being back in Civvy Street, but as the weeks went by, he became more and more restless.

'I miss the navy and the sea,' he said one day. 'If ever

you get the chance, Billy, when the war's over, you should join the navy. You'd love it.'

'I want to be a navigator in the RAF. It's always struck me as a miracle the way our bombers set off in the dark and arrive over their target – Hamburg, Dusseldorf, Berlin – right on time. I want to be the navigator who gets them there.'

'Better to be a navigator aboard a ship. If you were really good and got all your qualifications, you could end up as captain of your own vessel. Imagine that!'

'How would I get to be ship's navigator then?'

'You'd have to study very hard at a college of navigation to get your Board of Trade certificate. There's a college at Southampton and one at Liverpool.'

'You make it sound really great. Maybe after I've finished at Damian College, I could go to one of them.'

For the umpteenth time in his life, Billy knew what he wanted to do and what he wanted to be.

'Right now,' said Jim, 'I miss the adventure and the excitement, but most of all I miss my ship-mates.'

'Why not join the Merchant Navy, like you said some time ago?'

'That's exactly what I have done. I've signed on, but it's not easy to get a berth.'

'But I always thought the Merchant Navy was crying out for men.'

'Yeah, but the best berths on the best ships are snapped up by the old hands who are well in with the masters. I can always get a place on a tanker, though.'

'Why is that?'

'See, it's like this. In a convoy, the tankers are the most dangerous ships to be on, 'cos the U-boats pick 'em out for special treatment. If they get torpedoed when they're fully loaded, they go up in flames like a Roman candle.'

'Best to avoid them then.'

'I'll say. I'd have to be pretty desperate to sign on for one of those. Anyway, I've managed to get some work on a coal boat that's sailing from Liverpool to Cardiff tomorrow. It's a pretty dirty job but it's better than just hanging around the house all day long.'

He was away for nearly a fortnight. When he returned, he was black with coal dust from head to foot.

'Just look at the state of you,' Mam said. 'I'm not kidding, anyone'd think you'd been down the mines, never mind on a coal boat. Get all them clothes off, our Jim, and I'll give 'em a good scrubbing. If you wasn't so big, I'd give you one and all. You used to be so particular when you were in the Royal Navy. No wonder that Jean Priestley found another fella. Why did you go on a coal boat?'

'Finding a ship isn't easy,' said Jim. 'You have to take what you can get. As for Jean, I haven't seen much of her since they moved to Wythenshawe. Might be as well – she was getting too serious for my liking.'

'But she was such a nice girl.'

'I'm not denying that. But the family's very religious. One brother training to be a priest; a sister training to be a nun. And Jean was that holy, I felt as if I was going out with a saint.'

It was two days after Jim's return that everyone started scratching. Under the arms, around the groin and, most especially, between the fingers.

'I think this itching is gonna drive me up the wall,' said Mam, scratching madly at her stomach.

'It's that bloody Jim that's brought this into the house,' said Dad. 'I've got them bloody red spots all round the top of me legs, and when I'm at work in the market I can't even reach down there for a scratch or all the other porters'll think I'm bloody well playing with meself.'

'It's in between my fingers where I find it's worst,' said Billy. 'You can even see the little mites in the tiny white lines where they've burrowed in.'

At the surgery, the doctor took one look between Billy's fingers.

'Scabies,' he announced. 'Your whole family, Mrs Hopkins, will have to go to the Infectious Diseases Hospital at Monsall to be treated.'

'Even me husband?' asked Mam anxiously.

'I said the whole family,' said the doctor. 'Furthermore, all your bedding and clothes will have to be disinfected.'

'Oh, bloody hell,' Mam said. 'He's not gonna like this.'

The treatment at the hospital involved first a very hot bath, after which a nurse, wearing rubber gloves and a rubber apron, covered them from head to foot with a foul-smelling sulphur ointment. Billy's dad moaned all the way there and all the way back.

'He's picked up these bleeding bugs aboard that bleeding coal boat and passed them on to us. I tell you, Kate, I'm not gonna stand for it. He'll have to go.'

'Give the lad a chance, Tommy. It's not his fault. It could've happened to anyone.'

That night, Jim came home with a shipmate at two o'clock in the morning after a night's revelry in the town.

Billy was awakened by the sound of voices being raised.

'What the bleeding hell d'you think you're doing, cooking chips at two o'clock in the morning?' he heard his dad yell.

'I've just come back with an old shipmate and we were hungry – that's all.'

'Listen, Jim, I've just about had enough of you. You sit round the house all day making us all miserable, then you give us all bleeding scabies, and now you're waking up the whole bloody house, making chips. Don't you know I've got to be up at four in the bleeding morning to go to work. It's hardly worth me going back to bed.'

'You've been at my bloody throat ever since I came back from the navy, turning your back on me and making those bloody hissing noises,' Jim shouted back.

'Listen, if you can't keep decent hours like other people, you can bleeding well sling your hook.'

'I'd better go,' said Jim's nautical friend. 'I'm not bothered about any chips. Be seeing you, Champ.'

'Wait,' said Jim. 'I'll come with you. I'm not stopping in this dump.'

Jim went into the bedroom and switched on the light.

'Sorry to disturb you, our kid, but I want to pack a few things and then I'm off.'

'Don't go, Jim,' said Billy. 'Stay. He'll get over it. He always does.'

'Nah, not this time,' Jim replied. 'Anyway, come on, give me one of your bear-hugs before I go.'

Billy held him in a strong clinch, at the same time patting his back.

'I wish you'd stay. What am I gonna do when you've gone?'

'You'll be OK, and anyway, even if I did stay, it wouldn't be for long. I've got myself a ship.'

'That's great news, Jim. What's its name?'

'*Empire Light.*'

'What kind of ship?'

'A tanker,' he said. 'I got fed up waiting.'

Billy's heart froze.

'For God's sake look after yourself, Jim.'

'The same goes for you, our kid. Be seeing you. Right, Judd.' He turned to his pal. 'Let's go. Sorry to leave on this note, Dad. Hope you get to work on time. Ta-ra.'

Billy heard the front door pulled to and Jim was gone.

He never forgot that Tuesday when he came home from school. He turned the key in the lock, and the moment he entered the flat he sensed that something was wrong. There was usually somebody talking or the wireless was on, but today it was ominously quiet. He opened the living-room door and took in the scene.

Dad sat at the table, chin in hand, the picture of misery, and Billy could see that he had been crying. Before him there was a mug of cold tea – untouched. Mam sat bowed before the electric fire, weeping silently. Billy felt a tightening of his stomach and his throat, and his hair seemed to stand on end.

'Oh, God,' he said. 'Please. Not that. Not Jim.'

'We've had a telegram,' Dad managed to say between sobs. 'The *Empire Light* has been sunk. Jim's missing.'

It was a Sunday afternoon in March when the *Empire Light* had been torpedoed. The captain wrote Mam and Dad a lovely letter explaining how the tanker had got it in mid-Atlantic on the way across to America. The sea had been rough and choppy and, as the ship had started to sink, most of the crew had got into the lifeboat which, for some reason or other, had broken away and was unable to get back to the ship. The captain and another officer had searched the ship for injured survivors but there were none. A destroyer had broken away from the convoy and had come as close to the ship as it dared, and the two officers had managed to jump on to its deck. RAF Coastal Command had scoured the sea for many hundreds of square miles but no trace of the lifeboat or any survivors had been seen.

'*It is with the deepest regret,*' concluded the captain, '*that I have to tell you that your son, James, must be presumed to be lost.*'

A few days later they received another letter, this time from the King.

BUCKINGHAM PALACE
The Queen and I offer you our heartfelt sympathy in your great sorrow. We pray that your country's gratitude for a life so nobly given in its service may bring you some measure of consolation.
GEORGE RI

'I can't believe he's dead,' said Mam. 'I could accept it better if they'd found a body. But we'll never know what really happened to him at the end.'

'It's best not to think about it, Kate,' said Dad. 'I only wish I'd never had that bloody row with him, all over such a daft thing as cooking chips late at night.'

'Maybe he's not dead,' said Billy. 'P'raps he's landed on some desert island and he's not been able to contact us.'

'No,' said Dad, his voice flat and final. 'He's dead all right. We may as well face up to it.'

Eyes overflowing, Mam began going through Jim's things in the wardrobe.

'Remember this green suit, Tommy? The one that drove us round the bend,' she sobbed. 'I only wish he were here now to wear it again.'

'Stop punishing yourself, Kate,' Dad said, very near to tears himself.

'And here's his boxing gloves and all his boxing things,' she grieved. 'You may as well have 'em now, Billy.'

'I don't want 'em, Mam. He might want 'em himself when he comes back.'

But in his heart of hearts, Billy knew Jim wasn't coming back. Jim, his beloved brother, was at the bottom of the sea.

As he lay in bed that night, he wept silently and sorrowfully at the thought of Jim dying in an open boat somewhere in the Atlantic Ocean. He had seen Noel Coward's film, *In Which We Serve*, and he wished that he hadn't, for only too graphically had it painted the picture of what could happen to men lost in an open boat at sea. Possibly a slow, agonising death from hunger, thirst and exposure. How long had it taken for them to die? How long had they waited to be rescued? How long had it been before they had lost all hope? He prayed that death had come to Jim and his mates with merciful swiftness.

Then his mood changed from sorrow to anger as he thought about the deaths in his lifetime and all that had happened since Chamberlain had made that fateful speech in 1939. Young Teddy Smith – drowned in the Cut. His pal, Henry – dead. His hero brother – dead. Their Honeypot Street home – gone. Steve and Pauline's happiness – gone. The world was an evil place with people like Mrs Mossop, Kevin the airman and Brother Dorian in it.

What a rotten, rotten, rotten world we live in, he raged silently. Very well, God, if there is a God, if it's part of your plan that I spend my life in this lousy, filthy hole here in Crumpsall, if I am to live in a slum with the mad and the criminal, I'm gonna start acting like 'em. Up to now, God, I've taken everything you've thrown at me with no complaints. But tomorrow I begin getting my own back. So watch out, God! Bugger the war! Bugger Hitler! Bugger Churchill! Bugger Damian College! Bugger the ATC! Bugger navigation colleges! Bugger the savage, heartless sea! Bugger everything and bugger everybody! Tomorrow morning, I'll go and see Vinny Buckley and Mick Scully and see what they have in mind.

Chapter Twenty-One

When In Rome . . .

'Hiya Billy,' said Vinny when Billy called at the Buckleys' ground-floor flat. 'I knew you'd come round to our way of thinking in the end. Come in a minute, will ya, and I'll be ready in two ticks. Then we'll go and get Mick.'

Billy went inside and was nearly bowled over by the stench of stale sweat and urine, which he traced to the steaming, wet nappies draped all round the fireguard. A snotty-nosed, bare-bottomed toddler sucking on a dummy gazed at Billy curiously and then greeted him by throwing a small metal toy at him, which fortunately missed the mark. Vinny's mother, a hundred per cent sourpuss, was breast-feeding a mewling, puking infant. She looked up from the baby to Billy but did not acknowledge his presence with even so much as a nod or a grimace. With practised ease, she switched the baby over to her other pendulous breast.

'If you're going out with that bleeding Mick Scully again,' she squawked, 'don't go getting into bleeding trouble with the rozzers again. We've got enough on our bleeding plates with your father in Strangeways without you joining him.'

'Awright! Awright! Stop bleeding going on at me,'

answered Vinny. 'Come on, Billy, let's get out o' this bleeding hole.'

When they were outside, he said 'Bleeding old cow! She's allus going on at me.'

'I didn't know your father was in Strangeways, Vinny.'

'Oh, him! The old man! He's in and out o' clink all the time. Got done this time for house-breaking. He's that well known in Strangeways, they invite him to the staff dances. What about you, Billy? Are y'off school today?'

'Yeah – I decided to take the day off. I'm sick to death of all that Latin, French, geometry and all that crap. I'm gonna start enjoying meself.'

'That's the idea. We'll show you how it's done. Just stick with us and you'll be awright. Let's go and get Mick. He's a right card, is Mick. Doesn't give a bugger for no one.'

It took Mick all of five seconds to make up his mind when they called.

'I'll get me coat,' he said. 'Right, let's go. First off – we need some fags.'

'I've no money on me,' said Vinny.

'Neither have I,' said Billy.

'Who said anything about money? Did you hear me mention money?' said Mick. 'Come with me.'

He led them to a car park outside a large biscuit factory.

'If you want the very best fags, always try the good cars first.'

He went along the row of cars, trying the door handles.

'Locked! Locked! Locked! Not locked!'

He opened the door of the Daimler and there, in the leather pocket in the door, spotted three twenty-packets of Player's Please!.

'We're in luck,' he said. 'And so early in the day! Must be Billy here – he's a lucky charm. Right, lads, cop for these!'

He threw each of them a packet of cigarettes, then took out of his pocket a brand-new Ronson and lit everyone's fag.

'See this,' he said, indicating the lighter. 'Got this on me last house-breaking job. Somebody carelessly left it out for me.'

Puffing arrogantly on their cigs, the three renegades walked up Hazelbottom Road, looking for fresh adventure and fresh quarry.

'This is more like it,' said Billy. 'Much better than wasting me bleeding time learning a lot of French irregular verbs.'

'I should bleeding well think so,' said Vinny. 'No one ever got rich reading a book.'

They came to a row of shops.

'OK,' said Mick. 'We're going into that toffee shop to see what we can knock off. Right, Billy. You watch me and Vinny – two master craftsmen at work.'

They entered the shop and a middle-aged lady came through a door at the back, ready to serve them.

'Good morning, lads,' she said. 'What can I get you?'

'Could I have a quarter of them boiled sweets on the top shelf?' said Vinny.

She climbed up her little step-ladder and turned her back for a moment, and in that instant Mick Scully helped himself to a big handful of Caley's Double Six.

'Which ones?' asked the lady naively.

'No, not them,' said Vinny. 'I mean the humbugs in the jar next to them.'

The lady turned to get the jar down and Mick moved to take his second handful – this time Mars Bars.

The shopkeeper weighed and bagged the humbugs.

'That'll be threepence,' she said.

'Oh, heck,' said Vinny, feeling in his pockets. 'I've left

me sweet coupons on the table at home. Just save them humbugs for me, missus, and I'll be back in a minute.'

Outside the shop, Mick took out his spoils.

'Let's see,' he said. 'Four bars of Caley's, five Mars. Not bad, eh, Billy. And all free!'

'Bloody fantastic!' said Billy.

'But wait,' said Vinny. 'You were so busy watching Mick at work, you didn't see me grab these.'

Vinny produced three packets of sherbet, two bags of Pontefract cakes, and three Cadbury's Milk. Billy began to feel that he had found his true calling – a life of crime with all its attendant excitement and thrills, not to mention the haul.

After eating all their loot, they developed a monumental thirst.

'S'not so easy to swipe bottles o' pop; they're too big and bulky,' said Mick. 'It's best to get a drink at the fountain in the park.'

'That's OK,' said Vinny, 'as long as you don't use that cup on a chain. You never know who's been using that.'

After quenching their thirst, they made their way to the pitch'n' putt course which, at that time of the day and year, was deserted and unattended.

'Fancy a round of golf, old chaps?' asked Mick, indicating the locked hut.

'Why not, old boy?' replied Vinny.

Mick picked up a largish stone from a nearby rockery and tapped it gently on the window of the hut, breaking the pane. Another small tap and he began removing slivers of glass until he was able to put his hand in and open the catch. After that, it was an easy job to get inside, and Mick began handing golf irons and balls through the open window.

The trio processed through the park, whacking golf

balls for all they were worth across the spacious lawns, until they were out into Delauneys Road, where they continued their madcap game. They chortled in delight and triumph with every successful stroke until Billy hit a glorious drive straight into someone's front window, showering glass on the poor, unsuspecting occupants.

An irate householder appeared, shaking his fist.

'You stupid lot o' bastards, you. I'm gonna set the bloody police on you. You should be locked up, the bloody lot o' you.'

'Run! Run like hell, Billy!' Mick shouted. 'Or you've had it.'

They ran like the wind until they arrived, panting breathlessly, at Woodlands Road, where they chucked the golf gear over a hedge.

'So far today,' said Mick, 'we've had fags, chocolates and a game o' golf. But what we need is money.'

'So what do we do?' asked Billy.

'We do a house, that's what we do,' he answered. 'Are y'on, Vinny?'

'On,' he said.

'This is the plan,' said Mick. 'Can you whistle, Billy?'

'Yeah, I think so,' he replied, giving a demonstration.

'That's bleeding smashing,' said Mick. 'As good as Al Jolson. You can be the dog-out while me and Vinny do that house over there. If you see anyone coming, do your Jolson bit and give us time to make our getaway. Got it?'

'Got it.'

The two youths went across the road and rang the door bell several times. There was no answer and so, using a small brick, Mick broke a pane of the leaded-light window in the corner of the door, reached in, turned the Yale lock and within a minute they were inside. Aware of his responsibility, Billy kept vigil, looking alertly up and down the road, but there seemed to be no one about. Five minutes later, the two were out again.

'Eight quid,' said Mick. 'Left in a box on the dressing table. Daft buggers they are, leaving money about.'

'Told you it was easy,' said Vinny. 'Money for jam.'

'Right, Billy. That's two quid for you for dogging-out, and three for me and Vinny for doing the job. Fair enough?'

'Fair enough!' said Billy, thinking it really was the easiest money he'd ever earned.

'I think I'll call it a day,' said Mick. 'Not a bad haul, eh, lads?'

'Fancy going to the pictures tonight, anyone?' asked Vinny.

'Not me,' said Mick. 'I'm doing another job later with my older brother. We're gonna do a warehouse and we've even got a van to carry the stuff.'

'Understood, Mick,' said Vinny. 'What about you, Billy, fancy the pictures?'

'Yeah, why not?' said Billy.

When he got home that night, Mam said:

'Have a good day at school, son?'

'Not bad. I learned a lot. One day I'm gonna be rich and play golf, you'll see.'

'What next, I wonder? They're learning you some funny things at that school of yours.'

'I'm going to the pictures tonight,' he announced suddenly.

'No homework, then?'

'Not tonight,' he lied.

At six o'clock he called for Vinny again. There was the same smell of sweat and urine, but now there had been added the smell of baked beans, which made the stink even more obnoxious.

They decided on the Temple picture house, which was showing a Boris Karloff horror. They paid for their tickets, swaggered down the aisle and pushed their way along the row to two vacant seats, treading on toes and a six-inch layer of monkey-nut shells. They slouched back in their seats, put their feet on the seats in front, lit up their fags and were ready to make nuisances of themselves. Their chance soon came.

In one of the shorts, the Mills Brothers were crooning something about dry bones and how they connected.

'Rag bone connected to you,' Billy shouted out in the same rhythm.

This witticism seemed to cause amusement to most of the cinema except the usher, who came rushing down the aisle.

'Any more of that and you're out,' he said, flashing his torch at them.

'You wanna fumigate this bleeding place,' Vinny called out to him. 'The bugs are taking it over. I came in here with a pullover and I'm going out with a jumper.'

During the big picture, the hero said to his girl: 'I love you darling but I have only one worry.'

'Me glass eye might fall out,' shouted Billy.

Later the handsome hero was saying: 'There is only one thing I desire in life.'

'Ten Woodbines and a box of matches,' Vinny yelled.

'But that's two things!' Billy called out.

'That's it,' shouted the usher. 'You two, out! And don't bloody well come back!'

They found themselves on Cheetham Hill Road.

'It's only nine o'clock,' said Vinny. 'Let's go to Lorenzelli's Milk Bar and see if we can pick up a coupla birds.'

Lorenzelli's was crowded that night.

'Two hot Vimtos!' Vinny ordered.

They took their drinks and sat down next to two girls, about fifteen years old, one blonde and one brunette – both of whom were chewing gum and wearing long, dangling ear-rings. Vinny looked them up and down.

'Wharra you lookin' at?' Blondie said. 'Whadda you want – a photograph or summat?'

'Wouldn't mind a bit o' summat if you've got any to spare,' said Vinny. 'Anyroad, evening, girls, nice weather for this time o' the year.'

'Bloody hell,' said Blondie. 'He'll be asking if we come here often next.'

'Well, do you?' asked Billy mischievously.

'Do we wha'?' asked the brunette, who was the less pretty of the two.

'Come here often,' he replied.

'Depends what you mean by often,' she retorted.

It looked as if the conversation might continue on this semantic level for some time, but Vinny changed its direction.

'Wanna fag?' he said, offering his packet of twenty Players.

'Don't mind if we do,' they both said with alacrity, removing the chewing gum and sticking it under the table.

'I say, we *are* posh, smoking Players. Me and Doris can only ever afford Woodbines.'

'What do you both do, then?'

'We both work at Woolworth's. She's Toys and I'm Toffees. She's Doris and I'm Elsie.'

'Billy and Vinny,' said Vinny. 'Pleased to meet you. And if ever I wanna buy summat under a tanner, I'll know where to come.'

The chatting-up process continued on this level until ten thirty, when the milk bar closed.

'We'll see you both home,' said Vinny.

'You don't half fancy your chances, don't you?' said Elsie. 'All right, then. Wait outside and me and Doris'll just go to the toilet.'

Whilst they were waiting outside, Vinny said:

'Elsie's mine and Doris is yours. See, I think this Elsie fancies me.'

'Thanks, Vinny,' said Billy. 'So I get the ugly one.'

'You know what they say about not looking at the mantelpiece.'

The two girls reappeared and Vinny said:

'I don't know what it is you girls do in the toilet but you both look smashing. Fancy a walk in Manley Park or wha'?'

'Don't mind if I do,' said Doris, linking her arm into Billy's.

They found their way to Manley Park shed and the four of them sat there smoking Players, blowing the smoke across the glowing cigarette ends.

'Whadda you say we stay out all night?' suggested Vinny.

'I'm game if you are, Doris,' said Elsie.

'Awright, then,' said Doris. 'It'll be a bit of a laugh. But what about work tomorrow, Elsie?'

'Oh, bugger work,' she said. 'I'm fed up with the bloody job anyway. Let the supervisor try serving just for a change.'

So it was decided. But no one, except Billy, noticed that Billy hadn't been consulted. It looked as if he were outvoted anyway.

Vinny moved with Elsie to a dark corner of the shed, and Billy could hear lots of furtive fumblings, which lasted the whole night with murmurs of, 'No, don't, Vinny. Don't do that. I don't allow it on the first date.' Then, 'Ah, Vinny, that's better.'

As for Billy and Doris, they sat most of the night smoking Billy's fags.

'You can put your hand here,' she said, placing his hand on her breast. 'I don't mind.'

'Thanks very much,' he said.

He remained in that position for most of the night, his right hand round her shoulder and his left hand on her breast over her dress. He could feel nothing but a hard lump and the unyielding material of a strongly built brassière. He was tempted to go further but didn't because it was much too cold, the wooden seats were too hard and uncomfortable, and besides, he didn't fancy her. He would have preferred the blonde and he was annoyed that Vinny had simply assumed that he could automatically have the prettier girl.

They watched the dawn come up, and feeling utterly washed out, grubby and dishevelled, they parted company.

'Billy,' said Doris, 'I think you're a real gentleman. Anyone else would have tried it on, but I liked the way you kept your hands to yourself. I don't believe two people should go too far on their first date, do you?'

'Dead right, Doris,' Billy said. 'That's the way I feel.'

'Or, in your case, Billy, didn't feel. Anyroad,' she said, 'I hope we see each other again in Lorenzelli's.'

'Hope so, Doris.'

On the walk back home, Billy said:

'Eh, Vinny, I've found out two things about girls tonight. First, why do you think they wear brassières?'

'To stop their tits from falling down, I suppose.'

'That's one reason. The other is to give 'em a suit of armour so a lad can't get his hand in there. You'd have needed an acetylene lamp to get into that Doris's bra.'

'What's the other thing you found out?'

'The less you want them, the more they want you. And

the more you want them, the less they want you.'

'That gives us a problem, then,' said Vinny. 'It means we can only ever have it off with the girls we don't want it with.'

'That's right. So if we don't want it with 'em, we won't have it with 'em.'

'You've got me bleeding beat there, Billy. All this bleeding education stuff is over my head. I just hope that you're wrong.'

They got back to Gardenia Court at six o'clock in the morning, and Armageddon in the shape of his dad was waiting for Billy.

'Where the bleeding hell do you think you've been all night?' he bawled as Billy opened the front door.

'Just sitting in a park shed with Vinny Buckley,' he mumbled.

'You stupid bleeding get,' he said, striking Billy across the head with each word. 'Do you know we've had the police out looking for you? Do you know I've lost a day's work today because of you?'

'We haven't done any harm,' stuttered Billy.

'Haven't done any harm! Haven't done any harm! I told you to keep away from that bleeding Buckley family. They're bloody riff-raff and they'll take you down with 'em. After we've encouraged you to go to college to make summat of yourself, you want to end up with that bleeding lot who'll have you in Strangeways afore you know where you are. You've worried your mother out of her mind all night. Haven't we had enough trouble, being bombed out and losing our Jim, without you going off the rails and all? Anyroad, you come with me.'

He took Billy by the scruff of the neck and forced him down to the Buckley flat, where he banged noisily on the door.

Vinny opened the door.

'What the bloody hell . . . !'

Before he had finished his sentence, Billy's dad had grabbed him by the shoulders.

'If ever I see you near my son again, I'll belt the bleeding living daylights out o' you. I'll bleeding swing for you, d'you hear?'

'Yeah, Mr Hopkins. But we haven't done nowt wrong.'

'Whether y'ave or y'aven't, I don't care. Just keep away. And as for you, our Billy, get up to bed afore I really lose my temper.'

A week later, Mick Scully was arrested with his brother for burglary and sent to Borstal for five years. One month after that, Vinny Buckley was caught house-breaking and sentenced to three years in the same institution.

Dad's punishment was bad enough, but Mam's was infinitely worse. For a whole week, Billy got the fish-eye treatment and his mother became stony-faced whenever he tried to speak to her. For a whole week she froze him out with that glassy-eyed stare of hers, and if she spoke to him at all, it was in monosyllables.

'I'm very sorry about last week, Mam,' he said.

'Oh, aye,' she said, not taking her eyes off the potatoes she was peeling.

'I didn't mean any harm and it won't happen again.'

'So you say,' she said, slicing up the potatoes for chips.

'A funny thing happened today at school, Mam.'

'Oh, aye,' she said, without looking up from the stove.

'During the PT lesson, a lad threw a fit.'

'Oh, aye,' she said, all her attention on the chips.

'He was foaming at the mouth and talking a funny language.'

'I dare say,' she said, concentrating hard on the frying pan.

'The teacher had to hold his tongue down with a ruler.'

'Oh, aye,' she said, moving the chips around the pan.

'Then they sent for the ambulance and he was taken away to Prestwich Asylum.'

'Oh, aye,' she replied, focusing on the loaf of bread she was cutting up.

By the end of the week, Billy was almost climbing up the wall to get her attention.

'If I stand on my head and sing "I'm an Old Cow-Hand" will you forgive me and talk to me?'

She almost smiled.

'Come on, Mam, give us a smile. It won't happen again. Honestly. I promise. I've been in Coventry for a week and I can't stand any more.'

'Oh, very well, you daft little bugger. Come here.'

She gave him a big hug.

'Just make sure you behave yourself in future. Anyroad, what happened to that lad they took to Prestwich Asylum?'

'Oh, him. They found he was all right in the end, after his mam started talking to him again.'

'I'm not kidding, our Billy, you are a daft bugger. Sometimes, I think you *should* be in a bloody asylum.'

'As long as you don't freeze me out like that again, I'll be all right.'

'What you need is an interest apart from all that studying you do at that school. Where were you in class last time?'

'Eighth, Mam. And that's without killing meself. If I really got my head down, I could be in the first five.'

'I'll have to see if your father can get you some more fish from the market. Talking of your father, why don't you go and give him a helping hand sometime? He'd like that, and maybe you and him can get back on friendly terms again.'

* * *

The following Saturday, Billy was up at three o'clock in the morning to go and help his dad in Smithfield Market. He dressed quickly and Dad made a quick brew before they set off.

'I don't know how you do this every morning, Dad,' Billy said. 'I feel as if I've just gone to bed.'

'You get used to it. Anyroad, come on, we can't sit here all day. We've got work to do. And remember there's no buses at this time in the morning.'

They strode swiftly the four miles to Smithfield Market – Billy hardly able to keep up with Dad's rapid stride. They arrived at four o'clock, and even at that early hour the market was already a hive of noisy, bustling, chaotic activity as the giant lorries discharged their loads of fruit and vegetables brought in from every corner of England.

Dad unlocked his cart and pushed it to his normal pitch in the centre of the market, where he sat on it waiting for custom. He hadn't long to wait.

Ely Entwistle, Choice Fruiterer and Greengrocer of Bury, approached him.

'How do, Tommy. Can you pick up me order for me?'

'How do, Ely. Aye, go on then. What is it?' asked Dad.

'Six cod at Holbrook's, ten taters, five cabbage, four caulies at Deakin's, eight apples at Smith's, seven straw-berries at Keegan's, nine plums at Blundell's. Awreet?'

'That's a seven-an'-a-tanner job, Ely. Leave it to me,' replied Dad. Billy noticed that he wrote nothing down.

Like Stanley Matthews streaking down the wing, Tommy dodged and weaved his way through several bottlenecks of vehicles, whose drivers hooted and swore at one another in frustration.

Within an hour, Dad had loaded up all the orders and, with the strength of a donkey, pulled the heavily weighted cart along the cobbled market road.

'Push, Billy! Push!' he called to Billy at the back of the cart.

A few minutes later they found Ely's lorry parked on the edge of the market.

'You're a bloody good worker, Tommy,' said Ely. 'Here's ten bob. S'worth every penny. Will y'have a few things to tek home?'

'Aye, ta,' said Dad, helping himself to some fish and a selection of fruit and veg which he put into a canvas shopping bag hanging on the back of the cart.

'See you on Monday then, Tommy,' shouted Ely.

Billy and his dad then returned to his pitch to await further customers. They worked in this way all that Saturday morning – hard and fast – until eleven o'clock, when at last the pace began to slow down and the market became relatively quiet, by which time Billy was dropping with exhaustion.

'Here y'are, Billy, here's half a crown for you. You've earned it. You go on home and take these few things to your mother. I'll go and have a quick one or two in the Hare and Hounds afore I finish.'

'I never knew until now how hard your work was, Dad.'

'It gets easy when you've been at it for over forty years.'

Billy caught the 62 bus and made his weary way back home, carrying the canvas bag laden with fish, fruit and vegetables. As he walked through the door, he sang:

'*Show me the way to go home, I'm tired and I wanna go to bed.*'

He collapsed on to his bed and was asleep in ten seconds.

★　★　★

Shortly after that, following his mam's suggestion about taking up an interest, Billy decided to go for piano lessons. In fact he had taught himself to play by ear – mostly out of tune – on his sister Pauline's upright, driving the young Keenan family out of their minds in the process. His favourite piece was a distorted, discordant rendering of Rachmaninov's Prelude, complete with melodramatic commentary about a man buried alive in his coffin – which sent delicious shivers of horror down the spines of his two young nephews, Oliver and Danny.

> *'Now he's banging on the lid of the coffin.*
> *Now he's squirming, trying to get out.*
> *Now he's yelling for someone to help him.*
> *Now he's weeping quietly – almost given up.*
> *Now he's getting weaker.*
> *Now he's given up hope.*
> *Now he's dead.'*

'You could get a job in a pub playing that,' said Pauline.

'He'd soon empty it,' said Steve. 'They could use him at closing time instead of calling "Time, gentlemen, please." Just get him to play that piece and he'd clear the pub in thirty seconds flat.'

Billy thought it was time he learned to play properly, and it was with this in mind that he knocked on the door of Miss Lois de Lacy, LRAM.

'Do you give piano lessons?'

'I do, but I usually take on toddlers – just starting. How old are you?' said Miss de Lacy.

'I'm nearly fifteen but I'd like to start from the very beginning.'

'Very well, then. But I warn you, I'm more accustomed to teaching five-year-olds.'

At the first lesson, Miss de Lacy, all lace and dangly bits of jewellery, announced brightly:

'This is a piano!'

Acting the fool, Billy deliberately approached the sideboard.

'What – this?' he asked.

Miss de Lacy didn't blink or smile, thinking perhaps that she'd taken on a moron.

'No, this,' she replied, pointing to the piano.

'Got it!'

'These are the low notes,' she said, playing a bass chord. 'They sound like big bad bears, don't they?'

'And these are the high notes,' she said, playing a rippling arpeggio at the top of the keyboard. 'They are like little fairies tripping through the forest.'

'Got it.'

At the end of this introductory lesson he was given his first pieces of homework to practise. The first item required the playing of crotchets on one note – middle C – to the words of a song entitled 'Crunchy Flakes'.

'*Crunchy flakes! Crunchy flakes!*' he sang. '*Give you all – that it takes!*'

He played this over and over again as Miss de Lacy had instructed until he could execute it perfectly. Whilst he was practising and singing thus, Pauline decided quite suddenly and without any warning or explanation to take the children for a walk. When she returned, Billy had progressed to his second piece – a much more challenging number, entitled 'The Woodchuck'. The performance of this composition demanded singing and accompanying himself on two notes – middle C and G.

'*If a woodchuck could chuck wood,*' he trilled and played. '*How much wood would he chuck?*'

'If there's any chucking to be done,' said Pauline,

interrupting him, 'I suggest you chuck up learning to play the piano before you drive us all bonkers.'

'I can take a hint,' said Billy. 'But I like music, and as you know, we're not allowed to play musical instruments in the flats. If you'd let me practise here I wouldn't mind taking up the trombone or a trumpet, or maybe drums.'

'No, no,' she said hurriedly. 'Try something a bit quieter, like soft-shoe dancing. Wait a minute, I've got it! Ballroom dancing! That's it!'

And that was how Billy got himself into the world of Victor Sylvester and Harrigan's Dance Academy on Queen's Road.

Chapter Twenty-Two

Dancing In The Dark

Towards the end of 1943, things began to happen. General Eisenhower announced an armistice with Italy; the big three, Churchill, Roosevelt and Stalin, met in Tehran; Marine Sam Hopkins landed at Naples and had Mussolini on the run; young Les Hopkins, accompanied by the rest of the Eighth Army, fought his way up the boot of Italy; the bombing of Manchester ceased and the Blackpool evacuees, including the incorrigible Brother Dorian – as dictatorial as ever – returned to Manchester, the funny business at the Martindale bungalow forgotten; Flo at long last got her man and married Sergeant Barry Healey; and Billy learned to dance.

'Forward left foot – side right foot – close. Forward right foot – side left foot – close,' recited Billy, book in hand, as he practised his steps down the lobby of their flat.

'What is it you're doing now, our Billy? You're allus up to summat,' Mam said.

'Dancing, Mam. I'm learning the waltz from this book, *Ballroom Dancing Made Easy*. Forward left foot – side right foot – close. Wait a minute. I'm right up against the wall. What do I do now? This book doesn't tell you what to do when you come up against a solid object.'

'You'll never learn how to dance from a book, you daft ha'porth. You need to be learnt properly by a teacher, you need music, and most of all, you need a partner.'

'You're right, Mam. Lend us a coupla bob and I'll try Harrigan's Dance Academy on Queen's Road tonight.'

At seven o'clock, Billy turned up at Harrigan's and paid over his two shillings to a little old lady in the box office.

'Your two shillings covers the lesson and the dance afterwards,' she explained. 'Monday's the waltz, Wednesday's the slow foxtrot and Friday's the quickstep.'

'And Tuesdays and Thursdays?'

'They're for advanced only – South American dances, tango and rumba.'

Billy went through and saw several groups of men and women each being taught by different teachers.

'Over here!' called a giant of a man who, judging by his misshapen nose and his cauliflower ear, had once been a boxer.

Billy went over and joined a group of five other men.

'I'm Lofty O'Malley,' said the giant, raising both arms above his head. 'Your dance teacher. Tonight we're gonna learn the waltz. Get behind me and do just as I do. Ready! And – forward left – side right – close. Forward right – side left – close.'

Lofty waltzed forward gracefully and lightly like a butterfly whilst the six learners followed behind, walking stiffly like men trying out artificial legs.

'Watch yourself in the mirrors,' Lofty called over his shoulder, indicating the large wall mirrors which surrounded them.

Billy caught a glimpse of himself and was taken aback to see a tall, lanky boy of fifteen dancing behind Lofty.

'Gosh – is that really me?' he said aloud. 'I look so skinny and my nose looks as if it's outgrown my face.'

'That's you all right,' said Lofty. 'Don't worry about being on the thin side, though. That can only help your dancing. Look at Fred Astaire. Don't know about your nose, though; you'll have to wait for the rest of your face to catch up. But I'll swap noses with you any day.'

The rest of the lesson was taken up practising. Lofty took the girl's part, and he and Billy made a strange sight indeed as they waltzed round together – a gawky youth and a seventeen-stone bruiser.

After the lessons, old Mrs Harrigan, the lady from the box office, who looked even smaller standing up, announced through the microphone:

'And now you will have a chance to practise all that you've learnt this evening with our instructors, who are waiting in the centre of the floor to welcome you. We begin with the waltz. I'll come round and allocate the ladies and Lofty will do the same for the men.'

'Miss Lucy!' Lofty called, holding Billy's arm above his head like a referee declaring the winner of a boxing match.

Soon, calls of 'Miss Rosy!' 'Mr David!' 'Miss Joyce!' 'Mr Philip!' echoed all round the maple-floored ballroom until all the instructors had a learner each. The four-piece band struck up with the 'Fascination Waltz' and they were off.

Lucy was a young, slim sixteen-year-old with a pretty face, light-brown hair tied back with a ribbon, and a little attractive, turned-up nose.

'I hope I don't stand on your toes,' he said. 'I'm an absolute novice – so you'll have to be patient.'

'That's OK,' she smiled. 'That's what we're paid for, and I'm wearing me special steel-capped dancing shoes. First, place your right hand under me left shoulder blade.'

'Like this?' he said.

'That's it. No need to be shy about it. We're only dancing – you're not making love to me or anything like that. Now, take my right hand in your other hand and lift your arm to shoulder height. Does that feel comfortable?'

'Strange but OK.'

'Now, we move. Ready... in time to the music... And – one – two – three. Forward right – side – close. That's it.'

Together they began to move around the ballroom – Billy somewhat awkwardly, Lucy easily and gracefully.

'There's a big difference between dancing with you and dancing with Lofty,' he said.

'About ten stone difference,' she said. 'You know, you move quite well for a novice. You're quite light on your feet.'

'Well, like you, I'm not exactly a heavyweight. I used to do boxing and that teaches you to be light on your feet.'

'I think you could make a very good dancer if you put your mind to it. You never know, you might be another Fred Astaire.'

'Funny you should say that. Lofty just said I looked like him – a regular bag o'bones.'

'Well, that's a start anyroad.'

'You dance beautifully,' he told her. 'How long have you been at it?'

'I started just after leaving school. So it must be about two years now.'

'I wish I could reach your standard.'

'Nowt to stop you if you work hard enough at it.'

When the waltz had finished, Billy returned to his place and spent the rest of the evening simply observing.

'Now we have a demonstration of the slow foxtrot by Miss Lucy and Mr Lofty,' Mrs Harrigan informed everyone through her microphone.

Admiringly, Billy watched the couple glide across the floor so elegantly and so effortlessly to the tune 'I'll Be Seeing You'. As they floated by, Lucy gave Billy a broad smile which he returned with a surreptitious wink.

One day, he vowed to himself, I'll be the one doing that demonstration.

At the end of the evening, he met Lucy as she was about to leave.

'Which way do you go?' he asked, politely.

'I live in the flats.'

'So do I! Not Gardenia Court?'

'No, Hazlewood House.'

'Is it OK if we walk back together?'

'All right, I don't mind.'

'I'd love to be able to dance like you,' he said as they made their way along Queen's Road. 'You must have had private lessons, surely?'

'No, I didn't. I learned all me dancing in my spare time at Harrigan's.'

'I don't think I can afford to go to Harrigan's three or four times a week.'

'It is a bit dear, though not as dear as having private lessons with the top professionals like Frank Rogers or Archie Lamont. Don't you have a job?'

'No. I'm still studying at school. But I could look for a part-time job, I suppose.'

'Still studying at your age? I'm surprised anyone stays on after fourteen. Me, I hated school. Just seemed like a waste o' time. I could hardly wait to leave.'

'What do you do now, Lucy?'

'I work at the biscuit factory; it's a bit boring packing biscuits all day – that's why I took up dancing. At least I have summat interesting in my life. And the money I earn is good – it's helped me to pay for my lessons at Harrigan's.'

'I've got another year before I leave school.'

'You're lucky, if you're good at schoolwork. Not like me, a bit thick.'

'I'm sure you're not thick, but why do you say I'm lucky?'

'Well, if you go on to college, you'll end up in an interesting, well-paid job. Not like me – a skivvy in a biscuit factory.'

'But sometimes, school and all the studying I have to do seem like a waste of time. I'm always desperately short of cash and it's then I'm tempted to leave and take a job.'

'Don't talk daft. If you've got the opportunity to do summat useful with your life, don't throw it away. You could end up in a really boring job like mine.'

'It's just . . . well . . . when I see you dancing . . . like I did tonight, I'm tempted to jack it all in and start enjoying life a bit.'

'Look, dancing is the one and only thing I've got in my life. It's what helps me to get by. At work, we're like a bit of the machinery, having to keep up with it all the time. But at night, after I've got away . . . well, it's then I come to life. Dancing gives me a chance to express meself . . . to be me and not just part of a conveyor belt.'

'Still, I wish I could dance half as good as you.'

'Look,' she said suddenly, 'if you're really serious about wanting to learn, I could teach you at weekends.'

'Honestly? That'd be great. But where?'

'Why not on the rooftop of the flats?' she said, warming to the idea. 'I used to go up there sometimes in the nice weather – sunbathing. There's plenty of room for dancing – it's even bigger than Harrigan's dance floor. I could bring my portable gramophone and some Victor Sylvester records.'

'Lucy, you're marvellous. But why're you doing it? What do you get out of it?'

'I like teaching, that's all. And you never know, I might get Fred Astaire as a partner.'

'Thanks a lot, Lucy.'

'There's just one thing, though,' she said, turning serious. 'I mean dancing only, and no trying it on with me or anything like that.'

'Sorry, I'm not with you.'

'You know what I mean. Getting fresh and that.'

'Promise, Lucy. Cross my heart.'

They reached Hazlewood House.

'This is where I live. What's your name, by the way?'

'Billy or William – take your pick.'

'Billy's a nice name. I'll take that. See you on Sunday afternoon. Call round at two o'clock. I live at number ten.'

'It's a date,' he said. 'Good night, Lucy.'

'Good night, Billy. Be seeing you. Remember, though – just dancing and no messing about. No hanky-panky.'

'Hanky-panky? Never crossed my mind.'

'Not even once?'

'No, not even once.'

'Well, then I feel slighted and insulted,' she said, laughing.

'I'll never understand girls. Good night again, Lucy.'

Billy went home that night with a light step, a song in his heart and a whistle on his lips.

'How did you get on at Harrigan's, son?' Mam asked.

'It was great, Mam. I danced with a seventeen-stone boxer and a girl called Lucy. And I think I'm in love.'

'Oh, aye,' she said. 'Who with? The boxer or the girl?'

'Don't be funny, Mam. I think I know now what I want to do with my life.'

'You keep changing your mind every five minutes. One minute it's a boxer, then a writer, then a teacher, then a navigator. What is it today?'

'Professional ballroom dancer.'

'What next! Don't be so daft, you'd never earn a living as one o' them fellas wearing tights and prancing about the stage showing all they've got.'

'That's ballet, Mam. This is ballroom, and I'll tell you summat – it's a lot more interesting than all that boring stuff we're doing at school.'

'If you're going to be a teacher or a writer like you say, you'll have to stick it out at school and pass your exams. If you like dancing, keep it as your hobby. Anyroad, where are you going to get the money to keep going to Harrigan's?'

'Well, for a start, Lucy's going to teach me for nothing on Sunday afternoons. But you know, Mam, I get really fed up always being short of money. I think I'd be better leaving school, finding myself a job and getting a bob or two in my pocket.'

'You do talk barmy sometimes, our Billy. What was the point in us making all them sacrifices, pawning Granny's teapot and all that, if you're going to throw it all away just when you're nearly finished and the end is in sight?'

'Do you realise, Mam, that just at this moment I haven't got two ha'pennies to rub together?'

'I know. I know. I can't afford to give you any more. It's hard enough finding your bus fare every day. I know you don't like being without money in your pocket, but you could stop smoking for a start.'

'I smoke three Park Drive a day. That costs about tuppence ha'penny. I haven't even got that for tomorrow unless I walk the six miles to school.'

'There's a few empty mineral bottles in the cupboard. You could take them back. That'd give you tuppence ha'penny.'

'Right, thanks, Mam. That'll give me a smoke tomorrow, at least.'

'Why don't you look for a part-time job?'

'I could start chopping wood again, or deliver papers, I suppose.'

'No, I don't mean that. You could help your dad in the market on Sat'days. That'd give you a coupla bob.'

'But don't you see, Mam? It's just scrimping and scraping all the time. Cadging a penny here and a penny there just to keep going.'

'Well, no matter what you say, our Billy, you're not leaving school and that's that. Why don't you ask that pal you're allus going on about – Robin what's-his-name – if you can help him and his dad delivering tea on Sat'days?'

'You know, Mam, that's the best idea I've heard all week. I'll ask him at school tomorrow.'

Chapter Twenty-Three

Hands Across The Sea

The next day, Billy made a point of finding Robin at the mid-morning break.

'I'm looking for a part-time job, Robin,' he said. 'Any chance of me helping you and your dad with tea deliveries at weekends?'

'Funny you should say that, Hoppy. My dad just made a big delivery to the new American Red Cross canteen they've opened in St Anne's Square for American service-men from Burtonwood, and the manager was asking him if he knew of two likely lads for an evening job shining shoes in the men's barber shop.'

'Sounds interesting. What's the deal?'

'Hours four thirty to seven o'clock. No pay – tips only. But they should be pretty good as the Yanks are very well paid. Our troops are always saying they're over-sexed, over-paid and over here.'

'They're just jealous. I don't know about over-sexed and all that, but as for being over-paid, I read somewhere that a Yankee private is paid five times as much as one of ours, and that an American sergeant gets more than a British captain.'

'Do you fancy giving it a try then, Hoppy? Or do you

think cleaning boots is stooping too low?'

'No, I don't mind cleaning boots as long as I don't have to lick 'em. What about homework?'

'We get at least two private study periods a day. So we should be able to do homework then.'

'You seem to have thought of everything, Robin. We'll go down together and apply for the job.'

The two boys presented themselves to the GI barber shop after school and got the job on a trial basis.

'A smart khaki uniform complete with GI hat goes with the job,' the head barber said. 'The Yanks like their employees to look smart – and that goes for even the shoe-shine boys.'

'In uniform at last,' said Robin. 'And look at these swish shoulder flashes saying "American Red Cross" with the Red Cross emblem underneath.'

'People are going to think we're a coupla surgeons, Robin.'

'In a way we are. Foot specialists.'

The next night, the two of them turned up for their first stint of duty. The music being played through the PA system was Bing Crosby's 'Shoe Shine Boy'.

'Why, they're playing our song, Robin,' said Billy.

'That's OK, Hoppy, as long as it's not "Lazy Bones".'

It wasn't long before they got their first customers – two GIs in the Army Air Force.

'Hi, there,' one of them said, sitting in the raised chair. 'I'm Tex and this is my buddy Rick. How's about a shoe-shine, boys?'

'Sure thing,' said Robin, adopting the American idiom. 'I'm Robin and this here is my pal, Hoppy. We're both students.'

'Stoodents, eh? Working your way through college.

That's what we Americans like to see. Get-up-'n'-go. I hated school myself. Didn't seem to get the hang of it no-how. Now, every time I pass my old high school, I nearly matriculate. You hear what I'm saying?'

They placed their feet on the shoe-stand. Billy and Robin took one look at their boots and their spirits plummeted, for both soldiers had size 10s richly encrusted in thick mud. The two apprentice shoe-shiners took in a deep breath and began scraping off the mud.

'We just flew down from doing manoeuvres in the Scottish hills,' said Rick. 'Boy, that Scotland is some place, I tell ya. What kinda language do they talk up there? All that "och aye" and "hoots mon" stuff. Sure beats me – just Double Dutch.'

'It sure is good to get back to Lancasheer where we talk the same lingo, eh, Hoppy,' said Tex.

'We're two great nations divided by a common language.'

'Say, that's pretty cute,' replied Tex. 'Whadda you two guys studying?'

'Oh, the usual stuff,' said Robin. 'Maths, languages, English literature, Shakespeare – that kind of thing.'

'Oh, Shakespeare, you mean all that "Hey nonny, nonny" crap?' said Rick.

'That's right,' said Billy, now beginning to apply brown shoe polish to Rick's footwear. 'We're studying *The Tempest* and *Julius Caesar*.'

'Ah tell ya,' said Tex. 'Last month in London, Ah was shacked up with this real classy broad. She took me to the theatre to see this Shakespeare guy. *Hamlet, Macbeth* and then *King Lear*. Boy, did those guys have problems! By the end of each play, everyone was mincemeat. Worse than Al Capone's St Valentine's massacre, Ah tell ya. Y'know what I'm saying?'

'I reckon this Shakespeare guy is over-rated,' said Rick. 'Ya see one of his plays, you've seen 'em all. Say, I once knew one of these high-brow dames in New York – crazy about opera, she was. She took me to the Met to see an opera called *The Valkyrie* by a guy called Wagner.'

'Oh, yeah. What was that about, Rick?' asked Tex.

'Don't rightly know, Tex. But there was this big fat guy wailing something in German and some huge, big-assed broad, as big as a house, with a kinda kettle on her head screaming the same thing over and over again. Sounded like "I-will-I-won't-I-will-I-won't".'

'A guy told me that them operas last a real long time.'

'Long? Well, I tell ya, Tex. The show started at seven o'clock. Three hours later, I looked at my watch. It was seven-fifteen. You unnerstand what I'm saying?'

'Yeah. So I guess we'll just stick to the good old movies – Bogie and Edward G. Whatcha got planned for tonight, Rick?' asked Tex.

'Ah got myself a whole pack o' rubbers and I'm gonna get myself laid until I've used up the whole pack. Either of you two guys got any sisters?'

'Sorry,' said Robin. 'Can't help you there, fellas.'

'I've got two,' said Billy. 'But they're both married.'

'Hell, that don't matter none,' said Rick. 'I'd be willing to keep 'em both happy and satisfied if their husbands are away. Come to think of it – even if their husbands ain't away.'

'Sorry, can't help you there, Rick.'

The shoe-shining operation was in the final stages and both boys began cracking their polishing cloths and buffing the shoe leather for all they were worth.

'Well, Hoppy,' said Rick. 'You've made a darned fine job o' my boots. Why, you can see your face in 'em. How much is that, now?'

'That'll be threepence, Rick,' said Billy.

'Here,' said Rick, tossing over a half-crown. 'Keep the change, son. You've earned it.'

'Gee, thanks, Rick,' said Billy.

'I never could figure out this funny money o' yours,' said Tex. 'But the same goes for you, Robin. Keep the change and put it towards your studying.'

'Gosh, thanks a million, Tex,' said Robin.

The two soldiers got down from the stand.

'Be seeing you, guys,' said Rick. 'And remember, Hoppy, if them sisters o' yours ever need any special comforting, you let me know, you hear?'

When they'd gone, Billy turned to Robin and said:

'I think I'm gonna like this job. If we keep up this rate of earning, we'll be rich by seven o'clock.'

'Yeah,' said Robin, 'and I like the way these GIs talk to us as if we're adults. It makes me feel all grown-up.'

The music over the PA changed to Irving Berlin's 'My British Buddy'. The next two soldiers were already waiting.

'I'm Ev and this here ugly-looking guy with the cigar is Bob. Maybe you could fix him up with a new face. If not, we'll settle for a shoe-shine.'

'I'm Hoppy and this is Robin. Shoe-shines a-coming up right away – sir!'

Without preamble, the cigar-smoking Bob handed Billy a photograph, as if giving him a visiting card.

'Is this your family?' asked Billy in amazement.

'Yep, it certainly is, young sir,' Bob replied. 'That there's my wife, Lee, and that's young Robert junior, aged ten. The old guy is my pop. Ain't they a swell-looking family?'

'They sure are, Bob,' replied Billy, getting down to the mud-removing business.

'You said your name's Hoppy. Any relation to Hopalong Cassidy?' asked Ev.

''Fraid not,' said Billy. 'But I'm a distant relation of Buffalo Bill.'

'You don't say,' said Ev. 'How's about that? You hear that, Bob? This guy's related to William F. Cody. Good job you ain't doing the barbering around here, Hoppy, or you'd be taking a few scalps, I guess.'

'I heard what you were saying just now to Tex and Rick about us having a different language and all,' said Bob, 'and I reckon you've certainly got something there. I just came back from my hotel and when I asked the desk clerk to give me an early call, she asked me what time I wanted to be knocked up. I tell ya, don't know about knocked *up*, you could've knocked me *down* with a feather.'

'Here in Lancashire,' said Billy, 'we have a man who goes round the streets very early in the morning with a long pole just knocking people up. He's called a knocker-upper.'

'You don't say! Now that's what I call a real man's job. And this guy's got a very long pole, you say. I reckon he needs one with a job like that.'

'You know,' said Ev, 'we've been given a little booklet explaining things about you Limeys, Hoppy. Lemme read a little bit from it: "If British civilians look dowdy and badly dressed, it is not because they do not like good clothes . . . All clothing is rationed . . . Don't make fun of British speech. You sound just as funny to them." Do we sound funny to you, Hoppy?'

'Not funny, but different,' answered Billy tactfully. 'We pronounce words differently. For example, you say ske-dule and we say she-dule.'

'So instead of saying, "It's our scheme to be scholars

384

in school", you guys would say, "It's our sheme to be sholars at shool." '

Billy and Robin laughed.

'It just goes to show,' said Billy, 'how crazy our pronunciation is. But apart from that, we also use words differently. Look, I'll say a word and you tell me what you understand by it. Ready? Bum.'

'Hobo,' said Ev.

'For us, that means backside or arse,' said Robin.

'For "arse",' said Bob, 'we say "butt" or "fanny".'

'For the English,' said Billy, ' "fanny" is on the other side of the body. Try this – petrol.'

'Gas,' said Ev.

'That's indigestion or idle chatter for us,' said Robin.

'What about "sidewalk"?' said Bob.

'To us,' said Robin, 'that's the pavement.'

'And for us,' said Ev, 'pavement's the middle of the road. That could lead to really disastrous consequences given the wrong instructions.'

'Try this sentence,' said Billy. ' "I'm mad about my flat." What does that mean to you?'

'That means,' said Bob, 'I'm darned angry 'cos my automobile has a puncture.'

'For us,' said Billy, 'it means that I'm really excited about my apartment. So you see what I mean about two languages. You just used the word "Limey", Ev. What does that mean?'

'Why, that's a word we use to mean someone British. Comes from the time when the British used to drink lime juice to fight against scurvy on board their ships. We Yanks just called 'em Limeys, I guess.'

'And that word "Yank", that's a funny word as well,' said Robin. 'What's it mean? Anyone know?'

'There's an argument about that word, Robin,' said

Bob. 'Some say it means "Janke", or Dutch for "Johnny", from the time when the Dutch ruled over New York. It was called New Amsterdam then. Others claim that "Yankees" is the Red Indian way of saying "English". No one really knows.'

'Say, what is this?' said Ev. 'Some kinda college or a shoe-shine stand? I'm learning fast. But what gets me is the way you Limeys have everything the wrong way round. You pile all your food on to a fork with your knife. We just need a fork.'

'I must admit you've got me there,' said Billy.

'Yeah,' said Bob. 'And you go into a shop to buy something and everybody keeps saying thank you the whole time. I bought a candy bar in a store yesterday and had to say thank you four times before they'd let me outa the joint. And whenever I ask for directions, the guy always says, "You can't miss it." '

'Say, Hoppy,' said Ev, 'why do you British like bathtubs? Who wants to sit in his own dirty water? We Americans always like to take a shower. Don't you think it's more hygienic?'

'Well, we British like to make sure we're clean before we take a bath – then we just like to sit there and soak all our cares away.'

At this point the GI boots were being given their finishing touches with the polishing cloth.

'That's what I call a shoe-shine,' said Ev, handing over a half-crown to Robin. 'I learned a lot from you two guys tonight. Thanks a lot. One last question, though. Exactly what is the name of this country of yours? Is it England? Britain? Great Britain? Or just plain United Kingdom?'

'None of those,' said Billy. 'It's just plain United Kingdom of Great Britain and Northern Ireland.'

'How about that!' exclaimed Ev.

'That really is a great shine, and it's been most interesting talking to you, Hoppy, and to you, Robin,' said Bob, tossing a half-crown in payment for his threepenny shoe-shine. 'Keep the change, Hoppy. Worth every cent. Here's a coupla Hershey bars and a packet of rubbers.'

And he stuffed the items into Billy's top pocket before he could protest.

'Thanks for the Hershey bars, Bob. Don't know about the rubbers, though.'

'You mean you're still a virgin, or you don't use 'em?'

'Both, Bob.'

'It's about time you tried, boy. All you need is a pair of nylons and you're away.'

'Never wear 'em, Bob.'

'Huh, funny guy, eh? Tell you what I'm gonna do for you, Hoppy. Next time I see you, I'm gonna let you have a pair of nylons so's you can get yourself a piece o' tail.'

'Gee, thanks, Bob. You're a pal,' said Billy.

At seven o'clock, the barber shop closed up, and the two boys did a final count of the night's take.

'Thirty-seven shillings and sixpence,' announced Billy. 'I'm as rich as Rockefeller, and this is only one night!'

'Thirty-five for me,' said Robin. 'I'm off to order my Rolls Royce tomorrow morning.'

The boys parted company in a happy, jubilant mood. Billy arrived home at 7.30.

'Well, Mam, how much do you think I made?' he asked triumphantly.

'I don't know. Five shillings?'

'Nearly right,' he said, pouring out all his takings on to the dining-room table.

'I hope you haven't been out pinching money,' she said. 'How much is there?'

'All honestly earned by the sweat of my brow. Over thirty-seven shillings for one night's work. By the end of the week I should have about eight or nine quid. And here's a coupla American candy bars for you.'

He said nothing about the rubbers tucked away in his back pocket.

'Eeeh,' she said. 'That's a lot more than your dad's earning in the market.'

'We're in the money! We're in the money!' he sang, dancing round the table. 'First thing, I pay you something towards my keep after all these years. Next thing I buy will be a pair of really good dancing shoes – those with the shiny patent leather – and I'm really going to learn how to dance. You'll see.'

At the end of the week, his total earnings came to over ten pounds, and Billy felt that he had at last found his niche.

'You know, Mam,' he said, 'I like the idea of having money in my pocket. It makes a big difference to life. Without money, you're nothing. What's more, the people I work with treat me as an adult instead of a child as they do at school. I wouldn't mind leaving and getting a full-time job.'

'Look, Billy,' she said, 'I've said it till I'm blue in the face. You're not leaving school – not before you're sixteen. And you're wrong. Money isn't everything. "The greatest wealth is being content with a little." Your health and strength are much more important. And don't you forget it.'

Chapter Twenty-Four

A Little Learning

All that term, Billy worked as he'd never worked before. At school he studied Caesar's *Gallic Wars* in the original, Shakespeare's sonnets and Palgrave's *Golden Treasury* of poems; mechanics, magnetism and electricity; Tudor architecture; the short stories of Guy de Maupassant; quadratic equations, Euclidian geometry and a lot of other useful subjects. His academic progress over the last year had been good and he was vying with 'Oscar' Wilde for fifth place in class, but at maths he was in a class of his own.

His shoe-shining activities were so profitable that he had managed not only to buy his dancing shoes and pay for lessons at Harrigan's, but to save some money as well, and by the end of November, he had accumulated the princely sum of twenty-five pounds.

But it was in the field of dancing that he made the greatest strides and the greatest progress, moving up from novice to accomplished amateur in the space of three months. After work in the barber shop, he attended Harrigan's every night, including Saturday, learning the basic steps and the many beautiful variations in every dance. He moved through the waltz, the slow foxtrot and the quickstep, and on to the more advanced South American dances – the tango and the rumba. He mastered most of the subtle movements and absorbed the techniques of the natural and reverse turns, double reverse turns, the feather, the whisk and the chassé, the drag hesitation and the backward lock. At home he studied and practised all the advice and exercises given by Alex Moore in his standard work on ballroom dancing. Billy lived and breathed dancing until his movements became smooth, graceful and effortless.

The master class, however, was held every Sunday afternoon on the rooftop of Hazlewood House by Lucy, who took all the skills he had acquired at the dance academy and tuned and refined them to the highest level, until Billy was beginning to feel that he had been dancing all his life. As she had insisted from the start, the relationship with Lucy was strictly dancing and nothing else. On their third meeting in September, Billy had presented her with two Hershey bars.

'A GI gave me these candy bars, Lucy. They're all yours.'

'Are you sure? Good chocolate is so hard to get nowadays.'

'That's OK. He also gave me these.'

He showed her the packet of rubbers.

'Oh, yes,' she said, frowning when she saw what they were. 'So what? I do hope you're not getting any funny ideas.'

'No, no. I just thought you might be interested to know what these Yanks are like, that's all. That's not all he gave me.'

He showed her the nylons that Bob, as good as his word, had given him.

'Take 'em. I have no use for them.'

'Look, Billy, I thought we had things straight from the very beginning. I like you and I think you're very nice-looking and all that. But if you think you can buy me with a pair of nylons, you'd better think again, that's all. I'm not like that. I may work in a biscuit factory but I'm not crackers. Dancing only, and nothing more, remember?'

'OK, Lucy. But keep the nylons anyway, as a kind of fee for these lessons.'

'All right, I'll take 'em as sort of payment. Wait till the girls at work see 'em; they'll scratch my eyes out. Right then, so I'd better start earning them. Let's get to work! Slow foxtrot! My favourite dance! I want to see long, gliding, smooth steps from you. Try to make it look sort of lazy and easy.'

She switched on Victor Sylvester playing 'As Time Goes By' and they danced across the rooftop.

'Keep up on your toes on the feather step and don't forget what I told you about contrary body movement. It's a bit like you on your bike when you turn right. Sway over to the right a bit and stay relaxed. That's it. I've never known anyone to pick up dancing so quickly and easily.'

'What do you expect from Fred Astaire?'

'And I've never known anyone so modest, either.'

'My modesty's the thing I'm most proud of.'

Billy moved rhythmically across the floor, lightly and easily.

'Slow, slow, quick, quick, slow,' chanted Lucy in time to the music. 'Now the impetus turn. Move the left foot ever so slowly to your right and forward left. That's beautiful. We'll make a dancer of you yet. You'll see.'

Sunday after Sunday she added more and more refinements to his movements, until one day towards the end of November she announced:

'I think we're ready.'

'You mean for lovemaking, Lucy?'

'Stop acting the goat, Billy.'

'Huh! Very funny!'

'We're ready to enter a slow foxtrot competition at Harrigan's next Saturday. I think we're moving together quite nicely. It's amazing, really, to think that you began dancing only a few months ago.'

'That's me, Lucy. When I go for something, there's no half-measures. It's all or nothing at all.'

On the evening of Saturday 27 November, Billy put on his new dancing shoes and donned his dark-blue suit – which he had paid all of ten pounds for at Reid Bros in Market Street – a white silk shirt and a spotted tie. He spent a good deal of time Brylcreeming his hair until he had the quiff just right, and another ten minutes practising throwing his cigarette into his mouth from waist height until he got it on to the edge of his lip every single time.

'You handsome devil, you,' he said to his reflection.

'You remind me of that film star,' Mam said when she saw him.

'Which one?' he asked, throwing a fag nonchalantly into his mouth. 'Humphrey Bogart?'

'No,' she said. 'The one who's allus with him. Edward G. Robinson.'

'Stop taking the mickey, Mam. I need all my confidence tonight for this dance competition.'

At Harrigan's that night, there was a good crowd and it looked as if everyone was entering the competition.

'Don't be nervous, Billy,' Lucy said. 'Half this lot'll get knocked out in the first heat. Most of them ladies can't even do a proper heel turn.'

'And some of the men move like elephants,' said Billy

to boost his own self-confidence.

'The only pair to worry about is Freda Pritchard and Duggie Diggle over there, but I think we've got them licked.'

At nine o'clock promptly, Mrs Harrigan made her announcement through the mike.

'And now we come to our foxtrot competition for our regular patrons. Only those who have taken lessons with us are eligible. Please attach your numbers to the gentleman's back and take the floor for heat one.'

Billy and Lucy were given the number 17.

'My lucky number,' said Billy. 'We used to live at number seventeen, Honeypot Street, Red Bank.'

'I hope you're right,' said Lucy. 'I thought that's where you got bombed out.'

The Saturday-night five-piece band struck up with the song 'I Remember You' and the competition began. Billy and Lucy glided smoothly and effortlessly round the floor in perfect time to the music, Billy displaying a light feather step and a reverse wave with lots of contrary body movement. Freda and Duggie, numbered at 8, also swept beautifully around the room, making full use of the available space.

At the end of heat one, only six couples were called back – Lucy and Billy and Freda and Duggie among them. In heat two, Billy and Lucy began to show off their steps: the telemark, the open telemark, and the natural hover telemark, which brought a burst of applause from the spectators. Meanwhile, Freda and Duggie were giving a lovely display of light feathery dancing which brought gasps of admiration from their supporters. At the end of heat two, only three couples were brought back: Freda and Duggie, Rita and Roy and Lucy and Billy.

'At least we're in the first three,' said Lucy. 'But to win,

Billy, you'll really have to pull out all the stops.'

The band began to play 'It's a Lovely Day Tomorrow' and the three couples started to float their way around the ballroom, demonstrating the most intricate and subtle steps of the slow foxtrot.

Lucy and Billy put out all their best movements which they had practised so hard and so patiently all those Sunday afternoons. Billy performed the weave, the top spin and the outside swivel with grace and elegance. He and Lucy wore easy, relaxed smiles – 'the happy face' – as they flowed around the floor. Billy finished with a beautifully executed impetus turn followed by hover and on into the feather step and a reverse wave. Then it was all over.

Mrs Harrigan and Lofty went into a huddle for an eternity that was all of five minutes. The crowd waited tensely for the decision. Mrs Harrigan went to her mike.

'Here are the results of our slow foxtrot competition. In third place, number seven, Rita and Roy. In second place . . . number eight, Freda and Duggie. And our winners tonight . . .'

Her voice was drowned in the cheers of the spectators, while Billy found himself being hugged to pieces by an ecstatic Lucy.

'WE DID IT! WE DID IT!' she yelled. 'Billy, I think you're marvellous.'

'Ah know Ah am,' he said in his best Lancashire accent. 'Ah've 'ad a reet good teacher. And come to think of it, you're not so bad yourself, lass.'

The three couples went forward to receive their awards: a pair of small dressing-table mirrors for third, somewhat larger mirrors for second, and two superb gold-plated statues of a dancing couple for the winners.

'Congratulations to all of you,' said Mrs Harrigan. 'And Billy, could I see you for a moment after this dance?'

For Billy and Lucy, the rest of the evening was somewhat confused, as if they were in a dream come true – which they were. Lucy clung closely to Billy in every dance.

'I can't believe it's happened,' she said. 'After all our work! It's paid off! And as for you, Billy, I've never known anyone to pick up dancing so quick.'

'Right at the beginning, you told me I could be another Fred Astaire. I tell you this, Lucy. School, Caesar's *Gallic Wars* and quadratic equations seem a million miles away.'

'Remember what I told you, Billy? Your education's more important than dancing. Get yourself qualified and get a good job with good money and one that's interesting as well. How many more times do y'ave to be told, you daft devil? You can allus keep up dancing as your pastime. But don't end up like me in a lousy, monotonous job.'

'OK! OK! Keep your hair on. It's just that . . . well . . . I'm so happy that we pulled it off. It's all down to you, Lucy, and your teaching on the rooftop.'

Towards the end of that wonderful night, he went to see Mrs Harrigan in her office.

'Billy, you've made such astounding progress in dancing, I'd like to offer you a part-time job as instructor/host on the staff. The pay is three shillings per evening, and naturally, your admission to all dances would be free. Are you interested?'

'Interested? I'll say, Mrs Harrigan. When do I start?'

'You can start on Monday if that's OK with you.'

Billy and Lucy were so preoccupied, so full of their triumphant win that evening, that they failed to notice the glamorous and beautiful young girl who watched all their excited reactions with a curious, faintly amused smile on her lips. If they'd known what she had in mind, they might have paid her more attention.

*   *   *

On Monday evening, after his shoe-shining duties, Billy managed to reach Harrigan's just in time to start his dance-instructor job. Pretty soon he was absorbed in teaching a group of novices the steps that he himself had learned only a few short months ago.

The usual practice session followed the lessons.

'Mr David! Mr Duggie! Mr Roy!' Lofty called out as he circulated the room, allocating ladies to the male instructors. It sounded so strange and it took Billy a little by surprise when he heard his own name being called: 'Mr Billy!'

It was even more of a surprise when he saw walking towards him the most beautiful girl he had ever seen outside the cinema screen. She had obviously modelled herself on Rita Hayworth, for she had the same hairstyle, the same cheekbones, the same dreamy, come-to-bed eyes and even the same kind of sultry expression.

'Good evening, Billy,' she said softly, with a charming smile. 'My name's Adele.'

'Hello,' said Billy, gulping, his eyes popping out of his head. 'Nice to meet you.'

The band struck up with 'Sleepy Lagoon' and the couples began to waltz around the floor.

'One thing is obvious,' said Billy. 'You're no novice. You move beautifully.'

'Why, thank you,' she said. 'I have been dancing for a number of years, as a matter of fact.'

They danced on for a while. She really was exceptionally good – like a feather in his arms.

'I specially asked for you tonight,' she said.

'Oh,' he said, puzzled. 'And why was that?'

'I watched you in the slow foxtrot competition last Saturday. I think you're pretty good.'

'The compliments are really flying around tonight.'

'Notice I said "pretty good". But you could be outstanding if you went about it the right way.'

'You think so? What is this "right way" you're talking about?'

'Look,' she said, 'I hope you don't think I'm being too forward, but I came here tonight just to see you. Could we talk at the interval, after the quickstep?'

'OK,' he said. 'Fine.'

Lucy waltzed past with her novice partner.

'Catch you later, Billy,' she said, eyeing Adele suspiciously.

'Right,' said Billy. 'See you after this dance.'

'Who's that girl?' asked Lucy when they met between dances.

'Dunno,' said Billy, 'but she certainly knows how to dance.'

'Watch your step,' said Lucy ominously. 'She's set her cap at you.'

'How can you tell that, Lucy?'

'We girls can tell. Believe me.'

At the break between dances, Billy invited Adele across to the ballroom snack bar. As they sat together talking over a cup of tea, he noticed from the corner of his eye that Lucy was engaged in earnest conversation with Roy on the other side of the room.

'Sounds very mysterious, Adele – this wanting to talk to me,' he said.

'Nothing mysterious, Billy. I'll come straight to the point. I broke up with my dancing partner a couple of weeks ago and I'm looking for a new one. I wondered if you were interested, that's all.'

'But you are obviously a much higher standard than I am – in fact, semi-professional, I'd say.'

'You would soon reach the same level if you had private lessons with the right teacher.'

'Who would that be?'

'Frank Rogers at the Deansgate Dance Academy is one of the best in the country. He's the north of England professional champion. I've been going to him for over two years.'

'Everybody knows about Frank Rogers, but he must be very expensive.'

'You have to pay if you want the best,' she said. 'Look, I'll be here tomorrow night, and if you decide to accept my proposal, you could let me know. I should warn you, though, that when I see something I want, I go after it until I get it.'

'You mean me?'

'You got it – first time.'

After their chat, Adele went to the cloakroom, collected her coat and left.

When all the practice sessions for the evening were finished, the band packed up and went home and Mrs Harrigan put on Victor Sylvester records for the last half-hour. It may have been merely coincidence or the fact that Mrs Harrigan was a keen observer of her staff's behaviour, but the record she put on as Billy and Lucy danced a last slow foxtrot was 'Won't You Change Partners and Dance with Me?'.

On the way home, Billy told Lucy about Adele's proposal.

'And are you going to take it? To be honest, I didn't like the look of that girl,' she said petulantly.

'I'm very tempted, Lucy. After all, Frank Rogers is one of the top teachers in the country. And you can't condemn the girl just because she's glamorous.'

'You may not agree with me, 'cos you're just an

innocent little boy. But us girls can tell a baby-snatcher from fifty paces.'

'Who're you calling a baby, Lucy?'

'You are, Billy, when it comes to girls.'

'I think you're just jealous.'

'Me? Jealous! Right, that does it, Billy! You can bugger off with this glamour-puss.'

'Very well, I will, if that's the way you feel.'

'It's bloody unfair that after all my efforts on the rooftop, you should go off with this man-chaser.'

'But that was our agreement, Lucy, remember? Business only. Dancing only. This could be my big chance to get into the big ballroom competitions – not just the local hop.'

'Then you can bloody well get lost, Billy. You can piss off. And don't come crawling back to me if it doesn't work out with Miss Glamour Pants.'

Lucy stormed off and Billy wondered if he had done the right thing, for he'd only decided to accept Adele's offer when Lucy had pushed him into answering.

'Would you do something for me?' Adele asked at their first private lesson with Frank Rogers.

'Sure. Just name it, Adele.'

'It's your name. Change it. "Billy" reminds me of the tin kettle we used when camping in the Girl Guides. It also sounds like the name of a plumber or a bus conductor, not a successful ballroom dancer.'

'What do you suggest?'

'How about Edwin, or Grant? Wait a minute . . . I've got it . . . Julian! That's a lovely name. From now on, for me, you're Julian.'

'OK, if that's what you want. Julian it is.'

The lesson began. Billy had thought he could dance – until, that is, he had his first session with Frank Rogers at his dance academy.

'The very first thing we have to teach you, Julian, is how to walk,' said Frank.

'But I learned that when I was eighteen months old.'

'That was toddling. This is walking rhythmically. Let's try it in slow motion. Swing the left leg forward from the hip – heel skimming the floor, toe slightly raised. Good.

'Now, as the left foot passes the toe of the right foot, release your left heel so that it just touches the floor. Lower your left toe so that the foot is flat on the floor.'

'There's more to it than I thought,' said Billy.

'Let's try it with your partner. Place both hands on Adele's shoulders and walk together across the floor. Excellent. Lightly. Move from the hips.'

The lesson continued in this fashion. Frank worked them both very hard and certainly earned the high fee of ten shillings an hour that he charged.

Towards the end of the first lesson, he said:

'We'll try walking together with close hip contact. Hands behind your back. Right, Julian, see if you can guide Adele around the room using hips only. Ready now. Push your hips, Adele, as if resisting. Push forward, Julian. Excellent. Now we'll try it to music. No hands! Hips only!'

He switched on Victor Sylvester playing 'Once in a While' and Billy and Adele moved around the room with both hands behind their backs.

'I'm finding this hip-to-hip business very sexy, Adele,' whispered Billy when they were out of earshot of Frank Rogers.

'I felt as much, Julian,' she whispered. 'Behave and concentrate on the dancing.'

'One final thing before we pack up,' said Frank. 'I'd like to check out your hold.'

They took up their position.

'Good,' he said. 'You're just the right height for each other. You're going to look great when I've finished with you both.'

He fastened an elastic band around Billy's right hand.

'You have a slight tendency to splay the fingers. That elastic band should keep them together. Keep your left wrist straight. Perfect. Now let's see your slow foxtrot.'

He switched on the record and Billy and Adele glided smoothly round the studio.

The weeks went by and Billy fell into a very busy routine – school, shoe-shining, dancing. As for Lucy, she soon recovered from her initial anger with Billy, as she found her new partner, Roy, to be a skilful dancer and an amenable person. Despite that, however, she never forgave Adele for the way, as she put it, she had snatched away her partner and protégé from under her nose. Adele joined Harrigan's staff. The two ladies were at daggers drawn every night as they stood together in the middle of the floor, waiting for novices to be allocated to them.

'Eaten any more men lately, Adele?' hissed Lucy.

'Why, are you offering, Lucy?' spat Adele. 'That new partner of yours looks quite tasty.'

'You keep your thieving eyes off him,' Lucy snapped.

'I will, Lucy, if you'll tell him to keep his big goo-goo eyes off my breasts.'

'My dear Adele, it's no wonder he's staring at 'em. It's that bloody dress you're almost wearing.'

'Why, thank you, Lucy, I'm sure,' Adele cooed. 'I'm so glad you like it. And that C & A dress of yours is lovely too – it's dyed really well.'

'But not as well as your hair, Adele,' Lucy sniffed.

'You bloody bitch,' Adele rasped as, adopting her fixed

Cheshire cat dancing smirk, she moved off with her stiff-legged, robotic partner.

'Yes, yes. Come on! Come on! That's it,' she grunted to the unfortunate learner. 'Forward left, side right, close. Forward right, side left, close.'

'Good. That's very good,' Lucy said encouragingly with her best ballroom Mona Lisa smile to her beginner. 'And . . . one . . . two . . . three. One . . . two . . . three.'

The two couples hadn't got far when they collided unceremoniously.

'You clumsy bitch! You did that on purpose,' Lucy snarled, all vestiges of her smile gone.

'Piss off, you stupid sod,' Adele hissed through clenched teeth, the Cheshire cat now turned to a tigress.

Each night the ladies bickered in this fashion, but meanwhile, Billy's private lessons with Frank Rogers began to pay off and the standard of his dancing improved by leaps and bounds. One evening, Mrs Harrigan called Adele and Billy into her office.

'I've noticed that you two are looking very good on the floor. I want to ask you to become our demonstrators of the slow foxtrot on Wednesday evenings; it would show our novices just how it should be done.'

'I vowed that this would come off one day, Adele, and at last it's happened,' Billy said.

'But only after a lot of very hard work and determined effort,' she said.

That first Wednesday evening, Mrs Harrigan announced:

'And now we have a demonstration of the slow foxtrot by two members of our teaching staff, Miss Adele and Mr Julian.'

They went into their routine – Billy now a very confident performer. As they danced around the floor, they could hear the admiring remarks of the novice spectators:

'See that lovely heel turn.'

'That's an impetus turn. I've just learnt that tonight.'

'Did you notice the CBM in that reverse wave.'

'She made a clumsy heel turn there, Roy. Did you notice?' Lucy said happily in a loud stage-whisper.

Despite Lucy's bitchiness, Billy was ecstatically happy that evening, dancing with a beautiful girl to the admiration of the crowd. The flattering remarks were meat and drink to him and he thought how perilously close his life had come to taking off in a different direction with Mick Scully and Vinny Buckley.

At the interval, he and Adele sat close together in the bar, enjoying the tea, the cakes, and the adulatory glances which were cast in their direction.

'Good demonstration, you two,' Duggie Diggle called light-heartedly from the other side of the room. 'If ever you get fed up with him, Adele, I'm without a partner. So you know where to come!'

'Gercha!' said Billy genially.

'No chance, Duggie. What happened to Freda?' said Adele, laughing.

'The usual story,' replied Duggie. 'She's found somebody new.'

'I enjoyed your demo, Julian,' gushed a young female fan as she ordered a tea at the counter. 'You and Adele look fantastic together.'

'Why, thank you,' said Billy.

A dark-haired, well-built youth approached.

'Here comes another admirer, Adele,' said Billy.

'I don't think so,' she said. 'It's Cyprian, my ex-partner. Watch him, Julian. He's dangerous – has a fierce temper.'

'You – Julian?' sneered the ex.

'That's right,' said Billy.

'My name's Reggie,' he snorted, 'but she renamed me Cyprian. Didn't like the name Reggie. "Not good enough. Too common," she said.'

'You're pissed, Cyprian,' Adele said, 'as usual.'

'I want to warn you, Julian, or whatever your bloody name is. Have a care. She's all top-show. She'll give you a new name and a new image, but as soon as she's had enough of you she'll throw you away like an old sock.'

'Get back to the pub where you belong,' Adele snarled. 'It was the best bloody day's work I ever did – dumping you.'

'Same goes for me, Adele,' he growled at her. 'You used me – took me for a ride. Well, promised me a ride, anyway, but never came across with the goods. Watch yourself, Julian – she'll have a ring on your finger and one on your nose if she gets her way.'

'I've heard enough,' said Billy. 'Get the hell out of here. Insulting Adele and causing trouble.'

'Or we'll call Lofty to deal with you,' added Adele.

'Oh, call the bruiser, would you?'

'Just bugger off,' said Billy. 'You drunken sod.'

'Why, you bag o' bones – you streak o' piss, I've half a mind to clobber you one.'

'That's it,' said Adele. 'Lofty! Lofty! Can you come over here, please?'

Lofty detached himself from his seat near the bandstand and strode over.

'Trouble?' he enquired.

'Trouble?' said Cyprian/Reggie. 'She's the bleeding trouble. Miss Prick-Teaser there.'

'Right, pal. On your way,' said Lofty, frog-marching the unlucky Cyprian to the door. 'And if I see you near this dance studio again you'll go home with a black eye and a thick ear. Now – git!'

Cyprian was helped through the door with a shove that sent him sprawling outside on to the asphalt path.

'You can see now,' Adele said, 'why I dumped him. He was just a brute.'

'You were well rid of him, Adele,' Billy said.

From that night, their romance developed apace and their necking sessions in her front room became hotter and hotter and dangerously close to getting out of control.

Adele's front room was directly under her parents' bedroom.

'You'll have to whisper,' she said, as they went into a close embrace on the settee.

They settled down to several minutes' passionate kissing which threatened to carry them both away to never-never land.

'I'll love you till the end of time,' she said.

'I'll love you till each mountain disappears,' he sighed.

'I'll love you till the wells run dry,' she murmured.

'Till hell freezes over,' he breathed in her ear.

'Till the deserts bloom,' she cooed.

Billy was beginning to run out of unlikely eventualities to love her till, and so thought it best to change the subject.

'My mother stopped breast-feeding me too early and put me on the bottle,' he said.

'How do you know that?' she asked softly.

'I've been trying ever since to get myself off the bottle and back on to the breast,' he replied plaintively.

'You're a clown,' she said. 'But a lovable one.'

'I've always had one big problem, though,' he continued.

'And that is?' she whispered.

'I've never been able to get the hang of these brassières,' he said, opening the buttons of her silk blouse.

'There's no problem here,' she said, cuddling into his shoulder. 'I never wear one.'

After ten minutes, there came a knock on the ceiling.

'It's getting late, Adele. Time to say good night,' her dad called.

'OK, Dad,' she called back sweetly. 'Just coming.'

Given the excitement of Adele and the dancing world, all the academic stuff Billy was learning at school seemed boring and irrelevant to life and having a good time. He vowed to leave school at the first opportunity, get himself a well-paid, interesting job and continue with the lifestyle to which Adele had made him accustomed.

New Year's Eve. Billy had big plans for celebrating this particular festivity. Everything in the garden was looking rosy. Flo's husband, Sergeant Barry Healey, was home on leave and staying with them in the spare bedroom; at Harrigan's there was to be a big shindig, ticket-holders only, and all their crowd would be there. At the GI barber shop, he worked until 7.30 that night, and the tips were unbelievable as the doughboys unloaded some of their dough. He had bought Adele's ticket and his own – never mind the cost of five shillings a head, he could afford it. He had arranged to collect her around 8.30.

When he got back after work to the Gardenia Court flat, though, he sensed that something was amiss. Flo and Barry were getting ready to go out, but one look at his dad and Billy knew immediately what it was. He'd been on the booze – probably all day in the Hare and Hounds – as his way of bidding farewell to the old year. He had spent the afternoon and early evening sleeping it off and had awakened in a foul temper.

By eight o'clock, he was suffering from a mammoth hangover. Eyes glazed and bloodshot, face haggard and drawn, he sat hunched at the fireplace with his back to everyone. He hated visitors at the best of times and he made no bones about showing it. But when he was in his cups anything could happen, and the family had found it best to make itself scarce. Every so often that New Year's Eve he muttered incomprehensible curses and strange incantations, accompanied by weird hissing, shushing noises which sounded like a tyre being let down.

'Bleeding strangers in the house,' he mumbled to himself. 'Hiss-ss. Shush-sh-sh.'

'No bleeding peace,' he grunted. 'Hiss-ss. Shush-sh-sh.'

Eventually Flo and Barry were ready to go out.

'We're going to visit Barry's married brother, Mam,' said Flo. 'We'll be back about one o'clock.'

'Righto, Flo,' said Mam.

'Bleeding nuisances,' growled Dad. 'Hiss-ss. Shush-sh-sh.'

Billy knew there was going to be trouble. He busied himself grooming and primping himself up for the big dance. He washed and shaved carefully, having showered previously at the American Red Cross Club, applied his aftershave, dressed in his Reid Bros suit and his best white shirt. He was ready to depart to collect Adele.

Then all hell broke loose.

'You drunken swine! You bloody great bully, you!' Mam screamed at his dad. 'You've been hissing and muttering to yourself all bloody day.'

He turned his bloodshot eyes on her.

'Who the bloody hell d'you think you're talking to?'

'Hitler! Hitler!' she yelled.

'Hitler? Calling me Hitler?' he snarled, thumping the table with his fist.

'You drunken pig!' she shouted, her blood up.

He stood up and thrust his face at her.

'S'no wonder I get drunk. A man's house is no longer his own. Bloody strangers everywhere I look.'

The conflict was reaching fever pitch. They were both seething and spitting hatred at one another.

'It's the same every holiday,' she cried, now in tears of rage. 'You stink the whole house out with your drinking. I'm ashamed to have visitors in the place.'

'Then you can piss off out and sling your hook,' he bawled.

He came at her then, grabbed her by the shoulders and thrust her up against the wall. She screamed and fought to get free from his grip. She put her arm up for protection as he raised his fist to strike her.

'You stop that, d'you hear! Don't you dare hit her!' said a disembodied voice.

To Billy's amazement, he found that the voice belonged to him.

Dad's fist froze in mid-air. He turned and gazed at Billy in amazement.

'Who the bloody hell do you think you're talking to, yer cheeky little bugger?' he growled.

But his hand was stayed.

Mam let out a long moan of utter anguish and began sobbing and wailing uncontrollably – sounding like Aunt Mona when Uncle Eddy had assaulted her. Released from the bully's grip, she opened the front door and ran outside, still crying.

'Wait, Mam, I'll come with you,' Billy shouted, all hopes of collecting Adele and all thoughts of the big dance now banished from his mind.

He sat with his mam on a low wall at the corner of Gardenia Court. She was shivering from the cold and, racked with misery, she continued to weep, tears overflowing. Billy put his arm round her to warm her and comfort her.

'Don't worry, Mam, don't worry,' he said. 'It was the drink talking.'

'I've had enough living with this pig,' she moaned. 'It's the same every holiday time. He comes back from the pub stinking the place out with his beer, and hissing and snorting like a bull. I can't stand no more of it, Billy. I'm gonna chuck meself in Union Street Canal.'

'It's OK, Mam. It's OK,' Billy consoled. 'He's drunk. He doesn't know what he's doing or saying. He'll be better tomorrow.'

'It's no use carrying on, Billy. I've had to put up with him for years. Tonight's the last straw. I'm gonna do away with meself. Don't bother about me, you go off to your dance.'

'No, Mam, forget the dance. I'm staying with you. I can always go dancing some other night. Adele will understand.'

They stayed there for over two hours, the two of them, sitting on that low, bottom-freezing wall. The moon was up and the tenements were bathed in a great white light. They sat watching the silent, smiling moon gliding through the silver-tipped clouds. In some of the flats they were holding noisy, festive parties, and Billy and Kate could hear the sounds of singing and revelry as the residents of Gardenia Court gave a liquid welcome to the New Year. At twelve o'clock, ships' hooters and car horns sounded off in distant parts of the city, and the party-goers began their drunken rendering of 'Auld Lang Syne'.

'Nineteen forty-four, Mam. Happy New Year!' he said, kissing her on the cheek.

'Same to you, son. Let's hope we have a better year ahead of us than the one behind. And let's hope this drunk you've got for a father mends his ways.'

'Come on, Mam,' he said. 'We're going back in. He'll have gone to bed by now, I should think. If not, and he starts again, he'll have me to deal with.'

'What a way to see the new year in, eh, Billy!' she said. 'Almost as bad as the Blitz in 1940.'

'Well, there's one thing about being here tonight. I'll be the first one to open the door and I've got dark hair. So that should bring us good luck.'

Next morning, it was the old, old story. Dad had sobered up and was all humble and contrite, trying to win back her love – in fact, everybody's love.

'Happy New Year, Kate,' he said softly. 'And I've bought you this big box o' chocolates, luv.'

But he had blown it and was due for his punishment. Sentence – one week's fish-eye treatment. Billy hoped he would be man enough to take it on the chin. Mam looked through him with that stony-faced, unseeing stare of hers.

'You eat 'em, Hitler!' she said.

Once again, Billy began to feel sorry for his dad. He knew what it felt like; he'd had some of this glassy-eyed, non-person torture after the stopping-out-all-night incident with Vinny Buckley.

'Happy New Year, Dad,' he said when he saw him.

'And the same to you, son. Sorry about last night,' Tommy said quietly. 'I've got you this box of fifty Players.'

'Thanks, Dad. I don't know where you get them from with this cigarette shortage. They're like gold.'

'Oh, I have my little ways,' he replied, winking.

'You do and all, Dad,' Billy said under his breath. 'You daft bugger. You do and all.'

And even though Billy consulted a map of Manchester, he never did find out where Union Street Canal was.

* * *

He saw Adele at the New Year's dance later the following night and apologised for his failure to turn up.

'I understand, Julian,' she said. 'Don't worry about it. I managed to take a taxi to Harrigan's and I danced with Duggie Diggle most of the evening. He took me home. I hope you don't mind.'

'No, I don't mind, Adele.'

He was lying, of course.

Chapter Twenty-Five

Schooldays: Dear Old Golden Rule Days

It has been claimed – though the actual authority is never quoted – that most men have a brief sexual thought every six seconds. This means, of course, that there must be at least five seconds when they're *not* having a sexual thought. For the smokers' club of the Upper Fifth at Damian College – not so. They thought about sex all the time. Constantly. Even when doing maths, it was sex. English – sex. History – double sex. Physics – more of the same. None of the members had actually had it. Full sex, that is. Though Nobby Nodder claimed to have got very near it with a girl called Ronnie in the Regal cinema.

At dinner-time, the six foundation members of the club – Billy, Robin, Titch, Nobby, Oscar and Olly – plus the more recently accepted Pottsy took their daily constitutional through the back alley adjoining the school. They lit up their fags – Park Drive on a poor day, Lucky Strike if Billy or Robin had struck lucky at the American Red Cross. The topic of conversation was the same each day and they took a prurient interest in examining the numerous condoms left behind from the previous night's copulations.

'Just look at all these Durexes,' said Oscar, poking the

abandoned contraceptives with a stick. 'There must have been a lot of shagging going on down here last night.'

'Well, the Government is always saying there should be mass production,' said Nobby.

'Mass seduction's more like it,' said Oscar. 'There are so many bags, they must have had the pros lined up against the wall – like an assembly line.'

'And why not?' said Olly. 'Didn't Herbert Morrison say, "Give us the tools and we'll finish the job." Did you know that over ten million a week are sold in Britain?'

'Half of them seem to be here,' said Pottsy, 'judging by all these Durexes.'

'Surely,' said Billy, the Latin scholar, 'the plural of Durex is Durices. It goes like radix – radices – and matrix – matrices.'

'As far as I'm concerned,' said Titch. 'They're just bags.'

'That's a very oversimplified view,' said Robin. 'There are subtle differences between them. The Yanks call them "rubbers" and they claim their models are ten inches long.'

'Oh, come, come,' said Nobby, 'that's stretching it a bit far.'

'Why do they have little teats on the end?' asked Pottsy.

'You mean you don't know, Pottsy?' asked Oscar.

'No, honest.'

'Then you must ask one of your sisters,' said Robin.

'I don't think they'll know,' he said. 'We're not allowed to say the word S-E-X in our house. It's taboo.'

'Not many people know this,' said Olly. 'The erect penis varies in length from five inches to ten inches.'

'Well, I certainly didn't know that,' said Pottsy.

'Some African tribes,' Olly continued, 'make their young boys go about with weights hanging from their things to make them longer.'

'I trust,' said Oscar, 'that they take them off when they're adults and are on the job.'

'Let's hope so,' said Billy, 'for the sake of their womenfolk.'

'I read,' said Nobby, not to be outdone in the display of sexual knowledge, 'that they have now begun manufacturing different coloured bags.'

'Green for beginners, maybe,' said Pottsy.

'And, I suppose, red, white and blue for the patriotic,' added Titch.

'Red for hot sex,' said Robin.

'The nearest I've ever got to hot sex,' said Oscar, 'is having a wank in the bath.'

'That's a very dirty way of doing a clean thing,' said Titch.

'Or a clean way of doing a dirty thing,' added Billy.

'Hey, fellas, I was told by a GI,' said Robin, 'that you can now buy banana-flavoured bags as well.'

'What next?' commented Pottsy. 'How does the woman get to taste it, I wonder?'

'Use your imagination, Pottsy,' said Olly.

'I still don't get it,' said Pottsy.

'But the woman does,' said Oscar lecherously.

The Upper Fifth studied nine subjects and the curriculum of the school was heavily weighted towards formal academic teaching. The boys did their utmost to make the dry educational programme more entertaining by introducing witty, comical comments. With some masters this was well-nigh impossible, as they interpreted these attempts as challenges to their authority.

One such was Brother Sebastian – the geography master – who developed an immediate antipathy towards Billy from the word go. The brother walked into the classroom each day and began his lesson with a routine opening:

'And . . . er . . . the meaning of "hinterland" is, of course, er . . . er . . .' A smacking of his lips. 'Hopkins!'

'Hinterland, sir, is a region lying inland from a coast and served by a port city and its facilities. For example, Lancashire is the hinterland of Liverpool.'

'Right,' grunted Brother Sebastian, sounding somewhat disappointed that he had failed to catch Billy out.

On another occasion, when Billy was feeling somewhat out of sorts, the master strode into the room and began in the accustomed way.

'And . . . er . . . the meaning of "irrigation" is, of course, er . . . er . . .' Smacking of lips. 'Hopkins!'

'DON'T KNOW, SIR!' replied Billy defiantly.

'Why, you blasted, blithering idiot,' Sebastian bawled, making a beeline for him.

Before the master had reached his desk, Billy managed to blurt out:

'Irrigation is the supplying of dry land with water by means of ditches, pipes or streams, so making the land fertile.'

Sebastian stopped and listened to the definition, then said grumpily:

'Oh, so you do know then.'

Brother Zachary was another master it was best not to try it on with. He taught maths and Latin and he took his subjects very seriously. Billy was one of his favourites, as he was always first in maths and second or third in Latin. On only one occasion did they clash, and this was so rare an occurrence that Billy was deeply upset by the encounter. It happened that he was translating a Latin unseen from Horace.

'Caesar, as a young boy,' he translated, 'would often visit the home of his . . .'

Billy stopped at the word *avus*, not knowing it meant 'grandfather'.

This surely means 'bird', he said to himself, thinking of the Latin word *avis*. I can't possibly say: 'Caesar used to visit the home of his bird.' It'll bring the house down and everyone will roar with laughter at me.

'Sorry, Brother Zachary, it doesn't make sense,' he said.

'Yes it does, William. Go on,' Zachary urged his favourite.

Billy was now determined not to become the butt of everyone's ridicule.

'Sorry, sir, it doesn't make sense to me.'

'It makes perfect sense, you chump!' Zachary said angrily.

Billy blushed to his roots and his eyes filled with tears, for Zachary and he had a close mutual-admiration relationship. Fortunately, it was the one and only time that the two did not see eye to eye.

The most popular master in the school was Brother Ambrose, a dark-haired, olive-skinned master from South America who had a ready wit, a keen sense of humour and an unwavering sense of discipline. He could cause chaos and wild horseplay one moment and then quell it in an instant with one stern, forbidding look. He was another not to be messed with.

He invariably began his French lessons with:

'*Ouvrez toutes les fenêtres*. Open all the windows – there's a terrible smell in here!'

'There wasn't till you came in,' replied Oscar.

'Oh, is that so, Wilde?' Ambrose said slowly, with ominous good-humour.

There then followed a wild rough-house, with Ambrose chasing Oscar around the room with a cricket bat and the students clambering over desks to protect their friend. After everyone had let off steam, Ambrose simply turned to the class and in a quiet, menacing voice said:

'OK, that's enough now. Let's get down to some work. Start exercise ten.'

The proverbial pin could be heard.

Physics was taught by a Bart Jarvis, an absent-minded scientist who had no class control whatsoever, despite his breaking several long, scientific rulers on the bottoms of his badly behaved, unwilling learners. It was in one of their early attempts to introduce sexual implications into physics that the smokers' club members came to grief.

Bart was demonstrating the expansion of iron and had to set up his apparatus to show how the coefficient of this metal was arrived at.

'It's definitely got much bigger,' said Oscar.

'And longer,' said Billy.

'And thicker,' added Robin.

'Look at the bulbous bit on the end,' said Nobby.

'It looks like a poker,' said Titch.

'And can you see all that stuff bubbling and spurting out,' said Olly, indicating the boiling water in the retort flask.

Bart ignored the ribald comments and continued with the experiment. At the end of the lesson, however, he looked up from his notes and said:

'Class dismissed, but would the following remain behind: Gabrielson, Hopkins, Hardy, Nodder, Smalley and Wilde.'

'Uh-oh,' said Titch. 'Trouble.'

'I want all of you to know,' said Bart, 'that I understood every disgusting reference you made during my lesson. If it ever happens again, I shall report you to Brother Dorian and you will probably be expelled.'

Bart had no more trouble.

It was in English and history that the club extracted most of its fun and entertainment.

English was taught by a little, elderly, dull-eared brother, nicknamed 'Baldy' for obvious reasons, who seemed out of touch with all that was going on around him. When he had first made his appearance, the whole class had broken down in paroxysms of suppressed laughter and heads had disappeared under desks for a good five minutes.

'I'm going to test your knowledge of grammar,' he snapped, slapping his elbow to his side. 'Give me an example of an adjectival clause.'

Oscar raised his hand immediately.

'The bag which was found in the alley had not been used.'

'Excellent,' he said, chalking it up on the blackboard with a noisy sucking-in of his breath with every word that he wrote.

The class watched, hardly able to contain its delight that he had fallen for it.

'Next, a noun phrase as subject of a sentence.'

'The survival of this country depends on the high quality of its seamen,' offered Nobby.

'Very good indeed,' said Baldy, putting it up on the board with his loud siphoning noises. 'Now, can anyone give me a sentence containing an adverbial phrase of place?'

'In the forest, the two boys espied two beautiful big tits,' said Olly.

'Excellent,' exclaimed Baldy. 'I'm glad to see that you all know your grammar and your parts of speech. What about figures of speech? Give me an example of a hyperbole.'

'The boy tried to hide his secret but it stuck out a mile,' said Robin.

'Good. I can see that I am going to get on well with this class.'

He seemed to have but one method of teaching, which could be termed 'reading round the class', for he rarely attempted any explanation or exposition. The method might have worked had it not been for the farting noises and the snorting sounds of suppressed laughter which accompanied every reading. Titch found particular diffi-culty, as he was a giggler and the slightest suggestion of a snort was enough to set him off.

'Enter certain niffs,' announced Billy, substituting his word for 'nymphs' in the stage directions of *The Tempest*.

Titch, reading the part of Ariel, was unable to continue – much to Baldy's perplexity and annoyance.

But it was the attempts to read the poetry in Palgrave's *Golden Treasury* which were the real test of strength and character. Billy found himself having to tackle those lines in Gray's 'Ode to Vicissitude':

> *See the wretch that long has tost*
> *On the thorny bed of pain.*

He could get no further, however, for all round him the snorts and the snuffles started up. And poor Titch, as luck would have it, landed up with the poem 'Willy Drowned in the Yarrow' and was completely stymied and unable to read beyond 'Willy' before the stage-whispers of 'Willy? Willy 'Eck!' were being called all about him.

Pottsy was not normally a provoker of laughter in the form, since he did not altogether understand the subtle allusions or the clever innuendo – the pace was too fast for him. But came the occasion when the naive Pottsy was an occasion of loud guffaws. During a reading of *The Tempest* he was due to say the line: '*Are we to be cheated of our lives by drunkards?*' Instead he confounded Baldy and the whole class by reading: '*Are we to be cheated of our lives by seventy drunkards?*'

'Yes, Potts,' said Baldy. 'But how do you come to the conclusion that there were seventy of these inebriates?'

'Because it says so in my book,' said Pottsy.

It was Oscar who saw it first.

'The number seventy is the number of the line on the left-hand side of the page!'

A great guffaw went up from the class at this stupidity, and Baldy himself almost smiled. Pottsy wasn't the only one to make a *faux pas*. One afternoon, during a poetry-reading exercise, Billy was disconcerted when his answer to a sudden question fired at him from Baldy was greeted with great howls of mirth and derision.

The class was reading 'The Bard' by Thomas Gray and had reached the lines:

> *Hark, how each giant-oak,*
> *O'er thee, oh King!*
> *their hundred arms they wave.*

Billy was preoccupied thinking about Adele and their next dancing date when Baldy suddenly asked:

'Hopkins, what's got a hundred arms?'

Billy was nonplussed for a moment, then answered:

'Why, a centipede, sir.'

Even Baldy joined in the laughter.

But the finest hour in the Baldy saga belonged to Oscar, who agreed, on payment of threepence per head from everyone in the class – giving a total prize of over six shillings – to faint during the lesson. Billy was elected stake-holder. Throughout the reading of *The Tempest*, Oscar issued instructions.

'Move your desk a little further forward, Hoppy. Titch, a little to the left. Robin, give me a little more space.'

Billy, in the role of Caliban, was just saying:

Be not afeard: the isle is full of noises,
Sounds and sweet airs, that give delight, and hurt not

when Oscar put a hand to his head, gave a loud moan and keeled over.

For a moment, Baldy was stumped. Then he reacted.

'Give him some air. Loosen his collar,' he bawled, slapping his elbow to his side. 'I'll get some water for him.' And he shot out of the room.

As soon as he'd gone, Oscar opened his eyes.

'Has he gone? Right, Hoppy, that's six shillings and threepence you owe me.'

Billy paid up just before Baldy got back.

'Here you are, Wilde, drink this water,' the master said, holding Oscar's head. 'Do you think you're going to be all right?'

'Yes, sir, I think so,' said Oscar weakly, pretending to come round.

'You'd better get some air,' said Baldy, helping him to the door.

After ten minutes or so, Oscar reappeared.

'I think I'll be all right now, sir,' he said, full of self-pity.

'No, you'd better go home, I think,' Baldy said, not relishing the thought of having to deal with yet another fainting fit, or even, horror of horrors, vomiting.

'Yes, I think you may be right, sir,' said Oscar feebly, at the same time seizing the opportunity to give the class a big, broad wink.

Oscar left – much to the annoyance of the rest of the form, who had to remain and plough their way for the umpteenth time through *The Tempest*. They were even more annoyed when they learned later that he had gone off to the Odeon cinema on their money.

The choicest sexual observations, however, were reserved for the history teacher, a dedicated young lady with the unfortunate name of Edith Dunn, a graduate straight from university, who had little realised when she took the job on that she would have to work in a cage of lions and a pit filled with venomous snakes. The form just about broke her heart. She had no discipline whatsoever, and from the moment she walked through the classroom door, there was chaos.

'Quiet! Sit down! Turn round! Put that down! Stop that!' she screeched before she had even crossed the threshold. 'Make less noise or we'll all write up notes.'

No one took a blind bit of notice of her.

'Right! That's it!' she yelled. 'Start writing notes! Now!'

She turned to the blackboard and began scribbling furiously on the board. Detailed notes on the Congresses of Vienna, the foreign policy of Palmerston, Kitchener's action in the Sudan, the Jameson Raid and the Boer War. Nobody even bothered to read the incomprehensible jargon she was chalking up so energetically. Most continued with their own activities.

In the front row, Robin Gabrielson was acting out the grunting of the Nile boatmen as they towed Kitchener's barge down the river; Billy was playing Hangman with Oscar; Olly was compiling a dictionary of swear words and, having reached 'B', was finding that letter as fruitful as 'A', which he had completed during Edith's last lesson with words like 'abuse', 'adultery', 'anus' and 'arse', along with compound words derived from these like 'arse-kisser' and 'arse-licker'.

At some point in the lesson, Oscar began asking his historical questions.

'Miss, is it true that during the Sino-Japanese War the Japs forbade the importation of Chinese prose?'

The question he was most proud of was:

'Miss, yesterday, you were talking about the Boer War. Can you tell us please who's Krujer?'

And Miss Dunn would naively begin answering his question:

'You mean Paul Kruger, I think. Well, of course, he was the Afrikaner leader and president of the Transvaal.'

'Ah, now I see, miss. The Afrikaner leader. He's Krujer. Thank you, miss.'

Finally, as she was leaving at the end of the lesson, Oscar would call out to her just as she reached the door:

'Miss, when's your next period?'

But even Edith Dunn spotted the *double-entendre* and obligingly blushed for the class. If only she had taken a leaf out of Bart Jarvis's book and threatened them with Brother Dorian, she would have solved her problems in one go.

June the sixth 1944 was D-Day. A terse, low-key announcement from General Eisenhower's HQ told the world that the long-awaited invasion of Europe had at last begun: 'Allied naval forces supported by strong air forces began landing Allied armies this morning on the northern coast of France.'

It was also D-Day for the Upper Fifth. The School Certificate examination of the Northern Universities Joint Board began.

From the beginning, it soon became obvious that the

exam was to be a travesty. The students were ill-prepared not only by the final year's course but by the whole period of their grammar-school education, which had been completely disrupted by a world war.

Apart from this major factor, there were one or two local practices which did not stand up to scrutiny. In art, for example, Billy's sketching and drawing skills were extremely limited – but not so those of his exam neighbour, Robin, who possessed a genuine talent in this direction. The subject for the drawing-from-memory part of the art exam that year was an inspirational one – a shovel resting across a bucket. The two friends sat at the same exam table. A quick switch of drawing boards, a quick switch back again, and lo! Billy had a most beautiful, accurate representation of the subject on his drawing sheet. The architecture section of the tests followed, and the art teacher invigilated the students – checking to see that there was no hanky-panky. As he circulated the examinees, he stopped at the occasional desk.

'No, Wilde, you've got that buttress wrong,' he murmured. 'It should look like this. Here, let me show you.'

And he executed a quick, skilful sketch on Oscar's exam paper.

He moved on, reached Billy's desk and looked over his shoulder.

'That Tudor chimney isn't quite right. Don't you recall doing it last month? This little drawing should help you remember.'

He left his crib on the desk for Billy to copy.

'I'll be back in five minutes to collect my drawing,' he said softly.

But Billy wasn't only a recipient, he was also a giver, and with his friend Robin he had a quid pro quo arrangement.

'What did you get for number six, Hoppy?' Robin asked in the algebra exam.

'Um . . . $x = 69$ and $y = 73$,' whispered Billy.

And in the French and Latin exams, Billy was a ready source of information for vocabulary.

'What's the French for "nest"?'

'*Le nid.*'

'What's the Latin for "The boys were hurrying"?'

'*Pueri festinabant*,' Billy whispered.

Two minutes later, Robin called his attention again.

'Psst! Hoppy, quick! That sentence *Fraus est celare fraudem*. What's it mean?'

' "It is a fraud to conceal a fraud",' said Billy in an undertone.

Thus ended Billy's grammar-school education.

The results of the examinations were published in July. Taken as a whole they were mediocre, as were Billy's but he was the only one to pass in all nine subjects – including geography.

'Blame the war,' everybody said.

At the final meeting of the smokers' club in the back-street alley, the members strolled along, puffing ruminatively at their fags and kicking away the odd condom.

'Well, boys, that's the end of the year,' said Oscar. 'See you next September in the sixth form.'

'Not me,' said Billy. 'I've had enough.'

'But don't you want to go to college?' asked Robin.

'No thanks,' replied Billy. 'I can't see the point in any of it. I've just completed five years' grammar-school education. Some education! The whole thing has been a mockery and a sham. What have I learned? How to fend off a randy headmaster and how to cheat at exams. In addition, my brain has been crammed with a lot of useless facts. I know about the Congresses of Vienna, how to copy a Tudor chimney from a crib and how to conjugate irregular verbs in French and Latin. Indispensable bits of knowledge to survive in the modern world.'

'But you were top in maths, Hoppy. Surely you're not going to waste all that?' said Titch.

'Maths!' Billy said. 'I know about quadratic equations, how to solve problems about filling baths and papering rooms, and, oh yes, that any two sides of a triangle are greater than the third, so I cross a field diagonally, but then the village idiot does that.'

'What will you do then?' asked Nobby.

'I'm not coming back to school for more of the same old stuff, that's for sure. I'll look for a job.'

'What sort of job?' asked Oscar.

'Dunno,' said Billy. 'I'd like to try my hand at being a writer. Maybe a job on a newspaper is the answer.'

Chapter Twenty-Six

Gopher On The Guardian

The middle-aged, bespectacled man behind the desk at the Juvenile Employment Bureau studied Billy's job application card whilst Billy studied his face, thinking how much he resembled Dr Crippen with his small moustache and his wire-framed specs. The clerk looked up.

'What kind of job are you looking for, Mr Hopkins?'

'What kind are you offering today?'

'Well, let's see now.'

He consulted his box of tricks.

'Here's one. Lift operator at Dobbin's.'

'No. My brother tried that. We all felt he was getting a bit above himself.'

'A comedian, eh? I notice that under 'previous experience', you've put down 'shoe-shining'. How would you fancy a job in a shoe shop?'

'No thanks. I've had enough of the shoe trade.'

'There's a job here at Atherton colliery. What about a career in mining?'

'After a grammar-school education, I think that's a bit beneath me.'

'Your jokes are killing me. Let's be serious for a minute.

First I need to know if you're manual or non-manual.'

'I thought I'd like to be a writer.'

'Ah, at last. Now we're getting somewhere. A writer? I see. A pen-pusher. That's non-manual.'

'I would have thought pushing a pen was manual.'

'Look, don't try to tell me my job.'

'Sorry. I don't just want to push a pen. I want to write imaginative stories; stories that I've made up out of my head.'

'Ah, then you'll want a job on a newspaper.'

'I'd love one if you have one.'

'The best way to go about it is to start on a little paper like the *Cheetham Gazette* and write about local events, like football matches or what's on at the local flea-pit.'

'Good idea. I'll take it.'

'But unfortunately, we don't have any jobs like that just at the moment. I see you've written "ballroom dancing" as one of your hobbies. Why not a job writing about that on a paper like *The Dancing Times*?'

'Sounds great. Right up my street.'

'However, we don't have any such job on our books.'

'Look, this is ridiculous. What jobs do you have on your books?'

'There's one here working on the *Manchester Guardian*.'

'But that's the best quality newspaper in the country. Well, second, anyway, after *The Times*. I'm not ready to write for that yet.'

'Oh, it's not as a writer.'

'Well, what is it as?'

'A copy boy – a sort of messenger boy. But you'd be mixing with the top journalists in the land. Maybe you could work your way up the ladder.'

'If there's a chance of getting on the staff some day, I'm willing to start at the bottom. What's the deal?'

'Pay, thirty-five shillings a week,' he said, reading from the card. 'Hours five p.m. to one a.m. And you get Saturday night off.'

'I'll give it a go. But that's my ballroom dancing gone for a Burton.'

'Good. The job's yours. Take this card of introduction and ask for Mr Fogg, who's head of the post-room and will clear up any questions you may have. And good luck.'

Frank Fogg was a short, disabled old man with a pronounced, bouncing limp and a withered left arm.

'Are we pleased to see you,' he said. 'We've been short-handed for weeks now. It says on this paper that your name's William Hopkins. But that's much too formal. What do we really call you?'

'My friends call me Hoppy.'

'Then Hoppy it is,' he said, 'though I'm the one you should be calling Hoppy, eh?'

He pointed to the other copy boy sitting at the table in the centre of the room. A tall, handsome, fair-haired youth about eighteen years of age, he was impeccably dressed in neatly pressed flannels, white silk shirt, dark tie and smart sage-green jersey; well groomed right down to his manicured fingernails, and probably his toenails as well.

'This is Miles Harrison, your opposite number; you two will be working very closely together.'

'Hi, Hoppy,' said Miles, smiling and extending his hand. 'Good to know you.'

'Hi,' replied Billy shyly.

'Our job,' said Mr Fogg, 'is to act as a communication centre between the writers and the printers. We are their go-betweens.'

'You mean messenger boys?' said Billy.

'That's another way of putting it, I suppose,' said Mr Fogg.

'It's a crude way of putting it,' said Miles. 'We are essential cogs in the production machine. We are the conduit which facilitates the flow of communication and information between the various parts of the network structure.'

'What happens,' continued Mr Fogg, 'is that the tele-printers upstairs chatter out the news on every conceivable subject. It's then dropped down a chute to us and we make sure it reaches the right sub-editor, who then writes it up in King's English. Show him how it's done, Miles.'

Miles collected all the strips of news items from the table and placed them between different fingers.

'Home – Parliament,' he listed, 'Sport – Entertainment – Foreign – Local Government – War – Science. See, I have eight items in eight finger spaces. Now follow me.'

Miles led the way into a large room – quiet, with an atmosphere like a reference library – in which numerous sub-editors, eye-shades on their foreheads, were busily writing up the day's news.

'We now collect their finished copy,' Miles whispered, 'and we send that up on a pulley to the compositors working upstairs on their linotypes.'

Billy examined a piece of finished copy and found it a mass of strange wiggles and hieroglyphics.

'Is this in code, Mr Fogg?' he asked when they were back in the post-room.

'It is a kind of code between the sub-editors and the compositors – they seem to understand it well enough, though.'

'And that's all there is to the job?' asked Billy. 'Carrying bits of papers to and fro.'

'Oh, no,' said Miles. 'Along the main corridor – we call

it the Holy of Holies – there are all the VIP leader-writers – the editor, A.P. Wadsworth, the Miscellany writer, Gordon Phillips, the deputy-editor, J.M. Pringle and other big writers like Wainwright, Derek Senior, Crozier and the features editor, Miss Linley.'

'And what do we have to do with them?' asked Billy.

'We collect their leaders and so are privileged to be the very first in the whole of Britain to read what the *Manchester Guardian* has to say about current events.'

'Big stuff, eh? And is that it?'

'There's more,' said Miles. 'A.P. Wadsworth and Gordon Phillips always consult me and ask my advice as they're writing their main leaders. I'll show you later on in the night.'

'That reminds me, Miles,' said Mr Fogg. 'Isn't it time to collect those items from Miss Linley?'

'Oh, yes, Mr Fogg,' said Miles. 'Perhaps Hoppy could collect them as his first assignment.'

'Be glad to,' said Billy, anxious to contribute and be accepted as one of the team.

'Right then,' said Mr Fogg. 'Ask Miss Linley, who's in the fifth office along the corridor, if you could have the long stand and the big weight.'

'Rightaway,' said Billy, eagerly.

He soon found Miss Linley's office. He knocked lightly on her door.

'Come!' she called.

'Good evening, miss,' he said. 'Mr Fogg asked if you could let me have the long stand and the big weight.'

Miss Linley was a middle-aged lady with greying hair. She had obviously been very pretty when younger. She smiled happily.

'You're new here, aren't you?' she said. 'What's your name?'

'Yes, Miss Linley. New here tonight. Everyone calls me Hoppy.'

'Welcome aboard, Hoppy. I'm expecting an important phone call from London any moment now. If you could just stand outside and wait for a while, I'll be with you shortly.'

Billy took up his stance outside her office door. Half an hour passed by ... nothing happened. He stood his ground. Another quarter of an hour. Nothing.

'Strange,' he said aloud, shaking his head. Then the penny dropped. He knocked on her door again.

'Come!' she called.

'Thank you for the long stand and the big weight, miss.'

'You're welcome, Hoppy,' she said, laughing.

Back in the post-room, Mr Fogg and Miles were waiting. When Billy appeared, they both roared with laughter.

'What kept you?' chuckled Mr Fogg.

'Now we'll go and have a conference with the editor and the Miscellany writer,' said Miles, still chuckling.

'No tricks!' said Billy.

'No tricks, honest.'

They arrived outside the office of the big white chief, A.P. Wadsworth, and Miles tapped gently on the glass door.

'Yes,' barked Wadsworth. 'Come in.'

'I've come for the usual consultation, sir,' said Miles.

'That's the new copy boy, eh?' said the editor. 'Welcome to the *Manchester Guardian* staff. Right, Miles, what're you waiting for? Fire away, then.'

'Pies are on the menu for supper tonight, sir. Cheese and onion, meat and potato, steak and kidney, plus the usual veg.'

'Yes, yes. What do you recommend?'

'Cheese and onion looks good, sir.'

'Very well, then bring that for me. Oh, and collect tonight's editorial, will you?'

'See what I mean about the editor consulting me before he submits his editorial?' said Miles.

As they walked back to the post-room, Billy read the editorial hot from Wadsworth's typewriter.

'*Five years!*' it said. '*We look back today upon five years of the sternest struggle which the British people have ever fought, a war for our national survival, for the rights of free peoples and for the life of civilisation itself . . .*'

'This is pretty good stuff,' said Billy. 'I think he deserved the steak and kidney instead of that cheese and onion.'

'Right,' said Miles. 'But we must make sure there's some of that left for us at twelve o'clock.'

So Billy joined the staff of the *Manchester Guardian*, and it was not long before he had the routine practices of the job at his fingertips. After he'd been there over a month, he began to wonder when he might get the chance to write something.

'When I joined the staff here, Mr Fogg,' he said one day, 'I hoped to become a writer.'

'Yes,' said Fogg. 'I thought that might be the case. But you know, Hoppy, you're going about it the wrong way. You wouldn't believe it to look at me, but I too joined the staff here over thirty years ago with the same idea.'

'What happened, Mr Fogg?'

'Well, about twenty years ago my bicycle and I got into an argument with a GPO van which left me like this. But before that, I had big ideas about becoming the next C.P. Scott. And then I found out the truth.'

'And what's that?'

'All the writers on this paper, even the reporters, are time-served journalists. Most of them have honours English degrees, many of them Oxbridge. Working your way up from the rank of copy boy isn't on. Look at me – aged sixty and still a copy boy after all these years. The only thing I've got to look forward to is retirement, a gold watch and a nursing home. Do you really want to become a writer?'

'I really do, Mr Fogg – it's my one great burning ambition in life.'

'Then go and study for a degree. Become an expert in something so that you can write with authority and knowledge. Don't let anyone or anything distract you from that purpose. When you're young, you'll find all kinds of temptations around you trying to pull you off your chosen path. Don't let them. Stick with your goal. Don't stay as a copy boy all your life, taking restaurant orders from the leader writers and acting as a go-fer for the rest of the staff. Start as a door-mat – and you'll end up as a door-mat.'

'So there's no chance for me to become a writer on this paper?' said Billy miserably.

'Sorry to be so blunt, Hoppy. You may have some talent for writing but you'll never develop it as a messenger boy. I'm sorry for you, but it's for your own good. I'm really doing you a big favour telling you all this.'

'What about Miles? Have you told him the same thing?'

'Don't talk to me about Miles! He has delusions of grandeur and is living in cloud-cuckoo land. His real name is Harry Miles but he's switched the names around to Miles Harrison. Says it sounds posher and more impressive. That's Miles to a T. All image and no substance. He goes home at night looking more like the editor than the editor.'

This statement about Miles was true. Billy had taken to accompanying him on the same all-night bus after work. For these public appearances, Miles wore an immaculately tailored military-type raincoat, and a smart trilby; he carried a leather attaché case with the words 'MILES HARRISON: MANCHESTER GUARDIAN' blocked in gold letters on the side for all the world to see. When they boarded their bus, they each carried a fresh-smelling copy of the next day's paper straight from the presses, and talked to each other about the night's events as if they had written and produced it personally.

'Before APW sent up his copy to the compositors tonight, he asked my advice,' said Miles in a voice that all the bus could hear, 'and I told him the first option would be the one least likely to give him ulcers.'

'Yes,' said Billy, 'and I thought the Low cartoon tonight was particularly apt, so I told the illustration editor that she ought to go ahead with it.'

At that point, the bus conductor came round collecting fares.

'My son was hoping to become a reporter,' the conductor said, addressing Miles. 'What would you advise, sir?'

'Tell him to drop me a line with a small example of his work. That's me,' he said, pointing to his name on his case.

'Thank you, sir. Oh, no, never mind the fare. Have this one on me,' he said, giving a broad wink.

In fact, the idea of a copy boy writing for the great newspaper was not entirely barmy. Gordon Phillips welcomed stories for the tailpiece of his Miscellany column and a payment of ten shillings was made for a successful entry. Billy managed to get one published during his time there.

FEROCITY AT THE THEATRE

Emerging from the Opera House the other night after a performance of *King Lear*, two theatre-goers were overheard to say:

'Some say Wolfit takes the cake but is Giel-gud!'

'Yes, and some say Gielgud takes the cake but you should see Donald Wolfit!'

'Rather a ferocious contribution, I think,' said Gordon Phillips after he'd read it. 'Nevertheless, I'll accept it. You write rather well, by the way. Shows promise!'

This from the great man himself! God had spoken!

It was about this time that Adele began to make her feelings known.

'Look, Julian,' she said, 'if we're going to continue as partners, we need more practice. The odd afternoon session at the Ritz and the Saturday-evening hop at Harrigans – well, they're just not enough if we're going to get anywhere.'

'But it's my job, Adele,' he said.

'Some job! A glorified messenger boy! Sometimes you even dress like one. We need to get a decent suit and maybe change our hairstyle. Then we'd be getting somewhere. But I really do wish we would change our job. Can't we get one with decent hours so that we can spend more time together? And not just for dancing either. The settee and I are wondering when you're going to come back to us.'

'Funny you should say that, Adele,' said Billy. 'I've been thinking exactly the same myself. And as for my job, I had hopes of becoming a writer one day but there's no chance of coming up through the ranks. Not on the *Manchester Guardian*, anyway.'

'It's just a dead-end job for dead-beat characters,' she

said. 'You can get a job with better pay and higher status if you really look. My dad's always telling me that without money, you're nothing in this world and nobody'll respect you. And anyway, I don't want my friends saying I go round with a messenger boy.'

'Dead right, Adele,' he replied. 'At the *Guardian* I've learned how to carry bits o' paper between my fingers, carry messages, read out the menu every night till I can say it in my sleep. "And what would you like tonight, sir? Steak and kidney, meat and potato or cheese and onion? Yes, sir. Yes, sir. Right away, sir. Three bags full, sir." And all for thirty-five bob a week. I can see myself still doing it at sixty, like old Mr Fogg.'

'Now you're talking sense,' she said. 'So what are you going to do about it?'

'The only way to become a writer and to get on the writing staff of a paper like the *Manchester Guardian* is by going to college or university.'

'I hope you don't,' she said quickly. 'There's no money in books, study and all that. Besides, that would take you away from me. It's here that I need you – partnering me on the dance floor.'

'And on your front-room settee as well.'

'Trust you to think of that.'

' "In the spring a young man's fancy lightly turns to thoughts of sex", Tennyson said that.'

'And in your case, not only in the spring.'

'I think you're beginning to understand me at last,' he said.

At Christmas that year, Billy reached the end of his tether as general dog's-body and glorified waiter. Early in the New Year he handed in his notice at the newspaper and began to look for another job.

Chapter Twenty-Seven

It Takes Two To Tango

'Everyone thinks the tango is difficult,' said Frank Rogers, 'but it's actually easier than the other dances.'

'I love the tango music and rhythm,' said Adele, 'and I just adore the jerky head movements.'

'She loves South Americans,' added Billy. 'But where do the jerky movements come from, Frank?'

'The tango came from Cuba in the late nineteenth century,' said Frank, 'via Argentina, Spain and France. Unlike the flowing dances – the waltz, the foxtrot and the quickstep – it is a kind of static, stop-start dance with aggressive movements.'

'Why jerky movements, though?' asked Billy.

'The jerky movements are reminiscent of a strutting cockerel asserting his authority. But enough of the lecture, let's check your hold. Right arm further round Adele.'

'With pleasure,' said Billy, holding Adele on his right side.

'Behave, Julian,' said Adele.

'Bring your left hand slightly in towards yourself, Julian, and lower it slightly. Good. Now, let's try it all to music.'

He switched on 'La Cumparsita'.

'Ready – now!'

Adele and Billy began to dance the tango with perfect rhythm and expression, like two professionals.

'Remember all I've told you,' Frank called. 'Staccato movements. Crisp walk! Keep it sharp! Eyes . . . look at each other! That's it! Change direction – now! Body sway . . . good! Rock turn! Back corté! Promenade – turn! Outside swivel and sway!'

'That felt good,' said Adele.

'You know,' said Frank, 'you two are looking better on the floor each time I see you. You've got good appearance, excellent technique and fluent movement.'

'Do you think we're ready for competitions yet, Frank?' Adele asked.

'I've taken you both as far as I can,' he said. 'Now you need the experience of competitive dancing. You may not win straight off, but it would be good if you had a shot at it.'

'We're ready, Frank, as soon as you give the word,' said Billy.

'There's the Manchester Amateur Tango in a coupla weeks' time at the Ritz ballroom. That'll be the time to get you two launched.'

'Then I'd better start thinking about my dress,' said Adele. 'All those thousands of sequins to be sewn on. It's going to be hard work.'

'Yes, for your mother,' Billy said. 'I suppose I'd better start saving for the hire of my Moss Bros suit.'

Later, after Harrigan's Saturday-night ball, Billy and Adele got down to their regular snogging session on the front-room settee.

'Don't get carried away, Julian,' she whispered. 'Keep your self-control.'

'It's not me you should be talking to,' he said. 'It's JT down there.'

'JT?'

'John Thomas – he's got a mind of his own. Nothing to do with me what he decides.'

'That's the beast in you.'

'On the contrary, he always behaves like a perfect gentleman.'

'How do you make that out?'

'He always stands up in the presence of a pretty lady.'

'Sometimes I think you're crazy.'

'Yes, Adele. Crazy for you. When are we two really going to get it together? These necking sessions are driving me wild. You can't go on teasing me like this.'

'I don't want to go too far, Julian. If you made me pregnant, it would ruin everything.'

'We could always use something.'

'You mean a Durex. I've seen them advertised in the chemist's. I don't know how anyone could have the nerve to ask for them.'

'No need. I've got some left from the time I worked in the Red Cross. American rubbers.'

'I don't know. I don't really trust those things.'

'Look, Adele, we've got to do something or I'll end up as a babbling idiot.'

'Oh, I'm still not sure about it. But . . . well . . . look . . . I'm not promising anything, Julian, but sometimes my parents go out on a Saturday night to the Queen's Park Hipp. Maybe we could . . . maybe that'd be our chance . . . maybe . . . I'll let you know.'

'I'll love you, Adele, till the world stops turning.'

'I'll love you, Julian, till the stars lose their glory.'

'Till the birds fail to sing.'

'Do you have a handkerchief handy, Julian?' she whispered into his ear.

'It's late, Adele,' said the voice from the ceiling.

'Julian's just on his way, Dad,' she said.

'Back again already!' said the Juvenile Employment Officer. 'So what happened to our budding young Charles Dickens at the *Manchester Guardian*?'

'It wasn't Charles Dickens they wanted. It was Joe Muggins to run their errands and carry their messages.'

'And now I suppose you'd like me to find you another job? What kind would you like this time?'

'Anything that doesn't involve night work.'

The officer consulted his box and flicked through several cards.

'Do you have a good hand?' he asked. 'Only here's a job offering thirty-seven shillings a week for a good hand.'

'As a matter of fact, I've got two good hands. Does that mean double pay?' Billy said, holding out both hands as evidence.

'I remember you now,' said the officer. 'You're the one with the funny sense of humour and the ballroom dancing.'

'That's me summed up in two phrases,' said Billy. 'Does this job require special knowledge or anything like that?'

'No, it simply requires good penmanship, calligraphy – handwriting to you. You don't make blots or anything like that, do you?'

'No, I've tried to keep my copybook clean. I'm not an ink-spiller, provided I don't have to use a quill pen. Who's the job for – Dombey and Son?'

'Listen, Tommy Handley,' the man said. 'Show a bit more respect. The job is with the Inland Revenue. They're switching over to the Pay-As-You-Earn system and there's an urgent need for clerks to write up their new filing cards. Hours nine to five.'

'I think I can push a pen with panache,' said Billy. 'I'll take it.'

'Very well, then. Take this introduction card to District Three, Sunlight House, and ask for a Mr Albert Fiddler.'

'Fiddler? Inland Revenue. You must be joking!'

'Your corny sense of humour should take you a long way,' said the clerk. 'A long, long way.'

Billy found Sunlight House on Quay Street and took the lift up to the eighth floor. He went through the office door leading to the Third District of the Inland Revenue. There was certainly no sunlight there – not even fresh air. The office was a large, smoke-filled room with a great number of desks at which sat several wan, sad-looking tax officers studying mountains of paper and puffing away at their fags. There was an air of doom and gloom about the place.

Billy presented himself at the counter.

'May I please see Mr Fiddler?'

'What's your tax problem?' said the shrivelled-up old man on counter duty.

'No tax problem. I'm the new clerk.'

'God help you!' said the old man, shaking his head. 'Come this way.'

Albert Fiddler, a sour, sallow-looking individual, was the most miserable bloke Billy had ever set eyes on outside Gardenia Court. His mouth turned south at the corners, giving him a perpetual expression of disapproval. Strangers in the street put it down to a bad case of indigestion but the permanent frown frozen on to his features was more the result of a lifetime spent poring over ledgers and unravelling the financial affairs of countless would-be tax-dodgers than problems with his metabolism.

Let it be understood then – Albert Fiddler was not a happy man. He could never understand why his fellow-citizens seemed so unwilling to pay their taxes with a smile, as he himself did.

Billy wasn't the only recruit that Monday morning. There was also a young, fair-haired boy eagerly waiting to be instructed in his duties.

'We start here at nine o'clock prompt,' recited Fiddler in a bored monotone. 'If you're late, your pay gets docked fifteen minutes for every five minutes or part thereof that you are behind time. You get one hour for lunch and the same rules apply if you come back after one p.m. Any questions so far?'

'No, Mr Fiddler,' the two youths replied.

'Now, Hopkins and Fernley, as you were no doubt told at the Labour Exchange, we are changing over our whole system to PAYE. Your job will be to copy out the names and addresses from these big ledgers and transfer them on to con-cards.'

'Just that, Mr Fiddler? Names and addresses?' said Billy brightly.

'Yes, just that, Hopkins,' he sighed wearily. 'Our qualified tax officers will do the rest, the brain-work – sorting out code numbers, et cetera. You print the surname at the top followed by the other names, in legible handwriting. Addresses should be printed neatly underneath. Do you think you can manage that?'

'I think so, Mr Fiddler. How many names and addresses are there?'

'This first batch is the whole of the GPO in our catchment area. About five thousand, I believe. But when you've finished them, we have the rest of our district taxpayers, about thirty thousand in toto.'

'Yes, Mr Fiddler.'

'To avoid you getting bored, you can arrange the con-cards in strict alphabetical order when you've finished writing them up.'

'Yes, Mr Fiddler.'

Billy surveyed the waiting ledgers and the huge pile of blank con-cards, and his spirits plunged.

'My God,' he said to the other lad. 'The labours of Hercules.'

'His jobs were easy,' said Cliff Fernley. 'He had it cushy – killing a monster or two and cleaning out a few stables. Look at us, we've got thousands of cards to fill in.'

'And Hercules was made immortal at the end, whereas we just get thirty-seven shillings a week. No use moaning about it, though. We may as well make a start.'

After an hour, Billy said:

'In the Catholic Church, we have a prayer, "O God, send me here my purgatory." I think the prayer's been granted.'

'Who said this is purgatory? More like hell, if you ask me,' whispered Cliff.

Billy began singing softly to the tune from Gilbert and Sullivan's *HMS Pinafore*:

> *'When I was a lad, I served a term*
> *As office boy to an Attorney's firm,*
> *As office boy, I made such a mark*
> *That they gave me the post of a junior clerk.*
> *I served the writs with a smile so bland*
> *And I copied all the letters in a big round hand,*
> *I copied all the letters in a hand so free*
> *That now I am the boss of District Three.'*

'No singing whilst on duty!' said Fiddler, scowling.

Hour after hour they sat there, the two young men, copying, copying, copying until their hands ached. After ten days they finished the GPO staff, only to be given the employees of several large firms in the area. The days became weeks and the weeks became months and still they sat there, copying out the names and addresses from the big ledgers.

'My God, my God!' Billy cried out one day in anguish. 'Why hast Thou forsaken me? Cliff, this is worse than a term in prison. I'd rather be on a chain gang – at least they're out in the fresh air. This task we've been set is like writing out the London telephone directory. What have we done? What have we done to deserve this?'

'Perhaps we were murderers in a past life,' said Cliff, 'and this is our karma.'

'If you're right,' said Billy, 'then we must have been mass murderers to merit such a punishment. I'll say a prayer that this torture will come to an end soon.'

St Albert Fiddler must have heard him, for the next day he came to them.

'You two have done very well. You have completed more than twenty thousand con-cards between you. Time for a change. We don't want you becoming bored, and so I'm giving you a new task. I'm putting you on a creeping check.'

'Oh, thank you, thank you, Mr Fiddler,' exclaimed Billy. 'But what's a creeping check?'

'In the filing room, we have over thirty thousand files. Sometimes they get put back in the wrong order. Your job for the next few weeks will be to check through them all and make sure they're in the correct sequence. If they're not, put them right. It'll make a change from all those con-cards, anyway.'

'You've been praying to the wrong saint, Hoppy,' said

Cliff Fernley after a week of it. 'I'd rather be back on the con-cards. Look at the cuticles of my fingers, torn to ribbons.'

That night, when he got home, Billy said to his mam:

'I don't think I can stand much more of this job, Mam. I'll end up in Prestwich Asylum if I have to spend my life filling in con-cards and doing creeping checks.'

'Everybody has to work, son. And you can't expect to like your work. That's what you get paid for – for doing summat that you don't like doing. Otherwise they wouldn't pay you, would they? Stands to reason.'

'There are two things keeping me sane at the moment, Mam. One is my dancing. If it weren't for that, I think you could send for the yellow van.'

'And what's the other?'

'Reading and studying. I've started reading Plato's *Republic* just so's my brain won't seize up.'

'And what about your ideas of becoming a writer or a teacher? I hope you haven't given them up.'

'Just about, Mam. I've dug myself into a deep hole and I can't see any way out.'

'You never know, son, you never know. Life's funny that way. Sometimes when you're least expecting it, opportunity knocks at your door. What I allus say is – what has to be will be.'

'That's a very helpful saying, Mam, I must say. You're a fatalist. It means I may as well stop trying.'

'It means nowt o' the sort. It means that if it's meant to happen, it will, that's all. And I'm not that thing you just said I was – that fatalist thing. I'm a Catholic and proud of it.'

'Anyroad, as I was saying,' Billy added, 'it's being so cheerful as keeps me going. That, Plato and my ballroom dancing.'

★　★　★

'You look very smart, sir, if you don't mind me saying so,' said the man at Moss Bros. 'A perfect fit. Tailor-made for you, in fact.'

'Nice of you to say so,' said Billy.

'That'll be thirteen pounds altogether, sir,' he said as he folded up and packaged the outfit. 'Three pounds for the hire of the dress suit and ten pounds deposit – returnable if the goods come back undamaged.'

Billy came out of the shop carrying his precious parcel as if it contained the Crown Jewels. All the way home on the 62 bus, he nursed it like a baby, and managed to reach the flat without mishap.

'Well I never,' said Mam when she saw the evening suit hanging up in the wardrobe. 'Our Billy's joined the toffs.'

'That there is the uniform o' the Tories,' said Dad. 'Didn't I say a long time ago that he'd be getting ideas above his station?'

Billy could hardly eat his omelette-tea that Friday night because of the excitement.

'This is a big tango competition, Mam. The best amateurs in Lancashire will be at the Ritz tonight.'

'I hope you win, son.'

'Oh, we don't think we'll win anything, Mam. We've not got the experience and it'll all depend on what the judges are looking for.'

'Then why go in for it?'

'For the experience. If we get any recalls, that'll be a big success.'

'Oh, I see.'

When Mam said 'I see' like that, it meant that she didn't.

'Anyroad, Mam, I'd better start getting ready. I've ordered a taxi for seven o'clock and I'm picking Adele up at quarter past.'

'A bloody taxi! What next!' said Dad.

After a long bath, a close, careful shave and a thorough sprucing-up, Billy emerged in full array.

'Bloody hell!' said Dad. 'He looks like a waiter at the Midland Hotel. He's bloody well gone over to the enemy.'

'Eeh, I'm right proud o' you, son,' said Mam. 'In them tails you look just like Astaire in that picture, *Top Hat*. All's you need now is a cane, a big hat and Ginger Rogers.'

'Wait a minute, then,' he said and ran into the bedroom.

A minute later he emerged wearing Dad's pot hat and carrying his walking stick under his arm, began to waltz around the flat giving his best imitation of Astaire singing and dancing.

Then he took his mother in his arms and began dancing around the table with her. 'You're as light as Ginger Rogers, Mam,' he said.

'Get off with you,' she said. 'You daft ha'porth.'

There was a loud knock at the door.

'That'll be my taxi,' Billy said. 'Better not keep it waiting.'

'Best o' luck, son,' Mam called. 'Do your best! And put these rosary beads round your neck and tuck them under your shirt so's they can't be seen. You got them beads at the infants' school for answering your catechism. D'you remember? And they've been blessed by the Bishop o' Salford. They'll help you to win summat, you'll see. And try not to let the neighbours see you as you go out. We don't want them thinking we're getting stuck-up and above ourselves.'

'Aye – do your best!' said Dad, looking out of the window. 'But some hopes of the neighbours not seeing you. Nosy buggers are looking out already.'

'And you're looking out o' your window looking at

them looking out of theirs,' said Mam.

'Aye,' he said, 'but it's our Billy's taxi, not theirs.'

A taxi at Gardenia Court was a rare event. A small crowd had gathered round the black cab when Billy got to the foot of the stairwell. There were three or four bare-arsed, snotty-nosed toddlers with the inevitable dummies stuck in their mouths. A mongrel dog raised its hind leg and pissed on the rear wheel of the waiting car.

'Sod off!' yelled the taxi-driver, aiming a kick at it.

'Ockins! Ockins!' simple-minded Annie sputtered when she saw Billy.

'Evening, Annie,' Billy said.

'Bleeding hell!' screeched Mrs Pitts from her veranda. 'It's the bleeding Duke o' Windsor.'

'More like a bleeding tailor's dummy,' said Mr Pitts, who was standing next to her.

Billy ignored all the comments and waved to his mam and dad, who were gazing down at him from the top veranda.

'All the best, our kid,' called Mam.

'To Clifton Street, please,' Billy said to the driver.

Five minutes later the taxi pulled up outside the terraced house which was Adele's home. Billy rang the bell; the door was opened by her mother, a small, kindly, round woman in her mid-forties.

'She's almost ready, Julian,' she said. 'She'll be down in a minute.'

'Plenty o' time, Mrs Lovitt,' he said.

'I'm really glad you're taking her out like this,' said the woman. 'Adele is our only child and she gets a bit turned in on herself sometimes. A bit depressed, like.'

'I didn't know that, Mrs Lovitt.'

'She can also have a bit of a temper if she's rubbed up the wrong way. I know me and George have got to tread carefully sometimes. She's looking really lovely tonight, though, you'll see. Mind you, she ought to be. She took the day off work and has been dolling herself up all day.'

'What exactly does she do, Mrs Lovitt?'

'Why, hasn't she told you? She's on the cosmetics counter at Kendals.'

'Ah, that explains her skill with make-up.'

'She's always been fussy about her appearance and that. Oh, here she is now.'

Adele appeared and Billy's heart skipped a beat. She had excelled herself in her preparations. She looked like a fairy princess – a vision in pale-blue tulle with sequins and pearls sparkling on the fitted bodice of her dress and shimmering in her light-brown hair, which she wore tied back to emphasise the beauty of her face and neck.

'You look stunning,' he gasped. 'You take my breath away. I can't believe that you are actually going to the ball with me.'

'Why, thank you, kind sir,' she said. 'And why shouldn't I be going with you, Mr Astaire?'

'Best of luck to both of you,' said her mother. 'You make a beautiful couple when I see you together like this.'

'Don't wait up, Mother. We may be quite late.'

'No, I'll wait for you to help you off with the dress.'

'I said don't wait up, Mother,' Adele flashed, 'and I mean it!'

'Temper! Temper!' said Mrs Lovitt.

'You just make me so bloody mad sometimes, Mother, you do, honestly,' Adele snapped, 'always fussing.'

'Don't spoil all your nice make-up, dear,' said Mrs Lovitt.

'Oh, come on, Julian,' Adele said impatiently. 'Let's go.'

★　★　★

The Ritz ballroom in Whitworth Street was crowded that Friday night with exquisitely dressed, glittering competitors, along with their supporters and spectators. The twenty-two-piece orchestra struck up and began playing in strict tempo the sweet-sounding melodies of the day – 'I'll Buy That Dream', 'Laura', 'You'd Be So Nice to Come Home To' and 'Who's Taking You Home Tonight?'. What a wonderful, magnificent scene as the radiant couples arrayed in full feather glided across the polished maple floor of the spacious ballroom. And what a glamorous, romantic night for Adele and Billy as they merged into the crowd of whirling, elegant dancers.

'I hope we get at least one recall after all our efforts,' he said.

'Don't worry, Julian,' she said confidently. 'We shall. We've got Frank Rogers sitting over there ready to give us support and advice. Also, we've been given the number twenty-eight – the year of our birth. It's bound to be lucky.'

'I only hope it doesn't mean we're going to come twenty-eighth,' he replied.

'And now we come to the main event of the evening – the one you've all been waiting for – the Manchester Amateur Tango Championship!' the Master of Ceremonies announced through the PA system. 'There will be three heats in all. So would competitors now kindly take the floor for heat one.'

'This is it,' said Billy nervously.

The band began to play 'Temptation' and the thirty competing couples took to the floor. The three judges, clipboards in hand, stood at different points in the ballroom jotting down notes as the dancers swished past them.

Adele and Billy gave it everything they'd got,

remembering all that Frank had taught them. Smooth, flowing, skimming steps – then crisp, staccato changes of direction capturing the elusive tango atmosphere. They felt completely at home on the floor and almost forgot they were in a competition. Ten minutes and heat one was over.

'Well done, you two,' said Frank when they joined him at his table. 'Couldn't have done it better myself. I'm sure you'll get a recall into heat two.'

He was right. They found themselves called back along with eleven other couples.

'I just can't believe it,' cried Adele. 'A recall on our first attempt. I knew my instincts were right, Julian, when I first saw you at Harrigan's all those months ago.'

'Watch your timing, Julian,' said Frank. 'Remember what I said about rhythmic expression – steal a little time from one step and add it to the other – that's what makes it fascinating to watch. And Adele, when you turn your head in a change of direction, make it sharp and brisk. Now go on and make me proud of you.'

'Right, boss,' said Billy.

The band began to play 'Jealousy' and the twelve couples went into their routines.

Adele and Billy danced the tango as they'd never danced it before. They skimmed across the ballroom with flair and panache, every movement, every step, clean and crisp, every variation performed in fine, graceful style: the fall-away promenade with outside swivel and brush tap, progressive link, twist turn, and a flourishing bow as the music came to a close.

'That was superb, Julian,' whispered Adele.

'You were pretty good yourself, Adele – everything depends now on what the judges thought of it.'

They hadn't long to wait. Adele gripped Billy's arm

nervously when the MC began making his announcement.

'For the final heat, the judges have selected the following six couples: numbers six . . . nine . . . fourteen . . . seventeen . . . twenty-four . . . and twenty-eight!'

'OH, JULIAN! JULIAN!' Adele shouted excitedly, clutching even more tightly at his arm. 'I CAN'T BELIEVE IT! WE'RE IN THE FINAL!'

'I had a hunch you two were going to get in,' said Frank. 'That last performance was the best I've ever seen you do. But now you're up against the very best amateurs in the north-west. You'll need to pull out something really special. Remember the cockerel and the jerky movements!'

'We can only do our best,' said Billy, touching the outline of the rosary beads under his dress shirt.

At that moment he glanced around him and it was then that he saw them. Sitting up in the spectators' balcony. He couldn't believe his eyes. There was his mam and his two sisters watching the whole performance. How had they got there? They must have taken a taxi! They must have had it all organised secretly. He gave them a big smile and a cheery wave of recognition, to which they responded with an encouraging thumbs-up.

'We'd better do well now, Adele,' he said. 'I've got half my family up there in the visitors' balcony.'

'Oh, God! Here's hoping,' said Adele, as the music struck up with 'La Cumparsita'.

They gave a repeat performance of the tango, but the knowledge that the Hopkins women were now eyeing his every step lifted Billy's efforts to a new level. This time, their presentation surpassed even that of heat two in brilliance and finesse. In quick succession, one subtle variation followed another, giving a sparkling, lively interpretation of the Argentinian dance. Footwork, body turns, head movements, facial expressions – all combined to produce a fluent, streamlined performance which brought spontaneous applause from the onlookers. As the music finished, Adele, smiling happily for the judges, timed her final curtsey to perfection.

'Out of this world,' Billy whispered to her. 'The best yet.'

'Same goes for you, Julian. You were fantastic.'

'If you two don't make the first three, I'll eat my hat,' said Frank Rogers. 'You excelled yourselves there. What happened to you, Julian? I've never seen you dance as well as that – ever.'

'Fear, Frank, fear. With the women of my family watching every move, I just had to pull something out of the hat.'

'And now, here are the results of our 1945 tango competition,' announced the MC. 'In third place, couple number twenty-eight; in second place, couple number six, and in first place, and the Manchester tango champions . . . couple number fourteen!'

It took a moment or two for them to take it in.

'OH, JULIAN! OH, JULIAN! WE MADE IT! WE MADE IT!' Adele cried ecstatically, throwing herself into Billy's arms. 'You great big wonderful Fred Astaire, you!'

'I knew all along we'd do it,' he said with pretend nonchalance. 'Otherwise I'd never have paid three pounds for the hire of this suit.'

'You wonderful, crazy boy,' she said. 'I love you.'

'I'm proud of you both!' called Frank enthusiastically. 'It's moments like this that make the job of dance instructor worthwhile. Well done!'

They went forward and collected their engraved silver medals to the applause and whistles of the crowd.

'Come on, Adele,' he said, pointing to the balcony.

'Come and meet the Hopkins women.'

'I hope they like me,' she said anxiously.

'How could they not?' he said as they made their way through a congratulatory crowd of spectators.

'Adele,' he said when they'd found them, 'I'd like you to meet my mother and my sisters – Pauline and Florence.'

'Pleased to meet you, I'm sure,' said his mam. 'And I think your dancing was lovely – just lovely.'

'Nice to meet you, and congratulations,' said Polly.

'Likewise,' said Flo. 'You both looked marvellous on the floor. I think you two should've come first, though.'

'Thank you all so much. It's so nice to meet all of you,' said Adele, shaking hands with each of them in turn. 'Isn't Julian an absolutely wonderful dancer?'

'Julian?' Mam asked. 'Who's Julian when he's at home? My son here is called Billy – not Julian.'

'S'all right, Mam,' he said. 'It's Adele's pet name for me, that's all.'

'Pet name? What are you – a dog or summat? And what's wrong with the name you were christened with, I should like to know? I don't understand all this changing o' names. Polly is now Pauline; Flo is Florence; and now our Billy isn't Billy any more – he's Julian.'

'But Julian's a lovely name, Mrs Hopkins,' said Adele.

'I'm sure it is,' said his mam. 'For someone else – but not our Billy.'

'Anyroad,' said Billy, anxious to get out of an awkward situation, 'we'll get back to our dancing, Mam, and then I'll be taking Adele home.'

'Good night, everybody,' said Adele. 'Hope to see you soon.'

'Good night, Adele,' said the Hopkins sisters.

'Good night, Adele,' said his mam. 'And good night, our Billy!'

'Good night, Mam,' Billy called.

'Julian . . . bloody daft name . . .' Mam muttered.

After the last waltz, Billy took Adele home by taxi.

'It's after midnight, Adele,' he said at her doorway. 'So I won't come in. But thank you for the most exciting night of my life.'

'And thank you, Julian,' she said, kissing him on the lips. 'It's all been like a wonderful dream and I don't want to waken up. I never thought for a moment we'd win anything.'

'I did all along,' he said, opening the buttons of his shirt and showing her the rosary. 'I think these beads I've had round my neck all evening might have helped a little.'

'Rosary beads?' she said, frowning. 'Who gave you those to wear?'

'My mother told me to wear them for success and good luck.'

'I see,' she said. 'Sorry, Julian. I don't believe in all that hocus-pocus, that mumbo-jumbo stuff. And talking of your mother, I had the distinct impression tonight that she doesn't like me. She objects to me calling you Julian. I'll bet you find her a bit awkward to deal with. And I'm sure of it – she doesn't like me.'

'Oh, she's not so bad, Adele. And I'm sure that you're wrong about her not liking you. But never mind all that about my mother for a moment – you won't have to dance with her. What about us? When are we two going to . . . you know . . . get together, like?'

'I think I'd rather like to have some sort of ring on my finger before we thought about that.'

'We're a bit young for rings and things, Adele – we're only seventeen, for God's sake.'

'I don't mean a wedding ring – an engagement ring for a start would do.'

'I'll start saving tomorrow. But in the meanwhile, we've still got JT to consider.'

'Oh, him! I'd forgotten about him. The gentlemanly JT. Look, they don't know it yet – but my parents are going to the Queen's Park Hipp tomorrow night. I'll see what I can do. Call for me about seven o'clock.'

'But how do you know in advance that your parents are going to the Hipp?'

'Oh, I have my little ways of persuading them. They usually do as I tell 'em. You can rely on it – they'll be on their way out just before seven.'

'I'll count the hours, Adele. And JT has just heard what you said and has begun to act like a gentleman again. We'll both see you tomorrow. Good night, Adele.'

'Good night, Mr Astaire.'

Her front door opened and her mother appeared.

'I thought I'd better help you off with the dress, Adele,' she said.

'Look, Mother,' Adele rasped. 'I told you not to wait up. I can damn well get the bloody dress off myself. I'm not a little girl, you know.'

Billy heard this little exchange as he walked away, but it didn't really register. Perhaps he didn't want it to.

The next morning was Saturday and Billy returned the Moss Bros outfit to the shop in St Anne's Square and got back his ten pounds deposit. He spent the rest of the morning browsing through Sherratt and Hughes bookshop, but his mind was on other things – certainly not books, except maybe for the one or two he found in the health section. He picked one out entitled *Family Health*.

'*Priapism*,' it read, '*a persistent erection that cannot be made to subside. If you have an erection that persists for no apparent reason, do not waste time trying to get it down with*

457

cold compresses or other home remedies. Go to the nearest hospital at once.'

What a thing to have, he said to himself. Suppose a ballet dancer got it. He'd have problems all right.

He looked furtively around the shop and put the book back hurriedly in case the prim middle-aged female shop assistant had seen him reading it. He selected another called *Guide to Better Living*.

'*Condom*,' it said, '*made of thin rubber and unrolled over the erect penis. Should be used in conjunction with a spermicide. Reliability: 2–15 per cent get pregnant. Disadvantages – can break or leak.*'

Best not to read these things, he thought, returning the book to the shelf. Anyway, where am I going to buy spermicide in Manchester on a Saturday morning? And when it says 'can break or leak', it probably means British-made. I'm sure the Yanks make their things stronger.

As he left the health section, the lady assistant eyed him suspiciously and he was glad to get out of the shop. He spent the afternoon in a state of feverish excitement. He lay on his bed reading, trying to concentrate on following the convoluted arguments between Socrates and Glaucon on the meaning of justice, but they held no appeal for him. Would it never be seven o'clock? The hands of their mantelpiece clock seemed to have stuck at four.

He unlocked his private drawer in the dressing table to check. Yes, they were still there in his wallet, along with the ten one-pound notes from Moss Bros. The packet containing three new pink Yankee condoms.

They won't be new for long, he thought salaciously.

The clock hands moved slowly, but oh so slowly, round to five.

'Switch the immersion on, Mam,' he said. 'I think I'll have a bath.'

'But you had one last night,' she said. 'Why so many baths? You haven't got scabies again, have you?'

'Don't be daft, Mam. I just want to relax for a while, that's all.'

'I'll bet you're going out with that girl again. The one that was calling you Julian. Bloody daft name. I just didn't take to her – I don't know why. You be careful of her, that's all. Don't go doing anything you shouldn't or she'll have you walking down the aisle afore you know where y'are. Anyroad, I'm sure too many baths can't be good for you – they ruin the pores of your skin.'

After a long soak, Billy shaved and applied liberal quantities of stinging aftershave to his face and body, primped up his hair and dressed in his best bib and tucker.

'You stink like a bloody brothel,' said Dad.

'Here, how do you know what a brothel stinks like?' Mam asked.

'It's just a way of speaking, Kate, that's all,' Tommy said humbly.

'I should hope it is,' she said.

'Anyway, he does stink a bit, you've got to admit,' he said. 'Where's he off to then? Chasing the girls, I'll bet.'

'Just 'cos I'm all spruced up and smelling nice for a change, everyone in this house thinks I'm up to summat. I'm just going dancing at Harrigan's, that's all.'

At 6.45 p.m., Billy stationed himself in a secluded spot at the top of Clifton Street, from where he had a clear view of Adele's house. He patted the back pocket of his trousers to make sure he had not forgotten the rubbers. No, they were still there. He was now trembling with excitement and anticipation at the thought of what lay ahead and what she had agreed to. A little before seven o'clock, the front door opened and her parents appeared.

'We'll be back around ten, Adele,' her dad called back. 'If you go to Harrigan's tonight, don't be back too late. It was well after midnight before you got to bed last night.'

He pulled the front door to and strolled down Clifton Street with his missus linking him. Billy waited a good five minutes and then, with heart pounding, knocked softly at the door. Adele appeared almost immediately.

'Come in, Julian,' she said. 'They've both gone off to the theatre.'

'I know,' he said. 'I saw them go.'

'I hope you've not been up in a tree watching them like a sniper.'

'No, I saw them from the end of the street. I've been waiting all day for this moment, Adele. Look, I'm trembling like a leaf. Is it still on?'

'I suppose so, if you insist,' she sighed. 'Did you get the American thingies?'

'I've got 'em here. Three of 'em.'

'You'll not need three unless you're Errol Flynn. All right, we may as well get this over. Give me a minute.'

She left the room and went upstairs, and Billy took the opportunity to remove his clothes. He sat naked on the settee. In a moment, she was back.

'I see JT is the perfect gentleman again,' she said. 'Better turn off the light, and lie down on the fireside rug.'

She switched on the electric fire.

'Right then,' she said, 'let's get on with it.'

'What about the rubber? We have to put that on first.'

'Oh, all right, come here. I'll do it. It's like rolling on a silk stocking.'

'Have you done this before?' he asked.

'No. Like you, it's my first time.'

She lay back and lifted her skirt.

'OK, I'm ready. You can do it now.'

'But I can't do it without some help from you. Guidance, like.'

'You'll have to find your own way in, Julian. No hands. I'm not helping you.'

Adele lay back, her body tense and unyielding, whilst he made several unsuccessful stabbing attempts.

'You're making a pig's ear of it, Julian. You've no idea, have you? You've lost your way.'

He tried again – and again – but could find no way in.

'Look,' she said after a while, 'this isn't going to work, Julian. I don't think you're doing it right.'

By this time, he had begun to fear she was right and that he really did lack the necessary skill.

'Remember, this was all your idea, Julian, not mine,' she said.

'Sorry, Adele. Maybe it wasn't such a good idea after all. What do you say we abandon it for the time being? Maybe try it some other time. I'll read a couple o' books on the subject.'

'That'd suit me fine, Julian. Some other time. I don't think this is the time or the place.'

They both stood up. JT was no longer behaving like a gentleman.

'It's a relief anyway to know I haven't got one of those priapism things,' he said.

'I'll slip upstairs and replace a few garments,' she said. 'Then I suggest we go out to Harrigan's to do the thing we're really good at – dancing.'

'Agreed,' he said.

As they walked together down Queen's Road, Adele's arm through his, Billy sensed that, somehow or other, it was the beginning of the end.

'When we're engaged, Julian,' she said, 'then I'll give

you the help you were asking for. But you really boxed it up tonight, didn't you?'

'Suppose so, Adele. But JT really does need help. After all, he doesn't have an eye down there to see where he's going.'

'If we were to announce our engagement, I think you'd find JT would be able to see where he was going.'

'You think so?'

'Mind you,' she continued, 'after we were married, we'd have to clear up one or two things.'

'Like, for instance?'

'Well, I wouldn't want to see you wearing any of those funny things, those rosary beads that you had on the other night, and I definitely wouldn't want any of those crucifixes and holy pictures I've heard you Catholics hang on the walls.'

'Right. Now I'm beginning to get the picture.'

'My dad said that you lot worship statues and other holy objects you have round the place. Is it true?'

'Of course it's true. Every night I talk to the statues, and sometimes they talk back. I've found I've had the best results from talking to a teapot or a cup and saucer.'

'Now you're mad at me. I can tell.'

'No. Didn't your dad tell you? Us lot never get mad at anyone. It's against the fifth commandment.'

'I'm only thinking of what's best for us, Julian. You know, when we're married. I can see it now. A nice little house and maybe two lovely children – a boy and a girl would be nice. I wouldn't want a house full of dozens of kids like I've heard some Catholics have, would you?'

'Not really,' Billy said grimly. 'But one thing you'd better start doing from now on.'

'Oh, and what's that?'

'Stop calling me Julian and start calling me Billy. And

another thing. I do not hang holy pictures and crucifixes, but if I married you, the first item on the agenda would be to book you and me a nice pilgrimage to Lourdes, where I'd buy the biggest statue of the Virgin, the biggest picture of the Sacred Heart and the biggest crucifix I could find to hang in our bedroom. Then I'd have a great big painting of the Pope done on the ceiling so that you'd see it every time we were on the job. Next, I would make sure that you had about twelve kids and I'd bring 'em all up as Catholics and try to get a few nuns and priests out of 'em.'

'If you're going to talk to me like that, you can bloody well get lost and find another partner.'

'Adele, you're just a selfish, spoiled brat who should have been spanked across the backside years ago.'

'And you can piss off, Billy, and find yourself another partner. After tonight, I don't want to set eyes on you again. Now I'm off home, and please don't call on me again.'

'Thanks for a very sexy evening, Adele. I really learned something tonight. I hope the next man you try it with has a John Thomas that can see in the dark. I'll send you a coupla presents for Christmas – a torch and a sex manual.'

'Don't bother, lover boy. You're the one who needs a sex manual, not me. And if you go to that confession thing you lot have in your church, don't tell him you've had sex tonight, 'cos you haven't, and you never will till you learn a few basic facts of life. Good night and good bye.'

After that night, Billy's enthusiasm for ballroom dancing and teaching basic steps at Harrigan's went cold. He stopped going so often. He could not find the energy or the will to look for yet another partner with whom he could go through the same old routine all over again. On the odd occasion when he did visit the dance studio, the spectacle of the dancers looked hideous: the rictus smiles, the orange panstick and oil-slick hairdos, the bitchiness, and the stupid prancing about in time to the mechanical music; the whole scene had lost its appeal for him.

On the contrary, he had found a new interest, one that absorbed him and gave him greater satisfaction – philosophy! Reading Plato's *Republic* and attempting to follow the arguments of Socrates on the subject of justice and the ideal state became his chief preoccupation. Perhaps something at school had rubbed off on him after all, and perhaps his education had not been the waste of time that he had imagined.

Chapter Twenty-Eight

Jacob's Ladder

'I think we're in a corner of Hades,' said Billy as he copied out the umpteenth con-card.

'And Fiddler is chief Hell's Angel in this section, thinking up fresh tortures for us every day,' said Cliff Fernley.

'Nothing – but nothing – could be worse than that creeping-check torture he had us on for three weeks.'

'Don't you be so sure about that, Hoppy. He's got a vivid imagination.'

'Anyway, here's a stupendous piece of news for you. A really great piece of news. That con-card I've just filled in was the very last.'

'You really mean it? The very last?'

'The very, very last. The thirty thousandth. A bloke called Zechariah Zuckerman.'

'I can't believe it. We ought to celebrate it in some way. Any ideas?'

'Well, those whom God would destroy he first sends mad.'

'So?'

'See that large bottle of Waterman's ink we've been dipping into for the last three months?'

'The one with all the pellets of paper, dead flies, et cetera?'

'The very one.'

'Well?'

'I'll give you half a crown if you drink it,' said Billy, laying down a shiny new coin.

'Hoppy, you must think I'm mad!'

He paused and looked from bottle to coin like a spectator at a tennis match.

'Half a crown, you say?'

'He who hesitates is lost,' said Billy.

'Right on! Carpe diem!' he cried, then seized the bottle, took a long draught of the blue goo and ran out to the toilets.

He came back after a couple of minutes displaying a set of azure-coloured teeth and gums.

'Half a crown if you don't mind, Hoppy.'

'With pleasure,' said Billy. 'Worth every penny. But why so blue, Cliff? Why so down in the mouth?'

He had begun to croon 'Where the Blue of the Night' when Fiddler sidled up.

'I've told you two before. No singing on the job,' he growled. 'Get on with your copying.'

'Finished, Mr Fiddler,' said Billy brightly.

'What – all thirty thousand?'

'Yep – all thirty thousand.'

'In alphabetical order?'

'In strict alphabetical order!'

'Then your next job is to check that all the con-cards agree exactly in sequence and in details with all the files in the stock-room.'

'But that means sixty thousand items in total. That'll take ages and ages,' whined Cliff, grimacing and showing his pearly blues. 'That's a double creeping check!'

'More like a double-cross,' said Billy. 'No use wailing about it! Let's get on with it!'

'What a bloody rotten life it is, Cliff,' Billy said when Fiddler had gone. 'I live in a block of flats that I'm sure are worse than the Gorbals, I've got this bleeding lousy job under the Marquis de Sade, and I've blown it with my girlfriend.'

'Oh, things aren't so bad,' said Cliff. 'We can always get pissed on a Friday night. There's that to look forward to.'

'You mean a trip to Never-Never Land. Nah. What's the use? That doesn't solve anything. But Cliff, fancy having to do this job for the rest of our lives!'

'You're a miserable get, Hoppy.'

'You've room to talk. You're the one that's blue. Anyway, what I'm suffering from is divine discontent.'

'You mean you're depressed?'

'No, more than that. I just can't see the point of it all. Why we're here on this planet, I mean. A philosopher was once asked, "What's the best Fate that can befall a man?" and he answered, "First, not to have been born, and failing that, to die early." '

'I know why we're here,' said Cliff.

'Why?'

'We're here because we're here because we're here. There is no reason. We're just accidents of nature. The whole universe is an accident – a series of meaningless coincidences. God's sick joke.'

'At least you believe in a God.'

As they got down to the tedious task, on a sudden whim Billy raised his eyes to heaven as he'd seen Christ do in Pictures of the Garden of Gethsemane, fingered the rosary beads in his pocket and called out in an anguished voice:

'Is there anyone up there listening? Then hearken to me, oh God and all ye angels and saints. If you will send down a Jacob's ladder and haul me out of this bottomless pit, I'll believe in you for ever more. Let me do something better with my life.'

'And what about me?' complained Cliff.

'You pray to your own God and get your own bloody ladder!'

'Have a good day, son?' Mam asked when he got home that night.

'Don't ask!' he said. 'Good day? At the Inland Revenue? I should be so lucky! The only thing interesting that happened today was my friend drank a bottle of ink.'

'Well, wouldn't you think they'd give you coffee or tea – growing lads like you. You must have a very funny canteen, that's all I can say. Oh, there's a letter up there for you,' she said, pointing to the mantelpiece.

'Letter? For me? Who do I know that can write? It's probably a demand for money.'

He took it to read in the bedroom in case it was from Adele, threatening to come back to him or recommending a sex manual. He slit open the envelope and read:

Dear Hoppy,
How's it going in the world of commerce? Here at school, things continue much as they did in your day: Oscar still thinking up witticisms for our amusement; Baldy still as deaf as a post; Edie Dunn still on the verge of a nervous breakdown; Olly continues with his dictionary of obscene words and has now reached the letter 'P' and I leave it to your imagination to think of the words he's found; the smokers' club is still smoking itself

to death, mainly on Park Drive since our Yankee bonanza came to an end.

The point of this letter, Hoppy, is to tell you that we, the smokers, are all applying for places at a teacher training college in Chelsea, London. The college is opening up again after being closed since 1939 and has been used as a mortuary during the war. So if we get in, they'll simply be exchanging one set of corpses for another. Why not take a day off and come to see us? We still smoke in the alley at dinner times.

Your old shoe-shine pal,
Robin.

'Who was the letter from, son?' Mam asked as they settled down to their evening tea.

'That wasn't a letter, Mam. It was a ladder from my friend Jacob.'

'Sometimes I think that income-tax job has driven you barmy, our Billy.'

Billy took a day's leave to visit his old chums at school.

'Gosh, it's good to be back amongst you normal, sane people after some of the characters I've been rubbing shoulders with,' said Billy as they walked down Smokers' Alley.

'Us normal, sane people? Are you trying to insult us, Hoppy?' exclaimed Oscar.

'I mean it's great to be back in the old smokers' club alley. I notice there's been no let-up in the shagging down here, judging by the number of bags left lying about.'

'I suspect they're all left by one man,' said Titch. 'A latter-day Bluebeard who's trying to break some kind of record.'

'Yes,' said Robin, 'he probably goes into the chemist's and says, "Gimme a gross o' Durex – the usual week's supply."'

'Perhaps it's President Paul Kruger with our Edie Dunn,' ventured Nobby.

'No banana-flavoured bags yet?' asked Billy.

'We don't really know,' said Robin. 'No one's willing to stoop so low as to sample one. You're welcome to try, Hoppy, if you like.'

'No thanks,' replied Billy. 'Peaches were more my fruit. Remember Blackpool?'

'What about your sex life?' asked Olly. 'Still a virgin?'

'Yes and no,' replied Billy. 'It was all set up for me. I was invited, had an admission ticket, but when it came to getting through the doorway – well, it wasn't as easy as you think.'

The smokers' club was all ears for its street-wise, street-hardened member.

'These are all very penetrating observations,' said Oscar.

'Not easy, Hoppy?' asked Nobby. 'I've never had any problems. What went wrong?'

'The lady tending the door failed to show me the way in. I think that she thought that my old man could see in the dark.'

'Perhaps she thought it was a carrot,' said Olly.

'Or perhaps she thought it had a lighted bulb on the end,' said Oscar, 'rather like a miner's lamp.'

'What you needed,' said Robin, 'was foreplay.'

'Surely that's when you're teeing off on the golf course,' said Pottsy.

'Not quite,' said Oscar. 'Foreplay is when you're having it off on the golf course.'

'Did you know,' asked Olly, 'that according to the *Kama*

Sutra there are sixty-four ways of having it off?'

'I wouldn't mind trying any one of them,' said Pottsy. 'But I don't seem to be able to attract the girls to get them to do it.'

'Experiments have proved,' said Olly, 'that if you can get your tongue down a girl's ear, she's yours for the asking.'

'I've read,' said Robin, 'that there is a little spot on the base of a girl's spine that when stroked or touched sends her wild with desire.'

'Not what I heard,' said Titch. 'I've been told on good authority that if you can only get to fondle a girl's left breast, she'll do anything.'

'Just the left?' asked Billy. 'Not the right?'

'I'm only saying that's what I heard,' protested Titch.

'I would have thought that a girl's breasts were apolitical,' said Oscar. 'Are you claiming, Titch, that the breasts have political affiliations?'

'Why not?' said Titch. 'Maybe socialist girls respond to left-breast titillation and Tory girls to the right.'

'The next thing you'll be claiming,' said Oscar, 'is that a girl's left nipple is red and her right blue.'

'The nearest I've ever come to a girl's bosom,' said Pottsy, 'was when I saw my big sister's breasts as she came out of the bath. I nearly died of shock.'

'A case of "See nipples and die",' said Oscar.

'I've never actually been out with a girl,' said Pottsy, 'so how do I get to touch a girl's breast so that she can't resist me?'

'Try some of those blue-rinse ladies in your dad's Conservative club,' suggested Robin. 'Try their right breasts. I think they call them blue tits.'

'You lot are still as crazy as ever,' said Billy.

'We often envy you, though, Hoppy – leaving school

471

and getting yourself a job,' said Robin. 'How's that going, by the way?'

'Leaving school when I did was the biggest mistake of my life,' said Billy.

'But you were going to be a journalist on a newspaper,' said Oscar. 'What happened?'

'The first job, at the *Manchester Guardian*, was a calamity, but the second, the one I'm doing now at the Inland Revenue, is a disaster.'

'You're doing work and getting paid for it,' said Nobby, 'which is more than any of us is doing, surely?'

'I'm like one of those hamsters you see on a treadmill. Working like the clappers but going around in circles getting nowhere. If I don't get off the treadmill soon, I feel I shall go like one of those bags we've been talking about – bananas.'

'Sounds bad, Hoppy,' said Robin. 'Perhaps I wrote to you just in time – before you blew a fuse.'

'You certainly did, Robin. Now what about this college you're all applying for? What's the score?'

'We don't know too much about it, Hoppy,' said Robin. 'It made a sudden late decision to open its doors – which explains why it still has places.'

'The course is for two years initially,' said Oscar, 'but it's possible to go on to do London University degrees if you are bright enough and opt for a couple of extra years.'

'You lot will all have Higher School Cert – Subsid – by summer, whereas I've got only plain School Cert,' said Billy.

'But in nine subjects,' said Robin. 'And experience in commerce. I'm sure you'll get in, Hoppy. It'd be really great if the whole lot of us went together. Imagine it! The smokers' club in London – the bright lights, the theatres, the cinemas, the West End!'

'And we might even try to fit in some study too, if we can find the time,' said Titch.

'Surely all that's going to cost a packet. What about grants and things?'

'Tuition and boarding are covered by the Government – and Manchester may award a grant of twenty pounds a year provided you agree to teach for them when you've finished. And that's it!' said Olly.

'So we're looking at about two pounds a week for books, train fares, personal spends, et cetera,' said Billy.

'At least,' said Nobby. 'My dad worked it out at about two hundred pounds or so for the whole course over two years.'

'Then I'm just crying for the moon,' said Billy. 'My dad earns around five pounds a week. I don't see where we'll get two hundred pounds out of that.'

'But you won't need the whole amount all in one go,' said Robin. 'That's over a long period. About thirty shillings to two pounds a week should keep us going. And remember, we can always get jobs during the holidays.'

'If we can find jobs,' said Olly.

'It'll do no harm to apply, Hoppy,' said Robin. 'As for the money problem, why not cross that bridge when you come to it?'

'At this moment, Robin, I can't see any answer. Somehow I think I've had my chips. But it's my one and only hope – so I'll apply anyway, as a last desperate measure in case, as Mr Micawber put it, something turns up.'

Three weeks after submitting his application, Billy received an invitation to attend for interview at the Manchester Damian College office. The principal of the London college, Mr Michael Roberts, had agreed to make himself available for informal discussion and the answering of any questions that candidates might have.

'Please sit down,' Mr Roberts said. 'I'll just check your name first, if you don't mind, to make sure I'm talking to the right person. You are Mr William Hopkins?'

'Yes, sir. That's correct.'

'You have a name with poetic associations, did you know that?'

'Yes, sir. Gerard Manley.'

'Not related in any way, are you?'

'No, sir, I'm afraid not.'

'Have you read any of his stuff?'

'Yes, sir. I've read most of his poems, including his most famous – "Pied Beauty".'

'Good. Which one impressed you most?'

'I liked "Pied Beauty", of course, and also "Spring and Fall".'

'Yes. How does that last one go again?'

> *'Margaret, are you grieving,*
> *Over Goldengrove unleaving?'*

'You like reading, do you?'

'Very much, sir.'

'What are you reading at present?'

'I have two books going, sir. I'm reading Somerset Maugham's *Razor's Edge* and wrestling with Plato's *Republic*.'

'Excellent. And how are you finding our dear friend Plato and his teacher, Socrates?'

'Most interesting, sir. Though I think that Socrates often asks his students questions and then shoots their answers down in flames.'

Michael Roberts laughed.

'Quite true. He seems to enjoy letting them flounder a bit before he destroys their argument. Can you remember any of the arguments of his students?'

'A few, sir, though I'm only a little way into the work. There's Polemarchus, who argues that justice is rendering to every man what is due to him; there's Thrasymachus, who claims that "might is right" and that the just man always comes off worse than the unjust man.'

'Do you agree with that?'

'Oh, no, sir. The argument is like that of the Nazis we've fought the war against. It also reminded me of a little rhyme in the book of comic verse you've edited.'

'Oh, you've looked at my book, have you? Which rhyme did you have in mind?'

'The one by Lord Bowen, the one that goes:

> *The rain, it raineth every day*
> *Upon the just and unjust fella*
> *But more upon the just, because*
> *The unjust hath the just's umbrella.'*

'Oh, very, very good,' he said, laughing and slapping the desk.

'Thank you, sir,' said Billy, laughing with him.

'Yes. Very good,' he continued. 'Now, on your form I see you've been working for the last year. What made you leave school before the sixth form?'

'I hoped to be a writer, sir, and wanted to get some experience on a newspaper.'

'Well, newspapers don't come any better than the *Manchester Guardian*. Why did you leave after only three months?'

'I wasn't getting anywhere, sir. I realised that I needed better qualifications.'

'Yes, I see. And now you feel you'd like to be a teacher?'

'Yes, sir.'

'Why is that? Why do you want to become a teacher?'

'I feel that I may have something to offer, sir. I have had some experience teaching and entertaining my young nephews, and I've always found great satisfaction when I see they've understood something I've taught them or enjoyed a story I've told them.'

'But there's more to education than mere entertainment, Mr Hopkins. What do you think we should be teaching in school?'

'The basic skills to start with, and then how to live fully and morally, and how to cope with life's problems.'

'Good answer. But what sort of people do you think our schools should be turning out?'

'If we are to believe Plato and Socrates, sir, good citizens.'

'Yes, but that begs the question: what do you mean by a good citizen?'

'One who respects the laws of God and the laws of the state.'

'That's all very well. But how are we to teach them all those things?'

Billy was stumped and felt he was getting out of his depth. Then he had a sudden flash of inspiration.

'Why, sir, that's precisely why I want to come to your college! To find out!'

'Oh, good answer!' exclaimed Mr Roberts, slapping the desk again. 'Good answer! Well, thank you, Mr Hopkins, for a most interesting discussion. We'll let you know the results in the next fortnight, when we've finished all our interviewing.'

'Thank you, sir,' said Billy as he left.

Outside the office, the smokers' club members were waiting.

'How did you get on in there, Hoppy?' asked Robin.

'Couldn't have gone better. I'm sure he'll offer me a place.'

'Fantastic!' said Robin. 'London, open up dem golden gates, 'cos here we come!'

The following Sunday, there occurred a family gathering. Steve and Pauline came round with their kids for tea and to receive a report of the interview. Sergeant Barry Healey was home on a weekend pass, and so seven adults and two children gathered round the table for high tea. Mam opened a tin of West's middle-cut salmon, there was the usual tossed salad, and the inevitable pineapple chunks.

'I've been saving these two tins since before the war,' Mam said.

'What are we celebrating, Mam?' asked Billy.

'The end o' the war with Germany, of course, and I allus said to meself that I'd open these two tins when the lights went on again.'

'This is just like the old days,' said Polly.

'Not quite,' said Flo. 'Our Jim is missing and the two lads are still in the forces.'

'But surely they'll be home soon – now that Hitler's killed himself,' said Mam.

'You've never said truer words than them, Kate,' said Dad. 'It won't be long before the whole lot's over and we've got that bastard Churchill out of the Gover'ment. He's all right when it comes to fighting wars, but he's not the man to lead us in peacetime. There was one thing, though, I was sorry to hear.'

'What was that, Mr Hopkins?' asked Steve.

'They're going to try that Lord Haw-Haw for treason –

probably hang him. They'd be better giving him a job on ITMA with Tommy Handley.'

'That's true, Mr Hopkins,' said Barry, chuckling. 'He gave us all a good laugh during the war. But the war's not over yet. We've still got Japan to beat.'

'You're right there, Barry,' Dad said. 'We've just got that Mickie Doo fella to finish off and then we can really start celebrating. But I tell you, I'm more worried about him than I was about Hitler. I hope they don't send our two lads to fight him, that's all. They could be out in them jungles forever.'

'You're right about that, Mr Hopkins,' said Barry. 'The Japs are ready to fight to the very last man. They even consider it a great honour to die for their country.'

'That's right,' said Steve. 'They believe that if they die for their country they will be given a very high place amongst their ancestors in heaven.'

'I only hope that when I get to heaven, we don't have to mix with a lot o' bloody foreigners,' said Dad.

'And who said you're going to heaven? More like the other place for you,' said Mam.

'He thinks there's a colour bar in heaven,' said Billy. 'All the blacks and coloured in one place, and all the yellow folk in another. And God is an Englishman.'

'No, He's not,' said Mam. 'He's an Englishwoman.'

'I read the other day,' said Dad, 'that some of them Jap snipers can stay up in the trees in the jungle for weeks, living off rats and anything else they can find. It'll take a bloody miracle to get them to surrender.'

'Let's stop talking about war,' said Mam. 'Let's change the subject, for God's sake.'

'How did the interview go, Billy?' asked Steve eagerly. 'Did you remember what I told you about not being too clever? About throwing the ball back into their court if the questions got too rough?'

'I did exactly as you advised, Steve, and the interview went like a dream. Almost as if someone else was answering the questions. I'm sure they'll offer me a place.'

'They can offer you a bloody place if they like,' said Dad. 'But you're not going and that's bloody final.'

'What's the problem?' asked Steve.

'Money!' said Dad. 'That's the bloody problem. He may have got away with it going to that Damian College, but this is different. This is bloody big money.'

'How big is big, Mr Hopkins?' asked Steve.

'About two quid a week for two years. That's nearly half my weekly wage,' Dad said. 'And that's not counting that we'll have lost his wage as well.'

'If you stopped drinking,' said Mam, 'we could afford it. You're too fond of the bevy, that's what you are.'

'I've not even been accepted yet,' said Billy. 'So we may be talking about something that's not going to happen.'

'It sounds to me as if you're in,' said Barry, 'from what you've told us.'

'Look,' said Steve, 'Pauline and I have talked it over and we're willing to contribute ten shillings a week towards his expenses. Will that make any difference?'

'And Barry and I have talked it over and all,' said Flo. 'And we're willing to give ten bob a week as well.'

'There you are, Ma,' said Steve. 'What do you say to that? Can you raise a pound a week to send your youngest to college in London?'

'Of course we bloody well can,' she said. 'His lordship here'll just have to sup a few pints less, that's all.'

'I used to be bloody master in this house before the war,' said Dad. 'I don't know what the world's coming to when women start telling a working fella what to do.'

'Then it's settled,' said Mam. 'He's going to college and there's an end to it.'

'I think you lot are the best family anyone could ever hope for,' said Billy. 'When I go to college I'll try to be a credit to you all, and I'll never, never forget the sacrifices you're making.'

'You can have the job of looking after us all when we're old and decrepit,' said Polly.

Chapter Twenty-Nine

Bombshells

On Tuesday 7 August 1945, the Allies vaporised the city of Hiroshima, a town of twelve square miles on the Japanese main island of Honshu, killing more than seventy thousand people. Mr Churchill said, 'By God's mercy, British and American science outpaced all German efforts. The possession of these powers by the Germans at any time might have altered the result of the war and profound anxiety was felt by those who were informed.'

In Sunlight House, young people from the various offices, not fully understanding the gravity and horror of the event, walked about pulling their eyes into oriental slits and saying, 'Please, Mr Truman, you no droppee bomb on Hiroshima, please. We have great honour to surrender, please.'

'Here,' Mam said when Billy got home that night, 'isn't this the day that memory man in Blackpool said the world would end? Well, it hasn't. So he owes me a bob.'

'Maybe it's ended for him,' said Billy. 'Anyroad, you'd have a bit of a job finding him now.'

'I suppose I would,' she said. 'Oh, and by the way, there's an official-looking letter up there behind the tea-caddy from that there college in London.'

'Why didn't you say so?'

Impatiently he tore open the envelope.

'I'll bet it's from the principal, Michael Roberts, offering me a place.'

'Come on then, read it out,' she said.

'Dear Mr Hopkins,' he read. 'We regret to inform you that, following your recent interview, we are unable to offer you a place at the college for the coming year. We are aware that this must be a disappointment for you but you will realise that we have received more applications than we have places. We have therefore had to restrict our selection this year to those candidates with HSC. You may wish to submit a fresh application for our intake in 1946. Yours sincerely, Michael Roberts.'

Billy's face fell. Bewildered, he continued staring at the letter in disbelief and dismay, and he could taste the bile rising in his throat.

'That's a bombshell, Mam,' he said thickly. 'I don't understand it – the interview went so well.'

'P'raps it wasn't meant to be,' she said. 'Anyroad, it's not the end of the world.'

'In my case,' he said in a broken voice, 'it is. That memory man was right after all.'

'Come on, cheer up, our kid. It's not as bad as that – you've still got your health and strength.'

'You don't understand, Mam. That application was my last hope. Now I have nothing ahead of me but that soul-destroying job in the Inland Revenue. I can see my future rising up in front of me like a solid brick wall.'

'You can allus climb over a brick wall, son,' she said,

'and see what's on the other side. One day you'll meet a nice girl and settle down. You'll see.'

'What a rotten hand fate has dealt me, Mam. Born in the slums of Collyhurst, bombed out of Honeypot Street back into the slums – to this dump which is even worse than the Dwellings. I tried to be a writer on a newspaper and ended up as a toe rag. Now what have I got to look forward to? I'm chained like a slave in a civil-service galley. I give up.'

He went into the bedroom and lay on his bed, staring at the ceiling. All his friends from school would be going off to college in September. He could hear Robin Gabrielson's voice in his head.

'The smokers' club in London – the bright lights, the theatres, the cinemas, the West End! London, open up dem golden gates, 'cos here we come!'

The sun began to set, the light to fade, and soon he was in the darkness. Still he continued to stare – his mind numbed at the thought of his prospects and the life before him.

His mam tapped gently on the door.

'Come on, our Billy. Don't just lie there moping. Come and have a bit o' tea.'

With heaviness of heart, he got up from the bed and went into the living room.

'I've been thinking,' she said, 'you used to be happy dancing. Why don't you go back to Harrigan's and find that lovely girl you was going out with? What was her name?'

'Adele. But I gave up Harrigan's after I broke up with her.'

'Well, you can't just lie there being miserable.'

'All right, Mam. You may be right. I've got to try and cheer myself up. I used to feel on top of the world when

I was out dancing with her. I'll walk over and see her. I'll try to make it up with her. Maybe she'll have me back.'

He washed, spruced himself up, put on a clean white shirt and a smart tie, and began to feel a little better. He walked the short distance to Adele's home and rang the doorbell.

It was a good five minutes before she came to the door. She was wearing a silk dressing gown but she looked as beautiful as ever.

'Hello, Adele. Thought I'd just call and see how things were with you.'

She stared past him.

'What do you want, Billy? I'm pretty busy at the moment.'

'I had a piece of rotten news today and I wondered if you felt like going out dancing.'

'You must be joking after the things you said to me last time. Get lost, Billy. Go and find yourself a nice Catholic girl to bear you a dozen kids.'

A voice from over Adele's shoulder called:

'Who is it, Adele? Tell whoever it is to bugger off. We're busy.'

Duggie Diggle appeared, fastening his shirt buttons.

'It's OK, Maximilian,' she said. 'It's only an old flame, but he's just going.'

'Oh, it's you, Billy,' he said. 'Too bad, old son. Adele's partnering me now. You blew your chance with her.'

'Hello, Duggie,' Billy said. 'Maximilian. That's a nice name. I didn't know you and Adele had got together.'

'That's one way of putting it, I suppose,' he leered.

'Sorry to have disturbed you, Adele,' Billy said. 'Parents at the Queen's Park Hipp, I suppose. I hope Maximilian there remembered to bring a torch.'

'Look, Billy, just piss off,' she hissed.

Billy walked back home, hands in pocket, shoulders slumped.

'Well, did you see her?' Mam asked. 'Did you fix up to go dancing with her?'

'Just leave me alone, Mam,' he said, and went back into the bedroom, where he lay, hands behind his head, staring at nothing.

The next day, he went into work as usual. Cliff Fernley took one look at his face.

'What in God's name has got into you? You look like a Scotsman who's lost a pound and found a tanner. In fact, come to think of it, you're getting to look more like Albert Fiddler every day.'

'Sorry, Cliff. I heard that I failed to get into college and I don't want to talk to anyone today. I need time to get over it. Best thing is to leave me alone.'

'OK, Hoppy. If that's what you want.'

There were to be no jokes, no pranks, no laughs that day. Simply the solid, hard grind of civil-service routine. A little later that morning, Albert Fiddler came up to Billy's desk.

'You look as if you got out of the wrong side of the bed this morning, Hopkins.'

'Yes, Mr Fiddler.'

'Anyway, I've got a change of job for you. You're supposed to be good at maths. Here's the invoice book of a taxpayer we suspect of cheating. The itemised details on each foolscap page have not yet been added up. That's a job for you, Hopkins.'

'I only learned to do quadratics and Euclidian geometry.'

'Look, just get on with it, and less of your lip.'

His spirits drooping, Billy added up page after page of

bills for over three hours that morning. By dinner-time, he had completed the task and went off alone for his midday meal at Joe's Chop House. On his way back, he stopped for a little while at Lower Mosley Street bus station and watched the great luxury coaches leaving for their long-distance destinations – London, Penzance, Glasgow, Edinburgh. Well, he could watch but he wouldn't be going anywhere this year further than Gardenia Court and Sunlight House.

Still dejected, he returned at one o'clock to find Fiddler waiting for him with a scowl that spelled trouble.

'You're supposed to be the whizz-kid at maths! Those invoices you added up this morning! Every bloody one of 'em is wrong.'

'Sorry, Mr Fiddler. I've got things on my mind.'

'You might well say sorry. What bloody fools we tax officers would have looked if we'd accepted your figures when we're supposed to be investigating a tax-dodger. It's about bloody time you started to get your mind on your job, or push off and find another.'

Billy's lips turned pale and stiff.

'Yes, Mr Fiddler. Sorry, Mr Fiddler,' he said in a dull voice.

That night he got home from work at the usual time, had his meal in silence, and went to lie on the bed to continue his contemplation of his old friend – the ceiling. He had been there for over an hour when he heard a stir and the sound of voices outside the bedroom door.

'Where is he?' he heard Steve Keenan say.

'He's in there, Steve,' Mam said. 'Just lying there. I'm worried about him.'

Steve tapped gently on the door.

'Billy, do you mind if I come in for a minute?' he said.

'OK. The door's not locked.'

'What's all this I hear about you getting a letter from the college and then going into the slough of despond?'

'I had all my hopes pinned on going to college, Steve, and now . . . well . . . I've just given up.'

'Given up! You must be crazy!' he said. 'Did you ever read that speech Churchill gave to the boys of Harrow School?'

'Can't say that I did, Steve.'

'I can still remember some of it,' he said. 'I was so impressed. "Never give in! Never give in! Never, never, never! In nothing – great or small, large or petty. Never give in except to convictions of honour and good sense. Never yield!" '

'How does that apply to my case, Steve?'

'I'll show you how it applies! Give me that letter from the college and we'll appeal. Never give in, Billy! Never give in!'

True to his word, Steve composed and typed a letter to the principal purporting to come from Billy's dad.

Dear Sir,
A few weeks ago, you were kind enough to grant my son, William Hopkins, an interview for a place at your college for the coming academic year, commencing September 1945. We were most disappointed in the family to learn that you were unable to offer him a place because of lack of an HSC qualification.

May we appeal to you, sir, to reconsider his case? In 1944 he passed the School Certificate in all nine subjects and was the only student in his college to do so. During the last year, as an alternative to staying on at school for a further year, he decided to gain experience in journalism and the civil service. He worked at the *Manchester Guardian* where he gained valuable understanding of the workings of a modern newspaper. Today he is employed in a busy office of the Inland Revenue.

We feel, sir, that his year in the world of commerce amply compensates for the year he missed in the sixth form, since it has given him a background knowledge which should prove of inestimable value to a prospective teacher.

We trust you will give this appeal your earnest consideration.

Yours sincerely,

Thomas Hopkins.

'Well, if that doesn't do the trick,' said Steve, 'nothing will. That's all I've got to say.'

It was a memorable, never-to-be-forgotten Saturday morning when Billy picked up the early-morning post and opened up the letter from the college.

'I'M IN! I'M IN!' he called at the top of his voice. 'Mam! Mam! I'm in! I'm in! The college has reconsidered my position. I'm in heaven!'

He pulled her away from the toast she was buttering and waltzed round the flat with her, singing 'I'm in Heaven'.

'Mam! Mam! I'm over the moon. I must rush round and tell Steve Keenan right away,' he called excitedly. 'And then I'm going over to Rusholme to tell my pal, Robin Gabrielson.'

Billy found Steve and Pauline just about to go shopping with their two children when he arrived with his good news.

'I felt in my bones,' said Steve, happily, 'that you would get into college. I just knew it all along. Never give in!'

'We'll make it a family motto,' said Billy. 'Steve–Pauline – I cannot put into words how happy I feel at this moment. It's all down to you, Steve, and your tenacity. I'll never be able to thank you enough.'

'Yes you can,' said Pauline, laughing. 'Just don't take up piano-playing again.'

'Come shopping with us,' said Steve. 'The kids would enjoy your company.'

'Can't,' he said. 'I've got to get over to see my pal to give him the good news. He'll be as pleased as Punch.'

'Right you are,' said Steve. 'No more depressions, Billy – OK? Happy days are here again! Now you get off and see your friend.'

It was Mrs Gabrielson, Robin's mother, who opened the door.

'You must be Hoppy,' she said, 'the one our Robin did the shoe-shining with. I can recognise you from his description.'

'Tall, dark and ugly, that's me, Mrs Gabrielson.'

'Not quite true,' she said, laughing. 'But do come in. Robin will be really glad to see you.'

'Hoppy!' Robin said when he saw Billy. 'What brings you to this part of the world?'

'Good news, Robin! I'm in. I've just heard from the college.'

'That is the best news I've heard all year. Absolutely out of this world!'

'I'd just about given up Robin, I tell you. It was my brother-in-law's letter that pulled it off.'

'This means that all the smokers' club – one hundred per cent of us – will be going together. You know we were all very miserable when you got that awful letter from the college telling you there was no place for you. It wouldn't have been the same with one of us missing.'

'Exactly how I felt, Robin. Now it's London, open up dem gates! Oh, Robin, Robin, I can't describe to you my utter relief at getting out of this job in taxes – it's been destroying me.'

'We all sensed that in the smokers' club, Hoppy. We could see it was getting to you. Now all our prayers have been answered.'

'It's like a dream come true.'

'Do you realise, Hoppy, it's just a fortnight before we're on that train together?'

'Don't I know it! There's an incredible amount to do between now and then. I've got to buy new suitcases, clothes, books, and so on and so on.'

'Most of us have already done our shopping, and even some of our packing, would you believe it. We're so ahead of ourselves that Titch and I have fixed up to go walking in the Peak District next week. Why not join us? It'll be a chance to talk about our big plans for the future.'

'Can't, Robin, I'm afraid. I have to work at the office almost to the bitter end, as I need every penny I can lay my hands on. Which reminds me, I must get back this morning as I promised to give my dad a hand before he wraps up in the market.'

'OK. I'll pass on your good news to the others and we'll see you in a fortnight at the railway station. What a day that'll be, eh! The bright lights! The theatres! The . . .'

'I know! I know! The cinemas! The West End!'

'Be seeing you then, Hoppy,' Robin called happily as Billy went down the street.

The week following his visit to Robin Gabrielson, Billy was run off his feet. There were a thousand and one things to attend to in preparation for college: the purchase of books, writing materials, clothes, sports kit, toiletries and name tapes, as well as packing to be done, along with visits to the barber, the dentist and the doctor. Most of his buying expeditions had to be done in the evening after the daily grind at the Inland Revenue office. It was after one of these purchasing sessions that he arrived home, happily exhausted, and collapsed in an easy chair. Mam was cooking the evening meal, and as usual, Dad was busy devouring the *Manchester Evening News*.

'Only a week left, Mam. I've just about completed all my shopping and I'm packed and ready to go. I'm looking forward to saying goodbye to that office. If I ever see another con-card or another file, I shall throw up.'

'Here, Billy,' said Dad, 'what's the name of that pal of yours – the one you're going to college with . . . Robin something or other?'

'Robin Gabrielson? What about him?'

'There's summat here in the paper about him. You'd better sit down afore you read it.'

Billy had a sudden premonition of disaster. His stomach turned over and a shiver went down his spine.

'Let me see that,' he cried.

MISSED HIS FOOTING WHEN CLIMBING DOWNFALL

Student's forty-foot death fall on Kinder. When climbing the Kinder downfall, Kinderscout, Derbyshire, with a friend, Robin Gabrielson, seventeen-and-a-half-year-old student of Rusholme, Manchester, missed his footing and fell to the rocks forty feet below. He was taken to Stockport Infirmary where he died last night.

His friend, Richard Smalley of Fallowfield, said

that Gabrielson was about twelve feet above him. Smalley shouted to Gabrielson: 'I can't climb any higher here, I will try to work my way round.'

A moment later he heard a scream and his friend's body fell past him on to the rocks. Smalley wrapped Gabrielson in his coat and left him in a sheltered spot while he went for help.

With a gamekeeper, whom he met on the moors, he summoned assistance but it was six hours before the ambulance could reach Gabrielson. On arrival at the infirmary, he was found suffering from injuries to the back of the head and internal injuries.

Gabrielson had recently won a place at a teachers' training college in Chelsea, London, and was due to begin in a week's time.

Billy's mind went numb and a freezing sensation enveloped his whole body. There was a tight pain in his throat and his heart pounded against his ribs. He stared, speechless, shaking his head at the newspaper, entreating it to say it wasn't true. He put his head down on the table but the tears would not come. He could not take in what he had read. It must be some other Gabrielson, some other Smalley – not his friends, surely. They were all going to college together in a few days' time. They had their train tickets and were all packed and ready to go. The room went cold, a violent trembling racked him, and he crossed his arms and wrapped them round his chest as if trying to ward off the cold.

His mother felt his pain. She put her arms around him to try to comfort him and stop the shivering.

'Don't take on so, our Billy,' she said. 'It's all right. It's going to be all right.'

'Another disaster, Mam. Will they never end? He was my best friend. We were going to college together on Sunday.'

'I know. I know,' she said. 'But it's God's will.'

'Don't talk to me about God, Mam. He's no friend of mine. He's my enemy. He's gone too far this time. He has done nothing but rain death and destruction down on my head. This is the last straw. Now I just want to be left alone.'

Once more he went to his bed, this time covering himself with a blanket in an attempt to get warm and stop the shaking. He gazed up at that grey ceiling he had come to know so well. In the semi-darkness, he could see Robin, and hear his voice. As he recalled images of his dear friend, his eyes grew wet and the tears flowed endlessly down his face.

He was awakened from his mournful meditation by a gentle knocking at the door.

'Billy, son, don't just lie there. Come out now. There's another little item about your pal y'ought to see.'

He got up and went into the living room.

'This is it, on page eight,' Mam said, handing him the paper.

GABRIELSON – On 10 September 1945, result of an accident, Robin James, aged seventeen (*requiescat in pace*), dearly loved son of Joseph Paul and Catherine. Deceased will be taken into St Joseph's, Longsight, on Thursday. Requiem Mass Friday, 10 a.m. Interment Southern Cemetery. No flowers by request.

'I'll go to the funeral on Friday, Mam, but right now I think I'll go for a walk. Maybe call on Pauline and Steve.'

'Will you be all right, son? Do you want me to come with you? You're not going to do nowt silly, are you?'

'No, Mam. Don't worry. I'd rather walk alone to think – that's all. I shan't be late.'

The evening was damp and wet. A raw fog had descended and it was nearly dark. The streets were deserted and quiet. Billy stumbled on, unconscious of the drizzle, head down, shoulders hunched. As he passed St Anne's Church, he suddenly became aware of the rosary beads round his neck. The beads his mother had given him for luck in the dancing competition, and the very same beads awarded to him by Sister Helen in another age when, as a stupid, innocent child, he had taken in all their stories and their lies about a merciful God. An involuntary shudder convulsed him, and with a great cry of despair, he wrenched the beads from his neck and hurled them into the rain.

'Take them, God, if there is a God,' he cried. 'I'm finished with you and all those tales of your goodness and mercy. Where were you when Teddy White was drowned in the Cut? When Henry Sykes was blown to bits by that German bomb? When Jim's lifeboat was lost? When Robin Gabrielson fell on the rocks? A saviour they call you, but you're nothing but a fraud. You do nothing but destroy those I love.'

He had reached Pauline's house. He rang the bell. It was Steve who opened the door. No words were needed. One look at Billy's strained, tearful face told all – that some dreadful misfortune had befallen him.

'Billy! For God's sake, come in.'

'Billy, you look awful,' said Pauline. 'Let me make you a cup of tea.'

'I've just heard of the death of my best friend,' he said. 'We were going to college together. Now I'm not sure any more that I want to go. Fact is – I'm not sure about anything any more.'

'But that's terrible, terrible,' said Steve. 'Tell us in God's name what happened.'

'I'll tell you what happened, Steve, but not in God's name. I no longer trust or believe in Him. It was He who allowed my closest pal to be killed falling from those rocks.'

'What a tragedy! We're so sorry to hear about it, Billy. And now you're wondering about your own future and whether you should go to college without your friend. And you've lost your faith in God as well. All hope's gone, eh?'

'That's right, Steve. Robin Gabrielson's gone, and with him all hope. As far as I can see, life's just one big lottery and without meaning. The universe is just a series of pointless accidents. "*A chequer-board of nights and days/ Where Destiny with men for pieces plays./One thing is certain, and the rest is lies/The flower that once hath blown forever dies.*" '

'You are in a bad way, Billy,' said Steve, 'if you think that there is no point or purpose to the universe. Only God knows why we and the universe exist. You seem to think that the death of your friend was pointless and meaningless.'

'Well, wasn't it?' said Billy.

'If I remember correctly, Billy,' said Pauline, 'it was through this pal, Robin, that you got the idea of going to college in the first place.'

'That's right, Pauline. It was because of a letter that he wrote to me. We had such big plans for the future, he and I.'

'You had your plans and the man upstairs had His. And they weren't quite the same,' said Steve. 'Have you thought that that letter from Robin may have been part of God's plan for you? What you are suffering now, at this moment, may be God's way of showing you the way you must go.'

'I've thought about all the sufferings, all the deaths in my life and I no longer believe that there is a God.'

'Life is not simply the pursuit of pleasure,' Steve said. 'Remember that bit of the prayer – "To Thee do we cry, poor banished children of Eve, mourning and weeping in this vale of tears." That's what the world is, Billy, a vale of tears. You may not believe in God, but He believes in you. You may not be looking for Him, but He is looking for you all right.'

'I've thought about God and all that and cannot accept the arguments for His existence.'

'Well done! You've worked it all out by logic, eh?' Steve said. 'Listen, Billy. Faith in God has nothing to do with logical arguments. God is a supreme being who is beyond all reason and all knowing. You simply accept Him and there's no way we can unravel his divine plan or the way he treats us. Faith, you will remember from your catechism, is a gift and not something you arrive at by intellectual arguments.'

'Have you never doubted, Steve?'

'Of course I have. We all have. There is a prayer we used to say, "Oh God, I believe in you. Please help me overcome my unbelief." '

'Right at this minute, Steve, I feel that He has deserted me, and I am alone.'

'Don't you remember that story?' he said. 'How a man thought God had deserted him when he noticed only one set of prints on the sand at the very time when he was at his lowest. You will recall that there was only one set because at the most difficult time of his life, the Lord had carried him. And God will help you through this rough patch, Billy. Trust Him.'

'How do we know that? It doesn't seem that way at the moment.'

'Look, I don't want to go all heavy on you, but let me remind you of that passage in St Matthew. "*Come unto me, all ye that labour and are heavy laden, and I will give you rest. Take my yoke upon you, and learn of me; for I am meek and lowly in heart; and ye shall find rest unto your souls. For my yoke is easy and my burden is light.*" '

Billy walked home heavily that night in sombre, pensive mood. Steve had given him much to think about.

St Joseph's Church was packed that Friday morning for Robin's Requiem. Everyone who'd ever known Robin seemed to be there. Billy looked round the church slowly: Robin's grieving parents, his relatives, his teachers, his fellow-students, his neighbours filled all the benches to the very back. In the main aisle, at the front of the church, stood the oak coffin with the polished handles. From the choir loft a small group of Damian brothers sang the plain-chant Mass. Solemn-faced, the members of the smokers' club sat together towards the front of the nave.

Billy could not take his eyes off the coffin. Inside that box lay his closest friend, fast asleep in a dream from which he would never awaken. His eyes closed never to open again. His lips sealed never to speak or smile again. Past all help or need of it.

'Eternal rest grant unto him, O Lord,' intoned the priest.

'And let perpetual light shine upon him,' answered the congregation.

'May he rest in peace. Amen,' said the priest.

After the Introit, Robin's father began the first of the readings in a quiet, melancholy manner, and it seemed to Billy, as he listened, that the words were being directed specifically at him.

'*Death is nothing at all . . . I have only slipped away into the next room . . .*'

Mr Gabrielson's voice faltered; he paused and swallowed hard. For a moment it looked as if he might break down. He took a deep breath and in a low, grief-stricken tone continued:

'*What is death but a negligible accident? Why should I be out of mind because I am out of sight? I am but waiting for you, for an interval, somewhere very near, just around the corner . . . All is well.*'

For a minute or two there was a solemn stillness – not a sound in the church except for subdued sobbing, and the blowing of noses, amongst that anguished congregation. Then the brothers began to chant the Sequence of the Dies Irae and the Mass continued.

After the communion rite, a distraught-looking Titch went forward to give the final reading:

> '*Lead, kindly light amid th'encircling gloom,*
> *Lead thou me on, the night is dark*
> *and I am far from home, lead thou me on.*
> *Keep thou my feet; I do not ask to see*
> *The distant scene; one step enough for me.*'

There was a catch in his voice, and Titch broke down – unable to continue. Sorrowfully, he looked appealingly towards Billy, who nodded his understanding, walked forward and took over the reading of Newman's verses.

'*I was not ever thus, nor prayed that thou*

shouldst lead me on; I loved to choose
And see my path; but now lead thou me on.
I loved the garish day and, spite of fears,
pride ruled my will; remember not past years.

So long thy power hath blest me, sure it still
Will lead me on o'er moor and fen,
O'er crag and torrent, till the night is gone,
And with the morn those angel faces smile
Which I have loved long since, and lost awhile.'

At the end of the Mass, the coffin was borne out by
the pall-bearers, followed by a grieving procession of
mourners. The smoking-club boys, who had known
Robin best, stood together in a forlorn, melancholy
group. Mrs Gabrielson, her eyes red with weeping, came
up to them.

'Thank you, boys, for coming, and for those beautiful
readings,' she said softly. 'Robin so loved you all. And
now he won't be going to college with you after all. I can't
tell you how hard it is to take it all in and to accept that he
is dead. Everywhere in the house are hundreds of little
reminders of him – his clothes, his shoes, even his collar
studs and cuff-links. And his half-packed suitcase is still
in his bedroom, exactly where he left it. I haven't had the
heart to move it.'

She was about to break down, but recovered her
composure.

'Go to college,' she said, 'and, for the sake of his
memory, do well and succeed. That's what he would have
liked. He will be with you down there in Chelsea in spirit.'

They watched the cortège proceed slowly down
Plymouth Grove until it was out of sight. There was a
song which went round and round in Billy's head:

All the birds of the air
Fell a-sighing and a-sobbing
When they heard of the death
Of poor Cock Robin.

'When something like this happens,' he said, offering his cigarettes round, 'everything in one's life falls into perspective.'

'Too true,' said Oscar. 'You begin to get your priorities right. What's important and what isn't.'

'We spend all our time,' added Titch, 'worrying about exams, about money, about sex, about career, about tomorrow.'

'All the time taking it for granted that we're going to have a tomorrow,' said Olly.

'Poor Robin has no tomorrow,' said Nobby.

'We've got to take each day as it comes,' said Billy. 'Act as if each day was our last.'

'And one day,' said Oscar, 'we'll be right.'

'Robin's mother seemed keen that we should stick to our plans, go to college without Robin and succeed for his sake,' said Titch.

'I'm not so sure,' said Pottsy. 'Academic study, as you all know, was never my strong point. I'd like to go to college with you all, but my father wants me to go into his business to learn the ins and outs of the retail trade. I'll sure miss you lot.'

'That goes for me too,' said Billy. 'I'm not sure about anything any more.'

'Oh, surely not, Hoppy,' said Oscar. 'Don't say you're changing your mind about college.'

'It's enough the gang's going without Robin, without you pulling out as well,' said Nobby.

'I'm having second thoughts,' said Billy. 'College

doesn't have the same attractions now that Robin's dead. He was the one who encouraged me the whole time.'

'All the more reason you should go, surely?' said Titch.

'Well, the way I see it, I did an awful lot of moaning and complaining about my job – how boring it was and all that. That doesn't seem to matter any more. Life isn't all that bad. I've got my ballroom dancing, and if I worked hard in the civil service, I could end up as a fully fledged tax officer.'

'What about your ambitions to write and all that?' asked Olly.

'A pipe-dream, Olly, a pipe-dream. That's all it was. If I went to college, I'd have to consider the tremendous expense I'd be putting my folks to. That's apart from the fact that they would lose my weekly wage too.'

'We hope you change your mind, Hoppy,' said Oscar.

'I've not decided yet,' said Billy. 'Robin's death has got my brain in a whirl and I don't know whether I'm coming or going. I thought I might get away this weekend, say back to Blackpool for a couple of days, walk the beach at Cleveleys where we used to play together, and think things through.'

'But we're supposed to leave on Sunday,' said Titch.

'I know! I know!' sighed Billy. 'I'm just confused, that's all. Do I really want to go to college? Do I really want to be a teacher? I can't see the point in anything any more.'

'Well, just in case, Hoppy, here's my hand,' said Nobby. 'Goodbye, and we'll see each other when we see each other.'

'Same goes for me,' said Pottsy, shaking hands.

'Cheers!' said Olly, taking Billy's hand. 'But I hope to see you in a couple of days.'

'I'm not shaking hands,' said Oscar, 'because I just know you'll be going with us to London.'

'Neither am I,' said Titch. 'Please, Hoppy, be sensible and make the right decision.'

Sadly they parted company at the corner of Plymouth Grove and went their different ways.

Sunday afternoon. A taxi pulled in at the Central Station approach. Billy got out with his luggage, paid the driver and struggled his way across the station concourse. He consulted the large railway timetable board.

'Platform six,' he said aloud.

He handed his ticket to the collector at the barrier.

'Better hurry, mate,' said the man. 'That train's due out in a few seconds.'

He hurried as best as he could with his suitcase along the platform, looking for a particular compartment.

And there they were! Heads sticking out of the windows as if it were a cattle truck – the Damian College Smokers' Club.

'Trust you to be late, Hoppy!' called Oscar.

'Come on, Hoppy!' shouted Titch. 'Get a move on or you're going to miss the train!'

High Hopes

For my daughter Catherine

I find that the further back I go, the better I
remember things, whether they happened or not.

Mark Twain

High Hopes is a fictionalised autobiography.
Any resemblance to persons living or dead
is purely coincidental.

Preface

1945

There are certain dates in history which are indelibly imprinted on our minds: 1066, 1492, 1815, and 1914 to give but a few examples. To this list we must add the year 1945 for it witnessed the end not of one major war but of two: Germany capitulated in May, Japan in August. In human terms, the cost of the wars was estimated at 55 million dead. The year itself reads like the last episode of a great epic novel. It's all there: the final dénouement and the triumph of justice, the death of some of the main protagonists, and the events run the whole gamut of emotions from euphoria to horror.

Horror in February when we learned that Allied bombers had devastated Dresden, incinerating 130,000 people; horror again when we heard of the Nazi death camps with their gas ovens, the mounds of skeletal corpses, and the emaciated survivors; and yet a third time when, in early August, atomic bombs vaporised the Japanese cities of Hiroshima and Nagasaki, killing and maiming countless numbers of citizens.

Sadly, President Roosevelt died in April at the age of sixty-three on the eve of victory in Europe and was replaced by Harry Truman. Later in that month, Mussolini and his mistress were shot by Italian partisans, and strung up by their heels. Shortly after that Adolf Hitler and his new wife Eva Braun took their own lives in their underground bunker whilst Russian troops were virtually hammering on the Chancellery doors above.

The revered British war leader, Winston Churchill, survived in good health all right but received the shock of his life in July when the British electorate rejected him at the polls and gave the Labour party under the leadership of Clem Attlee a landslide victory.

It was also a year of great rejoicing. On 7 May, when it was announced that the war in Europe was officially over, thousands of people took to the streets around Whitehall to celebrate and to listen to the voice of Churchill who ended his speech by singing and conducting the crowd in 'Land of Hope and Glory'. And on 15 July when the lights of Britain were switched on once again after more than two thousand nights of blackout, euphoria knew no bounds. Families flung open their curtains and switched on every light in the house and it was this action more than anything else that brought home the fact that the war really had ended.

There was yet more joy to come when the defeat of Japan was proclaimed at midnight in London on 14 August. The government declared a two-day holiday which triggered off a wave of hysteria with a blatant cacophony of ships' sirens and railway train whistles, a relay of bonfires blazing across the country, and triumphant street parties in every town and village. In London's Piccadilly, the festivities continued well into the night with American GIs sporting carnival hats, waving the Stars and Stripes, leading im-promptu processions, beating drums, blowing whistles, and throwing fireworks.

2

But for many families, the jubilation was tempered by the pain of knowing that their loved ones would never be coming home. As for the survivors, the demobilisation scheme, with its provisions for staggered release, meant an agonising wait before they could be allowed to return to Civvy Street.

The war had left Britain almost bankrupt. With peace came an austerity greater than the country had ever known. Nearly everything was rationed: meat, fats, eggs, cheese, sugar, sweets, clothing, petrol. Towards the end of the year, the screw was turned even tighter when severe food cuts were announced – the fat ration (inclusive of butter, margarine and lard) was reduced from eight to seven ounces a week. Coal and other fuels were as scarce as they had ever been during the war. Bread with its greatly reduced wheat content was next to be rationed, whilst the importation of rice was halted altogether. Cigarettes – informally rationed by shopkeepers – were obtainable only for long-term, regular customers and were always kept 'under the counter'. The only things that were plentiful were job vacancies – there were five jobs chasing every worker, with the result that it proved well nigh impossible to fill the more menial tasks.

For many, the one bright note in that autumn of 1945 was the resumption of professional football and such was the enthusiasm that on one Tuesday afternoon in November, 85,000 fans turned up to watch Chelsea draw with Moscow Dynamo at Stamford Bridge.

It was against this backdrop that Billy Hopkins in Manchester was persuaded by his best friend, Robin Gabrielson, to quit his job as junior clerk in the Inland Revenue and go to London to train as a teacher, along with their other close school chums. It was to be an exciting

3

new start and his joy knew no bounds. Then tragedy struck one week before he was due to take up his place at the college. All Billy's hopes and dreams collapsed like a pack of cards.

Chapter One

Decisions, Decisions

Billy Hopkins sat alone in the church. The funeral was over and now all was quiet save for the muffled roar of traffic on Plymouth Grove.

He stared at the space where the coffin had rested less than half an hour before. He couldn't take it in – Robin Gabrielson, his closest friend in the world, dead. His mind was filled with disbelief. Surely, there'd been some mix-up or other, a case of mistaken identity that you read about in the paper sometimes. He couldn't be dead, surely to God. Taken so brutally and without warning.

The tears that would not come during the Requiem Mass now flowed freely.

He was so wracked with sobbing he failed to notice the old priest who had approached.

'Can I be of any help, my son?' he asked gently.

'I don't think so, Father,' said Billy. 'No one can help me. I've lost the best friend I ever had. I can't understand why God let it happen.'

'You mean the young man who fell so tragically to his death on the Derbyshire Hills last week?'

Billy nodded.

'Indeed, that was a terrible thing but you can't blame God for every human disaster.'

'Why not? He's supposed to be in charge. Where was He when He was needed? He could have prevented it so easily. Why didn't He do so?'

'Who knows? Perhaps your friend had completed his journey and was here on earth to kindle a light in the darkness. Your personal darkness. To show you the way you should go.'

'If that's true, why am I so confused? I can't get over the idea that it was Robin who persuaded me to apply for college. Now the war is over, this year was to mark a new beginning for us. We'd got it all mapped out. The way we'd study together, what we'd do, the places we'd visit, the things we'd see, the people we'd meet. And now – nothing. Our future plans gone for a Burton.'

'Someone once said, "The way to make God smile is to talk of future plans". You may have your plans but God has His and the two are not always the same. Robbie Burns said it best: The best laid schemes o' mice an' men/Gang aft a-gley.'

'But my friend was so young, Father. He was seventeen years old and his death seems such a waste.'

'Depends on how you view death. If we see it as an enemy, death causes anxiety and fear. But if we see it as a friend, our attitude is different. It's simply a transition from earthly life to life eternal.'

Billy and the old priest talked in the deserted church for over an hour, and when Billy finally left, he had much to think about. He had to make a decision – yes or no.

* * *

He caught the 53 bus home because it took the scenic route past Bradford Road Gasworks and Philips Park Cemetery – a long rambling route across the Manchester suburbs which would give him time to think things over. At Smedley Road he got off and began the long walk past the bomb sites, the dilapidated public air-raid shelters and the numerous blocks of tenement flats which had been thrown up pre-war by the authorities in a wave of optimistic slum clearance – Jasmine Crescent, Heather Close, Hyacinth House – until he reached his own building, Gardenia Court. Wearily he climbed the graffiti-decorated, malodorous stairwell, and arrived finally at his own front door. Before he could turn the key in the lock, his mam opened the door and looked up anxiously into his face.

'You've been crying, Billy,' she said.

'I wasn't the only one, Mam. The whole school was there and I don't think there was a dry eye in the church. It was so sad to see his mam and dad – so heartbroken. I don't think they've taken it in yet.'

'And what about you, Billy? Have you taken it in?'

'Not really. I'm still in a state of shock. I feel numb and can't grasp the fact that he's gone, never to be seen again. Titch Smalley feels the same way. I had to take over one of the readings when he broke down in the middle.'

'Titch Smalley? The lad who was with him when he fell on the rocks?'

'That's right. He's one that'll never get over it. Neither will I.'

'The family feels for you, Billy, and we're so sorry for your loss. But you know, you're going to have to put this behind you and move on.'

'Easier said than done. This death has changed things

so much for me. After the funeral, I had a long talk with a priest in the church. All the way home on the bus, I've been weighing things up and I've finally made up my mind.'

'And that is?'

'I'm not going to college. That's definite.'

She looked thunderstruck. 'Not going . . . but what will you do? I mean, what about your big plans of going to London and all that?'

'I can't see the point in any of that now. The big idea was that we'd go together, study and enjoy London life together. He was always painting a picture of the places we'd visit – the cinemas, the theatres, the West End, and . . .' There was a catch in Billy's voice and he was unable to finish the sentence.

'You can still do those things, Billy,' Mam said disconsolately.

'No, Mam. All that's changed. I don't want to go to London without him. I'll stay on at the Inland Revenue job and take my chances there. If I work hard, I could become a fully qualified tax officer in a few years' time.'

Dad, who had been pretending to read his newspaper all this time, looked up and, addressing the unseen companion he seemed to carry on his shoulder, said: 'At last the lad's come to his senses. Instead of taking money out of the house, he'll be bringing it in. Tax officer's not as good as a proper trade but it's better than going off to some lah-de-dah college where he'd learn all kinds of daft, useless things. And as for London, I've heard some right bad stories about it – he'd pick up a lot of bad ways from the toffs down there.'

'You've never been to London in your life and neither

have I,' Mam protested. 'So how do you know what it's like and what he'd be learning?'

'I've read about their goings-on in the *Evening News* and I hear it on the wireless.'

'Anyway,' said Billy. 'My mind's made up. I didn't get much sleep last night thinking about the funeral and all that. So I think I'll try to get forty winks after tea.'

It was turning dark when Billy was awakened by the sound of talking in the room next door. It looked as if Mam had organised one of her family 'conflagrations' for he recognised the voices of his two sisters Polly and Flo and their husbands, Steve and Barry.

Must be important, he thought, if they've gone to the trouble of arranging baby-sitters for all their kids. May as well go and face the music, he said to himself.

He went to the bathroom to freshen up before joining them in the living room.

He found them sitting round the white-scrubbed kitchen table, like a board meeting in session. Mam sat at the head, Polly and Flo to her left, Steve and Barry, to her right. The subject appeared to be Billy and the London college.

Steve was the first to speak.

'Billy, we're so sorry for this terrible tragedy. Today must have been hell for you.'

'I feel as if my whole world has come to an end,' Billy replied. 'The worst day of my life.'

'If you make the wrong decision,' said Mam, 'it *will* be the worst day of your life. Now your father's gone to the boozer, it's time to get down to brass tacks without him putting his spoke in.'

'But I think Dad's right in a way,' Billy said. 'Going to

college will cost a fortune not only in kitting me out and that but in keeping me supplied with spends. I've got too used to earning a wage and being independent.'

'Independent on thirty shillings a week!' exclaimed Mam. 'Listen, Billy. All of us here are prepared to make sacrifices to see you through. When I think back on what we've done so far – like pawning Grandma's teapot to send you to Damian College, all that you went through on evacuation to Blackpool ... it'd be such a waste if you gave up now. In so many ways all my hopes have been pinned on you.'

'Sorry, Mam,' Billy said, 'I don't understand. Why on me?'

'Look, our Billy,' she said. 'The one thing that's kept me going all these years has been the thought that at least one of us'll get somewhere in this rotten old world. You're the youngest in the family with a chance that none of the others had. If you throw it away, you'll be letting all of us down. Don't be such a fool. If you decide not to go, I don't know what I'll do. . . . If you can't understand that, I can't . . .' Mam broke down and began to weep.

Billy was dumbstruck. He could only watch helplessly. Mam crying was something he couldn't handle.

'I had no idea that my going to college meant so much to you,' he faltered.

'Of course it does, you great loon,' said Flo. 'Your success is our success. Don't you see that?'

'You've got this offer on a silver platter,' added Polly, 'and you're thinking of turning it down. You must be mad. Have you forgotten the letter Steve had to write to the college to ask them to reconsider when they turned you down the first time? What was all that for?'

'And think of your friend Robin,' said Barry. 'In a way

10

you'd be letting him down as well.'

'Not only that,' said Steve. 'Look at the job you'll be going into when you finally qualify. Teaching! One of the noblest professions. Imagine it! I can see you now in the classroom. Eager faces looking up to you, children hanging on to your every word. What a contrast to the stiff-backed, crusty old strap-wielding teachers we had to put up with as kids. I can see you refereeing football matches in the winter, umpiring cricket in the summer, taking your class on hikes at the weekends, a life out in the fresh air. Compare that with your present job sorting out taxes on the clerical treadmill in a smoke-filled office for the rest of your life.'

When Steve had finished extolling the teaching profession, Billy's mind was in turmoil. For over three months, he had carried around in his head Robin's vision of life in London until it had become part of reality. Now with Robin's death, the imagery had changed and he couldn't adjust to the new scene. London without Robin was too painful to contemplate and now here was Steve appealing afresh to his imagination, creating new scenes for him to envisage. Fine, Billy thought, but he could also see ahead a two-year stint of being permanently broke, of penny-pinching and trying to make ends meet. There was also another thought, one that he was reluctant to admit to himself. Was he capable of a course in higher education? His School Certificate results were nothing to write home about and going back to the tax office was a way out which let him forget the little snags gnawing at him. Then he thought – tax office, a way out? More like a cop-out.

'Hey, hey! Hold on!' Billy said at last. 'I'm taking a beating here. Outvoted! There are too many of you to argue

11

with. If you want the real truth, I'm not sure I'm cut out to be a teacher. Not even sure I have the brains for higher education.'

'Nonsense!' said Steve. 'Of course you've got the brains. Think positively and banish negative thoughts like "I can't". Stop talking defeat. Think "I can and I will".'

'These are great ideas,' Billy replied, 'but have you worked out how much they're going to cost?'

'Leave that to us,' said Steve. 'First we'll have a family whip-round. Sam's due to be demobbed from the navy soon, and I hear he's got marriage on his mind. But I'm sure he'll put in a few bob to help his kid brother. I think the same will go for Les even though it'll be a couple of years before the army releases him. Barry and I are ready to do our share.'

'How am I supposed to pay you back?' Billy asked.

'It'll be up to you to look after us when we're old and decrepit,' Polly laughed.

'Why use the future tense?' Billy answered in the same vein. 'But I didn't know teacher's pay was that good.'

'Don't forget the big pension you'll get at the end,' said Mam, thinking of the pittance she was due to receive in a few years' time.

'And look at the holidays you'll get,' Polly added. 'Three weeks at Christmas, three at Easter, six in the summer, and that's not counting the odd bank holidays and half-term breaks.'

'When I think of the time I'll spend not doing it,' said Billy, 'I think maybe teaching is the only job for a layabout like me. But suppose I do decide to go, what'll Dad say? He won't like it.'

'You leave your father to me,' said Mam darkly. 'I know how to keep him quiet.'

'One last thing,' said Polly. 'If and when you get to that college of yours, for God's sake, see if you can put some weight on. I hope the food is good down there because you're looking more like Frank Sinatra every day. No wonder they call him the "skeleton".'

'So I should look like Sinatra! So I should worry if I had his voice or his money,' Billy said, in the manner of their Yiddish neighbours.

It was the first attempt at a joke since he'd heard about the death.

'You're all very persuasive,' Billy continued. 'You've made so many thoughts whirl around my brain, I don't know whether I'm coming or going. The best thing is to sleep on it and then make up my mind.'

On that note, the family 'conflagration' broke up, with Billy promising to let them know the next day.

Before he went to sleep that night, he lay on his bed alone with his thoughts. His mind went back to that joyous day when he'd learned that he'd been accepted by the London college. He could hear Robin's voice in his head when he'd told him the glad tidings.

'Hoppy,' he'd said, using the gang's nickname for him, 'it's the best news I've heard this year. And what a year it's going to be! Nineteen forty-five! Just think about it! You and me and the gang together in Chelsea. A dream come true. And I'm so happy you're getting out of that terrible humdrum office job. We were getting worried about you. You were beginning to look like a dried-up, miserable civil servant. This offer of a place is a golden opportunity – don't mess it up, no matter what. Remember our motto: *carpe diem*! Seize the day! Opportunity knocks only once at every man's door. So make sure you open it when she calls.'

13

Exhausted by the day's events and the heated family debate, Billy fell into a deep sleep.

Next morning, he awoke with a fresh mind but Robin's voice was still echoing in his head: 'A golden opportunity – don't mess it up, no matter what.'

He went into breakfast.

'Well, Mam, I've slept on it and I've decided to go,' he said.

'Thank God, you've come to your senses,' she said. 'But that was a sudden change of mind, wasn't it? What happened? Was it what we said last night? You heard the voice of reason?'

'No,' he said. 'More like a voice from the grave. Or maybe it was that talk about the long holidays. I'll go to this college and at least give it a try. But if I don't like it, I'll be back before Christmas.'

Sunday afternoon – the day Billy was due to depart – he left the tenement with self-doubt still gnawing at his heart, not only about leaving behind the familiar and going into the unknown but wondering if he had what it took to make the grade and become a teacher. Was he making the right decision? Though he still wasn't a hundred per cent sure, it was good to have reached some kind of conclusion. And it would be good, he thought, to join his old school friends on this new adventure.

Dad shook his hand. 'All the best, son,' he said. 'Don't forget us and where you come from. Remember your home's always here if you change your mind. I know you think I've tried to hold you back but I only wanted what was best for you. And to show I'm behind you, here is a little present from me.' He handed Billy a Rolex Tudor wristlet watch. 'Take care of this, son,' he said. 'You'll need a watch when you get to that there college of yours. I bought it from a pal in the Hare and Hounds but I won't say how much I paid for it,' he added, tapping his nose. 'Ask no questions and you'll hear no lies.'

'Thanks, Dad. You couldn't have got me a better present.'

Mam wanted to accompany him to the station but he wouldn't let her. Her eyes were wet as she helped him lift his bulging suitcase into the taxi.

'Now, are you sure you've got everything?' she asked. 'Your money, your ration book and your identity card?'

'Don't worry, Mam. I've got them all here safe in my inside pocket.'

'You go off, Billy, and make something of yourself,' she said. 'I know you'll make us proud.' She kissed him on the cheek. 'Ta-ra, son.'

'Ta-ra, Mam. I'll do my best.'

As the cab drove off, she watched it till it had turned the corner of Gardenia Court and was lost from view.

Half an hour later, the taxi pulled in at the Central Station approach. Billy got out with his luggage, paid the driver, and, watched by several porters leaning against the wall, struggled his way across the station concourse. He consulted the large railway timetable board.

'Platform six,' he said aloud to himself.

He handed his ticket to the collector at the barrier.

'Better get a move on, mate,' said the man. 'That train's due out in a few seconds.'

He hurried as best as he could with his suitcase along the platform, looking for a particular compartment.

And there they were! His friends, their heads sticking out of the windows as if it were a cattle truck – the Damian College Smokers' Club.

'Trust you to be late, Hoppy!' called Oscar.

'Come on, Hoppy!' shouted Titch. 'Get a move on! Or you're going to miss the train.'

Chapter Two

To travel hopefully is a better thing
than to arrive . . .

Robert Louis Stevenson

Billy hoisted his suitcase onto the luggage rack; the train
lurched forward and they were on their way.

He looked happily round the compartment at the
adolescent gang that was such an important part of his
existence. They sprawled on the seats and puffed on
their Park Drives, full of *joie de vivre*, the arrogance
of youth and confident hope in the future. He'd spent
his life with them since the age of eleven when they'd
'passed the scholarship' and been accepted into Damian
College. He'd shared so many experiences with them,
happy and sad, that he'd developed a deep understanding
of and affection for them all. He had come to know every
nuance of their moods; knew precisely what each one
was going to say even before he knew it himself; knew
who'd tell which story, who'd laugh and for how long
over a particular type of joke; knew their foibles inside
out – who claimed to be what and why. To the outsider,

17

however, they were a motley-looking crew.

Each of them had his own particular nickname. Billy himself had been awarded the sobriquet Hoppy after subduing the class bully in a boxing match.

Tony Wilde had been nicknamed Oscar because of his name and his disposition and because of his efforts to emulate the great aesthete with his epigrams and his venomous wit. Billy, along with the rest of them, was wary of him and a little afraid of his vitriolic tongue. It was a moot point, though, whether Oscar's character was the result of his nickname or whether his nickname was the result of his character. One thing was sure, his physique in no way resembled the original Oscar, for he was tall, thin, and lanky – a regular beanpole.

Sitting at the window seat was Titch Smalley, born Dick Smalley, a name which had caused him a certain amount of inconvenience at school. He was the antithesis of Oscar. Small and down-to-earth. Happiest when miserable and believed things were going to get worse before they got worse. Titch came from a poor background and Billy was especially fond of him. Perhaps because they had one important thing in common – they were both stony-broke.

The third man in the compartment was Oliver Hardy – Ollie to them – a bit of a know-all who fancied himself as a walking encyclopaedia. At school he'd made it his life's work to compile the definitive dictionary of dirty words and phrases. He'd reached the letter 's' and was finding it a rich source of synonyms for sexual intercourse with such words as screw, shag, stuff, and the Yiddish *schtup*; his favourite phrase was *score between the posts*, an extraction from Australian folklore. He was a mine of useless information and could be relied on to chip in with the facts when nobody wanted them.

Fourth fellow traveller – Nobby Nodder, the lady's man and obsessed with sex. Claimed he'd had it off almost every night when he was going round with a nymphomaniac called Ronnie. 'She was so hot,' he claimed, 'she made the Kama Sutra seem like Hans Andersen.' But when he said 'almost every night', Billy was sure that 'almost' was the operative word. Almost on Monday, almost on Tuesday . . . They had to admit, though, he was a well-read student. He'd read the sex manuals and was an expert on perversions.

Finally, there was Rodney Potts or Pottsy as he was known, son of a well-to-do Manchester businessman; none too bright but he'd managed to scrape enough qualifications to get into college – even this college. The smokers' club hadn't accepted him into their clique at first but he finally made it when he told a blue joke – one about an elephant: 'There was this primitive early man wandering naked through the forest when he met an elephant. The elephant looked down at his thing, studied it for a while and said, "You'll not get much food with that, my lad".' Not bad, they'd said, and his joke was accepted as an entrance fee. Pottsy was a likeable, handsome lad, fair-haired, fair-complexioned, pale of eyelash, and uncomplicated. He'd turned down the chance to join his father's retail business and had opted instead for the training college, not because of any burning vocation to teach but for the companionship of his school cronies. As he had nothing but three older sisters at home, it was understandable. Billy felt a certain sympathy for him.

'For a while, Hoppy,' said Oscar when they'd settled down, 'we thought you'd changed your mind about coming.'

'I nearly did,' said Billy, 'but my family told me about the holidays teachers get and that clinched it.'

'Of course, you've been working in an income tax office for the last year,' remarked Titch. 'You must have found it hard to leave a good job like that.'

'Good job!' echoed Billy. 'You must be joking. As soon as they found I'd been to a grammar school and knew how to write, they set me the task of copying out the names and addresses of the entire British population from great ledgers onto things called con-cards – part of the new Pay As You Earn system.'

'What about those secretaries who work there?' said Nobby, lecherous as ever. 'I've heard they're hot stuff. The really randy ones wear an anklet chain as a sign they're up for it.'

'Dead right,' said Billy. 'Some of them were hot stuff. I tell you, it wasn't safe walking through the typing pool. A man was likely to lose his trousers. And the work was so monotonous we spent our time thinking about how we'd get off when we got off at five o'clock. But Nobby, how come you knew that stuff about the anklet chain? It's supposed to be a state secret.' Our secretaries were shrivelled up old maids, thought Billy, specially picked for their ability to curb lustful thoughts in the randy young male clerks.

'With so many glamorous girls around,' Billy continued, 'it was very hard to concentrate on the main task in hand, namely the transcribing – in our best copperplate hand of course – of a whole lot of dull details from stuffy old tomes.'

'Sounds Dickensian. I suppose you used quill pens and high desks,' said Ollie.

'Right,' said Billy. 'Only worse. I was bored out of my skull and I had resigned myself to a life on the treadmill. I was going quietly mad when Robin rode in like the US cavalry with news of this college. He wrote to me to ask if I'd be interested in joining you lot. What a question! Like asking a wretch being tortured on the rack if he was interested in a holiday in the South of France. As soon as I heard I was accepted, it took me around ten seconds to think it over and I handed in my notice on the spot. Then tragedy struck. End of our dreams.'

'It's going to be hard for us to come to terms with his death,' Oscar remarked. 'Especially you, Hoppy, as you were so close.'

'That's putting it mildly,' replied Billy. 'When Robin died, our big ideas took a nose dive.'

Titch said nothing. He seemed to have become suddenly engrossed in the book on his knee.

'Talking of London and college,' said Pottsy, who up to this point had been silently watching the receding country-side, 'has anyone here been to London before?'

No one had.

'I suppose you're going to tell us that you and your family have stayed at the Ritz,' said Ollie.

'Not quite,' replied Pottsy. 'But my dad once came down here on business and he brought me and my three sisters on a visit. We stayed at the Strand Palace.'

'Typical Pottsy! Staying in a palace,' Nobby exclaimed. 'So what's London really like?'

'Big and expensive,' Pottsy replied. 'And you've never seen such traffic – you take your life in your hands when you try to cross the road. When we went down two months ago, the place was in ruins. Bombed-out buildings every-where.'

'Still the same,' said Billy. 'But thank God the Germans never got the atomic bomb,' said Billy 'or there wouldn't be any London at all.'

'I suppose we'll be OK,' said Titch nervously. 'We were used to being away from home during the war when we were evacuated to Blackpool.'

'Nothing to worry about,' said Oscar, 'as long as we Mancunians stick together. We'll be in the mire together and we're used to that. We're bound to meet some awkward types with funny accents but we'll get by. At least *we* speak the King's English, which is more than we can say for some of these other provincials – yokels from Geordieland or Yorkshire. Why, I've heard that people from Cornwall speak a foreign language. But London! Think of it! It may be in ruins after the battering from the Luftwaffe but it's still the most exciting city in the world.'

'Don't tell me,' said Billy. 'I've heard it before – the bright lights, the cinemas, the theatres, the pubs, the restaurants, the West End! I can hardly wait to get there!'

'Don't get carried away,' Titch added, looking up from his book. 'I hate to be the fly in the ointment but there's still the little matter of money. Can we afford those marvellous things you're going on about?'

'No problem,' said Billy. 'You're talking to Rockefeller. I've got over five pounds in my pocket. So what's the worry? And my mam's promised to send me ten shillings a week as well. I've never been so rich.'

'Me too,' said Titch. 'I've got five pounds to last me the term and my mam and dad said they'd try to send me a few bob a week or whatever they could afford.'

'I've no money worries,' said Potts. 'My dad's opened a bank account for me and I can draw on that as long as I don't overdo it.'

'So we can borrow off you, Pottsy,' said Ollie.

'My dad warned me about that before I left,' said Pottsy.

'He said that in business and friendship neither a borrower nor a lender be 'cos you'll lose both your friend and your money.'

At that moment, the train pulled into Crewe station.

'Time for sandwiches,' said Billy, unwrapping his packed lunch. His mam had made up his favourite, cheese and pickle. Good old Mam, he thought. She must have used up a whole week's cheese ration on these sandwiches. He had a momentary vision of her as she'd waved to him from the veranda as he'd got into the taxi – she had looked proud but sad and anxious. He pushed the thought quickly from his mind. It wouldn't do to let the others see that he was feeling homesick already.

From their hand luggage, the rest of them produced a miscellaneous collection of provisions, making the compartment smell like a delicatessen.

'God knows when we'll get to eat again,' said Billy, munching away. 'We've been travelling for three hours. I thought this was supposed to be a non-stop express. So much for the LMS Railway. I'm sure we've been going backwards.'

'With the fuel shortages they keep telling us about,' said Oscar, 'we're lucky there's any train at all. Anyway, doesn't LMS stand for Laborious and Murderously Slow?'

'I suppose we'll get to the college some time today,' said Titch.

'Talking of the college,' said Nobby, 'it's happened so quickly, we've not had time to find out much about the place. I know it's in Chelsea but how did it get this weird name – Marjons?'

'Now he asks!' said Billy. 'I suppose you've been too busy weighing up the nightspots and where the birds'll be to think about the college. Anyway, it's in the King's Road.

23

Used to be two Anglican colleges – St Mark's of Chelsea and St John's of Battersea. When they joined together, they became the College of St Mark and St John. Marjons for short. We were lucky to get in, though, a bunch of Papists like us.'

'That's because the college had little choice,' said Oscar. 'After we were all turned down by St Mary's College at Strawberry Hill, I thought that was the end of our hopes of ever becoming teachers. Then I read somewhere that the new Labour government had ordered all training colleges to speed things up and start training teachers as fast as they could because there's such a desperate shortage everywhere.'

'I think it's this college that must be desperate if they took us lot in,' Titch said. 'We're not exactly out of the top drawer, are we?'

'Speak for yourself,' said Pottsy. 'Anyway, what's it mean when it says training college? Does it mean military exercises, drilling and long route marches? Or maybe circus training involving whips and chairs or leaping out of pools to catch raw fish.'

'Nothing as extreme as that,' said Ollie, always ready with information. 'To train is to instruct so as to make obedient to orders, like training an animal to perform simple tricks, for example teaching a dog to jump through hoops.'

'I'd never have come if I'd known I had to jump through hoops,' said Pottsy.

'I've heard that the college was used as a mortuary during the London Blitz,' said Billy. 'The cellars were used to store the corpses before burial.'

'I definitely don't like the sound of that,' wailed Titch. 'What sort of place are we going to? Dead bodies and jumping through hoops!'

24

'I presume,' said Billy, 'that the dead bodies have been removed by now.'

The conversation might have continued along these lines but they discovered, much to their surprise, that the train was pulling into Euston station. The two hundred-mile journey had taken six hours.

London at last! They had finally made it. Now they wondered how they were to get to Chelsea. No one had given it much thought. They got their luggage down from the racks and made their way along the seemingly endless platform.

As they lugged their heavy suitcases across the crowded concourse, the station porters, seeing there was no tip to be had, watched them indifferently like a row of owls perched on a wall.

Chapter Three

Will your Grace command me any service
to the world's end?

Shakespeare, Much Ado About Nothing

Outside the station, they got their first view of London. Their impression was of a grey city, much of it still in ruins and relieved only by the innumerable bright red buses which seemed to be everywhere. They found a friendly London bobby who advised them to catch a Number 73 to Victoria and then a Number 11 which would take them on to Chelsea and right up to the gates of the college.

They found the bus easily enough but the conductor wasn't keen on taking them with their luggage.

'You lot should hire a taxi,' he said.

'You must be joking, mate,' replied Titch. 'We're not made of money. We're students. Can only just about afford the bus fare.'

'All right, all right!' said the conductor. 'Pile in. Put your bags under the apples.'

'Apples?' queried Titch.

'Apples! Apples and pears! Stairs! 'Ere, what's up wiv you? Don't you unnerstand King's English? You must be from up North.'

They boarded the bus, put their cases under the stairs and dashed up to the top deck for a smoke. Billy opted to stay on the lower deck to keep an eye on the luggage. He knew about these Londoners. Hadn't his dad given him dire warnings about the London thieves and spivs who were waiting their chance to pick his pockets and make off with his stuff? 'And keep your eye on that new watch I've given you,' he'd said, 'or they'll have it off you soon as look at you. Can't trust them there Southerners.' He should know – he read the *Manchester Evening News* every night.

'Which college are you lot goin' to then?' the conductor asked Billy as he clipped his ticket in the little machine that was slung round his neck.

'College of St Mark and St John's in Chelsea. Marjons for short.'

'Marjons! Sounds more like that Chinese tile game the old ladies play. What kind of students are you then?'

'Going to be teachers.'

'Cor blimey!' the conductor said. 'The Chalk and Duster Brigade. Gawd help poor England!'

What strange expressions and what a funny accent, Billy thought. Like visiting a foreign country.

It was in Tottenham Court Road, however, that he became aware that he had truly left his roots back in Lancashire. They passed a signpost which bore the legend TO THE NORTH, which sounded like an ominous warning to all passers-by that up there in the North, the land of Blake's 'dark Satanic mills', there lived savages who still painted themselves in blue woad. But when Billy saw that sign and realised its significance for him, he felt a sharp pang of nostalgia for the people and places he'd left behind, as if they were so far away in a distant world that he'd lost them forever. All their hopes are resting on my shoulders, he thought. They've made so many sacrifices for me, I can't let them down – I must succeed.

The bus wound its way through the centre of the city – shells of bombed-out buildings everywhere. Billy gazed in awe at the passing scene – the unremitting roar of the traffic, the honking of the taxis, the endless lines of buses, trucks, and cars, the thousands of jostling pedestrians, many of them still in uniform, who thronged the streets, all combining to produce the chaotic sights, sounds and smells of the great metropolis that was London. There were the theatres and the huge hoardings that loomed up on every available space crying out their blatant slogans: FOR YOUR THROAT'S SAKE SMOKE CRAVEN A: 10 FOR 1/2d; VALET FOR LONG LASTING BLADES: 3d EACH; PHYLLIS DIXEY IN *PEEK-A-BOO* WITH HER VARGA MODELS AT THE WHITEHALL THEATRE; WESTMINSTER THEATRE: ROBERT DONAT IN *THE CURE FOR LOVE*.

One particular billboard which grabbed his attention pictured a voluptuous Jane Russell stretched out in the hay. The poster read: *THE OUTLAW.* A SCORCHER OF A FILM. ODEON LEICESTER SQUARE.

Like a magic carpet, the bus transported him through London's famous landmarks whose names he'd seen only on a Monopoly board: Strand, Northumberland Avenue, Trafalgar Square, Whitehall. And places he'd only heard about on wireless programmes like *In Town Tonight* when a man with a sergeant-major voice would bring London's traffic to a standstill with his ringing command, 'HALT! Once again, we bring you the personalities that are *IN*

TOWN TONIGHT.' Billy half expected to hear Eric Coates's rousing Knightsbridge March that always followed the introduction.

As the bus crossed the great city, he was treated to a flow of tourist guide commentary by the conductor in a Max Miller, cheeky-chappie voice.

'Charing Cross. Books, books, books. Poetry books, scientific books, saucy books. Foyle's the place for you lads.' He little knew how prophetic his words were. 'Trafalgar Square. See the lions over there? Made from cannons captured at Trafalgar. Nelson's Column, one hundred and sixty-seven feet high. Statue at the top, seventeen feet high. You got nothing like that up North, I'll bet.'

'We've got Blackpool Tower,' said Billy. 'The biggest phallic symbol in Britain – five hundred and twenty feet.'

'Gercha,' the conductor said.

They reached Victoria station.

'This is where you get off,' he called to the gang upstairs. 'Catch a Number Eleven. All the best, boys. But for Gawd's sake, don't come learnin' my kids that funny Northern accent. I want 'em to speak proper like the rest of us in Bethnal Green.'

'Thanks, mate. And thanks for the conducted tour,' Titch said as he stepped off the platform. 'Cheeky bugger,' he added as the bus moved off.

'Any time,' the conductor shouted back. 'Chalk and Duster Brigade! Cor blimey, that's a laugh!'

They caught the Number 11 bus close behind.

If the first conductor was Max Miller, the next was Buster Keaton, po-faced and gloomy, as if he carried the world's problems on his shoulders. He said nothing and betrayed no kind of emotion about them or their luggage.

The Charon of London Transport, Billy thought.

The bus drove on for a while. Suddenly their ferryman announced in a robotic, speak-your-weight voice, 'World's End.'

'I knew it! I knew it! My God! Has it come to this?' declaimed Oscar. 'Is this where we end our days? The World's End?'

'World's End,' the conductor repeated triumphantly. 'Next stop the Brewery, the Power Station.' Then with a feeble attempt at sarcasm added, 'Marjon's Holiday Camp.'

'Thank you, my good man,' said Oscar. 'And do try to contain your schoolgirl giggling.'

'I liked that man,' said Titch. 'In some ways he reminded me of my father.'

The Damian College Smokers' Club had arrived – at last. Up to this moment, the idea of living and working in the capital had been a mere dream. A life of bliss in London! They had thought and talked of nothing else for six months as they puffed on their Park Drives in the alley behind the school. Now they were here, they were feeling distinctly apprehensive. What had they let themselves in for? What did fate have in store?

They stood together on the pavement, a forlorn group nervously taking stock of the surroundings and soaking up the atmosphere. Behind them, silhouetted against a leaden London sky, rose the massive Battersea Power Station, its great finger-like chimneys pointing and belching thick black smoke into the heavens. Ahead, over the bridge, was the Nell Gwynn pub, conveniently placed for supplies as it stood next door to Watney's Brewery, which at that moment was emitting hissing jets of steam along with a powerful aroma of fermenting hops.

'The pub's handy,' remarked Billy. 'But at one and a

penny a pint, who can afford it? Anyroad, who needs the pub? We can simply stick our heads out of a window and sniff the air.'

It was the building across the road, however, which commanded their attention – the building on which they had pinned their hopes and their dreams and where they were to spend the next two years. The first impression was not favourable. The place had fallen into disrepair during the war. It was a dirty, depressing, tumbledown affair and clearly had not seen a lick of paint in a long time. The rambling, dilapidated edifices were surrounded by a crumbling high wall and approached by a large iron gate and a porter's lodge. Like the front of Strangeways.

'Do you know that this is the oldest training college in Britain?' asked Ollie.

'Who'd have guessed?' said Oscar.

'That conductor was right,' Billy said. 'This is the world's end.'

'Two years,' intoned Titch lugubriously.

'You make it sound like a prison sentence,' remarked Nobby.

'How long is two years?' asked Potts, blowing little bubbles from the end of his tongue, a revolting habit he indulged in whenever he was puzzled or lost in thought.

'An interesting question,' replied Ollie, ready with the answer. 'It depends. According to a wise philosopher – probably Einstein – time is relative. If you're enjoying yourself, time flies but if you're miserable, time drags.'

'How do you make that out? Time is always the same no matter what, surely?' protested Potts.

'Let's put it like this,' said Nobby. 'If you're on the job with a beautiful girl, a minute is nothing. But if you're

31

sitting on a red-hot stove, a minute is forever.'

'Then this next two years will be forever,' Titch groaned happily.

They crossed the road and entered the gates. Their new lives had begun.

Chapter Four

Day One

The first day was devoted to finding their way around. The small band of second-year students – twelve in number – who had been in residence since 1944 acted as guides and advisers. Before they set off, their particular second-year mentor introduced himself.

'My name is Bullock. I come from Taunton, Somerset,' he said. 'My friends call me Bovril. But you may call me Mister Bullock.'

'Why thank you, Mr Bovril,' replied Oscar. 'Your dialect proves my theory that the way we speak reflects our environment. Your intonation is that of a bull in a field.'

'Watch it,' Bullock snorted.

He took them on a tour of the facilities – the administration block, the library, the tiered lecture theatre, seminar rooms, the gymnasium, woodwork shop, art studio, and the science lab.

'As far as I'm concerned,' drawled Oscar, adopting his aristocratic pose, 'a science lab is a chamber of horrors consisting of foul smells and dripping taps. Hardly the place for a gentleman.'

'And this,' announced their courier proudly, 'is the college dining room.'

'The most important room in the college,' said Titch. 'When do we eat?'

'Your table's Number Six, of which I'm the head,' said Bullock, pointing to their allotted place and ignoring Titch's inquiry.

Any doubts they'd entertained about the age of the college were now dispelled by the decor of the oak dining room which was dominated by a large polished table on a raised platform. Around this were twenty smaller refectory tables complete with monks' benches. The oil portraits of previous principals looked down disapprovingly from the wood-panelled walls.

'I suppose we have to listen to plainchant whilst we eat,' remarked Oscar.

'And homilies in Latin,' added Billy.

Finally Bullock conducted them to South Block, the oldest part of the college. They climbed the stone stairs to the top floor where they came to a long, draughty corridor with thirty or forty rooms branching off.

'These are your study-bedrooms,' Bullock announced. 'Number Eighty-nine is for Robin Gabrielson.'

'He won't be coming,' said Billy quickly.

'Why not?'

'He died a fortnight ago in a climbing accident,' Billy replied.

'I'm so sorry to hear that,' Bullock said.

Titch had gone very quiet as he always did at the mention of Robin Gabrielson's name.

'Anyway, the room next door – Room Ninety. Hopkins,' Bullock continued.

The six students peeked into the room. One look and

their hearts sank. Dark and dingy were the words that sprang to mind. The room was a small, cramped box containing a narrow iron bed, a bookcase with a fold-down flap that served as a writing desk, and a small wardrobe. A prison cell.

'Are all the rooms like this or is this the one reserved for solitary confinement?' asked Billy. 'Have I unknowingly committed some crime?'

'They're nearly all the same,' answered Bullock. 'This is one of the better ones.'

'When I saw your dining room a few moments ago, I had my suspicions,' said Oscar. 'Now I've two questions for you, Bovril. First, when do we get our tonsures and second, where are the self-flagellation whips? I'd no idea we were joining a strict ascetic religious order.'

'I can see you fancy yourself as a comedian,' said Bullock. 'You'll soon get used to it.' Narrowing his eyes, he added in a Gestapo-like voice, 'And if you're looking for methods of punishment, Wilde, you'll find out soon enough how our system works. We have ways of dealing with jokers like you.'

Billy looked out of his window. 'At least I have a first-class view and smell of Watney's,' he called to the others as they were allocated their rooms along the corridor.

'I'm looking straight at Battersea Power Station,' Titch called. 'Just my luck.'

Next they were shown the bathroom which consisted of a curious arrangement of a large bath across which was stretched a wooden board with holes to accommodate three enamel basins – an ingenious device thought up by some enterprising carpenter to speed up student 'throughput' in the mornings. The kind of ingenuity that would have earned an Iron Cross in a Nazi concentration camp.

'Because of the national fuel shortage,' said Bullock, 'there may or may not be hot water but if you run the hot tap for five minutes, you'll soon find out. If there's a loud knocking sound in the pipes, you're in luck.'

'No doubt designed by Heath Robinson or one of his brothers,' said Billy.

'Thank you for your conducted tour of this five-star hotel, my man,' said Titch. 'But I repeat my earlier question – when do we eat around here?'

'Dinner's at seven thirty. That's in two hours' time,' replied Bullock, looking at his watch.

'Two hours! I'll never last that long,' moaned Titch.

'And what's this dinner-in-the-evening stuff?' protested Nobby. 'What kind of rum place is this?'

'In better class homes,' said Pottsy haughtily, 'dinner is always in the evening. At home we always dined at eight. At weekends, we even dressed for dinner.'

'And I suppose the rest of the week,' said Oscar languidly, 'you ate your meals in the buff.'

'No. In the dining room,' replied Pottsy, blowing his little bubbles.

'Obviously,' said Billy, 'we've joined the toffs. I don't know what my dad would say if he knew. Anyroad, a student, like the army, marches on its stomach. Let's hope that the college gets better marks for its food than its accommodation. I have strict orders from home to put on some weight.'

At seven thirty they trooped into the dining hall for their first college meal. They found their table easily enough, with Bullock sitting at the head. At the lower end was a rough-looking character around thirty-five years of age.

'Let me introduce the deputy head of the table,' Bullock

announced. 'Corporal Jack Elder of the Durham Light Infantry. Like you he is a first-year but, unlike you, he is a war hero.'

The Mancunian sextet could only stare dumbfounded. Billy was the first to move.

'Pleased to meet you,' he said and stuck out his hand in friendship.

'Likewise,' growled Jack Elder, grasping Billy's hand. Smiling maliciously, he gazed into Billy's eyes as he tightened his vice-like grip until Billy winced with pain. 'Sorry about that,' said Jack, grinning. 'Can't resist doing that. Like to see how hard I can squeeze a bloke's hand when I first meet him. Test his bottle, like.'

Billy grimaced as he wrung his injured hand. 'Very funny,' he managed to say. 'I like a firm handshake though, not the flabby kind. But what's a war hero like you doing in a college like this?'

'Always wanted to be a teacher ever since I got knocked about at school,' he replied. 'Thought I'd like to do the knocking about for a change. After I was wounded in Normandy, the gover'ment couldn't do enough for me. They gave me the Military Medal and a special grant. So 'ere I am.'

'You said wounded, Jack. What happened?' Billy asked.

'Hit in the stomach with flying shrapnel from a moaning Minnie. That stopped me in my tracks all right, I can tell you.'

Jack's little speech was interrupted by the entry of the academic staff who, in their flowing black gowns, processed formally through the dining room and up to the top table. The whole college rose to its feet. The principal rapped three times with his gavel and then intoned a blessing on the meal.

'*Benedictus benedicat per Jesum Christum dominum nostrum.*'

'Amen,' everyone answered and sat down.

Billy and his friends could hardly wait for the meal as it was seven hours since they had last eaten. There was an appetising smell of soup coming from the kitchen.

'I hope the soup's as good as it smells,' Billy remarked. 'It's certainly got the gastric juices flowing.'

'You bloody lot don't know what hardship is,' Elder sneered. 'I joined the army seventeen years ago and we had it rough. What were you lot doing seventeen years ago?'

'I was in bed with a woman,' replied Nobby. 'Breast-feeding.'

'Things haven't changed much then,' said Billy.

The kitchen servers wheeled out the trolleys with the tureens of steaming soup – one to a table.

'Good-o,' said Titch. 'Food at last.'

That was before he tasted the soup.

Bullock ladled out the glutinous liquid onto their plates. The concoction was so tasteless and watery that the only solution was to joke about it.

'Goes to show,' Titch said. 'Don't believe everything you smell.'

'What kind of soup is this?' asked Ollie.

'Don't ask!' replied Billy in his best Yiddish inflection. 'But if we can't eat the soup, at least we can eat the bread. Perhaps the next course will be better.'

The main course was worse. The potatoes were black and under-cooked, the beans stringy, and the meat – what little there was – turned out to be tough and gristly.

'I've seen tastier food on the floor of Belle Vue elephant house,' said Oscar.

'Too true. Only an imbecile would eat stuff like this,'

agreed Titch, tucking in. 'But I'm hungry enough to eat nails.'

'You should have tried bully beef in the army, son,' said Jack who was cleaning his plate with his bread.

'I'm still hungry,' whined Titch when the dishes had been cleared away.

'You could try Dirty Dick's café round the corner,' said Bullock. 'He's usually open till ten o'clock.'

'I'll bet he does a roaring trade from this college,' said Billy.

Grace after meals followed. 'We thank thee O Lord for your blessings and for your beneficence.'

After the meal, the gang repaired to Dirty Dick's and satisfied their hunger with cheese rolls and mugs of tea.

Later that evening when the group had dispersed and retired to their rooms, when the goodnights were said, when the joking and the bantering were over and the hollow laughter had subsided, Billy lay on his bed, hands behind his head, staring at the ceiling. The lights from the passing traffic on the King's Road cast flickering shapes on the walls around him. He could feel depression creeping over him like a mantle.

It's been a long day, he thought. A rough day. What have I let myself in for? What would Robin have thought about all this? Probably the same as I do at this moment. He should really be in the empty room next door and I'm sure he'd have been as dejected. What a dump we've come to! No wonder we got into this college so easily. That food tonight was straight out of Dickens's Dotheboys Hall. For Mam's sake, I'll stick it out for another fortnight and then I'll think about going back to dear old Manchester. Things could have been a lot worse there. I could probably get my old job back in the tax office and I could take up dancing again. Maybe I'll write to my old girlfriend Adele and see if she's free.

He lay awake into the small hours, thinking. He heard the distant hooting of an owl somewhere in the college grounds. Now his imagination ran riot and he began to fill the hush of the night with strange noises. He thought he heard the sound of quiet weeping somewhere. Was it the soft sighing of the wind round the building? Was it his imagination or the subdued sobbing of Titch – or someone – in one of the adjoining rooms?

He became aware that he was developing a stye on his eye – a sure sign of tension. Which made him even more downcast.

With these thoughts whirling round his head, Billy's brain shut down for the night.

Chapter Five

He that wants money, means, and content is
without three good friends

Shakespeare, As You Like It

On Monday, after a frugal breakfast of lumpy porridge,
they started their first week with registration. They were
signed up, documented, stamped, recorded and their existence formally and officially recognised. Two days of
choosing courses followed. The college had not yet acquired
a mathematics lecturer and as the Mancunians hadn't a
single scientist among them – a reflection of the education
they had received – they ended up opting for the same
subjects: English, History, French. Familiar territory, they
thought, but there was a snag – these particular arts courses
had enormous reading lists. In addition to academic
subjects, there were also professional courses like Education, Physical Education, Health Education, each with a
different set of demands.

'How can we buy the books they're insisting on?'
moaned Titch as they emerged from a history lecture. 'And
how can we read that lot? There won't be time to go to the
toilet.'

41

'Then forgo visits to the toilet,' said Oscar. 'According to you, every silver lining has a cloud. Stop building dungeons in the air, Titch. We'll get by somehow.'

In the final days of the orientation week, they had to choose a personal development course from Art, Music, Woodwork. As Billy was clueless in all three, he took what he thought was the easy way out and selected woodwork.

He turned up to the woodwork shop, along with other conscripts, for initial briefing. He started off badly.

'I know what this is,' he said, picking up a plane. 'It works like this . . .' and he ran it across a bench top. It was wonderfully satisfying to see thin shavings of wood come curling from under the plane.

There was a yell of anger from across the room.

'You bloody great idiot!' the voice bellowed. 'I've spent hours smoothing that desktop to an eggshell finish and you've bloody well ruined it in ten seconds.'

It was Jack Elder.

'Sorry, Jack,' Billy stammered. 'It was a genuine mistake. I'd no idea that you'd done so much work on it.'

'Sorry doesn't make it right,' he snarled. 'I've half a mind to kick you in the balls, Hopkins. You must be as blind as a bloody bat.'

'Look, Jack, I've said I'm sorry. What else do you want me to do?'

The apology was not accepted and Billy knew that from that moment, he had made an enemy of Elder.

He decided that discretion was the better part of valour and dropped woodwork, opting instead for art, about which he knew even less and in which he was even more clumsy. By such accidents are life's choices made.

* * *

On Friday morning, the new intake of 150 students took their seats in the steeply tiered lecture theatre and Michael Roberts, the principal, came onto the rostrum and addressed them.

'Gentlemen,' he began (this appellation was enough to make Billy's chest swell with pride. Gentleman – him?). 'Gentlemen,' he repeated in case they had missed it the first time. 'I welcome you to the college. You have been selected from the many applications we have received. It's a proud day for us because the college has been virtually closed since the outbreak of hostilities in nineteen thirty-nine. Peace has descended upon the world again after six years of a war which has devastated civilisation on a scale never seen before. Recovery will take many a year but the carnage has ceased and nations are free to turn to the tasks of reconstruction. You gentlemen are part of that reconstruction and we must begin the long, patient work of rebuilding our nation and our culture. You have been privileged to take up the task, the vocation of teaching and educating the next generation. It is a fearsome responsibility and the minds and morals of our young people – we might even say the future of civilisation itself – will be in your hands.'

Billy hadn't fully appreciated the solemnity of the task he'd taken on. The upholding of Western civilisation? Was he up to it? he wondered.

The principal went on to warn them about some of the great pitfalls in teaching.

'You must avoid at all costs,' he thundered, 'what Alfred North Whitehead has called "inert ideas" – that is, ideas which were significant once but have now been superseded. You must teach your children to think for themselves and you must avoid rote learning of incomprehensible concepts

43

like "The terrestrial core is of an igneous nature" and the arithmetic of the eighteen sixties with its gills, bushels, chains, and poles.

'To cram a lad's mind,' he went on, 'with infinite names of things which he never handled, places he never saw or will see, statements of facts which he cannot possibly understand and must remain merely words to him – this, in my opinion, is like loading his stomach with marbles.'

Billy was so inspired by this rhetoric he was beginning to forget about train timetables back to Manchester. Not now he knew he was a gentleman and that the future of Western civilisation was in his hands.

Michael Roberts turned to a contemplation of reality and an examination of Cartesian philosophy. Billy sat bewildered. Was he really there? the principal asked. Was anybody there? Did anything exist? How did they know? What irrefutable proof did they have? Billy didn't understand a word. He'd never before questioned his own existence. Of course he was there. They were all there. He could see them, couldn't he? Hear them, touch them. Definitely smell them! What nonsense! Of course they were there! They agreed wholeheartedly with Monsieur Desmond Cartes. 'I think, therefore I am.' The only trouble was Pottsy – he didn't think and therefore he wasn't.

Roberts left the rostrum and there followed a descent from the elevated to the commonplace when the domestic bursar, a sad little man, appeared like Moses with his tablets of stone.

'We are a civilised community,' he sighed, 'and therefore we have certain rules which we must abide by if we are to live in harmony together. First: female guests are not allowed in your study-bedrooms. They must be entertained in the Junior Common Room.'

'Well, that's a relief anyway,' whispered Oscar.

'OK for you, Oscar, but for me it's a tragedy,' murmured Nobby, flicking a comb through his locks. 'That's taken away my whole reason for being here.'

'Second,' the bursar continued, 'you must be in college by ten p.m. on weekdays and eleven p.m. on Saturdays. If you wish to stay out beyond these hours for special reasons – say a visit from your parents – you must get prior permission from your tutor who will issue an *exeat*. Late-returning students without *exeats* will be gated, that is, not allowed out the following weekend. This is checked by a signing-in procedure at the porter's lodge.'

'Prisoners on probation,' whispered Nobby. 'How am I supposed to pursue my love life with such restrictive hours? I'll have to climb over the walls to get back in.'

'Now for some basic rules. You must clean the bath and toilet after use. You must make your bed in the mornings as there is a great scarcity of domestic staff. You may have heard that the Minister of Fuel, Emanuel Shinwell, has imposed deep fuel cuts on institutions like our own and as a result you may find that more often than not the central heating and the hot water system are not working.'

'Shiver with Shinwell!' someone called out.

Billy didn't usually ask questions in public but he felt someone had to say something. He took a deep breath and asked, 'How are we supposed to study if we're shaking with cold?'

'You must wear extra clothing or get under the blankets.'

'May we run an electric fire if we can get one?' asked Pottsy, the letter to his father already written in his head.

'There are no electric points in your rooms. Only the electric light socket and you must not under any

45

circumstances run anything from that other than the light. Otherwise you may fuse the lights of the whole college.'

'What if we need to iron clothes – shirts and that kind of thing?' asked a Geordie student.

'We have a weekly laundry service for which there is a small charge and so there should be no need for ironing. One last point,' the bursar went on. 'Whilst we shall endeavour to supply adequate nourishing food, the cuts in rations imposed by the Minister of Food, John Strachey, have made things very difficult but we shall do our best.'

'Starve with Strachey!' the same heckler called.

Billy looked at Titch in dismay as the commandments were promulgated. Oscar raised his eyes to heaven. But the real blow was yet to come.

'Finally, I regret to inform you that it will be necessary to levy Caution Money, that is, a contingency fee of two pounds per student to cover any damage to property that may result during your time here.'

There was a general murmur of disapproval which really did sound like *rhubarb, rhubarb*.

'Why didn't you damned well tell us before this?' protested a lad with a Yorkshire accent.

'No need for bad language. This is an Anglican college, remember. As you know, the decision to open the college was made at the last moment and in our haste we overlooked the matter in the letter giving your joining instructions. The sum, less charges, if any, will of course be returned at the end of the college course.' With that, the bursar turned on his heel and left the rostrum.

Billy quietly absorbed the news. This last announcement was a blow that spelled disaster. Goodnight Vienna. No money. No course. QED.

'That's it,' he said with finality. 'The last straw. That lets me out. I'm left with three pounds, and from that I have to buy books. Can't be done. Unless I starve for the next three months. I can't ask my folks for any more money. They've already spent a fortune on me. Manchester, here I come.'

'I'm left with only two pounds to last the term,' groaned Titch. 'I knew that bad news was round the corner. Nothing but grey skies frowning on me.'

The rest were in similar straits.

'What in God's name are we to do?' asked Titch. 'I can't simply give up and go home. My parents wouldn't have it.'

'Well, we can't live on air,' said Billy. 'I need five fags a day. They cost one and four for ten and that's for Woodbines, the cheapest, when I can get them.' He did a quick mental calculation. 'That's almost half my weekly spends gone for a start.'

'You could always try giving up, I suppose,' said Titch sententiously.

'Easier said than done,' Billy replied. 'Anyway, I never smoke before noon.'

'Why's that?' Titch asked.

'I don't stop coughing till half past eleven,' Billy laughed.

'Do you always make jokes in the face of disaster?' Titch asked.

'Always,' Billy replied. 'It's a thing I learned during the war.'

'Look on the positive side, you two,' said Ollie. 'It's well known that initial demands by tutors are excessive. I think we can cut their lists right down and, anyway, we don't need all the books straightaway. The demand will be staggered, surely.'

'And we can share books if we can come to some agreement as to who buys what,' added Nobby.

'Not entirely true,' said Billy. 'Certain books in history need to be acquired rightaway. For example, *A History of the Common People* by Cole and Postgate. We have to have that for the first lecture. Cost – fifteen bob.'

'Here's another,' said Titch. 'Grant and Temperley, *A History of Europe*. Cost, seventeen and six. That's my money practically gone on two books. We're snookered. Don't see how we can carry on.'

'We could take up the twenty pound loan offered to us by Manchester Education Committee,' said Ollie, always ready with a solution.

'I don't fancy that one bit,' replied Titch. 'If for any reason we decided to pack up the course, we'd have to pay it back and that would mean trying to sell the books which would then be second-hand.'

'I agree,' said Billy. 'Over the two-year course, we'd then owe the MEC forty quid. Fancy starting your career with a massive debt hanging over you. It's just not on.'

Some Friday night! Instead of thinking about going out to enjoy themselves, Titch and Billy were sitting in the latter's study bemoaning their financial situation when the corridor outside became Petticoat Lane market. Students facing ruin began patrolling the corridor shouting out their wares like medieval town criers.

'I have a waistcoat watch and chain here for sale,' called Ollie. 'Going at a bargain price. A sacrifice at four pounds. Any takers? A family heirloom.'

There was an opening and slamming of doors as willing buyers traded with willing sellers.

Nobby's voice was heard next. 'I'm prepared to sell *The*

Joy of Sex by Havelock Ellis for a reasonable price. An indispensable How To Do It manual.'

Then a Geordie voice: 'New shoes, size eight, a give-away at a coupla quid.'

'A Waterman fountain pen – one pound! One only. A sacrifice. Hurry, hurry, hurry.'

Titch and Billy were about to join the mêlée – Billy had a spare pair of socks and the watch his dad had given him, Titch had a shirt – when their attention was drawn to another piece of merchandise.

'I have a dozen new copies of Cobbett's *Rural Rides* going at half price,' sang the voice in a Southern twang which they recognised as that of Rodney Brighouse (naturally nicknamed Bigarse as that was how it sounded to their Northern ears) from Basildon, Essex.

Titch and Billy were out in a flash. *Rural Rides* was a set book and at half price! They bought one each.

'How did you manage to get hold of twelve new copies?' they asked.

'Easy,' Brighouse answered. 'A trip to Foyle's Bookstore on Charing Cross Road – helped myself to a satchelful. The old geyser on the counter was half asleep. Piece of cake. Meet me there on Saturday and I'll show you the ropes. Easy as falling off a log.'

Back in Billy's room, they thought this was the answer to their prayers. But not a satchelful – that was greedy and asking for trouble. No, just a single copy of Cole and Postgate's *History* and a copy of Grant and Temperley.

They drew lots and Billy got the Cole and Postgate, Titch, the G & T – all 750 pages of it.

'Trust me to get the big heavy tome. I'm bound to get caught and that's the end of my short college career. But what choice have I got? It's like stealing a loaf of bread in the early nineteenth century but at least I won't get Botany Bay.'

Next morning was Saturday, the busiest time at Foyle's. The two would-be shoplifters, wearing their raincoats with the big pockets, met Brighouse outside the store at 119 Charing Cross Road.

'It's best to buy at least one book,' Brighouse advised, 'as a distraction. Then you can simply walk out with the big prizes. One last thing though, the chances of getting nabbed are absolutely so remote they're not worth talking about but if one of us did get nicked, we must promise not to squeal on the others.'

'Agreed,' the two apprentices said readily.

Billy and Titch decided to buy one book each – Billy, *Hamlet*, and Titch, *Much Ado* – to divert attention from the theft.

The three of them entered the shop and dispersed to different parts of the five-storey building.

Finding the Shakespeares was no problem as all the Warwick editions were shelved together in the literature section on the second floor. Locating the history books, however, was not so easy. They walked along miles and miles of shelves, searching for their booty, but no luck.

A young male assistant dressed like a tailor's dummy saw their difficulty and came forward.

'Can I be of any assistance to you gentlemen?' he asked obsequiously.

Both students turned a bright red.

'Er . . . we're looking for the history section,' Billy stammered. Titch looked down at the floor and shuffled his feet.

'That's on the third floor,' the assistant answered readily.

'Any book in particular? Perhaps I can help you locate it.'

'Er, as a matter of fact, we're looking for *A History of Europe* by Grant and Temperley and *A History of the Common People* by G.D.H. Cole and Margaret Postgate.' Billy wondered if he'd said too much and tipped the man off as to their felonious plans.

Evidently not, for the assistant replied, 'Ah, yes. You'll find both books on the corridor immediately above us. You see, our books are classified not according to authors as you find in other bookshops but according to publishers. It's a little eccentricity of our proprietor, Christina Foyle. Grant and Temperley is published by Longmans, and Cole and Postgate by Methuen.'

'Thanks for your help,' Billy mumbled. 'Perhaps we'll go up there and take a look.'

The young salesman strolled away, looking for other customers in need of help.

'I'll go first,' Billy hissed. 'You wander away from me and I'll help myself to Cole and Postgate.'

One look at Titch by any discerning shop assistant, Billy thought, would have picked him out immediately. He looked furtive and shifty-eyed as he went off browsing amongst the bookshelves along the corridor. He was whistling softly and tunelessly – a sure giveaway.

Billy selected a Warwick edition of *Hamlet* and then climbed the stairs to the history section. A quick look round and the deed was done. Cole and Postgate were stowed in his capacious pocket. Shaking like a leaf, sure that everyone in the shop was aware of the bulky protuberance in his raincoat, Billy joined the small queue at the first sales desk. He waited his turn. What was it that Ollie had said about time? Suffering slowed time down, that was it. This waiting to be served was eternity . . .

At last he reached the desk. The assistant about to serve him was no other than the helpful young man now obviously doing a stint behind the sales desk. Heart racing, his mouth dry, Billy presented his *Hamlet*, conscious all the time of the great heavy lump in his pocket.

The man made out a bill for the book.

'Will that be all, sir?' he asked.

'Er . . . yes . . . just the Shakespeare,' Billy lied.

The assistant eyed him closely. 'Did you manage to find the history books you were looking for?' he asked.

'Er . . . no . . . er . . I changed my mind,' Billy stuttered. 'I'll just take the *Hamlet* for the time being.'

'Certainly, sir. No problem,' the man said brightly. 'Here's your bill. Take it across to the cashier on the next desk and pay him.'

My God, will this queuing and waiting never end?

'How much?' he asked hoarsely at the cash desk.

The second assistant was so harassed, he gave Billy hardly a second glance.

'Seven and six,' he replied brusquely. •

Billy had to go into his trouser pocket for the money which made the bulge in his coat even more prominent.

ANY TIME NOW, HE'LL CALL FOR THE POLICE, his mind screamed.

'Thank you, sir,' the man said as he stamped Billy's invoice with the word PAID. 'Now, if you'll just take the invoice and the book across to the packing counter, my colleague will wrap it for you.'

'No need for that, thank you,' Billy stuttered.

'It's Foyle's policy to wrap the books,' the man said sharply. 'It's your visible proof that you've paid for the book.'

Billy joined the third line. My God, he thought, this is

becoming unbearable. Why is buying a book so bloody complicated?

The old man at the packing counter was in no hurry. Slowly and carefully, he made a brown paper parcel tied up with string. He obviously took pride in his work for each package had to have a fancy reef knot.

Billy was sure that his left cheek had acquired a twitch and that the whole store was looking in his direction. ANY MOMENT HE'LL CALL FOR THE OWNER AND THAT'S ME FINISHED.

At last his turn came. The elderly chap tried to engage Billy in friendly conversation while he created a masterpiece in paper and string.

'You'll enjoy this play, sir. I think *Hamlet* is probably Shakespeare's finest work.'

'Yes, yes,' Billy replied, 'I'm sure I shall.' I wish the old codger would get a bloody move on. He must think I've got all day to stand here talking about *Hamlet*.

'Yes, sir,' the man was saying, 'It was first performed in sixteen hundred and one. There's the story that Shakespeare himself played the ghost in one of the early productions.'

'Yes, yes, yes,' Billy mumbled. 'Very interesting.' Give me the bloody book, you old windbag!

At last the assistant handed over the book wrapped and tied in a neat parcel. 'There you are, sir,' he said. 'I've left you a little loop to carry it with.'

Billy took the parcel quickly and strode decisively towards the door for a quick getaway.

'Wait a minute,' the cashier called after him. 'Can you come back here, please?'

OK. It's a fair cop, guv, you've got me bang to rights, he was ready to say, wrists held out for the cuffs.

He returned to the check-out desk.

'You've forgotten your receipt,' the man said cheerfully. 'You'll need that in case you're stopped.'

'Thanks,' Billy muttered and slunk off. Out of the corner of his eye, he saw a jittery, suspicious-looking Titch about to join the first queue. Not far behind was Brighouse, his satchel bulging with books.

Outside, sweet relief flooded Billy's veins. He'd made it! Safe! Oh, what joy to breathe the free air! The beautiful, polluted, fume-laden London air! He was out – with a fifteen bob book! He could appreciate the thrill and the adrenaline-flow experienced by inveterate shoplifters after a successful job. But never again! He'd never make a thief. Too neurotic. He scurried along Charing Cross Road, and near Shaftesbury Avenue went into an amusement arcade. Now, it was only a matter of waiting for Titch.

He whiled away the time feeding a one-armed bandit with a few pennies but his heart wasn't in it.

What if they catch Titch with that heavy volume? He was too naïve to hide his guilt. Anyone with a modicum of sense would see that he'd swiped something. Poor Titch. This college course meant so much to him. And to himself, too, for that matter. Otherwise why was he risking everything on this crazy venture? What a stupid thing to do for a couple of books! He could imagine Titch with a nervous tic when he came to pay for his *Much Ado*. They'd see through him rightaway. The police would be called and that would be IT! In some ways, Titch would be glad to be found guilty. It would confirm his philosophy of life, namely, 'Best not to be born but, failing that, to die early.'

Billy had put his last coin in the machine when suddenly Titch was there – crimson-faced and breathless, glancing nervously over his shoulder to check he hadn't been followed – an obvious filcher.

'Got it!' he panted. 'I've got it! Grant and Temperley! Look!'

'For God's sake,' Billy said, 'put it away! Wait till we get back to college.'

There was no sign of Brighouse but that was no problem. He knew the ropes and how to look after himself. No doubt for him it would be yet another successful mission and he'd be selling his spoils on the South Block corridor that very night.

As they stood at the stop in Trafalgar Square waiting for a Number 11 bus, their hearts were filled with joy on their deliverance and they congratulated each other on their lucky escape.

Their euphoria was brought to an abrupt and shocking end when, in a police car which drove close by them, they caught a glimpse of Brighouse sitting between two uniformed policemen in the back. He looked pale and distraught, nothing like the arrogant, brash individual who'd been selling set books at half price. They hoped to God he'd keep his word and not grass on them.

Billy and Titch didn't steal again. They'd learned their lesson. Two nervous wrecks not cut out for a life of larceny. Besides, they reasoned later, they were supposed to be teachers in training, supposed to set an example to the young. How could they base their careers on theft? No, they'd manage somehow by sharing their resources with the gang, selling one or two personal items and, if it came to the pinch, taking up that £20 loan from the Manchester Education Committee.

'We'll get by somehow,' Billy said to a doubtful Titch.

Later that night, the story went round the college like a

forest fire. Brighouse had been caught outside Foyle's with his satchel crammed with copies of Aristotle's *Ethics*. He was expelled forthwith, putting paid to any teaching ambitions he might have had.

There but for the grace of God, they thought.

Chapter Six

A little learning is a dangerous thing

Alexander Pope

In the second week the students were thrown in at the deep end and it was down to business with a vengeance. Every day was filled with a round of lectures. In history, they set off on the long journey that would take them from the founding of Constantinople in AD 330 to 1914. Billy did not understand why their study of European history stopped at the outbreak of the First World War, and he never discovered the reason; Halsall, the young lecturer, said there was no time for questions or other distractions as they had so much to get through in two years.

In French, they were introduced to Pierre Loti's *Pêcheur d'Islande* and Molière's *Le Malade imaginaire* as well as poetry, composition and syntax.

English literature kicked off with *Hamlet*, Cobbett's *Rural Rides*, and Browning's dramatic monologues, with the promise of an endless stream of books and plays to follow.

Billy didn't know what had hit him.

Towards the end of the week, they were introduced to a

strange subject entitled Education. What was it? they wondered. They never did find out. The lectures were taken by a Robert Owen Travers, a short, excitable Welshman with ill-fitting dentures and unfortunate acronymic initials. He was, inevitably, nicknamed 'Taffy'.

The six of them made it to Taffy's first lecture by the skin of their teeth. They had tried to get to the toilet between sessions but in that crowded timetable, there was insufficient time to fit in such extravagances.

They scrambled into the stratified lecture theatre and found all the seats seemed to have been taken. They looked round bewildered but Jack Elder came to their rescue, pointing to vacant places in the front row.

'Thanks, Jack,' Billy called, though he was a trifle puzzled by this helpfulness. Maybe I've misjudged him, he thought.

'It's like Sunday church service where no one wants to sit in the front benches,' remarked Pottsy as he took his seat and spread his notebook, pen at the ready.

'Perhaps they know something we don't,' Titch said ominously.

Taffy bounced into the room all businesslike, spraying spit in every direction. After a severe bout of hawking, he began.

'Good morning,' he said breezily.

Everyone wrote it down.

'I am going to introduce this field of study with a few special samples to shed light on the nature of learning.'

With every sibilant, saliva rained down upon them. Billy looked down at his notebook. It was covered in flecks of spittle. He looked at his companions' books – they were the same.

'I want to begin,' said Taffy, 'by telling you a little story.

58

There were once two French peasants, a father and a son, who decided to give their goat its name. The baptismal ceremony took place in the village square and began with the father beating the animal across its backside whilst the son held it by its collar. The old man struck the beast over and over again, as if beating a carpet. With each blow he shouted "Napoleon" into the animal's ear. After some considerable time, he stopped and said, "*Eh bien*! That's enough! Now he'll remember his name." In order to make sure, the son walked across to the other side of the square and held out a large carrot, calling out to the beast, "Napoleon!" The goat trotted across to him immediately. "Yes," said the son. "He's got it. He knows his name now!" '

Travers now became excited and paced up and down the front of the room. He picked up a chair and walked about with it.

The students watched mesmerised, wondering what he was going to do with the chair. His output of mucus now became prodigious and they were compelled to cover their books from the splodges which rained down upon them.

'What does this story teach us?' Taffy hissed.

Pottsy raised his hand. His friends cringed.

'It teaches us,' Pottsy declaimed confidently, 'that the French are cruel to their farm animals.'

Taffy became apoplectic. 'Yes, yes,' he snorted. 'And what else?'

A student, Claude Evans – a Travers compatriot – offered an answer.

'It teaches us,' he announced in ringing Laurence Olivier tones, 'that the best way to teach animals and children is by the use of the carrot and the stick.'

'Nearly right,' sputtered Taffy. 'Perhaps it will become clearer if we take some other examples from the animal world. Pavlov, a Russian physiologist, found that a hungry dog salivated at the smell of food. He taught it to salivate by associating the food with the sound of a bell.'

'I always thought Pavlov was a Russian dancer,' whispered Pottsy.

'And obviously Taffy has no need of a bell to start salivating,' commented Billy.

'Can any student suggest the significance of all this?' Taffy sounded as if he himself wasn't too sure.

Ollie raised his hand. 'It teaches us,' he volunteered, 'that the best time to teach children so that they remember well is before lunch when they are hungry and the bell goes.'

'How do you make that out?' spat Taffy impatiently.

'I wouldn't let the kids go in to dinner until they'd memorised what I'd taught them.'

'No, no, no,' Taffy objected. 'The Pavlov experiment demonstrates how an animal can become conditioned to a stimulus such as a bell. We have another example from a psychologist called Edward Thorndike who trained a cat to escape from a cage. Whenever the cat pressed a bar, the door of the cage opened, allowing it to escape. He called this Learning by Association.'

'There is an alternative view,' said Billy, raising his hand. 'We could also say that the cat conditioned the experimenter.'

'How so?' Taffy exploded wetly.

'Perhaps the cat thinks, "I've really got this psychologist conditioned. Every time I press this bar, he opens up the cage." '

Travers gave up and switched from animals to children.

Ah, this is more like it, they thought. This is what we came to college for. Child psychology.

60

Taffy went on to describe an experiment where the psychologist placed a rubber ring on a young baby's head. He called this Stimulus 1 (S1). They jotted this down in their books. The baby cried, shook its head and the ring fell off. This was Response 1 (R1). The rubber ring was replaced (S2) and the baby cried even louder and shook it off again (R2). This was repeated to S5 and R5. They now had impressive-looking scientific diagrams representing all this – Billy's mam and dad would have been proud. In this way, the baby learned quickly how to deal with a rubber ring that a child psychologist had placed on its head.

Billy tried to imagine Miss Eager at St Chad's elementary school teaching her wards by this method. 'Rubber rings – on the heads – place! Shaking of heads – begin!'

They left the theatre baffled and made their way to the dining room.

'If that's psychology,' said Nobby, 'you can stick it.'

'A lecturer,' said Billy, 'is someone who talks during *someone else's* sleep.'

'And a lecture,' added Oscar, not to be outdone, 'is the means whereby the notes of the lecturer are transferred to the notebooks of the student without the subject matter passing through the minds of either.'

'Talking of matter,' said Titch, 'the next time we have Taffy, I'm going to wear oilskins and carry a large umbrella.'

Billy nodded. 'He was like a revolving garden sprinkler of pancreatic juices.'

'He'd be useful if ever there was a fire,' added Nobby. 'He could put it out by lecturing to it.'

On the way out, Elder met them.

'Hope you enjoyed the bath,' he sneered. 'Didn't you dumbheads hear about Travers' excess saliva problem? All

61

of us at the back admired the way you entered and sat in the splash zone.'

'Thanks to your useful directions,' said Billy.

They went into lunch.

Chapter Seven

Manners maketh man

William of Wykeham

In civilised society, a meal is an enjoyable activity, something to look forward to, a means of allaying one's hunger and of enjoying not only food but good conversation. At Billy's table, however, there was no hope of any of these pleasures.

The standard of the food, it must be said, was consistent. That is to say, execrable. Undercooked meat, black potatoes, stale bread, cold soup continued to be the order of the day. The aftermath of war, they said. Shortage of food, shortage of staff to cook it and serve it. Sometimes, the sight of the nauseating mess served up was enough to make their stomachs heave. Their table expressed its revulsion by sending the stuff back with little notes stuck in it: 'This is disgusting' or 'Feed this to the pigs and see if they'll eat it', 'Excrement par excellence', 'Garbage', 'Slops', 'Revolting Vomit', 'We want our ration books back!'

They vied with each other to produce phrases best describing the sickly hash that was dished up. Oscar's was voted favourite. 'This soup,' he announced one day, 'is a concoction of old fags and cabbage stumps stewed in the juice of boiled boots.'

'The soup tastes different today,' remarked Titch one bright Monday morning.

'That's because they washed the plates,' replied Billy.

The students were constantly hungry; not only were they served culinary disasters, there was insufficient bulk. On one occasion before dinner, Billy followed the usual '*Benedictus benedicat*' by treating the table to his own version of grace:

> 'Heavenly Father bless us,
> and keep us all alive,
> there's eight of us to dinner,
> and not enough for five.'

Fresh fruit and vegetables were still rarities, and eggs were almost unknown. Not that it mattered to Titch because for some crazy faddish reason, he couldn't eat eggs. One unforgettable Saturday night, poached eggs were on the menu. The Damian table spotted them at once as soon as the serving trolleys emerged from the kitchen. The whole table turned as one to Titch.

'Who's having your egg, Titch?' they chorused.

There was no need to ask.

Ollie gave the game away. He wore a Cheshire cat smirk, and with lowered head stroked his knife on the table in a circular sawing motion. It was revolting and the whole table responded by imitating this loathsome behaviour. Seven knives stroked the table with seven similar smirks. Ollie turned the colour of carmine with embarrassment and was never allowed to forget the incident. Time and again, it was re-enacted. In a moment of boredom, one of

64

them had only to ask, 'Who's having your egg, Titch?' in order to spark off the required response.

Elder didn't suffer the pangs of hunger like the rest as he had a generous War Office pension which enabled him to keep well supplied with provisions. He usually had a jar of peanut butter to supplement the meagre diet. He had the despicable habit of extracting a large quantity on his knife, watched enviously by his fellow diners like dogs observing their master, and spreading it thickly on a large crust of bread. When all was ready, he shovelled it into his mouth, belching loudly. He never offered any to his companions. They hated him for it. Little did he know that when he went to the Nell Gwynn for his nightly pint, his table companions would sneak into his room and help themselves to a slice of his currant cake, a few of his biscuits, and one or two of his Gold Flake cigarettes. He never suspected a thing. They never touched his jar of peanut butter; Jack kept a careful check on its contents and it was impossible to swipe any without detection.

One evening, to everyone's surprise, Pottsy became a source of information and a guide to correct behaviour.

'My mother always used to say,' he announced, 'that you can always tell a gentleman by the way he eats his peas.'

'And how do you make that out?' Titch asked.

'Well, you, Titch, turn your fork over and scoop them up. That's never done in the best circles. It's my mother's way of sifting the U from the non-U.'

'Your family's a bunch of snobs,' said Billy. 'How are we supposed to eat them?'

'Not snobbery but correct etiquette. You should try to spear a couple of peas and push a few more onto the back of the fork or take some other vegetable onto the fork and then add peas. Never eat them with your knife as you do, Jack.'

Elder looked angry for a moment, then as he stuffed his mouth with a peanut butter wad, he said, 'Yeah, I suppose you're right but we used to leave that namby-pamby way of eating to the officers.'

'Does any of this matter?' Billy said. 'I mean, the way we eat?'

'It matters a great deal,' said Oscar, anxious to get his two cents in. 'In Victorian and Edwardian times, there was strict adherence to formal behaviour, and elegance and refined manners reached a high point. If we ever attend such a dinner, we should know which implement to take up and which glass to use.'

'Some hopes of us attending such a dinner,' said Titch. 'Anyway, there's nothing wrong with our manners.'

Pottsy continued his instructions. 'I notice, Titch, that you drop bits of bread in your soup and you drink it drawing the spoon towards you. You're supposed to break your bread with your hands and eat it separately.'

'Have you done,' said Titch peevishly, 'or is there more?'

'Pottsy's right,' Oscar said, looking pointedly at Nobby. 'You're not supposed to drink soup noisily or belch when you've finished. I can't imagine Oscar Wilde making butties at a dinner party.'

'Then he didn't know what he was missing,' replied Nobby, munching away happily.

'What about fish bones or orange pips?' Billy challenged.

'You may spit them into the cupped hand or spoon but unobtrusively. If you choke over a bone, leave the table at once.'

'Yeah,' said Elder, 'you'll probably be carried off

unconscious. That should cause a cheer all round.'

Ollie said, 'I think I'm the only one here that eats properly. Is that right, Pottsy?'

'Almost, Ollie, except for your habit of picking your teeth with your penknife.'

'That's telling him,' said Billy.

'And you, Hoppy,' Pottsy went on, 'always put your knife and fork down wrongly when you have finished. I find it annoying when you slip your knife in between the prongs of the fork.'

'I'll try to do better,' said Billy sarcastically.

Billy had always considered himself smart and 'with it' but Pottsy had unknowingly exposed a yawning gap in his social behaviour. Secretly he promised himself that he'd buy or borrow a book on etiquette at the first opportunity.

He tried to change the subject. 'Correct dinner table behaviour is all very well,' he said, 'but what is the accepted way of sending disgusting food back to the kitchen?'

Food was a sore point; Billy was still hungry at the end of every meal. His greatest pleasure in life was to go for a meal of Vienna steak and chips at the Blue Star Café on the Fulham Road but since the meal cost two shillings, it was only on Friday night – allowance day – that he could afford it. During the week, he and Titch made do with a cup of tea and a cheese roll at Dirty Dick's. On Saturdays during the football season, Dirty Dick was run off his feet when the crowds descended on Stamford Bridge and swamped his establishment. On other days, things were quiet and they could get a little service. Money and their lack of it was the problem. Twopence for a cuppa and fourpence for a roll. On Thursdays, they couldn't afford even that as they were usually out of funds until their weekly allowance arrived on Friday.

On one of these Thursday afternoons when they had run out of money, Titch and Billy called at Pottsy's room to try and negotiate a loan.

'Sorry,' he said. 'I don't give loans – it's against my principles, remember. Neither a borrower nor a lender be, and all that stuff.'

'Come on, Pottsy, there's a pal,' Titch pleaded. 'Just fourpence until we get our allowance on Friday. Hoppy and I want to go for a cuppa.'

'Nothing doing. If I do it for one, I'll have to do it for everyone. You'll just have to go without.'

'You're a mean bugger, Pottsy,' Billy said. Then he added, 'Did I ever tell you how revolting I find your habit of blowing bubbles? It's said that many male fishes blow bubbles when they want to copulate. Did you know that?'

'I, too, can play the insulting game, Hoppy,' he replied. 'What about that spot on your face? You look hideous.'

'Look, Potts,' retorted Billy. 'Talk to us when you start to shave – why, your face is as smooth as a baby's bottom.'

With that, Billy and Titch turned on their heel and stalked out of his room. They descended three flights of stairs, crossed the quadrangle, and went through the porter's lodge. They hadn't got far along the King's Road when back at the college a window was thrown open on the top floor and Pottsy's face appeared.

'Hoppy! I say, Hoppy!' he bawled, waving and shaking his fist.

Several passers-by stopped and gazed up.

'Don't forget your Valderma ointment for your spots!' Pottsy always had to have the last word.

One Monday afternoon, Billy and Titch were lingering over their cups of tea as usual. Jack Elder was sitting alone on the other side of the café. The phone rang in the inner office and Dick went to answer it. In his absence, Elder whipped over to the counter, put his arm round the glass cabinet and swiped a cheese roll. Before Dick was back, he had, like Francis Bacon's books, tasted, chewed, swallowed and digested it. His two companions were disgusted by this pilfering of food from a poor man like Dirty Dick who could ill afford to lose even one cheese roll. And they told Elder what they thought of him. Besides, he hadn't given them any. The greedy bastard.

Every week, the students waited desperately for their allowance from home – in Billy's case, a ten shilling postal order. After the last lecture on Friday morning, there was a mad scramble to the hall where the post rack was located. The crowd round it was always six deep and it was a fight to reach the pigeon holes. Billy could see his letter in the slot marked 'G to H'. When he'd finally got his hands on it, he tore it open eagerly, read the brief note that his mam had so painstakingly penned.

•

Dear Billy,
I hope this letter finds you in good health and you are enjoying life down there and working hard to pass out as a teacher. We're not so bad though your dad still slips out to the pub for a quick half. More like half a gallon, if you ask me. Anyroad, your dad says you mussn't mix with them there Lunndon toffs or you'll pick up bad ways. Here's your ten shillings P.O. to help you through the week. The family give two shillings each.
　Keep smiling,
　　Your loving Mam & Dad.

'Good old Mam,' Billy murmured to himself. 'She never lets me down.'

He noticed Titch examining the few envelopes that remained in the S to T slot.

'Everything OK, Titch?' he asked. 'Vienna steak in the Blue Star as usual tonight?'

Titch looked ashen. 'Afraid not,' he mumbled. 'Nothing's arrived. No postal order. S'funny, they usually send me seven and six every Friday.'

'I shouldn't worry, Titch,' Billy said. 'I'm sure there'll be something in tomorrow's post. Delayed, that's all. But no problem, I'll stake you a steak tonight. I'm flush. Got ten shillings.' They had their usual Friday night feast.

The following week, Titch got his letter plus a postal order for a reduced amount. His dad, who had been a bus driver with Manchester Corporation, had been sacked for turning up to the evening shift smelling of drink. From that time on, Titch was on his uppers and only survived through the generosity of his cronies who each agreed to give him one shilling a week from their own resources. Pottsy was even more magnanimous and gave him one and six.

When Billy paid for Titch's Vienna steak, he left himself short that week and had to cut down his smoking from five to three a day. He could hardly afford to smoke even those. His dad, his brother Les and his old friend Cliff Fern at the Inland Revenue sent him an occasional packet to keep him going. But Billy was annoyed with himself at his weakness and every Sunday night he emulated Mark Twain and resolved to give up, to start a fresh week without nicotine. He got through the day on Monday reasonably well, though with a struggle; Tuesday he became intolerable, his nerves on edge. On Wednesday he turned vicious and, for the sake of his friends, gave up the unequal struggle and lit up again. What ecstasy to draw on that first fag! One Sunday, though, he was particularly disgusted with the wretched habit, and he took the three fags reserved for his Monday ration and flung them out of the window into the rain.

'That's it! I'm done with smoking forever. It's a dirty, filthy habit and I feel better already.'

Next morning, Billy could be seen in the bushes below searching for his three fags.

When Pottsy had given them lessons in etiquette, he had suggested that polite dinner table topics were important. Topics like illness, religion, sex and politics were strictly taboo, he had said. But Billy's table never ran short of subjects for discussion and there were no taboos.

It is said that when caged chickens are being taken to market, they begin to peck at each other's eyes. The same is true of companions in misfortune. At Table Six, mealtimes became battlegrounds, especially in the interminable delays between courses, when the diners used the time to find each other's weaknesses and expose them to the world at large. As they had no secrets from each other, this was not difficult and even things told in confidence were put on public display. Humiliation was the name of the game and Jack Elder proved to be a master. Perhaps in some previous age, Billy mused, he had been a torturer in a medieval dungeon. Be that as it may, he revealed a hidden talent for rooting out those vulnerable spots which hurt most. And Billy was his favourite target. Sometimes Billy dreaded going down for meals. The only defence was to be ready with a counter-attacking insult. He and Titch spent much time building up a quiver of suitable vitriolic arrows ready for use whenever the need arose – which was often.

Still at the head of their table sat Bullock, their second-

71

year mentor who was there not only to keep order but to indoctrinate them with the culture of the college, such as it was. At the lower end, Elder retained his position as overseer, with the Mancunians ranged along the monks' benches on either side of the table as befitted their inferior station.

One day when they were suffering a particularly long interval between the watery soup and the slop which constituted the main course, Oscar addressed the table.

'Are you aware that man is the only animal that blushes?'

'That's because he is the only one that needs to,' answered Ollie.

'Bloody right,' Elder said, and turned to a stranger at the next table. He tapped him lightly on the shoulder and, pointing to Billy, said, 'Have you seen this arsehole blush? Here, Hopkins, do us a favour and give us a blush.'

Billy felt a hot red tide rush into his face.

'There you are,' Elder leered. 'What did I tell you? Thanks, Hophead, for obliging us.'

'You great big oaf, Elder,' spluttered Billy. 'How dare you embarrass me like that. You tooth-sucking tosspot. May you dig up your father and make soup of his bones.' Billy had put considerable time and effort into thinking that one up.

Elder scowled menacingly. 'Don't push your luck, Hopkins, or I'll be coming for you one of these nights.'

'Is that so?' Billy said. 'One thing, Jack. We'd never stoop so low as to steal cheese rolls from a poor honest shopkeeper like Dirty Dick as soon as his back's turned. We've got higher morals than that.'

'Ah,' said Oscar languidly. 'Maybe so but he FOYLED the shopkeeper.'

Titch and Billy blushed with embarrassment, which gave

Elder yet another opportunity to draw attention to their predicament.

'Yeah, we all heard about that book-swiping expedition on Charing Cross,' the corporal hissed. 'I've half a mind to report both of you to the college authorities for theft. That'd bloody well put paid to your careers and no mistake.'

'Now, now,' said Ollie. 'This is becoming nasty. Let's keep things on a friendly basis.'

Which remark prompted the whole table to act out the 'Who's having your egg, Titch?' routine.

'Looking at you lot,' said Nobby, 'it's no wonder I prefer the company of women – they are more civilised and more polite.'

This was the signal for the whole table to switch from knife-stroking to combing their hair and wetting their eyebrows.

'Your brain, Nobby,' said Oscar, 'is between your legs. You trail about the world wondering who or what you can stick it into. You have the body of a man and the brain of a sexually perverted newt.'

So the entertainment continued until the execrable pudding brought the verbal jousting to a conclusion.

They retired to the common room for their post-prandial cigarette, whilst the lucky ones with money repaired to Dirty Dick's to supplement the meal.

On one or two occasions, they turned their malice exclusively onto Jack Elder. A dangerous thing to do.

'Is it true, Jack,' asked Billy mischievously one day, 'that your family have an estate in Durham?'

'What's it got to do with you?'

'You're not by any chance related to the rich farmers who invented elderberries?'

The suppressed laughter of Billy's mindless companions infuriated Jack.

'Here, watch it, Hopkins. Or I'll be comin' to blackarse you one of these nights.'

When Oscar saw that mud was being thrown about indiscriminately, he chose that moment to join the fray by venting his spleen on Bullock.

'In the first place,' Oscar drawled, 'God made idiots; this was for practice. Then he really got into his stride and made the second-years, producing a prize bunch of illiterate, inarticulate louts.'

'Right, that's it, Wilde,' said Bovril. 'You're for it. Tonight, we're a-comin' for you. You're due to have your arse blacked.'

'I'll join you in that arse-blackin' party tonight,' said Elder. 'Hopkins here has been asking for it.'

True to their word, half a dozen second-years plus the aggrieved Elder appeared that night on the corridor of South Block.

'Right, Hopkins first,' bellowed Elder.

Several study doors were flung open as the occupants came out to witness the arse-blacking.

'What's the matter with you lot?' Titch called out. 'Don't stand around. Do something. You're like prisoners in a concentration camp. No resistance. Come on, fight back!'

To no avail; the South Block residents were not willing to put their arses on the line.

The door of Billy's room was flung open and the seven assailants barged in and pinned their victim to the bed. Billy tried to fight back but was overpowered. His pants were unceremoniously removed and the seven attackers went to work with their Cherry Blossom, leaving Billy with an ink-black posterior. There was not the physical

74

suffering of a caning but the pain of the indignity was worse.

'Next,' yelled Bullock, 'that bastard Wilde. He's too big for his boots. We'll see how he feels with a buffed backside.'

Oscar was ready for them and took the wind out of their sails with his languid reception.

'Come in, gentlemen,' he called. 'Let us get this tedious business over and done with. With the minimum of fuss, if you please.'

Unconcerned and trouserless, with *derrière* already exposed, he lay face down on his bed reading a book, like a recumbent statue in a Norman church. Armed with tins of polish, the septet went to work on his backside and soon had a shine that would have been a credit to Billy and Titch back in their shoe-polishing days at the American Red Cross.

'Finished, gentlemen?' Oscar asked, looking up from his book. 'Then I'll bid you good evening. Please close the door as you leave.' He returned to his reading.

Their work successfully completed, the aggressors rushed off noisily down the corridor, no doubt to dispense their rough injustice in another block.

Billy lay on his bed recovering from the shock of the assault whilst Titch, who had witnessed both arse-blackings, berated the onlookers still standing around.

'You spineless lot, you gutless lot of worms. You're the kind who'd stand and gape if the Ku Klux Klan came barging down the corridor.'

'Well, what did you expect?' Potts shouted back. 'Did you expect us to take on the British Army?'

'No,' Titch yelled. 'But we didn't have to take it lying down.'

'Oh, I don't know about that,' they heard Oscar call. 'I enjoyed it.'

When the hubbub had died down, Titch and Billy met in the latter's study.

'That's it,' said Billy. 'I've had enough of this bloody college. I've just about hit the buffers. It's been a disaster ever since I came here – one thing after another. First, no money, then we came close to being arrested for shoplifting, boring lectures about kids with rubber rings on their heads, lousy food, bickering at the table, and now assault and battery. Elder has got it in for me.'

'I agree with everything you say, Hoppy,' said Titch. 'You know me, I believe life is divided into the horrendous and the woeful, but this once I think we should give the place a little longer, say until Christmas.'

'But you always say things get worse before they get worse.'

'That's right, my double worse theory. Now it's time for my double better theory. We live in the best of all possible worlds, I'm sad to say, and it's always darkest before the dawn and all that stuff.'

'You are a mixed-up kid, Titch – but very well. Until Christmas! And if things haven't improved, I'm out of here and back to Manchester and civilisation.'

'And I'll be with you,' said Titch.

Chapter Eight

Frailty, thy name is woman!

Shakespeare, Hamlet

When Oscar spoke facetiously of the ascetic life, he was not far from the truth, especially where Billy was concerned. The others had managed to get the occasional date with girls from Whitelands training college, but during the first few weeks, Billy had been completely without the company of the opposite sex. Nobby as usual claimed he was having it off every weekend with a girl called Freda. They didn't believe him but they were entertained by his stories of conquest, of how the girls couldn't resist him and how they were always dragging him off to their beds.

'You seem to be able to attract the girls easily,' said Billy one evening at dinner. 'So what's your secret?'

'Piece of cake,' he boasted. 'First, you must remember that women are different from men.'

'*Vive la différence!*' said Billy.

'Seriously,' Nobby said. 'A woman has a completely different nature. She likes to be wooed with flowers and sweet talk. More than anything, every woman wants to get a man but her nature stops her from coming out into the open about it.'

'Why is that?' asked Pottsy, emerging from one of his daydreams with a prodigious output of tongue bubbles. 'What makes them so reserved if they're so keen on hooking a man?'

'From the beginning of time, man has been the hunter, woman the hunted. She knows the rules of the game. She lets the man do the chasing while she pretends to be coy but in reality she enjoys being chased. Best of all she likes being caught though she can't admit it.'

'When it comes to women,' said Pottsy, 'I'm the one who should know about 'em. I've got three sisters at home. The one thing I can't stand about 'em is the way they always leave the lavatory seat down.'

'Well said, Pottsy,' laughed Billy. Then turning to Nobby, he said, 'But you're the one who seems to have a great knowledge of what makes women tick and to have mastered the art of catching 'em. So come on, let us in on this esoteric knowledge of yours. How do you do it?'

'Well, I'll tell you,' Nobby began but Jack Elder barged into the discussion.

'What do you young pipsqueaks know about women? I was going out with skirts before any of you were born. Pin your ears back and learn from the master. Now, most women have an inferiority complex about themselves. They think there's something wrong with them. They're too thin, too fat, too tall, too short. They're not happy about the shape of their nose, their mouth, their eyes, their ears. Even the glamour pants don't have a high opinion of themselves – they think they're not very bright or not very interesting.'

'It's probably the men who've sold them that idea,' said Oscar, 'with the advertisements telling them what they must do and what they must buy to make themselves more attractive to men.'

'Dead right,' answered Elder. 'So the best way to get round a piece of fluff is to make use of her inferiority complex by appealing to her vanity.'

'I'm not sure I like the sound of this approach,' Billy protested. 'But go on, how do we do that?'

'First, show you're interested in her. Hang on to her every word as if it's the most intelligent thing you've ever heard. Listen to her problems, let her talk about herself, show understanding and sympathy. Let her see what a nice bloke you are by being kind and good-mannered, and all that. Best of all, tell her a few jokes, get her laughing and you've as good as got her between the sheets. I tell ya, they're like trained seals – throw 'em a fish in the form of a compliment and watch 'em slap their fins together.'

'Jack, you're a cynical bastard,' Billy said angrily. 'Machiavellian. Don Juan hiding behind Sir Galahad.'

Elder narrowed his eyes and gave Billy a poisonous stare. 'Watch it, Hopkins. Don't push it. Remember what happened last time,' he said menacingly.

'So the idea is to flatter her?' Nobby said in an attempt to defuse things.

'Now you're getting it,' Elder chuckled. 'Tell her what she wants to hear, how lovely she is, praise her taste in clothes, lay it on thick. Compliment her on her hair and her dress though it's her pants and how to get into 'em that's on your mind. Make out you're interested in her intellect though it's her body you have designs on. Never fails.'

'Come off it,' Billy protested vehemently. 'That approach might work with the dumb blonde type but it wouldn't work with a beautiful, intelligent girl. She'd see through you right away.'

'That's another thing,' added Elder, ignoring the comment. 'For God's sake, don't pick the most beautiful girl in the room – she'll probably have a boyfriend already, and you may find she's vain and stand-offish. No, better to pick the fat one with acne sitting in the corner. She'll be so grateful for the attention, she'll soon be offering you crumpet for tea. And as for that flowers and chocolates shit, when it comes to the crunch, give it to her good and proper. "Wham-bam-thank-you, ma'am" as the GIs in Normandy used to say.'

Billy flared up. 'I've never heard such cold-hearted crap. You sound as if you've just fallen down from the trees. You're a nasty piece of work, Elder, to treat the fair sex with such contempt. One day, you'll meet your opposite number and you'll get your come-uppance. I only hope I'm around to see it.'

Chapter Nine

Dancing Lessons

During the week, a combination of college work, the early curfew and lack of funds ensured that they led a quiet life, and on most weekday nights they were in bed by 11 p.m. A visit to Dirty Dick's and the occasional treat at the Blue Star Café were all they could manage. Weekends were different and the Damian group managed either a walk to Putney or a visit to the pictures. For Titch and Billy, the flicks became an essential escape from the academic routine.

'Right, Titch,' said Billy one night. 'What do you say to ducking Travers' education lecture and going to see Celia Johnson and Trevor Howard in *Brief Encounter*?'

'A difficult choice,' replied Titch. 'Duck out of the lecture or take a ducking in the lecture. Johnson and Howard get my vote.'

This skipping of lectures became a habit and it's a moot point whether they learned more at films like *The Lost Weekend, The Way to the Stars, Les enfants du paradis* than they did in dry-wet talks on Watsonian behaviourism.

The film that made the greatest impact was undoubtedly *The Jolson Story* which the Damian lot saw several times.

The bathrooms of South Block rang out for many weeks with amateurish imitations of the great minstrel singer. Even Oscar the aesthete was infected with the craze.

'It's no use,' he proclaimed one night after a particularly puerile attempt to emulate the crooner. 'There is a certain silky texture to his voice which makes it inimitable.'

Most of the time at college, they were homesick for Manchester and Mancunian culture, which the Southerners declared was a contradiction in terms (an oxymoronic statement, they said). Billy often thought about his former girlfriend Adele and in his nostalgia for all things connected with home, he sometimes saw her in a more glamorous light than was actually the case. His relationship had come to an abrupt end when she had tried to lay down the law about what religious beliefs and practices she would and would not tolerate 'in our little home after we are married', as she'd put it. As for their first clumsy adolescent attempt at sex, it was perhaps best forgotten, but in the silence of his room, Billy could not prevent himself from playing the scene over again in his mind's eye.

Adele had been his dancing partner and together they'd had a few successes in local competitions. Their romance had also been making progress and they'd had one or two hot necking sessions on the settee in her front room. He'd enjoyed these all right but she'd got him so excited that he always went home feeling frustrated. Then she'd promised – reluctantly, he had to admit – to let him go all the way, to give him, as she put it, 'the full thing'.

He wouldn't forget that Saturday, not if he lived till a hundred. Most of his sex education had been acquired at school through his peers in the smoking club and he wasn't sure that they always had it right. They certainly had some weird ideas on how to stimulate a female – like fondling her left breast rather than the right, as if the left had special aphrodisiac properties. So he'd spent the afternoon in the Central Library reading sex manuals in an effort to fill the gaps in his knowledge. There was lots of stuff about contraception, sexually transmitted diseases, about things that could go wrong and the like, but he could find nothing about the best way to do it. He could leave that to nature, he supposed.

She'd pressed her parents into going out for the evening. From a distance, he'd watched them set off and when he'd judged the coast was clear, he'd knocked on the front door.

'Come in,' she'd said. 'Do you still want to go through with this?'

'Does a bird want to fly, does a duck want to swim?' he'd answered.

'Oh, very well,' she'd sighed. 'Let's get this thing over with.'

She stretched out on her back as stiff as a board and, closing her eyes, announced, 'Right, you can do it now.'

Just like that.

Hardly the most romantic invitation in the world but beggars couldn't be choosers.

She'd given him no help whatsoever and the evening had been a disaster. What had made it worse was that she had accused him of 'botching it up'. Not at all good for his macho self-image.

He shivered involuntarily at the memory of the fiasco.

Before setting off for Chelsea, Billy had made contact once more with her and they were regular correspondents. Now that Billy was at an Anglican establishment, she hoped that he'd drop that Catholic nonsense and become a normal apathetic type like the rest of her family. Her mother, though, felt that since he was studying to be a teacher – a respectable profession with a steady income, and a good pension at the end – he had become a 'good catch', Catholic or not. Besides, knowing her daughter and her ability to get her own way, she felt sure that in time Adele would bring Billy round to the family's agnostic way of thinking.

Their correspondence continued in the same vein as their former protestations of love and took the form of declaring the eternal nature of their adoration in such phrases as 'Yours till hell freezes over; till the wells run dry; till the deserts bloom'.

Billy had run out of improbable eventualities when he discovered a rich seam of unlikelihoods in the poetry of W. H. Auden and the songs of Vera Lynn. These enabled him to enrich his letters with further phrases like: 'Yours till the stars lose their glory' and 'Till China and Africa meet, and the river jumps over the mountain and the salmon sing in the street'.

Pottsy spent much time writing letters to his Rowena in Manchester and was forever singing her praises and drooling over her photograph. They would gather in a little group in his room to make toast, to keep warm by his electric fire and listen to Denny Dennis singing love songs on his record player – all plugged into an adaptor connected to his electric light socket. Inexplicably, the college fuses remained intact.

Pottsy and Billy developed the curious habit of standing in the bathroom together, their hands immersed in bowls of very hot water. Pottsy blew his little tongue bubbles, whilst Billy sang in his best Sinatra/Haymes crooning voice the romantic love songs of the day: 'Love Letters (straight from your heart)'; 'A Little Lonely on the Lonely Side Tonight'. But it was the sentimental ballad 'Saturday Night Is the Loneliest Night of the Week' that triggered a profusion of bubbles like a Monday morning washday.

The songs Billy chose always contained the word 'lonely' somewhere in the refrain – a sure indication that he was not so much lovesick as homesick. It was painful to be away from home but since it was more manly and grown-up to confess love for a girl than one's mother and her apple pie, they converted the pain into what they thought was love.

Not long after the black-arsing ordeal, when Billy was feeling particularly blue, he thought back to those happy days in Manchester when, with Adele as his partner, he had won third place in the North-West Tango Competition held at the luxurious Ritz Ballroom. He remembered that Frank Rogers, his ballroom dancing tutor in Manchester, had recommended an exclusive studio run by Alex and Carol Gibson, both ex-world champions, on Kensington High Street. For the first few weeks at college he had hesitated about turning up there for several reasons: he had been too busy settling in and, conscious of his dad's dire warnings about Londoners' so-called evil ways, he was nervous about introducing himself to such disting-uished people. One evening, Billy plucked up courage and presented himself there. 'Nothing ventured, nothing gained,' he said to himself, quoting one of his mam's many aphorisms.

'I remember Frank Rogers well,' said Alex Gibson. 'A first-class teacher. I hope he told you that we do not cater for beginners and we accept only members who have reached Silver Medal level. We should have to appraise your performance before we issue you with a membership card, you understand.'

'Why so exclusive?' Billy asked.

'As you can see, the studio is only big enough to

accommodate about eighteen people and so we have to restrict our numbers. Our advanced class meets every Saturday night and we encourage the highest performance standards. On this initial visit, perhaps you would demonstrate what you can do by dancing with my wife Carol.'

Carol came forward, smiling in welcome. 'Nice to meet you, Billy,' she said. 'You've certainly got the slim build of a dancer.'

Alex switched on the strict tempo music of Victor Sylvester playing 'Fascination'.

Billy took up his hold and Carol and he moved effortlessly and gracefully across the polished floor of the little studio. He tried one or two simple variations like the 'feather' and the 'hesitation pause'. Carol was an obvious professional as she responded skilfully and sensitively. He tried a few more advanced steps and found she was equal to everything he tried.

'Where did you learn to dance like that?' she said. 'You're obviously gold standard.'

Alex watched them flow around the room with grace and poise.

'No need to go on, Billy,' he said. 'Welcome to the club. You must be one of Frank Rogers's star pupils. I'm sure he was proud of you.'

'Thank you,' said Billy. 'That's praise indeed coming from two world champions. I should be honoured to become a member.'

'Fine,' said Alex. 'We meet every Saturday night at seven thirty and I'll introduce you to the others if you'd like to come. If you are interested in joining our Formation Team, you'd be most welcome.'

'I shall be here on Saturday,' said Billy, 'but I'm not sure about the Formation Team as college keeps me fairly busy.'

'We can look at that another time,' Alex said. 'Till Saturday, and welcome once again.'

'Goodbye and thank you,' added Carol.

Billy left the studio as light as a feather. After his unfortunate experiences at college, his visit to the studio was like a shot in the arm. I think I could survive London and the college if I could take up dancing again, he thought. It'll be like an oasis in a desert.

Come Saturday afternoon, Billy's companions took themselves off to Stamford Bridge to watch Chelsea Football Club being beaten yet again by some Northern team. Provided there was a supply of hot water, he spent the time soaking in a long hot bath, with the muffled roar of the football crowd undulating in the background. At six o'clock, he signed out for dinner, took a snack of a cheese cob and a mug of tea at Dirty Dick's and caught the tube to Kensington High Street.

At the studio, Billy found an elegant crowd already assembled there. Smiling broadly, Alex and Carol came forward and shook his hand warmly.

'So glad you could make it,' said Carol. 'Let me introduce you to one or two people.'

She conducted Billy around the company, presenting various people, but his attention was drawn to a pretty, slim, dark-haired young lady who was at that moment sitting alone in a corner of the room. Billy judged her age to be about twenty-four or -five.

'Let me introduce Doris Hartley,' Carol said, taking him over to her. 'You two should make a good partnership.'

Billy spent that first Saturday night dancing only with Doris. Every dance they tried – the waltz, the foxtrot, quickstep, tango – they seemed to glide across the floor as if they had danced together for years. Her movements were natural and elegant.

'I can see you've danced before,' she said.

'The same goes for you,' replied Billy. 'Are you a professional dancer?'

'No,' she laughed. 'I thought about it once but decided it was too risky. No, I work as a secretary at the Ministry of Education in Whitehall.'

'Ah, then you can advance my career for me. I'm hoping to be a teacher one day.'

'Afraid not. I'm a lowly stenographer without influence.'

Their conversation flowed as smoothly as their dancing, even at the interval when they continued talking over a cup of tea and a chocolate biscuit. Too soon, the evening came to an end and Billy had to excuse himself in order to get back to beat the college curfew.

Any romantic notions Billy might have entertained about Doris were soon dispelled when she told him she was married.

'My husband, Harry, is in the RAF and waiting to be demobbed,' she told him. 'At present he's stationed in Malta and we can both hardly wait for him to get home.'

'Doesn't he mind you going off dancing on Saturday nights?' Billy asked

'Not one bit. In fact he encourages it. Dancing was never his scene and he knows how much I love it. We have a very happy marriage and we get along fine. We both like the theatre, especially opera, and when he's home we're regular visitors to Covent Garden. You'd like him, Billy, and I hope you can meet him one day.'

'Hope so too,' Billy said, and he meant it. 'Thanks anyway for a wonderful evening, Doris. I can't remember when I last danced with someone as accomplished as you.'

'Thank you for the compliment,' she said. 'The same goes for me. See you next Saturday.'

Billy left the studio happy and contented. So there was a life outside the college walls after all.

Every Saturday night, Billy blew half his weekly allowance on the tube fare and the entrance fee to Alex Gibson's salon. Doris became his regular partner. They danced to the silky strains of Victor Sylvester and Josephine Bradley until they moved together as one. He learned that Doris and her husband had their home in Chiswick, and that they were both five years older than he was – not that any of that mattered. They danced, they talked, they had a cup of tea at the interval, they enjoyed each other's company and they parted at 10.30 as Billy rushed to catch his tube. They were both happy with the arrangement and for Billy a new dimension was added to his life, making it more tolerable.

Around this time, the college authorities, feeling that it was unhealthy, even dangerous, to deprive so many men of female company decided to demonstrate its liberal attitudes by organising a hop in the college hall. Women students, strictly chaperoned, from Whitelands College were invited across to cheer them up. The women sat on one side of the hall and the men on the other. There was little beauty or sexual promise and nothing to tempt the men across the gap. Most of their visitors were quintessential schoolmarm types, lisle stockings, flat sensible shoes, cheap perfume, and steel-framed spectacles.

Billy stood quietly on the sidelines observing the pathetic attempts of his fellow students to dance. Bullock, their mentor, was making a reasonable attempt to waltz but it was obvious that he possessed no more than rudimentary skill and knew only the most basic of steps. As for the rest, they moved like men trying out artificial legs for the first time. The affair was a minor disaster. Billy was gratified to note that Jack Elder, his tormentor, was one of the most inept. Some time into the dance, however, watched admiringly by his junior table companions, the corporal succeeded in luring a plump, blonde girl – a bespectacled Boadicea – up to his room.

'I pity that poor girl,' Billy said to Titch, 'when he employs his subtle hanky-panky love techniques on her.'

'Oh, I dunno,' Titch replied. 'She's a big girl and looks like the kind who can look after herself.'

At breakfast next morning Bullock commented on the pathetic dancing skills displayed by his fellow students. 'A disgrace,' he said. 'I don't know what Whitelands College must think about us. Our students danced like a bunch of clod-hoppers. I think we should organise dancing lessons for the lot of them.'

A little later that morning, Jack Elder came down to breakfast. He was wearing dark glasses but they failed to hide the fact that beneath them he was sporting two black eyes, a bruised cheek and a swollen ear. When Billy mischievously asked for a report on his amorous activities, he snarled viciously like a mad dog. It was some time before they learned that he'd got nowhere with his quarry, claiming that he'd been turned off when she sat on his knee. The girl weighed sixteen stone, was trained in jujitsu and had objected to his tender advances by giving him a practical demonstration of the art of self-defence. So much for Elder's theories about the opposite sex. It made Billy's day when he got the story.

A couple of days later, the following announcement appeared on the main noticeboard:

IF YOU WANT TO GET A GIRL,
LEARN HOW TO DANCE!

The recent 'hop' demonstrated an urgent need
for dancing lessons amongst our student brethren.
It is proposed therefore to hold dancing classes for
those wishing to acquire or improve their dancing
skills. Those interested should meet me in the
gym next Friday at 7.30.

YOU MAY BRING A DANCING PARTNER –
PREFERABLY FEMALE – BUT A NUMBER
OF WHITELANDS STUDENTS HAVE
EXPRESSED AN INTEREST. SO WHAT ARE
YOU WAITING FOR?

SIGN YOUR NAME BELOW

Terry Bullock, Second Year

The Damian crowd, including Billy, signed up for the class.

'If it helps me to attract even more girls, I'm for it,' remarked Nobby.

'I shall attend for the company only,' said Oscar. 'I'm not sure about the attracting girls bit. If there's a shortage of girls, I may have to have a male partner.'

Around three dozen students, including partners, turned up for the first Friday night session. Pottsy had agreed the loan of his record player and a few records of strict tempo music had been found.

Bullock opened the proceedings by announcing that students should partner off so that he could get a rough idea of individual standards.

'I noticed at the recent hop,' he began, 'that there are big differences in dancing skills. So in order to know where to begin, I suggest dividing you into different classes according to ability. Group one for absolute beginners and group two for reasonably proficient. Let's start with the simplest dance – the waltz. Could you start the ball rolling, Titch?' Bullock switched on the music of Victor Sylvester's 'Anniversary Waltz'.

Titch, who had chosen a partner of the same height, danced a few wooden-legged steps.

'Group one – beginners!' Bullock called out decisively. 'Next, Nobby. Let's see if you're any better.'

Nobby made a brave attempt with his beanpole partner but was little better than Titch.

Billy watched the proceedings quietly.

'Group one again!' Bullock announced. 'You're supposed to be dancing, Nobby, not pushing a wheelbarrow. I don't suppose you lot from the North have any acquaintance with the refinements and etiquette of the dancing salon. Jack, with your experience in the Durham Light Infantry, you should be light on your feet. Maybe you can show 'em how it's done.'

Jack Elder had obviously made peace with his pugilistic Boadicea for he appeared with her as his partner. Her actual name was Bertha and he proceeded to dance with her in a style more reminiscent of a regimental march than a light fantastic.

'It's supposed to be a waltz, Jack,' called Oscar, 'not a military two-step.'

'Watch your mouth, Wilde,' Jack grunted, 'or we'll be coming for you again.'

'Any time,' countered Oscar. 'Say the word and I'll be waiting.'

Whilst this exchange was taking place, Billy's partner for the evening arrived.

'Sorry I'm late, Billy,' she said. 'I was held up at work – a rush typing job.'

'That's OK, Doris,' replied Billy. 'I'm so grateful that you agreed to come.'

'Glad to be of help. I'm just glad to be busy until Harry gets home.'

'Great,' Billy said warmly. 'As you will see, Doris, it's going to be like missionary work taking culture to the uneducated masses.'

'Sorry, Jack. Group one,' Bullock proclaimed, 'but I think you show definite promise. Let's try one of our other clod-hopping brethren from Manchester. Right, Hoppy, hop to it! Another for group one, I'm sure. Have you peasants from Manchester ever heard of ballroom dancing?'

'My partner and I have done a little dancing together before though we're a little rusty and need more practice.'

'More for the beginners' group, I've no doubt.'

Billy and Doris took up their stance and moved with grace and poise in perfect time to Sylvester's flowing music. A hush fell over the assembled body and the watching students gazed open-mouthed as the couple danced smoothly round the room.

'If that's rusty,' gasped Titch, 'I'd like to see them when they reach top form!'

That was the night that Billy's fortunes took a turn for the better. Even Bullock had to defer and he handed over the organisation of the dancing classes to Billy. Doris agreed to give up some of her spare time to help with the ladies. Billy decided to arrange dancing lessons for the whole college and, to this end, recruited three or four students (Bullock included) who had demonstrated a modicum of skill. Regular classes were held for the rest of the term and in the evenings the gymnasium became a ballroom and passers-by could hear strict tempo music and the voices of the instructors: 'Forward left foot, side right foot and close . . .'

Some of the students reported later that it was the most useful thing they had learnt in their time at college.

As the weeks went by, Jack Elder became not only more enthusiastic but more friendly towards Billy, even defending him one day at the dining table.

'Hey there, Hopkins,' a bespectacled student at the adjoining table called. 'Give us another one of your blushes, there's a good fellow.' He smirked at his fellow diners and waited for the result. It was not quite what he expected.

Elder stood up and towered over the Billy Bunter type. 'Watch your mouth, four-eyes,' he snarled, clenching his fist. 'Hopkins here happens to be a particular friend of mine. Insult him and you insult me. Got it?'

The bewildered student turned his attention to his soup which appeared to have acquired a sudden fascination for him.

Things didn't stop there and whilst it would be an exaggeration to say that Billy and Jack became bosom friends, they certainly became good pals. The rest of the table was left in no doubt as to the change in the relationship because at one memorable breakfast, as the Damian crowd looked on in wonder, Jack slid his peanut butter jar across to Billy and said, 'Try some of that, Hoppy. It'll give your bread more taste than the college margarine.'

By the end of the term, Jack had become one of Billy's star pupils.

'Hoppy, I want to apologise for that attack on you,' he said at one of the sessions. 'I had you all wrong. We got off to a bad start in the woodwork class but there was more to it than that. You see, I've not had a grammar school education like you lot and, well, I thought you were all trying to take the Mickey and make me look a right Charlie.'

'No malice intended, Jack,' replied Billy. 'Let's forget it. It's in the past.'

The corporal held out a hand of friendship. Billy took it happily and while it was still a firm grip it was not of the crushing variety. Billy felt a surge of happiness flow through his veins. 'Right, Jack,' he said eagerly. 'Now let's take another crack at your feather step.'

An early return to Manchester was no longer on the agenda.

Billy was appointed chairman of the Entertainments Committee which had the responsibility of organising the end of term dance and that was to be a very different affair from the first primitive hop. A small band was hired, and the event was attended by all students – first and second years alike plus members of staff. The young ladies who came on this occasion seemed an entirely different type. Or maybe they were the same ladies better groomed and more glamorously attired. Billy invited Doris and she arrived in a most attractive cocktail dress.

'Doris,' he said, 'you look really nice tonight. Every eye in the room will be on you. Your Harry must be very proud of you.'

'Thank you, Billy, for those kind words. And good news about Harry. He's to be demobbed early next year. So you'll be able to meet him at last. I've written to him about you and he's beginning to wonder who this mysterious other man in my life is. I've told him that he has nothing to worry about.'

'Don't be too sure about that,' Billy grinned. 'With a beautiful wife like you, Harry had better keep on his toes.'

'Don't worry. Harry's not the jealous type,' she laughed. 'I'll invite you over to tea to meet him when he gets back home.'

'I'll hold you to that,' Billy laughed. 'Mention tea or food to me and I'll be there like a shot.'

The learner-dancers of Marjons seemed to have picked up the rudiments of ballroom dancing and on this occasion there was no sexual divide. Watched admiringly by students and staff, Doris and Billy glided skilfully across the floor. A happy and successful evening.

A couple of days later, Taffy Travers stopped him on his way to lectures.

'I see, Hopkins,' he said, 'that you are proficient in the art of propelling yourself across the ballroom floor. All very well in its place but don't let it interfere with the more serious business of studying psychology.'

Billy thanked him for his compliment. After he had gone, he wiped the spittle from the lapel of his jacket, and went on his way.

Apart from the arse-blacking procedure dished out to miscreants, the college had no traditions or customs to speak of. Or if it had, they had become lost during the war when a much depleted college had been evacuated to Cheltenham. One Saturday night, the second years made a brave attempt to create one. Pushed and jostled by the seniors, the whole student body assembled in the college grounds and began a slow march to Piccadilly Circus in single file, each student's hand on the shoulder of the one in front, and with one foot on the pavement and one foot in the gutter. A magnificent chorus worthy of a Welsh miners' choir arose in glorious harmony from one hundred and fifty throats – 'Lloyd George Knew My Father' to the tune of 'Onward Christian Soldiers' followed by a rendering of 'The Stars and Stripes Forever' with the words:

Be kind to our web-footed friends,
For a duck may be somebody's mother.
They live at the edge of a swamp
Where the weather is always damp.
Now you may think that this is the end.
Well, it is . . .

Somebody must have tipped off the police that a political demonstration was converging on the centre of London, for the procession was soon shadowed by a convoy of police cars.

When the march had reached Piccadilly, a huge circle was formed round Eros which, after a four-year absence during the war, had been restored to its place at the centre of the Circus. There the demonstrators chanted the college Maori-like war cry – which Billy had never heard before: 'I-zaka Zomba, Zomba, I-zaka Zomba, Zomba Zee. Yakaheema.' The chant finished with a great leap of a hundred and fifty students who shouted in one voice: 'Marjons!'

On the way back, the same curious marching style was adopted until they reached the home ground of King's Road and Cheyne Walk where a huge stone bust of some long-forgotten Roman emperor was appropriated from the garden of a deserted house and transported in a wheelbarrow back to the Junior Common Room. There, with due ceremony, the bust was painted with a red letter 'T' for Taffy and installed in a place of honour on a large marble mantelpiece.

For the first time, Billy felt truly proud to be part of such an august body of men. The idea of giving up the college course had been completely forgotten.

Billy had begun the course in September unsure about how well he would settle to study and the college routine after his year away from academic work. At the end of the term, he was relieved to find that not only had he passed his exams and the initial teaching practice but had achieved grades comfortably above average.

His cup was full.

Chapter Ten

Christmas at Home

The end of the first term came at last. For weeks, Billy had been counting the days. So many things had happened since he'd last seen his family and he'd so much to tell them – about college life, the food, the lectures, the teaching practice, the college ball, the crazy student march to Piccadilly Circus.

When he and his companions stepped off the train at Manchester's London Road station, it was indeed a joyful occasion. But after such a long absence and after so many exciting experiences, the town somehow looked strange and unfamiliar and he felt like an alien. After the hustle and bustle of London, it seemed smaller, quieter and less frenzied. The Billy Hopkins that emerged from the station was not the same Billy Hopkins that had set off for London in September.

The Damian gang parted company and Billy caught the 62 bus to St Luke's Church on Cheetham Hill Road. He struggled his way down Smedley Lane lugging his heavy suitcase, pausing every hundred yards or so to change hands. Manchester may look smaller, he thought, but this lane definitely seems longer. By the time I get to Gardenia

Court my arms will reach past my knees and I'll look like an orang-utan. Thank God it's downhill.

At the bottom of the lane, outside the Hyacinth House flats, he spotted his dad waving to him. Billy had never been so glad to see him even though he looked that little bit older.

'Hello, son,' he said, taking Billy's free hand in a firm handshake and following it with a tight bear hug. 'Good to see you again after all this time.'

'The same goes for me too,' Billy said warmly. 'It's three months since I was home.'

Dad said, 'Here, let me take that case from you.'

'It's heavy, Dad,' Billy warned.

'Heavy!' he said. 'As a market porter, I dare say I've lifted heavier things than that.' He took the case from Billy's hand. 'Bloody hell!' he exclaimed. 'It *is* heavy. What in God's name have you got in it – bricks?'

'Not bricks, Dad. Books.'

'What are you bringing a lot of bloody books home for? You're supposed to be on holiday.'

'Essays. I've got about ten essays to write. They don't let up at this college.'

They reached Gardenia Court and to Billy's eye it looked more squalid than ever. He noted the broken windows, the washing hanging at every veranda, the mongrel dogs which seemed determined to have a lump out of his ankles, and Annie Simpson, the simple-minded girl sitting on the low wall, saliva dribbling from her lips.

'Ockins! Ockins!' she babbled.

'I think she's saying welcome back,' Dad said.

They turned in at their stairwell and Billy's nostrils were assailed by the familiar malodours as they climbed the stairs: pickled herrings, steak and onions, curried

100

fish, rancid cheese, sour cabbage.

Mam was making a brew when Dad opened the front door.

'He's here,' he called. 'The one you've been waiting for – all the way from London.'

Mam came out from the kitchen wiping her hands on her pinafore.

'Billy,' she said. 'So you're home then.' She embraced him warmly. 'It's so good to have you back after all this time. The tea's made and your food'll be ready as soon as you are.'

'Food?' said Billy. 'What's that?' He had to turn his head away so that they wouldn't see the tear glistening in his eye. It was so good to be back in the bosom of his family.

Dinner that evening consisted of chips and two eggs plus copious amounts of bread and 'best' butter, followed by apple pie and custard. After the privations at college, Billy was in heaven.

At the table, they pumped him about the college. Did he like it? Did he get on with the other students? Were they sending him enough money? Did he understand the lectures? Were they feeding him right? Would he pass out as a teacher? Was he going back?

'Yes, yes, yes,' he answered to everything. 'I love it at college and I've made lots of friends. I've been made chairman of the Entertainments Committee. I've passed my first exams and I've settled into college life.'

They gazed at him proudly and drank in every word he uttered. They were enjoying his success as their own.

'You do talk posh,' Mam said finally. 'Like the news announcers on the wireless.'

'You mean like Wilfred Pickles?' said Billy.

'No, you daft hap'orth,' she said. 'Like that there Alvar Liddell fella.'

'It's to be hoped he's not getting above himself,' Dad said, addressing his invisible auditor, 'and joining them stuck-up toffs down there. Or he won't want to know us in a year or two.'

'Don't talk so daft, Tommy,' Mam said. 'He's our son.'

'What's happened to that watch I gave you when you went away?' Dad asked suddenly.

Billy flushed. 'It was pinched,' he lied. 'I was in the football crowd at Stamford Bridge and some pickpocket got it off my wrist.'

'Off your wrist?' Mam echoed. 'How did they manage that without you feeling it?'

Dad answered for him. 'Them thieving swine in London are that clever. I tell you, Kate, they'd pinch the stays off your back without you knowing or feeling a thing.'

'I'd like to see 'em try,' Mam answered. 'I don't think anyone's that clever.'

'Anyroad,' Dad said. 'I'll speak to my mate in the Hare and Hounds and see if I can get you another watch. You'll have to glue it to your wrist this time.'

Billy rigged up a little study in his bedroom and for much of the holiday spent his time writing essays and doing the required reading. One day his mam came into the room and looked at him fondly.

'I'm that proud of you, Billy. You're going to pass out as a teacher and you'll have a steady, respectable job in your hands and you'll never have to worry again for the rest of your life. And you'll get a pension as well. But I think you do far too much reading. One day your eyes'll pop out of your head if you're not careful.'

'I'll be OK, Mam,' he said. 'I've got to get through the assignments they've set me.'

'Assignments! That sounds important. What's that book you're reading now? Is that an assignment?'

'It is. It's French prose I have to study.'

'That doesn't sound very nice, Billy. Reading about French pro's. Let me see what it says.'

Billy showed her the first page of Maupassant's *Boule de suif.*

'What does that mean?'

'It means Ball of Fat.'

'How do you get Ball of Fat out of that? It doesn't sound anything like it.'

'It's not supposed to, Mam. It's French.'

'I don't know how you get your head round that stuff, I don't really. I suppose it's about French cooking, is it?'

'Not, it's about a French prostitute – she's a round little thing and that's why she's called Ball of Fat. It's supposed to be the best short story ever written.'

'It might be the best story ever written but it doesn't sound respectable. I do hope they're not learning you rude things, our Billy. Don't tell your father you're learning about French prostitutes, for God's sake, or we'll never hear the last of it. What else are you studying?'

'Well, I've got to write an essay on this poem, "Epistle to Doctor Arbuthnot".'

'That doesn't sound nice either. Epistle to this doctor fella. Who wrote it? Not another Frenchman, I hope.'

'No, this was written by Alexander Pope.'

'Oh, that's all right then.'

A few days later, Mrs Mulligan (''Er next door' as Mam called her) came to borrow a cup of sugar, 'Till Paddy, my husband, gets his dole money on Thursday,' she said. 'And how's that lad of yours doing at the London college?' she asked by way of conversation to justify the loan of the sugar.

'Tommy and me are right proud of him,' Mam answered. 'Though we worry sometimes that his head might burst open like a sausage one day, he's stuffing so much into it. At the moment,' she looked round to make sure there was nobody else listening, 'I want you to keep this to yourself – he's making a study of French prostitutes.'

'Ah, Mrs Hopkins,' she said, 'that doesn't sound nice. Now, why would he want to study that class of subject?'

'If he's going to be a teacher, he has to know about such things,' Mam said. 'They know what they're doing down there in London. Anyroad, he's studying some nice poetry about a doctor written by Pope Alexander.'

'That'll be one of them religious poems I've heard so much about. I'm sure the Bishop will be in favour of learning like that. I had an uncle who was high up in the Church and studying for the priesthood at Maynooth. He used to know about such things.'

'Not only that, he's reading something by that fella Shakespeare. A Danish play called Omelette.'

'Now that'll be a useful thing,' Mrs Mulligan said. 'My Paddy could do to take up a subject like that. For sure, he couldn't poach an egg without setting fire to the kitchen.'

When Billy walked out of their flat next day, he found he had been elevated to celebrity status in the district and was the talk of the tenements. He was sensitively aware of the heads that turned when he walked by. Housewives in hairnets and husbands on the dole stood around on their verandas smoking and calling to one another. Mrs Mulligan on the top store soon spread the news from one floor to the next.

'That's the Hopkins lad,' she cried to the Pitt family below. 'Sure, he's studying to be a teacher in London, so he is. Doing hush-hush research into French prostitution, and writing poetry about the papal father. Not only that, isn't he learning all about cookery as well and knows how to make Danish omelettes.'

The neighbours looked down from their eyries in awe and even the Jewish family with the three pretty but unmarried daughters were casting looks in his direction and wondering about possibilities. Now Billy had a pensionable job in view, they were prepared to forget his plum-dropping days when as a callow youth he had released succulent Victorias like bombs from the veranda onto their unsuspecting heads. They were ready to put it behind them and forge new friendly relationships. He might be a good catch despite his Catholic religion. Though some Jewish families might have considered his faith a serious disadvantage, they knew it could soon be rectified – a quick flick of the scalpel in the Beth Shalom synagogue would make him perfectly acceptable as a husband.

Billy strutted past the tenements with his head held high and tried to look intellectual and learned as befitted a local hero.

Christmas Day was a quiet affair. Billy went to early Mass with his mam, whilst Dad remained at home reading yesterday's *Daily Dispatch*. He had given up going to church a long time ago and he preferred to celebrate the birth of Christ in the Queen's Arms. Then, for Billy, it was helping to peel the spuds and to prepare the usual magnificent turkey dinner that would have graced the table of a king. At three o'clock, they listened to King George giving his speech to the Empire, after which the old couple retired to bed for a snooze whilst Billy dozed off, half listening to Henry Hall on the Light Programme.

In the evening, Mam applied a touch of lipstick and a smidgen of face powder and, dressed up in her new velvet blouse to which she had pinned her new brooch bearing the title 'MOTHER' (a present from Flo), in case anyone was in doubt as to her social status, she accompanied Dad to the local for a celebratory sing-song. Billy lay on their bright new rag rug with a box of chocolates trying to unravel the intricacies of Dryden's *Absalom and Achitophel*.

'Are you sure you're going to be all right, Billy?' Mam asked as they prepared to leave. 'I mean, it doesn't seem right you should be studying on Christmas night. You should be out enjoying yourself.'

'I'd rather be here, Mam, than anywhere else in the world. I have chocolates, a book and there's Tommy Handley in *It's That Man Again* on the wireless. What greater happiness is there?'

'Sometimes I worry about that lad,' she said to Dad as they descended the stairs.

'Nah, he'll be OK,' he answered, 'as long as he doesn't get ideas above his station.'

Christmas may have been quiet in the Hopkins household but Boxing Day saw a gathering of the clans. It was a great opportunity to catch up on everyone's news. Les was still in the army and hoping to be demobbed within two years. Sam had meanwhile married May Breslin, a beautiful girl from Ulster, and was planning to settle down in Belfast. Flo, his big sister, and her husband Barry, had brought their two children whilst Polly and Steve were with their four –

Billy was godfather to their youngest daughter, Kathleen. The small flat seemed to be bursting at the seams but that didn't stop the sing-song and the drinks from flowing, especially for Dad, who was putting it away like there was no tomorrow.

'I hate this stuff,' he said as he poured down yet another pint. 'I wouldn't give you a penny a bucket for it.'

'I'm sure we believe him,' Mam said, addressing the family gathered round the table. 'I'm not joking, he'd drink a brewery dry if he had the chance. When I win Littlewood's, I'll buy him a brewery and lock him up in one of the rooms.'

'Now, Kate,' he said. 'You know very well that's not true. I'd like to say a few words to the company here 'cos it's not often that we're together like what we are today. My son Billy's home from that there college in London and I want to say how proud we are of him today. I've always encouraged him to make something of hisself.'

'You've done nowt of the sort,' Mam interjected. 'You've always been against him going to college. If it'd been left to you, he'd be a mechanic's mate in Henery Wallworks.'

'Now, now, Kate. No need to be like that. There's nowt wrong with being a mechanic's mate, it's good, honest work. I know I've worked hard all my life – worked my fingers to the bone for this family.'

'And look what you've got to show for it,' she said. 'Nowt but bony fingers.'

'I've always tried to do what's best for 'em all, I have. I want my kids to grow up nice and friendly, and able to get on with other people. Not to get above themselves and think they're better than the rest of us. I don't want our Billy there to become a snob and go over to the enemy – the toffs. He mustn't get too big for his boots, that's all I'm saying. As long as he doesn't go giving himself airs, I don't mind him going to college. But in my opinion, book-learning never got nobody nowhere. It's skill with your hands that counts.'

'The only skill with your hands you've ever had,' she said, 'has been raising a glass to your lips. The whole family could've gone to college, even the girls, but you've been too fond of the bevy. You've drunk enough beer in your life to float the Royal Navy.'

'I've allus fed my family,' he protested. 'And I've never stole a penny from nobody and I could've stole thousands in my job, I could.'

'I suppose that's true,' she conceded. 'But you've never stole 'cos you've been too frightened of getting caught and being sent to the clink.'

'You're a hard woman, Kate. But you've been a good wife, a good 'un and I knew what I was doing the day I married you. I want to say to the company here today that getting a good partner is half your life. If you pick a bad 'un, your life isn't worth a light. And lastly, I want to wish everyone all the best for Christmas and a Happy New Year.'

'You're a bit late. Christmas has gone,' she said. 'And it's not New Year till next week so you're too early.'

Despite Mam's heckling, Dad's speech earned him a round of applause which made him so pleased and excited, he had to have one of his hated buckets of beer to calm him down.

At some stage, Billy found himself in conversation with Steve Keenan, the brother-in-law who had done so much to encourage him in his career.

'We knew you'd love college, Billy, once you got used to it,' remarked Steve, now a senior executive at Metro Vicks. 'It should be downhill from here to final qualification. I

108

can see we'll be coming to you to borrow money.'

'You were right about the college, Steve,' Billy replied. 'At first I found it strange and I didn't like it one bit but after a few weeks, I finally settled down. But I'm not so sure about its being downhill. There's still an incredible amount of work to do – our lectures are proper slave-drivers. As for me lending you money, I should live so long.'

Steve laughed at Billy's Yiddish mannerism. 'Incident-ally,' he continued, 'we now live in Clifton Street and there's a certain beautiful girl called Adele who's constantly asking after you. I'd say she's pretty keen. Maybe you ought to look her up.'

'I think Mam's been talking to you. She thinks I'm working too hard and should get out more.'

'Maybe she's right.'

On New Year's Eve, Billy dressed up in his best suit – his only suit – and wandered over to Harrigan's Dance Academy for the Hogmanay Ball. He treasured many happy memories of the place and he was excited at the prospect of meeting the old crowd again.

The place was heaving when he arrived but he soon found them. Oh, it was so good to see all the old familiar faces! Adele, as glamorous as ever, and Duggie Doyle; Lucy with her fiancé, Roy; Freda Pritchard and her boyfriend, Charlie Henshaw; Lofty O'Malley, the bouncer; and old Mrs Harrigan who seemed to get smaller each time he saw her. He waved and greeted them all happily.

'Great to see you all again,' he said warmly.

'Good evenin', Billy,' Adele said. 'We thought you'd deserted us and mixed only with the higher-ups now.'

'No chance,' Billy replied. 'I can't tell you how much

I've been looking forward to tonight and meeting you all again. I've really missed you lot. And thanks, Adele, for all those letters you wrote to me. In the early days at college, they were my lifeline.'

Freda said, 'You've lost your Manchester accent and no mistake.'

'He talks like a toff with a plum in his mouth,' Duggie said. He imitated Billy's so-called posh accent. 'In my orly days at college, they were my lahfline, don'cha know.'

Billy smiled good-humouredly and joined in the laughter. 'If I've lost my accent,' he grinned, 'it must have happened when I wasn't looking. I'll try to find it again.'

'Whatever you do, don't get toffee-nosed and stuck up,' Lucy added.

'As the actress said to the bishop,' leered Duggie.

This last aside caused a fit of giggles from the group.

'Oh, you are awful, Duggie,' Freda simpered.

'Nothing like that,' Billy said in answer to Lucy's remark. 'I'm training to be a teacher not the Prince of Wales.'

'I'll bet you find living in London exciting,' remarked Adele. 'Do you get out much to enjoy the bright lights and all that?'

'Not much but I've taken up dancing in a private studio in Kensington,' Billy answered. 'The standard's quite good and it helps to get me out of college at—'

'Yeah, yeah, yeah,' sneered Duggie, yawning loudly. 'All very interesting, I'm sure. I'm surprised you're even talking to country yokels like us.'

'I'm not like that,' replied Billy evenly. 'I'm a Mancunian and proud of it.'

'Hark at him!' leered Charlie Henshaw. 'Using big words – Mancunian! We're just elementary school types and don't understand words of more than one syllable, do we, Freda?'

'Don't ask me,' said Freda. 'I'm just an ignorant skivvy in a biscuit factory.'

'What subjects are you studying then?' asked Roy who seemed more serious than the rest.

'Books, reading and all that guff – women's stuff!' Duggie announced, barging across them.

'Various subjects,' Billy replied, ignoring Duggie's jibe. I've got to tread carefully here and play it down, he thought. Must avoid giving the impression of showing off. 'English, for one,' he said modestly.

'You mean Shakespeare and all that Hey Nonny Nonny crap?' Duggie snickered. 'Romeo, Romeo, wherefore art thou, Romeo? What bloody tripe it is.'

'I don't think Shakespeare is considered tripe by most people,' Billy said quietly, 'but we're studying more modern literature as well.' He didn't like the way things were going.

'You like to keep abreast of the times like,' he heard Duggie saying. 'Like Adele there.'

'Oh, Duggie!' Adele said, laughing heartily and digging him playfully in the ribs. 'You're a real card. Don't you think so, Billy?'

'He's a card all right,' agreed Billy, trying to look enthusiastic. 'The life and soul of the party.'

'All that studying,' commented Lucy. 'You must find it hard.'

'As the bishop said to the actress,' smirked Duggie. Like lightning with his wisecracks.

Another fit of sniggering.

'Not so hard,' Billy replied naïvely. 'Once you get used to it.'

'As the actress said to the bishop,' Duggie sneered.

The girls were beside themselves with laughter. Such a wit, such a wit.

If he mentions that bloody bishop or that actress again, thought Billy, I'll ram his yellow teeth down his throat.

'What other subjects are you doing, apart from English, I mean?' Roy asked.

'History and French.'

Duggie was in quick. 'So those things you were writing to Adele were really French letters?'

The group doubled up.

'That's a new one on me,' said Charlie Henshaw. 'As the monkey said when it scratched its back.'

More sniggering.

What's happening? Billy thought. They're shoving me out – giving me the elbow.

'Come on, Adele,' Duggy announced. 'Let's dance, for God's sake – all this highbrow talk's a bit too much for me.'

The music struck up with a slow foxtrot and two of the couples got up to dance, leaving Billy with Freda and Charlie.

'Anyroad, you guys,' Billy said to them, trying his best to play down any snooty accent he might unknowingly have acquired, 'you don't know how much I've longed for this night, just to be back in—'

'See that feather step?' Freda said abruptly, cutting across him and pointing to Adele and Duggie. 'Bloody useless. No contrary body movement. Duggie bends from the waist instead of using his whole body. Hasn't a clue. And as for Adele there, look at those terrible heel turns. She moves like a soldier on parade.'

'Yeah,' said Charlie. 'She's all over the place.'

Billy remained silent, unable to contribute to those spiteful comments. He was hurting at being snubbed so brusquely. Suddenly he thought, what the hell am I doing

112

here? I'm obviously not accepted any more. What's going on? I feel utterly lost.

Around eleven o'clock, he made his excuses.

'You mean you're not staying to see the New Year in?' Adele protested. 'You can't leave us now. Stay till twelve o'clock.'

'Sorry, Adele,' he said. 'I promised the old folk I'd let the New Year in at home – me being dark-haired and all that.'

'Let him go,' Duggie said. 'Let him get back to his French letters and his Shakespeare shit.'

Billy spotted Lofty O'Malley and old Mrs Harrigan at the other end of the ballroom and as he raised his hand to wave goodbye to them, he accidentally caught Duggie a smack on the side of his head. Billy had lost none of his old boxing skills.

'Sorry, Duggie,' he said. 'Hope I didn't hurt you.' As he was leaving, he added, 'As the bishop said to the actress. Goodnight, everyone, and Happy New Year!'

Outside, he put on his overcoat and raised the collar against a cold wind. He felt depressed. What on earth is happening to me? I so looked forward to this evening and to meeting my old friends again but I couldn't win no matter how hard I tried. Adele was perhaps a little more friendly but not much.

He walked down Queen's Road, bewildered and gnawed by self-doubt. I really got the cold shoulder tonight from the gang – I felt like the odd man out. And they made it abundantly clear that I no longer belonged. But then, where *do* I belong? I seem to be trapped between two worlds, my home background and the academic world in London, and at the moment I feel as if I don't fully belong in either – like one of those stateless people you read about sometimes.

113

Wait a minute, though. He stopped in his tracks. Perhaps, without realising it, I *am* becoming lah-de-dah! In God's name, I hope not 'cos that's *the* cardinal sin in my family – getting too big for your britches. He quickened his pace. No, not a chance. If I *am* getting above myself, Mam will soon put me in my place and cut me down to size. So will Dad for that matter, especially Dad. But *something's* happening and I don't understand what. Harrigan's the same place and it's the same old crowd all right – none of *them* have changed. But then, maybe *I* have.

Chapter Eleven

Soap and education are not as sudden as a massacre, but they are more deadly in the long run.

Mark Twain, A Curious Dream

The first term of the second year was devoted exclusively to the final teaching practice and the preparation for it. They had a brief introduction to schools in their first year but this had been mainly observation and not real teaching. Now all that they'd been learning was to be put into practice in a real school with real children.

In the run-up to the practice, they had many 'down-to-earth' lectures and there was no shortage of advice and warnings, all of which served to make the students even more nervous.

'Remember,' said Taffy, 'you are a model for your pupils; they will watch every move you make and imitate you. In morals, in your speech, in your demeanour, in your dress, you will be setting an example for them to copy. Not only the conscious things you do and say but the unconscious way you behave. If they see you smoking, they will ape you. If you say "Damn" when you drop something, they will emulate you.'

The student body listened spellbound.

'This means you must stop picking your nose,' Billy whispered to Titch.

'And Pottsy must stop blowing bubbles,' Titch whispered back.

'I cannot emphasise enough,' Taffy continued, 'the importance of body language. Avoid displaying weak body postures, such as slouching, or sitting on your desk swinging a leg or, worse, crossing your legs.'

'I certainly agree with the last,' whispered Nobby. 'It's been the worst feature of some of the girls I've met.'

'Imagine your first lesson,' said Taffy. 'The class haven't yet made up their minds about you. They are waiting for Jackie Green, the chief troublemaker and clown, to plumb your depths and sound you out. After the novelty of weighing you up has worn off, the test will come. It's like going into the lion's den. How will you deal with it? Will you be a lion-tamer or a Sigmund Freud? Assert your authority and control by adopting a dominant posture such as standing upright or with your arms akimbo. Fingertips touching in church steeple fashion illustrates a confident attitude.'

'I love dominant men,' murmured Oscar.

'We come now to the matter of dress,' Taffy said. 'I know schools can become grubby places but it pays to look as if you're efficient. Wear a suit. See that you haven't any buttons loose or undone, especially your flies; don't have clothes with stains on them and tone down your colour schemes.'

The student body became busy examining their dress for stains and loose buttons and they realised that something would have to be done about their grubby corduroys and faded shirts.

Taffy went on, 'Finally check your personal image. Avoid beards and moustaches. See if your breath smells – you will be leaning over children. Avoid mannerisms like chin-stroking, polishing glasses, juggling chalk and hand-rubbing.'

'We shall look like tailor's dummies,' remarked Billy as they filed out of the lecture.

Next on the agenda was role-playing teaching sessions.

'Introduce your lessons,' Jock Lenzie, the English lecturer, advised, 'by linking your subject to the children's immediate experience so that they can relate to your subject.'

Titch was first victim chosen to present a lesson.

'Very well, children,' he said, addressing his fellow students. 'What did you have for breakfast this morning?'

'Porridge,' Billy replied promptly.

'Bacon and egg,' answered Ollie.

'Bread and peanut butter,' volunteered Elder.

'Yes, yes, and what else?' urged Titch desperately.

'Tea and toast,' said Oscar brightly.

'Orange juice,' Pottsy offered.

'Milk,' said Nobby.

'OK, OK,' said Titch. 'Well, I'm going to talk about coffee, see.'

Towards the end of the term the allocation of schools for the final teaching practice was posted on the college noticeboard and there was a mad rush of students all eager to find out their fate. The college authorities had made special provision for the Catholic students and arranged places in denominational schools. Billy found he was to be with Jack Elder in a small Catholic school in Cadogan Square in the World's End district – a poor, rundown area

117

off the King's Road on the outskirts of Chelsea. It was an old-fashioned school in a ramshackle building with only three classes and all teachers were required to teach English, arithmetic, history, geography, drill, art and music.

They presented themselves at the headmaster's office on the first morning and even Elder, the D-Day hero, was nervous.

'I only hope the little buggers are well-behaved,' he said.

James Farrell, the headmaster, turned out to be a stern figure who looked and talked like Will Hay. He was, however, kindly disposed towards his two students as they were the first the school had ever received and he felt honoured that his school had been selected.

'I believe in firm discipline in my school,' he said. 'Without order and obedience, no teaching can take place. The children are not allowed to talk in class – not under any circumstances. When "Sir" is talking, they must sit still and listen.'

Billy was given a class of eight- to ten-year-olds. Mrs McBride, the class teacher, was a kindly, matronly old soul who took pity on him, a skinny eighteen-year-old, and did everything in her power to jolly him along and help him overcome his nervousness. The boys and girls were well-mannered and obedient, one might say docile, and their classroom was a homely affair with a cheerful fire warming not only his backside but also the daily crate of free milk that was deposited nearby to thaw out.

Billy prepared his lessons thoroughly and taught them all subjects.

When it came to history, he found that back at college there was a well-equipped visual aids library and so was able to enliven his lessons with colourful pictures. He taught

118

them about Perkin Warbeck and Lambert Simnel and captured their interest with stories about the Princes in the Tower. In the classroom next door, he could hear the gruff voice of Corporal Elder instructing his charges.

'Right, you little buggers, watch your step with me. You be nice to me and I'll be nice to you. You can choose the hard way or the easy way. If you want to play it rough, I can be rough as well. Now, we're going down to the school yard for drill and I'm gonna show you how we did it in the army. Now shaddup, you little bastards. I want some bloody 'ush before we move.'

The final inspection came towards the end of the practice.

Mr Farrell addressed Billy's class. 'Now we are going to have some important people visit the school and I want all of you to be on your best behaviour. You will sit still – there will be no fidgeting and no talking. As soon as the inspector comes into the room, you will stand to attention and say "Good Morning, sir." What will you say?'

'Good morning, sir,' they chorused.

'You will sit down when you are told to sit and when Mr Hopkins here asks a question, you will raise your hand and there will be no calling out. Give your best answer and don't forget to call him "sir". Woe betide anyone who is reported to me. Now fingers on lips while I talk to Mr Hopkins.'

The children placed index fingers on their lips.

'Now, Mr Hopkins,' said Mr Farrell. 'Give your best lesson for the inspector and if any of these children cause you the slightest trouble, I want to know immediately.'

'Right, Mr Farrell,' Billy replied, 'but I don't think you need worry on that score. Their behaviour is always exemplary.'

The inspection passed happily enough, with the children behaving beautifully and answering intelligently. A relieved Billy thanked the visiting examiner who complimented him on his imaginative teaching and hinted that he would be given an above-average grade.

'Well, how did it go?' asked the headmaster when the inspector had gone.

'Fine,' Billy answered. 'No problems.'

'Everyone well-behaved, I trust?' the head asked.

'Perfect,' Billy answered. 'The class answered well. One small boy was very bright when he queried one of the things I was telling them.'

'What happened?' he asked brusquely.

'It was good,' Billy said. 'I'd told them about the Princes in the Tower and how they were bricked up secretly by their wicked uncle. Then one of the boys raised his hand.'

'Raised his hand without being asked,' said Mr Farrell aghast. 'How dare he?'

'It was OK,' said Billy. 'He wanted to know how the uncle could brick them up without telling a bricklayer his secret and he might tell other people. His father's a bricklayer, you know, and that's probably why he wanted to know.'

'Give me the boy's name,' he demanded. 'I told them to speak only when asked a question. This is a breach of discipline.'

'It was nothing, Mr Farrell,' Billy protested. 'I was only too pleased that he'd asked the question. It showed he was thinking about it.'

'I must have his name,' he insisted. 'Suppose you hadn't known the answer. Why, he could have ruined your whole lesson. We can't tolerate even the slightest indiscipline. It must be nipped in the bud.'

He pressed Billy and then ordered him. Reluctantly, Billy gave the young boy's name, Martin O'Dwyer. Surely, Billy thought, Mr Farrell wouldn't punish the boy for daring to ask a question.

That afternoon Martin was called to the head's room and given a severe caning on both hands. The rest of the class looked wonderingly and accusingly at Billy and he felt like a traitor.

Young Martin's return to class was a scene straight out of *Hard Times*. The little lad came back with great tears glistening in his eyes and he looked at Billy with sadness and bewilderment that he had been punished so harshly for trying to join in the lesson.

His face haunted Billy for the rest of his time at college.

Despite that heart-wrenching event, the practice was a happy one and at the end of the Christmas term, Jack Elder and Billy went back by invitation to a joyous Christmas party with lots of cake, jelly and carol-singing. Mrs McBride gave him twenty Players, a smiling Martin O'Dwyer presented him with a pound box of Cadburys – a gift from the whole class – and Mr Farrell shoved a ten shilling note in his hand and told him to spend it on a good meal. Billy blew this small fortune on a dinner of Vienna steak and chips for Titch and himself at the Blue Star, followed by a visit to the Regal cinema to see James Mason in *Odd Man Out*.

Nineteen forty-seven came in with the worst winter of the century. The central heating system of the college was permanently out of action because of shortage of fuel and the students found it almost impossible to keep warm. There was no alternative but to get into bed and study with the blankets wrapped around them. Needless to say, Pottsy was the most popular student on the block because of his illicit electric fire and his record player. There was invariably a crowd gathered around his amenities until Pottsy, patient and generous though he was, had to lock his door to keep visitors at bay. 'Look, fellas,' he would call, 'give me a break. I have my own work to do.'

Despite the severe cold, Billy and his companions fell into a comfortable routine. During the week they worked hard to keep up with the reading and the endless stream of essays they were required to write. But at weekends, it was different. They relaxed. Billy became a familiar face at the Kensington High Street dance studio. He continued to dance with Doris and on one never-to-be-forgotten occasion in February he was invited back to the Chiswick flat to meet her husband, Harry, who had been finally released from the RAF. It was a happy occasion and Billy made short work of the mountains of scones with which they plied him.

Life was so busy that time flew by. The weeks became months, and the months a year. Before they knew it, the end of the course loomed up. Billy reviewed his two years. What had he learned? he asked himself. A bric-a-brac of facts.

He knew about Hopper windows and about the goodness of milk – tuberculin tested of course – which was reckoned to be the finest food in the world; about rickets, ringworm, adiposity, and the different kinds of mental defectives.

In a memorable lecture he and his companions had learned that there were different kinds of bad body posture.

'Note the different kinds of spinal abnormalities you should look out for in your pupils,' said Taffy. 'Kyphosis is a condition in which the back is hunched and bent. Lordosis, an abnormal convex curvature of the spine; and scoliosis, a lateral spinal curvature.'

'Kyphosis perfectly describes my condition,' said Billy as they left the lecture theatre.

'I claim Lord Osis,' Pottsy said.

'Nonsense!' Ollie retorted. 'What you have is Potts' Disease. Now me, I suffer from scoliosis – the result of scanning books sideways on library shelves.'

'I claim all three,' said Titch. 'They explain my peculiar gait.'

'None of these matters a damn,' said Oscar. 'Now, what I have is truly important, namely ankylosis of the sacroiliac.'

'Trust you to have a posh-sounding abnormality,' said Nobby. 'It's just a fancy way of saying backache. As for me, I'm pleased to announce that I have none of 'em. Which explains why I'm so attractive to the opposite sex.'

In their education course they heard about Sir Cyril Norwood, a classical scholar and ex-headmaster of Harrow, and his government report on secondary education. According to Cyril and his hero, the Greek philosopher Plato, human beings were of three types – golden, silver and copper. Golden children would go to grammar schools for an academic education; silver children with a practical bent would go to technical schools; finally the copper children – the vast majority of the nation's children – would go to secondary modern schools where they would receive a more concrete type of education.

'Obviously a school suited for navvies on a building site,' remarked Oscar.

For this last type, there would be no exams and the project method, that is building models or looking after animals, would be the best thing. Selection in this tripartite system of education would no longer be dependent on purse strings, pulling strings or the old school tie but would be determined by means of the new intelligence tests in an exam called the Eleven Plus.

What nonsense this snooty view of human nature is, Billy thought. None of it squares up with my real-life experience of children and schools. But although he and his companions had serious doubts about this doctrinaire guff, they had no choice but to comply if they hoped to be accepted into the teaching profession.

May 1947 was the start of a glorious summer but for the students it was a time to get down to the serious business of swotting for final exams. Titch and Billy learned prepared answers off pat and after dinner strolled round the college grounds reciting to each other parrot fashion what they had memorised.

'OK, Titch, you give me the role of William of Orange in the struggle of the Netherlands against Spain.'

Titch duly reeled it off. Then he'd say: 'Right, Hoppy, now you evaluate Garibaldi's contribution to the cause of Italian unification.'

Billy would comply and ask him the next question as they walked round the fields and puffed at their fags. Education for them meant regurgitation. How much easier the task would be, they thought, if they'd had some idea of the questions in advance.

Help was at hand.

The annual inter-college sports day came round in May, and that year was held at Borough Road College, Isleworth. Attendance at this event was always excellent by the sporting and non-sporting fraternity alike for the simple reason that it was the occasion for swapping inside information on the exam topics that were likely to come up. Students from St Mary's (Simmaries) of Strawberry

Hill had the hottest tips and they were listened to with great respect. After all, their priest/lecturers would hardly tell them fibs. Students armed with notepads and pencils wandered about like stockbrokers from group to group exchanging hints and clues, and bartering possibilities. Indeed, the whole affair had much in common with business on the stock exchange floor, for many of the transactions that day were based on hope, fear, and rumour. Scant attention was paid to the sporting competitions, though the Anglican Marjons wondered why the Catholic Simmarian high-jumpers insisted on passing a holy medal from hand to hand in the hope that angels might bear them that little higher over the bar. In the end, the event was won by the Marjon candidate who, whilst deficient in holy medals, had extraordinarily long legs.

They returned to college elated like fishermen with full nets. Pottsy, who had been gated for returning after 11p.m. at the weekend and had missed the sports meeting, sought them out eagerly.

'Have you got the questions?' he implored.

'No problem, Pottsy,' they said. 'We'll dictate them to you.'

'Oh, great,' he said, pen hovering over his notebook.

'Right. First in education,' said Titch. ' "Describe how you would organise a children's party in a deaf and dumb school. Your answer should give details of food and games required as well as the various roles to be played by members of staff." '

'Do you think we'll get that?' asked Pottsy doubtfully.

'A sure thing,' said Ollie. 'Next, "Evaluate the role of the caretaker's assistant in a secondary modern school in a deprived district." That's a definite.'

'I'm not sure I'd go for that question. It's got me stumped,' said Pottsy.

'The next one is easier,' Billy said. ' "How would you teach logarithms in the dark?" That's straight from the horse's mouth, from a Simmarian.'

'Finally,' added Oscar, 'the easiest one of them all. "How would you teach history backwards?" '

'Come off it,' Pottsy protested as the penny dropped. 'You lot never take anything seriously.'

Soon after the inter-college sports, it was time for examinations. Outside, the sun shone from a glorious blue sky, the college gardens were at their best with their superb billiard-top lawns, the air was scented by a profusion of flowers and beautiful plants, birds sang from every tree. But inside the musty halls, nothing was to be heard but the scratching of pens on paper as the students wrote their finals. Nerves and first-day anxieties were soon left behind as they poured out and regurgitated the vast amounts of knowledge they had spent two years stacking into their heads. At the end of three weeks, they emerged from the stuffy rooms punch-drunk, their heads reeling but feeling distinctly lighter having unburdened themselves of the facts and theories so painstakingly acquired over so many anguished days and nights.

From that point on, it was downhill, for there followed a wonderful last week in college. First a performance of Shakespeare's *Measure for Measure*. They loved the lines:

'What's he done?'

'A woman.'

And: 'Groping for trout in a peculiar river.'

In the chapel, a mixed choir of students gave a memorable performance of Handel's *Messiah* but the culmination of that last week came on the last but one night in Chelsea. Billy and his Entertainments Committee organised a magnificent formal college ball.

It was a black tie and evening dress affair, and a ten-piece orchestra was hired. The beautifully dressed young ladies from Whitelands graced the hall with their presence and as the dancers whirled about the maple-floored assembly hall, the scene was more reminiscent of a Viennese ballroom than a London training college. Doris appeared with her husband and Billy's heart turned over with pride when he saw her. She was dressed in a ravishing white evening gown and in her dark hair she wore a single white flower.

'I want to thank you, Billy,' said Harry, 'for looking after Doris for me whilst I was in Malta. I know how much she loves her dancing. As I think she may have told you, I'm no dancer, though from now on I hope to start learning. But tonight, she's all yours . . .' Then he added quickly, 'Just for the dancing, that is.'

Laughing, Doris and Billy thanked him and turned their attention to their dancing students and were gratified to see them gliding so easily and smoothly across the floor with their glamorous partners.

Jack Elder gave them both a smile of welcome and a thumbs-up as he danced lightly by with his Amazonian partner. From the way he moved and handled himself, he seemed to have become a different person. More of a gentleman than the man who had joined the college two years ago.

'Well, Doris, it looks as if our two years' instruction has paid off in the end,' Billy said.

'I've enjoyed every moment,' she replied.

Then, watched admiringly by students and staff, they

danced easily and gracefully across the floor to the melody of 'I'll Buy That Dream'. A truly wonderful and triumphant evening.

It was not the end of the final festivities, however. In the hope of making them forget the loathsome food they had suffered for two years, the college arranged an exquisite formal dinner with the menu printed in French which, despite their two years' study of that language, nobody fully understood though they made out that *Coupe Robert* was ice cream prepared by a chef named Robert.

Next day, there followed much hand-shaking, back-slapping, tearful farewells, and vows to stay in touch, and before they knew it they were on the train back to Manchester.

The journey back was something of an anticlimax – quiet and ruminative.

'And so – it's over,' Oscar announced to no one in particular. 'What *was* it all about?'

'We're teachers,' answered Pottsy. 'At least, I hope we are.'

'As the London bus conductor put it so beautifully,' said Billy, 'God help poor old England!'

Chapter Twelve

1947

The year 1947 was momentous in Britain's history. February saw the severest winter of the century and this, combined with serious fuel shortages and transport strikes, brought the country to its economic knees. Banks, government offices and even Buckingham Palace were candlelit. Food rations were cut to the bone and austerity was the rule of the day. In a complete bucking of the trend and in spite of clothes rationing, Christian Dior introduced his New Look with its hour-glass shape and extravagant use of material, much to the delight of the ladies (and most of the men) and to the dismay of Hugh Dalton, the Chancellor of the Exchequer. Meanwhile, under Lord Mountbatten, India was partitioned and granted independence after 163 years of British rule, and shortly afterwards Mahatma Gandhi was shot dead. The marriage of Princess Elizabeth to Mountbatten's nephew, the Greek prince Lieutenant Philip, was announced, and in that summer of brilliant sunshine, Denis Compton ended the cricket season with record-breaking runs and centuries.

It was in that same glorious summer that the Damian College crowd finished their teacher training and travelled back to their beloved Manchester, their Athens of the North as they liked to call it.

Titch and Billy began their long vacation by looking for jobs to fill in the time until their future plans were settled. Jobs were easy to come by in that era of postwar reconstruction and a bright future and great possibilities lay ahead. It was a time of great hope and happiness, and everywhere there was a buoyant, optimistic atmosphere. The war was over and the British lion was licking its wounds. The world was their oyster! What joy to be young! What joy to be alive!

In due course, they presented themselves at the Labour Exchange in the city centre. The clerk who dealt with them was the same man who had interviewed Billy in the Juvenile Employment Bureau all those years ago in 1944, now obviously promoted as here he was dealing with adults.

'So you're both looking for a temporary job?' he said.

'If possible,' Billy said. 'Two jobs – one each.'

He looked at him quizzically. 'I seem to know you from somewhere,' he murmured. 'Anyway, here's a temporary job at Sherman's.'

'You mean making tanks?' Billy replied. 'I thought the war was over.'

'Now I remember you. You were the comedian who went to work on the *Manchester Guardian*.'

'That's right,' Billy replied. 'Now my friend and I are looking for a couple of holiday jobs to fill in the time before we take up full-time occupations – probably in the army.'

'Right. Got it,' the clerk said. 'Tanks indeed. No, the Sherman's we're talking about are Sherman's Pools and

130

they're looking for one or two salesmen to promote their coupons. Pay is five pounds per week – no commission.'

'We'll take it,' said Titch quickly before Billy could blow their chances with a witty riposte.

They walked across Manchester until they reached a rickety old building which the Luftwaffe had not quite finished off. At the top of a wooden staircase, they walked along a dusty corridor to a poky little office where they found a hump-backed, bald-headed dwarf – most like Grumpy if one had to select one of the seven. In sepulchral tones, the old fellow recited the requirements of the job.

'Your task will be to persuade the punters to stop betting with Littlewoods and Vernons and to take our coupons instead. You have to collect two shillings from each punter. One shilling is tax, one shilling for the coupon. We pay you five pounds a week and we expect you to get at least five customers a day. We pay you on Friday but you hand your takings in to us every day at this office. Here is a supply of coupons. Good morning.' And he began to usher them out of his office.

'Wait a moment, slow down,' protested Titch. 'Do I understand you to say that we must sell the idea of Sherman's to new customers? And that we collect two shillings from each one of them?'

'Yes, yes,' he answered irritably, anxious to get back to Jane and the *Daily Mirror* crossword.

'And the minimum number per day for each of us is five customers, that is ten shillings per day,' added Billy.

'That is what I said,' he barked. 'You should wash your ears out.'

'And the weekly pay is five pounds a week?' asked Titch.

'Yes, yes, yes,' he snapped. 'Do you want me to give it

to you printed in red on parchment?'

'OK, OK,' said Billy. 'We're only checking. Keep your hair on.' Not that he had much to keep on.

Grumpy snorted and closed the door behind them as if they had disturbed him by being there, bothering him with stupid questions.

It was an attractive temporary job. They could choose their own hours, they were out in the fresh air, and it meant handling money – a new experience for both of them. Billy loved the feel of it and he hoped that some day he might have some of his own. They retired to a café for tea and toast and to lay out their plans for trapping unwary victims. The important thing, they guessed, in selling Sherman's coupons was to appeal to the customer's greed and to awaken visions of the untold riches which were waiting to be won every Saturday. Why Sherman's coupons, though? What did they have over their rivals? Answer: they were smaller and promised better chances. Their punters were buying dreams and fantasies for a couple of bob. We can't miss, they thought.

They decided to try their luck in Davyhulme along Lostock Road – cold calling, the trade called it. They descended on the unsuspecting housewives with their coupons. Titch had developed, after much practice before a mirror, the ploy of raising his newly acquired trilby, revealing his rapidly thinning hair which he thought gave him a look of maturity. He followed the hat-raising trick with a bright, 'Good morning, madam. I'm here to offer you a golden opportunity to make your fortune.'

He went into his spiel and explained fully and patiently what it was about.

'The reason you're being asked to pay this two bob is because of government regulations – nothing to do with us. Now, we're not offering these coupons to everyone down this road – there's some right riffraff here, I tell you. No, you've been specially selected as worthy of this honour.'

One or two comely wenches still in their nightgowns responded warmly.

'My husband's at work, luv. Won't be back till tonight. Do you want to come in for a bit – rest your feet, like?'

'Wonder what she meant by "bit",' Titch would remark.

It didn't happen often but the two young men were having none of that.

More usually they heard: 'Oh, I daren't take football coupons without asking my hubby. Come back after six o'clock.' They met with this response over and over again.

One or two were nasty and slammed the door in their faces. 'Bugger off,' they'd bawl through the letter box, 'before I set the dog on you.'

From such warm welcomes, they beat a hasty retreat.

After six hours' work and after calling on more than a hundred households, they had barely succeeded in making the day's quota of five coupons each. Triumphantly, they reported back to Grumps, each with their ten shillings.

'Only five customers each?' he grumbled after receiving their takings and giving them a receipt. 'You're not trying hard enough. But it meets the minimum requirement.'

With wobbly legs and aching feet, they retired to a café for a cuppa.

'Not trying hard enough. I like that,' Titch said. 'I'm sure I've worn my legs down. I feel like Toulouse Lautrec.'

They sipped their tea. Then the penny dropped.

'Wait a minute, Titch,' Billy said suddenly. 'We earn

five pounds a week and therefore we've earned one pound today. Are my calculations correct?'

'Correct.'

'After walking miles round Davyhulme, we have each managed to raise the required ten shillings.'

'Correct. So?'

'But we have earned one pound for our efforts.'

Titch smiled. 'So we don't need to use up all that shoe leather. We can simply hand in five names along with ten shillings and receive a pound for our trouble.'

'Exactly. Tell me an investment that will double your money every day.'

From that point on, they began their day in the local billiard hall where they consulted the telephone directory to pick ten names at random. After organising Sherman's coupons for the whole of Marjon's staff, they gave priority to names of the clergy listed under the churches, especially Nonconformists, since they knew that many ministers subscribed to Calvinist ethics and were opposed to betting on the basis that it was wrong to get something for nothing. 'By the sweat of thy brow shalt thou eat thy bread' was the rule by which such vicars lived.

That was precisely what Billy and Titch weren't doing – unless you count writing out ten names and addresses as sweaty work. After a week of this onerous calligraphic exercise, they went into town, collected their five pound weekly wage, and after celebrating their good fortune with the customary tea and toast, went their separate ways rejoicing.

Feeling flush on Fridays, Billy took to calling in at a specialist tobacconist on Peter Street to buy a twenty-packet of Passing Cloud because he liked the taste and oval shape of the cigarettes but also because of the illustration on the pink packet – the picture of the man having hallucinations.

It was on one of these Friday nights that he ran into Adele and her mother. They were waiting for the 62 bus in Albert Square and he joined them in the queue.

Adele gave him an enthusiastic wave and her mother smiled in recognition.

'Hello, Billy,' Adele called. 'Haven't seen you in a long time. Where've you been hiding?'

Adele looked as glamorous as ever in her bright red New Look coat and matching hat, with her auburn shoulder-length hair and her round blue eyes; she resembled the girl in a *Vogue* advertisement who was always being given expensive presents or stepping into the latest Rolls *coupé de ville* with a pedigree Pekinese under her arm.

'Oh, I've been pretty busy lately, working for a living,' said Billy.

'Why haven't you been to see me?' she pouted.

'I've only been back a week and my first need was to get some cash in my pocket. But I thought you were going around with Duggie Doyle. What happened to him and your dancing partnership?'

'Oh, with Duggie it's on and off. But I'm free now,' she added, giving her shy little-girl look.

'Why don't you ask Billy to tea?' suggested her mother.

'There you are, Billy. You've got an invite. Come back home with us.'

'Invite accepted,' Billy said. 'I'll have to tell them back home first though as they're expecting me.'

The two ladies alighted at Queen's Road and Billy continued to St Luke's Church. As he walked down Smedley Lane towards the Gardenia Court tenement, he wondered if he had done the right thing. Adele and he had corresponded

135

with each other whilst he was at college but that was no big deal. Did he want to get back with her now he was home? She was a beautiful and glamorous girl in the Hollywood mould but she was also something of a self-willed person- ality and liked to get her own way.

But it was only an invitation to tea. What harm was there in that? And he had nothing else planned, so what the hell!

At home, Billy explained to his mam that he'd been invited to tea with Adele.

'You be careful there, my lad,' she admonished. 'Now you're a teacher, you're a good catch for any working-class girl. I never took to that girl and the way she gave you that new name of Julian. Daft name. The stuck-up bitch.'

'I'm only going for tea,' Billy protested. 'Not to announce the wedding banns.'

'You mark my words, my lad,' she said. 'I know girls like that. She'll have you walking down the aisle before you can say Jack Rubenstein.'

Despite his mam's objections, Billy walked over to Clifton Street and to Adele's home. There he found Adele's parents – the mother he'd met and the father whom he knew only through his voice when he had knocked on the ceiling and in doom-laden tones had announced from above that the hour was late and it was time to bring proceedings to an end. Adele now made the introductions.

'Pleased to meet you, Mr Lovitt,' said Billy politely, 'though I feel I know you already.'

'Likewise, Billy. But please call me George,' he said, taking a firm grip on Billy's outstretched hand.

'And I'm Rita,' said Mrs Lovitt.

Formalities over, they turned their attention to the high

tea which had been laid out specially in his honour. Very different treatment from the last time I was here, Billy said to himself. What's happened in the meanwhile to change things? Though the Lovitts lived in a back-to-back terraced house, the interior was tastefully decorated and furnished. And for this occasion they'd pulled out their best crockery, cutlery, and glassware.

Just as well Pottsy taught me about etiquette and which implement to use, Billy thought.

They began with a VP sherry and followed with a delicious salad complete with a wide variety of dressings, the whole thing rounded off with an exquisite Lewis's trifle.

'That was a meal worthy of the Midland Hotel,' said Billy when they'd finished.

'Why thank you,' said Rita Lovitt. 'And do you know that Adele prepared that trifle herself? She's ever so good in the kitchen.'

I must try her sometime, Billy reflected. Mrs Lovitt seemed to have forgotten that he had seen them carrying the Lewis's food package.

'Oh, Mother,' said Adele coyly. 'You're embarrassing me with that talk about my trifle-making.'

Billy offered his Passing Clouds around, and they all puffed on them contentedly.

'You must be proud,' said Mrs Lovitt, 'to have passed your exams to be a teacher. Our Adele left school at fourteen but she was ever so clever at school. That's why she got such a good job at Kendal's on the cosmetics counter.'

'That explains your skill in putting make-up on,' said Billy, smiling at Adele who was acting all bashful. 'Maybe you should've got a job in a theatre. And you dress so elegantly as well. How do you manage it on the paltry clothing ration we have to put up with?'

'She uses our clothing coupons as well as her own,' said Rita Lovitt, answering for her. 'Also her granny's. It's so important for a young girl to keep up with the latest fashions and so we don't mind giving up our share. She's our only child, Billy,' she added proudly. 'We've always done our best for her and tried to give her everything she wanted. Always made sure she's never gone without. Sometimes we think she's a bit spoilt.'

For me, spoilt meant having an extra roast potato at Sunday dinner, Billy thought. Or maybe being given the rice pudding dish to scrape when everyone had finished.

'I wish you'd shut up, Mother,' Adele said ominously. 'I'm sure Billy doesn't want to hear that rubbish about me being the apple of your eye and that.'

'Well, our Adele, you're the apple of my eye whether you like it or not,' George said, looking fondly at his daughter. 'And so, young Billy sir,' he continued, changing the subject, 'you're now a fully qualified teacher in the service of Manchester Education Committee!'

'Well, not quite,' Billy answered. 'I have to wait another fortnight before we get the final results. And before I can teach, I'll have to do a stint in the forces – probably in the army.'

'But you'll be made an officer,' Adele gushed. 'I can see you now in your smart uniform, the Sam Browne belt, the riding boots, the pips on your shoulder.'

Now Billy had joined Adele in the *Vogue* ad along with the Pekinese dog and the flash sports car.

'You'll have all the girls falling for you,' said Mrs Lovitt playfully.

'There's no need for comments like that, Mother,' Adele snapped. 'We don't want to put such ideas into Billy's

138

head. Anyroad, he belongs to me, not other girls, don't you, Billy?' she simpered.

Billy didn't like the direction this conversation was taking.

'I didn't mean anything, I'm sure,' Mrs Lovitt apologised. Then she declared brightly, 'I wonder if Billy knows that we're related to the Lovitts of Altrincham who have the big grocery chain. One day, our Adele could inherit some of that wealth, Billy. That'd help if ever you were thinking of setting up home, wouldn't it?'

'I think you're running ahead of things,' Billy mumbled. Addressing George, he said, 'As for the army, Mr Lovitt, sergeant is probably the highest rank I'll be offered.'

'Still pretty good pay and allowances if I remember from my army days,' George rejoined. 'Lance corporal is the highest rank I managed. But teaching's a good job, Billy. Long holidays and good pension, eh.' Winking at Adele, he added, 'You'll be able to look after our little princess in the way she's been accustomed to. She likes the easy life, you know.'

The discussion went on in this vein for half an hour or so until Adele suggested that they go to Harrigan's Dance Academy and take up where they'd left off so long ago.

Unsure, Billy agreed and much to his surprise had a most enjoyable evening renewing old acquaintances and recalling their days of success in the world of competitive dancing. Happily, the crowd which had got his goat at New Year were absent and he didn't have to suffer the bishop/actress repartees. Adele, still a magnificent dancer, showed she'd lost nothing of her elegant style and her ability to attract the envy of other females and the lustful looks of their male partners. In the slow foxtrot particularly she glided effortlessly with perfect timing across the polished floor of Harrigan's ballroom.

At the end of a happy evening, Billy took Adele home. They reached the door of her home and Billy kissed her on the lips and said, 'Thank you for a great night, Adele. You're still as beautiful as ever and as for your dancing, you're incomparable. But you always were. It's been great getting back with you.'

'Why thank you, kind sir,' she said, making a small curtsy. 'I share your feelings. I don't want this evening ever to come to an end. But it doesn't have to yet. Come in and have a cup of tea before you make your weary way to your lonely bed.'

'Won't your parents still be up?'

'They won't when I give 'em their marching orders,' she laughed, narrowing her eyes.

They went inside where Mrs Lovitt was listening to the wireless. She switched it off as soon as she saw them arrive.

'We're in for a last cuppa,' Adele said, signalling undisguisedly with raised eyebrows that it was time for Mother to skedaddle. 'I'm sure you'll be wanting to get to bed.'

'Don't worry, Adele, I'm off,' Mrs Lovitt said helpfully. 'The kettle's boiled and so I'll leave you two lovebirds in peace. You do make a lovely couple.'

Coupling would be a better word for it, thought Billy.

When she had gone, Adele and Billy retired with their tea to the settee in the front room.

'Remember this settee, Billy?' murmured Adele.

'How could I ever forget?'

They set their cups down, forgot about their tea, and began kissing and embracing passionately.

'It was here that we promised to love each other till the end of time. Do you remember?' she whispered.

'I do indeed. It was until things like the wells ran dry and the mountains disappeared. Until, that is, one of us ran out of unlikely events to love the other till. It's a case of *déjà vu* all over again,' Billy replied.

'But in my case, it was true,' she said. 'Billy, I do love you. I know we once tried to make love and it didn't work out. I want you to know that if we were to become engaged, I'm more than willing to sleep with you. But the ring must come first.'

'Adele, don't remind me of that disastrous night. We – or at least I – made a complete pig's ear of it and it's an experience I don't want ever to repeat. As for engagements, I think we're both too young. We're only nineteen and there's plenty of time. Why do we have to wait until we get engaged before we . . . ?'

'If I became pregnant,' she said, 'it'd ruin everything and you'd feel that you had to marry me.'

'We could always use something.'

'I don't trust those things,' she said.

'I suppose you're right. And anyway, I'm a Catholic and it's against our religion to use them. But engagement is out for quite some time.'

'OK, if that's the way you feel, Billy. I'll go along with anything you say. I hope, though, that when we're married, you'll drop that Catholic superstitious mumbo-jumbo. You know how I feel – I couldn't stand having them holy pictures, statues and crucifixes in my house. We'll talk about that when we get engaged. But tell me that we're together again and I'm happy.'

When they parted that night, Adele seemed happy and content, but deep in his heart Billy felt troubled and uneasy. He didn't like that talk about Catholic superstition. They'd been through all that stuff before. Whilst he was no Holy Joe, he objected to anyone making fun of his church and he reserved the right to make up his own mind. There were other things. He had noted that the Voice of Doom had not spoken through the ceiling as it usually had in the past. Furthermore, he had the uncanny sensation that he was sliding down a slippery slope and he kept hearing the words of his mam: 'You mark my words, my lad. I know girls like that. She'll have you walking down the aisle before you can say Jack Rubenstein.'

At weekends, he continued to go dancing with Adele and at times their snogging sessions threatened to get out of control. They probably would have done had it not been for Adele's insistence on a ring. Billy was not overconcerned that they didn't go all the way as the image of that first disastrous try at sex still rankled, and he didn't want a repeat performance, or non-performance as the case might be.

Adele may be a little spoiled and self-centred, he thought, but she's the only girl around in my life at the moment. Perhaps my standards are too high and my ideal doesn't exist except in storybooks. Then again, maybe I'm not Adele's superman either. So, until our fairytale hero and heroine come onto the scene, I suppose we'll have to put up with each other. Sometimes if you hold out for the ideal, you end up with nothing. But engagement and marriage are definitely out. Anyway, apart from the question of finding the wherewithal to buy a diamond ring, there's the little matter of National Service. He was looking forward to that and Adele had awakened his imagination with her talk of a smart officer's uniform.

How his own family and the relatives would like that! A Hopkins lad from Collyhurst an officer!

It was inconceivable.

Chapter Thirteen

Sometimes a trivial thing can have dire consequences

A couple of weeks later, Billy heard that he'd obtained the Teaching Certificate of the University of London and was now a qualified teacher.

'Does this mean you know how to teach now?' Mam asked.

'Not really, Mam,' Billy replied. 'This certificate means that as far as they can tell, I won't do too much damage in the classroom if anyone appoints me.'

'That's more than can be said for some of the teachers I had at Board School,' she said.

The rest of the Damian crowd heard that they, too, had been successful. This had to be celebrated in the usual way and an alcoholic evening at the Sawyers' Arms on Deansgate followed.

The talk was about the coming spell in the forces which they would be required to do. The evening was supposed to be celebratory but in many ways it was tinged with sadness, for they sensed that fate would soon scatter them to the four winds, that they might part, go their separate ways and perhaps never meet again.

'I'd love to be in the army,' said Oscar. 'The thought of those virile soldiers taking their showers leaves me quite weak. Unfortunately, I doubt if I'll pass the medical because of my ankylosis – that's arthritis to you.'

'I'm really looking forward to it,' exclaimed Billy. 'Especially if we get commissioned. Good pay, the chance to go overseas and make new friends.'

'You know what they say,' added Ollie. 'Join the army, make new friends – and then shoot them.'

'I fancy the uniform,' said Nobby. 'Think of the birds we can pull. Why, they'll regard it as an honour to be shafted by an officer.'

'There's no guarantee that we'll get commissioned,' said Potts, 'but my dad reckons he can pull a few strings.'

'Exactly what does your father do?' sneered Oscar. 'I have the impression that he is a puppeteer in a circus.'

'I know I'll get posted to some remote outpost of the British Empire,' whined Titch. 'Far away from civilisation, and I shall spend two years wasting my sweetness on the desert air.'

So the conversation flowed, becoming progressively more ribald and noisy as the evening wore on and the alcohol began to take effect. There was an atmosphere of great anticipation and exhilaration and they thrilled at the idea that they were on the threshold of a new and exciting life. The worry and the constant studying for examinations were behind them and before them lay the prospect of new adventures, new places and new faces. As for teaching, well, that was something they could take up later. They'd cross that bridge when they came to it.

Shortly after their night out, they were ordered to report to Ardwick Green Barracks for the required army medical.

Nervous as kittens, they endeavoured to cover their anxieties with a stream of obscene and corny comments as they underwent the usual medical routine of being stripped, lined up, handled, felt, tapped, pummelled, and forced to bend down to have their innards and their anuses checked; they coughed on cue as the doctor cupped their testicles in his hand as if weighing them; they inhaled and exhaled; they read off the letters on the chart.

Throughout the procedure, they maintained a flow of what they thought were funny jokes about eye examinations and medicals in general, the 'I only came here to deliver a telegram' variety and the 'Doctor, doctor' type, like 'Doctor, doctor, how's that little boy doing, the one who swallowed the half-crown?' Answer: 'No change yet.' And 'Doctor, doctor, I keep thinking I'm a spoon.' 'Well, stand over there and don't stir.'

'I've heard them all before,' remarked the elderly GP, yawning.

Next, they were ordered to give a specimen of urine to demonstrate that they were disease-free and diabetes-free.

'You must urinate in my presence, if you please,' said the doctor.

'Piddling to order is easier said than done,' commented Titch. 'I drank a gallon of tea before I came out and now my bloody bladder refuses to co-operate. I never thought taking a slash would be so difficult.'

The six of them stood there in their birthday suits, straining to micturate into their jars. No use – none of them could make it.

Exasperated, the doctor said, 'You're like a bunch of shy virgins on their wedding night. Very well, we can't wait around here all day. Take yourself off to the toilets and come back when you've succeeded in splashing your boots.

And none of your tomfoolery, like swapping each other's urine around.'

Away from the tension of being under observation, the gang released awesome, Niagara-like streams of urine until the bottles were overflowing.

'What's this you're on, Billy?' remarked Oscar. 'Boddington's best draught?'

Titch, however, was still having problems producing the goods.

'You see,' he explained, 'when I was a little kid and my mam wanted me to do a wee, she always sang that nursery rhyme – the one about this little piggy...'

'You're not suggesting we sing it now?' exclaimed Billy incredulously.

'And why not?' said Oscar. 'Anything if it helps to hurry things along.'

Titch's five companions began to sing in unison:

> *This little piggy went to market,*
> *This little piggy stayed at home,*
> *This little piggy had roast beef,*
> *This little piggy had none,*
> *But this little piggy cried, wee-wee-wee-wee-wee,*
> *I can't find my way home.*

Success. It worked – Titch filled his jar.

Triumphantly, they presented the doctor with their precious gifts.

'I merely wanted a small specimen,' he wailed. 'Not a flagon of piss from each one of you.'

Doctors! they thought. They're never satisfied.

Finally, they had their ears checked and it was here that the examiner found an old lesion on Billy's eardrum dating back years to when his mother had accidentally poured water down his ear whilst washing his hair. He had a perforated eardrum of which he'd been unaware – his hearing was something he'd always been proud of.

'Though you've a small perforation on the eardrum, it seems to have healed,' the physician said, 'and I can see no reason why you shouldn't do your service in the army or the air force.'

But that small act of his mother's all those years ago dramatically changed Billy's life. It's truly food for thought when one reflects how the tiniest, apparently insignificant incident can alter the course of a personal history. Even the history of a nation, who knows? 'For want of a nail, the battle was lost . . .'

A couple of weeks later when Billy had returned home after a hard day in the 'Pill Hall' slaving over a snooker table writing out names and addresses, he found a letter in a buff envelope waiting for him behind the tea caddy on the mantelpiece.

Billy wasn't keen on receiving letters like this. His previous experience of them had not been happy and he'd long ago learned never to build up his hopes.

With trembling hands, he tore open the envelope and began to read. As he did so, the bile of disappointment rose in his throat.

'Well, Billy, what does it say?' his mam asked anxiously. He handed her the letter. She read:

Dear Sir,
NATIONAL SERVICE ACTS
Re. Your recent National Service medical examination held at Ardwick Barracks.
I am directed by the Secretary of State to inform you

that following your recent medical examination to determine your fitness or otherwise to serve in His Majesty's forces, you were classified as Grade IV and will not therefore be required to serve a period of National Service.

I should like to take this opportunity of thanking you for your attendance and for your co-operation.

I am, sir,

Your obedient servant,

Clifford Whitehead

For the Minister of Labour and National Service.

'Well,' said Mam, 'that *is* good news!'

'How do you make that out?' asked Billy bitterly. 'It's the same old story. As soon as I raise my hopes, they're dashed to pieces. I was looking forward to becoming an officer in the army. This letter is telling me I'm a right weakling. I feel like a cripple. Not even fit to join the army.'

'Nonsense,' she said. 'You've got a slight perforation of the eardrum, that's all, and even that's healed up. If there'd been a war, they'd have taken you right enough. Anyroad, I read in the paper the other day that that singer you're always going on about – Frank Sonata – was turned down for the American army because of a punctured eardrum. So you've got something in common. Look on the bright side – this is a piece of good luck.'

'Good luck! How can being told you're a wimp be a piece of good luck?'

'I believe in fate,' she answered. 'Who knows? You might have been sent to Palestine or some place like that and got yourself shot. No, count yourself lucky. Somebody up there is looking after you.'

Gradually Billy came to accept this latest turn in his destiny. Maybe his mam was right. At least his future was clear – no wasting time in the forces. There was some consolation perhaps in the news that Oscar, too, had been turned down, but not much. After all, he had a nasty-sounding deformity. But Oscar had always claimed that one day his arthritic disability would pay off.

The others of their group, Titch, Nobby, Ollie, Pottsy, were drafted into the Royal Army Education Corps. Not as officers – which was another crumb of comfort – but as sergeants.

There was another twist of fate shortly after Billy had his news about National Service. It may have been a coincidence but Adele decided that Duggie Doyle was her Prince Charming after all. A month later, they announced their engagement. Poor old Duggie, Billy thought, had fallen for her wiles and been lured into the honeytrap.

The Sherman's job came to an end and Titch went off to London to stay with relatives. It was a long summer holiday and there were still six weeks to fill. Billy was left at a loose end and was almost back to his adolescent game of dropping plums from the veranda on unsuspecting pedestrians below when he received a card from Titch. 'Pack your bags, lad,' it said. 'There are jobs galore down here. You can stay with me at my aunt's.'

Billy was off like a shot.

He caught the bus from Lower Mosley Street to Victoria where he found Titch waiting.

'I've found us two jobs already,' he shouted excitedly.

The jobs were as building labourers with Percy Bilton's, constructing a training centre in Perivale, not far from the Hoover factory. The foreman, a huge strapping Irishman, looked them up and down.

'You,' he said pointing to Titch, 'don't look strong enough to lift the latch of a gate let alone a bucket of mortar or a hod of bricks. You can have a job in the stores.'

Billy stuck his chest out and tried to look muscular.

'And as for you, you don't look much better. You remind me of that American crooner who's always going on about his daughter Nancy with the laughing face. But I'll give you a try on the gang digging a foundation trench.'

He handed Billy a huge pickaxe and fourteen-pound hammer and told him to join a line of Irish labourers. It was glorious weather and he stripped off his shirt to be like the rest of them.

'Will you take a look at this bag o' bones,' said Shaun, one of the labourers. 'How do you expect to do any digging with those muscles? Sure you could get a job in a circus as one o' them there freaks – you could go as the walking skeleton.'

This brand of sarcasm caused a great deal of mirth amongst his fellow Hibernians.

'Anyway,' he continued, 'the first thing we have to do is dig through the hard core of stone and cinders till we reach the clay underneath. Then we dig a trench four feet deep. Do you understand all that?'

'Got it,' Billy said, eager to show what he could do.

He lifted the big hammer which nearly wrenched his arms from their sockets. After five minutes, the sweat poured off him and he was exhausted.

'For God's sake, take it aisy,' said Shaun behind him. 'You'll not last an hour at that rate.'

Billy slowed the pace but he was still worn out, his back ached and his hands began to bleed.

'Shaun, if you could help me get through this hard core,'

he pleaded, 'I'm sure I can do the digging with a spade and my boots.'

'I'll do nothin' of the sort,' said Shaun. 'Sure I won't be gettin' your wages and so I won't be doin' any digging for you. You yourself will be collectin' the money on Friday. So stop your snivellin' and get on with it.'

'But my hands are bleeding,' Billy said.

'Ah, your hands'll get used to it in the end as it did for the rest of us. Piss on your hands to harden them up.'

At the end of that first day, Billy was in a state of collapse and every bone in his body screamed out for rest. But Shaun was right. After ten days, he had become used to the routine and his hands had toughened up.

After a while he was promoted to operating a piece of highly technical machinery – a wheelbarrow. He was entrusted to carry loads of liquid cement from the rotating mixer, across a narrow bridge of planks, and there to upend the squelchy mess into the trench.

And when the first morning tea break came round, what joy! He was so weak with hunger and thirst that he swooped ravenously on the huge pint pots of tea and the pavement-thick sandwiches which were brought round on a trolley at eleven o'clock and at dinnertime. Oh, sweet ambrosia and nectar, he thought. Whatever they tasted like to the Greek gods must have been something similar.

As the weeks went by, he became filled with admiration at the skill the labourers demonstrated getting a job done with the utmost economy of effort, and their ability to time a job to perfection.

One Friday afternoon, the foreman ordered Shaun and Billy to move a quantity of heavy paving stones, about ten in number, from one end of the site to the other. It was 4 p.m. and Billy reckoned they could move them in half an hour. They hoisted the first one into the wheelbarrow and Billy – now a skilled operator – started off with his load to the other side of the site. He was soon back for the next. Shaun, who was sitting by the stones, frowned at Billy and said, 'Sure don't be in such a feckin' great hurry. No need to break your feckin' back.' He set the timing of the operation and demonstrated the truth of Parkinson's great law, which stated: 'Work expands to fill the time available for its completion.'

Billy moved the last one into place at precisely 6 p.m. as the hooter was sounding.

'Time to knock off,' Shaun announced.

At the end of four weeks, Billy had become fitter and healthier than he had ever been in his whole life. He had acquired a deep tan and he glowed with health. Poor old Titch looked sallow, weedy, and positively ill after his incarceration in the windowless stores where there had been little to occupy him.

'Much to my surprise, I passed the army medical,' he said in his usual lugubrious tone. 'I must be better than I feel.'

Every evening, when the work was done, it was off to the local pub with Titch's aunt and uncle plus numerous Cockney cousins. There they consumed copious quantities of ale and Billy acquired a taste for gin and orange. This was indeed a happy time and the conversation and the jokes flowed easily and more noisily as the evening wore on. On one of these occasions, Titch's aunt looked at the two young men through an alcoholic haze and remarked, 'Look at the two of them there. There's my young nephew classified for the army as Grade One – he's as pale as a ghost and looks as if he should be in a TB hospital. And Billy sits there swilling his gin and orange and looking the picture of health with his golden suntan – he's Grade Four. It's a mad old world. I think the government has got its gradings mixed up. Are you sure you boys didn't switch the specimens of pee?'

Sadly, the holiday came to an end and it was time for the Damian gang to take their different paths – a true parting of the ways. With the rest of them, Titch went off as a sergeant instructor in the Royal Army Education Corps to teach illiterate soldiers the rudiments of reading. There were no exotic postings involved and he spent the whole period with the rest of them at Buchanan Castle in the north-east of England. As for Billy, it was time to start looking for a job. The prospect hung over his head like the Sword of Damocles and even the thought of it was enough to give him goose pimples.

Chapter Fourteen

He who can, does. He who cannot, teaches.

George Bernard Shaw

When he got back from London, Billy went looking for a teaching job. He was contracted to Manchester Education Authority as he had taken out a loan of forty pounds with them to get through college, and it had to be paid back from his salary.

Billy went to see his old head, Gus Thomas, at St Chad's for advice about which schools to apply to and Gus gave Billy his preferred order of schools – first St Aidan's, second St Anselm's. Billy arranged to see Mr Muldoon, the head of St Aidan's, but there was nothing doing there as the vacancy had been reserved for Potts pending the result of his Army medical. Obviously Muldoon had not got the news or perhaps Potts's dad, the puppeteer, was still hoping to fix an exemption for his son. Disenchanted, Billy took the bus across to Longsight and went to see St Anselm's school manager, Father Kelly. There was no interview as such.

In the private sitting room, Billy could smell a heady mixture of cigar smoke and malt whisky. Rosy-cheeked

Father Kelly gave every appearance of being comfortable.

'I see,' he began, 'that you have attended an Anglican college. What was wrong with our own college, St Mary's at Strawberry Hill, may I ask?'

Billy told him that the college had soon become full and no one from Damian College had secured a place that year.

'I trust you are a good Catholic,' he said. 'And that you attend Holy Mass and the sacraments regularly.'

Billy reassured him on these points.

Finally he said, 'You will have to pass the Catholic Teachers' Religious Certificate before we confirm your appointment. We don't want you teaching Protestant heresy to our children in the parish, now do we?'

Billy agreed with him of course and assured him that he didn't know any heresies to teach and even if he did, he wouldn't teach them – not to the children in his parish at any rate. He had become confused by the googly the priest had bowled him.

Father Kelly seemed satisfied by this garbled answer, for he said, 'Very well, I'll take you provisionally until you pass the Religious Certificate. You may start at the school next Monday. The school is on holiday at the moment but you should present yourself to the headmaster, Mr Francis Wakefield, on the first day of term.'

Billy's starting salary was £300 a year. He was delighted.

As Billy was about to leave, the presbytery doorbell rang and the housekeeper announced the arrival of a female visitor. She was a middle-aged woman, expensively dressed, decorated with lots of dangly jewellery, and wafting an aroma of exotic perfume. As he escorted Billy over the threshold, Father Kelly introduced her as Miss Andrews, the headmistress of the infants' school at Salop House.

'Mr Hopkins here is going to teach in the senior school,' he said.

'Ah, so you'll be working under Wakefield,' she exclaimed in a plummy voice. 'You have my sympathy. I wish you all the luck in the world – you're going to need it.'

'Thank you for those kind words,' Billy said as he departed.

What was he walking into? he wondered.

On the Saturday before he was due to start, Billy decided to do a recce of the route he would take and of the district itself – the so-called catchment area. He cycled over to Longsight and dismounted at Nelson Grove. As he strolled round the area pushing his bike, he noted the little two-up, two-down, privy-in-the-yard terraced houses – street after street of them, each named by some imaginative city planner after long-forgotten historical events and people. Hougoumont Grove, Waterloo Court, Blucher Street, Bulow Street. Illustrious names that seemed out of place in such squalid surroundings. He turned into Duke Street and was accosted by a young lady heavily made up and wearing an extremely short skirt.

'Lookin' for a short time?' she asked wearily.

'Short time?' Billy asked, puzzled.

'Yeah,' she said. 'A quickie, you know. I can show you a good time. Only a quid.'

'I don't think so,' he replied, getting the point. 'I'm not looking for a short time. I'm looking for St Anselm's School. Do you know it?'

'Know it?' she answered. 'I should do, it's my old school and my young sister still goes there. I think she's in the top class – name of Irene Moody. Look out for her, she'll eat you for breakfast. But there's no school building there now. Jerry put a bomb on it in nineteen forty-two. The best thing

157

he ever did. Anyroad, I think they're now in the Industrial School on Wellington Grove – best to ask there.'

Billy left the young maiden and walked along High Street, past the Corporation baths, past dingy shop fronts and cafés, second-hand furniture shops, a garage, until he finally reached Wellington Grove. At least he now had a rough idea of the district and the location of the school.

On the way back, he took a different route. He cycled some distance along Wellington Grove and then made a right turn into Regina Park Hill, a private estate and a different world. The park was a throwback to the Victorian era when prosperous Manchester cotton merchants, anxious to escape the hoi polloi, set up their large, commodious houses away from the common people. The estate retained a toll gate manned by a uniformed collector, no doubt to discourage traffic taking a short cut through the park. If this was the case, it was unnecessary because the state of the roads was an even greater deterrent – the deep potholes seemed designed to break the springs of any car doing over ten miles an hour. As the road climbed steeply, Billy dismounted and walked the rest of the way until he commanded a fine view of the surrounding district and the slums which nestled at the foot of this rich man's territory.

The estate was like an island of prosperity set in a sea of poverty. No two-up, two-down hovels here. Instead, there were wide, tree-lined lanes and large Edwardian and Victorian houses with drives, orchards, and manicured hedges. And the names of the roads and avenues delivered what they promised. Chestnut Avenue – broad and straight – was indeed lined with chestnut trees whilst Birch Grove, Lime Grove, Sycamore Avenue similarly manifested arboreal truth.

Billy doubted if many of the St Anselm's pupils hailed

from this area; no doubt most of the Regina Park kids would be packed off to private boarding schools or fee-paying grammar schools. He thought about his own background – a tenement in Cheetham Hill. Gardenia Court. That was a laugh; there wasn't a gardenia to be seen within a hundred miles of the place. Somehow, Chestnut Avenue became the symbol of Regina Park wealth and he saw his own district and its lifestyle for what they were – poor and restrictive.

Lost in thought, he cycled back to north Manchester.

Chapter Fifteen

Chalk and Duster Brigade

For the whole of the weekend, Billy was on edge. Monday morning came round and in this anxious state, he had no appetite, his breakfast consisting of a mug of tea and a cigarette. What kind of job was he going to? he wondered. What sort of surprises were round the corner?

'You should try to eat something,' Mam said. 'You can't do good work on an empty stomach. Remember that saying: "In the morning, eat like a king; in the afternoon, like a prince; and at night, like a peasant." You've got it the wrong way round.'

'I've got a touch of the collywobbles at the thought of taking my first class. I dare say I'll be better by dinnertime.'

'I've made up some cheese sandwiches, and I've included a nice apple. An apple for the teacher.' She sounded as nervous as he did.

He put on his best clothes, such as they were – a pair of new grey flannels, a white shirt and tie, and a double-breasted jacket borrowed from Les's demob outfit – without his permission, of course.

'Eeeh, you do look smart,' Mam said. 'Fancy! Our kid a teacher! You've done us right proud, son. Here's a little present me and your father clubbed together to get you. When you started at Damian College, I forgot to buy you a satchel. Remember? Well, we haven't forgotten this time for your first day at school.' She handed over a smart briefcase with his initials embossed in gold.

'Gosh, thanks, Mam,' he said, kissing her on the cheek – a rare thing for anyone in their family to do. They weren't the gushing type. 'It can hold my sandwiches and the apple for a start.'

'You make sure you teach 'em proper now. And do be careful on that there bike,' she called as Billy went through the door.

He carried his Raleigh into Smedley Road and pedalled his way through the morning traffic, breathing in bus exhaust fumes along the way. He reached Albert Square, then went along Princess Street to Longsight. He dismounted at Wellington Grove and turned into Grimshaw Street, a narrow back street which led to a massive solid Victorian edifice built in red sandstone. It had a forbidding, unfriendly aspect, as did the dilapidated noticeboard displaying the title: ST ANSELM'S INDUSTRIAL SCHOOL FOR BOYS 1888.

This can't be it, he thought. He had been led to believe that the school was a much smaller affair. He crossed a large quadrangle and found a smaller broken-down outbuilding labelled 'St Anselm's Elementary School'. Through the gateway came a beefy, rosy-cheeked lad. He has the map of Ireland written across his features, Billy mused. The boy was dressed in corduroy trousers, a threadbare shirt, and a cardigan that had seen better days. He was chewing gum vigorously.

'Can you tell me where I can find the head?' Billy asked.

'You mean Mr Wakefield? Yeah. His office is at the top of the fire escape,' he replied, his jaws working overtime. 'I'll show you where it is.'

'Right, thanks,' Billy said. 'What's your name, by the way?'

'Joe Duffy. Why? I haven't done nothing.'

'I didn't say you had, Joe. But why aren't you in class?'

'We haven't got no teacher – so I'm acting as Wakefield's monitor, like.'

'What does that involve, Joe?'

'Running his errands and that. Put on a bet. Go for his cakes or his fags, you know.'

Together they climbed the fire escape, their feet resounding metallically on the iron steps. At the top of the stairway there was a dirty brown door from which the paint was peeling and on which was pinned a card bearing in green ink the instruction: 'Headmaster's Office. Knock and Wait.'

Joe Duffy did as it said.

'Yes, yes, come in,' called an impatient, tobacco-cured voice.

'Someone to see you, sir,' Joe Duffy announced importantly.

The head looked up from the letter he was writing. 'Who is it, Joe?' he asked irritably.

'Don't know, sir. He didn't say,' Joe answered, glancing impishly at Billy.

'Tell him to come in, for God's sake. And Joe, you can go for my messages. Here's half-a-crown – get me twenty Players and three cream buns. And don't be all day about it.'

'Right, sir. Do you want me to put a bet on for you while I'm out?'

'Not now, Joe,' the head replied testily. 'See me at dinnertime.'

Joe gave Billy a conspiratorial wink as he departed on his errand.

Billy entered and found an extremely small office, bare except for a small table, behind which sat a powerfully built man with a pockmarked, weather-beaten face in which were set two protruding eyes like two poached eggs, and a small, misshapen pug nose. He'd have won no prize in a beauty competition but he was a perfect model for a Toby jug.

Frank Wakefield stood up and held out his hand. Billy felt the firm grip and the rough, flaky skin of his palm.

'You must be Mr Hopkins,' Wakefield said warmly as he settled back in his chair. 'Father Kelly told us to expect you. I'm Mr Wakefield, the head.'

'Pleased to meet you. Yes, I met Father Kelly last Friday. He's offered me a provisional appointment to be confirmed when I pass the Religious Certificate.' Billy was still unsure of himself.

'The Religious Certificate indeed! What nonsense! Just teach the catechism and you'll have no problems.'

'I had a good grounding in the catechism at my elementary school.'

'Very well,' he said, smiling with his eyes. 'What is prayer?'

'The raising up of the mind and heart to God.'

'Right! What is God?' He was still smiling that funny smile.

'God is the supreme spirit who alone exists of himself and is infinite in all perfections.'

'You'll do,' he said, nodding his head. 'Father Kelly doesn't live in the real world. Doesn't know what a shortage of teachers there is. As far as I'm concerned, you've just passed the Certificate.'

'I also met Miss Andrews, the head of the infants' school,' Billy added, still a little puzzled by the lack of formality. Wakefield scowled when he heard the name.

'Andrews! Don't mention that name in my presence. All top show and no substance. All fur coat and no . . . never mind. Best to change the subject before I blow a gasket. Anyway, welcome to the school. I'd ask you to sit down if we had another chair and even if we did, there wouldn't be enough room. Sit down on the edge of the table for the time being.'

Reassured by the warmth of his welcome, Billy sat down as directed. Offering a cigarette which Billy readily accepted, the head gave him a rundown on the school.

'We're a small school of two hundred pupils in eight classes. No school building as such, only a bomb site at present but there are big plans for the future.'

'Big plans?' Billy asked, leaning forward. It was the first he'd heard of them.

Wakefield puffed on his fag. 'The nineteen forty-four Education Act has decreed that we shall drop the Elementary School title and our senior department will become a Secondary Modern whilst the junior section will be housed in a brand new building which is still on the architect's drawing board.'

'Sounds exciting, Mr Wakefield. Will you be the head of one of these new schools?' Billy looked round for an ashtray but could see none. The ash on his cigarette was becoming embarrassingly long.

Wakefield's face became serious. 'Hope so. Miss Andrews has her eye on the junior school but I don't think she stands a chance. Who wants a headmistress that smells

164

like the Gaumont cinema? Anyway, that's in the future. Today we have no building.' Noticing the long ash of Billy's cigarette, he pushed forward the lid of a tobacco tin. 'Use this – it's all we've got.'

'What were the huge buildings I passed on my way in?' Billy asked.

'Not ours, I'm afraid. They used to be the famous, or infamous, Industrial School but now they're about to be taken over by the NFS – the National Fire Service.'

'So we are restricted to this small outbuilding?'

'We are split between this building and some new prefab huts. Half the school is here in this dump and it's a damned dangerous place to teach kids – we've got dangling wires and loose timbers everywhere. The other half is about ten minutes' walk away in the prefabs which were originally intended for domestic science. As you can imagine, we're not popular with Wellington Grove School since we've taken over their nice new huts but we have no choice. I suppose you'd still call us an All-Age School – our children range from seven to fourteen, though the school leaving age has, as you know, been raised recently to fifteen.'

Billy stubbed out his cigarette on the make-do ashtray and then raised the question uppermost in his mind. 'Which class did you have in mind for me, Mr Wakefield?'

'You will be given the top class of fourteen to fifteen-years olds – boys and girls.'

Billy's heart skipped a beat. He couldn't believe what he was hearing.

'The top class! Do you think I have enough experience, Mr Wakefield? I mean, I'm new to teaching. I'm nineteen years of age.'

Wakefield smiled warmly. 'Perfect,' he replied. 'You'll be only four years older than some of the pupils. You'll understand and relate to 'em better than any of us old 'uns.'

Still not sure, Billy asked, 'Which subjects will I be teaching?'

'All of 'em,' he replied, looking intently at Billy. 'Except art, which I shall take, and science – such as it is, since we don't have a laboratory – taken by Mr Grundy. This will give you two double periods free each week to get on with your marking and preparation. Now I'm going to be busy over here this morning and the rest of the week, so I'll let Joe Duffy, my monitor, take you over to the prefabs and show you where your new class is. I'll come over later and see how you've got on. You'll find books and stationery in the storeroom cupboard. Joe'll show you.' He stood up to indicate the discussion was over. Billy moved towards the door.

Wakefield stopped him for a moment. 'Here is a new register for you,' he said. 'Make sure you treat it with the greatest respect as His Majesty's Inspectors will want to examine it, if and when they come to see us. Fairly straightforward. Simply fill in the details. By the way, are you in the Boy Scouts?'

'No. Sorry,' Billy said, disappointed in himself as he wanted to please his new boss.

The Toby jug frowned his regret. 'Rugby? Do you play rugby?'

'No. Sorry,' he said again, feeling that in some vague way he'd let the side down by not being a rugby-playing scout.

'Pity,' Wakefield replied.

Billy wondered if he had any more strange questions or surprises in store for him. He had.

'One last thing. I have no office in the prefab annexe. I

166

hope you don't mind but I've set up my desk at the back of your class and will work from there.'

'You mean you'll be sitting in on all my lessons?' asked Billy, aghast.

'Not all of 'em but many of them. Maybe I'll learn something from you.'

The thought flitted through Billy's mind that he could still apply for another job since there was a general shortage. Some of the other schools in middle-class districts like Didsbury or Fallowfield had better buildings, better equipment, better facilities. St Aidan's had a vacancy as Potts had gone into the army. He dismissed the thought of changing as unworthy and decided to take his chances.

Still in a state of mild shock, he found Joe Duffy, back from Wakefield's errand, listening at the door. Joe had a ring of cream round his mouth and, after depositing the head's shopping and his change on the desk, joined Billy outside the office.

'Right, Joe, let's go,' Billy said, trying to muster some semblance of authority. 'Did you enjoy the cream bun, by the way?' Billy asked.

'Me? Cream bun? Not me! I haven't had no cake. The buns were for Mr Wakefield.'

Billy smiled to himself. It wasn't so long since he'd been an adolescent himself.

There was a drizzle in the air when they got outside. As they crossed the playground, they met a hefty, corpulent, bearded teacher dressed in a smart military raincoat. He was holding up a large umbrella and was surrounded by thirty children who were awaiting his instructions.

'Right,' he boomed, addressing the gang of kids, 'all of you, to that wall – run!' He pointed to a wall about four hundred yards away. 'You must be the new teacher,' he bellowed, spotting Billy. 'I'm Gregory Callaghan, class teacher to Junior Three. The kids here call me Calor Gas but you can call me Greg. For our sins, my brother Alex and I teach at this academy of learning. Nice to meet you.'

Billy accepted the firm handshake happily.

'You'll like it here,' Greg said, making it sound like a command. 'We're fairly easy-going. Don't stand on ceremony.'

'You're the PE specialist here, are you?'

He gave a loud guffaw. 'Good God! Me, PE specialist? We don't specialise here, old man. We are Jacks-of-all-trades. Polymaths. You name it, we teach it.'

'Doesn't the rain bother you?' Billy asked.

'Not at all. Doesn't bother any of us. We do our drill in all weathers. Toughens the kids up.'

By this time, his PT class was back, clamouring around him, waiting for the next order.

'Right! To that wall over there – go!' he barked, indicating the opposite wall about five hundred yards distant. Whooping like Red Indians, the class ran pell-mell to their objective. Billy wondered if Greg had ever studied the 1933 Syllabus on how to take a PE lesson.

'You'll find Wakefield is firm but fair, but don't get on the wrong side of him,' he roared. 'It would be a distinct advantage to your career prospects if you joined the Boy Scouts or played rugby for Wigan. Which class has he given you?'

'The top class, I think,' Billy answered diffidently.

'He's handed you the poisoned chalice! And may the Lord have mercy on your soul!' Greg bawled. 'Talk to you later in the staffroom at break.'

His wards were back tugging at his sleeve. Joe Duffy and Billy left them to it.

'Yes, yes,' they heard him growl. 'Now run over to the main gate and back.'

The objectives he set them appeared to be more and more challenging, more and more distant, and obviously designed less to provide health-giving exercise than to give him a longer period of respite from their clamouring demands.

They walked a little way down Wellington Grove, and Billy began to feel more and more nervous the nearer they got to the school annexe. He could feel his heart thumping against his ribs. He talked trivialities to Joe Duffy to hide his inward fear, his confidence ebbing with every stride he took. Greg Callaghan's benediction was the second time he'd been warned about what he had let himself in for. Would he be able to cope? he wondered. This wasn't any old teaching practice. This was for real. And what did he mean by 'he's handed you the poisoned chalice'?

They reached a small back entry, and veered left until they came to an open space and the prefabs. There were two buildings, one long, one short, but both resembling army barracks. Both were fully populated, the longer building by young children and their teachers, all of whom seemed hard at work. Through the windows of the smaller, it was a different scene, and it was into this that they now turned. As they opened the door, the racket of twenty youths bawling and shouting assaulted their ears. The young hooligans who were to make up his class were engrossed in their own occupations: two boys rolling on the floor appeared to be practising Sumo wrestling, another group had formed a pontoon-playing quartet; a couple of boys played hangman at the blackboard; several girls were employing the time primping up each other's coiffures whilst others simply sat around, feet on chairs, manicuring nails, reading comics like *Film Fun, Dandy, Girl's Crystal* or simply browsing through back numbers of *Picturegoer*.

As Billy entered the room, one or two pupils looked up lazily from their games, yawned, and resumed their activity. The word 'pupil' gave the impression they were children but young adults would have been more correct.

The young rowdies were not wearing school uniform and yet there was a sameness about their dress and appearance. For the boys, short, quiffed hair styles, T-shirts and corduroys were the order of the day, whilst the girls had adopted their own distinctive mode of tight skirts and jumpers with identical hairstyles based on the Hollywood heart-throb of the day, Rita Hayworth. There was one exception – one deviant girl had modelled herself on Veronica Lake with a peek-a-boo hairstyle.

The class continued to ignore Billy.

'Right,' he ordered. 'Sit down and be quick about it.'

The class looked up but made no move.

'Are you deaf or something? I said sit down!'

'Why should we?' a red-haired lad asked.

'Because I said so!' Billy yelled. 'That's why. Now move. Or maybe you'd like to go and see Mr Wakefield.'

'I'm petrified,' he said, grinning cheekily.

'I didn't catch your name,' said Billy.

'That's because I didn't throw it,' he answered, smirking.

Billy saw that he couldn't win this competition.

It was Joe Duffy who commanded their attention. 'Hey! Quiet, you lot! This is our new teacher.'

A plump girl detached herself from her manicuring clique and addressed Billy. 'Are you permanent or supply? Only we had enough of bloody supply teachers last year. Most of our teachers only come here for the money.'

Some money, Billy thought. Twenty pounds a month.

Five pounds a week – that's my salary.

The rest of the class now noticed his presence and abandoned their activities for the moment to examine him. Suddenly they were firing questions and comments.

'How long are you here for?'

'You're too young to be a teacher!'

'Are we having you instead of Grumpy Grundy? That'd be great.'

'If we'd got that bastard Grundy,' observed the red-haired boy, 'I definitely would not be coming to school. I'd play wag every day.'

Billy wondered if obscene language was a normal part of their vocabulary. On this occasion, he said nothing. He walked over to the single-seater high desk but did not sit down. He gazed out over the faces before him and waited until he had their full attention. Ever so gradually, the groups began to break up and return to their places, girls on one side, boys on the other. When everyone had settled down, Billy addressed them, hoping that his jittery nerves were not too obvious. He cleared his throat.

'I'm your new teacher. You'll address me by my name – Mr Hopkins – or if you prefer it, sir.'

'You mean you're called Sir Hopkins?' said the grinning ginger-haired lad.

'Very funny, I'm sure,' said Billy. 'Anyway, this is the way you spell it.'

He printed out his name on the blackboard, ignoring the dictum they'd drummed into him at college – 'Never turn your back on the class'. But he couldn't see the point in showing distrust so early in the game. He seemed to have judged right, for nothing happened. It's going like clock-work, he thought. Well, almost.

'Let me make one thing clear,' he continued. 'You will

cut out bad language and you will never make that bar-
barous row in my classroom ever again.'

They stared back at him defiantly.

'Who the bloody hell does he think he is?' somebody
said in a stage whisper.

'No talking,' Billy commanded.

'Get this guy,' said another lad. 'He's going to play the
hard man.'

Billy ignored the remark.

'Occupy yourself with something more worthwhile than
I have seen up to now,' Billy commanded. 'Then each of
you come up to me one by one and give me your personal
details for the register.' This isn't so bad, he thought. I'm
handling it OK up to now. Playing it by the book.

He spent the first part of the morning collecting their
names, addresses, and dates of birth, and entering them in
the new register, thinking to himself that calligraphy was
the one skill in which he could boast a great deal of
experience after his purgatorial period filling out con-cards
in the Inland Revenue office. He discovered that most of
the pupils hailed from the Napoleonically named streets
along Wellington Grove (with a mysterious concentration
in Victory Street) and that all had been born in the year
1932–3, making them fourteen to fourteen and a half years
of age.

When this chore had been completed, Joe Duffy raised
his hand.

'Mr Wakefield made me the class monitor.'

'Yeah, Wakefield's lap dog,' someone called.

'Enough of that,' Billy said sternly. 'What does class
monitor mean, Joe? Surely not more bets and fags?'

'I sit near the Aga boiler here at the back, and I have to
keep it going by putting in coal every hour.'

The Veronica Lake girl with the sleepy eyes raised her hand.

'And I'm the tea monitor,' she said. 'I make the tea for the staff at playtime and at dinnertime.'

'Your name is?' Billy asked.

'Irene Moody,' she answered huskily, giving him the glad eye. 'I'd better go and put the kettle on.'

'How old are you, Irene?'

'Old enough, sir,' she leered salaciously, flashing her eyes and grinning to her friends.

I can see the family resemblance, Billy thought, remembering her short-skirted sister who had propositioned him with a 'quickie' the previous week.

'Very well, Irene,' Billy answered, ignoring the innuendo. 'You may go and make the tea. I don't want to earn the hostility of the staff on my first day.'

It was an unusual classroom to say the least – well-equipped but not with the kind of equipment he could make use of. Along one wall were a number of sink units complete with running water and draining boards. On the other side of the room were four gleaming electric cookers spaced at equal intervals, and at the back in a small fenced-off section was the large boiler Joe Duffy had spoken of. It was obviously Joe's pride and joy. The classroom had been custom-built for domestic science and one could well understand the frustration of Wellington Grove School at being deprived of this state-of-the-art facility. But as a normal teaching classroom, it left much to be desired.

After filling out the register, he took out sheets of card from the storeroom cupboard, and spoke to the class.

'You know my name but it will take me some little time to learn yours. You can help me by filling in a card with your name and placing it on your desk like business executives. Fold it in half so it looks like a Toblerone chocolate bar – if you've ever seen one. Make sure you print clearly the name by which you like to be known.'

A forest of hands went up.

'Got no pen.'

'No ink.'

'Got no blotting paper.'

'Write in pencil.'

'Got no pencil neither.'

They're just trying to be awkward, Billy said to himself. Fortunately he had anticipated this eventuality and prepared a set of emergency pencils ready sharpened. He congratulated himself on his forethought. I'm in control of the situation, he told himself, but this lot really do need to be spoon-fed.

'Don't forget to return the pencils,' he reminded the recipients.

All heads bowed as they filled out their cards. Some frowned and bit the ends of their pencils. One or two had considerable trouble writing their names. They stuck out their tongues, screwed up their faces into Quasimodo expressions, and squirmed uncomfortably in their seats as they painstakingly printed out their titles. Like my dad, thought Billy, when he's writing one of his rare letters.

While they were busy, Billy sketched a quick plan of their desk locations, intending to memorise them that night as soon as he got home – one of the invaluable tips he'd picked up at college. At least he could avoid addressing them as 'you' or the 'boy in the blue shirt'.

He looked at his watch. It was ten thirty.

'Break time!' Joe Duffy suddenly called. 'I have to ring the bell.' He produced a large heavy hand bell from under his desk and without more ado went outside where he began swinging it up and down.

'Now would one of you show me the way to the staffroom?' Billy said, addressing the class.

'Yes, Mr Hopkins sir. I'd love to show you the way,' said a pretty girl winking at her cronies.

'Your name?' Billy asked.

'Vera Pickles and no relation to Wilfred before you ask.'

Billy dismissed the class. 'OK, Vera,' he said. 'Let's go.'

Chapter Sixteen

Meet the Staff

Billy opened the door of the staffroom and was met by a smell like that of a saloon bar on a Saturday morning – a mixture of stale tobacco smoke and body sweat. There was clutter everywhere. Several tables were heaped with untidy stacks of exercise books seemingly abandoned in despair by their markers; in a corner lay discarded sports gear – soccer boots, a half-inflated football, a collection of odd gym shoes, table tennis bats, and a couple of broken hockey sticks. Confiscated comics and overflowing ashtrays dotted the room, and on one wall there was a row of coat pegs on which hung an assortment of coats, hats, and umbrellas. Piles of textbooks perched perilously on the edge of a central table, round which were arranged four wooden chairs, and about the room were scattered five or six rickety armchairs.

Being the first to arrive, Billy opened a window, and with a sigh of relief sat in the nearest easy chair.

'Not there, old man,' bellowed a stentorian voice which he recognised as that of Gregory Callaghan, the erstwhile running instructor.

'Why not? Is there something wrong?' Billy asked.

'I'll say there is. That's Grundy's chair. He'll play merry hell if he sees you in it.'

Anxious to please and not antagonise Grundy, Billy changed chairs quickly.

'Who's Grundy?' he asked.

'You'll find out soon enough,' Gregory said ominously. 'Now let me introduce my older brother. Our mother had ambitions for us and named us after popes. Anyway, this is Alexander. Older brother but not wiser. And certainly not Great. Alexander the Sixth, the poisoner, is more his style.'

Alex gave Billy a big smile and a firm handshake. His horn-rimmed spectacles gave him a faintly disdainful, intellectual look but his facial expression was cheerful and hearty.

'Welcome to St Anselm's,' he said. 'Call me Alex. I'm in charge of the remedial class. When I came to the school, they took one look at me and could see I was the remedial type right away. Take no notice of my brother there. He's planning to get married early next year and the thought of bedding a woman has affected his brain. And don't be put off by his sergeant-major voice. I always said it was a mistake to send him for those elocution lessons – thinks he's addressing a multitude the whole time.'

Alex's warmth and sincerity came through easily and Billy took a liking to him immediately.

'In our family,' said Gregory, 'the only way to get heard is to shout. One needs a loud-hailer or a public address system.'

'Thanks for the welcome, Alex,' Billy said, laughing. 'I'm finding it a bit daunting but everyone assures me I'll get used to it.'

177

'You will in time – that's the trouble,' Alex smiled. 'But what do we call you? We can't refer to you as Mr Hopkins, that's too formal.'

'Well, my family calls me Billy but my friends call me Hoppy.'

'Then Hoppy it is,' he replied, offering a cigarette from his case.

Gregory said, 'Better take it, Hoppy. It's the only one he'll ever offer. Notice how the moths flew out of the cigarette case. As for me, I prefer an intelligent man's smoke.' He took out the meerschaum pipe on which he was endeavouring to shape his personality. Now Billy knew why the staffroom smelt so musty.

The door opened to admit a white-haired, bespectacled lady, elegantly dressed and with her hair coiled matriarchally at the nape of her neck. She carried the inevitable portmanteau which seemed to be an indispensable accessory for the schoolmarm role.

'Good morning,' she said softly. 'I'm Miss O'Neill, the deputy head. We are so pleased to see you here at this school. We count ourselves lucky to get you as there's still such a desperate shortage of teachers in the country.'

Before Billy could respond, a short middle-aged woman, around fifty and of mannish appearance, strode into the room. Her plain face was free of cosmetics, and her grey hair was cut in a short style, which matched her severe two-piece suit. She stood with legs apart, hands on hips.

'Let me introduce Miss Elizabeth Logie,' said Miss O'Neill.

'Pleased to meet you. Call me Liz,' the newcomer barked.

'Likewise. I mean, pleased to meet you. I'm Hoppy,' Billy answered.

'You'll have to speak up as she's a little deaf,' said Miss O'Neill.

'Nonsense,' snapped Miss Logie, lighting up a small decorated pipe which gave off the pungent aroma of Turkish tobacco. 'I can hear perfectly well when my deaf-aid is switched on. Besides, I can lip-read.'

Billy wondered how she coped in a school like this. The girls in the top class, he thought, would make mincemeat of her.

Next came Mrs Sybil Melton-Mowbray, tall, angular, hearty and bespectacled, with a red, scrubbed-looking face.

'I'm pleased to meet you,' said Billy offering his hand. 'Isn't your name—'

'A town in Leicestershire,' she said. 'My hubby's name is Melton and mine's Mowbray. When we met, he said it was fate had thrown us together and we were destined to be joined together. A marriage made in heaven. Jolly romantic, what?'

'Certainly unusual,' said Billy.

'Jolly nice to have a new face,' she chortled. 'Don't be put off by the staff comm – it's not very homey-from-homey, what? I know when I first came here I was jolly depressed when I saw it. The whole place is in need of a spot of jollification, if you ask me. Not like my old school – we had a spiffing den there.'

She seemed so out of place in St Anselm's, Billy wondered how she had come to be there.

She seemed to read his thoughts, for she said, 'Emergency trained, don'cha know. Ex-ATS and all that. Used to work in Cheltenham but moved up North when my dear old hubby was posted here. Came a year ago when old Wakefield interviewed me and appointed me as his third mistress. I teach Senior One and take the gals for netters.'

'Finally, let me introduce Miss Mackenzie,' continued the deputy head, moving on.

Billy turned to look at the young lady before him and his heart skipped a beat. She was the most beautiful girl he had ever set eyes on. A kind, gentle face, neat nose and mouth, dimples, and there was about her a quiet, refined elegance. Her soft nut-brown hair was tied back with a red ribbon. But it was her large, round, hazel eyes with their faint hint of sadness that captured Billy's attention – they seemed to reflect inner calmness and tranquillity. The kind of eyes that brought out his protective instincts.

'Laura is fairly new here,' whispered Miss O'Neill. 'She started at the end of last term when she was kind enough to help us out by taking Junior Two.'

Laura Mackenzie turned to Billy and gave him a warm, friendly smile. 'Nice to meet you and welcome to the school.' She held out her hand. 'I hope you'll be happy here.' She had a young, fresh voice with a hint of a Scottish lilt.

Like Dante's meeting with Beatrice, it was love at first sight. A hackneyed phrase but nevertheless true. Billy fell without a shot being fired and in that instant, all thoughts of Adele, ballroom dancing, worries about the new job and his unruly class were consigned to limbo.

He swallowed hard, and almost forgot to take her hand. 'So pleased to meet you,' he mumbled. Her hand was soft and warm. 'How do you like it here?' he asked. It was the best he could manage.

'I've only been here a short time,' she said quietly, 'but I like it very much – I've found the children and the staff easy to get on with.'

'You'll have to be careful what you say to Laura,' Liz

Logie said, laughing. 'Her father is a school governor.'

'Merely a nominal post,' said Laura Mackenzie. 'I don't think the governors have even met yet.'

Irene Moody entered the room carrying a large heavy teapot. Remembering college lectures on 'Teacher and the Law', Billy thought if she had an accident and scalded herself, there'd be hell to pay and this school would be sued for all it had got. Irene, however, didn't seem worried and even found time to give Billy the sleepy, slinky look he had seen earlier. That one could be big trouble, he said to himself.

'Help yourself to tea,' said Miss O'Neill.

'Any drink you want,' bellowed Greg, 'as long as it's tea.'

Billy went up to the table and joined the queue for tea. He looked over the selection of mugs and picked out an attractive one bearing an outline of Winston Churchill – it was one of the few not chipped.

'Not that one, old man,' bellowed Greg Callaghan.

'Don't tell me,' Billy said, a little exasperated. 'It's Grundy's cup.'

'Got it first time,' Greg laughed, slapping him on the back.

'How can you be so sure it's Grundy's cup?' Billy asked, his hackles rising.

'Because it says so underneath, old man. Look under the cup.'

Billy did so and there, printed on an Elastoplast strip, were the words: GRUNDY'S CUP. HANDS OFF.

Billy chose another cup – a chipped one. He wondered if he dared take a biscuit. Perhaps they were Grundy's. He decided to chance it and opted for a chocolate variety.

'Sorry again, old man,' said Greg, this time quietly –

that is, quietly for Greg, which was in fact loud.

'Grundy's biscuits?' Billy sighed resignedly.

'No, just for once. You have to join the biscuit club – chocolates are an extra threepence a week over the digestives. Sixpence a week will cover it. You have to tell Miss O'Neill which kitty you wish to join. You'll soon learn the routine.'

Billy was learning fast. Decisions, decisions, he thought. He determined to lash out and join the ChocBikky group.

He looked around for a teaspoon.

'There's only one spoon,' chuckled Alex, handing him a tannin-stained spoon. 'You have to wait your turn. Grundy has one of his own but he carries it with him in his waistcoat pocket.'

Billy wondered if it was the right time to inquire about arrangements for dinner.

'Most of the staff go out for dinner,' Miss O'Neill told him, 'but Mr Wakefield and I have sandwiches in the staffroom. You're welcome to join us.'

Then in he came – Grundy! The capitalist who had cornered the market in chairs and cups.

Billy didn't know why but he'd expected a big hairy man who would tower over everybody. He couldn't have been more wrong. Grundy was a diminutive man with a pencil moustache and a nervous tic. He smiled, showing a set of ill-fitting false teeth the colour of Cheddar cheese. Obviously needs a new set of dentures, Billy thought.

Grundy picked up his Churchill mug of tea, stirred it with his personal spoon, then collected a chocolate biscuit and flopped down in his chair.

'They're all daft,' he bayed. 'I don't know why we bother trying to teach 'em anything. Science – that's what I'm supposed to be selling. Waste of time.'

'What's happened now?' asked Greg.

'I've been trying to get across Archimedes' principle to Senior Three. I asked 'em why big heavy ships at sea don't sink. Tracy McFadden reckons it's because the sea is so deep and strong it holds them up. So I asked her how come that they float when they're in shallow dock. That's why they have to tie them up, she says. To stop 'em from sinking. We may as well try to teach nuclear physics to a bunch of chimpanzees.' He sniggered at his own wit.

He noticed Billy.

'Hello, hello,' he murmured. 'What have we here? New blood. Fresh meat?'

'I have been given a provisional appointment,' Billy said.

'Appointment, by George! Not an ordinary job like ours! And provisional, he says. Why provisional?' he asked.

'Provisional until I obtain a Catholic Teachers' Religious Certificate.'

'What nonsense! Wakefield doesn't mind what you teach as long as you remember to clear up the milk bottles and put the chairs on the desks at the end of school.'

'Why is that?' Billy asked.

'So that the caretaker can sweep the classroom. You can teach the Koran and the Torah if you like but whatever you do, don't forget to put the chairs up and to clear away the bottles. Wakefield's more scared of the caretaker than of HM Inspectors.'

'Understandably,' said Liz Logie, puffing heartily on her pipe. 'The caretaker has power over life and death. Get on the wrong side of him and there'll be no heat in the school and the wastepaper baskets won't get emptied.'

'Anyway,' continued Grundy, 'our new friend here has the

183

top class, so I've been told. What a bloody waste of time that is, raising the school leaving age for that dumb lot. Officialdom seems to forget that we are part of the elementary school system – the dustbins of the educational world. Our job is to keep the lids firmly closed on the bins and to keep the rubbish off the streets. The bright kids go to grammar or technical schools and we're left with the dross.'

Billy wondered how the staffroom would have reacted had he rushed at Grundy, tipped his chair backwards, gouged his eyes out, and plucked out the bristles of his revolting miniature moustache one by one with a pair of tweezers.

'Surely you're not serious,' Billy exclaimed.

'Oh, aren't I?' replied Grundy, a sneer curling his lips. 'Your college taught you that these kids are no good at academic things but they're good with their hands. Twaddle! We know what these kids would like to do with their hands all right. So some bright civil servants in Whitehall thought up these places and hired idiots like us to sit on the lids and keep 'em quiet. That's your job – keeping the lid on. Better to kick 'em out at fourteen and make 'em earn their living in the jungle out there is what I say.'

Rather than tear out his hideous moustache, thought Billy, it might be better to yank out his revolting false teeth and flush them down the toilet.

He resisted the temptation and instead said, 'People said the same thing when the government raised the school leaving age from twelve to fourteen in nineteen eighteen. Factory owners reckoned they needed the tiny hands to keep the wheels of industry turning. There was even a deputation of actors who claimed that Shakespeare plays requiring child actors would no longer be possible if the age was raised.'

'That was for children of twelve – now it's a different kettle of fish. They're fourteen.'

'Surely at fourteen they're still kids,' Billy protested. He could feel himself getting hot under the collar. 'They'll stand a much better chance of getting on in the world if they've had a better training, a better education.' What a surprise, Billy thought. Taffy's lectures on the philosophy of education are beginning to pay dividends at last!

'Watch out, watch out!' Grundy whinnied. 'Here he comes, the idealist straight out of college with his new-fangled ideas. I've only been teaching twenty years and so what do I know? Why, the ink on your certificate isn't even dry yet, mate. You wait till you've had Senior Four for a year, you'll change your tune.'

'If he ends up anything like you,' snapped Liz, her eyes flashing, her nostrils flaring, 'heaven help us. You keep your ideals, Hoppy. God knows we need a few people with ideals in this world of ours.'

'Huh, we know your teaching ideals, Liz,' sneered Grundy. 'Send out the kids to do your shopping for you on Friday afternoon. Practical maths, she calls it. It'll be God help you if one of 'em gets run over.'

'At least I don't belt the living daylights out of them like you do with that strap of yours,' Liz Logie snorted. 'You should have got a job in a concentration camp. And even with your whippings and your beatings you can't control your classes.'

'You know what they say,' Grundy retorted. 'Spare the rod and spoil the child.'

'That went out in the eighteenth century about the time we stopped drawing and quartering people,' said Miss O'Neill sweetly.

'A great pity they ever did,' said Liz, looking pointedly at Grundy.

'I can't believe the kids are anywhere as bad as you're making out,' Billy said, addressing Grundy. 'You have to give them a chance.'

'Great,' replied Grundy. 'By all means, give 'em a chance but never turn your back on them, that's all.'

'Well, I did this morning,' said Billy, 'and I'm still here to tell the tale.'

'Beginner's luck,' said Grundy. 'You took 'em by surprise – they weren't ready. Wait a day or two.'

'Take no notice of him, Hoppy,' said Liz Logie. 'He exaggerates and he's trying to frighten you. You've got to adjust your teaching methods to suit your pupils and you'll be fine.'

'That's a laugh,' said Grundy. 'There's no teaching or learning in this place. Our pupils don't want to learn. It's every man for himself. Survival of the fittest.'

'Or as Oscar Wilde put it,' said Alex, 'survival of the vulgarest.'

'I'm optimistic,' said Billy. 'I think adolescents respond to the right approach.'

'And the best of British luck,' said Grundy. 'How on earth did you end up in a dump like this, I'd like to know.'

'Influence,' said Billy.

This intellectual debate ended with Duffy's bell-ringing.

'The bells of hell go ting-a ling, ling. For you but not for me,' Greg sang. 'You see, I have a free period,' he added.

'Don't ask for whom the bell tolls,' declaimed Alex. 'It tolls for thee.'

'Best of luck with your class, Hoppy,' Laura Mackenzie called in a warm, friendly tone.

Billy's heart skipped a beat.

'Thanks, Miss Mackenzie,' he said. 'From what people have been telling me, I'm going to need it.'

Chapter Seventeen

Cold Reception

After break, Billy stood in front of Senior 4 and waited until they had settled down. I'll treat them as equals, he thought. Adopting a friendly, informal approach, he addressed them.

'As you know, I'm new to the school – new to teaching – and so I hope you'll have patience if I put my foot in it or say the wrong thing. I don't know anything about you and if I'm to teach you properly, I need to find out what you can do and what your abilities are. So I propose to give you some short tasks which will give me an idea of your capabilities.'

One of the boys, a tall, athletic lad, raised his hand. Billy consulted the cardboard tag on his desk.

'Jim Mitchell. What's your question?'

'Look, let's get one thing straight from the start. We hate this dump. Nearly everyone in this class would have left school this year if it hadn't been for this sodding government raising the leaving age to fifteen. My dad had a good job lined up for me as a decorator's apprentice and now I've got to waste another bloody year doing the same old thing. We're sick of it. We've learnt nowt at this school.'

This short speech prompted a series of shouts, cries, and catcalls which threatened to get out of hand.

'Quiet, quiet!' Billy called.

Vera Pickles, the pretty dark-haired girl, joined in the protest. 'I had a good job at Lewis's as a shop assistant and now I've lost it. We can't see the point in staying another year in this dive.'

There was a general murmur of agreement amongst the rest of them.

'OK, OK,' Billy said. 'Keep your shirts on. I get the point. But what do you want me to do? I don't make the laws of the country. But who knows? You might get an even better job at fifteen than at fourteen. No more arguments. Right now, I want to see what you can do.'

Jim Mitchell gave a deliberately loud yawn.

'Let's try reading for a start,' Billy said a little desperately. 'I notice you have copies of *Gulliver's Travels* in the stockroom. Joe, give them out.'

Joe Duffy got out twenty-five tatty, dog-eared books.

'Right, cop for this,' he shouted, flinging books along the rows. There was an opening and banging of desk lids, calling out of names and general mayhem ensued. Once again, the situation was getting out of control.

'I said give them out not throw them,' Billy shouted, taking the books from Joe.

Billy noticed a boy in the front row. He was smiling an idiotic, vacant smile and he stared back at Billy blankly.

'What are you grinning at?' asked Billy irritably. 'See something funny, do you?'

The lad continued smiling.

'What's your name?'

'Dempsey. I haven't done nothin'.'

'Well, Dempsey. What's the big joke? Why are you grinning like a jackass?'

'He grins all the time,' said Mitchell. ' 'Cos he's not all there.' He tapped his temple with his index finger. 'Nobody at home upstairs.'

'That's right. No use asking him,' added Tessie Shea, the tubby one. 'He's as daft as a brush. All the boys in this class are thick. Better to ask a girl.'

'Shut your ugly face, Shea,' bawled Mick Lynch, the red-haired lad with the pink eyes. 'You girls make us sick. All stuck up. Can't think of anything except doing up your hair.'

'Grow up, Lynch,' shrieked Nellie Wallace, a tall, gangly girl. 'You boys are like a bunch of snotty-nosed kids.'

Billy thought it time to intercede in this inter-sex slanging match. 'That's enough of that. If you're going to survive in this rotten old world of ours, you must learn to tolerate each other. Now I want to hear for myself what Alf Dempsey can do.'

Alf began hesitatingly and stumbled through each word by sounding it out syllable by syllable. It was painful to hear.

'HE p-u-t – PUT th-i-s – THIS en-gi-n-e – ENGINE to TO ow-er OUR ear EAR.' For Alf, reading was like stumbling through a minefield – every word an explosive danger. He had the reading age of a kid of six.

'How old are you, Alf?' Billy asked.

'Fourteen and a half, sir,' he replied.

'Did you have a job planned like the others?'

'Yeah. I was going to be a body builder and a boxer.'

There was a howl of laughter from the class.

'I think he means car body builder, sir,' said Des Bishop. 'And the only boxing he'll do will be in a biscuit factory.'

Billy tried two other boys' reading, Duffy, then Horner. They were equally bad. Every attempt was greeted by howls of derisive laughter from the rest of the class. He finally chose a bright-eyed, intelligent-looking girl by the name of Anne Greenhalgh.

She got to her feet, picked up the book and began reading clearly and fluently, her voice modulating beautifully to the sense of the passage. The rest of the class fell silent.

' "He put this engine (a watch) to our ears, which made an incessant noise like that of a water-mill, and we conjecture it is either some unknown animal, or the god that he worships; but we are more inclined to the latter opinion." '

'That's how it should sound,' Billy said quietly when she'd finished.

He had found out what he wanted to know.

He switched next to written English by giving them a simple dictation from the same book.

'This is an abridged version of *Gulliver's Voyage to Lilliput* by Jonathan Swift,' he announced. 'You'd enjoy reading about Lilliput,' he added.

His remark seemed to cause amusement, especially to two boys at the back who were convulsed with laughter. Billy wondered what he'd done that was so funny. He checked his flies – rule number one in college teaching practice sessions. He shrugged his shoulders. Perhaps the boys were simply moronic.

He read out the excerpt carefully in short phrases. ' "He,

the emperor, is taller by almost the breadth of my nail than any of his court, which alone is enough to strike awe into the beholders." '

Billy noted the great differences in the facility with which they did the exercise. For some, it was purgatory as with contorted facial expressions they twisted and turned in their seats in their effort to transcribe the passage. When they had finished, he collected the papers for marking that evening. The first of many home assignments to come.

Billy had half an hour left to dinnertime and he utilised this with a simple mental arithmetic lesson, using examples from everyday shopping.

'I went into a shop,' he began, 'and I bought a cabbage for sixpence ha'penny—'

'Then you were bloody well robbed for a start,' said Mike Lynch, interrupting him. 'Cabbages are only fourpence on my dad's barrow.'

The class rewarded his comments with the usual guffaws.

'Your dad's a costermonger?'

'A what? Wait till I tell him what he is. But yeah, I suppose that's what you'd call him. He's on Market Street, and I help him every Saturday, and God help me if I give the wrong change.'

'Don't question the prices, Mike. Simply add up the bill and calculate the change.' Billy continued with the arithmetic exercise.

Mike Lynch, whose reading was sub-standard, was like greased lightning when it came to working out a bill and the change due. Faster than Billy and there was a pause each time until he had caught up with him. This caused much amusement but Billy didn't mind. On the contrary, it was a cause for rejoicing that one of his learners could add and subtract so rapidly.

He kept them thus occupied until Duffy rang the dinner bell.

Lunchtime!

Deo gratias. Thanks be to God.

Billy told the class to stand for the Angelus but before he could begin, he saw that the two gigglers had raised the flap of their desk and were pointing out something inside to their immediate neighbours, causing great hilarity. Billy walked over and made them open the desk lid fully. The source of the helpless laughter was a copy of *Lilliput* magazine opened up at a picture of a nude with impossibly large breasts.

'We was only looking at our copy of *Lilliput*, sir,' leered Roger Horner, obviously the leader of the pair. 'You told us to take a look at Lilliput.'

'Put that disgusting magazine away,' Billy said severely, 'and I don't want to see anything like that in this class again. Otherwise . . .'

He left the threat unsaid. Mainly because he couldn't think of a suitable punishment and he also found it difficult in his heart to reproach Horner as sternly as he deserved. Billy had no room to talk – only five years earlier he had been going through a similar phase of adolescent development.

The class said the Angelus. 'The angel of the Lord declared unto Mary . . . And she conceived by the Holy Ghost . . .'

When the class had finally departed, Billy sat down at his high desk and put his head in his hands. What a morning, he thought. Resistance to his authority in his first encounter with the class. Could he last the pace?

Could he survive in this hostile environment?

Chapter Eighteen

Lunch Hour

In the lunch break, he walked over to the staffroom and found that Miss O'Neill had made dinner arrangements with a true woman's touch, having spread an embroidered cloth over the table and provided a small vase of flowers. She had laid three places with cutlery, plates and china teacups.

'Beautifully done, Miss O'Neill,' Billy remarked.

'Why, thank you,' she said. 'We try to make lunch a civilised affair and not like the free-for-all we seem to have at morning break.'

They sat down to lunch. Billy unwrapped his sandwiches and placed them on the small plate Miss O'Neill had provided. He lifted the top slice and was gratified to note that Mam had given him not only cheese but slices of tongue, specially bought for his first day.

Shortly after, they were joined by Frank Wakefield.

'Sorry I couldn't get across this morning,' he said, addressing Billy. 'Well, how did you get on with Senior Four?'

'Oh, not bad,' he replied. 'I know it's early days but I found out two important things about them.'

'And what are those?' he asked, now very interested.

'Well, first, there's tremendous resentment at being made to stay on at school for an extra year. I can well understand the way they feel.'

'Right,' he said, opening up his lunch box. 'And the second thing?'

'There are vast individual differences in their levels of intelligence and achievement. Some of the class are extremely bright but one or two of them are practically illiterate and innumerate. They'd have problems coping in the modern world. They could hardly read the instructions on the side of a can, or an electrical appliance, like a toaster or an iron. Could be dangerous in certain circumstances.'

'Some of them can't read very well because they have bad attendance records,' said Miss O'Neill as she poured the tea. 'It's hard to teach them anything if they're not here. When they come back after a long absence, the class has moved on and they're left way behind.'

'Everything you say is true but it's no good simply wringing our hands, we're stuck with the situation,' said Wakefield, slicing a tomato. 'More important, what do you propose we do about it?'

'Look, Mr Wakefield,' Billy said, 'I'm the beginner round here. I don't want to be thought arrogant trying to teach my grandma to suck eggs. Mr Grundy's already accused me of being an idealist with a head full of useless training college theories.'

'Never you mind what Grundy says,' retorted Wakefield. 'He's got problems of his own, has that one. He lives at home with only his aged sister and a cat for company. No wonder he's bitter and twisted. Sorry, Miss O'Neill, I wasn't implying that being unmarried makes you doolally but . . . well you know what Grundy's like. He's happy if he can make it to Friday at four o'clock without a confrontation. As for you being an idealist, Mr Hopkins, I'd take that as a compliment,' he said, munching his sandwich. 'But let's get back to the problem of Senior Four and their individual differences. Any ideas?'

'One thing's obvious,' Billy said. 'Class teaching is out. We have to devise a system which allows us to cater for the wide differences in their abilities. Whole class teaching means it's too easy for some and too hard for others.'

'I agree,' said Miss O'Neill, 'but we can't go round giving thirty separate lessons to each one of them. That would mean many of them would get too much attention and some would get none.'

'There's a plan I remember reading about at college . . . but I don't want you accusing me of trying to foist new-fangled ideas on you. It'd be hard work for me because it means drawing up an individual programme for each child – at least in the basic subjects of the three Rs.' Billy wondered if he was giving the impression of being a know-all.

He need not have worried, for Wakefield said, 'Sounds great. Can you work out some details for me to take a look at? To start things off, you'd better have a look at the syllabuses for your class – I'll let you have copies of them later.'

'Meanwhile,' Billy said, now warming to his subject, 'I'll give the class a few standardised tests in the basics and then go to work on producing work schedules for each pupil. I can see it will mean burning the midnight oil.'

'Great,' Wakefield said. 'Now let's stop this formality business of Mr Wakefield and Mr Hopkins. Call me Frank. What do we call you?'

'Hoppy,' chimed in Miss O'Neill. 'I heard Alex talking to you at break. And you can call me Norah,' she added bashfully.

'OK, Hoppy,' said Wakefield warmly. 'What about the other problem? Senior Four resentment. More intractable, I'd say. It's a case of motivation and low morale.'

'I may have one or two ideas on that but I'd rather hear your notions of what we can do to get them interested.'

Wakefield offered him a cigarette and they lit up together. Miss O'Neill began clearing away the dinner things.

'I'm not going to give you a sermon on education but I have definite views on what it's about. Education is so important. We've finished a world war and we know that to defend a country, you need an army, but to defend civilised values you need schools. Many of our kids come from poor homes where they're knocked about. I don't think we should simply continue this practice and so we keep corporal punishment down to an absolute minimum. Grundy, though, is the exception and I think he's too free with the strap. I know that kids can sometimes get up to serious mischief, in which case I don't hesitate to deal with it, but I think we should be sparing in the use of corporal punishment. The one piece of advice I want to give you is this. In the early days of your teaching, be strict. Be firm. Don't stand any nonsense from them. Show them who's boss from the start and you can relax the reins later.'

'The iron hand in the velvet glove?' said Billy.

'More like the velvet hand in the iron glove,' Wakefield laughed. 'Absolute firmness hiding a mild approach. These kids have to stay on an extra year and it's no use our doing the same things all over again. They have a right to expect something different, something more interesting and exciting. The word education comes from the root *e*, meaning out of, and *duco*, I lead. It means a leading out. For me education is a leading out of what is already there in the pupil's soul.' He offered Billy another cigarette and a light.

'I'm going to owe you a fortune in fags,' said Billy.

'Don't worry about it,' Wakefield replied. 'I know what it's like to be a young teacher starting out. For Grundy, education isn't drawing out but putting in something that's not there, and that's not education. If anything, it's intrusion from the Latin *trudo*, I thrust. Grundy's method is to thrust in a lot of data into the pupil's head as if they're empty vessels needing to be filled up; mine is leading out of knowledge, and that is true education.'

'In other words, developing their potential, bringing out the best in them,' said Billy, drawing on his cigarette.

'Exactly,' he replied. 'School isn't simply a place for stuffing their heads with facts and figures – which they'll soon forget anyway. No, it has more to do with preparing them for life on the outside and that includes their social and spiritual, as well as their intellectual, development. We've got to release their full potential, not just their mental abilities. In this sense, education is everyone's business and involves everything that living itself involves. Our job is to give them guidance in the greatest of all problems – the problem of living.'

'That's a pretty tall order,' said Billy, frowning a little in perplexity. 'How do we do all this in one year?'

'I'm not saying we can do it in a year but we can make a start by taking them out of the classroom and involving them with the world outside – show them the beauties of nature, the practices of other occupations, get them involved in the process of creating something, not merely imbibing useless information. There's more to teaching than mere instruction. The old idea was that children were so many receptacles and it was our job to cram the facts in.'

'Like Mr Gradgrind in *Hard Times*,' Billy said. ' "Now, what I want is, facts . . . facts alone are wanted in life. Plant nothing else and root out everything else." '

'That's it,' Wakefield laughed. 'What I should like to see with the top class is a situation where we take them beyond these four walls and out into the world – hiking in the hills, cycling in the country, visiting factories, and so on. Take them out into the community and bring the community in.'

'Wow!' Billy exclaimed. 'Are you sure I'm the man to do it, Mr Wakefield – Frank? I mean, I'm still wet behind the ears.'

'You're young and you're enthusiastic. I know you can do it,' he said earnestly. 'You're an idealist,' he added with a glint in his eye. 'And that's what we need, an idealist.'

'I hope I can come up to your expectations,' Billy said. 'From what you've been saying, it looks as if we need a two-pronged attack. First, individual work schedules, and secondly a programme of visits. This is going to keep me busy.'

'But very fulfilling,' said Wakefield. 'Now, this afternoon, I shall take your class for art in order to give you a chance to have a tour of the school and find your way around. I'm sure other members of staff will be glad to show you what's what.'

At least, thought Billy, I get a temporary stay of
execution before I have to face that bunch of savages again.

Chapter Nineteen

Grand Tour of the School

In the afternoon, as Frank Wakefield had suggested, Billy made a grand tour of the school by walking over to the NFS annexe. First on his list was Miss Logie.

'By all means, come in,' she cried when she saw him. 'Meet Senior Two. Show how polite you can be. Say good afternoon, Mr Hopkins.'

The class obeyed her instruction and Billy responded in kind.

'This lot are the daftest in the school,' she announced, looking affectionately at her pupils.

The boys and girls in the front row grinned good-humouredly.

'What are you?' she asked.

'Daft, miss. That's why we've got the daftest teacher,' one of them called loudly.

'That's enough from you, Morgan,' she replied. 'That one should have been a pirate like his namesake,' she said in an aside to Billy.

Liz obviously had an easy-going relationship with her wards.

'Here, Buccaneer Morgan,' she said suddenly. 'Show

201

Mr Hopkins that you're not a pirate and not as daft as you look. Go with Nancy there on to Stockport Road and do my shopping. Here's the list and the money. And make sure you get the change right. And don't get knocked down!'

The two pupils left the classroom with her shopping basket.

'As for the rest of you,' she shouted, looking from one side of the room to the other, 'get on with your compositions, "What I'd do if I won the Treble Chance", whilst I have a talk with Mr Hopkins here.'

'Don't you worry that the two shoppers might have an accident?' Billy asked.

'Accident? This lot? They're quicker-witted on the streets than the two of us put together. No, I believe in practical arithmetic. When they come back, we'll put the shopping list on the blackboard and they can calculate it as an exercise. Last week, I had them reading imaginary gas meters and calculating the bills.'

'You seem to have a good relationship with them,' said Billy, and he meant it.

'True, but don't let that fool you. I can be strict with them as well if necessary. What you saw is the result of many years' experience. I can be friendly with them but they know how far they can go. You see, I was brought up in this district myself and there's nothing they can tell me about it. Now you've got a tough job on your hands taking the top class. My advice to you is to sit on them right from the start. If you let them step all over you at the start, you'll find it hard to get control later. Whatever you do, don't try to curry favour with them or try to win the popularity stakes. Show them who's in charge and if you win them over, you can always ease up later on.'

'That's exactly what Frank Wakefield said,' Billy remarked.

'Great minds think alike. Be on your guard, though, especially with the girls – they're practically grown women and they know the ropes. You're a young, good-looking man and they'll try to take advantage. One last thing. Never, never lay a finger on any of them or they'll have you in court before you can say Sugar Ray Robinson.'

'I'll try to remember it,' said Billy as he left her classroom. 'I'll go and have a word with Mr Grundy.'

'You'll find Grundy's nasty with the kids. But one thing I'll say for him, he's always fair.'

'How do you mean, Liz?'

'He's equally nasty with all of them.'

Billy walked along the corridor until he reached Mr Grundy's classroom. As he opened the door, he noted the strange atmosphere – the absence of noise. Complete silence in a school classroom was not merely rare, it was unknown, unnatural even.

'Mind if I come in?' he called.

'Not at all!' replied Grundy. 'Always glad to put a newcomer straight and get him on the right track.' He turned to the class and hissed, 'Right, you lot, do Exercise Sixteen on percentages and I don't want to hear a word from any of you.'

At the front of the class, three boys were kneeling on the hard wooden floor before the blackboard. Another had his arms raised sideways as if playing at aeroplanes – though it was evident that he wasn't enjoying himself by the way his aching arms wobbled.

'Get those arms up,' Grundy commanded.

'What have they been up to?' inquired Billy.

'This quartet,' said Grundy pointing to the penitents, 'were talking when they should have been working. So, for their sins, they can experience a little inconvenience.'

'I see,' said Billy, meaning that he didn't. 'You believe in running a tight ship, as it were.'

'Too true. I'm a great believer in original sin – there's a lot of badness in these kids and it's up to us to knock it out of them. Some mornings I begin the day by strapping everyone in the class – one stroke each.'

'Irrespective of what they've done or haven't done?'

'Why not? It's just to let them know what'll happen if they try it on. You've got to keep on top of them, show them who's master if you're going to survive. Teaching in this school is like working in a zoo and these kids are like wild animals. The only way to keep control is by means of the whip.'

'You mean like dealing with a pride of lions?'

'More like a bunch of vultures watching a thirsty man in a desert. Turn your back and they'll have you. They can smell fear on a new teacher and so you have to stay on top if you're going to survive. Be tough from day one. They may not like you but they'll respect you and that's worth a lot more. Most of them come from broken homes and what they're lacking is firm discipline. They get belted at home but it's inconsistent. They never know whether they're going to get a pat on the head or a clip round the ear. It's my job to see that they get strict but predictable discipline.' He turned to the wobbly armed sinner. 'Arms up, I said,' he yelled at him. 'Excuse me a moment, Mr Hopkins,' he said suddenly.

'Hamilton!' he roared. He strode quickly across the room

and clouted a fair-haired lad across the head. 'I said no talking! I'll teach you to disobey me when I give you an order. I'll stand for no nonsense in my class. Is that understood?'

The luckless Hamilton went to the front of the class.

'Right,' Grundy snarled, 'now hold out your hand.' He produced a tawse from a drawer of his desk and proceeded to deliver a stinging blow to Hamilton's left hand. 'Now get back to your place, and remember to do as you're told. And another thing, Hamilton, if you're going to chat to your companion, try to speak English and not that diabolical Glasgow dialect of yours. And it's about time you bought yourself a satchel for your homework. What are you going to carry your books in, laddie? Your kilt? And we don't want the grease of your fish and chips all over the exercise books either.'

Grundy turned to Billy. 'There's a spare strap in my desk which I'll let you have. Only, when you use it, there are a few finer points to keep in mind. First, make sure they've got their fingers stretched right out and their thumbs out of the way. Don't let the strap touch their thumbs or you'll leave a mark. Next thing you know they'll be running home complaining to their parents. Another thing, always strap their non-writing hand unless they deserve more than one stroke – in which case you don't have any choice.'

Billy declined the offer, feeling he'd rather try more humane methods to keep class control.

'That Hamilton is a new boy,' Grundy explained. 'Straight from the Gorbals. We certainly get 'em at this place.'

'How do you like teaching?' asked Billy suddenly though he felt he knew the answer already.

'Like it! Like it! That's an irrelevancy. We're not paid to like it. In my opinion, it's a job and it helps to pay my mortgage and my gas bills. As I see it, kids are nasty, brutish, and short. They're evil, smelly little animals who must be trained in the ways of civilisation. Left to themselves, they would soon return to the savagery of the jungle.'

'Don't agree with you there,' said Billy. 'I believe with Jean Jacques Rousseau that man's nature is fundamentally good, that children are by nature moral beings, and it's our job as teachers to bring out the best in them.'

'I hope you succeed in finding something good in that class you've been lumbered with,' he sniggered.

'If you don't like it teaching here,' said Billy, 'why not get another job?'

'I tried once or twice in the early days,' he whined. 'But no use. Once you're employed in the elementary system, you're stuck. Like being a prison guard in Strangeways or Alcatraz.'

'Surely school isn't like a prison. You're dealing with youngsters with fresh, lively minds. Don't you find it rewarding to see their eyes light up when they have insight into something or when you awaken their understanding and interest in science?'

'Personally, I don't give a damn whether they're interested or not. They might not care a toss for Boyle's Law or for the bones of animals that have been dead ten thousand years. All I want them to do is to shut up and listen.'

'Maybe it'll rub off on some of them one day,' Billy said in an attempt to inject a note of optimism.

Grundy snorted derisively. 'In my twenty years at the coal face, it's not happened. As for that class they've dumped on you, you've got real problems. Hewers of wood and drawers of water, that's all they'll ever be. None of them wants to learn, all they're interested in is getting out and earning some money which they'll waste in the dance halls or the pubs. By eighteen, they'll be married and by nineteen, parents. The girls will look like ugly old washerwomen by the time they're twenty-one. Let 'em leave school as soon as possible is what I say.'

'That's easy to say but I'm faced with a *fait accompli* and so I have to get on with it.'

'True, true,' he guffawed. 'But I don't fancy your chances with that bunch of morons. I'll give you six months.'

'Anyway, thanks for your time,' said Billy and he moved towards the door.

'No problem,' called Grundy.

Billy left Grundy's class thoroughly depressed and wondered if he, too, would end up with the same pessimistic view of human nature after a few years in the job.

So that's the general advice from the old hands, he reflected. Be a hard-nosed bastard – wear a tough mask no matter how you feel inside. The trouble is you can become so harsh, you forget you're a teacher and you end up bitter and twisted like Grundy. No, playing the hard man wasn't his style. He desperately wanted to be a good teacher with a relaxed, easy-going manner, whose teaching was a pleasant and enjoyable experience, not a petty dictator or a prison guard imposing his will on a lot of youngsters who were forced to come to school by law.

His next visit was to the remedial class taken by Alex Callaghan.

'Hoppy, great to see you!' was Alex's greeting. 'Come into my kingdom.'

The atmosphere in the room was a complete contrast to the last one. This is more like it, thought Billy. The children were smiling and looked happy. They were involved in a variety of tasks. Some were counting on an abacus, some absorbed in assembling simple jigsaw puzzles, others building models of Plasticine, still others trying to cut card with the monstrously blunt standard school scissors, and a few were struggling their way through a simple reader.

'As I said at the break this morning,' Alex whispered, his eyes twinkling, 'Frank Wakefield took one look at me and knew my calling right away. The backward class.'

'What exactly does that entail?' asked Billy, gazing at the class of children.

'Well, one big advantage is that the class is small – only fifteen children – but they require constant individual attention. The ages in this class range from eight to fourteen. Teaching them requires incredible patience and even the smallest advance is a reason for celebration.'

'How remedial are they?'

'Let me give you an example.' Alex called to a dreamy-looking girl in the first row. 'Norma, come here to the front for a moment.'

She came forward with a fixed smile on her lips, and stood before Alex's desk.

'Tell Mr Hopkins here your name.'

'Norma Johnson,' she answered shyly.

'And how old are you, Norma?' asked Alex.

'Don't know, sir. I think I'm fourteen.'

'How many buttons are there on your coat, Norma?'

'Don't know, sir.'

'Let's count them together.'

Norma and Alex counted off each button. 'One – two – three – four.'

'Now, how many buttons, Norma?'

'Four, sir,' she replied with a triumphant smile.

'Well done, Norma. Now sit down and go on with your building bricks.' Alex turned to Billy. 'That may give you a rough idea, Hoppy. We progress in very small steps. If we were to ask Norma again in a few moments how many buttons are on her coat, she'd probably have forgotten, and we'd have to do the exercise again.'

'Are all the kids as remedial as this?'

'Not quite. Norma is probably the most retarded but all are fairly backward. If we can teach them the absolute basics, we count it as a success. One or two might even manage to read simple text and do simple calculations.'

'Will they get jobs when they leave school, do you think?'

'The less retarded might but for the severely retarded, prospects are probably bleak.'

Billy left Alex's class with much to think about. Maybe the task of teaching the top class wasn't so bad after all.

Last port of call at the Fire Service annexe was Miss Norah O'Neill's needlework class. As he stepped into the room, he noted the atmosphere of quiet industry. About a dozen girls were seated in a circle engrossed in their various sewing tasks. A couple of the girls were engaged in trying to thread their needles, with one eye closed, face screwed up, tongue darting in and out like a snake as they summoned up all their reserves of concentration. Another girl had been deputed to read aloud from *Anne of Green Gables* to the rest of the group. At the exciting bits, many of them had pricked their thumbs and, not wishing to waste the heaven-sent opportunities which had fallen into their laps, had utilised the drops of blood to adorn their work with interesting red-spotted patterns.

Miss O'Neill came forward smiling broadly when she saw him. 'Welcome to our sewing circle,' she said. 'Say good afternoon to Mr Hopkins,' she instructed the class.

They looked up from their work. 'Good afternoon, sir,' they dutifully chorused, smiling coyly at Billy.

'Good afternoon, girls,' Billy replied. He felt like a visiting bishop.

'These girls will never have to do any elaborate sewing,' Miss O'Neill whispered. 'The most challenging things they will ever have to do in real life will be darning socks and sewing shirt buttons for their husbands.'

'They seem to be doing well as far as I can see,' Billy said. 'If I need any little mending jobs on my clothes, I'll know where to come.' On Les's clothes, that is, he thought.

'I teach them the fancy stitches,' Miss O'Neill said, 'as it's part of the syllabus. Back stitch, hem stitch, single stitch, double stitch, and so on. In the end, I usually have to unpick their efforts and do them over again. Take this piece of work.' She picked up an example from one of the girls. 'The gussets are gigantic and her necklines not nice. Last week I had to unpick her tucks. Nevertheless, they like this class – it's one of the few places they can find a bit of peace in their lives.'

'My own class, Senior Four, could learn a thing or two here,' said Billy.

'We're so glad you came here,' she said. 'We consider ourselves lucky to get you. You're young and enthusiastic so you'll have a better understanding of the needs of the top class than anybody. I do hope you get on with them.'

'I've got my fingers crossed,' Billy replied.

He left the NFS annexe and as he crossed the playground he espied Sybil Melton-Mowbray – a whistle suspended from a lanyard round her neck – and her 'netters' class.

'No, no, you silly pie!' she called as she leapt after her 'gals'. 'Pass the ball to Janet! Now shoot, girl! Shoot!'

Billy gave her a cheery wave which she returned with great enthusiasm.

'You see what I have to put up with,' she called. 'No team spirit.'

Billy returned to the prefabs and found the classroom of the person in whom he was most interested. Junior 2 and the class of Miss Laura Mackenzie.

He knocked gently on her classroom door and entered. He was met by the quiet hum of activity – of thirty children busy at their various tasks. Laura Mackenzie was seated at her desk and was listening to a young boy read. She smiled brightly when she saw Billy, and signalled him to come to the front of the class.

'Well done, Mark,' she said, addressing the child. 'Now sit down at your place and go on with your reading.'

'I hope I'm not disturbing you,' said Billy, 'but Mr Wakefield suggested I might walk around the school and acquaint myself with the lie of the land.'

'You're most welcome,' she said. 'And I know how you must feel in a strange place for the first time. I felt exactly the same when I came last term.'

'Your class seems busy.'

'They're a bright bunch and I try to keep them at it. At

the moment, some of them are getting on with their Janet and John books and some are practising their Marion Richardson patterns.'

'Marion Richardson patterns? What are they?'

'They are lines of patterns which prepare the children for what they call "real writing".'

'They look like lines of squiggles to me,' he said, glancing at the blackboard. 'Wavy lines that go up and down, and up and down again.'

Laura laughed. 'I suppose they do but at the end of the day, they produce beautiful handwriting – genuine calligraphy.'

'You obviously enjoy your work,' said Billy. How easily and happily she laughs, he thought.

'I love it,' she said warmly. 'And I also like this school a lot, both the children and the staff.'

'The staff,' Billy smiled. 'There's a fascinating subject. Quite a few characters amongst them. One or two seem to have stepped right out of Dickens.'

'True,' she said, her eyes sparkling, 'but no Daniel Quilps or Bill Sykes among them, I'm glad to say.'

'I won't say who but we do have a Micawber and a Gradgrind,' Billy said.

'True,' she laughed. 'But apart from the friendly staff, another reason I like this school is that it's so handy for me. I live only a short distance away in Regina Park.'

'Don't tell me you live in one of those mansions on Regina Park Hill!'

'Yes, I'm afraid I do,' she said light-heartedly. 'Why, is that bad?'

'No, no, not at all,' Billy stammered. 'I cycled over there recently and I was most impressed with the estate.'

'Ah, so you're a fellow cyclist,' she said. 'I come to

school on a bike every morning – much against the wishes of my boyfriend.'

Boyfriend. This was like a thump in Billy's chest. She already has a boyfriend, he thought, and furthermore she lives in one of those posh houses. Out of my league. He banished any thoughts of dating this wonderful creature. He felt the disappointment rise in his throat.

'Yes,' she was saying. 'It takes me ten minutes to come to school as it's downhill but I usually push my bike back as I find the climb up the hill a bit too much.'

'Your boyfriend disapproves of cycling, you said. Why is that?'

'Oh, Hamish thinks the traffic is dangerous. Anyway, you can ask him yourself if you like as he's coming to meet me when we finish at four o'clock. Come over to the school gate and say hello.'

'Sure thing,' said Billy, lying through his teeth. 'I'd like that very much.'

After four o'clock, Billy collected his bike and his brief-case, said goodnight to Frank Wakefield and walked over to the school gate where a large crowd of parents were waiting to collect their children. As he approached, Billy thought he'd play a little game with himself and try to guess which one was Hamish. To have won Laura he must have special qualities. Did they show? Would these qualities be written on his face? Would he be tall? Dark? Handsome? There were several men who could have fitted the bill. He spotted Laura talking to a Robert Taylor type near the fence.

That's me out, he thought. I've no chance against opposition like that. I'll simply have to tough it out.

He adopted a cheerful smile and waved to Laura. She

213

waved back and beckoned him over.

'Let me introduce Mr Jarvis,' she said. 'Father of Tony in your class and Francine in mine.'

Billy shook his hand warmly. 'I'm truly glad to meet you,' he said. 'Tony is one of my brightest pupils.'

After a brief exchange of pleasantries, Laura suggested they go and meet Hamish. 'That's him over there,' she said, pointing.

Billy was five feet eleven but Laura's boyfriend was a good five inches taller. He was thin and couldn't have weighed much more than eleven stone. He had a long face with high cheekbones, bushy eyebrows, and mousy-coloured hair. His severe facial expression seemed locked in a permanent frown of disapproval. His dark clerical suit, buttoned up at the front, looked expensive and was smart enough but didn't seem to go with the bright Fair Isle cardigan he was wearing underneath.

Laura said, 'Let me introduce Hamish Dunwoody. Hamish meet Hoppy.'

'Glad to know you, Hamish,' said Billy, offering his hand.

The hand remained hovering in mid-air.

'Pleased to make your acquaintance,' said an unsmiling Hamish, 'But if you don't mind, I won't shake hands at this time. Influenza germs can be easily passed through hand-shakes, did you know that?' He had an unexpectedly high-pitched voice, out of place in such a long body.

'I didn't know that,' said Billy, returning his hand to his side. 'But I'll be careful in future.'

Hamish assumed control of Laura's bicycle and then took her free arm possessively, more in the manner of a police officer than a boyfriend. Together, the three of them set off, pushing their bikes along the pavement.

Hamish continued, 'I take a leaf from Louis Pasteur, the French chemist who pioneered the idea of pasteurisation. He was careful about his own hygiene and refused to shake hands because he knew better than anyone that you often carry cold viruses in the palms of your hands.'

'Is that a fact?' said Billy. 'But I always thought that a germ is not necessarily dirty or harmful – it's the name given to any small scrap of life.'

'Aye, that's true, but about seventy per cent of the living organisms in the world are bacteria and I don't believe in taking chances.' He released Laura's arm for a moment and, taking out a Vick's inhaler, sniffed noisily into each nostril in turn.

Laura said, 'Hamish's early studies make him wary of risk-taking. Tell Hoppy about them, Hamish,' she added proudly.

'I did three years of medicine at Glasgow but then decided it wasn't for me.'

'What made you change your mind?' asked Billy.

'I found work on the wards depressing and you can pick up all kinds of ailments in hospital,' he replied. 'They're like huge warehouses stocking a vast array of diseases. You can pick up anything from a common cold to an exotic tropical disease.'

Billy laughed. 'Like leprosy, smallpox or elephantiasis, for example.'

'It's no laughing matter, believe me,' said Hamish, cutting him short with a withering glance. 'It's well-known that as many as seventy-odd thousand patients develop a life-threatening disability as a direct result of being in hospital. The same goes for doctors' surgeries.'

'It sounds as if you've been lucky to escape with your life,' Billy replied politely. What on earth did Laura see in this moronic hypochondriac? 'What are you doing now?' he asked.

'Now I'm studying to be an actuary – I'm in my final year at Glasgow.'

Glasgow! That means he'll be away much of the time. That's a relief.

'Actuary?' said Billy. 'That's a new one on me. What does an actuary actually do?'

'An actuary,' said Hamish, as if reciting from a textbook, 'is one who calculates insurance risks and the probabilities of the occurrences of various contingencies, such as birth, marriage, sickness, accidents, retirement, and death. Give me a few simple indices of a person, like his social class, occupation, religion, and I can predict certain things about him.'

'Such as?' asked Billy.

'Which part of town he lives in, which newspaper he reads, what illnesses he's prone to, and the age at which he'll probably die.'

'Like fortune-telling?' said Billy.

'A lot more accurate than that. We rely on statistics, not reading tea leaves. I'm always telling Laura that travel by bicycle in Manchester is risky. Did you know, for example, that in Manchester alone, one person is knocked off his bicycle every three hours?'

'I'll bet this bloke's getting really fed up with it,' said Billy.

Laura's eyes twinkled and she began to giggle.

'No, no, you don't understand,' said a frowning Hamish. 'Not the same man, for God's sake. I'm speaking statistic-ally, do you see?'

'Oh, sorry.' Billy smiled.

They had reached the Regina Park toll gate.

'Well, this is where I leave you,' said Billy, mounting his bike. 'I'll chance it across to Crumpsall. I hope I don't become that three-hourly man.'

He pressed down on the pedal of his cycle and with a cheery wave, set off for home.

As he turned the corner, Billy dropped the act. His heart was sinking. So that's her boyfriend, he said to himself as he cycled down Stockport Road. A real neurotic if ever I saw one – obsessed with his health. Sounded as if he were worth a bob or two. Three years at Glasgow University, eh! And now studying to be a high-flying executive! What chance do I stand against that kind of competition? Laura's the most beautiful girl I've ever clapped eyes on but maybe she's way out of my class, belongs to a different world. Compare my Gardenia Court with her Regina Park estate.

She probably has a servant or two to run her bath and wait on her hand and foot. What've I got to offer a girl like that? A bike, my old stamp album plus a lousy teacher's salary, that's what. Maybe Dad's right, best to stick to your own kind and not get ideas above your station. Best to know your place. Nah, *I* don't go for this know-your-place and stick-to-your-own-kind rubbish. S'too late anyway for that 'cause I think I've fallen for the girl. But will she ever take a peasant like me seriously, I wonder?

He was so absorbed in these thoughts, he forgot to give a signal as he turned right at Devonshire Street and came perilously close to being knocked down by a 92 bus.

The driver slid his window back. 'You silly sod,' he yelled. 'Watch where you're going, can't you? What's a matter with you? Somebody stole your girl, or something?'

'Sorry, mate,' Billy called back. 'Must've been dreaming.'

217

Stole my girl, he thought? Not on your life. Then adopting a John Wayne drawl, he said aloud to an invisible audience, 'I don't wanna worry you, Hamish Dunwoody, but I'll give you till sun-up to git out o' town.'

Chapter Twenty

The Two Cultures

The longcase clock in the hall of the Mackenzie household struck five. For the umpteenth time that day, Grandma Mackenzie adjusted the silk mobcap on her silver hair as she sat rocking in her chair by the kitchen range in the capacious kitchen. In the corner, old Aunty Aggie snored gently as she dozed in her high-backed armchair. Her spectacles had slipped from her nose and the copy of *The People's Friend* had fallen from her lap.

Grandma, a small, wrinkled old woman shrivelled by her eighty years, her hands knotted with arthritis, was feeling out of sorts and impatient for her food – it had been three hours since she'd had that cup of tea and the arrowroot biscuit. But there was another half-hour before Duncan, the head of the house, got home and it was unthinkable that they could begin without him. From time to time her bird-like eyes shot accusing glances at Jenny, her granddaughter, who sat in the large winged chair at the other side of the hearth, daydreaming.

'You'd better not let your father catch you in that chair, young madam,' the old lady rasped. 'You may be eighteen years old but that doesn't entitle you to sit there.'

Jenny continued to stare into space.

'Did you say something, Grandma?' she asked eventually.

'Oh no. I'm a senile old fool and I like blabbing to mysel'. You must be half asleep, child. But you dare to stay in that chair, my bonnie wee lass, and your father'll soon give you a rude awakening.'

'Dinna fash yoursel', Gran'ma,' Jenny answered. 'I'll be out of it soon enough when I hear him come in.'

Louise Mackenzie entered from the scullery, carrying a large plate of freshly baked bread, a dish of butter, and a board containing a wide selection of cheeses. She was in her early forties and an attractive woman with her auburn hair, large brown eyes, and rosy complexion.

'You'd better stir yoursel', Jenny, and set the table afore your father gets home. Hurry now.'

Jenny tossed her head impatiently, causing the ringlets in her red hair to dance for a moment. She got out of the chair reluctantly and began laying places for eight.

'That lentil soup you're making smells awfu' good, Louise,' said Grandma.

'It should do, Grandma. It's good rich stock made from the lamb we had at the weekend. With food rationing getting tighter every day, we've got to make the most of everything we get.'

'I'm so hungry, I don't know if I can wait another half-hour. And that fish you're steaming makes the waiting even harder.'

At that moment, old Aunty awoke. She looked over her spectacles at Grandma.

'Do you think of nothin' but food, Meg?' she murmured. 'If you had my constitution, you wouldna be so bothered. I mind a time when I could eat an oatcake with the best of them. But now . . . well, I'm not long for this world.'

'You've been sayin' that for the last twenty years, Agnes,' said Grandma. 'If you're on your way out, you're certainly takin' your time about it. But I'm that peckish, I think I must have the appetite of a twenty-year-old.'

'You'll have to wait, Grandma,' said Louise. 'It isn't ready and you know how Duncan would react if he found we'd started without him. As for the fish, you ken full well that's for Duncan's sensitive stomach.'

They heard the front door open and close, and for a brief moment they tensed.

'It's all right,' said Louise. 'It's only Laura home from school.'

Laura came into the kitchen.

'You're home later than usual, Laura,' said her mother. 'Did you have extra work at school?'

'Sorry, Mammy. We didn't get out until four fifteen. We don't finish at half past three like nursery school teachers,' she said, flashing a smile at Jenny.

'I'll bet she's been blethering to Hamish Dunwoody at the gate,' Jenny said peevishly.

'No, Hamish and I have been talking to a young man who's joined the school staff, that's all,' she answered.

'A young man?' asked Jenny, pricking up her ears. 'Is he handsome?'

'Yes,' laughed Laura. 'He's young, handsome and he's free, as far as I know. But I think you'd have to move quickly, Jenny – he's the type that will be snapped up quickly.'

'Some hopes,' replied Jenny. 'I'd have to get Daddy's approval first. My last boyfriend didn't come up to scratch because he was only a railway clerk.'

'You're both too young to be thinking about such things,'

said Grandma. 'In my day, we didna walk out with a young man until we were twenty-one and even then we were closely chaperoned.'

'It's nineteen forty-seven now, Grandma,' answered Jenny. 'Things have changed. My friends don't have fathers who vet their boyfriends and check their bank accounts before they're allowed to walk out with them.'

'Your father only has your best interests at heart,' said their mother. 'Anyway, enough of this blethering, it's nearly half past. Laura, go and call the others and tell them to get washed before Daddy comes in. Quickly, quickly, he'll be here any minute.' Louise made a quick survey of the table for any impropriety of detail which might reflect on the thoroughness of her preparations. 'Let's see, bread, butter, soup plates, side plates, knives, spoons. Fish knife and fork for Duncan.' She made a few minor adjustments to the arrangements. All seemed in order.

Meanwhile Laura had gone into the hall and called, 'Hughie! Katie! Time for tea! Daddy'll be home soon! Better get washed right away!'

A young boy's voice called back from the drawing room, 'On my way, Laura! Just finishing my homework.'

This was followed by a little girl's voice from a bedroom. 'Coming, Laura!'

A few moments later, the three came into the room. Hughie was sixteen years old and tall for his age. He was a striking contrast to Laura, his eldest sister, for, like Jenny, he had blue eyes and red hair. Katie, on the other hand, was a pretty twelve-year-old with light-brown eyes and hair which cascaded down her back – a miniature version of Laura and her mother.

'Come along now, all of you,' Louise ordered. 'To the table.'

She glanced at the clock on the wall and having satisfied herself as to the exact time, poured the boiling water into the warmed teapot. Then she joined the others at the table.

The seven people sat at their places and waited. As the clock in the hall began striking the half-hour, there was the noise of a car in the driveway, and five minutes later they heard the lock of the front door turn. Next, the clatter of an umbrella being placed in its stand. Footsteps followed, the kitchen door opened and in came Duncan Mackenzie.

He was about fifty years of age, a tall man with red hair, blue eyes and a healthy, ruddy complexion. He was wearing a black jacket and striped trousers – the standard dress for a senior inspector in the service of His Majesty's Inland Revenue.

His entrance was greeted with a respectful silence. He walked silently over to the fireside chair, sat down, removed his shoes and put on the carpet slippers which had been left warming at the hearth.

'Shall I take your coat, Daddy?' asked Jenny. She helped remove his coat.

'Hang it up carefully in the hall wardrobe,' he said.

'I always do,' replied Jenny.

Mr Mackenzie went into the scullery and washed his hands. The rest of the family waited in silence. He emerged from the scullery and went over to the table and sat down in the carver chair.

'Let us say grace,' he said.

All bowed their heads.

'Bless us, O Lord, and these Thy gifts which we are about to receive from Thy bounty, through Christ Our Lord.'

'Amen,' they said.

Louise poured his tea into his special cup which he received with a curt nod of the head. These preliminaries completed, Louise got up and brought in a large tureen brimming with hot lentil soup, which she deposited in front of Duncan, along with a ladle and seven deep plates. Carefully – clinically – he doled out the soup which was passed from hand to hand round the table. Louise returned the tureen to the scullery. Duncan commenced eating, which was the signal that it was now permissible for the others also to begin. This first part of the meal was consumed in reverential silence, with Duncan indicating his need for bread or pepper by simply pointing at the item in question. Six pairs of willing hands reached out to meet his requirements. The only sound to be heard was from Grandma as she slurped her soup with obvious relish.

'Must you make that row, woman, when you take your soup?' Duncan snapped. 'Can you no' eat like a civilised human being?'

'I'm always telling her that,' said Aunty. 'God knows I have little appetite now without havin' to listen to that racket.'

'It's my old dentures, Duncan,' Grandma whined, ignoring Aunty's comment. 'They dinna fit as well as they used to.'

'Then you should buy yoursel' a new set,' said Duncan. 'God knows you've got a good pension and you live cheaply enough here.'

'I'm waitin' on the new National Health Service,' she replied. 'We're told that false teeth and spectacles will be free.'

The soup course finished, Louise collected the plates and took them into the scullery. She now spoke for the first time.

'I've managed to get you a nice piece of hake, Duncan. I've steamed it the way you like it with a thick parsley

224

sauce. We've got to be careful of that stomach of yours.'

'That's good, Louise,' said the great man. 'You know how fond I am of a bit o' fish.'

Grandma was eyeing his plate covetously.

'And I suppose you like fish, too, you old glutton,' Duncan said facetiously. 'Here, pass your side plate.'

He scraped off a small portion of his fish onto her plate.

'I only wish I could manage to eat like her,' said Aunty plaintively. 'But I'm no' long for this world.'

The company ignored her.

'Oh, thank you, Duncan,' Grandma simpered. 'You're a good boy. I've always said that.'

Judging the mood of the master of the house was not usually an easy matter but this act of generosity gave a clue as to his present humour which appeared to be amiable. It was all right for everyone to talk.

The rest of the family tucked in to the bread and cheese. While they did so, Louise took it as an opportunity to instil a little discipline.

'Katie, I hope you're going to eat up your crusts. We cannot abide waste in this house. There's many a poor family would appreciate the lovely bread you're leaving on your plate.'

'Yes, Mammy,' Katie said.

'And Jenny, don't slouch like that,' said Louise. 'Pull your shoulders back, girl. You're getting a terrible stoop. And you know your father doesn't like to see you hunched up like that. And you, Hughie, take your elbows off the table. How many times do I have to tell you?'

'Yes, Mammy,' the two Mackenzies chorused.

Duncan looked at his youngest daughter and his features softened as he said, 'Well, young Katie, are you still the brightest lassie in the class?'

'I don't know, Daddy. You'll have to ask Laura,' Katie answered shyly.

'She's doing well enough,' said Laura. 'Katie's holding her own but we don't have such fierce competition in the junior school.'

'Then you should,' snapped Duncan. 'The world out there is a competitive place and only the best come to the top. Have ye no read your Charles Darwin?' Then turning his attention to Hughie who had been trying to lie low, he asked sarcastically, 'And how's my genius of a son been getting on at school?'

Hughie flushed and looked uncomfortable. He shuffled in his seat. 'Not bad, Daddy.'

Duncan gave him a withering glance. 'NOT BAD! What does that mean, laddie? You're still first in class, I trust.'

'I'm still first in the sciences, Daddy – physics, maths, chemistry, and biology. Third in English and Latin but I'm having a struggle in French. It's all those irregular verbs and accents.'

'Then you'd better get your head down, laddie. If you want to get into medical school, you must have matriculation and that includes a modern language. Do you hear me?'

'Yes, Daddy.'

'You'll stay in every night and do your studying. I'll have none of this gallivanting off to the youth club, prancing about to that jazz music. Your career must come first. I'd be disappointed in you if you failed to get the necessary grades.'

'Yes, Daddy.'

'If he doesn't get into medical school, Daddy,' said Laura softly, 'he could become a teacher perhaps instead.'

'I'll not hear that defeatist talk in my house,' bellowed

226

Duncan. 'Teaching! Pah! All right for a woman – a nice respectable occupation until she finds a husband, but not for a man, not for the breadwinner.'

'There's nothing wrong with a man being a teacher,' replied Laura defiantly. 'It's a noble profession.'

'You hould your whisht. It's not nice to argue with your father like that,' said Grandma ingratiatingly. She was hoping she might get the remainder of the fish that Duncan appeared to be abandoning.

'I mind a teacher we had in Kirkintilloch many a year ago . . .' Aunty began.

The family took no notice of her soliloquy. They'd heard it before.

'Teaching – a profession! I've never heard such rot,' Duncan shouted. 'The only professions worth talking about are medicine, law, accountancy. They're the only ones with decent salaries. Now that boyfriend of yours, Hamish, has got his head screwed on the right way. An actuary is one of the best paid jobs around. You'll never starve if you marry him.'

'There's more to life than money,' protested Laura. 'There are things like caring for others, dedication.'

'You try paying the grocer with those,' scoffed Duncan. 'Perhaps you've heard the saying, "When poverty comes in at the door, love flies out at the window." ' With that, he rose from the table. 'I'm off to the study for a smoke,' he announced. 'Where I can get some peace from a lot of nagging women and their jabbering tongues.'

Before he left, he turned to Hughie and said, 'You remember, laddie, what I said. You'll stay in every night and do your studying. Get some work done on your French – your life and career depend on getting at least a credit.' He stalked out of the kitchen.

'You shouldn't have provoked him like that,' said Jenny. 'It's best to agree with him and do your own thing anyway.'

'He's always going on about money and security. As if they're the only things that matter,' Laura said.

'I mind a man in Dumbarton many years ago. Now he had lots of money but he wasna happy despite his wealth . . .' Aunty rambled off on a solitary stroll down Memory Lane.

'I'm all for keeping the peace,' said Louise. 'You've got to try and avoid rubbing him up the wrong way. You were talking a minute ago about altruism, service, and dedication. Here's your chance to put them into practice. The dishes are waiting for someone to wash up.'

Jenny and Laura laughed, went into the scullery, and rolled up their sleeves.

The rest of the family took up their own pursuits. Grandma dozed by the fireside, dreaming of the next meal of cocoa and cream crackers, Louise took up her embroidery, and the two youngest continued with their homework. Duncan smoked his Three Castles cigarettes, read the *Daily Telegraph*, and listened to the wireless. Around eight o'clock, he rose and went up to the bathroom, emerging fresh and ready for a night with his cronies at the Knights of St Columba on Princess Road. First he went into the kitchen where he found the Mackenzie womenfolk about their various activities.

'I'll just pay a visit to the club, Louise,' he said. 'I said I'd take a look at their accounts for them and there's a man I have to meet there to discuss some business.'

I know his business, thought Louise, it's a discussion of Manchester United's chances in the FA cup and the quality of Younger's bitter.

With Duncan's departure, a cloud of repression was lifted

228

from the house, and the family heaved a collective sigh of relief. For the first time that evening, the sound of laughter was heard in the kitchen.

Billy was exhausted when he reached home after his first day at school. Bike on his shoulder, he climbed the stairs to their tenement flat, taking in the familiar stale stench wafting from neighbours' open doors – boiled fish, sour cabbage, and yesterday's stew. There was the usual screeching and bawling from the Pitts family in the flat below as they fought another round in their never-ending dispute.

Before he had turned the key in the lock, Mam opened the door.

'Well,' she said eagerly. 'How did it go?'

'Tea first,' he said, depositing his bike in the spare bedroom. 'It's a long bike ride from Longsight.'

'Already brewed,' she answered triumphantly. 'I saw you coming from the veranda.'

Seated a little later at the table, cup of tea in hand, he recounted the day's happenings.

'First, they have no building and I've been given a domestic science room in a prefab with the top class of fourteen- to fifteen-year-olds.'

'You seem to spend your life in these here domestic science rooms. If I remember rightly, you were in one when you were evacuated to Blackpool. But what about the other teachers? What are they like? Are they friendly? Do you think you'll like it? What about the kids you'll be teaching – are they well-behaved?'

'Whoa, Mam!' he exclaimed, holding up both hands. 'One thing at a time. In reverse order. The kids are a bit bolshie but I think I can talk them round. They're hopping mad because they've been made to stay an extra year at school. I like the staff, though. The head's OK, a rugby-playing scoutmaster, and there are two brothers named after popes, a big woman with one of those posh, double-barrelled names – a jolly-hockey-sticks type – a deaf woman who smokes a pipe, and a bloke who thinks he's commandant of a concentration camp.'

'It sounds like a Prestwich loony bin, or the inside of a cuckoo clock, if you ask me,' said Mam, shaking her head. 'Do you think you're going to be all right?'

'I know I'm going to be all right for I've fallen head over heels in love with one of the staff.'

'Not the deaf one with the pipe,' she said with a straight face. 'Your father'd go mad if you brought her home.'

'No, this one is the loveliest creature I've ever clapped eyes on, a Miss Laura Mackenzie.'

'And I suppose you're going to tell me she smokes cigars and has a beard.'

'No, nothing peculiar about her. Simply beauty un-adorned, a vision of loveliness straight out of a Gainsborough painting. You know, like the one you see sometimes at the cinema at the start of the big picture.'

'I hope her clothes are more up to date than that woman with the big hat. But you sound as if you've been struck by lightning,' she said.

'I have,' he said. 'But no need to worry. She's my ideal but unattainable – unreachable. In a higher class. Anyway, she already has a boyfriend from a rich family – Hamish Dunwoody. I don't stand a cat in hell's chance.'

He was hoping Mam would contradict him and she did.

'Well, you know what they say,' she replied, looking right at him. 'A faint heart never won a fair lady. Is she engaged to this Hamish fella?'

'Not that I know of.'

'Then there's always hope.'

'And a cat may look at a king,' he said. 'Or in this case, a queen.'

Mam drank it all in, enjoying the experience vicariously.

After Billy's account of his first day, she said, 'Well, anyroad, apart from that – falling in love, and deaf women smoking pipes – your dad and me are right proud of you. It's a real feather in our cap to have a teacher in the family. You should have seen their faces in the corner shop when I told them our lad was a teacher. Green with envy, they was. "Oh, he'll be that rich," the neighbours said. "Teachers get good wages, good holidays, and a big pension at the end. You're a lucky woman, Mrs Hopkins." So there you are, I feel as if we're somebody at last.'

'Why does everyone keep telling me about my pension? I've only just started the job. I don't plan to retire for another forty years,' he laughed.

But Billy was glad she was happy about his new status. He himself was less sure. He had that top class to deal with and he could smell trouble.

Chapter Twenty-One

Trouble in't Classroom

The next morning, Billy was up bright and early, ready to face his first real day of teaching. The euphoria and the excitement he felt were shared by Mam as if she were undergoing the experience with him. As she pushed his packed lunch into his hand, she gave him a big hug and said, 'Go and make us proud, our kid.'

Now where had he heard that before?

He reached school forty-five minutes later after the usual struggle weaving through the Manchester morning rush hour. As he crossed the grass between the prefabs, a leather football shot through the air, narrowly missing his head.

'You stupid bugger, Horner,' he heard a voice call.

'Piss off, Lynch. You should get out of the way, you fat get!' Horner replied.

'Hey up, here comes bloody Hopalong Cassidy!' another one cried.

So he'd been given a nickname already.

He entered the classroom, his head still buzzing with Wakefield's pep talk from the day before. His idea was to tread water until he had formulated some firm plans for his pupils. He decided to spend the first part of the day testing their level of English. The quickest way was to get them to write something.

'I'm going to start today with composition.'

There was a loud groan from the class.

'All right! All right!' said Billy. 'Take out your pens. I want you to write on this subject, not in your books but on the paper I shall give out.' He turned to write on the blackboard. As he did so, a pellet struck him on the back of the head. He knew it was a waste of time to ask for the name of the culprit. He ignored it but continued to write – sideways: WHAT I THINK AND WHAT I HOPE.

'OK. Start writing and let's see what you can do. One further thing, tell me what you really feel. No one else will see what you write except me.'

'Got no pen,' Mitchell yelled.

Billy had anticipated this and quickly supplied him from the spares he had ready.

'Need a new nib,' shouted Horner.

'Right, cop for this,' called Joe Duffy, throwing one across the room.

'You stupid bastard!' yelled Irene Moody. 'Look what you've made me do. I've spilled ink over my book.' She threw her exercise book at him.

'You crazy cow!' bawled Alf Dempsey. 'That bloody well hit me.' He threw the book back.

'You gormless git,' screeched Nellie Wallace. 'Now you've spilt my inkwell over my desk.'

Billy blew his top. 'Stand up, all of you!'

Slowly they dragged themselves out of their seats, scraping their chairs noisily across the floor. There was a banging of desk lids. They glowered back at Billy insolently.

'Did you throw a pen, Duffy?'

'Me? Me?' he said, protesting his innocence and appealing to the rest of the class. 'I haven't done nothing. Don't pick on me.'

'Right,' said Billy, exasperated. 'That's enough of this nonsense. Now get on with it.'

The class sat down and scowled at him. One or two of the brighter ones – Tony Jarvis, Anne Greenhalgh – got down to work but the rest were determined to have some fun by riling him, questioning his authority and generally causing as much trouble as they could.

'We can't write with this bloody ink, Duffy,' complained Mick Lynch. 'It's like bloody water.'

'Shut your gob, Lynch,' hissed Duffy. 'You're always moaning about something.'

'Get stuffed, Duffy,' Lynch retorted.

'You wait till break, you red-haired get,' snarled Duffy. 'I'll kick your balls in.'

'You and whose army?' growled Lynch.

So the lesson continued. A disaster.

At the end of the morning, Billy collected their efforts, such as they were. During the lunch break, he took a quick look at their writing. Most of it was execrable – a hotchpotch of blots, scratchings-out, misspellings, for the most part the work of illiterates though there were exceptions. Ignoring the messy style, he skip-read through them to see if there were any nuggets of gold to be mined from so much dross. He noted that there was a common theme running through them all. Without exception, they complained about the harsh methods of Mr Grundy. A typical example was that of Mick Lynch.

I cannt wate to get out of this skool

I reely haite skool and have allways hatied this dummp. Speshially Grumpy Grundy who shud get a job in 1 of Hitlers consentrashun camps, he is crooel and likes belting us, if he ever trys to hit me agen, like he did last turmm Ill thump him 1 in the gob. I hope he brakes his legs on the way home from skool, the new teecher Hopperlong is allrite but I think hes two soft.

And from Irene Moody:

I think are new teachers dead smashing but hees not tuff enuff, not like other teachers who our dead rotten. The worst of the lot is grundy as hees all ways giving us the strap even the young girls, I think hees a saddist and get pleshur from it an I hope that 1 day he will fall down a manwhole, I think he secrettly would like to get off with 1 of the girls. We sing a song about him: mister grundys a very good man, he goes to church on Sunday, prays to god to give him strengt to belt the kids on Monday.

The morning session had set a pattern of rowdiness for the day and the rest of the lessons continued in the same vein. The class were set on wrecking all his efforts. At dinnertime, Billy did not report their behaviour to Frank Wakefield.

This is my problem, he said to himself, and I must solve it for myself. But one thing is obvious, Grundy is not very high in the popularity stakes, and if the pupils' hopes and wishes come true he will be spending a considerable part of his life in traction. But I've got to find some way of getting through to these kids, something that will make them see sense and start behaving like civilised human beings. But what?

Next day, there was a change in their behaviour. They were talking when he took his first class in the morning but they went to their desks at once. The room became silent immediately. Silent as a tomb.

Great, he thought. That's the way I like it. They've come to their senses.

'OK, Joe,' he said. 'Give out the *King's English* books.'

Duffy distributed the books quietly and efficiently.

'I want to check up on some of the common mistakes in English that I've heard you making. When I know where your faults are, I should be able to help you. Speaking correct English can be important to your job prospects.' He spoke frigidly and without emotion.

He waited for the usual repartee from someone – 'What, me – a bricklayer? What good's correct English to me?' But no one spoke. They continued to stare at him wordlessly.

'The questions are pretty easy and I'm sure you'll have no problem with them. Turn first to page thirteen and look at Exercise Seven. It says, "Fill each space in the sentences with the correct word from the list." Got it?'

Nobody answered. The quiet was somehow strange and unnatural, and Billy was finding it disconcerting to be met by this wall of silence. But then, he supposed, that was the general idea.

He continued regardless. 'The first example is done for you. "When he met the lady he (rise, rose, raised) his hat." The answer is of course "raised". Now, Mitchell, do number two, using the correct part of the verb go.'

Mitchell pushed his chair back, scraping the floor noisily,

and stood up. He studied the sentence for a while and said: 'She had went for a walk.'

Billy glared at him. Then he saw the light in the eyes of the rest of the class as they exchanged glances. Still no sound.

'No, that's not right, Mitchell. The answer is "She had gone for a walk".'

Mitchell shrugged his shoulders impassively.

'Vera Pickles, try the next one.'

'He seen his uncle yesterday,' she replied.

A few members of the class snickered.

'If you go on answering like this, I'm going to create a scene all right. Next one, Lynch.'

'The old man has fell asleep in his chair,' he answered coldly.

' "Fallen",' said Billy wearily. 'Try the next, Tessie Shea.'

She answered the instant she heard her name. 'He was awaked by the noise,' she said, looking round the class triumphantly.

Billy saw what they were up to but there was nothing he could do about it. They had switched their tactics from rowdiness to bloody-mindedness. He listened to the rest of their botched answers.

The bell rung just after I had wrote the letter.
The picture was drew by a famous artist.
I have knew him since he was small.
The tree had fell across the road and many of its
    branches were broke.

'Obviously,' said Billy, 'you find correct English usage difficult. So I want you to finish the rest of the exercises at home tonight. I shall mark them tomorrow when you bring them in.'

This announcement was greeted with a howl of protest. For the first time that day, the silence was broken.

'Can't we just write out the answers?' Anne Greenhalgh asked.

'No, you will write out the complete sentences. Each and every one of them.'

'But there are forty of them,' protested Tony Jarvis.

'Good, it'll be good practice for you.'

'I've got to do my paper round,' Roger Horner called. 'I can't do it.'

'Got to help my dad on his barrow,' cried Mick Lynch.

'I serve in a shop,' said Tessie Shea.

'I've got to deliver my mam's washing,' screeched Nellie Wallace, 'I haven't got no time for no homework.'

'You should've thought about that when you were planning to ruin my English lesson,' said Billy.

I'm building a barrier, a wall of hostility between the class and myself, he told himself, but there seems to be nothing I can do to demolish it. The process seems to have a momentum of its own. I desperately want to teach and teach well but this lot won't give me a chance. I have to find a way of breaking this chain of events.

In an all-out effort to win their interest, he spent the whole of Wednesday evening at home drawing a colourful, detailed map of the school district showing the important landmarks and places, and – very important – the streets where his wards lived. This ought to attract their attention, he thought, if anything will. He rolled up the map and inserted it into a cardboard cylinder, ready for school next day.

'I hope you're not going to spend every night working,' said Mam when she saw him poring over the dining-room table. 'All work and no play makes Jack a dull boy.'

'This isn't work,' Billy replied. 'It's more than that. It's survival.'

Next day, he proudly unfurled his work of art in the geography period. There was a gasp of admiration as he pinned it up on the board. There was an immediate response.

'Hey, there's our street.'

'And the corner shop and the chippy.'

'There's my dad's pub,' exclaimed Mitchell.

'And our house!' squealed Nellie Wallace. 'And there's the houses where I take me mam's washing.'

It's working, thought Billy. At last they're interested in something.

At the afternoon break, as he went off to the staffroom for tea, there was still a small crowd of pupils around the map identifying various features in their little world.

When Billy returned ten minutes later, he found the classroom strangely hushed. They sat in their places expressionless and quietly waiting for him. He soon discovered the reason for their unusual demeanour. His map was a mess. During his absence, someone had ruined it by throwing a bottle of red ink over it. Billy looked despondently at his masterpiece, over which he had laboured for so many hours. Turning his attention to the class, he lowered his voice and spoke quietly and menacingly. The kids at the front could see how he narrowed his eyes and tightened his lips.

'You morons! I won't ask who did this because I know it'd be a waste of time. I'll simply say that if I ever find out, I'll take the law into my own hands.'

The class continued to gaze back at him coldly. On some faces, there was a look of stubborn defiance, on others a look of sad regret.

On Thursday evening, as Billy cycled home, he took stock of his first four days of teaching. Catastrophic. The class seemed to have gone through several phases. First, the bloody-minded phase with the slamming of doors and desk lids, followed by the awkward squad stage with many of them losing their pens, pencils, rulers, exercise books; next, the dumb insolence stage where every request or command was met with a scowl or an impudent reply. The last straw had been that afternoon, the vandalisation of his visual aid. He was in despair and ready to give up teaching for good. Maybe Grundy was right in his assessment. Perhaps they *were* unteachable.

At home over a cup of tea, he outlined his problem to Mam.

'These kids I'm trying to teach are angry, not with me but with Rab Butler and his Education Act. With the government for raising the leaving age and stopping them from going out to work. But they're taking out their anger on me and I'm having a bumpy ride. I really want to teach but they won't let me. There's nothing worse than a bunch of bolshie adolescents.'

'Eeh, I'm right glad,' she said, 'that you grew up before they invented all this adolescence. Most of your scholars are nearly grown up, nearly as old as you. I left school at the age of ten but today they're young adults not school-children.'

'They don't act like adults, Mam,' said Billy.

'P'raps that's because you don't treat them like adults,' she said. 'Give a dog a bad name and hang him. If you treat 'em like kids, don't be surprised if that's the way they behave.'

'Maybe I'm too young for them, Mam. Maybe they should have someone older and tougher.'

'P'raps you are too easy with them,' she said. 'They might be better off with that fella Grundy you're always going on about. I'll bet he'd give 'em what for.'

'That's pipe-dreaming, Mam. They're my class and they're my problem. I must admit, though, I don't know how to get control of them. Punishment is no good – that'll only make them into enemies. But there must be some way, some *thing* that I can hold over them. They must have a pet hate, something they detest. Something that'll scare the daylights out of 'em.'

'Well, whenever you or any of the lads gave me trouble, I always threatened you with your father. "Wait till your father gets home," I used to say. It always worked.'

'That's all very well, Mam, but I can't threaten them with that.' Suddenly, Billy had an idea. Vague at first, no more than a glimmer of light, but the more he thought about it, the more it seemed that it might be the answer. 'Wait a minute though, I think I can see a solution. Mam,' he said, kissing her on the forehead, 'you're brilliant. A genius. I think I know how to bring my young savages into line.'

'If it was something I said,' she replied, 'I'm sure I don't know what it was.'

'You know, up to now, I've been treating them with kid gloves. It's time they learned how it is when I come out fighting. If it's a scrap they want, they're going to find out they're up against the kid from Collyhurst. So they'd better watch out.'

241

Chapter Twenty-Two

The Ultimatum

Friday was the last day of the week and Billy could hardly wait to get to school to talk over his idea with Frank Wakefield, for its success would require his co-operation. He would have to play his cards right because today could be a very important day. Make or break day.

The first period of the day began with the usual insolent behaviour from Senior 4 – noise, raucous laughter, sullen looks, glowering and sulking. At the mid-morning break, Billy sought out Frank Wakefield.

'I've been giving a little thought to the problem of Senior Four, Frank,' he began, seriously understating the time he'd lain awake in the early hours, his preoccupation at breakfast and along the route to school, 'and I think I may have the remedy.' He explained his plan of action.

The head readily agreed to give it his fullest support.

After the tea break, Billy returned to class. His pupils slowly returned to their places with their customary rowdiness and shuffling of chairs. Billy bided his time. Then he went into action. He banged his fist on his desk. He began pacing the front of the room like a nervous

242

leopard in a cage. Every pair of eyes in the class followed him.

'Look, you bad-mannered louts!' he thundered. 'I've had it up to here with the lot of you. Everyone has advised me to get tough with you. "Give 'em hell," they said. But I'm not like that. This is my first year of teaching and I looked forward to teaching you – the top class. Top! That's a laugh! The dregs, more like it! This class should be setting the example and the pace for the rest of the school but look at yourselves. A bunch of ragamuffins. I tried treating you like adults and what was my reward? You've acted like hooligans ever since I got here – banging doors, desk lids, throwing books, swearing, scowling. But when you threw ink on my map yesterday, that was the last straw. I've had enough of you and so I've decided to ditch you. DO I MAKE MYSELF CLEAR?'

The class went quiet and, for the first time that week, were all ears. The boys glowered but some of the girls looked enraptured. Irene Moody gazed at him admiringly.

'You've done your best to sabotage everything I've tried to do for you. I've tried to treat you as responsible beings and your response has been that of a bunch of apes. Well, that's it, I've run out of patience. I've spoken to Mr Wakefield and he has agreed that starting on Monday morning, this class will be taken by Mr Grundy and I shall take his class, Junior Four.'

Silence. The class looked shell-shocked.

Then Jim Mitchell was up on his feet. 'Wait a minute, you can't do that to us. We hate Grundy. I for one won't be coming to school if we get Grumpy Grundy.'

'You will have to come to school, that's the law,' answered Billy calmly. 'Play truant and your parents will be prosecuted.'

'You don't mean it,' said Anne Greenhalgh, smiling nervously. 'You're bluffing. You wouldn't do that to us!'

'Try me,' Billy replied. 'I can assure you, it's been agreed. There's only one solution, I'm afraid.'

'Well what is it?' Tony Jarvis demanded. 'I tell you, the idea of spending my last year with old Grundy sends shivers down my spine.'

'Here it is,' said Billy. 'I'm leaving this class in about ten minutes and I shan't be back until one thirty after dinner. It's up to you. Here's your first exercise in taking responsibility. You've got to decide for yourselves. I want a solemn undertaking from each and every one of you that the hooligan behaviour I've seen in my first week will cease for good, starting Monday morning. Everyone must agree – no exceptions. Otherwise, I walk. And I mean it. It's been settled.'

Senior 4 was still in shock.

Billy left the room and walked over to the staffroom. His hands were shaking. He lit a cigarette and marked books until dinnertime.

As he ate his sandwiches with Frank Wakefield and Miss O'Neill, he wondered if he had done the right thing.

'Don't you worry about it, Hoppy,' said Frank. 'If they don't come round to their senses, I'm moving Grundy in with them, whether he or they like it or not. After all, he gets paid as a senior teacher. He can damned well earn it for a change. But this is Senior Four's first taste of democracy and somehow I think you'll find they see the light.'

'Hope so,' said Billy. 'Things came to a head when they destroyed my map. Obviously we couldn't continue along that course. Something had to give and it's not going to be me. They're up against Billy the Kid and I'm going to come out fighting.'

'That's better. That's the way to talk,' said Frank, adopting a Wild West tone. 'Them's fightin' words, pardner.'

At half past one, Billy returned to class. He found them in their places. He walked to his desk and sat down.

'Well,' he demanded. 'What have you decided?'

The class looked at him with cowed respect. Jim Mitchell stood up.

'The lads and me have talked it over and we're agreed we've been giving you a rough time lately and they want me to say we're sorry. If you'll give us another chance, we'll try to behave and do as you say. We don't want Grundy as our teacher. Anything but that. Tell us what you want us to do.'

The boys nodded their affirmation of what Mitchell had said.

'OK. Fair enough,' said a much-relieved Billy. 'Now, what about the girls?'

Anne Greenhalgh was on her feet. 'The girls in the class have elected me as their spokeswoman,' she said, 'and like the boys we want to apologise for our disgusting behaviour. We want you as our teacher and we're willing to stop messing about and do as you tell us. Only don't send in Mr Grundy or we won't know what to do. We'll do anything you say to stop that.'

There was a murmur of agreement from the girls.

'Right,' said Billy. 'Apologies accepted. From now on we all turn over a new leaf and start again. Pretty soon, you'll be leaving school and taking jobs. You'll be expected to behave like adults, which is what you are. So let's start right now in this class. I'll treat you not as kids but as grown-ups. After all, I'm not much older than you myself.'

The class laughed good-humouredly.

'These are some of the things I want you to do. First, no more swearing in my class. I don't want to hear the obscene words that have been thrown about in the last week. Secondly, treat each other with respect. I don't like this war between boys and girls as if you hate each other's guts. From now on, you call one another by your first names. When you start your first jobs, you'll find that the people in the workplace have respect and friendship for one another and they usually refer to each other by first names. So, we'll do the same.'

'What about you?' asked Tony Jarvis. 'What do we call you?'

'I'm your teacher and the office I hold should be respected. Call me Mr Hopkins or sir – take your pick. You should also have respect for other teachers in the school.'

'You don't mean old Grundy, surely, sir,' exclaimed Mick Lynch.

'I do indeed,' said Billy. 'What he does in his classroom is his own business, not ours. He is a teacher and has his own methods. No more nasty remarks about him, got it? Now, I have an obligation to you to try to make my lessons relevant and worth your while. You have the right to expect that from me. But on the other hand, you have the duty to pay attention and give of your best. Start behaving like grown-ups and that's the way I'll treat you.'

As he was speaking, the door shot open and Nellie Wallace burst in and sat down at her desk.

'I had to deliver me mam's sodding washing – that's why I'm late,' she announced to the class. She looked around the room. 'Why's everyone so sodding miserable?'

The rest of the girls frowned meaningfully in her direction.

'Here's our first example,' said Billy. 'Nellie, go out of the room and come in properly.'

'What the hell's going on?' Nellie shouted.

'Just do it!' snapped Irene Moody.

Nellie shrugged her shoulders, got up and went out of the room. A moment later, she walked back in with a book on her head and with the deportment of a Christian Dior model.

The whole class burst into spontaneous laughter. Then applause.

'Sorry I'm late, sir,' she said curtsying. 'I had to do some errands for me mam. May I please sit down?'

'By all means, Nellie,' said Billy, laughing despite himself.

Nellie's tomfoolery helped defuse a tense situation.

By special concession granted by Frank Wakefield, Billy dismissed his class early at 3.30. As he cycled home at the end of his first week, he was elated.

'I've cracked it! I've cracked it!' he repeated to himself all the way up Cheetham Hill Road.

Chapter Twenty-Three

New Deal

That weekend at home, Billy burnt the midnight oil working out a programme for his recalcitrant class. By Sunday night, he had the details clear.

If this works, he reflected, teaching the top class is going to be a joy instead of a penance. He went to bed happy but with a bonnet buzzing with a billion bees. He had a restless night with so many ideas turning over in his mind. Next morning, he awoke still tired but nevertheless looking forward eagerly to putting his scheme into action.

Monday morning began with the usual hymn-singing practice for the whole school, but when Billy faced his class in the second period, he noted a different atmosphere. Somehow they looked tidier and their faces shinier. All eyes were focused on him. He had their full attention.

'Well, Senior Four. For us, this is a fresh start – the first day of the rest of our lives. We shall see how it goes till Christmas. Then we'll review the situation.

'Remember this: you are the senior class in this school, the so-called top class. It means you must set an example at all times. The youngsters look up to you and their little eyes are watching everything you do and say. If you swear and curse, they'll do the same; if you push and shove, so will they; if you come to school looking like tramps, don't be surprised if they imitate you. Up to now, you've not set a very high standard but from today, all that's going to change. Starting now, you've got to show that you are indeed the top class in every way – in behaviour, manners, bearing, and actions. If I'm to be your form master, I want to be proud of you. From what I've seen of you, I know you've got it in you to be a great class – the finest this school has ever seen. It's up to you.'

Jim Mitchell had raised his hand. 'This is all very well, Mr Hopkins – sir – but you've got to see it from our point of view. We should have left this year and we don't want to go on doing the same old things we've been doing for the past three years.'

Billy noticed the respectful 'sir'. Things looked promising.

'I hear what you're saying,' said Billy, remembering his college lectures on counselling. 'I have a programme which I think you'll like. It's different from anything you've ever done before. When I drew it up, I was thinking that you'll soon be leaving school and it was time that we started to take that into account by preparing you for it and teaching you some of the things you'll need. In other words, a preparation for life.'

'What kind of things will we be doing, sir?' asked Anne Greenhalgh, intrigued.

'As I see it,' Billy continued, 'the mornings will be devoted entirely to work in the basic studies – reading, writing and arithmetic plus history and geography. But with one difference, the lessons will be designed for your individual needs. Each of you will have a specially tailored programme to suit your own particular requirements. I'll show you what I have in mind a little later.'

'Did you say the mornings for the basics?' asked Tony Jarvis. 'But what do we do in the afternoons?'

'Afternoons will be given over to social and recreational skills.'

'What are those, sir?' asked little Josey Parker.

'Well, for example, Monday afternoons will be for games as usual, the boys go to football or cricket, and the girls to netball – those parts of the timetable will remain. The other afternoons will be different. They will be given over to some aspect of learning about life outside school. Tuesday afternoons, we shall go out to visit the local library to do our own study and research.'

'Research – us?' asked Nellie Wallace. 'What kind of research? I mean, do we wear white coats and that, like they do in a Frankenstein picture?'

There was general laughter, which Billy joined.

'No, Nellie. It'll be research into books and encyclopaedias. But one thing at a time. On Wednesday afternoons, we'll either go out to visit some place of interest, like a factory, a hospital, or the fire station, or even a police station, to see the people at work.'

'If we go to the police station, some of us might not get out again,' said Roger Horner.

More laughter.

'I live in a pub,' said Jim Mitchell. 'My dad could fix up a visit to a brewery.'

'I'm not sure about that,' said Billy. 'Some of you might not want to go home.'

More merriment. The pupils of Senior 4 were enjoying themselves.

'Anyway,' Billy went on, 'sometimes, we shall bring in an expert to talk to us, like a doctor, or a policeman, or a nurse, or an engineer, people who can tell us about their jobs. Thursday afternoons, we shall learn some of the social graces and the time will be given over to ballroom dancing.'

There was a gasp of amazement from the class. They turned to each other in excitement. Billy gave them a moment to digest this news.

'But who will teach us, sir?' asked Irene Moody when order had been restored. 'Most of us can't dance – especially the boys.'

'I shall have that honour,' said Billy. 'I've taught dancing for a few years. Mr Wakefield has given us permission and the school will lend us its gramophone, and I can arrange to borrow a few records.'

'Fantastic,' exclaimed Tessie Shea.

The class was having difficulty in taking all this in. So different from anything they'd experienced before at school.

'That leaves Friday afternoon and you'll be free to pursue your own activity provided you've reached your target and finished your programme of work.'

'You mean we could play football in the yard?' asked Joe Duffy incredulously.

'If you've done all your jobs, yes.'

The class looked stunned by this revolutionary curriculum.

'Look,' said Billy. 'You'll get into the swing of things as we go through the term – it'll become routine. Right now, let's have a look at one of our basic subjects. Arithmetic. What is it and why do we need it?'

'Who knows and who cares?' replied Mick Lynch, causing the usual ripple of merriment around the class.

'Arithmetic! How I hate it!' exclaimed Vera Pickles.

'Why do you hate it?' Billy asked.

'Because I'm no good at it. I'm hopeless.'

'Look,' Billy said, getting hot under the collar. 'Let's have one thing clear in this class. You never, never say "I'm hopeless" or "I can't do this or I can't do that". If you keep feeding yourself with negative thoughts, telling yourself you can't do something, how do you expect to be able to achieve anything? You've already made up your mind you're no good at it. Always tell yourself positive things like "I can do it" and "I will do it". Then we'll get somewhere.'

'Yes sir,' she answered, 'I'll try to remember it. And, sir, I like it when you get mad.'

Billy sighed. This wasn't going the way he'd planned.

'OK,' he said. 'I'll try to get mad to please you. Now, what about arithmetic? I need to know how much you know about it so I can start teaching you at the right level.'

'It's about numbers, adding and subtracting, measuring things, and that,' said Tony Jarvis.

'Good answer,' Billy said. 'And why do we need it?'

'So we can get the sums right and not cheat each other,' replied Anne Greenhalgh.

'Right. Give me some examples.'

'When I'm working on my dad's barrow in Market Street,' said Mick Lynch, 'God help me if I don't give the right change when I'm selling someone potatoes or apples.'

'Good. Let's look at money.'

Billy tested them on money tables, pennies in a shilling, shillings in a pound, shillings in a florin, shillings in a guinea, pennies in half-a-crown. They seemed to know their tables well enough.

'What other things do we measure?'

Joe Duffy raised his hand. Good, Billy thought, we don't get many answers from him.

'Please, sir,' said Joe, 'it's time to put coal in the boiler. I have to do it every hour.'

'OK, Joe,' Billy said disappointed. 'Do your job.'

At this point, Wakefield came into the room and began working at his desk at the back of the room.

Billy had been led to believe that the classroom was the inner sanctum of a teacher, a private place not subject to scrutiny and observation except by inspectors or by invited guests. He'd have felt nervous teaching in the presence of any of his colleagues or of an outsider. But the head! A hundred times worse. He felt he was destined to have a permanent critic weighing up every word he uttered.

'Now, as I was saying,' Billy continued uneasily, 'what other things do we measure?'

'How heavy things are,' answered Vera Pickles.

'Right – weight. What do we measure weight in?'

'Tons, hundredweights, pounds, ounces,' she answered.

'There you are. And you said you didn't know arithmetic.'

He checked their knowledge of weights – most of them had a firm enough grounding.

'How do we weigh people?'

'In stones,' answered Tessie Shea, the tubby girl. 'Don't I know it!' The class rewarded her with the usual laughter and Billy couldn't help joining in. It was good that she was able to laugh at herself.

'How many pounds in a stone?'

'Fourteen,' Tessie answered gloomily.

'If anyone here is worried about their weight,' said Billy, 'be comforted by the fact that the heaviest man in recorded history is an American called Hughes who weighed seventy-six stone.'

The class was suitably impressed.

'What's the lightest any grown-up has ever been?' asked Josey Parker, the small slip of a girl.

'I believe it was once again an American – this time a woman. She weighed forty-nine pounds. How many stones is that?'

'That's only three and a half stone,' Anne Greenhalgh gasped.

'So much for weighing things. What about measuring liquids? They can change their shape so easily.'

'Gallons, pints, gills,' Jim Mitchell said right away.

'He should know, sir, his dad runs the Waterloo Arms,' said Tony Jarvis,

'I'll bet you don't know, sir,' said Jim Mitchell, 'how many tots in a bottle of whisky.'

'You've got me there, Jim. But I'm willing to learn.'

'We measure tots in an optic and we get thirty tots and a bit from each bottle. They call the bit that's over "the barman's tot". Every so often, we get a visit from an Inspector of Weights and Measures who comes round to check our measures. I can show you if you come to the pub some time. You can even have a free pint.'

'Thanks, Jim. I may take you up on the offer. Now these measures we've been talking about are used here in Britain and are called imperial measures. If you ever go abroad to the Continent, you'll find they operate on a different system called the metric. But you won't ever need to worry about that unless you go to live over there. The last thing I want to test you on is time. How do we do time?'

'By going to prison,' Roger Horner called out.

When the giggles had died down, Billy said, 'How do we measure it? And don't say by chalk marks on the prison cell.'

'In seconds, minutes, hours, days, weeks, months, years,' answered Anne Greenhalgh.

'Good. There are twelve months in a year. Why twelve?'

'Hasn't it something to do with the moon going round the earth, sir?' said Tony Jarvis.

'That's correct, Tony.'

'Why do we have leap year every four years?' Irene Moody asked suddenly, giving Billy that look of hers.

'Because it takes three hundred and sixty-five and a quarter days for the earth to go right round the sun. This means that we have a quarter of a day left over. So every fourth year we add a day to February.'

'I remember Mr Grundy telling us about that in science,' said Roger Horner, grinning and looking round the class. 'Wasn't it a fella called Copper Knickers who worked that out, sir?'

'You mean Copernicus, I think,' Billy replied. My wild days in the Upper Fifth are coming back to haunt me, he thought.

'Isn't the leap year the time when a woman can propose to a man, sir?' Irene asked, darting a knowing look at the other girls. 'And isn't the next leap year next year in nineteen forty-eight?'

'Why, yes, so it is,' he said, falling for it.

'I'll be back next year, sir, to see if you're free,' she said, fluttering her eyelids.

Once again, the class enjoyed the joke. They were beginning to see that school could be fun.

'It's rough on anyone who has their birthday on February the twenty-ninth,' remarked Des Bishop. 'They only get to celebrate it every four years.'

The lesson was interrupted when Mr Wakefield sitting at his desk at the back raised his hand.

'What about horses, Mr Hopkins?'

'Sorry, I don't get you, Mr Wakefield. Horses? What about horses?'

'How do we measure them?'

'I believe it's in hands but I don't know much about it.'

'A hand,' said Joe Duffy, making his first real contribution, 'is the width of the hand from thumb to little finger – it's about four inches.'

'Good lad, Joe,' said Wakefield. 'It's exactly four inches by decree of Henry the Eighth. Sorry, Mr Hopkins, I thought you might like to know that.'

'Why thank you, Mr Wakefield. Most interesting. If I need information about horses, I'll know where to come.'

This informative exchange brought Billy's first 'arithmetic' lesson to an end.

'Hey, sir,' said Vera Pickles in a surprised tone, 'I enjoyed that lesson. If they're all like that, I think I'm going to like arithmetic.'

'Well, the way I see it,' Billy said, 'is that you think you've had a raw deal by having to stay at school for an extra year. But give me a chance to prove to you that school is the happiest time of your life. Give me three months, till Christmas, say, and then see what you think.'

The boys and girls of St Anselm's were not accustomed to being spoken to as young adults like this and they didn't know what to make of it.

'The programme you've fixed up for us, sir, sounds great,' said Tony Jarvis. 'We've got to come to school by law and so we may as well make the best of it. At least we don't have Grundy as our teacher.'

Billy finished his first afternoon of teaching by reading the first chapter of their set book, *A Christmas Carol* by Charles Dickens, an old favourite which would take them to the end of term and the start of the Christmas holiday.

When the class had departed, Billy began packing the various papers he'd need to begin lesson preparation –

textbooks, syllabuses, schemes of work, assignments for marking. A chore that was to last more than forty years.

Billy reached home at five o'clock, his new briefcase bulging with papers.

As usual, Mam had already prepared tea.

'Well, Billy, how did it go?' she said solicitously as she poured out his tea.

'Pretty well, Mam. I'm teaching a class that's only four years younger than me and I think I've already had a proposal of marriage from one of my pupils. To be timed for leap year.'

'It sounds as if you've made a good start. They must like you if they want to marry you already.'

'And I've got enough work on my plate to keep me busy till twelve o'clock every night,' Billy said.

'Fancy,' she exclaimed. 'I still can't hardly believe it. Me with a son a teacher. And think how rich you'll be when you get your first pay cheque at the end of the month. That'll give your dad something to think about, him and his rubbish, always going on about you getting a trade in your hands.'

In that second week, Billy initiated the first part of the two-pronged programme for his class. He worked as he had never worked before and was never in bed before midnight. Apart from the vast amount of marking and lesson preparation that the job involved, he drew up individual work schedules to match the attainment level of every pupil. Each one had a custom-designed set of objectives both in arithmetic and English, and each pupil recorded his own achievement on a grid chart after each lesson. The individual programmes involved exercises in arithmetic to be completed correctly, or certain English tasks – learning about conjunctions or full stops, writing a letter or a composition, learning a spelling list. The plan relied heavily on individual or small group teaching. At the end of the week, those who had achieved their objectives were released from the classroom to play football or netball in the school yard.

'How's it going?' Frank Wakefield asked one dinnertime.

'Too early to judge,' replied Billy, 'but one big advantage is that each pupil works at his own pace and even if absent misses no important lessons. He simply takes up where he left off before the absence.'

The pupils began to respond to this new way of working and even the slower pupils worked hard at their own standard to complete their jobs to win free time at the end of the week.

'I like this way of working,' remarked Tony Jarvis. 'I can work at my own speed and I feel as if I'm learning something at last.'

'I'm starting to like school and even arithmetic,' said Vera Pickles. 'Before, I was always being made to look stupid in front of the others. Now I get on with my own work at my own speed and I don't bother about what the others are doing.'

Nellie Wallace and Alf Dempsey, too, began to make progress with their reading as Billy had encouraged other members of the class to listen to their reading efforts. They were both keen to win their freedom on Friday afternoons.

It was the ballroom dancing that was the biggest success. At first, there was a good deal of shyness on both sides but gradually this receded. To the strains of Victor Sylvester, the top class of St Anselm's learned to move gracefully across the floor. Further, there was great progress in the cultivation of social graces and the art of relating to the opposite sex. When it came to inviting a girl to dance, in the early stages boys had simply beckoned a girl onto the dance floor by jerking a thumb, to which the girls responded with a 'Get lost!' The boys soon learned that they got better results by approaching a partner and politely asking, 'May I have this dance, please?'

As time went by, Billy's relationship with his class got better and better. A happy, friendly atmosphere developed and, furthermore, the pupils began to take a greater pride in their appearance and their status as 'senior' class. Their behaviour became less strident and more civilised. They were growing up.

On the way home, Billy got into the habit of walking with Laura Mackenzie up to the toll gates of Regina Park. Hamish had returned to his studies at Glasgow University and so the two of them were able to talk without benefit of actuarial statistics. Their conversation flowed easily and amicably and Billy found Laura had a quick wit and a ready sense of humour. Much of their time was spent laughing about some of the funny happenings at school and the eccentricities of some of the staff.

'I liked the way Greg announced in ringing Gielgud tones to his junior art class: "Dear boys and girls, I prefer you put the paint on the paper and not on your faces," ' said Billy.

'As if Junior Three could appreciate irony!' she chuckled.

'At first I didn't think I was going to like this school but things have settled down and I now enjoy teaching. Senior Four is a delight to be with and I think I'm getting somewhere with them.'

'Somehow I always felt you would,' she said.

But things weren't always plain sailing. One Thursday dinnertime, Nellie Wallace appeared at the staffroom door.

'I've told you that we don't like to be disturbed at

dinnertime. It's the only peace we get,' Grundy barked. 'Well, what do you want?'.

'Please, sir,' said Nellie, 'I've come for the school record player and the Victor Sylvester records.'

'The what?' Grundy exploded. 'What on earth's going on?'

'It's OK,' said Billy, coming to the door. 'It's for our ballroom dancing lessons.' He handed the equipment over to Nellie.

'Ballroom dancing lessons!' Grundy shrilled. 'Whatever next! This is supposed to be a school, not a dancing academy. We're here to educate them not mollycoddle them.'

'Depends what you understand by educate,' Billy replied. 'Education isn't simply book-learning and instruction. It involves a wider concept like learning adult behaviour and some of the social graces. Besides, for the eighteenth-century gentleman, dancing was an indispensable part of his broader education. You should try reading Jane Austen.'

'This is an elementary school, mate, not a finishing school for ladies and gentlemen,' he sneered.

'I don't see how you can object to the top class learning useful social skills and good manners,' Billy replied hotly, becoming more and more exasperated by Grundy's sarcasm and derision.

The rest of the staff had been listening to this exchange and now Liz Logie joined in.

'It wouldn't do you any harm to learn some of the common courtesies,' she said to Grundy.

'I've noticed a definite improvement in the dress and deportment of the top class,' said Alex. 'They seem more mature somehow. Less horseplay and fooling about.'

'Whatever you're doing to 'em,' added Greg, 'keep on

doing it. Maybe I'll come over one Thursday and learn ballroom dancing myself.'

'Any success I've had with the top class is down to Mr Grundy,' said Billy. 'Because of him, I was able to establish control and win the co-operation of my class.'

Mr Grundy preened himself. 'I'm glad you listened at least to some of my advice,' he said smugly.

'You'll never know how much you helped me,' Billy replied, smiling.

Chapter Twenty-Four

Plans

On one of the research visits to the local library, Billy had set the class the task of finding out about their own street names and their own locality. They had spent the afternoon delving into the various encyclopaedias and local documents, and writing up their findings in the special notebooks provided. Next morning back in class, they were bubbling with enthusiasm about what they had discovered.

'I live in Waterloo Court, sir,' gushed Josey Parker. 'It's named after a famous battle.'

'And our pub,' added Jim Mitchell, 'is the Waterloo Arms – that's named after the battle as well. Didn't we beat the French in eighteen fifteen, sir? Is that where it got its name?'

'Absolutely right,' said Billy. 'Any other findings?'

'Wellington Grove,' answered Tony Jarvis. 'Named after the Duke of Wellington who led our troops against Napoleon.'

'Our house is in Blucher Street,' Nellie Wallace squealed fervently. 'And Blucher was a Prussian general at that battle as well. And I take my mam's washing to a lot of the streets I found out about.'

'We live in Victory Street, sir,' said Irene Moody eagerly. 'Did it get its name 'cos we won at that battle?'

'That's right,' said Billy, nodding his head earnestly. 'Obviously you've been working hard at the library. I congratulate all of you. First-class research.'

The eyes of his class shone with happiness at their success.

'And I live in Napoleon Street,' said Joe Duffy. 'Trust me to live in a street named after the loser.'

'It must have been a great day after the victory was announced, sir,' said Anne Greenhalgh. 'Like the end of the war in nineteen forty-five when the newspapers had headlines like "Victory in Europe" and "Japan Surrenders".'

'Why don't we do the newspaper like it was?' asked Jim Mitchell, his interest suddenly awakened. 'Pretend, like, that we're living in eighteen fifteen and reporting on the battle and that.'

There was a murmur of approval from the rest of the class.

'Let's do it, sir. It'd be great fun, sir.'

Billy felt the pride rise in his heart. This is what it's all about, he told himself. Ideas coming from them, not me stuffing their heads with things they don't want to know.

'OK, OK,' he said glowingly. 'A few years ago, I worked on the *Manchester Guardian* as general dogsbody and I can show you how we could organise it.'

From that point on, there was no stopping them. Anne Greenhalgh was voted editor-in-chief. In discussion with Billy, she agreed to arrange the editorial staff into special-ised teams. One group of girls opted to cover a 'Woman's Page' and female fashion of the early nineteenth century; two boys, Jim Mitchell and Tony Jarvis, chose to cover details of the battle; Mick Lynch and Roger Horner selected arms and weapons of the period; a mixed group ran a 'Letters to the Editor' column; and two boys who had shown some skill in art settled on cartoons, graphics and maps.

The project sparked off a wave of enthusiasm and participation. Billy found himself inundated with questions on every topic and a new lively atmosphere developed. Often when Joe Duffy got up to ring the bell for break or dinner, a small crowd of pupils, disinclined to leave, lingered behind, wanting to carry on. Sometimes, Frank Wakefield joined in the discussion and added his knowledge and opinion to the topic being considered. He was pleased to see the new developments and the direction the curriculum was taking. For Senior 4, school had become a happy and a valuable experience.

In the midst of one of these discussions one day, Anne Greenhalgh remarked wistfully, 'It's all very well, writing up about these things, ladies' fashions and that, but all we've got are pictures and drawings. It'd be much better if we could see the actual things themselves. Isn't there a museum or something we could visit, sir?'

Jim Mitchell nodded his agreement. 'It's the same with writing about the battle and the kinds of weapons they used. What does a flintlock look like? And how did they fire it? What kind of bullets did they shoot? What's the difference between a flintlock, a matchlock, and a musket? We'd have a better idea if we could see the real thing instead of just pictures.'

Billy promised to look into it and discuss the matter with the headmaster.

'There's a first-class exhibition at Tatton Hall in Cheshire,' Frank Wakefield replied. Shaking his head doubtfully, he added, 'But the difficulties in taking a mixed group out there are insuperable. First, there's the question of transporting twenty-five adolescents and there's also the little matter of accident insurance. I can't see Manchester Education Committee agreeing to it. I'll look into it but I don't offer much hope.'

Surely, thought Billy, there was some way out of the impasse. It would be a great pity to dampen his pupils' fervour at this stage. But part of the growing up process was the ability to take life's ups and downs. The sensible thing to do was to discuss it with them.

'Tatton Park,' he began when he met them, 'would have been the ideal place to visit but there is the problem of getting there since there is no direct bus or train service there.'

There was a groan of disappointment.

'We could go by bike, sir,' Alf Dempsey suggested.

A great roar of scornful laughter greeted this crazy idea.

'Where are we going to get twenty-five bikes?' sneered Roger Horner, looking round the class for support. 'Use your brain, Dempsey, if you've got one.'

'It's not such a daft idea, sir,' said Tony Jarvis slowly. 'Many of us have got bikes. Some of us have sisters or brothers with bikes. We could borrow them for the day.'

'Sometimes, radical notions pay off,' said Billy thoughtfully. 'Let's have a show of hands. How many have bikes?'

Seventeen hands were raised.

'How many can get an extra bike?'

Five more hands.

'That leaves us three short. Any ideas?'

Silence.

265

'Either we all go,' said Billy, 'or none of us goes. We can't leave some members of the class behind whilst the rest of us cycle off to Cheshire.'

At that point, Frank Wakefield came into the room. He took one look at their faces.

'This place looks like a funeral parlour,' he said. 'What's happened? Who died?'

'We're short of three bicycles,' Billy answered, 'for our projected trip to Tatton Park.'

'I think I could borrow a bike for you,' Wakefield said slowly, 'but you've a long way to go before you set off on such a hazardous safari. As I said earlier, we have to get permission and insurance. I can't promise anything at this stage.'

Such was the look of anticipation on the faces that it would have taken a heart of stone to turn them down now. And the one thing that Frank Wakefield did not have was a heart of stone.

'I'll see what I can do,' he said, smiling encouragingly.

'I think I know where I can borrow the other two bikes,' said Billy. 'But first I'll have to ask them. The people concerned are not aware at this moment that they are going to offer us a loan of their bicycles.' He had in mind his brother Les and Laura Mackenzie.

'Hey, sir!' said Jim Mitchell warmly. 'You know, I think it's going to work!'

Nellie Wallace raised her hand. She looked distraught. 'Please, sir, even if you do borrow a bike for me, it's no use. I don't know how to ride one. I've never had a bike to learn.'

'No problem, sir,' said a beaming Joe Duffy. 'If we get the bikes, I'll teach her on Friday afternoons.' Irish eyes really did smile.

The pupils of Senior 4 now went into action. The rest of the week saw the appearance of a motley collection of bicycles, bone-shakers and crocks, from the sit-up-and-beg variety to the latest racer with ten gears. Billy expected a scooter, a three-wheeler, or at least a penny-farthing to be brought in any day. Every dinnertime, a team of boys could be seen outside the prefabs repairing, servicing, oiling, greasing and updating the miscellaneous machines which were brought in from back yards and cellars. Several boys, Alf Dempsey among them, showed a marked aptitude for mechanics. Terms like Schrader valve, cotter pin, lubrication points, rod brakes, rim tape, trigger control could be heard being bandied about. Repairs to punctures, gears, brakes, wheels, sprockets were carried out as a matter of routine. Joe Duffy gave Nellie Wallace training and practice every dinnertime until she was reasonably proficient and no longer wobbled about. As their Wednesday afternoon visiting speaker, Billy invited the traffic adviser from the city police, who gave lots of tips about cycling safety.

'As a cycling club, you may cycle in pairs but keep well over to the left, always signal clearly and in good time, make sure your bike is in good order, especially brakes. At junctions, your teacher should control the traffic to let you pass through.'

The class looked expectantly in Billy's direction.

Billy extracted the maximum education value from the projected trip. The form was set the task of planning and calculating the route – distance, time required to reach their destination, places of interest on the way and, most important, what they expected to see at Tatton Hall itself. Jim Mitchell was elected by popular vote as route leader.

'As far as we can calculate, sir,' said Jim, 'it's about thirteen miles from here and it should take us about one and a half hours including stops to get there – maybe longer if we have any mishaps, like punctures or breakdowns.'

Came the day when Frank Wakefield reported the results of his inquiries to Billy.

'Good news and bad news,' he announced, looking steadily at Billy.

'OK, Frank,' said Billy anxiously. 'Let me know the worst.'

'No, I'll give you the good news first. The Education Committee has granted permission provided we can get ourselves insured. That shouldn't present any problem.'

'And the bad news?' Billy asked, searching his face.

'There must be two teachers to accompany the party. One male for the boys, one female for the girls.' His eyes twinkled as he said, 'I thought we might ask Mrs Melton-Mowbray. What do you think?'

Billy couldn't hide a slight grimace. 'Fine,' he answered. 'But I don't think she has a bicycle.'

'Is there anyone else we could ask? Any of our female teachers with a bike?'

'I suppose we could ask Laura Mackenzie,' Billy said carefully as if it had taken profound thought to reach such a conclusion, 'though I was hoping to use her bicycle for one of the girls. But she did say when I mentioned the matter to her that she might be able to borrow her sister's bike as well for the day. But who would take her class while she was away?'

'I think that can be arranged,' Wakefield said, now smiling broadly.

At four o'clock, Billy escorted Laura to Regina Park

gates. As they wheeled their bikes along, Billy broached the subject.

'It looks as if our projected trip to Tatton Park is on. And Frank Wakefield has given me his OK to ask you if you'd like to accompany me, I mean . . . that is . . . us . . . Senior Four, on the visit.'

'I'd love to, Hoppy. I feel greatly honoured to be asked. But why didn't you ask Mrs Melton-Mowbray or Liz Logie?' she asked teasingly.

'Well, of course, we thought of them first,' he said in the same vein, 'but they don't have bicycles.'

'Incidentally,' said Laura, changing the subject, 'are you aware that half the top girls have been shadowing us all the way from school and have been doing so every day? I don't know what they're expecting to see.'

'Perhaps they're hoping for some indiscretion one of these evenings.'

She gave him a mischievous look. 'I wonder what kind of thing they have in mind,' she said, deadpan.

Chapter Twenty-Five

Cycle Trip

Next morning, Billy gave the news to the class. There was a loud cheer.

'We shall set off in a week's time, next Wednesday morning at nine o'clock prompt. So no one must be late or they'll find we've gone without them. Remember to bring a packed lunch – sandwiches and whatever you like. I'm glad to say that Miss Mackenzie has kindly agreed to go with us to chaperone the girls.'

'Chaperone! We're not a bunch of kids, sir,' complained Irene Moody. 'Do we have to have a chaperone?'

'Afraid so. Not that I believe any of you need an escort but that's the regulation.'

'Anyroad, I'm glad she's going,' grinned Tony Jarvis impishly. 'She's a stunner. I'll bet you're glad she's going as well, aren't you, sir?'

Billy looked at him quizzically. Was the boy able to read his mind?

'Shut your face, Jarvis,' Irene snapped angrily. 'What do you know?'

'Now, now, Irene,' answered Tony patronisingly. 'Don't get them into a twist. We know what's in your mind. And by the way, it's not Jarvis, it's Tony, if you don't mind.'

On the morning of departure, Billy made the usual trip across Manchester and arrived at school at eight forty-five. As he entered the classroom, he was taken aback by the sight that met his eyes. His wards were already at their desks, packed lunches much in evidence, notebooks at the ready. There was a sense of excitement and a new, radiant look about them. They were truly prepared for the excursion, spruced up, scrubbed, groomed and gleaming, and also dressed as if they were to take part in the Tour de France cycling race. Many of the boys were wearing shorts and jerseys, others had their trousers held by bicycle clips. It was the girls, however, who had excelled themselves with their long skirts and woollen jumpers, their hair tied back in ponytails, looking for the world like a bevy of Hollywood beauties. A few had applied a smidgen of red to their lips.

'I can't believe my eyes,' exclaimed Billy. 'Is this my class of pupils I see before me? Or is it a group of fashion models dressed up for the catwalk?'

The class basked happily in his delight.

'My dad has sent a pile of fruit for everyone,' Mick Lynch announced. 'An apple and an orange each.'

'Hope they're not faded rejects,' retorted Tessie Shea to everyone's amusement.

Billy called the register, to which the class responded clearly and quickly, impatient to be on their way. As he reeled off the names, it soon became obvious that there was one person missing. A person they could hardly forget.

'Wait a minute,' said Billy, looking round the room. 'Where's Nellie Wallace? We can't go without our Nellie. Not after all her practice with Joe there.'

271

At that moment, the door burst open and Nellie barged into the room.

'Sorry I'm late again, sir,' she panted. 'I had to take Mrs Ormeroyd's dinner round to her house for warming up later on. But I'm ready now, sir.'

'Ready' was the right word. There was a gasp of incredulity followed by happy laughter when they took in Nellie's costume. She was attired in wide pyjama-legged culottes, a thick woolly jersey and a bright red beret set at a saucy angle.

Mick Lynch was first to react. 'We're going to look at old-fashioned clothes,' he guffawed. 'You weren't supposed to get dressed up in 'em.'

'Quiet, Lynch – I mean Mick – you're only jealous,' she rejoined, tossing her head.

'You look fabulous, Nellie,' said Billy. 'But where did you get such a beautiful outfit?'

'Me mam give me it, sir. She used to go bike riding and that when she was a young girl.'

'She must have gone cycling with Victoria and Albert,' smirked Mick Lynch who had to have the last word.

Laura Mackenzie arrived. Many of the boys could not restrain a wolf whistle. She wore a calf-length tartan tweed skirt, a knitted jumper with matching cardigan, and on her head a tammy with a large red bobble.

'Good morning, everyone,' she said brightly, looking around the room. 'I can see everyone is prepared for safari.'

'You look smashin', miss,' exclaimed Tony Jarvis. 'Doesn't she, sir?'

'She certainly does, Tony,' Billy agreed enthusiastically. 'A little touch of Scotland to help us on our way.'

'Why, thank you, kind sirs,' said Laura.

'And did you bring your bagpipes with you, miss?' asked

Irene Moody archly, glancing slyly at her female friends.

'No, Irene,' Laura smiled back. 'Unfortunately they wouldn't fit into my saddle bag, but I did bring a little haggis for lunch.'

'Haggis for lunch?' said Alf Dempsey. 'I always thought haggis was a lot of ugly old women.'

'Maybe that's what she eats,' was Irene's catty rejoinder.

'No, no,' said Des Bishop. 'Haggis is a Scottish musical instrument like a sweet potato pipe.'

'Like an ocarina?' suggested Billy.

'I can see that you've got a lot to learn about Scotland,' Laura laughed.

Frank Wakefield, who had been busy settling Laura's class down to some work, now made his appearance and cast an inspectorial eye over the assembly. He obviously approved, for he said, 'It makes me feel proud to see you dressed so smartly for the occasion. I know that your behaviour for the rest of the day will be exemplary. Remember, you are representing the school. If this visit is successful, there's no reason why we shouldn't arrange more of them. Take care on the road and obey everything that Mr Hopkins and Miss Mackenzie tell you. Now off you go and enjoy yourselves. Oh, and don't forget, this is an educational visit. So make sure you learn something useful.'

The class divided into pre-arranged partnerships. Girls on the inside, boys on the outside. Joe Duffy, who had taken responsibility for Nellie's safety, now made a point of escorting her. Jim Mitchell as route leader rode at the front of the convoy with Laura at his side. Billy accompanied Anne Greenhalgh at the back.

Soon they were moving smoothly through Regina Park and along Birchfields Road towards the two-lane Kingsway. The traffic was light for a Wednesday morning. They were overtaken by the occasional 40 bus and every now and then by a new Morris 8 or an Austin 7.

Lucky blighters, Billy thought. They must be very rich or have special privileges to own a car, especially since petrol is still on ration.

Every now and then they passed a billboard which asked in large letters: IS YOUR JOURNEY REALLY NECESSARY?

In the case of Senior Four, yes! Billy said to himself.

Free from the formality and the constraints of the classroom, Billy found that his pupils unburdened themselves, seizing the opportunity to tell him about the things that were on their minds.

Whenever traffic allowed, Billy moved along the rows like a sheepdog checking that all his wards stayed in line.

As he passed along, Tony Jarvis called out, 'Hey, sir, this is better than school, isn't it?'

'This *is* school,' Billy called back as he came abreast of Joe Duffy and his protégée. 'Joe,' he said, 'could you drop back so that I can talk to Nellie there and see how she's getting on?'

Joe complied and Billy turned to Nellie.

'Well, Nellie, how's it going?'

She beamed happily. 'Everything's fine, sir. I love school now and I'm enjoying this trip out. I'm glad of the rest.'

'You work pretty hard at home, don't you?'

'I'll say, sir. Me dad walked out on us last year – he ran off with a younger woman and left me mam to fend for herself. There's five of us in the family and I'm the eldest. We're always dead short of money, sir, and me mam has to take in washing, ironing, sewing and darning from the neighbours in our street. We even cook for some of them and donkey-stone their steps to earn a few coppers.'

'And you help your mam out?'

'That's right, sir. That's why I'm late for school some-times. But I'll try to do better.'

'You've got a lovely name, Nellie. Do you know you're named after a famous music-hall star?'

'Yes, sir. That was me gran. She saw her a few times at the Ardwick Empire and so because me dad's name was – is – Wallace, she gave me the same name.'

'Let's hope you become as famous one day,' said Billy, and he cycled on to draw up alongside Alf Dempsey.

'Enjoying yourself, Alf?'

'S'great, sir. I love being out in the open air – hate being cooped up in the classroom all day. But you've changed all that.'

'You're keen on the great outdoors, I can see that. Also keen on sport.'

'Yeah, that's right, sir. Especially boxing.'

'How come?'

'Me dad used to be a boxer, sir. Won dozens of cups and medals, and that. But he drinks a lot, now he's retired from the ring. Comes home every night from the pub drunk. Gets nasty sometimes and turns on me and me mam.'

'Sorry to hear that, Alf.'

'S'all right, sir. He doesn't do it so much now – I'm getting too big for him. And if he tries to hit me mam again, I'll belt him one.'

'So that's why you want to become a boxer!'

Alf grinned. 'Yeah, that's part of it, sir.'

The group had now reached the roundabout on the main Altrincham Road where they had to turn right. Billy rode to the front of the line and ordered everyone to stop.

'OK,' he called. 'We'll adopt the routine we've practised. I'll go on to the main road and stop the traffic coming from your right and when I give the signal, make your right turn towards Altrincham.'

The manoeuvre was executed without a hitch. Not that there was much traffic to deal with anyway. Then it was on through the leafy lanes of Cheshire to Bowden and then Bucklow Hill until they had their first glimpse of Tatton Hall. And what a thrilling sight it was! They felt like Livingstone when he first espied Victoria Falls. Their eyes beheld the magnificent mansion as they approached it through a beautifully landscaped park complete with lakes, woodlands and deer. The boys and girls were mesmerised as if they had entered a fairyland – which they had.

When the bicycles had been parked at the back of the mansion, Billy gathered his class outside the main entrance for an introductory briefing.

'Well, Senior Four, here we are at last. Congratulations on your cycling skills and your road manners and behaviour. Our routine today will be as follows. For the rest of the morning, we shall be taken on a conducted tour of this wonderful building. Ask the guide as many questions as you like. We'll meet again at half past one this afternoon when you'll be free to conduct your own research for our newspaper. We shall leave at three o'clock. We are asked to help preserve this historical monument by not touching any of the exhibits but I'm sure there's no need to tell you that. And Duffy – no smoking!'

When the laughter had died down, Duffy retorted, 'And the same goes for you, sir.'

Billy took his class in to meet the guide who had agreed to take them on a tour of the Egerton home. As if in a dream, the visitors tagged on behind, gazing in silent awe at the paintings, the portraits, the decorated ceilings, the furniture and the furnishings, listening to their guide's animated account and also to the ticking and melodious chiming of the many ancient clocks that were distributed throughout the hall. Billy's chest swelled with pride when he heard the flow of questions being directed at the guide.

'When was this building first put up?'

'How many servants did the Egerton family have?'

'Does the park grow its own food?'

'Is the Egerton family connected with Egerton Road in Manchester?'

Laura circulated among the little groups, directing their attention to unusual exhibits, or pointing to a particular painting or an interesting sculpture. She certainly won over the boys who hung on her every word.

Is this the same group, Billy mused, that was so rebellious only a few weeks ago? Is this the class that Grundy wrote off as useless? Only yesterday in the staffroom he had dismissed the whole idea of an outing as 'rubbish and merely an excuse to get out of the classroom and avoid doing work'. What would Grundy say if he could see them now, completely absorbed in the guide's explanations, questioning, note-taking, drawing, sketching?

Dinnertime soon came round and teachers and pupils had built up healthy appetites. The young students wandered off to discuss their reactions to the visit and, no doubt, thought Billy, to enjoy an illicit smoke. He decided to let it go this time. After all, in seven or eight months' time, they'd be masters and mistresses of their own fate.

At some distance from the mansion, Laura and Billy found a picnic spot giving a panoramic view of the undulating parkland. At a table near a fountain containing a statue of Cupid, they settled down to eat their lunch.

'This is an idyllic spot,' Laura said as she unwrapped

her sandwiches. 'Thank you so much for inviting me, Hoppy.'

'You're the one doing the favour,' he answered, pouring coffee from his thermos. 'Incidentally, Hoppy is a nickname my pals at school gave me and I got stuck with it. OK for school and for my cronies but I'd be glad if you would call me Billy.'

'Then from now on, Billy it is,' she said warmly.

He felt a tingling of his scalp when he heard her use his first name like that.

'That's that settled. You know, Laura, it's funny how an outing like this, when we're away from the formality of school and playing the role of teacher, we relax and simply be ourselves. We stop acting a part, as it were. On the way here, pupils have been pouring out their problems in a way they never would or could back in the classroom. I felt like Sigmund Freud.'

'I know what you mean, Billy,' she laughed. 'Perhaps there's something about you that makes people want to confide in you. But I had a little taste of it too. On the road here, Jim Mitchell gave me his life story and some of the difficulties he has living in a pub. Like the Saturday night knees-ups and the fist fights. Makes you realise that we're not merely teachers but social workers as well. I must say I like the idea.'

'That's right. Not merely instructors but sympathetic listeners too. But then everyone's got problems, I think. Though to be honest, you always look so cool, calm and collected, Laura, I can't imagine you with a problem.'

'Don't take everything at face value, Billy. Maybe I don't have any major problems, but I do have little things which niggle. Only pinpricks, I suppose.'

'Like for instance?'

'There you go, Billy. Playing at Sigmund Freud again. The thing that's on my mind is my younger brother. I'm a little worried about him. He's doing important exams soon, and my father is pushing him a bit hard. Daddy's a wonderful man but he rules the roost with a firm hand, brooks no argument, and knows all the answers. We love him very much but he does tend to be a bit bossy.'

'I know the problem, Laura. I've got a father like that myself. You said "we" just now. Who's "we"?'

'The rest of our family – my mother, younger sisters Jenny and Katie, and my brother Hughie. Oh, and I nearly forgot, my grandmother and old Aunty Aggie.'

'So, four children plus two old 'uns in your family. Almost as big as my own – there are five of us. And I'm the baby. And spoiled, so they tell me.'

'I'm sure you're not,' she laughed. 'But what about your father? You said he was a bossy-boots as well.'

'Bossy only when my mother gives him permission to be so. He's more mellow nowadays though – has to be or my mother would give him what for. On balance, I'd say she's in charge in our family but she's developed the knack of letting my dad think he's in control.'

'She sounds quite a character, Billy. As for my father, he's a creature of his Scottish background, I think. In Scotland the man reigns supreme and he expects everyone, especially the womenfolk, to obey him without question at all times.'

'Surely your dad admits that he can be wrong sometimes. After all, he's only human.'

'Never, I'm afraid,' she laughed, and poured herself a cup of coffee. 'There are two infallible beings to his way of thinking – God and Duncan Mackenzie. Sometimes God is wrong but never Duncan. It's a matter of saving face. If ever he's wrong, he cleverly reverses the argument so that it appears that you were the one who was mistaken.'

Billy chuckled. 'Sounds to me as if he'd make a good politician – even Prime Minister. What does he do for a living, Laura?'

'Senior inspector in the Inland Revenue,' she said apologetically.

'Inland Revenue! Don't mention that term to me!' Billy exclaimed. 'I used to work – I use the term loosely – in an income tax office as a serf. The senior clerical officer was bad enough. He had his desk in the main office and was regarded by everyone as a minor deity but as for the senior inspector! He occupied an office away from us lower mortals and we rarely caught sight of him. If your dad was one of those, then as far as I'm concerned, he is God and no mistake.'

Laura laughed. 'Tell him that and he'll love you forever. The trouble is that he has fixed ideas about education. Once again based on the Scottish system. If you don't have a degree, then you're not fully educated. Preferably a degree with honours written after it.'

'That lets me out,' sighed Billy. 'I'm a lowly peasant with a rubbishy Teacher's Certificate.'

'Same as me,' she said. 'But in my case, it's OK because I'm a woman. I have to wait until a member of one of the acceptable professions with an honours degree falls in love with me.'

'Like Hamish, I suppose.'

'Oh, Hamish! His family and mine have known each other since the beginning of time when we all lived in Dumfries. Hamish and I grew up together and our family have always had an understanding that we'd marry some day when he's qualified. Of course, for my father, Hamish can do no wrong – he's Scottish, he's studying for honours, and his subject is actuarial studies which everyone assures me is very lucrative.'

'Family understanding, you say. What about love? What about Cupid over there,' Billy said, indicating the statue on the fountain. 'Doesn't he come into it?'

'Afraid not. Not unless he's a doctor, a lawyer, or an accountant with a degree and a professional qualification from the University of Glasgow.' She sounded contempt-uous of the whole system.

'Don't let yourself get trapped, Laura, into doing something you don't want. Life is too short. There's more to it than having a secure future. Love and happiness are more important. Oops, there I go doing my Sigmund Freud again.'

'I'm sure you're right, Billy, but going against family wishes, especially my father's, is not as easy as you think.'

As the conversation proceeded, Billy's heart sank slowly deeper and deeper into his boots. Honours degrees? Noble professions? Scotland? Bagpipes? Haggis? He didn't stand a chance with this beautiful, beautiful girl with whom he'd fallen in love.

'But we seem to be talking only about me,' she com-plained. 'What about you? Do you have a girlfriend? I'd be surprised if you didn't,' she added.

'What makes you say that, Laura? I mean, how do you know I like girls?' he said with a mischievous grin.

'My instincts tell me,' she smiled. 'You're quite nice-looking, so I'm sure the girls queue up to go out with you. I've noticed anyway that the top girls have a crush on you. They obviously think the world of you.'

'What's your evidence for saying that?' he asked, pleased by the implied compliment.

'I suppose it's the way they genuflect when you go by,' she laughed.

Billy joined in her laughter. Maybe she's not out of reach after all, he thought. She's handing me a small bouquet.

'But you must be careful, Billy. Those girls will eat you for breakfast. Especially that Irene Moody. I've seen the coquettish way she looks at you. That girl could give Veronica Lake a few pointers. There's something about that girl . . . I don't know what it is but she acts a bit too grown up. Anyway, to get back to the subject. I was asking you if you had a girlfriend.'

'Not really,' Billy answered reluctantly. 'There was a girl called Adele but I think she's now engaged to be married to someone else and so I don't have anyone at the moment. I used to do a lot of ballroom dancing and Adele was my partner for competitions.'

'You said you think she's engaged. Is it not definite then?'

'Knowing Adele she could always change her mind. I hope it's definite though,' he laughed, 'or she might come knocking at my door.'

Was it his imagination or did he notice a flicker of concern on Laura's face? He didn't mention the necking in Adele's parlour every weekend. That was in the past. What would she care anyway if he had a string of girlfriends?

'The only dancing I've done,' he heard her saying, 'is Scottish dancing – eightsome reels.'

Billy had a fleeting vision of Laura hopping about with a bunch of brawny Jocks dressed in kilts.

'But the Scots,' she went on, 'are more concerned with educational qualifications than dancing the Highland fling. This Scottish obsession with the great paper chase is enough to drive one round the bend. As I said earlier, I'm concerned about young Hughie. Only sixteen and about to take his School Certificate. He is expected to go in for medicine. He's doing well enough in science subjects but having a struggle with his French which he has to have to complete the required matriculation. My father's putting the pressure on him and I'm getting worried about him – Hughie, that is, not my father.'

When he heard this, Billy saw a faint glimmer of hope – and it was no more than a glimmer. Maybe this was his chance. He heard himself saying, 'French? Maybe I could help him, Laura. I don't have an honours degree but I have studied French and am qualified to teach to School Certificate standard.'

'Oh, would you, Billy? I'd be so grateful. We'd pay you of course.'

'Pay? I don't know what my Jewish friends in Cheetham Hill would say but your gratitude is pay enough. We'll fix up something tomorrow. I'll give him a passage to translate from English to French so I'll know where to make a start.'

'Billy,' she said warmly, 'you're a wonderful person. I could kiss you for that.'

'So what's stopping you?' he said, holding out both hands and adopting his best Yiddish accent.

'Mainly the fact that your class is on its way back for the second session,' she giggled.

In the afternoon, the form divided into their different editorial teams – fashions of the early nineteenth century, sports, furniture, and weapons and artillery. For ninety minutes, they inspected different parts of the mansion like young professional journalists going about their business, writing up notes, discussing findings, sketching items which caught their interest. At three o'clock, it was time to bring the visit to a close.

On the way back, the class was full of it, jabbering away like a cage of monkeys.

'Did you know, sir, that some of the women had pinched-in waists, sir – only seventeen or eighteen inches,' exclaimed Vera Pickles. 'It must've been murder, sir. They used to squeeze themselves into tight-laced corsets and stays.'

'And so did the men!' added Anne Greenhalgh. 'In fact, they used to spend more time than the women primping themselves up.'

'And those dresses they wore! Even the men's clothes! They looked so small,' commented Tessie Shea. 'They wouldn't fit people today. I know I couldn't get into any of those gowns the women wore.'

'Quite right, Tessie,' said Billy as he cycled alongside. 'People were smaller and shorter in the past. For example, the average height of a man in the Middle Ages was only five feet six inches. Today, it's around five feet ten inches.'

'The Egertons had over forty servants, sir,' said Josey Parker. 'And did you see the terrible kitchens they had to work in? Up at half past five in the morning and working till ten o'clock at night – even later if there was a banquet on.'

Further along the formation, discussion was on military matters.

'Wellington's army used grenade launchers, sir,' Jim Mitchell called out breathlessly as they climbed a small incline in the road. 'Many of Napoleon's troops were still using swords and lances against muskets.'

'And Wellington used infantry squares against the French

light infantry,' added Mick Lynch. 'The French were clobbered.'

All along the line of bikes, the pupils pedalled on with a constant stream of enthusiastic chatter about all they'd seen and heard. Billy had now become the final authority in settling disputes and here and there he heard his name being quoted as the last word. 'Hopalong said . . .' 'I asked sir and he said . . .' For Senior 4, Billy had become God.

With a strong wind behind them, they made good time back. Laura left the convoy at the corner of Regina Park Hill and Billy took the rest on to school which they reached shortly after four thirty. The school was deserted. Four o'clock at St Anselm's saw a mad dash for the gates and it was usually a toss-up who got out first, children or staff.

Billy's own class seemed reluctant to depart but he dismissed them and they finally cycled off, still twittering excitedly.

Billy went into his classroom to collect his belongings. A successful day, he said to himself. I think everyone got a lot out of it.

As he was about to leave, he had one last visitor – Irene Moody who had waited outside the classroom until everyone had departed.

'I came to get my things, sir,' she said huskily, giving him her slinky look. 'That was one of the happiest days of my life. And, sir, I want you to know that if there's anything – and I mean anything – I can do for you, you've only to ask.'

Laura was right, thought Billy. I have to watch my step with this one. She's a sensitive adolescent. I like her and I don't want to hurt her by ridiculing her but dealing with her is like walking on eggshells.

'That's nice of you, Irene,' he said tactfully, moving

towards the door. 'I'll remember your offer. And I'm glad you enjoyed the day. We learned a lot. It's been a long day and now I think it's time to make tracks. It's all very well for you, Irene, you live close by. I still have to cycle across to Cheetham Hill.'

'Yes, sir. Goodnight, sir. And thanks once again.'

Billy mounted his trusty mechanical steed and pedalled off.

Chapter Twenty-Six

Model Lessons

The morning after the Tatton visit, Billy arrived a little late for school. The traffic along Princess Street had been particularly heavy that morning, and he cursed the trams, the cars, and the traffic lights as he was held up at junction after junction. If I had my way, he said to himself, I'd ban cars and trams from the city centre and allow only bicycles and pedestrians. Maybe a few buses but that's all.

When he finally pedalled through the school entrance it was five past nine and his pupils were already in their places. As he stepped through the door, the whole class rose as one. There was a smile on every face.

'Good morning, Mr Hopkins,' they chorused.

'Good morning, everyone,' Billy said. 'Please sit down. You're embarrassing me.'

The class grinned back.

There was something about them, an eagerness in their expressions, and from that day forward, there was a different atmosphere. The Tatton excursion had somehow released a new energy and a new spirit of co-operation. Billy was euphoric about this development for it meant acceptance and recognition that he was their teacher and had earned their respect.

The class got down to the job of producing an historical newspaper. They called it *The Morning Post*, and the front-page headline was 'VICTORY AT WATERLOO', followed by an account of the battle by 'our special correspondent' Jim Mitchell. The rest of the paper contained contributions from every member of the class, including Alf Dempsey and Nellie Wallace. Billy's job was to print it, which meant writing it out in Indian ink with the authentic layout of a national newspaper. The result was proudly displayed on the school noticeboard and every break a crowd of children gathered around to read it. The senior class was justly proud of their effort and woe betide anyone who even thought of defacing it.

The class fell into a happy routine. Mornings were devoted to hard graft – the basic curriculum of the three Rs, science, art, and social studies. The afternoons were given over to broadening their horizons through a series of outside visits and invited speakers, plus their weekly ballroom dancing lessons.

One morning, Tessie Shea raised her hand in class.

'Yesterday in our research afternoon at the library,' she said, 'I was reading about a man called Ebenezer Howard who built a new town called Welwyn Garden City.'

'That's good,' answered Billy. 'You happened to see his name in the library, did you?'

'Not really, sir,' she replied. 'I saw his name first on the back of a packet of Shredded Wheat and so I looked him up in an encyclopaedia.'

'So what's your point, Tessie?'

'I had an idea, sir. Why can't we build a model town like his in class, showing the way our town ought to look.'

'I have an uncle and an aunty who live at Port Sunlight,' added Anne Greenhalgh who had obviously been discussing it with her. 'That's a model town as well, built by Lord Lever. We could build our model town on a large board. On one side, we could show our district, all black and dirty, as it really is, and the other as it could be – the town of the future.'

'I like the idea,' said Billy, 'but what do we build it out of? It's a big project and we have little in the way of funds.'

'Out of matchboxes,' suggested Tony Jarvis. 'When I was a nipper in the infants' school, we used to make things out of old boxes. I remember matchboxes were the best.'

'You'll have to show us,' said Billy.

At morning assembly, Frank Wakefield appealed to the whole school to bring in matchboxes. A large cardboard box was placed outside the classroom for this purpose. The response was overwhelming. Matchboxes poured in from every conceivable source and of every shape, size and with every kind of illustration on them – cats, camels, sauce recipes, Red Indians, trains, Russian dolls.

Billy supplied the class with pictures of all kinds of buildings but left the actual construction to the pupils, to their imagination and their handicraft skills.

The class had been divided into groups, each with responsibility for a particular section. The various groups gathered the motley collection of matchboxes – Puck, Captain Webb, Swan Vestas, Bryant and May – onto their desks and puzzled out how to make use of them. They turned the boxes this way and that in an effort to create a house similar to the picture before them. Some houses, like the slum houses of the Industrial Revolution, were relatively easy, but others, like the circular modern houses and public buildings, were more challenging and required much creative imagination. Billy wandered around the class making suggestions and giving help and advice where it was required.

One day, two window cleaners appeared at the windows and as they were polishing the panes, they were distracted from their task by what they saw as bizarre educational practice.

'Hey, Bert,' one of them called to his companion. 'Come 'ere and have a butcher's at this.'

Bert complied and gazed spellbound at twenty-five adolescents playing around with a lot of boxes.

'Bleedin' hell,' he exclaimed, shaking his head. 'It's like a bloody asylum in there. If that's modern education, you can stuff it.'

The result at the end of the term was a magnificent display entitled 'Buildings: past, present and future'. On one side were depicted the slums and factories of the Industrial Age whilst the other provided a contrast illustrating how a modern town could be laid out, complete with roundabouts and ring roads.

This wasn't the end of the matchbox episode. Tony Jarvis discovered not only a new word – *phillumeny*, or the love of matchboxes – but a whole new world and a new interest which was to occupy him for the rest of his life. For the remainder of that term, he went around telling anyone who was willing to listen, 'I'm a phillumenist.'

Billy's classroom became at times like a marketplace. Wakefield had his 'office' at the back of his classroom and there was a succession of visitors to see him during Billy's lessons. Most of them were quiet and peaceful enough, though on one occasion Wakefield had to deal with Alf Dempsey's father who had arrived the worse for wear from drink, which he had no doubt needed to give him Dutch courage. For Senior 4 it made an interesting diversion from arithmetic exercises.

'You kept our Alf behind after school, Wakefield, for being late, di'n't you? We need 'im to 'elp at 'ome, see. Keep 'im behind again, you bastard, and I'll be round to duff you up.'

'Right, on your way, pal,' said Wakefield, helping him forcibly out of the room.

'Oh, so it's a fight you want,' shouted Dempsey senior, taking up a professional boxing stance.

Frank Wakefield was no lightweight and he grabbed Dempsey round the shoulder to push him out. They both fell to the ground, grappling with each other. It was the son who came to the rescue and resolved the contest.

'Get home, Dad, before I belt you one. You're showing me up in front of my mates. Now piss off home.'

This seemed to do the trick, for the older Dempsey looked at his son through his alcoholic haze and some notion of the commotion he had caused penetrated his brain.

'Right, son. I was only looking out for you.'

'Well, don't!' Alf yelled, ushering him out of the room.

The interruption provided an interesting diversion which Billy exploited by instructing his pupils to write an essay describing the event.

Every Tuesday afternoon at 3 p.m., Mr Stanley Cashman, a clerk from the Education Offices, appeared to check and pick up the savings which the Head had collected from the schoolchildren during the week. He stood beside Wakefield's desk at the back of the room reconciling the various sums of money he had come to take away. Most of his attention, however, was given over to Billy's series of lessons on the early explorers and he hardly gave a glance to the accounts books he had come to examine.

Flattered by the attention he gave every week, Billy prepared his best lessons for him and an unspoken mutual understanding sprang up between them. On these occasions, Billy became oblivious of the rest of his class and there were only two people in the room – Billy and the bank clerk. Every Tuesday afternoon they set off together on their perilous journey of exploration and as the weeks went by they became seasoned travellers.

There developed between them a special bond of comradeship, and why not? After all, had they not come through some hazardous journeys together? Had they not sailed together with the Vikings in their longships from Scandinavia to Iceland and points further west; journeyed with Marco Polo across the roof of the world to meet Kublai Khan in Xanadu; in 1487 set out in three caravels and rounded the Cape of Good Hope with Bartholomew Diaz; and in 1497, after a hair-raising voyage round Africa in which they had almost come to grief, finally made it to India in the company of Vasco da Gama. They looked forward to the next episode, to their trip across the Atlantic in the *Santa Maria* when they would discover America with Christopher Columbus at the helm.

Often Wakefield had to bring Stanley Cashman back to reality by reminding him of his purpose in the school.

A procession of tradesmen and artisans also came through Billy's class regularly. Most of them became absorbed in the lessons being taught and occasionally one or two of them would join in, forgetting that they were no longer pupils but had come to fix something or other or to install a piece of equipment.

One morning Billy was taking an English literature lesson and was reading *The Invisible Man* by H.G. Wells aloud to the class. They were engrossed in the story and had reached the point where a villager's snarling dog attacks the Invisible Man and tears his trousers. Fearenside, the owner of the dog, tells his friend of the incident and recounts how strange it was that there was no sign of pink flesh showing but only a black void where the leg should have been. He ends up by referring to the Invisible Man as 'piebald'.

Tessie Shea raised her hand. 'What does piebald mean, sir?' she asked.

Now at college, Billy had been trained never to answer such a question directly. 'Never tell your pupils anything,' he'd been instructed. The correct approach was to engage one's learners in dialogue and encourage them to follow a train of thought, the so-called Socratic method, by which they'd be led along a sequence of questions and arguments until they stumbled on the correct answer – much as Socrates himself had done when he strolled around the marketplace in Athens engaging his young followers in disputation and logical thought.

'Think of the word "pie",' Billy suggested. 'Can anyone think of its use in another word?'

The answers came thick and fast.

'Apple pie.'

'Potato pie.'

'Meat pie.'

'No, no,' Billy said. 'You've got the wrong pie. This "pie" means different colours.'

'Rhubarb pie!' shouted Des Bishop. 'That's different colours.'

'How about blueberry pie?' suggested Jim Mitchell.

Billy was getting desperate. 'Look, think of a man who had "pie" in his title.'

'Ah, now I know, sir,' said Tony Jarvis triumphantly. 'You mean the one Simple Simon met when going to the fair. The "pieman".'

'Sometimes me mam calls me dad that when he comes home blotto,' said Horner.

'How do you mean?' Billy asked, puzzled. 'How does "pie" come into it?'

'Me mam belts him with a rolling pin and shouts, "Drunken bugger! Pie-eyed again." '

Billy was about to give up on the Socratic approach and resort to old-fashioned instruction when Alf Dempsey of all people raised his hand. Most unusual, Billy thought. Alf never answered anything but maybe, just maybe, he had the answer this time.

'Ice pie!' he called.

Billy and the rest of the class were baffled by this contribution.

'Ice pie, Alf? I don't get it,' he said.

'It's a game, sir, that we play at home when there's nowt to do.'

'He means "I Spy",' said Jim Mitchell.

When the guffaws had died down, Billy felt it was time for a more direct approach.

'The word "pie" means dappled or marked in spots, patches, or blotches of a different colour or shade.'

'You mean speckled, sir?' said Anne Greenhalgh.

'That's right,' Billy said.

'The Pied Piper,' she said. 'He was dressed in clothes of different colours.'

'Now we're on the right track,' Billy said. 'And there's a common bird that has the word "pie" in its name.'

'You mean blackbirds baked in a pie, like?' asked Vera Pickles, trying to be helpful.

'No, no,' Billy almost screamed. 'This bird is known for its habit of pilfering and hoarding. Sometimes it's taught to speak.'

'How about "magpie"?' called Mick Lynch. 'That's black and white.'

'Good! Got it at last,' Billy exclaimed with a sigh of relief. 'So now can you tell me the meaning of "piebald"?'

'Excuse me,' said a voice from somewhere under the floor.

Billy looked around bewildered.

The plumber emerged from under the sink and announced in ringing tones, 'Why don't you bloody well tell 'em and have done with it? Piebald means black and white; roan means grey and white; skewbald means brown and white. I know 'cos I place a bet on the horses every dinnertime. I've got a bob each way on one today and it's a piebald. Awright?' With that, his head disappeared back under the sink.

Billy could only mumble, 'Why, thank you very much for that information. We'll try to remember it.'

The class looked at Billy puzzled. Should they listen to him or the oracle from the underworld?

So much for the Socratic method, Billy thought. From now on, I'll simply tell 'em. It's simpler and quicker.

It was not only the general public who joined in. Frank Wakefield sitting at the back of the room couldn't resist putting his oar in from time to time.

In one lesson, Billy had got on to figures of speech – a favourite with the class. They had dealt with similes – as blind as a bat, as fierce as a lion, pleased as Punch, as smooth as velvet, ignoring the smooth as a baby's bottom suggested by Des Bishop – and had finally reached onomatopoeia, the imitation of natural sounds in words.

Billy wrote up the words 'bang, blast, boom, bellow' on the blackboard. 'Look at these words,' he said, 'and tell me what they have in common.'

'They all begin with B,' said Mick Lynch immediately.

'What about these?' he said, writing up 'crunch, gurgle, plunk, splash'.

'They give the sound of what's happening,' said Irene Moody.

'Good. We call this onomatopoeia.' He wrote it up on the blackboard.

'What do we call this figure of speech, Alf Dempsey?'

'Tomatopie,' answered Alf.

Trust Alf to produce the malapropism, thought Billy. He should come and meet my mother some time.

'Not quite, Alf. Can anyone give me the word that indicates the sound of coins?'

'Jingle,' said Anne Greenhalgh.

'Good. Now the sound of heavy chains.'

'Jangle,' said Roger Horner. 'Like in a filum about Alcatraz.'

'Paper being crumpled up.'

'Crumple,' said Alf Dempsey.

'Well done, Alf! And another word for the same?'

'Crinkle,' from Tony Jarvis.

'Excellent,' Billy said. 'Now horses' hoofs on a pavement.'

'Clatter,' said Tessie Shea.

'Yes, well done!' he said. 'Now . . .' Billy noticed that Wakefield, sitting in his usual place at the back of the room, had raised his hand. 'Sorry, Mr Wakefield. Anything wrong?'

'No, no,' he replied, 'but wouldn't "clippety-clop" do there, Mr Hopkins?'

Billy thought about it for a moment. He had to be careful here.

'No, not really, Mr Wakefield. Clatter is a better word, I think.'

'Why? What's wrong with "clippety-clop"?'

'Nothing really wrong but it's like saying "gee-gee" for horse.'

'Oh, very well,' he said, 'if you say so.' With that, he went back to his correspondence.

Frank Wakefield did not forget the incident. He bided his time and got his own back a little later. Revenge is a dish best eaten cold, was his philosophy.

Billy was giving a lesson on Christopher Columbus, and was enjoying himself. He had both the class and the bank clerk eating out of his hand.

He had explained how Columbus had sailed across the Atlantic in his ships *Nina, Pinta* and *Santa Maria*, how he had the idea of proving the world was round by reaching Cathay by sailing west, how he hoped to make his fortune and at the same time convert the Chinese to Christianity, how the crews were superstitious and had become more and more terrified as they sailed into uncharted territories. As they journeyed on without any sight of land, they became panic-stricken, imagining the horrors which lay ahead – boiling seas, monstrous sea serpents, the constant fear of falling over the edge of the world into a bottomless void. The idea grew that they would never return to their wives and their families back home in Spain. Billy's story was reaching its climax.

'So there they were sailing where no man had ever been before – into the unknown,' Billy declaimed. 'They'd been at sea for months and still there was no sign of land. The sailors began to mutter amongst themselves. There was murmuring and mumbling and talk of mutiny.'

'If Columbus had hand-picked men, surely they wouldn't mutiny,' said Jim Mitchell, caught up in the suspense. 'They'd be loyal to their captain, surely.'

'Good point, Jim,' Billy exclaimed, nodding his head vigorously.

The bank clerk signified his agreement about the shrewdness of the question and gave a thumbs-up.

'But you must remember,' said Billy, 'that many of the crew were criminals who had been given a pardon by Queen Isabella provided they sailed with Columbus on his hazard-ous voyage. Apart from that, they had mouldy food, stale water, damp clothes, cramped quarters – life on board was rotten and unhealthy.'

The bank clerk had abandoned the work of accounts and had become an active participant in the lesson, for he now raised his hand.

'How many men were on these ships, Mr Hopkins?' he asked.

Billy had prepared his work well, knowing that Mr Cashman would be in his audience.

'The *Pinta* and the *Nina* were small ships – forty and sixty tons only. On the *Pinta*, there were eighteen men on board, another eighteen on the *Nina*, but on the *Santa Maria*, which was one hundred tons, there were about sixty crew.' He turned back to his class.

'Anyway, as I was saying. The crew were fed up to the back teeth – they had been at sea for six months. On the eleventh of October, fourteen ninety-two, Slit Gizzard Jack, the bosun, yelled to the crew gathered on the foredeck: "I've worked it out, lads, and we'll never get back to Spain. Come on, let's take over the ship afore we fall over the edge of the world."

298

' "Aye," they shouted. "Mutiny! Mutiny! Let's kill Columbus!"

'They began to move towards the captain's cabin but as they did so, from high, high up in the crow's nest,' with a flourish Billy pointed towards the ceiling, 'a voice called out . . .' he paused for dramatic effect and was about to bellow 'Land ahoy!' when with consummate timing Wakefield interrupted with an urgent cry from the back of the room.

'The boiler's gone out back here, Mr Hopkins!'

Touché.

Sometimes, embarrassing situations arose for teacher and pupils alike. Billy could never forgive the writer of one textbook who had devised examples without examining the implications for young adolescents, especially girls, who had to deal with them. The book also taught Billy an important lesson, namely the need to check out material before presenting it to his class.

The English class was employed on parsing and analysis and everything was going well for the first ten minutes.

Jim Mitchell began with the first sentence. ' "John saw the red squirrels." "John" – proper noun and subject of the sentence. "Saw" – active transitive verb. "The" – definite article qualifying "squirrels". "Red" – adjective qualifying "squirrels". "Squirrels" – common noun, object of the verb "saw".'

'Very good, Jim,' said Billy. 'You've obviously done your homework. Next, Vera Pickles. Parse the next sentence.'

The class turned to the next page and to the next sentence. Vera was confronted with: 'Great tits sang in the trees.'

Both Vera and Billy turned a bright red when they realised what was in store. The class stared at the book unbelievingly. Several heads submerged under desk lids.

'Yes, make a start, Vera,' said Billy, determined that they should plough ahead regardless. Vera looked at Billy pleadingly.

'Must I, sir?'

'Yes, why not?'

Vera began. You could have made toast on her cheeks – and on Billy's.

' "The" – definite article qualifying "tits". "Great" – adjective qualifying "tits". "Tits" – common noun, subject of the sentence. "Sang" – intransitive verb. "In the trees" – adverbial phrase of place.'

Needless to say, the class had dissolved into uncontrollable giggling. Billy wished he could find the author of the book so that he could slowly and enjoyably pull each one of his teeth out with a pair of pliers.

However, the most potentially embarrassing predicament was to come. After the morning break one day, Billy returned to class to find everyone in place and ready for the lesson to start.

Nellie Wallace was in the front row and chewing gum vigorously, reminding Billy of a matronly cow chewing the cud. All businesslike, Billy strode into the room.

'Come on, Nellie. You know the rule. Into the wastepaper basket!'

Billy ordered the class to take out their exercise books and he walked down the central aisle, examining their work as he did so. A strange hush fell over the room and his wards stared at something ahead which had captured their attention. Tony Jarvis's head had disappeared into his desk and his shoulders heaved with uncontrollable glee.

Puzzled, Billy turned round and could not believe his eyes.

Nellie had stepped into the wastepaper basket and was standing there, gawky girl that she was, still chewing, the colour mounting her cheeks. She was having trouble maintaining her balance. She looked at Billy appealingly with a look that said: 'I've obeyed your instruction. Now please get me out of this.'

Billy was in a dilemma. He realised that one sarcastic remark, like 'Not you, you silly girl! The chewing gum!' would destroy her and she'd never forgive him. The class waited in anticipation for Billy's response, ready to explode into laughter at the smallest encouragement. Billy was determined not to give it to them.

'OK, Nellie,' he said. 'Step out of the basket. Drop your chewing gum into it. Remember that's where your chewing gum should be. Now go back to your place.'

'Yes, sir. Thank you, sir,' she said quietly.

The class sighed collectively in disappointment. They were not sure whether Billy had intended she step into the basket.

Later, Billy thought, Nellie doesn't understand elliptical speech but by God what discipline! If I'd said, 'Jump, Nellie!' she'd have asked 'How high, sir?' only when she was in mid-air.

Chapter Twenty-Seven

French (Ici on parle School Certificate Français)

The following Monday Billy had his first date with Laura. Not the romantic kind. It was business. He'd arranged to accompany her home to start the series of French lessons for her brother Hughie.

'I think he might be a little nervous at first,' she said as they wheeled their bikes up Regina Park Hill. 'So I hope you'll not be too hard on him if his French isn't up to scratch.'

'He's not the only one who's nervous,' said Billy. 'I feel as if I'm entering the exciting world of the rich and famous, like Beverly Hills.'

Laura laughed. 'You have a slight tendency to exaggerate. We're neither rich nor famous.'

They had reached the top of the hill. There were some open fields and a few large houses set back from the road. In front of them was one of the biggest private houses Billy had ever seen – practically a mansion. They stopped at the front gate, an imposing wrought-iron affair.

'This is it,' she said. 'Home.'

'Not rich and famous, you say? What about this?' said Billy, pointing to the plaque on the wall. It read: LOUISE

MACKENZIE, LRAM, TEACHER OF MUSIC AND SINGING.

'Oh, that's one of Mammy's interests – she takes on a few pupils. She used to be a professional singer in Scotland before she married.'

'Ah, is that all?' He swallowed hard. This was a very different world from his own.

They opened the gate and walked along a winding drive through what estate agents call a mature garden of trees and shrubs – rowanberry, elm and rhododendrons.

'We can leave our bikes in the garage,' she said.

She opened the door of the porch and turned her key in the front door. The hall smelled of lavender and beeswax and there was a large porcelain flowerpot containing an arrangement of chrysanthemums on a half-circular walnut table. He could see the reflection of the flowerpot in the cushion-framed looking glass – the whole setting resembling an illustration from *Ideal Home*. The Persian carpet gave it the finishing touch.

Billy helped Laura off with her coat and then took off his own. She hung them up in the hall wardrobe.

'Hughie!' she called. 'Mr Hopkins is here.'

A tall, good-looking boy appeared from one of the rooms off the hall. He was smiling. Billy wasn't sure whether the smile was one of welcome or a nervous grimace.

They shook hands warmly.

'Nice to meet you, Hughie,' he said. 'Laura has told me about you – all to the good, I might add.'

'Glad to know you, Mr Hopkins,' said Hughie, still smiling. 'Thanks for agreeing to help me with my French.'

'Don't call me Mr Hopkins, it keeps us at a distance. Billy will be fine.'

'We've arranged for you to take the lessons in here,' said

Laura, opening one of the doors. 'In the drawing room, if that's OK.'

'That's fine,' said Billy. Drawing room? Where he came from, they called it 'the parlour', and they didn't even have one of them in the flat.

'Is it OK if I smoke?' he asked.

'Of course,' she answered and brought him a heavy glass ashtray from the other side of the room.

My God, he thought, even the ashtray is a collector's item.

'I'll leave you to it, Billy,' she said. 'If you need anything, I'll be in the kitchen across the hall.'

Billy and Hughie went into the drawing room, and, for Billy at least, into a different domain. Billy looked around him at the Pye radiogram – not only a radio but incorporating a record player that could play 33.3 rpm, a whole symphony on two sides! – the decorated firescreen, and a good deal of elegant period furniture. What caught his attention in particular was the mahogany Bechstein grand piano which stood in front of the large bay window. On the fold-down music stand, someone had left a book of Chopin Nocturnes opened at one dedicated to Laura Duperré. A portrait of Beethoven glowered down from the wall.

'We can work here,' said Hughie, indicating a writing bureau, 'if that's OK.'

'Suits me fine,' said Billy, thinking it's the first time I've ever worked at a Queen Anne bureau. 'How did you get on with the unseen passage I sent over for you?'

'Not bad, I think, I'll let you be the judge, Billy. I should warn you, though, that I'm not very good. Hamish, Laura's boyfriend, told me that my real ability was on the science side and that I have no aptitude for languages.'

'No aptitude for languages! What nonsense!' Billy exclaimed vehemently. 'Everybody's got aptitude for languages. We master our first by the time we're five at our mother's knee. Anyway, let's take a look at your effort.'

Hughie handed over his work and watched Billy's face anxiously as he gave it the once-over. Billy noticed immediately a considerable number of errors but he looked up and smiled.

'Not bad, not bad,' he said. 'Good for a first effort. English into French is never easy. A few errors but I can see no reason why you shouldn't get a distinction by the time the final exams come round.'

'I'd be so grateful, Billy,' he said. 'Daddy has been putting on the pressure lately. Forbidden me to go out at night. I have to get at least a credit to matriculate.'

'You remind me of an American friend,' said Billy. 'He hated school so much he was always saying that every time he passed his old High School, he used to matriculate.'

Hughie laughed for the first time that day.

At that point they were interrupted by Laura bringing tea on a silver tray.

'Oh, it's so nice to hear Hughie laughing,' she said. 'Music to my ears. I thought you'd both like a cup of tea to get you started. And Billy, you're invited to join us for a meal when you've finished, if you have time. You can meet the rest of the family.'

'Love to,' replied Billy, at the same time feeling a little uncomfortable as he wondered if his table manners were up to it.

'Now, let's take a look at some of your basic errors,' he said when Laura had left. 'First, learn to spell *beaucoup* and avoid those *beacups*. I notice, too, that you have written *dans Paris*. I know that in English we say "in Manchester"

305

or "in America" – the word "in" can apply to nearly every situation. In French, not so. They like to distinguish between the different "ins". Learn this sentence: *Quand on est à Paris, on est en France*. The word "in" is *à* for towns and *en* for most countries.'

So the lesson continued and their hour together soon passed.

'I think I've learned more French this evening than I have in the last month,' said Hughie, finishing off his notes.

'Remember all we've said this afternoon, Hughie, and I'm sure you'll soon be producing error-free translations.' Then Billy added, 'The funniest attempt I ever came across was from a boy at my old school who translated *Non, merci, ma chérie, je ne veux pas acheter un appareil cinématographique* (No, thank you, my dear, I don't want to buy a cine camera) as "No sherry for me, thank you, I'm appearing at the cinema".'

Tears of merriment sprang to Hughie's eyes.

Laura appeared once again at the door. 'Time for tea, you two. From the noises coming from this room, it sounds as if you've been telling jokes instead of working.'

'Not at all,' said Hughie. 'Laughing and working at the same time. I think I'm going to enjoy these French sessions.'

'Don't forget, Hughie, to do the second unseen for next week's lesson.'

'Thanks for everything, Billy,' said Hughie.

'And that goes for me too, Billy,' said Laura earnestly. 'Now, perhaps you'd like to freshen up before you come and meet the family. The bathroom is upstairs, along the landing and second on the right.'

As Billy climbed the stairs, he couldn't help noticing the thick red carpet, the stained-glass window on the first landing, the small pictures in their gilt frames hanging on the walls of the passageway. Botticelli's 'Spring', Manet's *'Déjeuner sur l'herbe'*, and a Millet country scene. The only art Billy was acquainted with were the flying ceramic ducks which his dad had acquired with cigarette coupons.

The bathroom was in keeping with the rest of the house, that is to say, large and luxurious. It was fully tiled in pink, had a kingsize washbasin, gold-plated towel rails and taps, a large mirror extending the length of the bath, a separate shower cubicle, a WC and a kidney-shaped basin with taps, which Billy surmised was designed for washing the feet. On the third wall was a large reproduction of Bellini's 'Young Woman at Her Toilet'. Everything was spotlessly clean and smelt of freshly laundered towels and soap scented with attar of roses.

Billy compared it with the little cramped bathroom at home with its one pair of swivel taps that served both bath and washbasin, the noisy cistern that had drying under-clothes forever clinging to it like barnacles, and the narrow windowsill that served as bathroom cabinet. As he saw it in his mind's eye, he became acutely aware of his place in the social hierarchy. The more he thought about it, the more it reinforced his notion that he was inferior. He washed his face, flicked a comb through his hair, and went downstairs to meet the Mackenzie family.

As he walked across the hall to the kitchen, his nostrils were assailed by the smell of freshly baked scones and bread. He knocked and entered when a voice softly called, 'Come in, Billy.'

Laura was at the small kitchen table rolling pastry. She had a smudge of flour on her nose and at that moment Billy fell in love with her all over again – with an overwhelming feeling of tenderness. Like William Cobbett, who had determined on his bride when he first saw her 'scrubbing out a washing tub in the snow', Billy knew that there could never be anyone else in the world for him but Laura Mackenzie.

She put down the rolling pin, wiped the flour from her hands on her pinafore, and came forward.

'Let me introduce my family. This is Billy,' she announced. 'And this is my mother, my sister Jenny, my sister Katie, my grandmother, and Aunty. Hughie you already know of course.'

After hand-shaking all round, Louise said, 'You are very welcome, Billy. And thank you for agreeing to give Hughie tuition in French.'

Not only a music teacher, Billy thought, she has a musical voice as well, like her eldest daughter. Or should that be the other way round?

'No problem, Mrs Mackenzie,' he said. 'I love teaching and Hughie is such a talented student, he is a pleasure to deal with.'

Katie gazed at him shyly. She'd seen him at school along with the other teachers and she was in awe that one of their teachers was here in the family kitchen and talking to her mother and sisters.

'Are you any relation to Douglas Hamilton Hopkins of Kirkintilloch?' asked Grandma.

' 'Fraid not,' answered Billy. 'I think I'm of Irish extraction.'

Grandma didn't reply but looked disappointed that an Irish type had managed to infiltrate the family kitchen.

'This is a lovely big farmhouse kitchen,' said Billy, looking round the room. His eye took in the Servis washing machine, the Prestcold refrigerator, the Aga cooker. 'So warm and inviting.'

'It's big,' said Louise. 'I think too big sometimes. It was all right I suppose when there were lots of servants to do the hard work. Notice we've still got the servants' bells up there on the wall but no servants.'

'Now she's got her daughters,' Laura laughed.

Aunty had been staring at him all this time, wondering if she might chance retailing one of her many anecdotes about the old days. He might listen to her.

'You remind me of my younger brother Jamie,' she began. 'I mind a time, ye ken, when—'

'I'm sure Billy doesna want to hear your stories,' Grandma snapped.

Anxious not to be seen as impolite, Billy began paying Aunty close attention but this was interrupted by Louise who said, 'What would you like for tea, Billy? We are having homemade scones and preserves or perhaps you'd like a couple of boiled eggs?'

'That sounds wonderful, Mrs Mackenzie,' Billy said. 'Boiled eggs would go down very well.' Was that the right thing to say? he wondered.

'I'll put them on now. We always wait for Mr Mackenzie before we begin,' she added. 'He should be here fairly soon.'

The mention of Mr Mackenzie's name sent an involuntary *frisson* down Billy's spine.

They sat down at the large dining table.

'I'm not long for this world, Billy,' Aunty began, 'but I mind a time, ye ken, when my brother Jamie came back from the war and . . .'

Billy nodded attentively but his mind was on the layout of the table as he examined it for unfamiliar implements that might cause him problems. It was not like the table at home. For one thing, the bread was not pre-cut. He noted a

309

breadboard and knife – obviously here one cut one's own. There was a dish of butter and he verified that he had a butter knife. Was one expected to pour one's own tea and, if so, did one put the milk in first? What about the boiled egg? Oh, how he wished he had opted for simple bread and jam. Was it the done thing to cut bread soldiers and dip them in the yolk? Pottsy in his etiquette tutorials at college hadn't covered these matters because they'd never been served boiled eggs.

Aunty was still relating her story of how Jamie had returned after a spell in the trenches, and of her family connections to the great John MacCormack, when her soliloquy was interrupted by the sound of a car coming up the drive.

'That'll be Mr Mackenzie now,' said Louise.

Billy froze but the family went into action. Louise put the finishing touches to the boiled fish she was preparing, and took Billy's eggs from the water. Laura infused the tea, Jenny arranged the great man's slippers before the fire. The hall clock struck five thirty and they heard the key turn in the lock.

A minute later, Duncan Mackenzie entered the room. Billy stood up when he saw him.

'This is Billy,' Laura said quickly.

Duncan looked at Billy intently as if he were assessing a taxpayer for possible tax evasion. After a pause, he gave a curt nod and took Billy's hand in a firm handshake.

'How d'you do?' he said.

'Pleased to meet you,' answered Billy, equally economical with his greeting. It came out as *Pleasetameetcha*.

'Your slippers are warmed, Daddy,' said Jenny.

'Your tea is poured, Daddy,' said Laura.

'And your fish is ready whenever you are,' added Louise.

Duncan went into his evening routine. He removed his coat, put on his slippers, washed his hands while the family waited in silence. He sat down in the carver chair at the head of the table. The rest took their places round the sides – Billy next to Hughie and opposite Laura and Aunty. All bowed their heads as Duncan said grace. 'Amen,' they said when he'd finished.

Billy felt that he was taking part in a James Bridie play.

Louise brought on the cooked meals for the men. Fish for Duncan, eggs for Billy.

Duncan pointed to various articles on the table, first the cruets, then the bread. The rest of the family reached out swiftly to minister to his wishes. Billy had the impression that there was a competition going on to anticipate the next requirement, the winner being the first to seize the desired object. Maybe there were points for the various items and a prize at the end for the one who got most right – six for the salt, five for the pepper, four for a teaspoon. Billy became so absorbed by the family ritual, he found himself trying to guess the target of Duncan's index finger. There was little conversation and what little there was had to be addressed to the head of the table for evaluation. However, there was something in Billy's nature that found long silences painful. He had to say something.

'I'm sure we'll soon have Hughie speaking French like General de Gaulle,' he said.

'As long as it's de Gaulle's accent,' added Hughie, 'and not Winston Churchill's.'

All eyes turned to Duncan for assessment of these remarks. Were they funny? Was it OK to laugh? Were they to be treated seriously or with contempt?

Billy felt that a signboard such as was used to prompt reactions from a studio audience might not go amiss here.

311

LAUGH! GROAN! APPLAUD! HISS!

Duncan cut short any snickering with a cold stare. 'Hrrumph' was his response.

Billy turned his attention to the eggs and the implements for dealing with them. He had a choice. He could cut the top of his egg in one deft slicing movement with his butter knife. Was that the done thing? Or he could tap the shell with his spoon. Watched by the family, he opted for the latter. It was the wrong choice. It involved peeling off tiny bits of shell and some of these clung unfairly and tenaciously to the thin membrane of the egg. Now there was the question of what to do with the debris. Oh, how he wished he'd chosen the scones and the preserve! The family continued to watch fascinated as Billy struggled to resolve the conflicts in which the eggs had involved him. He realised that bread soldiers were out and he could tell that his decision to go for buttering half slices was the right one by the relieved expressions on the watching faces – though he was aware that he had lost points in his hacking of the bread. How would they have reacted if he'd sliced up the egg and made butties? he wondered. That would blow his chances with Laura and no mistake.

'And so,' Duncan began finally, addressing Billy, 'you've come to give Hughie there a few French lessons. How has he got on?'

Hughie looked at Billy pleadingly.

'An excellent start, Mr Mackenzie. I think he'll get at least a credit next summer, if not a distinction.'

The gratitude showed in Hughie's eyes.

'I'm glad to hear it,' Duncan said. 'I think the laddie needs a kick in the backside to get him working. How much shall we owe you for this tuition? I'm a man who believes in paying his way, ye ken.'

'Nothing, Mr Mackenzie. I'm glad to do a service for a colleague,' said Billy, looking at Laura who smiled and gave him a Gainsborough lady nod in acknowledgement.

No fee, Billy thought. Just the hand of your daughter in marriage.

'That's the kind of fee a Scotsman likes to hear,' said Duncan, grinning. 'Especially one who works in taxes, as I would have to add such a fee to your income for tax purposes.'

'On my pittance,' replied Billy, 'I'm barely within the tax range, despite the fact that I've taken part-time work in a youth centre to supplement my income. By the way, did you know, Mr Mackenzie, that I used to work in the Inland Revenue?'

'Is that a fact? Which district was that?'

'District Three in Sunlight House. I was a T3.'

'Everyone has to start somewhere, I suppose,' he chuckled.

'What's a T3?' asked Laura. 'It sounds like a mysterious job in the Secret Service.'

'Hardly,' said Billy, 'T3 means temporary clerk, grade three, and it's the lowest rank possible, slightly above office cleaner, in the civil service.'

'You're now a teacher,' said Louise encouragingly. 'So obviously you've risen in rank since then.'

'Not by much,' Billy laughed. 'I'm now a junior master in charge of the senior class at St Anselm's. Still at the bottom of the heap.'

'Not quite true,' said Laura. 'By all the accounts that reach my ears, you're a good teacher and you should go a long way one day.'

'All the way to Timbuktu according to the wits in my form.'

The family laughed together. An unusual thing for them to do at the dining table.

'You have a degree of course?' said Duncan.

' 'Fraid not,' answered Billy. 'I went to a teacher training college and as it was at the end of the war, they weren't really geared up for degrees.'

'To get anywhere in this world,' Duncan pontificated, 'you need a university degree, especially in teaching. In Scotland, if you were to teach in an academy, that's the secondary school, you'd have to have a degree. Those who teach at the higher levels must have honours.'

'In a secondary modern like St Anselm's, we're not academic,' answered Billy.

'Doesna matter. Things are going to get competitive in the future and only university graduates will stand a chance. Take a leaf out of Laura's boyfriend's book. Hamish is studying for his degree in actuarial studies at Glasgow.'

At the mention of Hamish's name, Billy felt the bile rise in his throat.

'I think Hamish is a bright man,' said Jenny. 'He knows which side his bread is buttered on all right.'

And bread never falls but on its buttered side, thought Billy. I hope Hamish falls on his face.

'Perhaps you two men would like to go into the study for a smoke,' suggested Louise, 'whilst we clear the table.'

'Good idea,' said Billy, thinking it was the best idea he'd heard all night. But there was another word. Study!

Duncan and Billy retired for their smoke.

The study was a long room, with a varnished wainscot and lined with leather-bound books from floor to ceiling. There was a log fire burning in the fireplace. The Parker-Knoll Camden armchairs completed the picture.

Duncan took out a box of cigars, guillotined the ends of two with his cutter and offered one to Billy, lighting it for him with his desk lighter. Billy puffed happily at his smoke. This was gracious living indeed. All he needed now was a brandy in a balloon glass and his contentment would be complete. Then I shall have joined the Tory Party, he thought. Wonder what my dad'd say to that.

As if reading his thoughts, Duncan poured two brandies into balloon glasses.

'This can be your fee,' he said, drawing on his cigar. 'Napoleon brandy – the best.'

Billy looked round the room in awe – he had never seen so many books outside a public library. The titles and authors of the volumes were equally impressive: Jane Austen, R.M. Ballantyne, Hilaire Belloc, G.K. Chesterton. He had reached the works of Charles Dickens when the study door opened and Laura joined them.

'I love the smell of cigars – reminds me of Christmas,' she said.

'That and tangerines,' added Billy. Returning to his examination of the books he said, 'You have a fine collection of books here, Mr Mackenzie.'

'Yes,' he agreed. 'Many of them inherited from mine and Louise's parents. But there's one book I feel is better than the rest put together. Which one would you say it was, Billy?'

Now here was a dilemma. Billy favoured the works of Robert Browning but he was sure the answer would be more esoteric.

He hazarded a guess: 'St Augustine's *Confessions*.'

'No,' said Duncan. 'Try again.'

'The Oxford English Dictionary?'

'No,' said Duncan, picking out *The Path to Rome* by Hilaire Belloc. 'This one.'

Billy determined to read it at the first opportunity. Earning the approval of Laura's father was going to be a full-time job. He must try to make Duncan like him and if one way of doing that was to read Belloc's *Rome* book, so be it.

'Would you be prepared to lend me the book for a little while, Mr Mackenzie?' he asked.

'Certainly. Always glad to enlighten a young man like yoursel'.'

Billy determined to study it thoroughly in case there was a *viva voce* exam on it the next time they met.

'I see, Mr Mackenzie, that you have the complete illustrated works of Charles Dickens,' Billy continued.

'Ah, so you like the works of Dickens,' said Laura warmly. 'So do I! We have something in common.'

'Not only am I a fan of Dickens's work but also that of his first illustrator, George Cruikshank.'

'Ah, you mean Boz,' said Duncan. 'All the sketches in Dickens's work were done by Boz. That was Cruikshank's pen name. Did you not know that?'

'Are you sure, Mr Mackenzie?' said Billy, puzzled. 'You must be thinking of Dickens's first novel *Sketches by Boz*, which was published in serial form. Cruikshank illustrated both this first book and *Oliver Twist*. Cruikshank was never known as Boz.'

'I'm surprised that a secondary school teacher – and an English teacher as well – could get a thing like that wrong. Boz was the pseudonym of Cruikshank, I can assure you.'

'I made a study of Dickens at college, Mr Mackenzie,' Billy argued gently, 'and I think you'll find I'm right. I had to write a long essay on him as part of my finals.'

Laura was making little danger signals to Billy with her eyes.

'I'm not a betting man,' said Duncan, 'and so we'll not wager on it. But we'll settle the matter here and now with the *Encyclopaedia Britannica*.'

He went over to the reference section and pulled down the volume marked Decorative to Edison.

Uh-oh, thought Billy. Trouble. How am I going to get out of this one? Whatever happens, Duncan mustn't lose face. He looked to Laura for help but she simply raised her eyes to heaven in supplication.

Duncan had found the required entry. 'Ah, here we are. Now, we'll see who's right. I'll read out what it says. "In 1833, Dickens began contributing stories and descriptive essays to magazines and newspapers: these attracted attention and were reprinted as *Sketches by 'Boz'* in February 1836. Illustrations were done by George Cruikshank." So you see, Billy, you were wrong. Boz was the name adopted by Dickens for his first book, d'you see?'

'Ah, now I see, Mr Mackenzie,' agreed Billy warmly. 'Boz was the name for Dickens, not his illustrator. What does the encyclopaedia say about Cruikshank?'

'Let's see,' Duncan said. He began to read from another volume: ' "Cruikshank, George (1792 to 1878) British caricaturist and illustrator whose large output included the illustrations for Dickens's *Sketches by 'Boz'* and *Oliver Twist* where he was known simply as Cruikshank." '

'I stand corrected, Mr Mackenzie,' said Billy, though he was hurting inside.

There was a glow of triumph in Duncan's eyes as he said, 'So, you've learned a thing or two about Dickens tonight, Billy. I'm always glad to pass on a little erudition to a young man like yourself.' Savouring his intellectual 'victory', he turned to Laura and said, 'Perhaps Billy might enjoy our musical evening next Sunday night. What do you think, Laura?'

Laura pursed her lips and looked dubious.

'Well, would you, Billy?' Duncan said. 'We hold a musical "At Home" once a month – it's very informal. Just a few friends and family. I think you'd enjoy it. We usually put on one or two little efforts, bits of music, recitations and the like. You may be able to join in the fun here and there. What do you say?'

I've really got my feet under the table now, he thought. Eating a meal with the family and attending a musical *soirée*. Hamish Dunwoody, you got till sunup to get out o' town. I don't know what this musical evening entails but I can always find out from Laura at school. If it means an opportunity to be near her, count me in.

'Yes, I'd love to come,' he heard himself saying.

'Good,' said Duncan. 'It might give us another opportunity to broaden your education.'

There may have been triumph in Duncan's eyes but in Laura's it was a different look. Not only gratitude but a new bond of understanding between them.

As the Mackenzie clock struck seven, Billy felt it was time to take his leave. He said goodnight to the family and Laura accompanied him to the door.

'Billy,' she said as he went to the garage to collect his bike, 'I don't know how to thank you for all you did tonight – for Hughie and for the way you helped Daddy save face. That took real guts.' She kissed him on the forehead. 'Thank you so much.'

Billy's heart leapt for joy.

On the way home that night, he said to himself, in that

argument with King Duncan, I lost the battle but I won the war.

And one piece of poetry suitably modified went round and round in his head.

> *Say I'm weary, say I'm sad,*
> *Say that health and wealth have missed me,*
> *Say I'm growing old, but add,*
> *Laura kissed me.*

Back at the Mackenzie household, Billy was assessed as a 'likeable young man'. But it was Aunty who gave him the highest accolade when she said, 'I think he's a wonderful young gentleman. He's the only one who ever listened to me.'

Chapter Twenty-Eight

If Music Be the Food of Love

In the staffroom next day, Laura seemed highly amused when Billy asked her about the projected musical 'At Home'.

'I don't get it,' he said. 'What's the joke?'

'You,' she answered. 'You do let yourself in for things without weighing up what's involved. Impulsive isn't the word for it. First, tutoring Hughie in French. I'm sure you took that on without thinking about the work it involved. Then you've accepted Daddy's invitation to one of our *soirées*.'

'If I'm impulsive, that's because my astrological sign is the crab. We're supposed to be an impulsive lot. Anyway, I see nothing wrong in volunteering my services to help Hughie. I enjoy teaching. As for the evening, I assume it'll be conversation and listening to a few classical records on your magnificent radiogram. I haven't heard a 33.3 player yet. At home, we're still struggling with an old HMV wind-up gramophone. On that, the music sounds as if it's being performed with a nest of snakes hissing in the background. I've borrowed your father's copy of *The Path to Rome* and I'm hoping we can have a discussion about that.'

'Our musical evenings involve a lot more than that,' she laughed. 'They vary but there's usually poetry reading, piano playing, singing, and Daddy may even perform a Highland fling or a sword dance.'

'Singing? What kind of singing?'

'Some solos, duets, madrigals, part songs – that kind of thing. Whatever takes our fancy. Do you have a party piece, Billy?'

'Not that I'm aware of, though I once danced like Fred Astaire in the infants' school. But surely you haven't got to do something. I'll simply come and watch.'

Laura raised both eyebrows. 'Perhaps you're right,' she said. She didn't sound sure.

'Who'll be there, Laura?'

'The family and an old friend of ours, Monsignor Guerin. And oh, I almost forgot, Hamish. He expects to be home for half-term.'

When he heard the name Hamish and the news that he'd be there, Billy felt a pang of anguish like a knife in his heart. He hid his feelings.

'Laura, please find out what the programme is likely to be so I can start inventing my excuses.'

Greg sidled up puffing a great cloud of nauseating smoke from his hideous pipe. 'You two look as if you're hatching up a plot,' he guffawed. 'You'll have people talking.'

'Do keep it quiet,' whispered Billy. 'We were thinking of putting a bomb under Grundy's chair.'

'Not a bad idea,' Greg roared. 'I came over, Hoppy, to enlist your help,' he continued. 'As you know, I'm getting married, and Emily and I have managed to find an apartment in High Lane, Chorlton, but it's in a poor state of repair. Flats are as rare as gold dust and so we don't have much choice. I wondered however if you'd be willing to help Alex and me decorate the place.'

'Sure thing,' laughed Billy. 'Why not? I can see that fate is guiding me into my true vocation – painting and decorating. It might be a good career move. I'm sure it would mean better pay.'

'I'll hold you to that pledge,' said Greg. 'When we get the key to the flat we might roll up our sleeves and get to it.'

'OK. Count me in,' said Billy.

'There's the crab in you again,' remarked Laura. 'Don't you ever say no?'

'Yes,' Billy answered.

The following Sunday, Billy cycled over to Regina Park for the Sunday *soirée*. He took off his cycle clips, deposited his bike in the garage, and rang the doorbell. Jenny answered it.

'Good evening, Billy,' she said warmly. 'Everyone's already here and we've been waiting for you with bated breath.'

'That's what comes from eating too many bates,' he replied. What a weak joke, he thought.

Jenny laughed. 'Laura told me you're something of a comedian,' she said as she showed him into the drawing room where they were all waiting – the Mackenzie family plus Hamish and a priest wearing the purple vest of a monsignor.

'I think you know everyone here,' said Laura, 'except Monsignor Guerin who is a long-standing friend of the family.'

'Though at the present moment, you're sitting down,' Billy joked. He was nervous.

Monsignor Guerin acknowledged the greeting and the drollery by shaking hands and laughing heartily.

Duncan glared at Billy. 'Hamish here was telling us about his university course,' he said, ignoring Billy's attempt at wit, 'and an interesting course it sounds. It should lead to a good, well-paid job. Deservedly so.'

'I think I have a job lined up already, Mr Mackenzie, with the Caledonian Mutual in Edinburgh,' Hamish simpered. 'They're offering me nine hundred pounds a year to start.'

Billy thought bitterly about his own paltry salary as a young teacher at the bottom of the scale.

'Fantastic, Hamish!' enthused Jenny, and she could not prevent herself from exclaiming, 'Lucky Laura!'

'Excellent, Hamish,' Duncan purred, glancing in Laura's direction, 'and I suppose you'll have big plans if you pull that off.'

The significance of these exchanges was not lost on Billy.

'I've no doubt that I'll be coming to see you then about a serious matter, Mr Mackenzie,' Hamish said. Looking at Laura, he asked, 'How does the idea of living in Edinburgh appeal to you, Laura?'

Laura flushed. 'I'm not sure about that, Hamish. Manchester's where my home and my job are and I'm loath to leave them at the present. But we can cross that bridge if and when we come to it.'

Good for you, Laura, thought Billy. Don't let them push you into something you don't want.

'Enough of this serious talk,' said Louise brightly. 'We're here to enjoy ourselves. It's a musical At Home, not a debating club.'

'Quite right,' said Duncan. 'I thought we might start the

evening's entertainment off with a part song. I found a beautiful Victorian piece by Walter MacFarren when I was browsing in the Henry Watson Music Library at lunchtime on Friday. His name sounds Scottish and so it's bound to be good.'

Huh, Billy thought.

Duncan handed out copies of a composition entitled 'You Stole My Love'.

'Before you came, Billy,' Duncan said, 'we agreed that Louise aided by Katie will sing soprano; Laura and Jenny, alto; Hamish and Hughie, tenor; and Billy, if you wouldn't mind singing bass with Monsignor. Our two senior members over there will act as observers and critics.'

Billy looked enviously at Grandma and Aunty, who sat comfortably by the fireside having been granted exemption because of their age.

'I used to sing alto in a choir, Billy,' Aunty croaked, 'but that was many years ago. Now, I'm not long for this world. I'll no' last another year.'

'Sing us another song, for heaven's sake,' snapped Grandma. 'And besides, when you were in a choir, I ken you had a terrible squeaky voice.'

Billy had already asked Laura to pass on the message that he couldn't read music but either there had been a breakdown in communication or his protestations had been swept aside.

He looked at his copy. The black squiggles on the paper were no more than a collection of lower case ds and ps – some upright and some upside down like a series of clay pipes in a shooting gallery. From his early musical training at St Chad's Elementary School, though, he knew that some of the notes went up and some down but the crucial question was exactly how much up and how much down. He was relieved to notice that there were no passages of solo bass singing.

The priest was standing behind the piano, and Billy joined him, thinking it was going to take every ounce of his working-class guile to get through this one.

Louise struck a chord. There was a droning sound like the humming of a swarm of angry bees as the singers cleared their throats and found their notes.

Duncan raised his long index finger which seemed to have been specially designed as a pointing stick and a symbol of his authority. Billy was half tempted to grab the finger and bite it but resisted.

Duncan held the digit aloft and with a 'One, two, three', brought it down smartly, and they were off, singing with gusto:

> *You stole my love. Fie upon you fie*
> *You stole my love fie, fie ah.*
> *Guessed you but what a pain it is to prove*
> *You stole my love, fie fie ah*
> *Fie, fie, Fie upon you fie.*

Billy found that by singing a milli-second behind Monsignor he was able to create the impression that he was sight-reading the music. For his part, Monsignor had the strangest feeling that he was in an echo chamber but being a courteous cleric, said nothing. The group continued in this fashion for a good ten minutes and Billy lost track of the number of 'fies' he had sung.

As they flicked over the pages, the pace quickened, the volume rose and the stream of 'fies' multiplied until they reached the last sheet, when the instruction *accelerando e fortissimo* released a flood of angry 'fie upon yous' from the whole company. Hamish seemed to be especially vehement in his denunciation of the Victorian Lothario as he raised his high tenor voice to fever pitch, and Billy had the distinct impression that his particular 'fie upon yous' were being directed at him personally. In the final bars, the 'fies' flew thick and fast and furious, bouncing off the walls and ceilings until Duncan's commanding forefinger was raised aloft and then swept sideways in a scything movement to bring the performance to a smart and unified conclusion. That is to say, almost unified. Billy had been so intent on watching Hamish's angry accusations that he missed the signal and when everyone snapped their mouths shut in disciplined fashion, he found himself singing one extra 'fie' not provided for in the music.

The whole company collapsed in laughter. Everyone seemed well satisfied and flushed by the entertainment, adjudging it 'great fun'.

'Excellent,' enthused Duncan. 'A perfect performance except for the supplementary 'fie' at the end but that's best forgotten.'

'Sorry,' said Billy, 'there were so many "fies"! I lost my way.'

Louise now took over the proceedings.

'I'd like to sing a song specially dedicated to my son and to the memory of his first day at school – which seems like only yesterday to me. A day I'll never forget.'

Accompanied by Laura on the piano, she sang 'Wee Hughie' in a soprano voice. But beautiful as Louise's voice was, Billy's attention was riveted on her accompanist and the graceful way her hands moved across the keyboard as her mother sang:

> *He's gone to school, wee Hughie*
> *And him not four*
> *Sure I saw the fright was in him*
> *When he left the door.*
> *But he took a hand of Daddy*
> *And a hand of Dan*
> *Wi' Jo's ould coat upon him,*
> *Och the poor wee man.*

Jenny was second in the programme with a wistful rendering of a Chopin Nocturne. She played slowly and sensitively, leaving her audience sad and thoughtful.

'That was a beautiful performance, Jenny,' said Hamish. 'You seem to get better and better each time I hear you.'

Flatterer, Billy thought.

'Why, thank you, Hamish,' murmured Jenny warmly. 'I never realised you were listening so closely. But it's Mammy's teaching you should be praising.'

For Billy, however, it was Laura's rendering of Haydn's song 'My Mother Bids Me Bind My Hair' that provided the highlight of the evening. Her gentle, lilting voice seemed to go to the core of his being and he felt an overwhelming love for her.

'Magnificent,' he said, when the polite applause had died away. 'Mr and Mrs Mackenzie, you really do have a most talented family.'

'Why, thank you, Billy,' said Duncan. 'But wait, there's more. You have yet to hear the younger end. Hughie, let's hear your piece.' It sounded like a command.

Hughie stood up, looking nervously towards his father. 'I can't sing but I've learned a poem, Daddy. I hope it's all right.'

327

'Yes, yes, Hughie. No excuses now. Let's hear your effort.'

Hughie cleared his throat. ' "The Charge of the Light Brigade" by Alfred, Lord Tennyson.

> *Half a league, half a league,*
> *Half a league onward,*
> *All in the valley of Death*
> *Rode the six hundred . . .'*

As Hughie recited, Billy rummaged through the jumble in his mental attic for a suitable ballad which would go down well with this company. He knew a few lines from a similar military verse but all he could remember was that each stanza ended with 'Sam, Sam, pick up tha' musket'. Then again he half knew a Lancashire monologue called 'Albert and the Lion' but it was not quite the thing for this distinguished assembly. As for the bawdy poem he'd heard in the college common room, all about the exploits of a certain Eskimo Nell, that was definitely out. He had in his inside pocket a possible contribution but he would use it only as a last resort.

Hughie completed the Tennyson ballad without a mistake.

'Well done, Hughie!' Billy called. 'You have a remarkable memory. I thought you might have given us a poem in French. But nevertheless, well done!'

'Not bad, not bad at all, I suppose,' said Duncan grudgingly. It sounded as if it had cost him great deal of effort to make the admission. 'Time for one more before we pause for a break. Any volunteers?'

Nobody moved. Nobody spoke. Billy shuffled uncomfortably in his seat. He could feel the net closing in. The

328

situation was saved by Monsignor Guerin who now stepped forward into the breach both literally and metaphorically.

'I could give you the famous speech from *Henry V* if that would be acceptable,' he said.

The cries of 'By all means' and 'Yes, let's hear it' gave him sufficient reassurance to walk to the centre of the room and begin declaiming with arms outstretched to an invisible audience.

'*Once more unto the breach, dear friends, once more*;
Or close the wall up with our English dead! . . .'

'First class, Monsignor,' Duncan called when the priest had finished, 'though when you speak of English dead, I take it you mean British dead. British citizens object to the use of the term English when it means the whole population of Britain. Remember that in *Henry the Fifth*, we had a captain from each nation: Fluellen, Gower, Jamy, and Macmorris.'

'You're right there, Mr Mackenzie,' Billy exclaimed, anxious to earn a few points after his *faux pas* in the 'Fie Upon You' madrigal. 'During the war I always thought that Ivor Novello's patriotic song "There'll Always Be an England" excluded the Welsh, the Scots and the people of Ulster. Hardly fair when all Britain was fighting the Nazi menace.'

'I agree,' Monsignor Guerin said. 'But I think the word England is used in a loose sense to include all the people of Britain.'

'Then they should say so,' grumbled Duncan. 'There's nothing wrong with "There'll always be a Britain, and Britain shall be free." '

'Sorry to interrupt this high-falutin' debate,' said Louise. 'It's time for a break. The ladies will retire to the kitchen and bring on the tea and buns, though I don't see why one of these nights the men can't take over that particular chore. After the break, perhaps we can hear what the rest of our company can provide in the way of entertainment.'

When he heard this, Billy felt a pang of alarm. He wondered how he could get out of it. Perhaps if he announced some excuse for having to depart suddenly, like 'I've just remembered it's my mother's sixtieth birthday today and the family's arranged a special surprise party – they're expecting me at home. Slipped my mind.' Somehow it didn't ring true. He'd have to think of something else.

'If anyone would prefer a glass of wine,' Duncan announced, 'I have a Blue Nun in the fridge.'

Billy didn't bat an eyelid when he said, 'That should liven things up good and proper.' If the nun was in the fridge, was it any wonder she was blue? Anyway to him, 'Blue Nun' sounded distinctly lewd like the title of a pornographic movie.

The ladies filed out to fetch the food.

While they were gone, Billy hoped the conversation might switch to a discussion of Belloc's *The Path to Rome* which he had spent the week studying in the hope of winning credits with Duncan for diligence. He was ready to submit to an oral examination on the subject, but no luck. The half-time discussion took a different direction.

'That was indeed a fine rendering of the *Henry the Fifth* speech, Monsignor,' said Duncan. 'Worthy of Laurence Olivier in the recent film.'

Ah, good, thought Billy, here's a subject I know something about. Perhaps in lieu of Belloc, I can earn a little credit on this new subject. He spoke up confidently.

'Olivier's *Henry the Fifth* was one of the finest films to come out of Pinewood Studios. Interesting the way Olivier brought Shakespeare's poetry to life within the Globe itself and on the rolling hills of Agincourt.'

'Of course,' added Hamish not to be outshone by this working-class peasant, 'since it was made as a morale booster during the war, it could not be shot at Agincourt itself. It was filmed in Hampshire in nineteen forty-three, forty-four.'

'Quite right, Hamish,' agreed Duncan. 'Agincourt itself was impossible, Billy,' he explained patiently, 'because of the war. As Hamish said, Hampshire was the actual location.'

'Sorry,' said Billy, 'but at college we had to make an intensive study of *Henry the Fifth* and I can assure you the film was shot not in Hampshire but in Ireland of all places, on the Enniskerry estate, to be exact. So the English bowmen were really Irishmen and the English soldiers falling out of trees onto the French were straight from the bogs of Ireland. While showing his Irish extras how to drop twenty feet from a tree to attack passing horsemen, Olivier sprained his ankle. I read somewhere that he directed one hundred and eighty horsemen and five hundred footmen from the Irish Home Guard.'

'Nonsense!' bayed Hamish. 'Where did you hear such drivel?'

'It never ceases to amaze me,' added Duncan, 'how people can pick up such wild ideas. We can soon test it out, however. Hughie, go to the study and bring me the book entitled *Fifty Years of Cinema*. We'll settle it once and for all.'

Billy remained quiet. He was in a spot. Again. He knew he was right but he was a guest in the Mackenzie home and it would be the height of discourtesy to cause Duncan loss of face. Hamish he didn't mind about. It was time he was taken down a peg. But what was the use in winning a debating point if it meant embarrassing Duncan and losing Laura?

Hughie returned with the film book already opened at the section on films of 1944.

'It says here,' he said, hardly able to keep the glee from his voice as he read from the book, ' "The film Henry V was produced and directed by Laurence Olivier and the film was dedicated to the Commandos and Airborne Troops of Great Britain, the spirit of whose ancestors it has been humbly attempted to recapture in some ensuing scenes.

' "Interior scenes were shot at Denham Studios but the actual battle of Agincourt gave the film-makers severe problems. In the early stages, an attempt was made to shoot the film on location in Hampshire but there was so much disturbance from the noise of the warplanes passing overhead that Olivier decided to move the location to Ireland where he employed many Irish extras who were cheaper as they were non-union men. Thus many of the English warriors and bowmen were in fact Irishmen." ' Hughie looked up triumphantly.

'Ah, so we were right,' said Duncan. 'The film was originally shot in Hampshire as we said. It was only later that the film-makers moved it to Ireland. Now do you understand our argument, Billy?'

Billy realised that he could never win a debate with Duncan.

'Ah, now I see,' he uttered diplomatically. 'I'd no idea that the film was shot at first in Hampshire. Thank you for pointing that out, Mr Mackenzie.'

'Always glad to pass on the wisdom of age,' said Duncan, never for a moment accepting that he'd changed his argument.

If ever Laura and I marry, thought Billy, I shall remind her that the price I had to pay to win her was the surrender of my intellectual pride.

'It's always best to be sure of your facts before entering into a debate,' added Hamish sententiously.

'My thoughts exactly,' said Billy, bringing the verbal jousting to a swift if unsatisfactory conclusion.

The smell of hot, buttered home-baked scones and ginger cake heralded the approach of the Mackenzie ladies who arrived with two trolleys laden with tea, crockery, and scones, along with a new delicacy of their own creation. 'Nutty nibbles' they called them.

'Ah, here comes the food at last,' said Grandma. 'About time too. I'm famished.'

'All very well for you,' whined Aunty. 'I don't think I could eat a thing – my digestion isn't up to it.'

'I'm sure I can cope with your share,' rejoined Grandma eagerly.

'These nutty nibbles,' said Billy, 'look most appetising. What exactly are they?'

'They're a sweet biscuit made from oats and syrup,' answered Laura.

'I think you should patent them,' said Billy, biting into one. 'You might make a fortune. You must give me the secret formula, though, and I'll pass it onto my mother.' He wondered whether it was the done thing in the Mackenzie household to dunk them in his tea.

Billy's mind went back to the time when in his etiquette seminars Pottsy had dealt with the subject thoroughly. How long should one dunk a biscuit to achieve the perfect consistency and to avoid its collapse into a gooey mess in one's tea? Research physicists, using an X-ray machine, an electron microscope, sensitive weighing equipment, a little gold and a complicated mathematical formula, had worked out that most biscuits would survive 3.5 seconds, though this varied with the viscosity of the drink. There was also a correct way of holding the biscuit as it was dunked, namely a shallow angle with the imprinted surface down.

The dilemma now facing Billy was whether to dunk at all. To dunk or not to dunk, that was the question. The matter was resolved when Grandma took her nutty nibble between two fingers and thumb and dunked. That was good enough for Billy. He imitated her and was relieved to see that the whole company had begun dunking.

The break was soon over and the second half began with crunch time coming a little nearer for Billy. He could feel the noose tightening.

Duncan stepped forward when the tea things had been cleared away.

'I'm no singer as everyone here is aware but I'll start the ball rolling,' he proclaimed, 'with an old Scottish ballad.'

Duncan's admission as to his lack of singing ability was the under-statement of the evening. In unmelodious tones Duncan cackled his way through 'Wee Cooper of Fife':

> *There was a wee Cooper wha lived in Fife,*
> *Nickety Nackety noo, noo, noo.*
> *And he has gotten a gentle wife*
> *Hey Willy Wallacky, hoo John Dougal*
> *A lane, quo Rushity, roue, roue, roue.*

For Billy, Duncan's rendering of this ditty was not only tuneless but also pure gibberish. Nevertheless he joined in the applause when Duncan finally sat down.

The queue's getting shorter, he thought. Nemesis is at

hand. Like waiting to be executed and no chance of a last-minute reprieve. Could he feign a sudden attack of laryngitis or perhaps throw an epileptic fit? On balance, not a good move; it might get him out of the present predicament but he'd lose any chance he might have with Laura. The family wouldn't welcome a schizoid hypo-chondriac in the family – though if Laura married Hamish, that's what they'd be getting.

'Well, that's the finish of the contributions from the Mackenzie family,' Duncan said. 'Now perhaps we can look to our guests for a contribution.'

'Wait a minute though,' said Billy. 'What about young Katie here? We haven't yet heard from her.' Anything to put off the dread moment.

'Very well,' said Duncan, eyeing Billy balefully. 'I dare say young Katie there can show us how it's done. Come along now, Katie, the family honour's at stake.'

'Yes, Daddy.' Katie whispered, 'but I'm too shy and so I'll have to say it from under the piano.'

What a splendid idea, thought Billy. Now why didn't I think of that? Wonder if I'll be allowed to perform from the same vantage point.

Katie settled herself under the Bechstein and recited softly the William Blake verse:

> *Little Lamb who made thee*
> *Dost thou know who made thee*
> *Gave thee life and bid thee feed?*

Her brave performance was rewarded by spontaneous approval.

'Well done, Katie!'

'Brave little girl!'

'Beautiful recitation!'

Hamish now threw his hat into the ring. He gave Billy a look of triumph as he said to the waiting assembly, 'I suppose there's no getting out of this. So I'll sing a song of Robbie Burns.' He took out a throat spray and began squirting a loathsome mist into his mouth.

This should settle his hash, Billy said to himself. I'll bet he can't sing a note on key.

Hamish began singing of all things Burns's 'Ae fond kiss'. To Billy's chagrin, Hamish demonstrated a pleasant tenor voice, if a little too sweet. Billy noted with quiet satisfaction that his voice had a touch of vibrato, poorly controlled. His choice of song, too, hardly seemed appropriate given his phobia about the transmission of diseases by coughs, sneezes and kisses. He finished with ringing emphasis:

> Ae fond kiss, and then we sever;
> Ae fareweel, and then for ever!

The applause and acclamation with which the end of the song was greeted was meat and drink to Hamish's ears but poison to Billy's. Hamish sat down with a look of elation in his eyes. He glanced triumphantly in Billy's direction. 'Beat that,' his expression said.

'Magnificent,' said Duncan.

'You've obviously had your voice trained,' said Louise. 'It shows in your breath control – no doubt about it.'

Hamish preened himself.

'You'll have me greetin' in a minute, Hamish,' said Jenny warmly. 'That song went straight to my heart.'

'That was good,' said Laura warmly.

Apart from Grandma and Aunty who had now dozed off

before the warm fire, there was only one person left. Billy prayed fervently that the floor would open up and swallow him but God ignored his plea. Why can't they force the two old ladies up from their chairs? he wondered. Wake 'em, shake 'em and make 'em do something.

'Well now,' said Duncan, 'that concludes our evening at home, I think, unless . . .' He looked towards Billy.

'What about Billy there?' said Hamish slyly. 'Is there not something he could do to amuse us?' He laid stress on 'amuse'.

Billy heard a voice saying, 'I think I could perhaps offer a little party piece to the company now.'

It was his own voice doing the speaking.

'I'm not sure if my contribution is suitable,' he said diffidently, 'but anyway I've brought the music for it.'

'Let me see it,' said Laura eagerly. 'I'll be glad to accompany you.' She looked at the music and smiled broadly. 'This should make the party go with a swing,' she said.

Billy stubbed out his cigarette, went to the middle of the room, and cleared his throat. Laura played the introductory chords and Billy began to sing. It was a modest enough opening, all about how nice it was to go roaming, how the sun was shining and the birds singing until the wanderer got further away from home . . . then he would have only one thing on his mind . . .

The audience watched fascinated, wondering what was coming next.

Billy then broke out into his best imitation of Larry Parks imitating Al Jolson singing 'My Mammy' in *The Jolson Story*. With great feeling he sang the refrain about his mammy until he reached the middle part of the song. At this point he dropped to one knee and with great expression added his own dramatic recitative.

'Mammy! My little mammy. It's my mammy I'm singing about, nobody else's!' Then pointing to an imaginary mammy in the sky, he implored: 'Mammy, look at me! Ah, don't you know me? Don't you recognise me? It's your little baby boy – Billy, the Collyhurst kid, come home to see you once more.'

The song finished with a great flourish with Billy down on one knee and hands outstretched in supplication as he sang with great emphasis:

> *I'd bike to Argyle*
> *To see your smile*
> *My mammy!*

The silence which followed was deafening. All eyes turned to the Emperor for final judgement. Would it be a thumbs up or a thumbs down consigning Billy to be eaten by the lions? The silence was not more than twenty seconds but to Billy it was eternity as he gazed anxiously at Duncan for evaluation.

Then it was over. Duncan's face lit up with a dazzling smile.

'That was stupendous!' he exclaimed.

The rest of the company took the cue and applauded enthusiastically. Hamish's face clouded over but who cared about him.

Billy was in!

Nobody was willing to follow the Mammy song and so the evening's proceedings came to a close.

Laura and Jenny accompanied the two young men to the door.

'Thank you both for a lovely evening,' Laura said and

planted an affectionate kiss on both men's cheeks. 'It's an evening I shall treasure forever.'

'The same goes for me,' said Jenny, imitating her sister's actions.

Hamish appeared to have forgotten his kissing phobia.

When the door had closed behind them, the visitors walked down the path, Hamish to his parked Morgan sports car, Billy to his bicycle in the garage.

'You don't stand a chance with Laura, you know,' Hamish hissed. 'Duncan would never accept a tyke like you.'

'I see. Duncan! Don't Laura's wishes come into it? But what makes you say that, Hamish? Why are you so nasty?'

'I didn't like the way you were looking at Laura this evening. Making sheep's eyes at her. I'm giving you fair warning. Stay away from her. If you're looking for a girlfriend, why not try Jenny? Laura's *my* girl – you just remember that.'

'You make her sound like a piece of property, a chattel.'

'You may think what you like,' Hamish snarled, 'as long as you bear in mind that Laura belongs to me. We've been going around with each other for a long time and there's been an understanding between us and our two families for years. In other words, it's not just a flirtation but a serious match. Laura and I will marry in two or three years' time when we've got enough money together. I doubt if you on your teacher's salary can afford to keep her in the style to which she is accustomed. Anyway, steer clear. You'll only create trouble for yourself and for Laura as well. Think about it.'

'I'll do my best to keep it in mind,' said Billy, 'but you make it sound like a political alliance rather than a love match. As for keeping away from Laura, I can't promise anything.'

On that sour note, they parted company.

It was drizzling when Billy cycled off but he didn't notice the wind against his cheeks and the rain in his hair. To the rhythm of his pedalling and the theme of Tchaikovsky's Fifth Symphony, he hummed the same phrase over and over again, 'I love you, Laura. I love you, Laura,' all the way home.

Chapter Twenty-Nine

Billy Hopkins, RA

A week after the *soirée*, Billy took up painting. The decorating kind. At Greg's flat.

Tennyson has said that in the spring a young man's fancy lightly turns to thoughts of love. In the case of Greg Callaghan, his thoughts turned to decorating his newly found apartment – which amounted to the same thing, for his wedding date had been fixed for the coming July.

After school one evening, the two brothers and Billy cycled over to the Alexandra Park district of Whalley Range.

'First, we'll go and meet my folks and have a bite to eat,' said Greg, 'and then we'll wander over to High Lane and start splashing on the paint.'

The Callaghans lived in a Victorian semi-detached house in Demesne Road. The house had large rooms and lots of them but the family spent most of their time in the spacious kitchen-cum-dining room.

Greg introduced Billy to his mother and father.

'Very pleased to shake your hand, Billy,' said Greg's father. 'Any friend of my sons is welcome in my house. You may call me Packy as everyone else does.'

'And the same goes for me,' the mother said, 'though indeed my name is Edna and not Packy. Wait now while I wet the tea and we'll soon have a brew ready for you boys. I'm sure after all that talking you do at the school you'll be ready to moisten your dried-up tongues.'

Edna infused the tea in the biggest teapot Billy had ever seen. He wondered why it had to be such a size. His question was answered when he saw the giant mugs which were each big enough to empty a normal teapot.

Alex offered his cigarettes round and everyone lit up except Greg who ignited his foul-smelling pipe.

'Now, young Billy,' began Packy. 'That name Hopkins is a common one in the west of Ireland. Are your parents Irish, by any chance?'

'I believe my maternal grandmother came originally from the old country,' Billy replied.

'Is that a fact now,' said Edna, thrusting a great mug of tea into his hands. 'What was your grandmother's name?'

'Lally.'

'Well, would you believe that?' she exclaimed. 'When I was a headmistress of a national school in Limerick, wasn't the school superintendent himself named Lally? Now that's a coincidence.'

'Most interesting, Mrs Callaghan,' said Billy politely.

'Hopkins is a much respected name in the west of Ireland,' continued Packy. 'My old friend Patrick Hopkins was once evicted from his cottage by an evil English landlord.'

'Ireland has had a troubled history,' Billy commented.

'Sean Lally, his name was,' said Edna. 'A grand man he was too. Proposed marriage before Packy came along.'

'Amazing, Mrs Callaghan,' said Billy.

342

'Some of our Irish peasants suffered terrible persecution at the hands of the English aristocracy,' Packy continued, ignoring his wife. 'Now Patrick Hopkins, there was a man for you.'

'Glad to hear it,' said Billy.

'Sean Lally was a handsome fellow,' Edna went on. 'I wonder sometimes if I made the right choice marrying Packy here.'

'The flat we're going to paint,' said Greg, blowing noxious clouds in every direction, 'is at the bottom of High Lane in Chorlton. Emily and I were lucky to get it.'

'Flats are not easy to get nowadays,' said Billy agreeably.

'You know, young Hopkins,' Packy continued, 'Benjamin Franklin visited Ireland in seventeen seventy-two and remarked on the opulence and affluence of the English noblemen and gentlemen of the time.'

'Anyway, Packy came on the scene and won my heart,' said Edna. 'He had no money but we were young and we thought love was all-important.'

'I asked Frank Wakefield today if he could give me a greater allowance for the retarded class,' said Alex, now joining in. 'We urgently need extra money for equipment for backward children.'

'Emily has chosen a class of green paint for the walls,' said Greg. 'I'm not too sure about it myself.'

'Franklin was appalled by the straitened condition of the bulk of the people who were tenants and extremely poor.'

'I think Sean Lally broke his heart when we parted,' said Edna dreamily, holding her steaming mug of tea with both hands. 'I don't think he ever married.'

'You know there are three more brothers that you haven't met,' Greg announced suddenly. 'Clement works for an

Irish shipping line here in Manchester. He doesn't get home till around seven o'clock.'

'That's been the problem of Ireland for the last three hundred years,' said Packy. 'Impoverished peasants and absentee landlords. A polarised society.'

'Frank Wakefield is tight with the allocation of funds,' said Alex.

'The other two brothers are Sylvester – he's a Benedictine monk and probably the only one who stands any chance of becoming Pope – and Calixtus who is the eldest and lives in Dublin.'

'I sometimes wonder if I might have prospered better if I'd married Sean Lally,' sighed Edna.

Billy looked from one to the other, trying to digest four conversations at the same time. It's like watching a Mozart opera, he thought, where the performers are intent on singing their own particular recitatives. Not easy to follow and even more difficult to respond to each separate speaker. A conductor might have helped, co-ordinating the performances, bringing each speaker in on cue.

The four-sided conversation continued throughout the delicious meal of bacon and eggs which Edna conjured up, a cigarette dangling from the corner of her mouth.

'I suppose you'll be wondering where we get bacon and eggs in these times of austerity.' Touching her nose, she answered her own question. 'Sure, we have special contacts across the water.'

'The peasants lived in the most sordid, wretched conditions,' Packy was saying. 'In dirty hovels of mud and straw, and clothed only in rags. Is it any wonder the lower orders considered themselves plundered and kept out of their own property by the absentee land-owning aristocracy?'

'We'll begin by painting the ceiling white,' said Greg, 'and we'll go for green on the walls.'

'It's impossible to teach a class of backward children without the necessary equipment,' Alex continued.

Everybody smoked throughout the meal.

Finally it was over.

'I felt you had a most sympathetic ear,' said Edna. 'With a name like Lally in your background, is it any wonder?'

'It was grand talking to you, young Hopkins,' said Packy. 'Come again – any time. You obviously have sympathy for the downtrodden. It's a long time since I had such an intelligent conversation.'

Alex, Greg and Billy cycled across Chorlton to High Lane.

They climbed a narrow staircase to Greg's flat and changed into their old togs. It was comfortable, if basic, accommodation comprising a large lounge, a small kitchen, a bathroom, and a large bedroom which Greg described as 'the most important room in the house'. Maybe some day Laura and I could start off with something like this, Billy thought.

Every night for a whole week after school, Billy slapped the paint onto Greg's walls and a goodly proportion onto his furniture. The colour chosen was *eau de nil*, a pale green colour supposed to resemble that of the Nile but for Billy it bore a closer resemblance to the water in a horse trough. The pungent smell of gloss paint turned his stomach and he came to hate the colour so much that he made up his mind never to visit the Nile if he ever won Littlewood's Pools. Not that there was much chance of that since he didn't bet on the pools.

Towards the middle of the week, as Alex and Greg were busy wiping up the sploshes of paint which had somehow

345

missed the walls and landed on the carpet, the conversation turned to the subject of marriage in general.

'I have no intention of ever marrying,' said Alex. 'Your friends like you and they accept you for what you are; your wife loves you but is forever trying to change you into somebody else.'

Billy had to have his say. 'Didn't some sceptic say: "Marriage is the price men pay for sex, sex is the price women pay for marriage"?'

'You're a couple of cynics,' said Greg. 'Remember the old saying: it's better to marry than to burn.'

'Not everyone would agree with that,' answered Alex. 'Burning might be preferable.'

'And what about you, Billy?' said Greg, ignoring his brother. 'I have the distinct impression that you have your eye on Laura Mackenzie.'

'What makes you say that?' said Billy, flushing. So people had begun to notice!

'You must be joking,' Greg guffawed. 'Why, it's obvious, man. The way you look at her, the way you hang on her every word, that soulful expression that appears on your face whenever she enters the room.'

'I had no idea I was so transparent,' said Billy.

'The whole staff is aware of it,' added Alex. 'The question now remains, what are you going to do about it? We're waiting on tenterhooks.'

'I don't think I'm going to do anything about it,' Billy replied. 'Laura Mackenzie is out of my class.'

'You're worried about that tall Scotsman she goes around with,' said Greg. 'What's his name?'

'You mean Hamish? I suppose I am in a way. He talks down to me. He called me a tyke the other day. Thinks I belong to the peasantry.'

'He shouldn't be a problem – he's studying at Glasgow University, isn't he? You should get in there while he's away. Besides, I think the reason you don't like him is plain jealousy,' Alex said.

'I suppose you're right. I don't like the way he considers that he has a natural right to claim Laura as his own. She goes about with him because there's some kind of long-term understanding between the families. I'm not so sure that she goes along with all that. I think I might stand a chance with her if I tried.'

'Then for God's sake, do something about it!' bellowed Greg. 'Phone her, ask her out. She's not engaged to this Hamish fellow and you're still a bachelor. So what's the problem?'

'I'm afraid I might be rejected, sent away with a flea in my ear.'

'Nothing ventured, nothing gained,' said Alex. 'You sound as if you're in love with the girl.'

'And how's that supposed to sound?' Billy asked.

'For one thing, you talk about her as if she's a mysterious being; you've surrounded her with a mystical aura and put her on a pedestal.'

'And another, you sound as if you want to take her to bed,' added Greg.

'I don't think of her like that,' said Billy quickly. 'I wouldn't dream of trying it on with Laura. If it's love at all, it's the romantic, chivalrous variety – the courtly kind like Lancelot and Lady Guinevere, like Abelard and Héloïse. I believe that perfect bliss is found only in unattainable love, when it's just out of reach.'

The two brothers roared with laughter.

'We've heard that one before,' boomed Greg. 'You've been reading too many books about King Arthur. Look,

347

our knight in shining armour, we'll set it up for you. We'll arrange a hike during the Easter vac – just the four of us – to the Peak District. We'll make sure you get plenty of opportunity to talk to the girl about chivalry and gallantry.'

Greg was as good as his word and approached Laura in the staffroom.

'I'd love to go,' she said. 'A chance to get away from it all and I'm fond of walking in the Derbyshire hills.'

The four of them arranged to meet one Monday morning during the Easter holidays at Lower Mosley Street bus station to take the bus to Hayfield.

The agreed time was nine o'clock but Billy made sure he was there at half past eight. Laura turned up just before nine o'clock. She was wearing the same outfit she had worn for the school bicycle trip, including the tammy with the large red bobble. She looked more beautiful than ever and Billy told her so.

'Greg and Alex aren't here yet,' he said. 'I hope they're not too late as there's a bus leaving at nine thirty. The next one is an hour later.'

They hung around the bus stop glancing anxiously in the direction from which they expected the brothers to appear. Nine thirty came and went and so did the bus.

At ten o'clock, Billy said, 'Well, Laura, it looks as if they're not coming. They don't have a phone so there's no way we can reach them. What shall we do?'

Laura didn't hesitate. 'I think we should go without them. I'm all set for a ramble in the country. I have my sandwiches and my flask and, well, I don't feel like going home again.'

'Do you think so?' Billy said, trying not to sound too

eager. He suspected she knew what Greg and Alex were up to.

They caught the next bus and ninety minutes later were in Hayfield.

'Let's walk to Jacob's Ladder,' Laura suggested. 'There's a glorious view of Kinderscout and Hope Valley from there.'

Together, they set off and the conversation flowed easily as if they had known each other all their lives.

'I loved the way you did your Al Jolson act at our musical evening. It brought the house down,' she said, chuckling at the memory of it.

'I thought at the end it was going to bring the house down about my ears.'

'Daddy loved it. It was such a contrast to the other efforts. You saved the evening from becoming stuffy.'

'When your dad said he had a Blue Nun in the fridge, I could hardly keep a straight face,' Billy laughed.

'I noticed,' she giggled. 'I don't think the rest of the company cottoned onto the double meaning though.'

'I was nervous about coming at first but I enjoyed the evening. You have a talented family.'

'Why, thank you, Billy,' she said. 'One thing I should tell you though. You've made a big hit with Aunty Aggie.'

'Only with Aunt Aggie? I'd rather make a big hit with you.'

Laura flushed.

They were passing Edale Cross and Billy pointed towards Kinder Downfall. 'That's the place where my closest friend Robin Gabrielson died in nineteen forty-five,' he said sadly. 'Only a week before we were due to go to college.'

'I heard about that. How tragic it was. The kind of

thing in your life you never get over.'

'None of the Damian gang ever did. When we reached college in Chelsea, his name was still on many of the administration lists. He was even due to get the room next to mine.'

'How sad it must have been,' she said, taking his hand.

They walked on together hand in hand until the path seemed to come to an abrupt halt. Laura ran ahead a little.

'My heavens! Come and take a look at this, Billy.'

They had reached the Jacob's Ladder escarpment and together they gazed at the panoramic view of the Peak District spread out below.

'It's breathtaking,' said Billy. 'Have you ever seen such magnificence?' He pointed to the distant scene. 'Over there to the left is the majestic Kinderscout and to the right Rushop Edge.'

Laura rested her head on his shoulder. 'It really is beautiful,' she murmured, nestling into him. Billy looked down into her eyes. 'And so are you,' he whispered and kissed her on the lips. Not a long kiss but a soft, gentle touch. 'I love you, Laura,' he said quietly. 'I love you very much. Ever since that first day when I set eyes on you in the staffroom, I have loved no one else. You were wearing a blue dress and your hair was tied back with a red ribbon. I didn't sleep very well that first night and haven't many nights since.' A feeling of unutterable sweetness and tenderness swept through his being. The lines from Keats echoed through his mind: 'O, the sweetness of the pain! Give me those lips again!'

For a while they stood at the top of Jacob's Ladder clinging to each other so closely they could feel each other's heartbeats.

'The same goes for me, Billy,' she said. 'I think I've

loved you ever since that day when Miss O'Neill introduced us in the staffroom.'

'But why didn't you give me some hint of how you felt?'

'A respectable girl doesn't go up to a man and say simply "I fancy you". When we were at Tatton Hall, you talked about ballroom dancing competitions and your partner – Adele, I think you said her name was. I imagined a glitzy, glamorous world of beautiful girls in shimmering, sequin dresses. Girls by the dozen at your beck and call.'

'I should live so long,' he said, holding out his upturned hands. 'I imagined you dancing the Highland fling surrounded by big, porridge-eating, caber-tossing Scotsmen. What chance did I stand against that kind of competition? Besides, you were going around with Hamish, the family favourite!'

'Hamish!' she exclaimed. 'I'd forgotten about Hamish! I don't know how he'll take it. But we'll cross that bridge when we come to it.'

Hand in hand, they set off back to Hayfield.

Chapter Thirty

Coppélia

Later that week, Billy walked to the public telephone box at the corner of Gardenia Court. He picked up the phone, listened for the gentle purr, inserted two pennies, then rang Laura's number. It was Jenny who answered.

'Rusholme two seven six four,' she answered brightly. Billy pressed button A and heard his coins drop. 'Could I speak to Laura, please?' he asked.

'Oh, it's you, Billy. What have you been doing to Laura? I've never seen her so bright and so chirpy. She's going around the house singing. She's in the shower at the moment and she's still singing.'

The image of a naked Laura singing in the shower flashed through Billy's mind. Attractive though it was, he dismissed it quickly. He didn't want to think of her in that way. For him, she was Lady Guinevere, Maid Marian and Snow White rolled into one. Laura was sexually desirable but despite the cynical comments of Greg Callaghan, his love for her was more spiritual than carnal, more Agape than Eros.

'Wait a minute though,' Jenny continued. 'Here she is. She must have heard the phone and come running.'

'Billy,' Laura said breathlessly. 'I thought it might be you.'

'Laura. It's twenty-four hours since I saw you last and every hour has been painful. Can we meet at the weekend? I can get two tickets for *Coppélia* at the Opera House for Friday, if you'd like to go.'

'Billy,' she said, 'is it really twenty-four hours since we last met? Of course I'd love to go. I'll meet you in the foyer at seven o'clock.'

'What about Hamish? Have you given him the good news yet?'

'Look, I'll tell you about it when we meet. Daddy's just coming and so I'll ring off for now.'

'Very well, Laura. I understand. One thing at a time, eh? I'll count the hours till Friday. I love you.'

'Me too,' she said hurriedly. 'Goodbye till Friday, Billy.'

Billy put the phone back in its cradle. What was happening? he wondered. Why did she sound so worried about the appearance of her father? If Laura was his fairytale princess, perhaps there was a dragon or two to slay. There was Hamish of course but he was a minor threat in the lexicon of dragons. There was probably a more fiery example in the person of Duncan, her father. He hoped there were no more.

On Friday night, Billy got to the Opera House in Quay Street at six thirty and anxiously paced the thick red carpet of the foyer. He was there with borrowed things – Les's demob raincoat and ten shillings from Mam for the five-shilling seats in the stalls. There remained a few bob in his pocket in case they had a drink at the interval.

'I don't think the ballet is a nice place to take a respectable girl,' Mam had said when he'd told her. 'All those men in tights prancing about and showing all they've got.'

'It's not that sort of show,' he'd explained patiently. 'This is a story about a toy shop and how the dolls come to life.'

'I hope you're right,' she'd said doubtfully.

Billy glanced around him. There was something about the atmosphere of a luxurious theatre that made him feel uncomfortable and inferior. Perhaps it was the smell of Havana cigars and the exotic perfume, perhaps it was the other theatre-goers who always looked and sounded so posh, as if they belonged there by right – the burly men in their Reid Brothers suits and their plump, bejewelled wives in their fur coats, gloves and hats. He was expecting to be unmasked at any moment by the big commissionaire in the Cossack uniform who seemed to be eyeing him suspiciously.

He wandered over to the display of photos advertising previous productions – Ivor Novello's *Perchance to Dream*, Noel Coward's *Private Lives*. He hoped Laura wouldn't keep him waiting too long. A horrible thought struck him. Maybe she wouldn't turn up. Maybe Duncan had put the kibosh on their meeting and forbidden her to go out with him. It had been obvious that he preferred Hamish as a suitor. After all, what could he, Billy Hopkins, offer his daughter? Nothing but a life of drudgery and penury. He was an impecunious, non-graduate teacher in a secondary modern school. Some prospects!

As these maudlin thoughts ran through his brain, suddenly she was there smiling at him, radiantly beautiful and wearing a new hat – a velvet, plum-coloured affair. Her appearance gave him confidence and security, for she looked as if she belonged naturally in this milieu. She was his admission ticket to this élite theatre society.

'Laura,' he exclaimed, taking both her hands and kissing her on the cheek. 'Am I glad to see you! For a while there I thought you weren't coming.'

'Sorry I'm late,' she said. 'I had to wait a long time for a bus. But wild horses wouldn't have kept me away. I haven't forgotten our walk in the Peak District. My memory isn't that short.'

'Anyway, you're here now, that's all that matters.'

As they went into the theatre, he said, 'It's a ballet about Charles Lamb's policeman brother by a bloke called Leo Debility.'

She looked puzzled for a moment. Then her eyes sparkled and she burst into laughter. '*Coppélia* by Leo Delibes. You are a bit daft, aren't you?'

'At last you've realised it,' he grinned.

The theatre lights dimmed, the orchestra struck up and they sat enthralled by Delibes' music and the superb choreography of the visiting Sadlers Wells company. From time to time, Billy glanced at Laura's enraptured face as she followed every movement of the dancers and took in every nuance of the music. A shiver of joy ran down his spine and he felt a bliss he had never known. If only time could stand still. Making this girl by my side happy, he thought, will be my life's ambition.

At the interval, they went to the crowded, smoke-filled bar.

'Isn't this expensive?' she asked. 'Seats in the stalls and now drinks in the bar.'

'No problem. I took out a mortgage before we came out. What is your pleasure, mademoiselle?'

'A pineapple juice would be fine, Billy.'

'A nice inexpensive drink. I'm beginning to like you more and more.'

Billy managed to push his way through the throng at the bar and soon came back with two Britvic juices. They had cost a bob each which he thought was daylight robbery.

'Now, tell me what's been going on. Have you given Hamish the good news?'

'Yes. I phoned him on Monday and told him that our courtship was over.'

'And how did he take it?'

'He sounded angry. Said he'd suspected that you'd had designs on me and that you'd taken advantage of his absence.'

'Do you agree with that, Laura?'

'Of course I do, Billy. Thank God you did have designs on me, and as for taking advantage of his absence, if Hamish and I had truly loved each other, absence would have made the heart grow fonder. But it didn't. One strange thing though. My sister, Jenny, seems pleased about developments. I think she's set her cap at Hamish and, well, who knows? The only trouble is, Daddy hasn't accepted that Hamish and I are through. And you know better than anyone how he likes to get his own way.'

'I hope that on this particular occasion he doesn't get it.'

'No need to worry on that score, Billy. As far as I'm concerned, Hamish is the past. You are the present – and the future,' she added.

'I'm so happy to hear you say that, Laura. Your father could be a problem though. I think he's of the opinion that I'm the poor man at the gate. He's the emperor, you're the princess and I'm the swineherd daring to have ideas above my station.'

'But you'll remember from the Hans Andersen story that the swineherd turned out to be a prince in the end. I think Daddy'll come round eventually. He thinks money's the most important thing for a secure marriage and that Hamish is a sound commercial proposition. I happen to think there's more to life than money. Anyway, you're not going out with my father, you're going out with me, and don't you forget it,' she said, giving Billy a friendly dig in the ribs.

'OK, boss,' he said. 'I defer to your orders.' But the talk of her father and his ambitions for her had sewn disquiet in his heart.

'On a different subject,' he said cheerfully, 'how do you like the ballet?'

'I love every moment of it. How the ballerinas manage to pirouette so gracefully on the points of their toes, I'll never understand.'

'I think they must have hammer toes to execute those fouettes and maintain those arabesques.'

She laughed. 'You sound knowledgeable about ballet, Billy. Have you seen many?'

'This is my first. But I looked up one or two ballet terms in *The Bluffer's Guide to Ballet* in order to impress you. Anyway, if you say my name carefully, it sounds like Ballet. Only one vowel different.'

They enjoyed the second half of the show even more than the first. It ended with tempestuous applause and cheering. Billy and Laura clapped with the rest until their hands grew tired.

'You know,' Billy said, 'one day, I shall invent a pair of automatic hands, like a football rattle, which will do the clapping for us. We'll simply press a little button and sit back.'

They collected their coats from the cloakroom and Billy helped her on with hers. She linked her arm in his and held onto him tightly as they walked to Albert Square to catch the 89 bus.

At the gate of her home, they stood talking for a while,

about this and that, about school, about their families, about anything – the subject didn't matter. Simply being together was all they needed. They were aware of Jenny, Hughie, and Katie watching them from an upstairs window.

'They're hoping to see something,' Laura murmured.

'Let's not disappoint them,' he said and kissed her lightly on the lips.

At that precise moment, Duncan came upon them suddenly. He was returning from his nightly visit to the Knights of St Columba.

He nodded curtly at Billy and, addressing Laura, he said, 'Don't you be too long out here. It's time you were indoors. Has neither of you got the brains to notice the weather? It's raining.'

'Goodnight, Laura,' said Billy quickly. 'And goodnight, Mr Mackenzie,' he called.

'Hrrmph,' came the reply.

That weekend, Billy wrote a letter to Laura.

My dearest Laura,
Thank you for the most wonderful night of my life. Why must you torment me so? You have invaded my brain and I can think of nothing or no one but you. Everything I do is for you. I wash in order to please you; I spend hours cultivating waves in barren hair for your delight. I eat for your edification. I listen to music for you. You have inhabited my soul. May your residence be permanent.

You looked so beautiful in your new hat, I felt I had to mark the occasion with a verse. Forgive my puny effort.
All my love,
Billy

AN 'AT FOR AN ANGEL

Cities quake;
Bells peal;
Houses shake;
Dogs squeal;
Babies cry;
Sun blushes;
Birds fly
Into bushes;
Bells clang;
Buses crash;
Doors bang;
Windows smash;
Sinners pray;
Women shriek;
Horses neigh;
Mice squeak;
Cats spit;
Pups growl,
Throw a fit,
Start to howl;
Cars stop;
Pets escape;
Eyes pop;
Mouths gape;
Oh begorrah
Gossips chat;
They see on Laura
A bran' new 'at.

Chapter Thirty-One

Walking Out

They became sweethearts in a tender, old-fashioned way. They met each weekend and spent their time walking in Fletcher Moss Gardens, boating on the Mersey and on Heaton Park lake. Billy was becoming a proficient oarsman.

'Do you think Oxford would have me in the next boat race?' he asked.

'I'm sure they would,' she said. 'After a little more practice perhaps. And if they reject you, I'll have you on my team.'

They attended performances of the Hallé conducted by Sir John Barbirolli in the King's Hall, Belle Vue; on Saturday nights, they went to the Apollo cinema on Ardwick Green, cuddling on the back row as they half watched Spencer Tracy and Katharine Hepburn doing their stuff in films like *The World and His Wife*. They made love but not the wild passionate kind – they hugged, kissed, and embraced, and that was it. To sit on a park bench with Laura's head on his shoulder was for Billy perfect happiness. Not that they didn't desire each other physically; but the idea of snatched, furtive sex in a dark corner held no appeal for them. Such goings-on would have made her

360

unhappy and Laura's happiness was the most important thing in the world as far as he was concerned. Besides, there was always the possibility of an unwanted baby and the disgrace that that would entail. Physical love would wait until after they were married. For the present, simply being with each other was enough.

Frank Wakefield took a cigarette from the packet, put it between his lips and lit it from the one he'd just finished. My God, he thought, I'm becoming a chain-smoker. He sat in his little cramped office in the NFS annexe.

'Come in, Hoppy,' he called when he heard the knock. 'Come in and sit down, if you can find room, that is.' Wakefield smiled nervously. He wasn't looking forward to this – not one bit.

Billy wondered what it was about. At the end of his lesson before break, he'd received a message that the head wanted to see him. Most unusual, he'd thought, as he always saw Frank Wakefield at lunchtime when they shared their sandwiches. Have I gone wrong somewhere? he wondered. Done something I'm not supposed to?

'Coffee?' asked Wakefield, plugging in the kettle. 'It's only Camp coffee but I think you'll find it a little higher standard than that noxious brew they have over there in the staffroom.'

'Thanks a lot, Frank.'

'Cigarette, Billy?' he said offering his Players.

'Thanks again, Frank.' Billy didn't like the sound of this. What was this strange preamble leading up to? As far as he knew his record was OK.

Wakefield pulled on his cigarette and swung his chair sideways so that he was looking at the chart on the wall.

'You've been with us a year now, Hoppy. I thought it was

time you and I had a little private chat to review things. You've settled in here wonderfully well.'

'I made a false start, Frank, but then I think I got the hang of it,' Billy replied, still puzzled.

'More than the hang of it, Hoppy. Your projects and your organisation of visits have been exemplary and the HMIs have said as much in their probationary reports.' He stubbed out his fag in the ashtray and began playing with the ruler on his desk. He didn't look at Billy. He was finding it hard to say what he had to say.

He cleared his throat and said in a rasping voice, 'This school is not like other schools, though. Mind you, things are not as strict as they used to be. Why, before the war, if a woman married, she had to leave the profession. It was the same in the civil service. Did you know that?'

'No, Frank, I didn't know that.' Where was all this leading?

'You have to remember it's a Catholic school, Hoppy, and we have to set the highest example at all times.'

What the devil was he getting at? Billy asked himself. Surely he wasn't referring to his torrid affair with Adele. That had finished a long time ago.

'You have to bear in mind, Hoppy,' Wakefield went on, 'that this is a small parish and gossip easily goes the rounds, becoming more and more exaggerated as it does.'

'Sorry, Frank,' Billy said anxiously, 'you've lost me. Has someone been complaining about me?'

'No, no,' he exclaimed hurriedly. 'Nothing like that. It's just that . . .' He hesitated and hawked again. 'After a recent school governors' meeting, Father Kelly did happen to mention to me that he'd heard on the grapevine that there was a romance going on between two of his teachers in the school.'

362

Billy's heart skipped a beat. So that was what this was about! His romance with Laura! He felt his hackles rise.

'So what! I would have thought that that was a private matter between the two teachers concerned and not a matter for idle chatter.'

'Yes, yes, I agree with you, Hoppy,' Wakefield said quickly. 'But in our profession, we've got to be careful not to create scandal. We're like members of the clergy. The adolescents we're teaching are very impressionable.'

At that point, Greg Callaghan knocked lightly on the door and entered.

'Could I see you for a moment, Frank, about the playground duty roster?' he asked, glancing quizzically from one to the other.

'I'll see you later about that, Greg, if you don't mind.'

Greg withdrew diplomatically.

Wakefield turned to Billy and looked him straight in the eyes for the first time. 'The top class thinks the world of you, Hoppy, and if they saw or heard anything untoward between you and Miss Mackenzie, it wouldn't go down too well.'

'But there isn't and never has been anything untoward, as you put it, in our conduct. Look, Frank. I'm a bachelor and Laura Mackenzie is, as far as I'm aware, a spinster of this parish, to coin a phrase.'

'Look at it another way,' Wakefield said. 'Suppose you two fall out, have a lover's tiff. What happens? You're both not talking to each other and you create an uncomfortable, tense atmosphere in the school. Why, one of you might even decide to leave the school and then we're short of a teacher. School romances usually mean problems for everyone all round. Why, we'd be at sixes and sevens if we all started falling in love with each other. Take it from me,

Hoppy, it doesn't do to form close relationships in school, they nearly always lead to trouble.'

'Trouble? Laura Mackenzie and I are very much attracted to each other. Where's the trouble in that? I think you have a vivid imagination, Frank, and you're anticipating things that will never happen.'

'I'll tell you where the trouble might be, Hoppy,' he said, his hands visibly shaking. 'You have to be very discreet. You're young and inexperienced in the ways of the world. Your prospects – and mine as well for that matter – at this school are in the hands of the managers. They have the power to hire and fire, and the power to promote and demote. It's not a matter of whether you've done anything wrong or not, it's a matter of the way *they* see things. I've found it's best to keep your nose clean if you're going to get anywhere in the world of education. Look, let me be blunt. If you're looking for a girlfriend, why not pick someone from outside the school?'

Billy bristled. 'What business is it of yours or of anyone else who I choose for my girlfriend! And by keeping your nose clean, you mean doing exactly what the managers dictate. Is that it? And isn't Mr Mackenzie on the management board? He's a big noise in the KSC and the Catenians. I think I see what's going on here.'

'Whoa! Hold your horses, Hoppy!' Wakefield exclaimed, holding up both hands as if warding off an assault. 'Who said anything about Mr Mackenzie? I'm simply talking about a chance remark from Father Kelly, that's all. I'm not even sure he was serious. Don't go jumping to conclusions.'

Billy's rage, however, was on a roll. 'Look, Frank, I wasn't born yesterday. I can put two and two together. When you talk about promotion, I suppose you're thinking of your own chances and the new headship. The whole thing stinks. It makes me sick. You can tell Father Kelly – and Mr Mackenzie, if he's somewhere in the background – that they can take a running jump. What Laura Mackenzie and I do in our private lives has nothing to do with them. As for promotion, they can stuff it.' He got up to storm out of the office but Frank Wakefield stopped him.

'Hold it right there, Hoppy. Take it easy! I knew you'd react the way you did. I'd have been disappointed in you if you hadn't.'

'I can assure you, Frank, that my intentions towards Laura Mackenzie are entirely honourable,' he said, cooling down a little. 'I have a sneaking feeling that Duncan Mackenzie is somewhere behind this attempt to put me off. He thinks I'm not good enough for his daughter.'

'What rubbish! Perhaps he doesn't see the potential in you that I do.'

Billy began to laugh. 'I think he'd like a kilted, bagpipe-playing Caledonian with a first-class honours degree for a son-in-law. Instead he's maybe going to get a gormless Lancashire lad from Collyhurst.'

'That's more like it,' said Wakefield, joining in the merriment. 'You go ahead and live your own life and I'll back you to the hilt.'

Billy returned to the staffroom where he found Greg alone, puffing on his ubiquitous pipe.

'What in God's name was that about, Hoppy?' he bawled. 'Has the old man had you on the carpet? Hauled you over the coals? Read the riot act? I must say, he looked more nervous than you did. What was he going on about this time?'

'Giving me advice on affairs of the heart,' replied Billy.

'He's the last person I should go to for advice,' said Greg.

'Well, there's only one thing to do when you're given good advice,' said Billy.

'And what's that?' asked Greg.

'Pass it on to someone else as soon as possible.'

'Fine,' said Greg, 'as long as you don't have me in mind.'

Chapter Thirty-Two

Farewell

The end of Billy's first year of teaching came round all too soon. There was little formal teaching in the last week at school. Frank Wakefield was heavily involved in issuing Leaving Certificates and school references and Billy found himself at a loose end. Youth employment officers came to visit the school to talk to the class about openings and opportunities in the local district, mainly in the building and motor trades for the boys, shop work or clothing work for the girls. Much of the time was taken up with interviews, though many of the pupils had already secured jobs through their own families.

For much of the term, the class had been talking excitedly of leaving school at last, of going out into the big, bad world, of getting a job, earning money, buying the latest gear, and generally enjoying themselves. In the final week, though, the atmosphere was quiet and their enthusiasm muted as they realised that D-day was fast approaching. How would they fare, they wondered, and would they be able to cope?

Mick Lynch was fixed up to help his father in the costermongering business on Market Street. Jim Mitchell had finally arranged to take up the job in a decorating firm – postponed from the previous year. Vera Pickles found her post at Lewis's store was still open. Tony Jarvis landed a plum job as a messenger in the GPO, Joe Duffy would be a trainee bricklayer, and Alf Dempsey an apprentice motor mechanic. Nellie Wallace was going to be a machinist in a raincoat factory. Billy hoped that she'd remember not to obey orders literally and so avoid stepping into any more wastepaper baskets. Des Bishop signed up as a junior in a seminary with a view to joining a foreign mission later on. Irene Moody was undecided as to her future career.

'I don't want to spend my life in a boring job, sir,' she said huskily. The Veronica Lake persona seemed to have become a permanent feature of her character. 'Standing behind a counter at Woolworth's or being a waitress in a café – they're not for me. Besides, the wages in those jobs are terrible. No, I want to have plenty of cash in my pocket when I leave. To buy nice clothes, have nice holidays and that. My sister has her own little business and she said she might show me how to make some real money after school. So, I might join her.' She obviously didn't know that Billy was aware of the nature of her sister's business.

He couldn't help thinking what a strange job this teaching business was. There was no way of judging the effect one's teaching was having, if any. People in jobs which involved production of goods could see the results of their labours. At the end of the day, there was something to show for their exertions – a motor car or a bicycle – and they could say, 'I helped to make that.' Even doctors could say, 'I cured that person,' or if the patient died, 'I failed that time.' There was something concrete to see or to measure. But in teaching, no such thing – it was impossible to gauge the results. If one of the pupils made good, did a teacher claim him or her as a success? If so, what about the failures? Did he disown them and say, 'Nothing to do with me – not my fault'? In the case of Bishop, the school had helped produce a missionary priest. Did they claim him as one of their triumphs? If so, what about Irene Moody who looked as if she was about to join her sister in the oldest profession? Did they wash their hands of her and say, 'Too bad, it was her environment that caused her downfall'? A nice alliteration, he thought, a priest and a prostitute from the same form.

In the final week, everyone was present every day, as if they felt it was their last opportunity to share in something that they had taken for granted all year. On the last day but one at school, the class began recording everything that happened as 'The last time we shall . . .' Billy called the register. 'Do you realise,' said Nellie Wallace, 'that this is the last time Sir will call our name in the register?' They drank their milk: 'The last time we shall have our milk at school.' The boys played football at the break. Their last football in the school yard. The girls went for their needlework class. Their last needlework with Miss O'Neill. No wonder there was an air of gloom about the place. As if they were to be executed the next day.

On the morning of the last day itself, there was a final assembly of the whole school. Miss O'Neill and Laura played one of Schubert's *Marches militaires* piano duets as the various classes filed into the NFS hall. When everyone was in place, Frank Wakefield awarded money prizes from his own pocket for various achievements in class: half-a - crown for first place; two shillings for second, and one shilling for third. Various other awards were made, such as Best Effort, Best Attendance, and Best Improvement. Wakefield called out the names and shook the hands of the lucky individuals and congratulated them on their success. The whole school applauded.

Billy felt sorry for the children who came away with nothing. Had it been left to him, he'd have awarded a prize to everyone.

Then came the sad moment when the head distributed the Leaving Certificates. As he called their names, the leavers came forward to receive their piece of parchment. Every girl wept copiously as she walked up onto the stage, and even the boys looked as if they were having problems holding back the tears.

What a contrast, Billy thought, to the class he had taken over less than a year ago. Then they'd been angry at having to stay on an extra year and ready to take it out on him. Now here they were, sad and weepy at the thought of being released.

How appropriate, Billy thought, if Wakefield had used the line from a Hollywood police film at this point: 'Hey, you guys. Be careful! It's a jungle out there, I tell ya!'

Wakefield settled instead for the singing of a goodbye hymn:

> *Sweet Saviour, bless us ere we go,*
> *Thy word into our minds instil;*
> *And make our lukewarm hearts to glow*
> *With lowly love and fervent will.*

Throughout that term, the top class had been collecting for their farewell party, arranged for the evening of the final day. After assembly, there was a great deal of coming and going, and Billy spent much of his time in the staffroom, deeming it best to keep out of the way.

The boys were seen with sweeping brushes, mops and

buckets, and there was a great deal of moving of furniture. The buffet tables were put in place, the record player and a wide selection of records were taken over in readiness for their big shindig.

At six o'clock, the festivities began and the whole staff attended – including even Grundy who had spent much of the term whingeing about the waste of time it was and how 'education was going to the dogs'.

The pupils began arriving a little after six and Billy's heart swelled with pride when he saw them. The boys were a joy to behold in their best suits, collars and ties, gleaming shoes, and their hair slicked down with brilliantine – though it failed to hold down Joe Duffy's errant locks. Tony Jarvis and Mick Lynch sported tiepins and cuff links, and Alf Dempsey boasted a carnation in the buttonhole of his lapel.

'I hope you're not going to try and put coal into the boiler tonight,' remarked Frank Wakefield to Joe Duffy. 'Not in your best suit.'

'Only if you order me, sir,' he replied, 'and if it's in the middle of Mr Hopkins's lesson.'

'Here, Joe,' Wakefield said, taking out his packet of cigarettes, 'I know you smoke – have known for the past year. Have a decent one after those dimps you've been dragging on.'

'Thanks, sir. They were usually your dimps I smoked anyway.'

The arrival of the girls in a bunch caused a great stir. Their entrance was worthy of a Busby Berkeley parade and the eyes of the staff – and many of the boys – popped out of their heads. The girls had spent considerable time at each other's homes primping themselves up for the big party and the results were delightful. Their bouffant hairstyles, the judicious use of cosmetics, their New Look dresses and high heels – all had blended together in such a way as to transform them from gawky, leggy schoolgirls into young debutantes. No longer school kids, thought Billy, but highly attractive young ladies.

'I hope none of them are wearing those copper knickers Hopalong was telling us about,' Horner whispered to Dempsey.

The dancing began with the music of Victor Sylvester and Billy's pupils demonstrated what they could do.

'Well, I never!' exclaimed Grundy. 'I can see the education this class has been getting and it's not the academic variety.'

'Somehow, I think they'll find ballroom skills of more value in their world,' Wakefield rejoined.

It was Nellie Wallace who stole the show. Her dark hair was combed high on the back of her head and tied with a red silk ribbon. Her black silk dress must have meant many laundry chores for her mother.

'That girl has turned out to be a real swan,' remarked Laura. 'I'll have to watch my step with some of these girls. I think I may have competition.'

'Hardly,' said Billy, squeezing her hand. 'They're beautiful all right but young kittens and hardly in your league.'

The music started up with Sylvester's 'You're Dancing On My Heart' quickstep and Nellie came over to Billy's table.

'May I have this dance, sir?' she said.

'My pleasure,' answered Billy and together they glided across the floor in perfect time in strict tempo.

'You know, sir,' she said, 'when you first came to the school, we decided to give you a hard time. But after that bike ride to Tatton Park, well, things seemed to change. This has been the best year of my life and it's one I'll never forget.'

'That's fine, Nellie,' said Billy, 'but remember, don't obey orders literally by stepping into wastepaper baskets.'

'That's something I do want to forget,' she said. 'And thank you, sir, for not embarrassing me in front of the class. They were waiting to laugh at me and you didn't let them.'

The rest of the evening slipped by quickly and soon it was time for parting. The party had been fixed to end around ten thirty, and as that time approached, Frank Wakefield stepped to the front of the room and called for attention.

'I want to say how much we on the staff have enjoyed tonight and I hope all of you – former members of the top class – feel the same. You have been a great class and we're proud of you. We only hope that the next top class is half as good as you. Remember that although you are leaving us, you can always come back to see us any time. Now I think Jim Mitchell has something to say.'

Jim Mitchell came to the front. 'I'm not much good at making speeches but we're sorry we gave Mr Hopkins a hard time at the start of the year. Anyroad, we're grateful for all he's done for us and the top class has had a whip-round and we've got him a little present.' He nodded to Nellie Wallace who came forward with a package. Billy went forward and received it from her. He was overcome with emotion.

'I don't know what to say,' he mumbled.

'Then it's the first time!' Tony Jarvis called out. 'Open it, sir.'

Billy removed the wrapping and found a pewter tankard

with the engraved inscription: TO OUR TEACHER. THANKS A LOT, HOPALONG.

Billy looked up, his eyes moist. And for the first time in his life, he really was stuck for words.

Chapter Thirty-Three

Absence Makes the Heart Grow Fonder

When the summer holidays came round, the staff of St Anselm's departed in all directions to their holiday destinations, Greg to his mysterious honeymoon and the rest to various places on the continent. Laura, along with her sisters, Jenny and Katie, had fixed up to stay a month with an uncle in Ayr, while Alex Callaghan and Billy had arranged to take a three-week cycling holiday round Ireland. In many ways, Billy was not looking forward to it for it meant a whole month's absence from Laura.

'I don't know if I can stand being away from you for a whole month,' Billy told her the night before departure. 'But I suppose your dad will be glad to see us apart for a lengthy period.'

'I shouldn't worry about Daddy. He hasn't fully grasped yet that the understanding between Hamish and me is over for good, but he'll come round to it slowly but surely.'

'I hope and trust that he does. Whatever happens don't let him persuade you to go back to Hamish while we're apart.'

'Don't even think about it,' she said, taking both his hands. 'Hamish is history. You're the only one for me and

I'll make sure Daddy gets the message whilst you're away. Anyway, you've gone up in his estimation lately.'

'Oh, and why is that?'

'Hughie has just learned that not only did he get his Higher School Cert but also his credit in French giving him the modern language he needed for matriculation. He's been accepted by Sheffield's Medical School after he's served his National Service. We're all very grateful to you, Billy.'

'Aw, shucks, I didn't do nothin',' Billy drawled in his best John Wayne accent. 'But ah tell ya, pardner, ah'm sure gonna miss you like hell these next few weeks.'

'Absence makes the heart grow fonder,' she murmured, putting her head on his shoulder.

'As long as it's not a case of absence makes the fond heart wander,' he said. 'Have you ever noticed that for every one of these sayings, there's an opposite? For example, "Look before you leap" but "Faint heart never won a fair lady" and "He who hesitates is lost".'

'What about "The early bird catches the worm" and "Better late than never"?' she laughed.

'And as for absence making the heart grow fonder, remember also "Out of sight, out of mind", but that will never happen to us. The idea of not seeing you for four weeks fills me with heartache. I shall write to you every day.'

'The same goes for me, Billy,' she said, 'but I can't write to you as you will be on the move the whole of the time. But you'll be in my thoughts every moment of every day that we're apart.'

'There is one saying which is so true, there is no opposite, and that is, "Parting is such sweet sorrow".'

They kissed goodnight at the doorstep. If the rest of the

family was watching from an upstairs window, Laura and Billy were past caring.

The Gladstone Dock in Liverpool was a hive of activity when Alex and Billy arrived there to take the night ferry to Dublin where they were to spend the first leg of their travels with Calixtus, Alex's eldest brother. They reported to the customs shed and an officer came out to examine their luggage and their bikes to assure himself that there really were two bikes and that the two suspicious characters before him were not smuggling contraband to the Emerald Isle. Though what goods England might have that were worth smuggling across the water, they couldn't imagine.

Having run the gauntlet of immigration and passport control, they arranged for the cycles to go into the hold, after which they boarded the steamship *Pride of Erin* and established themselves on deck.

'I've always found it best to stay on the top,' Alex advised. 'That way, you avoid seasickness as you won't feel the ship's roll half so much.'

This was Billy's first adventure abroad and he felt a great sense of excitement as, leaning over the rail, he watched the boat cast off.

A big red-faced Irishman chose this moment to start an argument with a fellow national on the dockside.

'You have a donkey's arse for a face, so you have,' the big man bellowed, 'and if this boat weren't goin' out, I'd knock your feckin' head off into the middle of next week, so I would.'

'You thank your feckin' lucky stars the boat *is* going out,' the docker yelled back, 'otherwise I'd have your guts for garters, you feckin' ignorant bogtrotter.'

The two knew perfectly well that there was no chance of

either of them carrying out the threats as the distance between them was widening with every moment.

The boat ploughed along the Mersey and soon the Liver birds were silhouettes in the distance.

They found a comfortable cubbyhole and settled down for the night. The gentle rocking of the boat soon lulled them to sleep and they looked forward to a peaceful crossing.

It was not to be. About midnight their peace was shattered. The giant of an Irishman, with the red face and shock of matching hair, a bottle of Guinness stuck in each of his jacket pockets, and shirt wide open to reveal a colourful tattoo of His Holy Mother The Church, began serenading the sleeping deck passengers.

The lament he had chosen contained around ninety-six verses, each of which ended with the invocation: 'Glorio, glorio to the bould Fenian men!'

As if disturbing the slumber of the travellers wasn't enough, he proceeded to go around the deck demanding alms, for what charity or cause he didn't say, and his requests were couched in such terms that no one had the temerity to ask. Like the rest, Alex and Billy dug into their pockets and made a contribution. As a reward for their generosity, the minstrel treated them throughout their journey with all verses of 'The Boys of Wexford' several times over.

It was a tired and baggy-eyed pair of travellers that finally reached the Kingstown Harbour in Dublin where Calixtus was waiting to take them home for their overnight accommodation. Calixtus lived with his wife and two children in a comfortable semi-detached in the suburb of Blackrock, just south of the city.

After a breakfast of bacon and eggs – why was it called

378

a full English breakfast, Billy wondered, when no one in England had the wherewithal to provide it? – they pushed back their chairs and everyone lit fags. Sweet Afton was the name of the cigarette produced – why the Irish had adopted the name of a poem by the Scottish bard as their most popular brand was another puzzle. Pointless trying to find a rational explanation to these conundrums. Calixtus's children sat at the table with them and Billy remarked how well-behaved they seemed. They didn't, however, come up to Calixtus's exacting standards and he spent much of his time hitting or threatening to hit them with a rolled-up newspaper.

'Will you stop picking your nose, Patrick, or do I have to hit you again with this?' he called, brandishing a cylindrically shaped copy of *The Irish Times*. Or, 'Mary, give over biting your nails or do you want a taste of the front-page news?'

Fascinated, Billy drank it in. All part of cultural learning.

Their first day in Ireland was one of rest and sleep in preparation for an early start next morning.

At eight o'clock they set off, past Phoenix Park and on their way to Cork – 160 miles distant. After thirty minutes of hard pedalling, they reached Clondalkin on the outskirts of Dublin. They stopped at the first post office so that Billy could pen a postcard to Laura in Ayr. It was to be the first in an endless stream of cards that would land on her doorstep. All with the same message of love.

'At the rate we're moving,' said Alex, 'it'll take us maybe two days to reach Cork but we're in no hurry.'

At that point, a small open truck roared past and screeched to a halt about a hundred yards down the road. The driver got out of his cab and beckoned to them.

'Where are you headed, lads?'

'Cork,' answered Alex.

'Hop on the back, lads, I'll have you there in two shakes.'

They caught up with him quickly and clambered aboard, bikes and all.

The truck set off like a rocket. With the wind rushing through their hair, they watched the Irish countryside shoot by. Naas, then a short time after, Portlaoise. On through Tipperary to Cashel and an hour after that they hurtled into Cork. The whole journey had taken a little over two hours.

Billy and Alex got out of the truck elated.

'I think you were trying to break the land speed record,' said Billy to the driver. 'Can we buy you a pint of porter to show our gratitude?'

'I don't see any reason why not,' their Irish Sir Malcolm Campbell said. 'Haven't I a mouth like a dry crust?'

They went into a nearby bar and ordered three pints of porter and stood there talking about their driver's chances in a round-Ireland truck race. After a short time, he left and Alex and Billy remained at the bar where their unorthodox cycling dress of open shirt and baggy white shorts attracted the attention of their fellow drinkers.

'Are you on a cycling holiday, lads?' asked an inquisitive bystander sipping his pint and pulling on his clay pipe.

'That's right. We're cycling right round Ireland,' Billy replied, sticking out his chest and drawing on his Afton. He couldn't resist boasting a little.

'Now, is that right?' said an old man in the corner of the room. 'How far have you come today, lads?'

'From Dublin,' answered Alex nonchalantly.

'That's a fearful long way on a bike,' said another. 'What time did you set off yesterday?'

'We left this morning at eight o'clock,' said Billy truthfully. 'We came at a good speed.'

'Bejabers!' said the speaker. 'And it's only half past eleven now by the bar-room clock. You must be cycling champions. Will you take a pint o' porter with us?'

At two o'clock in the afternoon, the two travellers rolled out of the bar to find a boarding house for overnight accommodation.

Cork turned out to be a popular town and every place they approached was full. They tried St Christopher's Boarding House, St Patrick's, then St Agatha's but there was no room at the inn.

'I appreciate how St Joseph and Mary must have felt,' remarked Alex.

They sought help in a corner shop.

'Have you tried St Finbar's?' said the owner.

'We've tried the whole litany of the saints,' said Billy.

They eventually secured places in Mary O'Shea's lodging house: 'Clean rooms guaranteed,' the sign said. They deposited their luggage, locked up their bikes, and went out to get a meal and explore the town.

'This is a beautiful little spot,' remarked Alex. 'Like a picture postcard.'

That was the wrong thing to say for it triggered the need in Billy to send a card winging its way across to Scotland. They retired to Skiddy's Almhouse where Billy wrote his message:

My dearest Laura, I'm here in this beautiful little town but without you here to see it, it doesn't mean a thing. If I spot something lovely, my first thought is that I want you here to share it with me. Missing you every hour of the day. Alex talks but I hardly pay attention as I'm lost in thought about you. As you know, we're men of few words and so tomorrow, we

381

go to Blarney where we shall kiss the stone and see if
it helps us to get over our shyness and our taciturnity.
All my love, Billy.

There was a strong wind blowing when they left Cork the
next day heading west for Glengarriff via Bantry Bay. They
made slow progress and as a distraction from the struggle
with the elements, they sang, or rather panted, all the Irish
songs they knew. 'Shake Hands With Your Uncle Mike, Me
Boy' and 'Star of the County Down' with its chorus line:

> *From Bantry Bay up to Derry Quay*
> *And from Galway to Dublin Town,*
> *No maid I've seen,*
> *Like the brown colleen,*
> *That I met in the County Down.*

'It's about sixty-five miles,' said Alex, 'and if we go through
Skibbereen it's going to take us all day to reach Bantry at
this rate.'

'Is it any wonder?' Billy gasped. 'We're cycling into the
teeth of an Atlantic gale.'

Four hours later, they reached Skibbereen exhausted.

'Time for a break,' said Alex, pointing to Molly Malone's
Tea Rooms. 'I think we deserve a cup of tea and a smoke.
It's been tough going so far, Billy.'

'We need another racing driver like the one yesterday,'
laughed Billy. 'Have you noticed, by the way, that nearly
every place we've passed through since we came to Ireland
has either had a mention in a song or had a whole song
devoted to it?'

'I have indeed. Like Dublin, Tipperary, Blarney, Cork,
Bantry.'

'And later, we'll be going through Tralee, Killarney, Derry, and Galway,' added Billy. 'Why haven't our own towns in Britain had songs written about them?'

'Well, a few have. Like places in London or Glasgow. But who would want to write about Salford or Wigan or Manchester or Dukinfield?'

'I suppose you're right,' said Billy. 'Imagine a song about "Rose of Salford Docks" or "The Star of Trafford Park". Hardly places of great beauty like the ones we're passing through.'

'That explains it. Is it any wonder they're commemorated in music – we've come through some glorious scenery.'

'I'm afraid I've not been good company in this respect,' said Billy. 'If I see a wonderful scene or view, I want to share it with Laura Mackenzie and without her being present to see it with me, I can't fully appreciate it.'

'Instead of sending her these picture postcards, why don't you phone her and describe the places to her?'

'I'd love to, Alex, and I have her phone number in Ayr but so far I've not seen a single phone box. Do they have phones in this part of the world?'

'Of course they do,' he laughed. 'Ireland's not as backward as that. Since every Irishman is born with a silver tongue, they have to have phones to accommodate their vast vocal output. Probably best to try a hotel in the next town.'

'I will at the next opportunity,' Billy said eagerly. 'I don't know why I didn't think of it before.'

'You've fallen for that girl, haven't you?'

'Ah, so you've noticed,' Billy grinned.

'Noticed! You must be joking! You light up like a neon sign when you hear her name. The whole staff has noticed. We'd have to be blind as bats not to. She's a lovely girl.

You'll be a lucky man if you win her.'

'Were you never attracted to her yourself, Alex?'

'I was and I am but we're too much like each other.'

'I always thought that being alike and having things in common was a good thing.'

'True, true. You must share common values and interests, have a similar level of education, have a similar outlook on important things like religion, how to raise kids, and that type of thing. Otherwise you'd never be attracted to each other. The more things like that you have in common, the better. But when it comes to personality and temperament, that's a different matter.'

'What makes them different?'

'Take you and Laura. You couldn't be more different and that's why you're ideally suited.'

'How do you mean, "ideally suited"?'

'I have a theory about what makes a good match. Not everyone agrees with me – in fact some people think it's daft but I believe that opposites attract.'

'I suppose you're going to say next that she's beautiful and I'm grotesque. She's Esmerelda and I'm the Hunchback.'

'Be serious for a minute. I reckon some people are natural talkers and others natural listeners. When two people with this combination get together, you've usually got a good match. Each partner's happy, talking and listening the amount that suits their personality.'

'You reckon then that Laura and I are a match made in heaven?'

'Well, made at St Anselm's at least.'

'A great theory. You ought to write a book on it.'

'Maybe I will one day. Now, I've done more than enough blathering to fill my day's quota. If we're going to make

Bantry before dark, we'd better get a move on.'

The road took a northerly direction but the gale did not let up. After five miles of it, cycling with heads down, they turned into a hedge, and lit up their fags. They had been there only five minutes when an old farmer came along with a solitary cow. From time to time he struck it lazily with a long cane. When he saw the two cyclists sheltering in the hedge, he stopped and in a loud voice inquired, 'Where are you headed, lads?'

'Bantry,' Billy announced.

'Are you going on through the storm?' he asked in ringing tones that would have done justice to a Shakespearean actor at the Globe.

'We are!' proclaimed Billy in the same vein.

'Ah, ye'll never make it! Ye'll never make it!' he trumpeted, raising both his arms to heaven. With a sudden movement, he stuck a cigarette butt in his mouth and lowering his head close to Billy's ear, muttered, 'Have you got a light there?'

Billy obliged him with a light, and asked, 'Which is the best road to Bantry, would you say?'

'Well now, if I were trying to get to Bantry myself . . . well, in the first place I wouldn't start from here. But you see that road to the left?'

'We do,' they said.

'Well, don't take that one – it goes nowhere.' With his half fag ignited, he strolled off into the wind, still striking the unlucky beast.

'That man would knock John Gielgud and Donald Wolfit into a cocked hat,' remarked Billy as they watched the farmer's retreating figure.

Two hours later, they rode into Bantry Bay, found a cheap boarding house, and collapsed onto their beds completely tuckered out. An hour's rest and they were ready to explore the town.

'First, I must find a phone,' Billy said. 'It'll be so wonderful to hear Laura's voice again.'

'It's only a few days since you saw her,' Alex protested.

'To me it seems like eternity.'

They asked their landlady, Mrs Kathleen Quinlan, if she knew of any place that might have such a thing as a telephone.

'Ah, now,' she said, 'there's a very interesting question. I myself wouldn't have such a contraption in the house. I don't hold with such dangerous technology. Did I not read in the *Bantry Gazette* only yesterday that putting an electric gadget like that to your ear can give you every class of disease.'

'That's news to me,' Billy said. 'What kind of disease?'

'Deafness, for one thing,' she replied. 'And then the radiation passing through your head is sure to soften the brain and cause madness. Apart from that, you could pick up some terrible infection from the earpiece. Who's to say that the last one to use it didn't have leprosy or some such thing. Anyway, you could try the Tim Healy Hotel across the road – last I heard they'd installed one of them new-fangled inventions.'

The hotel looked a likely bet. At the reception desk, they found a leprechaun of a man – the image of Barry Fitzgerald. Billy gave him details of his requirements and the number in Ayr. 'We do have a telephone,' he said, eyeing them suspiciously as if they were English spies. 'We don't get much call for it, you understand, but I'll check with Bridget O'Hara, the town telephonist.'

He cranked the handle on the telephone vigorously and blew into the mouthpiece.

'Is that yourself there, Bridget?' he asked. 'How are you, me ould flower? And the family and the wee bairns? Good, that's good. Now I have a couple of Englishmen here who want the use of the telephone to talk to someone in Scotland.' He made Scotland sound like the Kremlin. 'Would that be possible now?' They heard Bridget squawking some kind of answer.

'She said it might be possible though she'll have to look up the procedure and the cost of such a long-distance trunk call,' he answered eventually.

'I take it the call will be private,' Billy said. 'Only I want to talk to my girlfriend in Scotland without the whole of Ireland listening in.'

'Jabers, how could you ask such a thing! Do you think we've nothing better to do with our time than eavesdrop on your idle chatter? Of course your call will be private.' This is going to provide me with a story for the regulars in Houlihan's Bar tonight, the midget thought. 'Twill be worth at least two pints, maybe three.

After a fifteen-minute wait, the phone rang again and Bridget made contact with Billy.

'I have Scotland on the line for you, caller,' she said. 'Hould on, please whilst I try to connect you.'

There followed a series of weird noises which sounded as if a tornado was raging at the other end of the line, then a succession of blips, burps, farts, and whistles, finally a chain of tut-tut-tut-tuts. Then silence. Billy was about to give up when over the ether he caught the faint sound of a human voice. It was Hamish.

'This is Ayr two oh eight five,' he called querulously. He seemed to be a million miles away. 'Who is this?' he kept repeating.

Heart pounding, Billy called, 'Hamish, this is Billy. I'm

speaking from Ireland. Could you put Laura on, please?'

There was a pause. The tornado over in Scotland seemed to be getting worse. Then Hamish's voice came back.

'Billy, you're no' welcome here. Laura is out walkin' with her sisters and I'm sure she doesna want to speak to you. You're no' wanted here. As for me, I dinna want to hear your voice ever again. Is that clear?' There was a clicking noise and the phone went dead.

Bridget came back on. 'I take it your call is now finished,' she said. 'There was no call for him to talk to you like that. None whatsoever. He had the tongue of an adder.'

Billy turned his anger and his frustration onto Bridget. 'I thought my conversation was supposed to be private,' he barked.

'Of course it was private,' she said. 'I didn't hear a single word that was said. All the same, he'd no right to speak to you like that. The bad-mannered, bad-tempered ould bugger. Let me try again.'

Bridget made several more attempts but to no avail. Hamish had taken the phone off the hook.

The call worried Billy to the core. Why was Hamish back on the scene? Had Duncan's views prevailed? Was Laura back with him? He felt like abandoning the whole tour and somehow getting across to Scotland. Hardly fair on Alex, though, he thought. This was his summer holiday and he'd so looked forward to it.

Before they set off for Tralee the next day, he sent off his daily postcard. He tried to make light of the phone call but deep down he was hurt.

My dearest Laura, Alex thinks you and I are ideally matched because we're so different in temperament etc. that we complement each other. For example,

388

I'm a man and you're a woman; you play the piano and I do not; you like marmalade and I do not; you're like Maureen O'Hara and I'm like Charles Laughton. I won't elaborate. Every moment without you is painful. Tried to phone you but all I got was Hamish. What's going on? All my love, Billy.

The rest of the tour took them through some of the most picturesque places in Ireland and in every one of them, Billy sent a picture postcard to Ayr. In every town he tried to find a phone but they were as scarce as haystack needles.

For the sake of Alex, Billy pushed his worries to the back of his mind and lustily joined in the songs about the places they were passing through. In Killarney, it was,

'By Killarney's lakes and fells/Em'rald isles and winding bays.' Then on to Tralee: 'I strayed with my love near the clear crystal fountain/That stands in the beautiful vale of Tralee.'

On the tenth day of the tour, they arrived in the city of Limerick. They found a lodging house as usual and then explored the town – the magnificent cathedral and King John's Castle with its five drum towers. As they crossed Sarsfield Bridge, Billy turned to Alex and said, 'I must try to phone Laura again. I'm really concerned about things. What was Hamish doing in Ayr? I'm sure her father is trying to push me out of the picture. The trouble is, Laura can't phone or write to me as we don't know where we're going to be from one day to the next.'

At Cruise's Royal Hotel, there was no difficulty contacting the operator and getting through to Ayr, but the number was reported as unobtainable. Now to Billy's anxiety was added the frustration of a breakdown in communication.

'Sorry to be such a wet blanket, Alex,' he said. 'It's the not knowing that is driving me crazy. It's like a sword over my head.'

'No news is good news,' Alex replied. 'Don't jump to conclusions. I'm sure there's a good explanation for Hamish being there. Why not wait till you get home?'

'Right, Alex. I'll try to cheer up. But the thought of Laura over there in Scotland with Hamish or surrounded by a bunch of young, brawny Scotsmen ... I'm afraid I might have lost her.'

'You've got too much of a vivid imagination, Hoppy. Try to forget it and look at the beauty of this town we're in.'

Billy was so taken by the glorious sights of the city that he was prompted to write two cards instead of the usual one. One of them read:

Dearest Laura, We're here in Limerick and there's something in the air that makes me go about spouting verse. Here's one for you.

There was a young fella called Billy
Whose face looked stupid and silly.
When asked why it was,
He said it's becoz
I'm in love with a beautiful filly.

Don't groan when you read it. I did warn you that I'm mad. Still can't get through to you on the phone. Hope everything's OK. All my love, Billy

Before they left England, everyone, that is to say the Callaghan family, had insisted that they visit the Cliffs of

Moher, 'The grandest coastal stretches in the British Isles,' they'd said. So after their two-day sojourn in Limerick, they headed towards the town of Ennis on the road to the cliffs. The town was a 'twister' of streets, many of which were named after Irish patriots, like Parnell and O'Connell. They noted, too, the statue in the main street and its dedication to 'the Manchester Martyrs who were judicially murdered by the English Government'. It was Fair Day and all available accommodation had been booked up. The only lodging they could find was over a shop and it meant sharing a large Victorian double bed in a vast bedroom which boasted three washbasins.

Before turning in, they visited the local hostelry, the Fergus Inn, and sank a few pints of porter. At half past ten, the landlord called out: 'Come along now, gentlemen, time to close up the place. So finish up your drinks and go home.' Billy and Alex swallowed the last of their pints and made ready to depart. They returned their glasses to the bar and wished the barman goodnight.

'If you'll hang on a few minutes, young sirs,' he whispered, giving them a wink, 'there'll be an extra drink for you.'

The lights were switched off and candles lit, giving the bar a mysterious conspiratorial atmosphere.

'Sh-sh,' hissed the landlord, finger on lip.

He proceeded to draw the illegal pints for his customers. Billy and Alex had not intended drinking more but the air of intrigue made extra drinks irresistible.

'Two pints of porter,' Billy whispered, handing over his money. Stolen sweets are always sweeter, thought Billy.

There was a sudden movement outside the window. The whole bar froze like a tableau in a West End play.

'Quiet. It's the Garda,' gasped the barman.

There was the sound of voices outside the door. The landlord came in with a uniformed police officer.

Caught in the act, he thought. Now we're for it.

'Give Michael here our best pint,' the landlord said to the barman. 'On the house,' he added, slapping Michael, their Garda guardian, on the back.

There was an audible sigh of relief from the regulars of the Fergus and everyone went back to their secret drinking.

Around midnight, Billy and Alex got into the big double bed, settled down, and, as a result of the porter and a hard day's biking, were soon fast asleep. At three in the morning, the room was suddenly flooded in bright light, and half a dozen big, rubicund Irishmen burst into the room and began shaving at the three washbasins.

'Mornin', lads,' called one of them cheerfully, as if it was the most normal thing in the world to begin their ablutions so early in the day. ' 'Tis a grand morning and the sun'll soon be up.'

The two cyclists felt there was no use in trying to go back to sleep and so they arose and began shaving along with their fellow lodgers.

'When in Rome . . .' said Billy wearily. 'But right now, like W.C. Fields, I'd rather be in Philadelphia.'

Three miles west of Liscannor, the Cliffs of Moher stretch for five miles – giant black rocks which far off in the mists of time had thrust themselves out of the sea in a massive primeval cataclysmic convulsion. Of all the sights they had beheld in Ireland, this was the most awesome and the most terrifying. From the top of O'Brien's Tower, they gazed across the wide expanse of the Atlantic Ocean and watched the rippling waves dash themselves angrily against the jagged rocks below.

'If you were ever thinking of committing suicide, this would be the place to choose,' said Billy in hushed tones.

'I'll remember that,' said Alex, 'if ever there's another Wall Street crash, not that I own any shares. But a sight like this fills me with a sense of foreboding and makes me think of the great power and majesty of God.'

This pious thought must have penetrated deep into Alex's subconscious for when they reached the little town of Lahinch on the Saturday night, he suggested that it was time he went to confession. It was in this little town that the close association between Church and secular organisations was so dramatically demonstrated. Billy agreed to join Alex at confession and, after finding the usual five shillings B and B lodgings, they went together to St Patrick's.

Three priests were hearing confessions and there were long queues for two of them. The third, however, Father Sean McCabe, seemed to have no one waiting and it was to him that Alex presented himself. It would be hard to say whether his choice was made out of compassion for the poor unpopular priest whom no one seemed to want or whether it had more to do with the fact that they were in something of a hurry to sample the local hostelry. Whatever the reason, Alex was in with the McCabe cleric for a good ten minutes and when he finally emerged he looked distinctly discomfited and flushed.

Strange, thought Billy, they don't come any more innocent or guiltless than Alex.

Apprehensively, Billy entered the box.

'Bless me, Father,' he began, 'for I have sinned. It is three months since my last confession.'

'As long as that!' the priest snapped. 'You should get to

confession more often than that! Suppose you'd been struck by lightning yesterday. It would have been straight to hell with you. Now tell me your sins.'

'I have given way to impure thoughts.'

'Tut-tut,' muttered Father McCabe through the grille.

'I've neglected prayer and the sacraments and I've been uncharitable in thought and deed.' Billy didn't get any further.

'You know that Christ gave the instruction to his apostles: "Whose sins you shall forgive, they are forgiven. Whose sins you shall retain, they are retained." This means I have the power to refuse you absolution.'

'I know that, Father.'

'Well, I don't believe you are contrite,' the priest hissed.

'I'm as contrite as I've ever been,' Billy replied.

'That's not saying much. Anyway, I don't believe that you are truly contrite. And so you must leave the confessional immediately and pray to God for forgiveness.'

Bewildered, Billy left the box, looking, he supposed, like Alex had when he'd emerged a few moments ago. He tapped Alex lightly on the shoulder.

'Let's go,' he said, 'before they throw us into the dungeons.'

'Gladly,' replied Alex, executing a quick genuflection.

Outside the church, they took one look at each other's mortified expression and broke into laughter.

'I feel as if I've had a session with Torquemada, the monk in the Spanish Inquisition,' chuckled Billy.

'Instead of burning at the stake, I think we deserve a drink,' Alex said.

They repaired to Gerry Hanlon's Bar and over two pints swapped notes.

'The blighter refused me absolution,' said Billy. 'Said I

wasn't sorry. So he quoted the bit about "Whose sins you shall retain, they are retained".'

'Oh, he forgave me,' said Alex, 'but he gave me one helluva penance. Two hundred Hail Marys and a hundred Our Fathers. He made me feel like Old Nick himself.'

'You're lucky,' said Billy. 'Me, he refused to forgive at all. So if I get hit by a bus tomorrow, it's the eternal flames of hell for me. Maybe I should chuck myself over the Cliffs of Moher.'

'I think the problem was that you sounded too English.'

'What's my nationality got to do with it?'

'You sound too matter-of-fact, too stiff-upper-lippish, cold and unemotional. The priests like to hear the true penitent strike his breast and proclaim: "Jesus, Mary and Joseph! God help me! I'm a terrible sinner and I deserve to burn in hellfire," etcetera.'

'You mean talk like that old farmer with the cow on the road?'

'Exactly.'

'Drink up,' said Billy heartily. 'Time for another, I think – that is, if you don't mind drinking with a sinful soul like myself.'

'The way I'm feeling,' said Alex, 'I'd drink with Beelzebub himself.'

'Perhaps you are drinking with him,' Billy rejoined. 'But don't forget you need a long spoon.'

They stayed drinking and discussing their sinfulness in Gerry's Bar until ten o'clock when the grumbling of Billy's digestive system reminded him that they had not eaten for some time that day.

'Most cafés will be closed at this hour in a little town like this,' said Alex. 'We could try the big hotel over the road, I suppose. Perhaps we can get something over there though it's a four-star hotel.'

'Who cares how many stars! Surely they wouldn't turn away two miserable pilgrims like ourselves.'

They crossed the road and entered the richly carpeted foyer of the hotel. The reception staff eyed them with suspicion but, fortified with Dutch courage, they entered the restaurant. It was a grand affair and several of the tables were still occupied by late-night diners. An obsequious waiter came forward, showed them to a table and hovered over them, ready to take their order.

'I think coffee and some cream crackers would suit me fine,' said Billy. 'What about you, Alex?'

'The same.'

'I take it you are residents of the hotel, sirs?' inquired the waiter.

'But of course, my man,' Billy assured him.

The waiter went off to get their order.

'Liar!' hissed Alex.

'I've already been shown today to be an unrepentant sinner doomed to be cast into the outer darkness for all eternity. So what difference will a little white lie make? We'll own up when we've eaten and then pay the bill.'

The waiter soon returned with the coffee and biscuits and a form asking for their names and room numbers. They ignored the request and tucked into the small snack hungrily.

Billy signalled to the waiter who had been watching them from a respectful distance.

'We're not resident. We were so hungry that we told you a fib. We're ready to pay the bill.'

The waiter looked angrily at both of them in turn as if they'd told him his mother was a whore and he was poncing off her.

'Can you wait here for a moment, sirs, whilst I consult the manager. This is most irregular.'

The manager, a little runt of a man, came waddling over and they could see from the way he was belching steam that he was not pleased.

'You have no right to come in here with your lies and your deceit. This restaurant is for residents only. Can't you read the sign on the main doors?'

Billy couldn't explain that through their alcoholic haze, they had failed to notice the sign.

'Look, give us the bill and be done with it,' growled Billy.

The manager did as asked and slapped down the bill on the table.

Alex took one look at it and turned white. 'He wants ten shillings each,' he said. 'That's more than our lodgings. It's daylight robbery.'

'Not really,' said Billy. 'It's now eleven o'clock and so it's night-time robbery.' Turning to the manager, he said, 'Ten shillings each for a coffee and a couple of cream crackers is outrageous. We refuse to pay. You may call out the Garda if you wish, but I'd sooner spend a night in jail than submit to such a bare-faced swindle.'

'That goes for me too,' said Alex.

They folded their arms and prepared to sit and wait for the police.

'Get out! Get out!' the manager exploded. 'I don't want to see either of you in this hotel again.'

The pair thought it best to depart whilst the going was good.

It was a shamefaced Billy and Alex that turned up at St Patrick's church next morning for eleven o'clock Mass. They went into the porch and joined the small queue of

397

worshippers who were introducing themselves to a church warden sitting at a table in the doorway.

'Terence Dugan, diocese of Galway, two shillings,' the apparitor called out. It sounded like an entrance fee.

'Mary Feeney, diocese of Cork. Two and six.'

When they got nearer, they saw the warden was no other than the manager of the hotel.

Billy and Alex signed the visitors' book.

'Hopkins and Callaghan, diocese of Salford. Ten shillings each!' the little manager called. 'That'll be one pound, if you please.'

The pair paid up without a murmur.

Touché, Billy thought.

The rest of the Irish holiday went by quickly, with flying visits to Galway and Connemara where Alex issued dire warnings not to reveal their English origins.

'Connemara is a Gaeltacht where Gaelic is the accepted language,' he said, 'Best to let me do the talking or these fellas will push you into the Corrib as soon as look at you.'

From Galway, Billy made his third attempt to contact Laura but with the same result. Number unobtainable. He sent off his last postcard, a picture of a sunset on Galway Bay.

My dearest Laura, You will be happy to know that this is my last postcard – you should have enough to paper a whole room. Soon I shall be on my way home to Manchester and to you. I count the days and the hours. It's been a great holiday but throughout I've experienced the constant heartache of missing you. Some day, we shall tour Ireland together. What's happened to your phone? Has your uncle forgotten to pay the bill?

Hope you don't find any spilleng mistakes in this. Sometime I think I'm seffuring from lysdexia. All my love, Billy

Then it was the tedious ride across the girth of Ireland, through Athlone and back to Dublin docks and the night boat to Liverpool. Billy left Ireland with mixed feelings – regret that a wonderful holiday had come to an end and yet elation that he'd soon be back with his Laura. But the elation was tinged with concern, and he hoped and prayed he hadn't lost her to Hamish. One thing was sure – he knew beyond the shadow of a doubt that there could never be anyone else for him but Laura Mackenzie.

Chapter Thirty-Four

Home Sweet Home

Billy hated Gardenia Court from the first day he'd laid eyes on it – its squalor, its malodorous stairwell, the rough neighbours and their constant blasphemous bickering. But now after the holiday in Ireland, after having gazed on the panoramic views of Kerry and the magnificent mountains of Mourne, Billy loathed the tenement with a new disgust. Sometimes, he wondered about the so-called benefits of going away on holiday, of seeing new sights, having new adventures, meeting interesting people. All very well, but when it was over and one had to come back to a dump like this, it seemed infinitely worse than when he'd left it three weeks ago. In some ways, it would have been better not to have gone. How he missed Honeypot Street and the house they had had there before the Luftwaffe put a bomb on it.

He climbed the stairs gloomily, bike on his shoulder. Mam was in the kitchen as usual preparing Dad's tea of tripe and onions. This flat of ours, he thought, as he went through the door, may be in a slum tenement but Mam keeps it so neat and tidy, it's like an oasis in a desert.

'Welcome home, son,' she called as soon as she saw him. 'Kettle's on.' It was good to hear her voice again. Always cheerful and welcoming.

Three mugs of tea later and after he had related his adventures, he said, 'Now I have something good and something bad for you. Which do you want first?'

'Definitely the good,' she said. 'Always think positively, is what I say.'

Billy handed her the present he'd carried all the way from Limerick – the one the Liverpool customs had wanted to confiscate.

Smiling in pleasure like a little girl with a Christmas toy, she unwrapped the gift carefully so as not to spoil the silver paper.

'Oh, Billy,' she exclaimed. 'You shouldn't have. You can't afford it.' It was a set of antimacassars in Irish linen.

'We've got an Aunty Cissie and an Aunty Hetty but I've always wanted an Aunty Macassar. And you're always going on at me about Brylcreem spoiling the backs of the chairs.'

'Oh, they're much too good to use. I'll put them away for a special occasion. Now, what's the bad news?'

'Only this,' he grinned, and he handed her his bag of dirty washing.

Billy had to wait a whole week before Laura came back from Ayr and it seemed like forever. The days of the calendar were marked off, oh so slowly. The week of purgatory ended when they met again in Fletcher Moss Gardens.

'I missed you every hour and every minute of the day,' he said, holding her close. 'So much so that I could not enjoy the holiday and there was a dull ache in my heart the whole of the time. The one thing that came out of the parting is that absence really does make the heart grow fonder. I love you now more than ever.'

'The same goes for me, Billy,' she murmured. 'Not for a single second were you out of my mind.'

'What a burden for your mind to carry around!' he murmured. 'Your companions in Ayr must have thought you slightly mad.'

'I think they did at times when I seemed lost in thought.'

'I was desperate to talk to you but I couldn't get through. And when I heard Hamish answer the phone, I thought I'd lost you.'

'That will never happen, Billy.'

'What was he doing there? Is he still hanging around?'

'He was there for only one day,' she answered. 'He came down from Glasgow.'

Billy felt a pang of jealousy strike at his heart. 'Does he think he's still in there with a chance?' he asked hoarsely.

'No need to worry on that score,' she said, hugging him tightly. 'Guess what? It looks as if Hamish and Jenny have hit it off. They spent a lot of their time together and they seem to have a special affinity.'

What sweet relief to hear those words! Laura was still his. His torment had been for nothing.

'I'm happy that things are turning out for the best,' he said. 'Maybe Hamish and Jenny are made for each other. I suspected that at your musical evening. The way he sang about "ae fond kiss" and the way Jenny looked at him, and how she reacted to his news about a possible job in Edinburgh. But I wonder what they have in common? Perhaps they're both hypochondriacs and study the medical encyclopaedia together.'

'You may be right,' she laughed. 'But remember that even hypochondriacs sometimes get ill. I think Hamish's 'career prospects may have more to do with it.'

'Anyway, here is my gift from Ireland to you,' he said, and he handed across a tablecloth in Limerick lace. 'It's big enough to cover a six-foot table,' he said proudly.

'Wonderful, Billy. I'm sure it'll look good on the Mackenzie table.'

'I wasn't thinking of the Mackenzie table,' he said. 'I had in mind the Hopkins table.'

'Sorry, Billy. I don't understand,' she said. 'Have I misunderstood? Is the cover for me or your mother?'

Should he ask her now? he wondered. He'd been thinking about it all the way round Ireland. What if she said no or demurred? His whole world would collapse round his ears. It was a risk he had to take.

'No, Laura, I meant for us, for our table.'

She looked puzzled. 'Our table?'

'What I mean to say,' he stammered, 'is, will you marry me?'

Laura burst out laughing.

He looked at her nervously. His life was in her hands and here she was laughing at him.

'Our table! No joking, being with you is like trying to solve a crossword puzzle sometimes.' She smiled warmly. 'Of course I'll marry you. I've been wondering when you'd get round to it or, should I say in your language, when you'd start talking table linen.'

He took her in his arms and they stood together overwhelmed by the emotion of it all. Then Laura laughed.

'That must be the most original proposal ever. You give a girl a linen tablecloth and then ask if she'd like to share your table when you get one.'

'You didn't want me to go down on one knee, I hope, and do a Charles Boyer,' he grinned.

'Don't see why not.'

He knelt on one knee and said in his best Boyer imitation. 'Laura, come away with me to the kasbah. Together, we shall escape from the world and love each other forever.'

'Right,' she answered, 'you've swept me off my feet. When do we leave?'

Chapter Thirty-Five

Meet the Folks

Laura and Billy's romance took up where it had left off before the holidays. At weekends in the hours they were away from each other, Billy watched the clock, waiting agonisingly for the time when they'd meet again. Every few minutes he checked his watch – the hands hadn't budged. Time stood still. When at last they met, they went on their usual long walks and boating outings, with Laura sometimes opting to take the oars.

'Laura, you're so strong,' he kidded. 'I know you'll look after me and protect me from harm.'

'Come off it,' she said.

It was after one of the rowing sessions at Heaton Park that Billy took her home to meet his folks. When he told his mam he was bringing Laura home, it was as good as an announcement in the *Manchester Evening News*, for there was an unwritten if not unspoken rule in the Hopkins household that the one you took home to meet Mam was the one you were going to marry. No exceptions. It meant that the liaison was serious. Taking the intended home sealed it.

Billy had planned it with military precision. It was a

Sunday afternoon and that meant his dad would be having his nap after his dinnertime boozing session in the Junction Hotel. If he timed it right, he could take Laura round to meet Mam, have tea and be out before Dad appeared.

It had often occurred to him that the sight of Dad emerging from the bedroom after one of his drinking bouts was enough to terrify the bravest heart. His face resembled the ugliest gargoyle on a church buttress: red-rimmed eyes, dentures absent, giving his features a collapsed Frank Randle look, his braces hanging down loosely, the top of his long johns showing. And to round it off, possibly a foul temper as well. Billy was anxious to avoid a confrontation; all his protective instincts came to the fore. Apart from that, Laura might even believe, God help us, that when she viewed his dad, she was gazing at a possible future Billy.

Laura looked particularly pretty that Sunday; the rowing had brought colour to her cheeks and given her a fresh, country-girl look.

'You look so attractive,' he said. 'You must take me rowing more often. But when I see you against the background of these dreadful tenements, you remind me of the phrase about a beautiful flower growing on a dunghill.'

'Thank you, Billy. But right now I feel nervous as if I'm going to be examined under a microscope, as it were.'

'No need to worry,' he replied. 'They'll love you. As I do,' he added.

They got to Gardenia Court around half past four. Billy was acutely conscious of how it must look to Laura. There was a dog barking from the ground floor flat. On the various verandas of the block, were the usual sights and sounds: a window frame stuffed with cardboard; the Pitts having their usual screaming match; curious women in pinnies and curlers leaning over the balconies, cigarettes dangling from their bottom lips. From the windows of the four storeys above them, poles stuck out with ropes supporting drying clothes.

As they mounted the stairway, Billy became aware more than ever of the odours emanating from the other flats: the privy smell on the first floor, the pickled herrings from the Finkelsteins, the sauerkraut from the Weinbergs. An assortment of stenches, individual foetid malodours mingling with carbolic as they reached Billy's home where they halted. Billy opened the Yale lock with his key.

'Well, this is it,' he said anxiously. 'Welcome to the Hopkins residence. One day, Laura, I hope you will take me away from all this,' he joked in an attempt to hide the tension.

Mam came to meet them when she heard the key turn in the lock. She, too, looked edgy.

'This is my mother,' he said. 'Mam, meet Laura.'

'Very pleased to meet you,' Mam said, reaching out her hand. 'Billy's told us all about you. He talks about nothing and nobody else. You're every bit as pretty as he's said.'

'Thank you so much, Mrs Hopkins, and it's so nice to meet you at last,' Laura said, her voice soft and mild. 'What a beautiful flat you have here. It looks so cosy and inviting.'

The flat looked immaculately clean. It ought to, thought Billy. Mam has been scrubbing it from top to bottom for the last week in anticipation of this visit. Good old Mam, she never lets me down.

'I've got a nice tea ready for the two of you,' Mam said. 'Would you like a swill before we sit down, Laura?'

'A swill?' Laura inquired gently, looking to Billy for an explanation.

Somewhere we've played this scene before, Billy mused, thinking of the time his sister Polly had brought home Steve Keenan, her future husband.

'A swill,' explained Billy in typical schoolmaster fashion, 'is a Lancashire expression meaning a little wash, a gentle rinse. When we were boys, it meant a little dash of water on the face but not the neck, as opposed to a full-scale wash which involved the turning in of the shirt collar and a thorough dousing, including the neck. Important to distinguish between a wash and a swill. Having a swill is what the middle classes would call freshening up.'

'You'll have to excuse our Billy,' Mam said. 'Sometimes I think he's not right in the head. If you'd like to freshen up, Laura, as Billy puts it, the bathroom's there at the end of the hall.'

'Thank you, Mrs Hopkins.'

'Well, what do you think, Mam?' Billy asked when Laura was out of the room.

'I think she's a lovely girl.'

Laura returned from her swill and they settled down at the table where Mam had prepared a high tea consisting of an egg salad: lettuce, cucumber, tomato, spring onion and beetroot, plus a red middle cut of West's salmon, and miscellaneous condiments, including pickles and piccalilli. As a dessert, she had gone up-market and, instead of the usual pineapple chunks, had invested in a tin of the more expensive peaches and apricots. And of course the buttered bread had been cut diagonally as was usual and appropriate for Sunday tea.

They were joined by Les who had been reading in his bedroom.

'We don't stand on ceremony here,' Mam said. 'Help yourself to whatever takes your fancy.'

'Thank you very much,' Laura replied. 'What a beautiful spread, Mrs Hopkins. You really have gone to a great deal of trouble.'

'It's only what we allus have on a Sunday,' Mam said. 'I believe in getting in something tasty for our high tea.'

'And in your honour, we're to have peaches and cream instead of chunks,' said Les. 'If you marry our Billy, Laura, it'll be back to chunks if you can afford even them.'

'Now, our Les,' said Billy. 'Don't you go making out that I'm poor and can't afford things.'

'Poor!' he replied. 'Has he told you, Laura, that he goes to school wearing my demob jacket?'

'Yes, he has,' Laura laughed. 'He says you never wear it.'

'That's right,' added Billy. 'I've got to keep up appearances. I belong to the noble profession of teaching.'

'It may be a profession but the pay is lousy,' Les rejoined, helping himself to copious amounts of piccalilli. 'Do you know what his monthly take-home pay is, Laura?'

'Not precisely,' she said, 'but I know it's not great. Remember, I'm a teacher too.'

'His net pay,' said Les, warming to his subject, 'is twenty pounds, no shillings and threepence.'

'And that goes on his upkeep, and his cigarettes,' said Mam, unable to resist adding her bit to the financial debate.

'At least I'm left with the threepence,' Billy joked. 'But you've forgotten about the few pounds I earn from the Youth Centre work.'

'His pay is more than mine,' said Laura. 'I get only nineteen pounds. I'm a woman, you see.'

'I've noticed that,' said Billy, 'and it meets with my strongest approval. But if you and I joined forces, Laura,

409

why, we'd have forty pounds a month. A prince could live on that.'

'Sure,' chuckled Les, 'provided the prince lived in a tent. I'm a watchmaker by trade and I earn nearly forty pounds by myself.'

'And is your mother a teacher like you, Laura?' Mam asked, changing the subject.

'She's a private teacher of music, Mrs Hopkins. She teaches singing and the piano.'

'Our Billy could benefit from a few singing lessons, Laura,' said Les. 'You should hear him in the bathroom. Reminds me of Jerry Colonna, that film star with the foghorn voice.'

'It must be nice to have a mother a teacher of music,' said Mam wistfully. 'I've allus been fond of a bit o' music myself. My favourite's Handel's Lager.'

'I'd rather have Boddington's bitter,' said Les, chuckling. 'But talking of Handel, I saw a notice on a billboard outside Cheetham Town Hall the other day. It said: "Tonight. Handel's Organ Works". Somebody had written underneath, "So Does Mine – Every Night".'

'These two lads are allus trying to get me confused,' Mam said. 'Our Les sent me to Lewis's last week to book tickets for that big Italian fella, the one they call Benjamin Giggly. I felt proper daft when I asked for the tickets – the girl started laughing at me.'

'Laughing or giggling?' asked Les.

'I think they're called malapropisms,' laughed Billy. 'She calls the American crooners Kerry Pomo and Bim Crosby.'

'Well, I nearly got them right,' Mam chuckled, joining in the fun.

This brand of conversation helped to relieve some of the early tension and Laura laughed and began to relax and enjoy the company. The banter would have continued in this vein but their voices must have carried through to the adjoining bedroom for sounds of movement heralded the imminent arrival of Billy's father.

Uh-oh, here comes trouble, Billy thought.

Mam rose quickly from the table. 'Leave him to me,' she said. 'I'll tidy him up a little before his public appearance.'

She met Dad as he emerged from the room and steered him off to the bathroom.

'If you are so foolish as to marry our Billy here,' continued Les, obviously enjoying himself, 'I should warn you that he's a Cancerian, that is, subject to sudden changes of mood.'

'In what way?' Laura asked.

'One moment he's jolly and joking, and the next he can be crabby or in a melancholy mood.'

'I'm a Gemini, born under the sign of the twins,' Laura answered. 'We're supposed to have changeable personalities too, so we should get on well together.'

'Well said, Laura,' Billy replied. 'Anyway, I'm only crabby when Les won't lend me his jacket and I have to pinch it.'

'Whatever you do, Laura, if you do decide to take him on as your husband, make sure you have a cigarette for him first thing in the morning. Otherwise, he's like a bear with a sore head. Now, if you wanted to swap him for a handsome, even-tempered man, I'm available.'

'Huh! Laura is a woman of taste and discernment, which is why she has chosen me,' Billy replied.

At this point, Mam guided Dad into the room. Whatever she had done, she'd made him reasonably presentable. He had washed his face and, in the terminology that public toilets sometimes couched their sartorial request, he had 'adjusted his dress'. His dentures were in place.

'This is our Billy's girl, Laura,' she said.

Billy liked that phrase 'our Billy's girl'.

Dad said how pleased he was to meet her and, after shaking her hand, sat down at the table where he proceeded to prepare a massive salad butty containing everything on the table. By some gigantic movement of the jaw, he managed to make his first assault on the mountainous sandwich. Billy's nightmare was taking place before his very eyes. Should he take Laura by the hand and make a quick exit before matters got worse or should he hang on and hope things might improve? He opted for the latter.

As Dad continued to champ on his butty, he struck up a conversation with Laura.

'So what does your father do, Laura?'

'He's an Inspector of Taxes, Mr Hopkins,' she said modestly, unable to hide her feeling of awe at his lusty eating style.

'I'll bet he earns good wages at that job,' Dad commented. Then he added, 'But I'll bet it doesn't go down too well with his pals.'

'I don't think he brings his work home with him,' said Laura, springing to the defence of her father.

There was a momentary silence whilst Dad ransacked his mind for something to say. His eye alighted on the beetroot.

'During the war,' he said, 'young ladies used beetroot in place of lipstick. Did you know that, Laura?'

'No, I didn't know that, Mr Hopkins. That's most interesting,' Laura said bravely.

'There was such a terrible shortage of everything,' Dad

went on. 'A bath, if you had one, that is, couldn't be more than five inches of hot water.'

'I was too young to remember most of that,' said Laura, 'but I can still recall that we were allowed only one little bar of soap a month.'

'Things was bad,' Dad continued. 'Why, women even used soot for eye make-up and there was such a shortage of silk stockings, they used gravy browning to paint their legs and pencilled in a black line down the middle for a seam.'

'You shouldn't have been looking at women's legs,' was Mam's contribution to the discussion of wartime deprivation.

'Still, I'll bet the gravy-stained legs attracted an enthusiastic following amongst the neighbourhood dogs,' said Billy in a brave attempt to introduce a little levity into the conversation.

There was a lull in the debate as Dad constructed another gigantic gastronomic delight.

By some strange convoluted process of reasoning, he got it into his head that Laura, being a member of the middle classes and a teacher in a Catholic school, was in some way connected with the Church because his conversation now acquired a singularly ecclesiastical flavour.

'I see that St Thomas of Canterbury Parish in Salford is holding a Mass for the sick and the housebound next Sunday,' he announced suddenly.

The company didn't know how to respond to this disclosure and so there was silence as they absorbed it and tried to assess its significance.

'I notice too in the paper, Laura,' he proclaimed, 'that the Bishop of Salford will be giving confirmation at St Dunstan's Church in Moston next Sunday.'

Laura took in this news as if it was the most fascinating thing she'd heard that day.

'That's very interesting, Mr Hopkins,' she said warmly. 'That'll be Bishop Heenan, won't it?'

As the name of the bishop had not been given in his copy of the *Evening Chronicle*, he was unable to give an intelligent answer and so responded by making inroads into his pavement-thick sandwich. He soon followed it with other equally intriguing pieces of news.

'Did you know that Pope Pius the Twelfth spoke fluent German, Laura?'

'I didn't know that, Mr Hopkins,' she said politely.

'Many people say that he was on the side of the Germans during the war, but I don't believe it. He hated war and in nineteen forty he tried to stop it.'

It suddenly dawned on Billy that his dad had prepared for this meeting by memorising choice morsels of church news to impress Laura – despite all his protestations about being against the middle classes. Though the morsels were inappropriate, Billy was touched by the fact he'd made such an effort.

He could see though that he was ready to offer yet more intriguing titbits of information about the clergy from his store of information on the church calendar and Billy decided it was time to make a move.

'We'll have to go now, Dad,' he said. 'I promised to get Laura back home at a reasonable hour tonight. We both have school tomorrow.'

'Thank you, all of you,' Laura said. 'I've enjoyed meeting you. I do hope we can get together again soon.'

Billy helped her on with her coat and they were ready to depart.

'Goodnight, everyone,' she called. 'And thank you once again.'

'Goodnight, Laura,' they said in chorus.

As they descended the stairway, Billy asked, 'Well, Laura, what did you think of 'em?'

'I think they're wonderful,' she replied immediately. 'Really entertaining – all of 'em.'

On the second landing, she turned to Billy. 'Well, how did I do? Am I accepted?'

'Laura,' he responded, 'you were stupendous. The soul of tact and I know they liked you a lot. But now I'm not sure we should get married – I didn't know you had such strong connections with the Church.'

'Very funny!' she said, digging him playfully in the ribs.

After school the following day, Billy faced both his parents over a cup of tea, anxious to have their reactions to their meeting with Laura.

'I think she's a lovely girl,' said Mam. 'She talks real posh like the toffs. Mind you, I thought she was a bit on the quiet side.'

'She could hardly get a word in, with you lot talking so much,' Billy countered. 'Anyway, you have to remember she was nervous, meeting all of you like that.'

'I suppose you're right,' Mam said. 'But you're such a noisy devil with so much to say for yourself, I wonder how you'd get on, that's all.'

'But that's just it,' he said. 'We're perfect for each other. One counterbalances the other. According to my friend Alex at school, it wouldn't do if we were both big talkers or we were both quiet. Anyway, God made us with two ears and one mouth which is about the right proportion we should use 'em. More listening than talking.'

'I'm sure you know what you're doing,' she said. 'Remember the saying though: "Marry in haste, repent at leisure." '

Dad had remained silent up to this point but he now felt it was time to deliver his judgement.

'You don't often ask my opinion, Billy,' he said, 'but choosing your life partner is a bloody serious business and you've got to think about it very carefully. Marriage makes or mars a man, they say.'

These weren't the answers Billy wanted to hear. He said, 'Look, we can all go on quoting proverbs about marriage. "Marriages are made in heaven" or "There's more to marriage than four bare legs in a bed" or "Marriage is a lottery" but what I want to know is what you really think.'

'Laura is a real fine-looking lass,' he said slowly. 'But she's not of our class. Why, her father's a high-up civil servant, an Inspector of Taxes, for God's sake. The sort I've been up against all my life. As I see it, the world is like a building made up of different storeys and different rooms – some above and some below, some big and some small. Everyone has his place and position in the building and the parts don't mix together.'

'That's out of date, Dad. You seem to see the world as made up of Us and Them. Those who are not with us are agin us. According to you, there's only two levels in society, like in that old Protestant hymn "All Things Bright and Beautiful":

> *The rich man in his castle,*
> *The poor man at his gate,*
> *God made them, high or lowly,*
> *And ordered their estate.'*

'Too bloody true,' he replied vehemently. 'The rich are all in a click and they're out to do the working man down. When you went to college, I had to go to one of them there tax offices. They made me sit on a hard wooden bench for a couple of hours. They treated me like muck.'

'But Laura isn't like that,' Billy protested.

'They're all in it together, son. Take gambling, for example. When our Jim was alive, he used to play pitch and toss with the other lads but let the police catch 'em and they were for it. If I want to put on a bet, I have to break the law by going to a backstreet bookie. But I'll bet if this Mr Mackenzie fella wants to bet, he's only to pick up the phone.'

'So because of your problems about putting on a bet, I'm not to think of marrying Laura?'

'It's not only that. Can't you see? She leads a different life from ours. They're not the same as us, I tell you. They're brought up differently, they eat different food, and are not governed by the same laws. The Mackenzies live in Regina Park, the snootiest district in town, where the wealthy cotton merchants used to have their big houses. Why, we couldn't afford to live in their garden shed. The nearest our class ever gets to them is as labourers or servants.'

'By gum, that's true,' Mam agreed. 'I spent my early adult life in service, so I ought to know.'

'The classes don't mix, it's a law of nature,' Dad argued. 'Oh, you can marry all right but you'd soon find that you don't do things the same, don't think the same. You'd have nothing but trouble, Billy, I'm telling you.'

'You're about a hundred years out of date, Dad. This is ninety forty-nine. I think you're talking rubbish. Of course we'd get on.' Billy was feeling less sure of himself.

'She's used to having nice things about her. You couldn't

afford half the things she's used to. Why, I bet her father's even got a car and a piana. You take my advice, son and marry your own kind.'

'I don't know what you're getting so het up for, Tommy,' Mam said. 'We're a respectable family in this house, we keep ourselves to ourselves, and we've never been in trouble with the police or owt like that. We don't owe nobody nothing and we can hold our heads up anywhere. So I think our Billy's good enough for any girl – posh or not.'

'I'm not saying he isn't,' Dad answered. 'I'm only thinking of what's best for him. Why can't he find a nice working-class lass who'll make a nice home for him and bring his kids up nice? Why does he have to go mixing with the bloody middle class? That's what I want to know.'

'Maybe you've forgotten,' said Billy, vehemently, 'that I've gone over to the bloody middle class myself by becoming a teacher. I've joined the enemy.'

'No need to talk like that, Billy,' said Dad. 'You're young and you can't always see what's best in the long run. It's only your happiness I'm thinking of.'

'I give up!' Billy exploded, and flounced out of the room and into his bedroom.

Quivering with anger, he lay back on his bed, arms behind his head. What bloody, bloody nonsense! he said to himself. The very idea that I should give Laura up because I might be marrying out of my class. It's medieval.

But Billy's dad had given voice to a feeling of inferiority he had harboured ever since he'd set eyes on Laura's home in Regina Park – a feeling he was reluctant to admit even to himself. Nevertheless his dad had planted a small seed of doubt in his mind where it began to germinate.

That night he slept fitfully, tossing and turning in his bed.

Chapter Thirty-Six

Parting Is Such Sweet Sorrow

It was the first day of the new term. Billy's reputation as a lively, exciting teacher had preceded him and the new Senior 4 sat at their desks looking at him eagerly. Unlike the first class of pupils that he'd faced, this fresh set had come to accept the idea that they were to stay at school until fifteen. They also knew that this Hopalong character taught not only the usual subjects but had introduced activities like ballroom dancing, cycle trips, and outside visits to places of interest. On the first morning, however, they were disappointed because it was a tired-looking Billy who turned up at school. He got through the morning somehow but his teaching was dull and uninspired.

At break time, Laura noticed the drawn, careworn expression.

'Billy,' she exclaimed solicitously, 'you look worn out. Are you feeling all right?'

'I'm fine, Laura,' he replied. 'Didn't sleep too well last night. Got things on my mind.'

'What sort of things? I hope I didn't put my foot in it yesterday when I met your family.'

'No, no. Nothing like that. I worry about money matters sometimes, that's all.'

'We're going to the flicks on Friday night, Billy. So we've got that to look forward to but if you're worried about money, we can go in the less expensive seats. And we can go Dutch. I'll pay for the seats if you're broke.'

'There's more to it than that, Laura,' Billy said evasively. 'We'll talk about it on Friday when we've got more time.'

'It sounds serious,' she said, now looking concerned.

'We'll go to the early show at the Apollo. It finishes around nine o'clock and so we can walk home and talk things over.'

'It sounds very serious,' she said. 'Can't you tell me now what's on your mind?'

'Best to leave it till Friday.'

The feature film at the Apollo was *Brighton Rock*, an adaptation of one of Graham Greene's best novels featuring Richard Attenborough, but they hardly noticed this detail. They sat in their usual double seat in the back row but Laura noticed painfully that Billy neither put his arm round her nor held her hand as he always did. Something was troubling him and she picked up his misery like a cold.

After the show, Laura put her arm through his and they walked in silence for a while along Stockport Road.

'Billy,' she said, 'you look so unhappy. What is troubling you? Why so sad?'

'I've been thinking things over,' he said slowly, 'and I'm no longer sure that you and I are meant for each other. Perhaps we're not suited.'

Laura went white and her heart skipped a beat.

'Not suited!' she faltered. 'How do you mean, not suited?'

'It's like this. You and I live in completely different worlds. You come from a well-to-do family and I'm from . . . well you saw on Sunday where I'm from. I don't think it's going to work out.'

'Is it something I've done? Something I've said?' she gasped.

'Nothing like that, Laura. I still think you're the most wonderful person in the world.'

'Well then? What's wrong? What's changed? I don't understand.'

'Laura, you're used to a certain lifestyle. One that I couldn't even begin to offer you. To paraphrase Churchill, I have nothing to offer you but tears, toil, sweat and penury.'

'Oh Billy, Billy. I don't care about lifestyle. It's you I want. Can't you see that?'

'That's all very well, Laura. You know the saying, when poverty comes in at the door, love flies out at the window.'

'Only too well,' she said ruefully. 'My father's always quoting it. But there's another saying which I prefer – love conquers all. Billy, we have something good here. Don't throw it away.'

'To put it bluntly,' he said, 'we belong to different social classes. You are middle class and I'm working class. I don't think the two mix easily.'

'I don't understand that. I thought the notion of social class was dead. Surely that's what the war was about – to end social class divisions.'

'Class is very much alive and kicking, Laura. Britain is a class-ridden society. It's everywhere. Think about the jubilees and coronations when the different orders and ranks are on display for all to see. Why, you'll find social class even in the cemetery.'

'I think you're making too much of this social class

thing. We're different personalities and that's good. But we have so much else in common. We have similar tastes in music and literature. We both like children. And, most important, we have the same sense of humour and that means a lot. What does that "you're middle class" business mean?'

'It means that you inhabit a different world from mine. There are so many things in your life that you take for granted as if you and your family possess them by some God-given right.'

'For instance?' Her hackles were beginning to rise.

'A Bechstein piano, a telephone, a motor car, beautiful paintings on the walls, grapes on the sideboard when there's nobody ill, a Pye Black Box gramophone. I could go on. If we marry, I can offer you practically nothing, except a penny-pinching existence. I'm a non-graduate, elementary schoolteacher and we'd have to eke out a living on a pittance.'

'But Billy, I don't give a damn for these material objects you're listing. Are we to part because we happen to have a piano, a telephone, and a Pye Black Box? They're not my fault. Am I to be jilted because we have flowers and fruit on the sideboard? That's ridiculous.'

They had reached Laura's gate. The faces at the bedroom window would see no kissing tonight.

'I'm sorry, Laura,' Billy said. 'I'm not happy with this but I think it's for the best in the long run. One day, you'll find a man with more money and better qualifications who'll provide for you in the manner to which you are accustomed. That should make your father happy at least.'

Laura broke down and began to weep. 'Billy, Billy. You couldn't be more wrong.'

With that, she ran into the house crying. Billy made his

sorrowful way to the 53 bus and back to Gardenia Court.

Laura was absent from school the following week. There was a haunted look about Billy, and those around him could sense that something was amiss.

'I anticipated this,' Frank Wakefield said at lunchtime. 'I saw it coming when you and I had our little chat. You two have had a lovers' tiff and now Miss Mackenzie's off sick.'

'It's more than a tiff, Frank,' replied Billy. 'We're definitely through. At last I've come to my senses.'

'Oh,' he said, 'and what does that mean?'

'Laura Mackenzie and I inhabit different planets. I live in Cheetham Hill and she lives in Regina Park. And ne'er the twain shall meet.'

'That sounds like a lot of sociology claptrap, if you ask me,' he replied.

'But it wasn't so long ago that you were warning me off.'

'You will remember that my concern was for the school's reputation and harmony in the workplace, not your social status with regard to Miss Mackenzie. If you want my opinion, and you probably don't, if I were in love with Miss Mackenzie, I'd move heaven and earth to win her. In life you get only one chance at happiness and you must seize it with both hands when it presents itself. *Carpe diem!*'

'That's all very well, Frank. But love doesn't pay the grocery bills. You know my salary. What could I offer her?'

'Love will find a way,' he said.

'If anyone else quotes another proverb about love,' exclaimed Billy, 'I shall throw a fit. For every proverb, as I keep telling my English class, there's one that contradicts it.'

'You are in a prickly mood,' he said. 'All I know is that

this new development in your amatory relationship means I'm a teacher short and I'm having to take Junior Two myself. So please come to some conclusion quickly so we can all get on with our work.'

Laura returned to school the following week but she looked pale and drawn. She had obviously spent much time weeping and there was a grief-stricken air about her as if she was in mourning for someone close.

They could not avoid each other in the staffroom nor did they wish to. They nodded to each other politely and exchanged the usual greetings and pleasantries as they did with other members of staff. Billy tried to go about his business normally, teaching, conversing, joking with colleagues, but in his innermost being, he felt a great sense of despair and of loss.

It was around this time that Titch came home on Christmas leave. Naturally they had to celebrate the furlough with a few pints in the Sawyer's Arms.

'Well, Titch, your National Service is up soon,' Billy said when he'd got the drinks in. 'Time has certainly flown.'

'It may have flown for you, Hoppy, but it certainly hasn't for me and the rest of the gang. But it's right, thank the Lord, we finish in summer – provided we don't get put on a charge that is, because for that they can add another three months.'

'You'll all have to keep your noses clean, then.'

'Too true. We're all watching our step.'

'So, what's everyone got planned?'

'Pottsy has decided to join his father in the retail business. When he saw what teachers get paid, that was enough for him.'

'Pottsy never had his heart in teaching,' said Billy. 'I

think he came to college just for the fun of it. What about the rest of them?'

'Ollie, too, has come to the conclusion that the class-room is not his scene. He's been studying for the ALA examination while in the army and he's obtained a librarian's job in Dewsbury.'

'And the other two?'

'Nobby's taken a commission in the Army Education Corps. It seems he was right about the uniform pulling the birds. He has them queuing up to get into his bed. At least, so he says. But you know Nobby and his slight tendency to exaggerate.'

'Typical Nobby. And Oscar?'

'As you probably know, Oscar found a post last year in a boys' boarding school in Yorkshire. Last I heard, he was happily settled there.'

'All great news, Titch. And what are you going to do with yourself?'

'I've managed to get a job in a secondary modern in Altrincham. Can't be much of a school though 'cos I was the only applicant.'

'Still the same old Titch,' Billy laughed. 'Always looking on the gloomy side.'

'Prepare for and fear the worst – that's our family motto. How's life been treating you, Hoppy, while we've been living it up in the army?'

Billy gave him a summary of all that had happened since they last met, the initial trouble with his class, the odd characters in school, especially Grundy. He told him about Laura and the way his dad had reacted to their engagement, how they had parted because Billy believed he wasn't good enough.

Titch listened to the whole story with rapt attention and

without saying a word. When Billy had finished telling him about the latest turn of events, he spoke for the first time.

'Hoppy,' he said, 'you're mad. Mad as a hatter. From what you've told me and from the way you've told me, it's obvious that you and this Laura are meant for each other. This is your big chance, you idiot, to achieve happiness. I've never said this before to anyone but this kind of certainty comes but once in a lifetime. Don't let it slip between your fingers. If Laura's the one, don't let her get away.'

'You've become quite philosophical in your old age, Titch.'

'That's what the army does for you.'

They parted company vowing to keep in touch now that they would both be living in Manchester. Later that night when Billy was alone in his bed, he thought over everything that Titch had said. Somehow he'd touched a nerve with his talk about not letting Laura get away. Now he wondered if he could get her back.

Next day at school, he greeted Laura in the staffroom. She returned his greeting but she was remote. She'd been hurt and she wasn't going to repeat the experience in a hurry.

Now Billy began to kick himself for his stupidity and all that nonsense about social classes and hierarchies. He'd let his dad lead him up the garden path all right. Up to now only his pride had stopped him from going up to her and saying, 'Please forgive me. Come back to me.' But Titch's little speech had hit home and he felt he had to do something to win back her love. Easier said than done, for he had the impression that Laura's sorrow had somehow turned to impatience with him and he was fearful that if he approached her again, she'd tell him to take a running jump.

I think I've screwed up well and truly, he said to himself. I doubt she'll have anything to do with me again. I suppose her father will be pleased about that and Hamish the hypochondriac is probably back in the running.

The rest of the term went by in routine fashion and Billy began to be reconciled to a cool, aloof relationship. No use, he thought, I've blown it for good.

Chapter Thirty-Seven

Deep Throat

It was after Christmas and the start of a new term. Billy put his personal problems behind him and poured his energy into his teaching in an attempt to forget his troubles. His new class were an eager bunch.

During a lesson on David Livingstone, Billy was going big guns on the adventures of the Scottish explorer. He had the class in the palm of his hand and they were hanging onto his every word. Stanley Cashman, the bank man, was spellbound and even Frank Wakefield looked up from his accounts from time to time. The atmosphere was electric as everybody in the room, pupils and adult observers alike, paddled their canoes through rivers infested with alligators and hippopotamus, waded through malarial swamps seething with crocodiles, slashed and macheted their way through dark forests and on towards central Africa. They had reached the mighty waterfall which the local tribes called Mos-oa-tun-ya, the smoke that thunders, and which Livingstone christened the Victoria Falls in honour of his queen. Billy hoped that the headmaster would not break the tension he had so carefully built up with some fatuous remark about the boiler needing replenishment.

'Picture the scene,' he said. 'Livingstone has abandoned his steamboat on the Shire River and now, frail and sick, he is being carried on a *kitanda* stretcher by his faithful porters. They come across a slave caravan surrounded by armed men. Livingstone detested the slave trade and orders his men to attack immediately. The guards run away and Livingstone frees eighty-four slaves. On they go, fighting their way through the impenetrable jungle, searching for the great lake which Livingstone believes to be the source of the Nile. They had given up hope when Chuma, his loyal six-foot African servant, pointed through the trees and called.' Billy raised his hand dramatically and pointed to the horizon, calling out, '*Huko bwana – nyasa!* Over there, boss – the lake!' At least, that is what Billy had intended to call but instead of a full-blooded cry, there emerged from his throat, not the roar of the African giant but a high-pitched, mouse-like squeak.

His classroom audience gazed at him nonplussed.

He tried again with the same result. A squeak.

What in God's name was happening? If the truth be told, Billy was proud of his voice – several friends had commented favourably on its rich timbre. He tried a third time and was highly relieved to find that his full voice had returned – but not for long. As he continued his narrative, it changed without warning from baritone to tenor. Perplexed, he decided to ignore the change of key and, clearing his throat, went on with the story. A minute later, it happened again, only this time he modulated to coloratura soprano. Strange, he thought. My voice broke about ten years ago. Perhaps I'm having a second adolescence.

His listeners by now had lost interest in David Livingstone and were finding greater entertainment in the changes of vocal pitch Billy was producing. Enthralled, they thought it was some trick he was employing in order to win their attention.

It was no trick. He soldiered on with his account of the scramble for Africa, alternating as he did so between Paul Robeson and Lily Pons until Sammy McGrath, Joe Duffy's successor as the head's monitor, mercifully brought the lesson to an end with his bell ringing. A bewildered class filed out of the room quietly but once released from control, began a vociferous post-mortem.

'What's gone wrong with old Hopalong?' asked Lily Malone, the new tea girl.

'He's going through a sex change, that's what,' said Sammy McGrath.

'Nah, he's having us on. He'll do anything to grab our attention.' This from Vito Clarke.

Several of the more ambitious pupils began telling each other stories, adopting roller-coaster vocal intonations in imitation of Billy's octave leaps. 'So this bloke Livingstone went down in the valleys and up amongst the mountains, down to the bottom and up to the top.'

Billy was at a loss to explain the phenomenon and there seemed nothing he could do about it – the modulations happened of their own accord. But it could be serious, for without a voice, he was out of a job. Speech was his stock in trade and whilst sudden sound jumps in his narrative accounts might lend a certain dramatic effect to the telling, it could for some listeners prove a distraction.

At home that night he told Mam about it, who as usual was optimistic.

'It's nothing. Just a sore throat,' she said. 'You've been talking too much. Overdoing it. Don't worry. It'll be all right.'

It would have been more comforting if Mam had been a

430

member of the Royal College of Surgeons or at least had held a recognised medical degree.

'Try gargling with TCP,' she said. 'That'll move the frog from your throat.'

Billy went into the bathroom and did as he'd been advised, the gurgling noises emanating from his throat resembling the coffee percolating machine in Luigi's trattoria on Cheetham Hill Road.

He tried singing. It should be explained here that the Hopkins bathroom had a curious plumbing arrangement. In the interests of economy, some corporation engineering genius had devised a system whereby the hot and cold water taps could be swivelled ninety degrees so as to flow into either the hand basin or the bath. The channel through which the water ran proved to be a perfect resonant amplifier for any would-be crooners or singers who happened to be washing their hands. It was into this improvised device that Billy now tried out his freshly gargled vocal cords with his best rendering of 'Nancy with the Laughing Face'. No use. He was still singing as a duet.

When he came out, his brother Les remarked, 'You know how we've said you sound like Sinatra? Well now you sound like Flanagan and Allen, both of them together.' Les could always be relied on for the encouraging remark.

Something very peculiar was happening to his vocal output. There was only one thing for it, *The Home Doctor*, the fourth volume in a Book Club series entitled 'The Home Expert' which Mam had bought in instalments through *John Bull* magazine. The other titles were *The Home Entertainer, The Home Handyman, The Home Gardener*. These were missing from the Hopkins collection as Mam had decided to discontinue payment mainly because, as a family, they did so little entertaining,

Dad was a useless and expensive handyman, and since they lived in a flat on the top floor, they were lacking a garden.

Titch had once borrowed *The Home Doctor* and returned it in a fit of depression when he had become convinced that he had every disease in the book from Achilles tendon and acne to xerophthalmia and xerosis. He had concluded that he'd been suffering from encephalitis lethargica since childhood.

The Home Doctor covered double vision all right and Billy noted the term for it was diplopia but there was nothing on double voice and unintended key changes. He turned to sore throat – even though his throat was not sore. He read out loud:

> May be result of excessive smoking or talking or may be part of body's early warning system that the throat is being invaded by germs. Antiseptic gargles are usually enough to combat the infection. The throat never becomes sore by itself – something makes it sore and that something could be something danger- ous. If the soreness does not clear up after two or three days, despite gargling, consult a doctor.

'What did I tell you,' said Mam. 'Too much smoking and too much talking.'

'Suppose you're right as usual, Mam,' he said. 'But I don't have a sore throat.'

He consulted the learned tome once again and then he found it. Aphonia. He read on: 'Loss of the voice or of the ability to speak normally, though may be possible to speak in whispers. May result from excessive use of voice or may be caused by paralysis of the vocal cords. Sometimes occurs also as a symptom of Hysterical Reaction.'

'That doesn't sound like you,' she said. 'I've never known you to go historical.'

'I'm sure my class at school would agree with you. Listen to this.' He continued reading: 'Another cause of aphonia is cancer of the larynx or voice box. Removal of the larynx (laryngectomy) may be necessary. Techniques have been developed to retrain people so that they can learn to speak again after such an operation using what is called oesophagal speech.'

'Glory be to God,' she said. 'Let's hope it isn't that, our Billy. Never trouble trouble until trouble troubles you, is what I always say. The best thing you can do is cut down on the cigarettes, try not to do so much talking, and go on with the gargling.'

'Yes, doctor,' he said.

Next day, he cut his fags from ten a day to five. At school, he avoided as far as possible using his voice and when he had to speak, did so in a whisper to avoid strain. This meant organising his teaching so that his classes were required to do an inordinate amount of written work, which didn't please his wards too well.

'I think I'm getting writer's cramp,' remarked Sammy McGrath.

'And my pointing finger is half an inch shorter,' added Vito Clarke.

'Don't you morons understand?' snapped Lily Malone. 'Mr Hopkins needs to rest his voice.'

'OK, OK,' answered Sammy. 'Keep your hair on. We know you have a crush on him.'

'I do not,' she snapped back. 'You lot are so thick, you can't see that he might lose his voice completely if he's not careful.'

433

In the staffroom, his colleagues remarked on his condition.

'From what I've heard,' sneered Grundy, 'you try too hard in class declaiming and over-dramatising things. This is a school, not a theatre. We're teachers not actors. A little more discipline and you wouldn't have to use your voice so much. You should sit on 'em and keep 'em quiet. Then you wouldn't have to rest your voice so much.'

'I wish one or two people round here would imitate Hoppy and give their voices a rest too,' barked Liz, her eyes flashing. 'Speech is silver but silence is golden.'

'And more people have repented speech than silence,' added Alex Callaghan.

'And some wit said that speech was given to man to disguise his thoughts,' said Greg, determined not to be left out of the sententious discussion.

'It's not as bad as that,' replied Billy quietly. 'I'm just trying to give my vocal cords a chance to recover without recourse to the medical profession. If nothing can be done for me, I can always look for another job where vocal gymnastics are an asset.'

'What about a job in a circus as a freak in a side show or perhaps you could join a choir? There can't be many singers who can achieve five octaves,' Greg guffawed.

'And virtually none who can sing both melody and descant at the same time,' added Alex.

'Demand for *castrati* dried up some time ago because of its illegality and cruelty,' said Liz Logie, not to be outdone in the facetious comments stakes, 'but maybe there's still some opportunities for counter-tenors especially as the music of Henry Purcell is becoming popular.'

Laura approached Billy, concern written over her face. 'I do hope it doesn't turn out to be anything serious,' she said. 'I'll get my class to say a prayer that it isn't. And old Aunty, who is a great fan of yours, says she is offering prayers to St Blaise, patron saint of sore throats.'

Billy was deeply moved when he heard this. What a first-class idiot I've been, he thought, to let this wonderful, gentle person get away. 'Thanks,' he said. 'No need to worry. The only ailment I don't have is hypochondria.'

She laughed. 'That's what I've always loved . . . liked . . . about you, Billy, your eternal optimism and your ability to laugh your cares away.'

'I don't believe in meeting trouble halfway,' he said. 'As for its being serious, I try not to think about it. We can make ourselves ill thinking we are ill and the imagination can run riot. Imagined fears are usually worse than reality. Incidentally, did I hear you say a moment ago "that's what I love about you . . ."?'

'I meant "like",' she said blushing. 'That's supposed to be over and done with. We're different social classes, remember.'

'I haven't forgotten,' said Billy ruefully. 'But you used "love" for "like". Your Freudian slip is showing.'

This slight indisposition of mine, Billy thought, is paying dividends. For one thing, there was the attention he was attracting and he'd definitely won the sympathy vote in the staffroom. But now here was the best prize of all, the possibility, faint though it was, that Laura might be coming back to him. Maybe she was willing to forgive him.

Three days passed and the throat trouble had not gone away. Reluctantly, Billy concluded it was time to seek medical advice. On Thursday evening, he called on Dr Reuben Glass, his local GP.

'What can I do for you?' the doctor asked, looking over

his bifocals. Glass had a face that was screwed up into a permanent grimace, a feature no doubt acquired over the years by dint of sharing and sympathising with the pain of so many patients. Billy described his symptoms to him.

'For some odd reason, my voice has begun modulating between basso profundo and coloratura soprano,' answered Billy. 'It's completely unintended and I'm at a loss to explain it.'

'Have you had any throat trouble before?' he asked.

'Not really but when I get a cold, it always seems to go to my throat in the form of tonsillitis.'

Glass placed a spatula on his tongue and a small mirror to the back of his throat. He looked down into the dark depths.

'Can't see anything. Tonsils seem OK. No sign of any inflammation. Do you have any pain or discomfort?'

'None.'

'Do you smoke heavily – I mean, you're not a forty-a-day man, I hope.'

'Nowhere near that many,' said Billy. 'With my salary, I can hardly afford five.'

'Any difficulty in swallowing?'

'None except when I have tonsillitis.'

'Do you sing a lot? Are you a member of a choir, for example?'

'The answer again is in the negative. I sing in the bathroom but my family would say the word "sing" is an exaggeration.'

'There's most likely nothing to be concerned about,' he said. 'Your trouble is probably due to overstraining your voice in the classroom.'

Billy didn't like the sound of that vague word 'probably'. What did it mean? Good grounds for belief? A good chance that there was nothing to be concerned about? Not definitely. Not sure.

'What about laryngitis or pharyngitis or tonsillitis?' said Billy. I'm being unfair on this doctor, he thought. After all, although he has completed a long course of medical training, he most likely has not studied *The Home Doctor* as I did last night. I hope my suggestions are of some help to him.

'The absence of inflammation leads me to believe otherwise,' said Glass.

'You don't think it's something serious?' asked Billy. 'Like cancer of the larynx?' There, the C word was out.

'I do not think anything of the sort,' replied Glass, giving his grimace an extra tweak. 'Go back to school but avoid overtaxing your voice if you can. Meanwhile, I'll make an appointment for you with a throat specialist at the Ear, Nose, and Throat hospital. There's a good man there – Mr Levy. He has an international reputation and has published many learned papers in *The Lancet*. He'll run a few tests on you.'

Good man at the ENT, learned papers in *The Lancet*? Run a few tests? To Billy, it sounded like the death knell. Do not ask for whom the bell tolls . . .

'What kind of tests?' he asked nervously.

'Don't get alarmed. A few tests a little more elaborate than I can run. It's nothing.'

'If it's nothing, why do I have to go to the ENT hospital?'

'Stop worrying. I want to rule out one or two items, that's all.'

'Like what?'

'Look, it's nothing. Trust me, I'm a doctor.'

Billy reported back to Mam. 'If they take away my voice

box. That's it. I'm going to be struck dumb. I don't know what I'll do,' he said.

'But they didn't say they were going to take away your voice box,' Mam said.

'Obviously they're not going to come straight out with it. Nervous types would go to pieces.'

'Not like you. Anyway, I keep telling you, there's nowt wrong with you.'

'If there's nowt wrong with me, why do I have to see a specialist?'

'Look, they want to be sure it's not . . .' she hesitated.

'Cancer,' he said.

'You said it, not me,' she replied.

'I don't mind *saying* it,' he replied, 'because it's my birth sign. I just don't want to *get* it, that's all.'

'I don't know what you're going on about, you don't have any of the symptoms.'

'I have *all* the symptoms – it's a textbook case of a throat tumour.'

At school, Billy continued to keep up the hail-fellow-well-met front in the classroom and in the staffroom.

'I think you're simply amazing,' said Laura at the end of the day. 'The way you keep joking and laughing care away. Everyone on the staff thinks so too. If I were in your shoes, I'd be scared out of my wits.'

'No point in worrying about something that hasn't happened,' Billy lied. 'I once saw a prayer in Chester Cathedral. It went:

> *Give me a sense of humour, Lord,*
> *Give me the grace to see a joke,*
> *To get some happiness from life*
> *And pass it on to other folk.*

That sums up my philosophy of life.'

' "Give me the grace to see a joke" – I like that. You should make it your family motto.'

'I believe in looking on the bright side. I'm inclined to hope rather than fear.'

'I agree with you about that, Billy,' she said. 'It's always best to hope. And I know you're not worried about the strange things happening to your voice but, well, Hamish is coming over to meet Jenny. He did three years of medicine at Glasgow and so he might be able to reassure you. I'll ask him to come over after school.'

'That'd be great,' said Billy. He hoped his lack of enthusiasm for the idea didn't show through. Hamish was the last person in the world he would have chosen to talk things over with.

At Laura's request, Hamish was waiting at the school gate.

'Hamish, I wonder if you could give Billy here the benefit of your medical knowledge,' she said.

Hamish glowered at Billy. 'I'm surprised that you should approach me of all people for medical advice,' he said bluntly. 'I'd like to make it clear that I'm doing this at the request of Laura and for no other reason.'

'And I'm listening to you for exactly the same reason,' Billy said quickly. 'Personally, I'd rather have consulted Dr Crippen.'

'That's it,' Hamish exploded. 'You'll no' get a free medical consultation from me.'

'Wait a minute, you two,' Laura said. 'This could be a serious matter. Don't let personal considerations stop us from using our brains. This throat trouble could be nothing but then again it could turn out to be life-threatening. So for all our sakes, calm down both of you and act sensibly.'

'OK,' Billy said. 'I'll take it easy though I don't think my throat merits this attention.'

'I'll see if I can be of any assistance,' Hamish said peevishly, sniffing at his nasal spray, 'though I canna help thinking you'd be best consulting a specialist.'

'My GP has arranged for me to see a Mr Levy at the ENT but it may take a little time.'

'I've heard of Levy,' Hamish said. 'He has worldwide standing so you'll be in good hands. Anyway, let's hear your symptoms and I'll offer my opinion.'

This reference once again to Levy's international repute, far from reassuring Billy, worried him even more. Why did he need to see such a celebrated specialist? He briefly explained his condition to Hamish.

'So what do you think?' Billy asked when he had finished describing his strange vocal experiences.

'Could be an inherited weakness or disposition,' suggested Hamish. 'Or it could be due to heavy smoking or overstraining your vocal cords.'

Billy nodded. 'I know that. But that's not so bad, right?'

'I suppose the dark side of the picture could be a malignant tumour on the larynx,' Hamish said gravely.

'Oh, really, you don't say,' replied Billy calmly though his heart was fluttering wildly. 'But I've felt no pain whatsoever.'

'Doesn't matter,' said Hamish cheerfully. 'Tumours can grow slowly and the sufferer may scarcely notice anything at first.'

'Sounds awful,' said Laura. 'I'm sure Billy doesn't have anything like that.'

'So what's the treatment,' Billy asked, 'for a malignant tumour?'

'Radiotherapy or even removal of the larynx, that is a

laryngectomy,' Hamish replied in sepulchral tones 'But sufferers can usually be taught to speak using the oesophagus. I believe there are approximately two thousand cases in Britain each year.'

'What about benign tumours? I suppose they are more common,' said Laura hopefully.

'Afraid not,' said Hamish. 'Oddly enough, benign cases are less common.'

'It's a good thing you're not the panicky type,' Laura said.

'That's right,' said Billy. 'Always look on the bright side, that's me. Anyway, Hamish, thanks for your help and advice.' Billy cycled off.

'Anytime,' Hamish called, smiling sinisterly.

Chapter Thirty-Eight

The Lionised Levy

Several weeks later, Billy was summoned to meet the illustrious Mr Levy at the ENT hospital in All Saints, Manchester. He presented himself bright and early at the reception desk where a pretty young lady wrote down his details – name, address, occupation, name of GP, next of kin, and finally his religion.

'My religion?' he asked. 'Why do you need to know this?'

'In case we have to inform your next of kin of any developments or summon a minister in case of emergency.'

This definitely sounded ominous.

'If you'd go through into the waiting room,' she said, 'the nurse will call you soon.'

Billy went through the swing doors and found a room crowded with pale, sick-looking, hollow-eyed people, all wearing the same rainbow-coloured bathrobes. It resembled the scene from a concentration camp after the Allied forces had liberated it. He sat down on one of the hard wooden benches and looked around at some of the terrible cases which had congregated in this depressing, ramshackle waiting room. All looked in far worse shape than he did and he felt he was something of an impostor being there. Here was a man with a huge mastoiditis; there was another with an unbelievably large swelling of the nose. What was he, Billy, doing here amongst these sick people? There was nothing wrong with him except a newly acquired ability to speak and sing in five octaves.

Poor devils, thought Billy. They're obviously in-patients who've been brought down from the wards for examinations, clinical tests, X-rays, and the like. Since they live here in the hospital, time is not so important to them and I suppose a trip down to the test centre injects a little excitement into the dull hospital routine. That nice-looking receptionist seemed pretty impressed that I was a teacher, though. Probably doesn't see too many healthy specimens in here. No doubt she'll realise I don't have as much time to spare as these other patients. I wouldn't be surprised if I didn't get priority.

He picked up a tattered copy of *London Illustrated* and began reading about the Jarrow marchers. He hadn't read far when there appeared a formidable giant of a nurse in full regalia complete with an assortment of badges and a blue belt (was it for judo?). Her starched uniform squeaked as she walked.

'William Hopkins,' she announced in a Lady Bracknell voice.

I was right, Billy thought. They can see that I'm a professional and I'm to be given a speedy processing through the system.

'Kindly follow me,' the nurse ordered. 'Now go into the changing room and put this on.'

It was a rainbow bathrobe.

'But it's my voice that's to be examined. Why do I need to put this on?'

443

'Kindly do as you are told,' she commanded, 'or the doctor will not see you.'

Billy obeyed the instruction, hung up his clothes, and joined the others in the waiting room. Was it his imagination or were they smiling at him in quiet satisfaction? Now he, too, looked like a concentration camp victim. Two hours later, after Billy had finished reading in the *Daily Telegraph* the full account of Chamberlain's successful negotiation ('Peace for our time') with Hitler at Munich in 1938, the same terrifying nurse appeared, announced his name, and signalled him to go into Levy's surgery.

Mr Levy turned out to be a small man with a funeral director's face set in the fixed smile of one who delivers a mixture of good news and bad news. He was dressed in a black coat and pinstriped trousers and he wore a carnation in his lapel. He could have come straight from a wedding reception – or a funeral – except that growing from his forehead there appeared to be a contraption that looked like a miniature miner's lamp or an alien's antenna.

Billy gave him the rundown on his condition, feeling that through repetitive practice the account was acquiring a certain fluency and piquancy.

'Uh-huh,' Levy said. He was obviously a man of few words. 'Let's take a look and see what we've got. Open your mouth wide.'

Taking a small linen napkin, he took a vice-like grip on Billy's tongue and yanked it out. Up to that time, Billy had never realised that his tongue was made of elastic; it now came out at least a foot like a piece of bubble gum. Levy put a small mirror to the back of Billy's throat and gazed down into the interior with his miner's lamp.

'Uh-huh,' he said triumphantly. 'Curious. Curious. Most interesting.' He released Billy's tongue which recoiled into place with a twang.

'Is it bad, doctor?' Billy asked anxiously.

Levy ignored him and picked up his phone and spoke into it. 'Max, could you come over here? There's an interesting case you should see.' He continued to gaze at Billy as an interesting specimen as if he had found a new species of insect. Perhaps he saw a Nobel prize there.

His colleague, Max Gluckman, a tall thin man in the same civil service dress, appeared within a couple of minutes. As a team, Levy and he could have appeared in the music halls, like Flotsam and Jetsam or the Western Brothers.

'What have we got, Sam?' Max asked.

'A larynx. See for yourself, Max. Take a look.'

Taking Billy's tongue, Max demonstrated that its length was not a foot but a foot and a half. He peered into the depths with his brow lamp.

'Ah-hah,' he said. 'Most interesting. Most interesting.'

'Thought you'd like it, Max,' smiled Sam Levy.

'What is it, for God's sake?' cried Billy, alarmed by their ah-hahs and uh-huhs and their use of words like 'curious' and 'interesting', yet at the same time secretly pleased that he had caused such interest and excitement for these two distinguished gentlemen. Maybe he'd get his name in *The Lancet*.

The two practitioners turned to look at Billy, surprised that their larynx had uttered words. Body organs on the dissecting table were not supposed to speak or ask questions. Larynxes were not normally attached to brains.

'We have detected several small curious growths on your

445

larynx,' Levy said. 'They need investigating.'

Billy's heart leapt. Were these two gentlemen giving him the black spot? God, he was only twenty years of age. Not a very long life.

'Why was my voice jumping around the octaves?'

'The best analogy I can think of,' answered Max Gluckman, 'is that of a musician playing a violin with several knots in the strings.'

'Can you come back this afternoon and we'll take a small sample for a biopsy?' said Levy. 'It will mean a local anaesthetic only. Meantime, don't worry. You may find that the growths are benign. The growths may be papillomas or polyps, harmless and easily removed without ill effects.'

'And the likelihood of cancer?' Billy asked with trembling voice.

'Remote,' said Gluckman immediately. 'Most cases are nearly always in heavy smokers. How many cigarettes do you smoke, by the way?'

'Used to smoke ten a day but am now down to five.'

'I wouldn't describe that as heavy smoking. Thirty a day and upwards I would define as heavy.'

'Is it true that benign tumours are not common?'

'They're fairly common. But my colleague and I were surprised to find them on your larynx. They're more commonly found in the nose. And we usually find benign growths in people like singers who misuse their vocal cords. It's a good thing that you have come to see us so early so we can check any development. Anyway, let's take this one step at a time. We won't make any decisions until we have all the data in front of us.'

'How soon will I know?' Billy asked.

'We shall take a small snick out of your larynx this

afternoon and send it to the pathological department of the university for examination. It's not painful and it won't take long. We should have the result in a couple of days. Meantime, you can go back to school and go on as usual.'

Go on as usual! Billy thought. Some hope! Everyone was sure he was laughing boy who never worried about anything. How little they knew him. OK, take it easy, he said to himself. Nobody said you had cancer. They found a few little growths on your larynx. So what? Could be nothing. Stay cool – no need for panic.

He decided not to go home at dinnertime. No sense in worrying his mam and dad. He went for a light lunch in Woolworth's cafeteria but he had no appetite and his toad-in-the-hole was left uneaten.

He tried to suppress any thoughts of malignancies. The idea of being struck dumb was too awful to contemplate. He'd rather die than spend the rest of his life voiceless and unable to communicate except by sign language. He put such notions out of his mind. Best to wait for the results of the biopsy – to put everything on hold until he knew something definite. He'd get by – he'd always got by. After all, he was young and healthy. Then there was the beautiful Laura. He knew that he was in love with her but if the news turned out to be bad, he'd abandon all hopes of winning her back.

It was good news that Levy had fixed up a test so soon, it would avoid a long and painful wait to know his fate – only two days. At the same time though, the fact that Levy was willing to set up a biopsy test so soon must mean that he was concerned. But it was so difficult to get straight answers from these physicians. 'Probably' was the word they were fond of using, or the phrase 'the chances are'. Well, what else could they say? They could only use indefinite verbs like 'may' or 'might' until they had some definite evidence in front of them.

He walked round the streets of the city centre – Oxford Road, Portland Street, Market Street, Cross Street, Deansgate, King Street – until it was time to return to the ENT.

The afternoon session was quick and simple. A local anaesthetic, Levy took a small sample, and that was it. No pain. No problem.

'Let's see,' Levy said. 'Today is Thursday. We should have the result on Monday afternoon. Come back around three o'clock.'

'Let's hope it's good news,' said Billy.

'I hope so too,' said Levy. 'And I must say how much I admire the calm way you have taken it all.'

With that, Billy was on his way home. It had taken forty-five minutes. Now the time of waiting began.

Billy sat on the 62 bus, to all appearances calm and composed. But within his brain a storm raged and a hundred voices called out the word CANCER! His mind was in a turmoil and as the bus crawled up Cheetham Hill Road, he thought he was going to keel over. The world about him was functioning normally and people were going about their normal business unaware, indifferent and uncaring that he was faced with the prospect of losing his voice and his speech. It was unthinkable. Everyone believed he was always cool and collected, little realising the inner fears he often experienced, like when he'd had to face the top class at St Anselm's. Inside he had been sick with dread and apprehension but to the outside world he had presented a picture of tranquillity and serenity.

He reached home at last and entered the flat quietly.

'Well, what happened at the hospital, Billy?' Mam asked anxiously.

'Nothing to worry about,' he fibbed. 'Clean bill of health.'

'Thank the Lord,' she sighed. 'My prayers have been answered.'

'I don't pray much,' said Dad, 'but this time even I said one for you.'

Billy closed his eyes to hide the tears that sprang up when he heard these words. There was no point in making them suffer with him. They'd know soon enough the result of the biopsy.

He retired early to bed that night. He usually turned in around eleven o'clock but tonight he made it ten. As he lay there in the darkness, he was oppressed by the thoughts he'd kept at bay during the daylight hours. He wanted to cry out: 'Everyone sees me as a joking, laughing, carefree individual but I'm nothing of the sort. I'm really a frightened little boy and I'm scared out of my wits at the idea of losing my voice for good. They're carrying out a biopsy to confirm what they already know. I've got cancer of the larynx.'

He gulped hard. Was it his imagination or was there a hint of pain as the saliva slid past his epiglottis? He could feel the tumours on his voice box. He knew now that he had cancer. He'd be speechless and voiceless and he didn't want to go on living. What would be the point?

'Look, God, I'll strike a bargain with you. Take away – something I've got two of . . . No, not those, I might need

449

them some day . . . I was thinking more of an eye or an arm but please, not my voice. I don't want a laryngectomy. I'd rather die.'

The hours of darkness passed slowly and not for one second did he sleep or banish the dread which overwhelmed him.

The next day, he went into school as usual and kept up the pretence that everything was normal, and in the staffroom he indulged in the usual good-natured banter. No one suspected the dreadful turbulence which raged within. He listened to the 'Doctor, doctor' jokes of Greg and laughed with the rest but not for a moment did he forget the awful predicament into which destiny had thrust him.

'You've not been eating these last few days,' Mam said. 'Is there something worrying you?'

'Nothing, I tell you,' he replied exasperated. 'I'm not hungry.'

For the next four nights, he did not sleep. He looked pale and sallow, his face drawn.

'Something *is* troubling you,' Mam said. 'I know you well enough to see that you've got something on your mind.'

In the quiet of the small hours, he could see himself in the ENT hospital. Levy was bending over him in the operating theatre. 'Sorry, but we've had to remove your larynx,' he was saying. 'But don't worry, we'll teach you to speak using your throat muscles.'

Then he was in the ward after the operation and patients in the other beds were pointing him out to their visitors. 'See that poor lad over there? Used to be a teacher till they cut out his larynx.'

He saw himself straining to speak but only able to

produce inarticulate guttural noises. No, he'd rather be dead than go through that.

But time and the hour ran through Billy's roughest day.

Chapter Thirty-Nine

Crunch Time

On Monday afternoon, he caught the bus to All Saints and presented himself to the receptionist at the ENT shortly before three o'clock. He hadn't long to wait.

Mr Levy came out to greet him. 'Please come this way, Mr Hopkins.'

They say that a prisoner in court can tell the verdict by studying the jury's faces. If that were true, it was a foregone conclusion because Levy looked serious and sad. He gazed at Billy for what seemed to be an interminably long time and then he smiled broadly.

'Good news. No trace of cancer – you're in the clear. The tumours are polyps which we can remove with a simple operation. Congratulations. I hope you've not been too worried over the weekend.'

Billy stared at him incredulously. Slowly the news sank in to the core of his being and a great wave of elation passed over him. Pure, unadulterated joy!

'Thank you so much, Mr Levy, for all you've done,' he said ecstatically. 'What happens now?'

'You come in next week for a small op, we remove the little growths and you will have your normal voice restored to you. Who knows, maybe an even better voice. It means a week as an in-patient.'

A week later, Billy found himself in a bed between the mastoiditis and the incandescent nose.

'We three are hospital symbols,' he joked to his two fellow patients. 'You're the ear, you're the nose and I'm the throat.'

Next day, he was wheeled into the operating theatre. As the anaesthetist injected his stuff, Billy said, 'Whilst you're at it, how about giving me a voice like Benjamino Gigli or, better still, Frank Sinatra?'

'We'll see what we can do,' he laughed. And that was the last Billy heard that afternoon.

He awoke around six o'clock and tested the result. 'The day war broke out,' he began with his brilliant imitation of Rob Wilton.

A nurse came running over. 'Good news and bad news,' she said. 'Good, you must take a week off work. Bad, you are not permitted to speak,' she said. 'You must rest your voice for at least a week.'

In the afternoon, Mam appeared at his bedside.

'So you're not allowed to talk,' she said. 'For a change, you'll have to lie back and listen.'

He nodded his assent. 'It's not as bad as that. I can talk a little but I have to conserve my voice for a while until it gets stronger.'

'Right. I can do the talking for a change. I think your father was wrong about that girl Laura.'

'Then why did you agree with Dad when he was going on about how we were working class and Laura was middle class?'

'I've found it's always best to keep the peace. It doesn't

453

mean I don't have my own opinion. We used to have a saying in Collyhurst: When a woman's convinced against her will, she'll have the same opinion still.'

'So you think Laura's the right girl?'

'She's a lovely girl with a lovely personality. If you think you've found Miss Right, you must not give her up, no matter what anyone says.'

'What about Dad? I don't think he'll accept it somehow.'

'You leave his lordship to me. I'll make him see sense. He's always against anything new at first but he comes round in the end. Remember how awkward he was about you going to college. He bought you a watch – no, two watches – at the finish.'

'I hope you manage to talk him out of that daft idea of the classes not mixing. I know Laura's the only girl for me, and his notion about her being upper and me being lower seems like a lot of hooey. The only problem is money and the lack of it. We can't get far without it.'

'If you're short of money, I have a bob or two put aside and it's yours for the asking. It's only sitting there in the Co-op Bank. I'd much rather it was out helping you and doing some good. We'll see you don't go short.'

'I'll remember that, Mam, if Laura and I get back together.' Billy was close to tears; he knew that her 'bob or two' had been accumulated by scrimping and scraping over forty years of marriage.

When Mam had gone, he lay there thinking deeply about his life and the direction it was taking. Somehow life without Laura did not seem worth living.

Later that same day, Laura came to see him.

'Laura, can you ever forgive me for my stupidity?' he said.

'Billy, oh, Billy, don't you know me at all? I've been

worried out of my mind about you. I do love you, Billy, no matter what.'

'Even if I'd lost my voice?' he said quietly.

'I said no matter what. I'd even give up the Bechstein piano and the Pye Black Box for you. There, now, that's saying something.'

'But what about the telephone and the grapes on the sideboard?' he joked.

'Those too,' she laughed. 'I've brought you the grapes from the sideboard as nobody in our house is ill.'

'Lying here in the hospital,' he whispered, 'you get to thinking about things, about your priorities, about what really matters.'

'I've never wavered for a moment, Billy.'

'Trust the middle classes to recognise a bargain when they see one,' he jested.

'Rest your voice and listen,' she said decisively. 'I don't want to hear that rubbish again about social classes and that they don't mix. When you get up out of this bed, I think we should tell everyone that we're walking out, that we're courting, or whichever way you want to put it.'

'You mean announce our engagement?'

'I mean exactly that and blow the consequences.'

'What about your father and honours degrees and so on?'

'You're getting engaged to me, not my father,' she said. Her determination impressed him. 'Besides, he's already married.'

Laura talked until the visiting bell rang.

'I have to go now, Billy,' she said. 'When we were apart, I wrote out this poem by Elizabeth Barrett Browning. Read it and think about it. It says more beautifully what I feel than I could ever say it.' She embraced him, kissed him on the lips and was gone.

A little later when the ward had settled down and all was quiet, he turned to the poem.

> *If thou must love me, let it be for naught . . .*
> *But love me for love's sake, that evermore*
> *Thou mayst love on, through love's eternity.*

For the first time since a child, Billy wept for his own stupidity and the thought that he might have lost Laura, had it not been for her sound common sense.

On her next visit, Billy apologised for his puerile behaviour and the shame he had felt for his own background.

'I felt,' he said, 'that I wasn't good enough for you. I've put you on a pedestal and I worship you. You are the princess in an Andersen fairy tale, the heroine in a tale of chivalry, the beautiful maiden in a Lehar musical.'

'I don't like being on a pedestal,' she said. 'It's cold and lonely there.'

'I was so naïve. I shudder to think that I almost lost you. You left me the Browning poem and I found it most moving. Now I return the compliment with my own choice – a poem from *Love's Philosophy* by Shelley.'

Laura read the poem quietly to herself. She stopped at a particular point.

'I love this part,' she murmured, tears sparkling in her eyes. 'I shall treasure it as long as I live. Let me read it so that only you can hear.

> *The fountains mingle with the river*
> *And the rivers with the Ocean*

The winds of Heaven mix forever
With a sweet emotion.
Nothing in the world is single
All things by a law divine
In one spirit meet and mingle
Why not I with thine?'

Every day, Laura went to see him after school to give him the latest happenings and the latest gossip in the staffroom. How Grundy had blown his top when Greg had provoked him by drinking from his cup and sitting in his chair. And every day they planned their future and their love grew stronger.

'When they let me out of hospital,' he said, 'we'll go, you and I, to Saqui and Lawrence in St Ann's Square and choose an engagement ring. We'll tell the world that we're betrothed.'

He had been condemned to be something of a Trappist monk for seven days – an impossible requirement for Billy. No teaching. No school. No talking. Heaven and hell at the same time.

'I suppose,' he managed to add, 'the correct protocol demands that I go and ask your father's approval and he will give me the third degree as to my income and my prospects etcetera.'

'Why not, if it makes you both happy, but I'm sure it's not necessary,' she said.

'One other thing,' he said. 'My old college is having a reunion in London at half term. Do you think he'd let you accompany me to London?'

'You mean for one of those weekends?' she said in feigned coyness. 'If you have designs on me, Mr Hopkins, for that you will definitely have to ask his permission.'

457

'No, I do not mean one of those weekends. Everything will be above board. Have you ever been to London, Laura?'

'Never.'

'Then I want to be the first one to take you on a tour of the capital. We could book one or two shows and get a taste of the high life.'

'Sounds exciting. We'll ask Daddy's permission but we'll go no matter what. We're both nearly twenty-one.'

After his release from hospital, he returned home and continued the period of enforced taciturnity. He managed to get through the period and he suspected that Mam thoroughly enjoyed the respite and a rest from his endless school anecdotes, his moaning about what a rotten day he'd had, his analysis of current events, and his jokes. She was able to tell him what she really thought and he was unable to reply as fully as he'd have liked. However, he was building up a great reservoir of observations and when his day of release came, the words came pouring out like a dam which had burst its banks. He talked non-stop – mainly rubbish – and although he didn't have a Sinatra or a Gigli voice, the resonance and the timbre had returned. He was back in business.

He felt as if he had discovered the perfect ailment – no pain, a minor op, lots of sympathy, and a week off work thrown in. Further, Laura had visited him every day in hospital and there was no mistaking the look of sheer, unbridled happiness that she manifested when she knew he was not to lose his voice.

There was a corollary. Levy maintained that the polyps were the result of voice strain and misuse of the vocal cords. He recommended two courses. First, lessons in voice training and singing, and secondly, a course of speech therapy.

The first part involved going to Laura's mother for an intensive course of singing lessons. In the Mackenzie drawing room, he went through Benché exercises and learned to sing the part of Mozart's Sarastro. First he tackled 'O Isis and Osiris' and 'within these sacred portals' from *The Magic Flute* and as a party piece 'The Hippopotamus Song' which had been made famous by Flanders and Swan. This part of the course was successful in that it introduced him not only to singing but later to the wonderful world of choral music when he joined the Holy Name Choir and met Denis Glynn, the conductor, who was something of a musical genius, utterly devoted to his field. The Holy Name Choir opened doors to a magical world of polyphony. Polyps to polyphony, thought Billy. He came to know the music of Tallis, Palestrina, Lassus, Vittoria, Britten, and, best of all, William Byrd. Choral music became one of the most important aspects of his life.

So, the first part of training recommended by Levy worked. The second, speech therapy, was not so successful.

Billy was sent to the Wythenshawe hospital and was directed to the special voice training unit where he found the therapist waiting. She was about twenty years of age, dark-haired, big blue eyes, gleaming white teeth, and she had the most beautiful reassuring smile. She looked like Ava Gardner.

'Good morning, Mr Hopkins,' she purred. 'Do sit down and make yourself comfortable. It's my job during these sessions to teach you how to project your voice without putting strain on the larynx. Most important, you must learn how to relax. First your whole body and then your throat and finally your larynx.'

Billy crossed his legs and began tracing a complicated geometrical pattern with his right foot. As she spoke, she surreptitiously watched his foot and began taking furious notes. Billy surreptitiously watched her surreptitiously watching his foot. He stopped the foot fidget and began stroking imaginary dirt from the back of his hand. She took more notes. Forcing Billy to relax was going to be uphill work.

'Look,' she said, 'I think the best way of getting you to relax is to provide a quiet, calm atmosphere. Take off your shoes and lie on the couch.'

Billy did as he was told.

She drew the curtains and, in the half-light, she looked even more attractive. She put on a record of Mendelsohnn's Hebridean Overture, *Fingal's Cave*, and began reading poetry about the sea and about how she must go down to it again, to the lonely sea and the sky . . .

The more she read, the more tense Billy became until he was as taut as a bar of steel.

She lifted his right arm to check the level of relaxation achieved. It stayed rigid in mid-air.

'It's no use,' she said. 'It's not working. I think we had better try again on another day.'

She was right. It wasn't working. She little guessed the reason. Billy had removed his shoes as instructed but he'd forgotten that in the right foot of his socks there was a big hole which he had intended bringing to Mam's attention some time. His big toe jutted out like the rock of Gibraltar.

Billy discontinued the speech therapy and concentrated instead on the Mozart arias.

Chapter Forty

Engagement

In the study of his home, Duncan Mackenzie sat in his favourite wing chair with a copy of the *Manchester Guardian*. He had lit his third cigarette of the evening – one more than he normally allowed himself at this time – and the newspaper remained unread on his knee.

In the drawing room, Billy Hopkins was being put through his musical paces by his wife Louise, and the strains of a Mozart aria rang through the house.

Duncan was lost in thought about his daughter Laura. It could not be said that he had a favourite child, though Laura, his firstborn, had a special place in his heart. But when did she grow up so quickly? It didn't seem that long ago since she'd looked up to him – he'd been her hero and whatever he'd said was accepted as Gospel truth. Came the day when she put on her first lipstick, had her first hair-do, and went out to her first dance. That was the beginning of the end. She'd brought home one or two callow youths with spots and weird hairstyles and they were no problem. It was a relief to see that she could attract boyfriends – it would have been more worrying if there'd been none, he'd have wondered what was wrong with her.

The years had flown by unnoticed and she'd grown from the leggy adolescent into the beautiful young lady she now was. For a number of years there had been an understanding with their good friends, the Dunwoodys, that their only son Hamish and Laura would make an ideal match. Hamish was a nice boy with tremendous career prospects even if something of a hypochondriac, but he'd grow out of that. He offered security and she'd never starve if she married him, that was for sure. But then she'd met this Billy Hopkins character at school – a good-looking boy, very polite and he'd certainly helped Hughie with his French, but he wasn't in the same league as Hamish when it came to earning power. This business with Billy had developed so quickly – it was only six months since the night of the musical evening when he'd sung that Al Jolson song. With hindsight, it had been pretty clear then that Laura had set her cap at him but he'd been blind to the obvious. There'd been something about her – she'd looked different somehow, her eyes brighter and aglow, as if lit up from the inside.

At the table, she'd been full of him. It was 'Billy said this' and 'Billy said that'. You'd think this Billy character was Solomon and Einstein rolled into one. It was then that he'd begun to realise that he, Duncan, had been relegated to second place whilst King Billy reigned on high.

He'd tried to put her off him but he'd had to play his cards carefully. Too much pressure would have driven her straight into Billy's arms. No, he'd had to be more subtle about it. A little nod in the right direction, a word in the right ear, and he was sure that Laura would come to her senses and see which side her bread was buttered. Then what he'd hoped for came about.

She'd come home broken-hearted from one of her dates with the new monarch, and there'd been nothing he or

Louise could do to console her. Inwardly he'd rejoiced that common sense had triumphed in the end. Sure, Laura was upset but she'd get over it eventually. But when her sorrow turned to melancholy, and seemed to get deeper, they became concerned. And now they were back together again.

Tonight, things had come to a head. She'd broken the news to him in such an offhand way. He'd come home as usual and sat down at the table. Jenny was late and he'd inquired about her whereabouts.

'She's out on a date with Hamish,' Louise had said.

'She should be here at the table with the rest of my bairns,' he'd said. An innocent enough remark, he thought. But Laura had reacted strangely with a sudden furious outburst. The conversation was indelibly printed on his mind.

'We're no longer bairns, Daddy,' she'd snapped. 'Jenny's nineteen now and old enough even to be married.'

'Nonsense!' he'd said reasonably. 'Nineteen's much too young. Why, I didna marry your mother until I was twenty-six.'

'That was in the Dark Ages,' she'd said. 'Besides, Mammy was only twenty from what I've been told.'

'Then it was different,' Duncan said, but a little less sure of himself.

'Billy said that young marriages have a lot to recommend them. A young husband has a great incentive to work hard and improve himself. Besides, babies are better looked after if the parents are young and healthy.' She had a reply for everything.

'And does this Billy say who's going to support these adolescent marriages?' he'd countered. He thought that was a pretty shrewd remark.

'Anyway,' Laura continued. 'Billy and I want to talk to you tonight after his singing lesson.'

'You're no' thinkin' of marrying this pauper?' he said.

'We've talked about it.'

'And exactly when are you hoping to get married?' Louise had asked anxiously.

'We've not decided,' she'd answered. 'That's what we want to talk to you about. We need to give it some thought. It's up to Billy.'

For Duncan that was the last straw! It's up to Billy! The very idea! He blew his top.

'I hope this wonderful Billy of yours doesna think he can keep running to me for money whenever he's short of funds. If he does, he can think again.'

'Look, Daddy,' she'd retorted, 'there's no need to get hot under the collar or play the outraged father. Billy and I are both adults and I'll tell you something. We've got our pride and would rather die than come begging to you for help. Not if we were homeless and starving in the gutter. We'd rather live in a shop doorway than come to you.'

And that had been that. Now he sat waiting for the music to stop and then they'd face the music together.

He heard Louise play the final chord of the aria. He lit a fourth cigarette. I must cut down on this smoking, he thought.

A few minutes later, Laura and Billy came into the room.

'You remember, Daddy, that Billy and I want to talk to you.'

As if he could forget.

'You make it sound mysterious,' Duncan lied, offering Billy one of his Three Castle cigarettes, 'but I have a shrewd idea what it's about.'

'Very well, Mr Mackenzie,' Billy said nervously, accepting the light that Duncan offered. 'There are two things we want to ask of you. I'll get straight to the point. First of all, Laura and I love each other very much and we'd like to announce our engagement. Before we do, we'd like your permission of course.'

'I guessed as much,' he said. 'How old are you Billy?'

'I shall be twenty-one next birthday.'

'I think you're both too young to be talking about engagement but I suppose it's useless my saying that. I dare say you'd go ahead with or without my permission.'

The couple said nothing but the expression on their faces gave him his answer.

'More important,' Duncan continued, 'supposing I were to give my permission, when did you have in mind for the wedding?'

'We hadn't got round to thinking that far ahead,' Laura answered quickly. 'But I suppose about two years or so. We'd need to save a fair sum of money.' She looked to Billy for approval. He nodded agreement.

'You never said a truer word,' Duncan said. 'You'll have an uphill job saving the money you're going to need to set up home. I reckon that a minimum of five hundred pounds is necessary nowadays before you can even think about marriage.'

On my salary, Billy thought, it would take forever to save that amount, and as Jimmy Durante says, 'I can't wait that long, I got only one change of clothing.'

'How much do you have at present in the bank, Billy?' he heard Duncan saying.

'Laura and I have opened a joint bank account, Mr Mackenzie, and we have almost fifty pounds saved,' Billy answered proudly.

Duncan looked aghast for a moment. Recovering his composure, he asked, 'What's your annual salary?'

'Three hundred and fifty pounds per year. Net I receive around twenty-two pounds per month.'

'Good God!' he exclaimed. 'How can you expect to marry on that? It's hardly enough for a vagrant to exist on, let alone a married couple.'

'We'll have my salary too, Daddy,' Laura chipped in. 'Together we should have about forty pounds a month.'

'And if you had a baby in your first year, as many young couples do,' Duncan argued, 'what then?'

'We'd manage somehow,' protested Laura.

'That seems like a vague answer to me. If you want to start married life in a house, you'll need a substantial down payment and a mortgage. Also furniture. I can't see you doing it on your limited funds.'

'We've worked it out, Mr Mackenzie,' said Billy enthusiastically. 'I could increase my hours at the Youth Centre, and Laura says she'll work at a Play Centre. So we should be able to save about twenty pounds per month, and in two years that would come to enough to make a start. As for furniture, there's always hire purchase.'

Duncan frowned and said, 'Shakespeare knew what he was talking about when he made Shylock say in *The Merchant of Venice*, "Neither a borrower nor a lender be; for loan oft loses both itself and friend".'

Billy didn't think it was the right time to tell him it was Polonius in *Hamlet* who'd uttered the immortal words to his son Laertes.

'Don't worry so, Daddy,' Laura said. 'I'm sure we'll get by.'

Duncan remained unconvinced. 'You said there were two things you wanted to discuss. What was the other one?'

Billy reddened. Laura followed suit.

'Next month I shall be going to London to attend a reunion at my old college in Chelsea,' Billy stuttered. 'I'd like your permission to take Laura with me.'

There was a long pause while Duncan took this in. He looked black. He gave a Beethoven-like scowl.

'You mean take my daughter to London and stay in the same hotel?' He had difficulty in phrasing the question. He managed to make 'London' sound like Sodom and Gomorrah.

'We'd have separate rooms of course,' Billy faltered. 'It's just that, well, Laura has never seen London and I'd like to be the first one to show it to her.'

'The first one to show it to her.' Witheringly. 'Would you now?' Duncan sneered. 'Yes, I'm sure you would. But isn't that courting temptation? I hope you don't have in mind violating my daughter. Jumping the gun, as it were.'

Billy's red face turned crimson. He has a funny way of putting it, he said to himself. 'I have the highest respect for your daughter, Mr Mackenzie. I'd not contemplate such a despicable act, and I resent your even suggesting it.'

'Daddy, I don't know how you can even hint at such a thing,' Laura exploded. 'Billy and I don't think about such things and won't until after we're married.'

No need to phrase it so strongly, Billy thought, but she was right about putting such ideas on ice until after the ceremony.

'I know human nature,' said Duncan. 'St Paul says somewhere, if you meet temptation, run a mile – or words to that effect. Going to London together, well, you're walking straight into it.'

Billy thought this might be an appropriate time to play the Scripture card he had prepared so carefully the night before. He hoped he wasn't overdoing it. 'Doesn't the Bible say, "Blessed is the man that endureth temptation: for when he is tried, he shall receive the crown of life"?'

Laura raised her eyebrows and looked at Billy quizzically.

'Absolutely right,' said Duncan, 'provided he does endure it and does not give way to it.'

'You'll have to trust us,' said Billy.

Once again, Duncan seemed unpersuaded.

As Billy took his leave at the door, Laura grinned, 'I liked the way you got the Biblical quotation in. That was clever, though I thought you were laying it on a bit thick. You were starting to sound like a Jehovah Witness.'

'Sorry about that, Laura, but you didn't do so bad yourself with that stuff about "we never think about such things". I hope you were speaking for yourself and not for me. But when I quoted the Bible to your father, I was only telling him what I thought he wanted to hear. The one thing that concerned me, though, was that your dad agreed with me. And when he does that, I'm sure I must be wrong somehow.'

Duncan wasn't the only one to raise objections to the engagement. Billy's dad was vehemently against it despite Mam's efforts to bring him round.

'I've got to speak my mind,' he said. 'Marriage between different classes is doomed from the start. It just won't work – oil and water don't mix. Laura Mackenzie's a very nice girl and all that, but how can our Billy afford to keep her in the lifestyle she's used to? Oh, they'll be luvvy-duvvy at first but when the gilt's worn off the gingerbread, what then? I'm warning you, there'll be trouble. Billy should marry one of his own kind, a nice, respectable, working-class girl.'

Later, when talking to Flo, Mam said, 'I think deep down your dad's worried about mixing with the higher-ups. He's frightened of them and nervous in their presence.'

Billy, Les and the rest of the family went to work on him but he wouldn't move an inch.

'You mark my words, they'll rue the day,' was all that they could get out of him.

'So be it,' Billy declared. 'It may be a long time before we marry but when we do, it'll be with or without his blessing.'

The week following the interview with Duncan, Billy and Laura went to Saqui and Lawrence in St Ann's Square and chose a beautiful solitaire diamond ring, paid for out of their savings. There was no formal engagement party but there were many cards of congratulations from friends and colleagues. One card was a surprise. It said 'To the two trend-setters, from Hamish and Jenny'.

At half-term, it was a radiantly happy, excited couple that took the train from London Road station to Euston.

They booked two separate rooms at a small hotel in Chelsea.

'Staying apart is going to be difficult,' said Billy, 'but we gave our word to your folks. I shall have to take a cold bath every time the mood strikes me. Perhaps I should simply stay in the icy water.'

'I feel the same way,' Laura said, 'but I think I'll forgo the cold baths all the same. When we get back to Manchester, maybe we should take up rug-making. It'll keep your hands busy.'

'I believe winding wool serves a similar purpose.'

'So I should take up knitting.'

'No. Both of us should take up knitting.'

Billy showed Laura around the sights of London and he himself re-lived the excitement of seeing the famous landmarks for the first time as he watched Laura's euphoric reactions. She was innocent and artless and he loved her for it. She was content and happy with the simplest of things, like a little girl viewing a Christmas tree for the first time.

On the first evening, Billy went off to the Nell Gwynn in King's Road for his men's college reunion. It proved to be a disappointment as most of his year group were serving out their time doing National Service. Billy was not over concerned as he knew that Laura was waiting for him back at the hotel.

Around eleven o'clock, he returned and found Laura reading quietly in her room. At the sight of her lying there so relaxed and content, his heart overflowed with tenderness and love.

She looked up from her book and smiled happily when she saw him. 'You've been away three hours and I've missed you so much,' she said, holding out her arms.

They embraced and held each other tightly. Soon things threatened to get out of control but sensing the urgency of his need, Laura said, 'I love you so much Billy. I want and need you but if we gave in to our passions now, it would ruin everything, spoil our plans.'

'Right now,' he said hoarsely, 'I'm inclined to agree with Oscar Wilde when he said "I can resist anything but temptation", but even though I want to make love to you, I can see the sense of what you're saying. There is one thing we could try, however.'

'And that is?'

'The Welsh have a courting practice which they call *bundling*.'

'What on earth is that? It sounds like wrapping up parcels.'

'It has certain similarities. I sleep here in the same bed with you but we are separated by different layers of bedclothes. That way, we can hold each other closely without going all the way, as they say. I promise to stay in my own section though I can't promise the same for my arms and my hands.'

'Sounds a little crazy to me,' she laughed.

'It could be worse. Sometimes it involved tying up the girl in a sheet or even tying her feet together.'

'I think we'll forget this weird Welsh custom and all its variations. Sharing a bed even in this strange manner would simply be tempting providence. I love you, Billy, but I think we'd be better in separate rooms.'

'You're not sure that I can resist temptation?'

'No, Billy. I'm not sure that *I* can.'

Billy gave her a last kiss and a final embrace and, with a sigh of resignation, retired to his own room.

The rest of the weekend was a joy. They visited the Victoria Palace and laughed at the antics of The Crazy Gang in their farce *Together Again*, and revelled in the music of Irving Berlin's *Annie Get Your Gun* at the Coliseum featuring Dolores Gray, but the highlight of the weekend was the performance of *Madame Butterfly* at the Sadler's Wells. As the tragic story unfolded reaching its climax in act three with the suicide of Butterfly, the strains of Puccini's poignant music filled the theatre. The tears ran down Laura's cheeks, and she reached for Billy's hand. He didn't exactly weep but he swallowed hard a couple of times and there was certainly a lump in his throat.

On their last evening, they had supper at a Lyon's Corner

House to the music of a string quartet and served by a 'nippy' waitress in Edwardian uniform. They returned to their hotel and in Laura's room kissed and cuddled as closely as they dared without going fully overboard.

'This weekend has brought home one thing clearly to me,' said Billy as he held Laura closely on the final evening.

'I think I know what you're going to say,' she murmured. 'And on this point we are fully as one.'

'Even if we are not in the flesh,' he laughed. 'I most definitely cannot wait two years before we join forces, as it were.'

'You have a funny way of putting things,' she said.

'Or not putting things,' he commented suggestively. 'Laura, let's get married this year and blow the consequences. I'm sure we'll manage the money somehow or other.'

'And throw caution to the wind?'

'Completely.'

'But we shall require a tremendous amount of money and at the moment that's the one commodity we're lacking.'

'We can take on a few private pupils and with the extra evening work at the Alfred Street youth centre, we should be able to save another hundred pounds. With the savings we already have, that will give us something approaching a hundred and fifty pounds. That's not a bad sum to make a start.'

'And I could do another night at the Ross Place play centre. Oh, Billy, do you think we can do it?'

'I'm sure we can. Together, we can overcome any difficulties. I know that if we have to wait two years, I shall be no use to you because I'll be resident in the lunatic asylum.'

'OK, Billy. I don't want to have to spend my life visiting

you in the Prestwich Hospital. Let's do it. But be prepared
for a storm of disapproval and resistance.'

Chapter Forty-One

Wedding Preparations

As Laura had predicted, there was an unholy row when they announced their intention to marry in the summer. The objections came thick and fast.

Not enough time to make the arrangements. Where will the reception be held? Not enough time to prepare speeches. What about the catering, the drinks, the flowers, the organist, the bridesmaids, the priest, the trousseau, the car hire, the wedding suits, the photographer? Who will pay for it all?

Not enough notice for many of the relatives to attend. Many have already fixed their holidays. What about Hughie who is in Malaya doing his National Service? Not enough time to get our outfits.

What about the children who will demand to come?

Then there was the other school of thought. Are you sure this isn't a shotgun wedding? We'll be counting the months to your first baby. Couldn't resist each other, eh? Nudge, nudge, wink, wink. It was that dirty weekend in London that did it. More elbow-nudging and winking.

The two fathers worried themselves sick.

'You know, Louise,' Duncan said, 'life's a strange thing.

I did my utmost to encourage Laura to marry Hamish as the one with the best prospects, and instead she wants to marry the one with the worst.'

'No need to worry, Duncan,' said Louise in an attempt to reassure her husband. 'They'll get by. They're young, healthy and resourceful, and very much in love. I'm sure they're going to be very happy. And as for Billy's prospects, I think he may surprise you one day.'

'I hope you're right, Louise,' he murmured. 'Only time will tell.'

As for Billy's father, he refused to countenance the marriage.

'This is one wedding I won't be going to,' he said decisively. 'Include me out. I think the marriage will be a disaster. You just wait till the honeymoon's over, that's all.'

'You miserable old devil,' Mam said. 'We'll just have to hold it without you. I know you though. You're just terrified of meeting up with the Mackenzies 'cos you think they're toffs and you'll put your foot in it.'

'Nonsense,' he replied, not too confidently.

For weeks before the wedding, Laura was involved in detailed planning for her trousseau and bridal outfit.

'We've managed to find a dressmaker who will be making my wedding gown,' she told Billy enthusiastically. 'It'll be made of ivory satin crepe with a full train. And we're using real flowers in the head-dress, the same as my bouquet. What do you think?'

'Great – simply great!' a bemused Billy mumbled. 'Sounds really exciting.' He didn't understand a word of it and besides, he had other things on his mind at that moment, for Duncan had raised more important matters.

'In case you're wondering,' he'd said, 'I've arranged a

good dowry for Laura but I plan to give that to you when you're both ready to buy a house of your own. Meanwhile, you just about have enough money to pay for your share of the wedding and go on a honeymoon. In my opinion your top priority is to find an apartment to rent.'

'Don't worry, Mr Mackenzie,' Billy had said, ever optimistic. 'That matter's well in hand. Laura and I have spotted a few likely looking places in the local paper and we'll be going to check them out after school.'

'If you can't find a place to live,' Duncan warned – almost hopefully – 'I think you should consider postponing the wedding until you do.'

Finding a flat wasn't as easy as Billy had imagined. The two likely addresses they had jotted down were situated on Stockport Road. The first was on the top floor of a Victorian mansion. To reach it, they had to climb three flights of stairs, passing rubbish bins on the way. The capacious stairwell not only reeked of the usual cooking odours but was decorated with assorted graffiti written by Kilroy ('Don't clean this hallway – plant something. Keep this hall tidy – throw your rubbish out of the window') and advising readers in choice language where they could go and what they could do when they got there. One look was enough.

'If we came here,' Billy said, 'it would be like home from home for me. Gardenia Court to Stinkwood House.'

The next flat was a little better but not much. Though it was opposite Pownall's massive warehouse, it had the advantage of being situated on the ground floor.

'You have your own kitchen and living room,' the proprietor told them, 'but the bathroom is on the first landing and is shared with the other floors. If you want a bath, you'll need a shilling for the geyser.'

Billy couldn't resist asking, 'Which flat does the geyser live in?'

Laura inspected the minuscule kitchen.

'I couldn't work in there,' she whispered to Billy. 'It's about the size of a broom cupboard and has no windows. When I'm in the kitchen, I like to look out on the world outside.'

'Doesn't look too hopeful,' Billy said when they emerged. 'Flats are like gold at the moment.'

'I do hope we don't have to go in with the in-laws,' Laura said, 'like so many couples do today. It's usually disastrous.'

'We've not found anything yet,' Billy said, 'but I have a Micawber-like faith that something will turn up.'

It did.

A fortnight before the wedding, Mrs Mackenzie reported that her friend, Mrs Sheila Dobson, a nurse at the Manchester Royal Infirmary, had a flat vacant. Whilst it was nothing to write home about, consisting as it did of a large lounge, a bedroom, a small but reasonable kitchen, and a shared bathroom, for them it was ideal. Mrs Dobson had had the first floor of her house converted into a furnished flat for her son and his wife but his job had taken him to the south of England, leaving the apartment vacant – a stroke of luck for Billy and Laura. There was a further bonus in that Mrs Dobson was away on duty most of the time which meant they'd have free run of the place.

The wedding was fixed for the glorious twelfth of August. 'The day when grouse shooting begins,' remarked Billy.

The wedding was to be held at St Anselm's church and would be presided over by the Reverend Father O'Flynn, aged eighty-two.

'Let's make it a quiet wedding with only the immediate families invited,' said Billy.

'Exactly my sentiments,' agreed Laura. 'A nice quiet wedding. I'm all for it.'

'Better still, why don't we simply elope?' Billy suggested. 'We could marry quietly at Gretna Green. Look at the money and the trouble we'd save.'

Laura looked aghast. 'And miss out on the greatest day of our lives! No, we'll organise the wedding at home and it'll be quiet but I'll still need a trousseau.'

'What's that?' asked Billy. 'I know from my French studies that a trousseau used to be a small bundle that the bride carried under her arm to her new home. I think we can run to that.'

'I should like two bridesmaids – Jenny and Katie,' Laura went on, ignoring his attempt at levity. 'They'll need special dresses. And it's customary for you to buy each of them a present.'

'What type of present?'

'Oh, small mementos.'

'I think I can afford a bag of Mintoes each.'

'Not Mintoes. Mementos! Like a pearl brooch each for example.'

Billy could see the hundred and fifty pounds they had saved rapidly melting away.

'What else am I to pay for?' he asked apprehensively.

'Well, it's customary for the groom to pay for things like church fees, the organist, bouquets and buttonholes, and rings.'

'Is that all?'

'I think so, though don't forget the two boys who pump the organ.'

'Can't be much of an organ if it needs pumping,' Billy said.

'I'll ignore that,' Laura said. 'We'll keep the bouquets simple. I should like to carry a bouquet of roses, carnations and cornflowers. And the bridesmaids similar. They shouldn't break the bank. One last thing. At Easter, Mammy and Daddy went to Rome. They've brought back the Papal blessing for us.'

'How much?' asked Billy.

'That's for free – compliments of Pius the Twelfth.'

Billy wondered what the Pope would have made of his experience at the barbers' shop. On the way home, Billy was accustomed to call at a hairdressing salon outside Victoria Station and he'd become a regular at the establishment of Len and Ken. Every fortnight, he swapped stories and the latest jokes with the two barbers. The establishment was the kind of male stronghold that would have interested anthropologists like Margaret Mead.

Ken started the ball rolling as he trimmed a customer's hair. 'Have you heard about the fella who thought that mutual orgasm was an insurance company?'

The regulars waiting their turn split their sides for the tenth time in the past ten minutes. Another great joke – we are all men here. Women just wouldn't appreciate the humour.

When Billy announced he was to be married the following weekend and would appreciate a special haircut, he was treated to a stream of blue stories about bridegrooms on their wedding night.

As he snipped Billy's locks, Len took up the comedian's role. 'Someone told the new husband that in sex it was essential to begin with foreplay – so he invited the couple next door to join them. Then there was this newly married bloke who told his bride, "I must warn you, darling, that I like to get up early every morning." "Yes," she replied,

"I've noticed that you're an early riser." '

Once again, bawdy guffaws all round the shop.

Finally, Len turned to serious matters. 'I suppose you'll be wanting a supply of these,' he said, indicating the box of contraceptives on the shelf. 'And not merely as "something for the weekend, sir", but on a regular basis. We can give a good discount for a box of twelve – that would be a week's supply for you, I suppose,' he grinned.

Billy turned a bright pink.

The waiting customers were agog for his answer.

'No, no . . .' Billy mumbled. 'They're against our religion and the Pope won't allow 'em.'

'I see, sir,' Len replied. 'Going in for a family are we, sir?' He made it sound like an investment in shares or the purchase of furniture from Lewis's.

All agreed that it would be a quiet wedding, a small modest affair with only the immediate families attending.

That was before the extended family got wind of the development. On the Hopkins side, there was no chance that a celebration and a family knees-up would be forgone.

'You can't leave out the children,' protested Billy's sisters. 'The wedding of their Uncle Billy is an affair never to be missed. It'll be something that they'll treasure for the rest of their lives.' Flo had three children and Polly four. When Sam in Belfast heard that their children were being invited, he insisted that his two be included as well. More distant family members heard about the planned marriage on the grapevine and since they regarded both weddings and funerals in the same light, namely opportunities to get together for the mutual exchange of news and gossip over drinks, it was vital they be included on the invitation lists.

By the time the list was finalised, there wasn't a skeleton left in the cupboard. The only shadow over things was Dad's refusal to attend.

Similar considerations applied to the Mackenzie family, and remote clans in the Highland glens of Scotland abandoned their mountain goats and sheep and prepared to make the journey South to celebrate the marriage of one of their lassies to a Sassenach. Bagpipes were a *sine qua non* of their baggage.

Duncan Mackenzie was awakened early in the morning by the excited babble of voices and a pattering of feet round the house. He'd slept badly, his slumbers disturbed by wild, worrisome visions. In his nightmare, it was raining heavily; he had lost his daughter Laura and was searching the streets of Manchester for her. He ran hither and thither looking in derelict buildings and back entries but to no avail, there was no sign of her. At last he'd found her, along with Billy, her intended. They were dressed in wedding outfits and were huddled together in the doorway of Lewis's store on Market Street.

'It's raining and you'll catch your death of cold. Come awa' home with me, both of you,' he'd said.

'We'd rather die of starvation here in this doorway than accept your help,' he'd heard her reply.

Still shivering at the memory, he sat up in bed and listened to the clatter. What on earth was going on? He rubbed the sleep from his eyes. Then it came to him. How could he have forgotten after his nightmare? There was to be a wedding.

There seemed to be panic everywhere with people rushing about the place, the house resounding to frenzied female voices demanding use of the bathroom, frantic inquiries as to the whereabouts of various items, calls for help with this and that.

Sounds like pandemonium, he said to himself. Thank God I have my own bathroom *en suite*. He gazed at the neatly pressed kilt in the Mackenzie tartan that was folded over the chair. This is a proud day for the Mackenzie clan, he thought, and it was up to him to uphold tradition.

He washed and shaved, dressed with particular care, and descended to the kitchen. There was chaos everywhere as the Mackenzie females fussed over dresses, flowers, and coiffures. To add to the confusion, a couple of helpers from the local church ran to and fro putting the finishing touches to the buffet breakfast which had to be ready immediately after the wedding ceremony. One table had been set in the kitchen for the many children who would be attending whilst the main buffet was to be in the study.

Finally, the ladies were ready. Grandma and Aunty both smelt faintly of mothballs and were dressed in costume more suited to a Gilbert and Sullivan opera. They twittered their way out to the waiting limousine, where Katie and Jenny in their silk and satin joined them. Louise, in a massive Ascot-type hat, brought up the rear.

Before they drove off, a delighted Duncan gave them the once-over.

'I'm proud of you,' he said. 'You bring honour and beauty to the Mackenzie clan.'

But if Duncan was proud of the advance party which set off for the church, he was bowled over when he caught sight of his eldest daughter. His heart leapt for joy, gladness and tender paternal love.

'Laura,' he said, 'you're truly a bonnie lass. You look wonderful, simply wonderful. When I see you now all ready to be married, you mind me of your mother and the day we wed. She looked so bonnie too.'

'Thank you, Daddy. And you look so smart in your chieftain's outfit, you'll create a stir when we walk into the church. But I hope you won't think I'm stupid when I tell you I'm as nervous as a kitten.'

'There's nothing to be nervous about, Laura. The married state is perfectly natural.'

'It's not being married that scares me, Daddy. It's that walk down the aisle with all those people there. We were hoping for a quiet wedding but it's got a bit out of hand and the thought of the long walk from porch to altar gives me the collywobbles. I hope I don't collapse and you have to carry me on your back.'

'Don't you worry your head, Laura. Remember I'll be there to support you – always have been ever since you were a little girl. Lean on me.'

'You're amazing, Daddy. Nothing ever seems to rattle you. You're always so calm and collected.'

Duncan said nothing about his nightmare.

In Gardenia Court, Billy and his family sat waiting for the wedding car.

'This is supposed to be a joyful day,' remarked Les, looking at the anxious faces around him. 'Yet everyone looks as if they're going to a funeral instead of a wedding.'

'I was thinking,' said Billy. 'Brides get dressed up in white, the colour of purity and joy. But men get dressed up in black. Is that a suitable colour for a wedding? We hired these morning suits from Moss Bros and I'm not sure how they'd spell the word "morning". Maybe it's "mourning".'

'You never said a truer word, Billy,' Dad pontificated. 'The suits and the limousine are black. Just the right colour for this occasion.'

'Take no notice of him, our Billy,' Mam said. 'He's a real Jeremiser. Only happy when he's miserable. Weddings are of course happy occasions,' she added, her eyes misting over, 'but for a mother it's always sad as well. In a way, it *is* like a funeral.'

'What makes you say that, Mam?' asked Billy anxiously.

'After today, you'll be gone from here, Billy. Your bedroom will be there empty and we'll miss you. You won't be coming back here no more from school. No more carrying your bike up the stairs. No more asking my advice and sharing your problems.'

'Don't be surprised if he's back in a few weeks for good,' said Dad gloomily.

'It's not as bad as that, Mam. I'll come back to see you regularly.'

'You say that now but you'll soon have your own home and your own family to keep you busy.'

'It's the same for Laura's mother, I suppose,' Billy said.

'No, it's not. You know the old saying, "My son is my son till he has got him a wife; but my daughter's my daughter all the days of her life." There's a lot of truth in that.'

'Don't worry,' Billy reassured her. 'I'll be back all right, when I want to borrow some money. And even though Dad isn't coming to the wedding, I hope he'll still get me those under-the-counter cigarettes.'

Dad nodded sadly.

Billy himself was not feeling as confident as he sounded. Up to this point, he hadn't thought deeply about the ramifications of getting married and of what it really meant. He'd been so busy and so run off his feet what with one thing and another that he hadn't had time to consider the gravity of the step he was about to take. So far it had been exciting fun and games – arranging this and organising that. Now he was all dressed up to the nines, ready to go for a ride in a posh limousine, followed by a church service, a slap-up meal and off for a fortnight's honeymoon in Devon.

He'd been worried and preoccupied about bringing his family into contact with the Mackenzies. The meeting of two social worlds, he'd thought, with himself at the friction point of them both. He'd tried to minimise the possible difficulties by arranging an early nuptial Mass, a quick wedding breakfast, and a train to Exeter for 2 p.m., after which each family would celebrate in its own customary way. Dad might not be at the wedding ceremony but he wouldn't miss the family knees-up for anything.

But now for the first time his mam's words brought home the seriousness of what he was going to do in church that morning. He was quitting home for good and after today he'd be returning to a new life in a furnished flat – a comfortable little apartment but nevertheless strange and unfamiliar. Whilst he wouldn't be sorry to see the back of Gardenia Court and its squalid surroundings, at the same time he felt a pang of regret that he was leaving his old life behind and going on a journey to face whatever fate had in store. Right at this moment, he thought, Laura must be thinking along the same lines. Pre-nuptial blues, the books called it. Today she would be parting from her parents and her family to embark on a risky life adventure with a relative stranger.

'The car's here,' announced Les who'd been looking out of the window. 'Time's up. Time to go.'

'No need to make it sound like the summons to the gallows,' said Billy.

As they emerged from the stairwell, he gazed up at the tenement verandas which reminded him of theatre boxes at the Albert Hall. Every single one of them was occupied by a neighbouring family – women still in their curlers, the men with their braces dangling down. Dad looked down forlornly from their own veranda. A solitary, melancholy figure.

'It's not too late to change your mind, Dad,' Billy called. 'Come on down, we'll wait for you.'

'No, my mind's made up, Billy. You go on without me,' he said sadly.

From one of the stairwells, a mongrel dog appeared, sniffed at the car, and then lifted its hind leg and began peeing on the rear wheel.

'Piss off,' the uniformed driver yelled, giving it a well-aimed kick up its backside.

'Look at the stuck-up 'Opkins lot,' Mrs Pitts screeched. 'They've joined the bleedin' toffs.'

'All the very best to you, son,' Mrs Mulligan called down, 'and don't forget to cook them there Danish omelettes for your good lady.'

Feeling like royalty, Billy waved back to them in acknowledgement.

'Goodbye, everyone,' he shouted, 'and the very best of luck to you all.'

The Daimler engine started up and, accompanied by a pack of mangy, snarling dogs which were bent on devouring the back wheels, the limousine soon left Gardenia Court behind.

St Anselm's Church was already full when the wedding car pulled up outside. Billy and his companions entered the church and surveyed the forest of flowers and outlandish hats. As they made their way to their places, Billy stopped many times to shake hands and exchange greetings with the numerous friends and colleagues who smiled and nodded encouragingly. Towards the front, he spotted the school staff and the whole contingent of ex-pupils from his first class, many of the girls with tears in their eyes, as they sat waiting and whispering impatiently for the ceremony to begin.

Billy stopped to talk to his headmaster.

'Thanks for coming, Frank. You seem to have brought half the school with you.'

'I couldn't keep them away,' Frank said. 'Especially the girls. I think this wedding's going to break a few hearts. All the best to you both, Billy. Don't forget I expect to see you both back at the beginning of the new term. Monday, September the fourth in case you've forgotten.'

'Have no fear, Frank. We'll both be there.'

Billy moved on and had a few words with his old chums from the Damian Smokers' Club who were also much in evidence.

'Thanks for making the effort to support me in my hour of need,' he joked. 'But when I see you all together like this again, I can't help but feel sad that our old friend Robin Gabrielson is not with us here today.'

'I'm sure he *is* here in spirit,' said Titch. 'Well, this is it, old pal. You're the first of the gang to get married.'

'And I shall probably be the last,' added Nobby in his smart lieutenant's uniform complete with Sam Browne belt.

'I doubt it,' smirked Oscar. 'I rather think that honour will be mine.'

'Don't forget,' said Pottsy, 'if you buy your groceries in one of our shops, I can offer you a twenty-five per cent discount.'

'I'll remember that,' laughed Billy. 'Laura and I will probably hold you to it. Maybe we can all meet up some time and go for a drink.'

'That's if your new wife gives you permission,' Ollie grinned.

They gave him the thumbs-up – at least, he interpreted it as such though knowing their scurrilous minds, the gesture probably had other significance.

On the right side of the church sat many of the Hopkins family with their children, along with a number of older relatives whom Billy had not seen for years – Aunts Cissie and Hetty, Uncles Matt and Eddie.

When they reached the front bench, Billy and Les sat down and waited for the ceremony to begin. Les kept casting glances back at the extended Mackenzie family gathered on the other side.

'I don't know what kind of rum family you're marrying into, Billy,' he whispered, 'but all those blokes over there are wearing women's skirts.'

'Keep your voice down, Les, they'll hear you. Have you ever noticed how the bridegroom comes into the church unnoticed – no music, no fanfare, no fuss, as if he has only a minor part to play in the marriage?'

'That's about the sum of it,' Les answered. 'You say the marriage. But marriage isn't a word, it's a sentence.'

'Now he tells me. Did you remember the ring?'

'But of course. Were you hoping I'd lost it?'

Their exchange was interrupted by the sound of the congregation scrambling to its feet and the organ playing Handel's 'Arrival of the Queen of Sheba'.

Murmurs of 'Oooh, isn't she lovely' could be heard over the music.

'Into the valley of death rode the six hundred,' recited Les in a feeble attempt at humour.

'Theirs not to reason why, theirs but to do and die,' replied Billy bravely.

Then a radiant Laura was beside him, in her beautiful bridal gown. His fairytale princess come true.

'Laura,' he whispered. 'You look absolutely stunning. How do I look?'

Laura smiled back nervously. 'Be serious,' she said.

Duncan Mackenzie and the two bridesmaids stepped back and old Father O'Flynn came forward.

'Dearly beloved,' he intoned, 'we are gathered here together in the sight of God, and in the face of this congregation, to join together this man and this woman in holy matrimony. Matrimony is an honourable estate and therefore not to be enterprised, nor taken in hand, un-advisedly, lightly, or wantonly, to satisfy men's carnal lusts and appetites, like brute beasts that have no understanding. Hear our prayers for Willibrord and Lorna, through your son Jesus Christ, our Lord, who lives and reigns with you and the Holy Ghost, one God for ever and ever. Amen.'

Billy and Laura walked to the altar with the priest and knelt at the prie-dieux reserved for them.

Father O'Flynn went on: 'Brethren, let women be subject to their husbands as to the Lord, for the husband is head of the wife as Christ is the head of the Church.'

Billy stole a surreptitious glance at Laura, smiled and gave her a big wink. She pulled a face in return.

'For this cause shall a man leave his father and mother, and shall stick to his wife,' Father O'Flynn continued.

There was the sound of subdued sobbing in the body of the church. It sounded like Billy's mam.

'Let every one of you in particular love his wife, and let the wife fear her husband.'

Laura was now definitely frowning. She pursed her lips and adopted a mock frightened expression.

'Thy wife shall be as a fruitful vine on the sides of the

house. Thy children as olive plants round about thy table.'

The rest of the nuptial Mass flowed easily and without a hitch. They reached the marriage vows.

'Willibrord and Lorna, I shall now ask if you freely undertake the obligations of marriage. Willibrord—'

'Billy,' whispered Billy.

Father O'Flynn looked perplexed for a moment. 'You'll be given the bill at the end of the ceremony,' he said, frowning. We've got a right one here, the priest thought. 'Repeat after me. "I, Willibrord Hopkins, take thee, Lorna Macmillan . . ."'

Billy repeated his words: 'I, William Hopkins, do take thee, Laura Mackenzie . . .' And went on to vow, 'To have and to hold from this day forward, for better for worse, for richer for poorer, in sickness and in health, to love, to cherish, till death us do part, according to God's holy ordinance; and thereto I give thee my troth.'

The subdued sobbing continued throughout the vow-taking and reached a crescendo in the 'for richer for poorer' bit.

Billy continued, 'With this thing . . . ring, I thee wed, with my body I thee worship, and with all my worldly goods I thee endow.'

'There goes his bike,' Mam said in her inimitable stage whisper – the kind that the whole church could hear.

The ceremony was over when Father O'Flynn said: 'Willibrord and Lorna, I now pronounce you man and wife. Willibrord, you may kiss the bride.'

The wedding bells rang out. Mendelssohn's triumphant march was played *fortissimo*. Confetti and rice were thrown as the newly marrieds ran the gauntlet. The wedding car whisked them away. There followed a mad rush to get back to the house for the free drinks.

For the bridal couple, the ceremony seemed surreal, as if it was happening to two other people, and before they knew where they were, it was all over.

At the house, guests were welcomed in by the sound of several bagpipes played by various visitors of the Mackenzie clan. They might have sounded better had they agreed to play the same tune. For the Hopkins family, however, it was all one. Caterwauling.

'Do you like the sound of bagpipes, Billy?' Steve Keenan asked.

'Let's put it like this, Steve. I prefer to listen to the sound of a chorus of alley cats serenading at two o'clock in the morning.'

'I take that as a no,' Steve said.

The hordes of children were settled at their special banquet in the kitchen and were soon feeding their faces. The adult feast did not go so smoothly. The Hopkins family, lacking familiarity with the concept of 'The Buffet', had seated themselves round the buffet table, napkins tucked into collars, knives and forks at the ready. There was nothing for it but for the other thirty guests to squeeze in and find places at the table.

Meanwhile, Uncle Eddy had been helping himself liberally to the port and sherry which were readily at hand

'You're not in your Greengate boozer now,' remonstrated Aunt Mona. 'You're not supposed to drink sherry from a pint pot.'

The effect of the fortified wine soon became obvious and it wasn't long before he had forgotten where he was.

The meal was proceeding smoothly when Eddy turned to Laura's mother who was sitting opposite him, and said in a voice all could hear, 'You want to get some of this grub into a paper bag to take home. Don't let the waitresses get it all.'

Uh-oh, Billy thought. Here we go.

Later, when Uncle Eddy was looking for the toilets, he addressed Duncan and asked, 'Excuse me, sir, but where's the gents?'

'Sorry,' Duncan replied, perplexed. 'The gents?'

'You know, your back? Your urinal?'

'Oh, you mean the toilet. There's a cloakroom off the hall and one upstairs if that's occupied.'

'Thenk you very much, sir,' he replied. 'Great party – it's a belter.'

At least Mam seemed to be getting on well with Grandma and Aunty. They talked ten to the dozen and even Aunty was running out of anecdotes – almost.

Came the time for the speeches. As was customary, the bride's father was called on first.

'I'm a man of few words,' he said. 'My task today was simply to give away the bride. After paying for this wedding breakfast, the bride is about all I have left to give away. But I'd like to say this.

'Laura and Billy are going to start their married life in a rented furnished flat and with very little money. I hope they know what they're doing. I only wish they'd managed to buy a house but it's no use crying over spilt milk. What's done is done and it's too late now. But when they do finally get round to buying a house of their own, I want them to know that I shall be there to give them my fullest support. I'll simply finish by asking you to join in drinking a toast to the happy couple. We wish them all the luck in the world – they're going to need it.' With that he raised his glass, drank the toast and sat down.

'Miserable old bugger,' Eddy whispered in an aside to

Louise. 'He should give them the money now.'

Next to speak was Billy.

'I know I can speak for Laura when I say this is the happiest day we have ever known, for it means the start of a new life together. Today is a day to rejoice and this I do with all my heart. I'm only sorry my dad is not with us on this otherwise perfect day – he has his own reasons and I'll have to respect those though I do not agree with them. And even though he's not here, I want first to thank him and my mam for looking after me up to now. Then thanks to Mr and Mrs Mackenzie for giving me their daughter's hand in marriage. I know that like my own father they're unsure about the wisdom of the step Laura and I have taken but I can promise them that I shall love and cherish their daughter for the rest of my life. Have faith in us. We've only just begun.

'I could fill this speech with jokes and funny lines but I'll leave that to Les who no doubt will tell you my jokes and funny lines anyway. I'm grateful to him for agreeing to act as best man. Blood is thicker than water and Les is thicker than both. I must say, though, that I'm not altogether sure that Laura and I are legally married for Father O'Flynn today seems to have married two other people – Willibrord and Lorna. No matter. I hope they'll both be very happy whoever they are.

'I liked the reference to the Gospel instruction, "Wives, be subject to your husbands", and the part which advised wives to "fear their husbands". Good, sound advice. Did you notice that in the marriage vows, the bride is told that she must obey her husband but no such instruction was given to the bridegroom. No problem 'cos Laura and I have solved the question of who'll be boss and we've come to an amicable understanding. I'll make the major decisions for us, like our attitude to the government's foreign policy, our answers to the economic crisis, and so on. Laura will make the minor decisions such as where we shall live, who our friends will be, where we shall go on holiday, and what I shall wear.

'Those of you who were watching the ceremony closely may have noticed that when the priest asked me, "Do you take Laura to be your lawfully wedded wife?" Laura gave me a nudge and answered for me. "He does!" she said before I could get a word in.

'Thank you to the rest of the company for the wonderful wedding presents you have given us. Especially the toasters. Making toast has long been one of my specialities consisting of the burn-and-scrape method but now the various toasters you have presented us with will raise our culinary standards to new heights. Thank you also for attending this ceremony as I know many of you have travelled great distances to be here. Some from as far away as Stockport and Salford.

'Let me finish by saying that I'm sure Laura and I have made a good marriage and that we shall be happy for the rest of our lives. I know it to be true because Laura just told me to say it. Now, please join me in drinking a toast to our beautiful bridesmaids, Jenny and Katie.' With that, Billy sat down to the applause of both families.

It was the turn of the best man to make his speech and Les stood up to oblige the assembly. He began by reading the many telegrams – one from Hughie serving with the Royal Army Medical Corps in Malaya – offering congratulations and best wishes, though there was one with the strange greeting from the Damian College Smokers' Club: 'Lang may your lum reek.'

'A "lum" is a chimney,' explained Les with a grin at

Billy, 'and roughly translated the message is, "Long May Your Chimney Smoke".'

Les cleared his throat and began his speech.

'I'm not used to making speeches so please excuse any mistakes I make. I've not prepared anything and so I can hardly wait to hear what I'm going to say. I congratulate Billy on an absolutely adequate speech. He's never been an easy one to follow. I know personally I can never follow a word he says.

'Laura wanted a simple wedding, and she got what she wanted – you've only to look at the bridegroom. One thing I will say about him, he's always willing to give you half of whatever he's got. And since he's got nothing, it means half of nothing.

'At school though he was always bright – he learned to read at the age of four. Trouble was, he didn't always understand what he was reading. Whenever he saw cautionary notices like "wet cement" or "wet paint", he thought it was an instruction to act. One day Sister Helen, the headmistress of St Wilfred's Infant School, warned the youngsters, "Remember, children, that in the school hall, there is a sign – Wet Floor. So be careful and don't forget." You guessed it. I was called out of class to take Billy home for a change of pants.

'But now, he has left home for good, Billy's career as a bachelor is over! We're going to miss him. He can always come back if he wants to borrow something, like my demob suit for example. I'm not sure but I think he may be wearing it today.

'It's usual at these affairs to warn the bride of the groom's bad habits. In actual fact, he hasn't got that many faults, but he makes full use of those he does have. Take smoking, for instance. He has to have a cigarette first thing in the morning. He gives up smoking every week, usually on a Monday, but by Wednesday he's so bad-tempered he does you a favour and starts again.

'One piece of advice I offer the newly married couple is this: never go to bed after an argument – stay up and finish it off. And for Billy: I hope you learn how to do the washing up, and remember the best time to do it is . . . straight after she digs you in the ribs.

'Ladies and gentlemen, it's now my pleasant duty to thank Billy on behalf of the bridesmaids Jenny and Katie for his generous words. It's a real pleasure to act as spokesman for such a lovely duo. Like everyone here, I wish Laura and Billy long life and happiness. Their long life will be our happiness. Let's drink a toast to the new Mr and Mrs Hopkins – Laura and Billy.'

When Les sat down, Billy looked at him admiringly. 'I never knew you had such hidden talents and powers of oratory,' he said, shaking his hand.

There followed the cutting of the cake, the photographs, the applause, the throwing of the bouquet – deliberately targeted at Jenny – after which it was time for the happy couple to retire to a bedroom to change into their 'going-away' outfits. This they did to the accompaniment of ribald remarks from the assembled company.

'No shenanigans in there.'

'The honeymoon doesn't start till you've reached your hotel, remember.'

'You haven't time for any messing about.'

The taxi to take them to the station arrived honking noisily. The entire wedding party congregated outside the house for the final farewell. More throwing of rice and confetti, more teasing. Billy helped Laura into the limousine but just before he went inside himself, he stepped onto the running board and gazed fondly back at his large family gathered at the gate to wave goodbye. He owed so much to them – for all they'd done for him, and for their unfailing support and encouragement. In his heart, there was a mixture of joy and sadness for he knew that he was leaving the past behind and embarking on a new life with a beautiful bride by his side. A life filled with adventure, promise, and high hopes.

Then he saw him – his dad! Elbowing his way through from the back of the Hopkins crowd. He was waving his wedding-cum-funeral pot hat.

'All the best, Billy lad,' he cried. 'Good luck to you both! I wish you every happiness.'

'Thanks a lot, Dad, for coming,' Billy called, his eyes glistening. 'It means a lot to us. I knew you'd make it in the end.'

'You just make sure you look after that new missus of yours, and come over and see us when you get back.'

'I will, Dad, I will,' Billy shouted. 'I'll have to come over to collect my bike. Half of it now belongs to Laura.'

The tranquil air of Regina Park was abruptly pierced by an agonising moan from sundry bagpipes as they tuned up with 'We're no awa' to bide awa', which the whole Mackenzie clan now sang out with great gusto. Not to be outdone, the Hopkins side struck up with a lusty rendering of Gracie Fields' 'Wish Me Luck As You Wave Me Good-bye'. There was a slamming of car doors, the revving of an engine, the rattling of tin cans tied to the bumper, and to the strains of the polyphonic medley, the cab moved off, turned the corner into Wellington Grove and, quite suddenly, they were gone.

Going Places

Billy Hopkins

It's the 1950s and Manchester is still suffering from post-war austerity, but Billy and Laura Hopkins are in seventh heaven as they return from their honeymoon. Their euphoria evaporates as they find themselves desperate for money and soon, with a baby on the way, they yearn for more than Billy's teaching salary can offer them.

Then Billy hears an appeal for Education Officers in Kenya. The glowing description of life in the colony, together with the many financial incentives, make it a tempting prospect. But what about the recent Mau Mau rebellion and the inevitable culture shock? After much hesitation Billy and Laura set off on a BOAC Argonaut for Nairobi and an exotic new life.

Filled with humour and warmth, *Going Places* is the compelling story of one family's journey to a land of dreams, challenges and heartache thousands of miles from home.

Billy Hopkins' novels have been warmly acclaimed:

'Hopkins is a fascinating author . . . He has few, if any, peers' *Manchester Evening News*

'In one moment you cannot help but chuckle, in the next you are wrestling with a lump in your throat, hoping that no one will notice' *Warrington Guardian*

0 7553 0220 6

headline

Kate's Story

Billy Hopkins

'Dad, it's the happiest day of my life,' Kate said. 'I wish time would stand still and it could be today forever.'

It's June 1897, and Kate is celebrating her eleventh birthday on the day of Queen Victoria's Diamond Jubilee. But Kate's joy is shortlived for tragedy strikes and, before long, her family is evicted from their home in Ancoats, Manchester. With no wages coming in, a mother unable to cope, and the threat of her siblings being split up, Kate has to grow up fast.

Through the ensuing journey of hope and heartache Kate learns to fight against the odds with determination. An indomitable spirit and bright sense of humour help her to survive the hardships of the workhouse and the sorrows and losses suffered during the Great War. But will they be enough to eventually bring her the happiness she lost as a child?

Nostalgic and poignant, *Kate's Story* is a truly heart-warming read, rich in Billy Hopkins' trademarks of warmth, laughter and triumph over adversity.

'I have just finished *Kate's Story* amidst tears and laughter . . . I will treasure this book for the rest of my life' Mrs Edna Wright, Manchester

'*Kate's Story* is excellent . . . A truly magnificent book' Dr Gus Plaut, Essex

'This is to tell you how much I enjoyed reading *Kate's Story* – a lovely mixture of humour and pathos' Dr John Spence, West Midlands

0 7472 6852 5

headline